The Great War Against Terrorism

by

Peter J. Michael

The Great War Against Terrorism

Turning The Wheels Of Justice
    Madness Takes Its Toll
Maniac Surrounded
    Detective's Investigations Into The Mysteries Of The World: Secrets
Unravelled
    The Figure Of Death
The Final Offensive

ISBN-13: 978-0-6459562-9-0

Published by Peter J. Michael

THE COMPLETE WRITTEN WORKS OF THIS ENTIRE BATTLE SAGA IN CHRONOLOGICAL ORDER ARE:

TURNING THE WHEELS OF JUSTICE

MADNESS TAKES ITS TOLL

MANIAC SURROUNDED

DETECTIVE'S INVESTIGATIONS INTO THE MYSTERIES OF THE WORLD: SECRETS UNRAVELLED

THE FIGURE OF DEATH

THE FINAL OFFENSIVE

THE WAR OF GOOD AGAINST EVIL WILL NEVER DIE!

JUSTICE HAS ITS MEANS!

THE GREAT WAR AGAINST TERRORISM

"I wrote Turning the Wheels of Justice, previously published as the Game of Kings," says Peter J. Michael, "because I was fascinated with subjects concerning power – and the conflict of power. Good versus evil, law enforcement versus corruption. In crux, it is a story very similar to the world itself: opposing methods, opposing beliefs and opposing armies; similar to the principles of Chess!"

Madness Takes its Toll is a spin-off novella from Turning the Wheels of Justice by Peter J. Michael. It explains the detailed events which took place after Crime Boss Domenico Armando escaped his New York City jail cell – until his first onslaught delivered against his marked targets, beginning with his bankrolled Senator, Ron Bishop. Also highlighting the fervent attempts made to catch him by New York City's top cop, Robert Stewart!

Maniac Surrounded is the sequel to Madness Takes its Toll.

Detective's Investigations into the Mysteries of the World: Secrets Unravelled, The Figure of Death and The Final Offensive conclude the epic war battle between the two powerful forces.

For crimes to be solved, law enforcement officials must take every one of them personally!

The enemy is evil. Evil pretends to be clever. But how clever can he be if he needs to cheat his way through life!

The devil works through the Hitler's of the world! Believe no wolf in sheep's clothing! Trust no wolf in sheep's clothing! The mind will remain more serene!

Contents

The Great War
Against Terrorism

PREFACE

Robert Stewart, a professional New York police detective was assigned to investigate the Chess Player and his nefarious conspiracy labelled, 'The Power Project'. The harmful and unlawful menacing plan became an international incident by the proper authorities.

The conspiracy had involved underworld investment into police and political corruption at an entirety. By orchestrating the elimination of those law-enforcement officials not influenced by them - and replacing those with their own handpicked recruits. To infiltrate the police departments by joining the academies as rookies and slowly obtaining promotions to take over the police power completely; until the Chess Player had controlled the local, state and federal powers.

And the same goal was legislated within the political arena. Sending handpicked men to become District Attorneys, Mayors, Senators, Judges and run for Presidency. In crux, these police and political groups of individuals who operated in the Chess Player's cities and territories who were not of Mafia allegiance were placed on a shockingly long target list, marked for termination. To be replaced by the Chess Player's own handpicked recruits to take over the police and political power in the United States.

And the same procedure was cast forward for their global-offshore territories, in various other countries across the world, with the cooperation of the entire global underworld; the absolute criminal commission that was controlled by their Boss of Bosses, code-named, the Chess Player.

Robert Stewart had vowed to do whatever necessary to protect his family, his colleagues and society in general, all at risk by this very evil and dangerously determined tyrant. Hence, Robert Stewart and his number one enemy became embroiled in a chess game war against the other. As two Kings or leaders in their own world who fought against each other's intrusive belief system; where only one of them was destined to survive. Thus, Turning the Wheels of Justice was formed.

1

TURNING THE WHEELS OF JUSTICE

BOOK 1

CHAPTER 1

'Success has its price'.

Robert Stewart proved a pioneer in crime fighting when he had arrested Giuseppe and Rowan Castalone in the year 1987, on the 1st day of July. The scheme between the police lieutenant and the underworld figures was a viciously dangerous, but extremely necessary action for the preservation of society. Robert's goal was to bring the entire Castalone organisation to justice. He had accomplished that by appearing to have turned corrupt as a person and renege on his obligation to serve the police force correctly. His primary objective was to gain the family's trust by making them think that he would betray his former law-enforcement colleagues by accepting bribes in exchange for offering his services of police protection. Robert was operating as an undercover police officer during the Castalone assignment. Robert's usual role had served the Detective Division of the local Brooklyn Police Department, 25th division precinct station house, of the state of New York.

Robert Stewart had spent many months in his role of setting up the Castalone family for the tumble; to remove them from the streets entirely. It was a ploy, a charade on his behalf. He entered the inner circle of the family by using his police profession as his powerful weapon, portraying himself as a rogue cop. His true intentions were kept to himself, top secret. He undertook a leave of absence from the police force, and landed himself a job of manual labour in a construction firm owned by the Mob's rival, Alfonse Lorenzo. Alfonse, being part of the conspiracy against the Castalones, as a current war between the two families had waged, had granted Robert an opportunity to approach the Castalone family via the many informants Robert knew had infiltrated segments of his organisation.

Talking against the force, with known Castalone informants who penetrated all Lorenzo factions as double agents; such spies had reported to Giuseppe of this man known as Robert Stewart. He was heard saying: "It seems as though all those against the law are the ones making all the money." That he resigned

2

from the police force because he had not favoured the notion of going to work everyday wondering if he was going to be killed by the very criminals he had supposedly gotten tired of fighting. It proved a losing battle. And instead of fighting them, why not join them. After all, they were getting all the perks. He had put forward the idea that he simply wanted to return to being a normal civilian. To undertake a 9-5 day job, so he could spend more time with his family. Before long, he obtained such work by making good relations with the foreman, who was impressed with his credentials. Thus, anyone would employ someone with qualifications to that of a former and highly decorated police official - and a good-tough one at that. Thus knowing the foreman was a Castalone spy, he was the one to approach. The foreman had seen Robert's proposition with far greater foresight than that of a construction worker. He came in handy when warding off Mob rivals who feared him; a good man to have on their side. So it appeared as though he had sold his soul, and obtained the position.

In not too long a period, he was offered a job to rejoin the police force and continue his policing role. Thus - to earn a greater salary through helping them. He accepted.

As a loyalty test, Robert was asked to assassinate his police partner, Sergeant John McCallum. The reasoning behind this was simple. John McCallum was not a member of the underworld clan. And hence, the commission wanted him removed. He was too aggressive. But in exchange; Robert wanted a ticket inside the organisation, to obtain a piece of the action. It was a guarantee. So Robert set up his death. He appeared to have killed his best friend that would swear his devotion to the Castalone family. Giuseppe hinted that killing a friend for the family would singe his trust. So it appeared as though Robert had shot him in the face. Robert had orchestrated it as such so the face could not be recognised. He obtained a dead body in the morgue which resembled John, bearing similar build, dark complexion and almost exact height; a gang member whose face was blown off in a dispute with rival gangs. For Robert had much required it to appear as though he had shot him in the face. And the body was picked up only the night before by the morgue police. And consecutively, Robert had toe-tagged the corpse as John McCallum.

So he had faked John's death and kept him hidden in a Specialised International Government Agency (SIA), local safe house. Thus, following the arrest of Giuseppe Castalone, John was notified by an SIA agent who was guarding him, in direct radio contact with Robert, okaying his release. That it was safe for him to roam the streets now. Giuseppe was in prison.

Meanwhile, at John's so-called funeral, no one was to know he was truly alive. It had to appear convincing. And the wisest method procured in achieving that was when his own mother in attendance was seen grieving for her own son; a much public display of grief. Of course, the obvious scenario

3

was that either Giuseppe or his people would be at the funeral to report of its event. And as it was the death of a respected police official, high profile to the public, reporters were scheduled to be within close proximity. So Giuseppe, who preferred being there personally to assess any passing of a test given, that promised an important promotion to a star recruit entrance inside his inner sanctums, of course, could not risk being seen by the reporters. Questions would be raised as to the relevance for his attendance that could give himself away as the culprit responsible. The public had long suspected his Mafia dictatorship role. So instead, he sent a very trusted long-serving enforcer to report back to him, posing as a reporter at the funeral.

So when family members of the deceased had attended the funeral and showed their grief; convinced it was John, despite a closed coffin scenario for obvious reasons, it was assured that the task was accomplished - and well. Following the funeral, Giuseppe, with his henchmen had gone to see Robert at his home.

Robert invited him and his four-man bodyguard entourage inside, though Giuseppe signalled them to wait outside. This meant Giuseppe trusted him implicitly. And the fact that Robert invited him inside his home was a sign Giuseppe would perceive also as equal sound faith. A friendship was always sealed by a man's invitation into his own home, his family's home. When the housemaid had left the room to make some coffee for everyone, Giuseppe said to Robert, "I knew after that Sergeant's death you were in. But now, I want to seal it. I want you to have more responsibility, more money. Today I realised that my faith in you has been confirmed. It takes a long time – but, yours has paid off, so to speak. You passed the test with colours that are as beautiful as my daughter Renee – I am sure you have noticed!"

Robert smiled closemouthed. Giuseppe's visit to his home this day meant that Robert would take orders directly from him - only Giuseppe Castalone, and not his son Rowan. No middlemen. No buffers. He would become his right-hand man.

Though one thing was certain, Robert knew that failing the loyalty test meant that his life and his family's lives were the ultimate price for such a failure. And having appeared to be a man to serve the Castalone Mob in any way; thus executing his own police partner, John McCallum, became the ultimate testing ground to achieve his loyalty. That had presented him with an invitation into the inner sanctums of the Castalone private office.

Meanwhile, as Robert had cut himself off from his family, he was introduced to the Castalone daughter, one of the powerful family's heirs. And old man Giuseppe Castalone surely wanted him as his sworn son-in-law. This proved as an additional weapon for Robert to obtain entrance inside the family's inner circle; and learn of their movements as a trusted friend.

Robert, using much proven cunning had succeeded in what he had set out to accomplish. He would be called to the waterfront docks to meet with couriers of the Castalone family group. And, given payment of thousands of dollars cash, concealed in an envelope, to allow protection for a shipment of drugs to come through. Then when he and his co-conspirators in the police force were made aware that a drug deal was scheduled, it would appear to the Castalone family as though Robert had given them a false time of its arrival - and a completely different location. To establish, that when police had arrived at the scene, someone must have tipped the enemy off.

As part of the ploy, Robert had to mislead and lie to his trusted friends on the police force who were kept in the dark of the entire operation. All the while, Robert was monitoring the Castalone drug importing routes and local shipping distribution networks. Gathering the necessary information which included the locations of their warehouses the drugs were then transported to once inside the country. He learnt the names of all their contacts and offshore suppliers and couriers; all their key people. He as well created his secret dossier which included the names of all their middlemen, in order to obtain all the necessary information against the family to present to authorities, his superiors. To present them with names, dates and places for final confiscation of their illegal imports. Then he would wait for the Castalone family to plan their major drug deal with enough ammunition to send them all behind bars for a very long time. Police Chief Commissioner Gordon, Robert's sole co-conspirator and accomplice in the operation, could not stress enough the importance of secrecy. Only he and Robert were in on the plan to crucify the Castalones.

The reason for the war between the Lorenzo and Castalone Family was unique. Alfonse's father, Anthony Lorenzo, Italian-New York crime boss, decided to turn himself and his entire world over to the police and government. For the first time in Mafia history, a higher-ranked Mafioso, in fact the head of a crime family was willing, quite enthusiastically to 'rat on his friends'. In the past, low-level soldiers had been forced to cooperate with the police, when it served their purpose. But a shock to the entire national underworld was established when one of their own high-ranked colleagues; a man who sat in with them during high-placed top secret discussions had decided to disclose their secrets to the outside world. To break their traditional law of silence, the Omerta, and turn his life entirely against their own: the 'Honoured Association'.

Of course, law-enforcement officials were sceptical at this. It was virtually impossible for a former Mafia commander to suddenly, as if struck by a bolt of lightning, to transform his otherwise, bloody ways and reform himself to divulging his sordid life's secrets to the proper authorities. Also, what became problematic, was the likelihood, if genuine, that he may not live out his new era of reform. In fact, his former compatriots may get to him somehow, before he divulged everything he now swore, in sincere desire to tell those authorities, against his once 'partners in crime!'

At the time of his reform; he fled the American syndicate and continued his business operations in his hometown in Italy. He continued business in Naples and Rome, before he turned himself over to the authorities, and was kept under twenty-four hour close guard in a secluded villa on the outskirts of Naples. Then, shortly thereafter, he was extradited to the United States under heavy guard.

Anthony Lorenzo's betrayal to the American and global syndicates had naturally angered, and shocked the entire international underworld!

It was evident that the greatest reason he did so, was all the talk of the commission's present lack of honour, dignity, and self-restraint from affecting masses of innocent lives caught in the crossfire of their murderous incidences and heartless plans of infamous, and limitless proportions. He also decided to turn informant in order to save his life and that of the future of his family. Being forced to participate in the all-evil police and political mass murdering 'Power Project', proved the last straw of his tolerance.

That same day, on that same night, when the truth had spread, Lorenzo's high-level counsellor and his son Alberto Lorenzo, with four bodyguards were gunned down in their own farmhouse, by a terror-driven group of men, all wearing black ski masks, covering their heads and faces, except their eyes. The assassins had stormed their Naples residence, executing everyone in sight, all the bodyguards, until they located the Lorenzo high-placed pillars of the organisation and massacred them with machine gun bullets to death. They did not stop there. When it became tragic enough that they made Alberto Lorenzo's wife a widow, and his newly-born son fatherless, they did not leave the farmhouse until they located the upstairs room where they hid. Inside, the small army of assassins had entered, holding their machine guns in gloved hands, and they found his weeping wife, holding their three-month-old son in her hands, weeping in terror in the corner of the room. Without a moment's thought, without a word spoken, they turned their weapons at them, in perfect aim and fired, until the dead corpses lay sprawled in a blood pool on the carpeted floor of the bedroom, before their heavy, steel-capped boots.

Naturally, the authorities were devastated of this occurrence, and only interpreted it as a warning, not only to Anthony Lorenzo, but to anyone who broke the criminal commission's code of silence. Anthony Lorenzo mourned terribly the loss of his beloved son, and his son's family as he resided in witness protective custody with the government now serving also as his guards. He mourned, he screamed, he wept. But, soon his sadness turned to further bitterness. He became more motivated, more driven, more focused, with the same zest and power of his youth, which had enabled him to build his empire, now, using the same energy that flooded into his veins, from his anger; he was willing to dismantle his entire empire and his entire former life of crime, giving the instruction manual, so to speak, to the government, to do so. To have his entire criminal world, and that of his former compatriots crumble with the same vigour and power as they used to amass their worlds from the ground up, also in their youths. He wanted them all to pay. He wanted to spill his guts, before they eventually found him and got to him also. He knew his days were numbered. And he also knew his government protectors understood that, even without admitting that fact to him. But before they found him, he wanted to publicise as much about his enemies to the government as possible. He wanted those former 'friends' and partners of his, now to suffer! All those bastards! Every son of a bitch one of them!

Robert Stewart, assigned to investigating the Lorenzo-Castalone agenda, had landed a case in Rome investigating the Lorenzo family operation. He had issued Anthony Lorenzo, the kingpin of the crime family with smuggling charges, exporting illegal drugs from Brazil into the United States. However, evidence had shown that he was forced into the illicit drug trade by the commission, whom arbitrarily decided they could reason with him, instead of killing him. And also, he was charged with gunning down two suspected Castalone soldiers, two months prior his entrance into the governments' hands, responsible for the death of one of his grandsons.

It was only a short time thereafter, that the desire for Mafia vengeance, and, in the hopes of clearing his name, had he turned himself over to the proper authorities. And he became informant. Though the police long suspected, and were able to prove his innocence in the illegal drug world; however forced by the underworld commission, they could still prove the murders he committed against two Castalone soldiers then in New York who killed his grandson prior in Italy. Despite Lorenzo crying foul in all this - that the murders were really only in self-defence against the very individuals who killed his grandson, as a means of strong-arm tactics imposed on the Lorenzo family, to cooperate.

It was his eldest son Alberto's five-year-old son. They killed him, without word or warning as he was in church with one of the family's bodyguards. The child insisted that his bodyguard take him to church, to pray for his family. And inside the local family Italian church, as they sat on the right of the aisle, on a Wednesday, the church deserted, the young boy prayed to the power above... His prayers had not finished... His words had not all been spoken... The church had blown up and exploded its entire existence to flames and ashes, with the two humans inside it. One of them was the five-year-old boy... Anthony Lorenzo's precious grandson!

It was within that hour, when a man rushed to Anthony inside his Italian home. And he whispered to him so the others could not hear of the news: "Your grandson, little Jeremy, he's disappeared. He's dead!"

7

Anthony Lorenzo broke out in a sudden outburst of cries. "No. This cannot be." And the rest of the family and its neighbourhood friends in attendance at his home that day understood, and they began to weep. The hysterical family could not believe it.

There was no question as to who was responsible for the atrocious and unconscionable bombing of a young boy and the church. And the day he lost his grandson was the day Anthony Lorenzo swore to put his life wholeheartedly against his evil compatriots, and soon after became informant. It was even very rare for low-level soldiers to turn against their Mafia employers, so, when Anthony Lorenzo, quite openly and enthusiastically declared his new allegiance to the proper government, against the otherwise bullet-proof omerta, naturally, the authorities were taken aback, beyond words.

And Anthony Lorenzo, with solemn assurance, with composure, clarity, and deadly-seriousness, had diffused their initial scepticism, that he, as a high-level Mafioso, changing allegiance to their corner was literally pronounced by the government as 'impossible'. He insisted upon his enthusiastic disclosures, that he in fact could not convince them enough to the real truth of the matter!

Robert Stewart, with the prosecuting district attorney and other law-enforcement officials could see Lorenzo was not their enemy. As he, in complete self-control, opened up secret revelations with composure, clarity, and utmost seriousness. Lorenzo was a Mafia of the old school. He resented the new breed of Mafia. They were mass murderers, even killers of women and children; bombers of churches!

He documented proof of how Italian and American Mafia strongholds had made inroads in infiltrating America's political parties. That they had in fact penetrated both political and police circles in all levels, and its activities were widespread in America and Sicily. He explained that its leaders were clever, cunning and impossible to detect, until now, and that they had controlled the police, the government, the business community and unions.

Though Robert Stewart, in his position, had always looked to legislatures, to judiciary, to be creating new laws; more severe penalties. And incorporate their part in phasing it out; as he enlisted the cooperation of his many connections and friends in law and politics. Robert understood that only a few police officers would put themselves out to genuinely help the innocent. To truly bring those evil powers causing them all dismay to justice. But as far as he was concerned, if nobody had fought it, it only strengthened financially, and increased its power and influence.

And Anthony Lorenzo, helping now as an ally to government authorities, was for reasons that he was forced to participate in the lethal and historical conspiracy to in fact murder the police and harm the government. And he could not close his eyes to it any longer. Apparently, authorities knew his greatest secret buried deep inside of him he was not revealing. Fear of his family's life if he revealed the identity of 'The Chess Player'. The criminal mastermind who forced his involvement in the dreaded conspiracy had made him tremble in silence. Already, his counsellor and best friend was murdered. And with one son, one daughter-in-law and now, two grandsons' dead, he did not want to lose the rest. For he knew revelations of 'The Chess Player' would automatically warrant the death of both himself and the remainder of his family. Oblivious, at that very moment, that the same revelations he made enthusiastically against the criminal syndicate, concerning the evil 'Power Project', would merit the same result; as the underworld commission would bind together as it affected them all. And he and his family would be hunted until in fact they were sworn dead.

But that aside, Robert and his comrades could see the real motive for all the outspoken revelations and disclosures he made. Lorenzo had a very personal score to settle. He wanted justice against the people who killed his son, his daughter-in-law and his two grandsons, and endangered his life, and that of his entire family. And mentioning the culprits responsible for his son's, his daughter-in-law and his two grandsons' deaths; and bringing forward evidence of their handiwork, Robert familiar with the crime family, then began his crusade that resulted in the Castalone downfall, their incarceration.

Lorenzo, in a series of conversations over five months, covered a replicated large novel of documented proof, incriminating the Mafia. And he was able to offer a history of unsolved murders of the Italian-American crime families that went back as far as 1940. Even the man responsible for the attempted assassination of the United States President two years ago, he let it slip. He as well revealed bits and pieces of salient information that authorities were able to paint out a very clear picture involving a conspiracy to all the police murders. But he never would reveal who the 'Chess Player' was. That was a no go. He said he did not know. Even though it was evident he was just too scared to make such a crucial revelation. He volunteered details of crimes unsolved that the government had long suspected, but never were able to prove.

Lorenzo wanted to cleanse his soul for his family and put them out of danger from the risky business, as it already had cost him a son and two grandsons and a daughter-in-law. Though he loved his mini power base, he was going to forget it. And put his family first. As he openly declared: "I will forget about the bloody power. What is power when it costs you your family? What is money when you have no one to share it with?"

Nonetheless, the indictment of Anthony Lorenzo for his crimes had possibly prevented a bloody New York war between him and the Castalone family group after he had lost his first grandson. And it also brought an abrupt end to Giuseppe Castalone's rapid rise.

Anthony Lorenzo, to this day, yet remained alive and resided in protective custody, currently in hiding in the United States. The day the Castalones waged war on the Lorenzo family, that became a territorial dispute to take over the Lorenzo family empire, with an attempt also on Senior Lorenzo's life, was the day it was made believe Anthony Lorenzo had died in a further bomb explosion, then planted inside his initial witness protective custody hideout in Italy, orchestrated by the evil family. All were made to believe he was dead by Robert Stewart and the government agency, the SIA, which had ensured his safe smuggling thereafter into the United States. Even Alfonse Lorenzo was none the wiser to his father's true safe-keeping. It was the only way to ensure his safety. And of course, Alfonse held the Castalones responsible for his father's 'supposed' death as well as an equal desire for vengeance against his brother Alberto, his brother's wife and his two nephews' murders.

Following the loss of his father and brother, his sister-in-law and two nephews, Alfonse took over in the running of his father's empire, then based in New York, as head of the family, mixed with an urge for justice on the man responsible for crippling his family line, so barbarically. But Alfonse's wife interceded and went to see Robert Stewart. She approached him with a request to help her save her husband as she knew the Castalones were also attempting to kill him. Scared for her husband's safety, and a bitterness he developed, she feared it would get him killed. An outcome she knew was inevitable if he had vowed to fulfil his need for justice on his own, in the old ways; which he was taught when his family's lives were in danger. She immediately approached the one man who could be trusted to intervene and help. Robert Stewart.

Robert, following his investigation into the Lorenzo family had his attention then focused to the true real enemy; the Castalones. He had arranged a meeting with Alfonse inside his office. He made Alfonse an offer so tempting he could not refuse.

Robert explained that already he had infiltrated the Castalone organisation by taking bribes from them in exchange for police protection. That he mainly dealt with drugs and arms. He would seemingly turn a blind eye whenever a drug deal was instigated. And he asked Alfonse to make the peace with the Castalone family in an attempt to gain their trust, in order to save any further lives that would be lost in an ongoing war. Especially civilian lives lost in the crossfire. And to also assist him in performing his duty which would also satisfy Alfonse's craving for justice. In the process, Alfonse would be able to assist Robert by supplying him documented proof also of the Castalone family's illegal business transactions. Since he was part of the organisation, he knew a lot of things: Names, dates, places and amounts. All of which could destroy the Castalone family. In the end, the offer was too tempting for him not to agree with Robert's plan.

Alfonse accepted the lieutenant's offer, knowing it was the right course of action. He also understood that if he killed the Castalones on his own, of course, the police would rate him as the number one suspect; seemingly, being a candidate with a strong enough motive to want them dead. Also, the agreement could spare the lives of his wife and the rest of his family liable to be lost in a war.

When Robert entered the covert undercover operation, he also had to ensure that his friends and family were not at risk because of his association with the Mob. He kept them at arm's length as if to portray to have cut ties with them altogether, for a family more promising; The Mafia, in order to protect them. A lot had to be sacrificed to destroy the Castalone family. He cut himself off from his family, his friends, and his casual acquaintances.

It was not long thereafter when a celebration was formed at the Castalone household, with Alfonse Lorenzo as one of the guest of honours, to commemorate the peaceful resolution of their two families, now working together. It was then when Robert was asked to kill his police partner, John McCallum. Robert had toe-tagged a dead man's body at the morgue as John's. It was a body that was just found dead in gangland territory - the ghettos in the Bronx. And when the handiwork was checked at the morgue prior to the funeral, the Castalones were impressed. They even congratulated Robert for blowing the man's face off, very clever. Shooting him in the face had made it more difficult for the police to identify. And at the funeral, when spies reported witnessing John's immediate family, with his mother there weeping over the death, crying out her son's name, they were convinced that Robert had completed his task with flying colours. And that was his ticket inside the organisation. By killing John, he proved his loyalty to the Castalone family. They could not help, but trust him now. Robert had spent a long time setting up the Castalones - and then it had paid off.

Even after the death was staged, which won him immediate passport inside the organisation, Rowan and his father decided to still keep a very close eye on Robert Stewart. A procedure they conducted with all their new recruits. It was necessary to ensure that they were not trying to deceive or manipulate them, particularly, any situation that brought them together for that matter. Giuseppe called a private meeting with his son and insisted that Robert be put under the Castalone microscope, to keep tabs on him. To make sure that their new friend was just that, their new friend. One thing Giuseppe taught Rowan was, "Never trust your friends, the same as your enemies. Always keep your eyes on them."

Rowan planted a listening device, known as a 'bug', in Robert's car and his house and his phone. "You better not be playing any games with the big boys. If you are, your days are numbered!"

And all along the Castalones put him through the grinder mill of tests to prove his trust. They requested access to government, top secret information, which Robert had modified, by not supplying the complete harmful information, but only the simplified basic form. Of course, Robert understood that Giuseppe already knew the information that was given to him on computer printout, accessed from the secret files of police headquarters. That he was using this to also test Robert. Only to make sure that he gave him the complete correct information, and exposed him to any file he requested, until he could gain his complete trust. Robert, again, would show him parts of the file, a few harmless pieces through contacts in the FBI, and DEA - all top secret highly classified documents. That mainly outlined the authorities' knowledge and staking out of routes of the East and South American connections — and whilst highlighting the activities in the South, the information particularly noted the Colombian connection on cocaine smuggling. Giuseppe grunted, as he now knew what routes to instruct his ships not to take, and established new ones when importing his merchandise into the country. Basically, Robert came to understand very rapidly that there was very little that Giuseppe Castalone did not know. It was all a test. And as a token of good friendship, Robert handed Giuseppe the file the FBI had on him through contacts higher up he said, leaving it at that.

Giuseppe responded by saying, "As in your profession, I must keep a low profile on my operations in business as well as personal. Every time a ship is intercepted, a contact could be apprehended and arrested, that draws my name in the newspaper." Giuseppe needed to explain no further. Robert smiled and gave a nod in total understanding and seeming complete agreement.

One week later, the Castalones held a meeting in a public restaurant. Already, Giuseppe informed Robert of the drug and arms deal being planned. Giuseppe wanted Robert's cooperation once again, this time only for a classic drug and arms deal. The instructions were laid out: "Friday, Dock 52. The merchandise will be transported on the last ship scheduled to dock that night."

Robert was seemingly impressed. It was a large deal. The shipment had contained arms from the Middle East and heroin from Sicily. Of course Giuseppe insisted that Robert arrange to have his fellow police officers remain as far as possible from the evening's activities.

Robert, even found amusement in such words, which were not even necessary to point out. "Well, I certainly will not be issuing out any invitations!" They both laughed.

But Rowan just revealed a sly grin. Of course, he also insisted that Robert be there himself personally to make sure that the operation ran smoothly. Giuseppe and his son also would be in attendance to supervise the exchange. When Robert parted company from them, he knew that this scam was coming to a head, that this was the greatly-large sting operation that was going to cast the Castalones into oblivion.

Sicilian-born, ageing, underworld Mob Boss, Giuseppe Castalone said to his son inconspicuously, as he motioned his eyes around all the guests of the restaurant, watching to see if anyone was looking at their direction, "Robert is a strong man who has proved to us his loyalty, even charmed us into believing in him. But one thing we must remember when dealing with Robert is, never to underestimate him. Both his cunning and his charm must be always seen as traps." Here he began to ponder the stories that people used to say about Robert: Causing so many seizures of their operations via numerous raids. Destroying so many crime bosses; and creating so many big sting operations. His rise in the police department was sworn to be spectacular. But believing in himself, wholeheartedly, that he was the only man who could convert Robert Stewart; he saw truth in what people used to preach. That: 'Everyone had a price'. - Even a man as Robert Stewart. There was no exception to that rule.

Once the waiter approached their table and asked for their menu, Giuseppe ordered a bottle of red wine, claret, and two dishes of spaghetti bolognaise. As soon as he finished writing their orders and paced himself away from their table, Giuseppe stared at the waiter suspiciously at the same time as he added, "Stewart has escalated swiftly through the ranks to the top of his police profession, not because of his smooth jokes and charismatic manner, but because he is a professional in his field. He is a very clever and dangerous man, a man with many friends. Even in politics. Robert's men and his acquaintances are especially loyal and dedicated to him. We must never overlook any loophole where he is concerned. We must account for everything; every possible trap meanwhile that could be set up for us. I mean, who knows, perhaps the restaurant staff could be his plants, we must always be on guard; anybody anywhere could be that man's ally!" He stared at the waiter with cold malicious eyes; when he disappeared inside the kitchen to inform the chef to prepare two orders of spaghetti bolognaise, before Giuseppe had revoked the stare to his son. "In fact, where a man like Stewart is concerned, one must even suspect his own children."

Rowan, who did not take offence, as the thought was inconceivable, painted a picture in his mind of the true meaning of his father's comment. Renee. For Robert had won her with his charm - and with that alone, Robert would be a dangerous man should he turn traitor.

Rowan replied, "Yes. Stewart is certainly a master at his profession. He has certainly convinced us of his 'apparent' goodwill. But as you said father, no matter how smooth and no matter how clean he appears from the surface, we will never remove our eyes from him, never!"

Giuseppe nodded in agreement. "Yes. He is one outsider who has come close to winning my trust, which is a virtual impossibility for any outsider to accomplish. We must never lower our guard for even a moment where he is concerned!"

And now knowing what he had to know, Robert Stewart and Alfonse Lorenzo met secretly to discuss particulars of the bust planned to go without a hitch. And whilst the deal was going through, suddenly the dock would be surrounded by police back-up witnessing the exchange. And the back-up would then coordinate the dirty work of all the arrests and seizures.

Robert, inconspicuously aware of the Castalone surveillance imposed on him, checked for bugs constantly. And as a professional, found the bugs planted, but never removed them. He never hinted that he knew. It only aided his cause. When he knew his home and car were bugged, he spoke to his co-conspirators; Chief Gordon and Alfonse outside. And inside, he would speak of his undying friendship and loyalty to the Castalone family. And would even be heard cancelling functions with his children to tend to more important business, the Castalone business.

And once he learnt of the drug deal coming through, he had arranged a secret meeting with Alfonse in an abandoned warehouse on the Brooklyn dock; Robert briefed him on everything. "We must be extremely careful. I don't want Giuseppe to be tipped off in any way and suddenly change piers on us for the drug bust."

And following the Castalone family arrests, the daughter Renee was in fact more relieved than anything else. She never really participated in the family business, nor approved of it. Though attempts were made to keep its truth from her, she could not help but be aware of it all, especially when she accidentally listened to unscrupulous conversations taking place with perky looking hoods that came to the house to meet her brother and father, behind closed doors. Only her brother was close-linked to the family operation. But she never interfered. For her father's mind had worked differently to others, a trait rubbed off on Rowan. If people in business who were not blood-related betrayed him, the ultimate result was death. And it made her think twice how seriously he would take a betrayal in the immediate family. His temper was ferocious and lethal. And when this temper was aroused by those petty little men on his payroll, she only felt frantic to the possible reaction if one of his own children turned traitor and put their life against his. He would not say that he did not want to know her, or that she was dead to him, despite all his talk that she was his princess. He would have her killed without a moment's thought.

Giuseppe was scared of no one. He had killed one police officer in his lifetime; perhaps, he killed even a hundred, even police captains and commanders. Without even a hint of concern over the risk, or the uproar a high-ranking police officer's assassination would cause.

Following such deaths, should more police commence breathing down his neck, he would shrug it off. As if their entire investigation would prove faulty. And if they did not stop, he would say, "Well, I'll kill them all."

She knew this by what he did to her mother. Giuseppe's wife, though forced into the arranged marriage, thought she could change him. She could not help, but learn of his evil ways. With refusal to tolerate them, she left him, wanted to divorce him. He then refused permission for any of the children to see her ever again. If they disobeyed his orders, he pointed out that they would be punished. He even destroyed all pictures of her that he had in the house; in photo albums, in the children's bedrooms. If anyone ever mentioned her name to anyone, especially in his presence, they would live to regret it.

The day Giuseppe's wife left she first told her children the story that she had of their father. She wanted to warn her children to never follow in their father's footsteps. So they would never become like him. She knew after this day she would never be able to see her children again, so she could only hope to give them one last message. That was concerning an event which took place a long time ago, when their grandfather was alive, Frank Castalone. He was very sick. He was old. Already suffered two serious heart attacks, and he had only six months to live. By now Giuseppe was groomed to take over the family business. But Giuseppe was impatient. He did not want to wait six months to claim his rightful power in the family business as heir. Giuseppe was forty-two at the time. He considered that he was already starting his power late and did not want to get any older.

So he had hired two killers to threaten Senior Castalone with guns in a violent struggle. Not to kill him with the guns, but to force that weak heart of his into another attack. And this one was fatal. And after he died, Giuseppe was now the new boss. And when he was greeted inside his own home by all such important rich men whom she read in the newspapers were crime bosses, their faces plastered everywhere; who lowered their heads down at him in greeting, as if they considered themselves less powerful, she knew he was the man who killed his father. Especially when he had waited one month after the fact to prepare his father's funeral, leaving his corpse to remain frozen in a box for weeks, as his soul must have been turning. And then she approached Giuseppe and said, "You killed your own father. You forced him into another heart attack to cover your tracks and claim your power right away."

Frank Castalone was much like a father also to her. He was the only father she knew. And without any concern to make denials, Giuseppe grabbed her jaw with his right hand to cut her ravings and brazenly shouted. "Enough. You should feel very lucky that I feel for you what I do, because if a man said that to me, he would not be able to talk again." Anyway, she learnt of the horror that her husband was, and of course, as any concerned mother, she warned her children to keep clear away from him. By then, they were still young teenagers, still impressionable. He was a man who was capable of killing his own flesh and blood; his own wife and children.

15

As she sought her independence far away from him, Giuseppe's people had soon located her and returned her to his house. He kept her as a prisoner in their own home for over five years and defied her attempts to leave him. He put locks on the doors in a separate compartment away from where their children could reach her. It was similar to an annex type facility. He also fixed the room so that it was fully manned and soundproofed, with a guard tending to her food. She was under a watchful eye, twenty-four hours a day. And at night, her bedroom door would be locked. And he made sure that any conversations with the children, only to be conducted under strict supervision, spelled good words of him. And that she was to tell the children that the evil story she told of him was a lie.

One time the door was left unlocked. She left the house for one week only to return to say goodbye to the children. She knew divorce was out of the question. He would never be seen in court over such petty disposition, he would right off as a little shameful act.

Having been inside the study, one of the bodyguards alerted him of her presence, when Giuseppe told her to let go of the children. That she was never to see them again. He instantly slammed the door on her face. His driver then escorted her to a mysterious destination, where after that day no one heard of her again. When the children asked where their mother was, Giuseppe only shrugged his shoulders, as if answering it were a chore, and said coldly, "She left. She's no good. You have no mother." Her worst fears had come true. She could see from an early age a lot of Giuseppe in Rowan, but not Renee. She thought of herself and her pure angel-faced daughter as two rabbits that had fallen prey to a bunch of wolves. Giuseppe was the master wolf and Rowan was formed into the same spit as his father. And now her children were going to grow up with Giuseppe, under his influence. And the inevitable evil that they would consecutively be succumbed to thereafter was irrevocable.

And it was recently that Renee could see the truth of her father in what her mother told them before she left. And she now felt safe that there was some good powerful force out there that freed her from the life of seclusion and fear and loneliness she was thrown into.

And these were the series of events which led to the Castalone family arrests - scheduled to face trial. Where if convicted, they could face up to life imprisonment, which made Robert Stewart a force to be reckoned with, and secured his promotion to Captain. New York, being the major city in the country torn by guerrilla warfare and underworld strife, had driven Robert Stewart's primary goal to destroy these criminal elements' internal secure empires, and to create a Mob-Free environment for the city and the nation as a whole.

16

CHAPTER 2

Robert Stewart had taken extra precautions on his safety as well as the safety of his family pending the Castalone trial. He insisted that round-the-clock police guards be placed on all members of his family. He also checked to make sure that reliable undercover plainclothes police guards were posted outside his home and his children's school, keeping an eye out for their safety. They would remain inconspicuous, so not to alarm the children of their presence. And having Alfonse Lorenzo's people in addition, coordinating security on his family was a great comfort knowing their safety was secure on that end too, prepared for any Castalone retaliation. That was possibly being prepared meanwhile, until he could come home and be with them. For he spent hours overnight debriefing the police reports of the Castalone case with the district attorney, at the 25th division downtown station house precinct. He missed his children terribly.

Robert also arranged for his door locks to be changed, and his windows resecured. And he would check his phones and home for listening devices that could still be planted by the nervous Castalones, edgy that the authorities had closed in on their turf, penetrating their security. That was all cautious paths a wise law-enforcement official as Robert always eventuated.

Robert left the station house precinct to go to his home after work, where the children made plans to stay at friends this evening, to study for upcoming school tests. When he dropped them off on 6th Avenue, Robert kissed each of them, who embraced their father proud of him and his recent promotion. And before he said a word, Robert's son stated, knowing it was Robert's forceful habit or cliché to ask, nonetheless, answering the question before it was put forward, "We'll be fine dad. We'll take care!"

Robert put his arm around his son's neck in a fatherly embrace, and rubbed his knuckles on his hair and said, "I keep saying it because no one loves their kids as much as I do!"

His daughter then embraced him and said, "We love you too dad!"

Robert, prior driving home said to his son, "You take care of your sister now!"

Renee Castalone had prepared a surprise celebration for Robert over his promotion as Captain for once he returned home. She found out about it when she called the station house precinct earlier to speak to Robert; she was told by the desk sergeant that he was also tied up with the new commissioner concerning a promotion. And she waited outside in her car, and when Robert arrived at his home, she made herself be known, holding a cake she baked for him. Which she too had it known that she rarely cooks for anyone. So Robert should feel flattered.

They each had a couple of slices of chocolate cake and sat down beside the open fireplace Robert had fixed inside the living room, and she comforted him as he explained his preoccupied state of mind. His numbness towards his family's security in matters such as Mob-related cases, which had his promotion marred somewhat, by the fear of his family being in danger. As over the years he lost many good friends on the police force in supposed freak accidents. The most recent loss became Commissioner Gordon simultaneously with the city's Mayor, who were gunned down outside City Hall by a drive-by shooting. The assailants left the scene unapprehended. Witnesses reported the car registration number plates were laminated, unrecognisable. And before that day was through, seven further traffic cops were gunned down in cold-blood, in various other districts in Brooklyn as well. All on the same day, whilst performing their rounds - killed in similar fashion by a drive-by shooting. And the assailants before long were arrested; and to everyone's surprise, they even confessed to the specific double killings. And made no denials to the further police deaths reported that day as well. Some gun-toting, reckless, stoned punks, it was alleged, were responsible for the killings of such high-profile members of the community. It appeared just a random senseless mass slaughter. It was just too unbelievably clean and open-and-shut. The case was wrapped up far too easy. Nonetheless, with so many of his police and political colleagues being wiped out over the years, through one means or the other, Robert developed much suspicion over the true cause to such mysterious deaths. And they also discussed the preliminary hearing of her father scheduled tomorrow morning.

The next morning was Giuseppe and Rowan Castalone's preliminary hearing. From the local prison lockup facility, Robert and armed police escorted the two defendants' downtown in a police squad car to the Brooklyn Supreme Courthouse for the hearing.

The Castalone defendants', in suit and tie, met with their defence attorney, and Robert and Alfonse were seated in the prosecuting section of the courtroom among the District Attorney and his assistant, who had their heads buried in a stack of reports made out of the case, to bring forward to the judge.

Though the evidence was mounted against the Castalones, Robert had seen it happen a lot in his experience as a police official. People he knew were innocent were sent to jail, and even those he knew, beyond any doubt, were guilty, went free. And it was because of the system that was created to be followed, that led Robert to mounting pressure via his friends in politics to be constantly reviewing old, inadequate laws - and look to strengthen legislatures

18

against its many loopholes; to further his progress in nailing criminals as these who mocked the judicial system, time and time again.

In the hearing, the judge found enough substantial evidence to warrant a trial for the two defendants', whom, despite attempts by the Castalone defence attorney present, had lost the bid, in which the judge ruled Giuseppe would be held in custody without bail, until a trial date would be set.

Though his father was to be remanded in custody until the trial, Rowan Castalone was out on bail. His defence attorney made it a point that Rowan, close-mouthed to his father's business, was not a threat to society, as Giuseppe was accused of being. And that his actions were only that of self-defence for his father. And he was not responsible for the founding of any illegal activities, nor a willing participant to any of them. And despite a strong case being presented, the prosecution lost its bid to keep Rowan in custody as well, without bail, pending the trial.

Because there were no witnesses who could swear that Rowan Castalone had in fact committed murder as accused, and no one had seen him, he was to remain free until the trial.

Robert eyed Alfonse, who made his disagreement in the judge's decision there known. Robert concurred, though displayed a cooler approach to the decision, and sobered Alfonse to act as such. And not give those criminals the satisfaction of any displays of anger. Besides, they got the old man locked up on enough sufficient evidence, where in the trial, they would both have to be struck with the devil's luck alone to avoid receiving life sentences each, with Alfonse as a star witness for the prosecution, against the defence.

But, even with Rowan out on bail, and Giuseppe still in prison, it yet posed a great threat. Unfortunately, the district attorney was unable to convince the judge of it.

Rowan would be able to see his father and still carry out his orders on the outside. And there was the likeliness that Rowan would skip bail, leave the country entirely following his likely retaliation, and not even attend the trial.

And the judge took all this into consideration and because of the severity and seriousness of the charges, the judge set bail higher. It was set at ten million dollars, and would only be returned following Rowan Castalone's presence in the courtroom for that trial. Robert, in himself, scorned at the judge. For no price of bail was too high for such a criminal. Ten million or one hundred million dollars was negligible. It made no real difference. The Castalones had enough money and influence, yet, of their own, at their disposal, despite its sizeable losses incurred so far via the police raids and whatnot, to recoup such losses in no time, and start afresh, only a new base of criminal operations, if only given the chance.

Once they were escorted back to the local station house lockup facility, Rowan was taken to the prison conference room, a room where clients were able to confer with their attorneys in private, where the police guard gave him some papers to sign. His lawyer was present, with a cheque already made out in Rowan's name. The guard handed Rowan a bond release form to sign, agreeing to all the conditions. The guard said, "If you skip the trial you forfeit the ten million!"

After Rowan signed the forms the guard had taken them, Rowan looked at him, "It's all signed, meaning I'm free to walk, right?"

The guard gave him his copy of the forms, and before he left he said, "See you in court." And his lawyer patted Rowan on the back as they both followed suit, only to find Robert posted in the hallway staring at him coldly. And without any word said, Rowan made a swift exit.

The next night, Rowan Castalone went to see his father in prison. Now being on the outside, watching his father in prison blues, definitely he found were not his style or colour. They were separated by a large iron soundproofed glass window, only to be heard by a prison phone on each side. Rowan knew it was up to Robert to release and drop the charges against his father. But since he would not, he was keen on retaliating.

"I promise you father, when the time is right, I will kill him. And then I am going to take care of all the witnesses, because there is not going to be a trial. And there isn't going to be a conviction. In the meantime, I will do whatever I can to get the business off the ground again, so when you get out, things are a little bit pleasant. But our loss of millions from the purchase, from the raids and in seizures, well, the business is hardly a business anymore. Our powerbase is weak. We cannot even fight our enemies. Father, the Castalone family and its allies may become for sale to another family. That's how weak we have become, no thanks to Stewart, who will be finished just as quickly as he has finished us!"

Before long, Rowan, who was thinly built, though dynamically stoic in appearance had arranged a meeting with his key lieutenants and soldiers. He explained that since his scaring tactics did not work, to be prepared for the signal to spring out more bloodshed. Targets were the trial witnesses against the Castalone family. If the charges were not dropped before the commencement of the trial, then all the witnesses must be made to die before that trial begins, so there would not be a trial. And his father would be released from prison on insufficient evidence, and there would be no case against the Castalones.

The people on trial, being proven to be a threat to society, and all that was just, have been making threats against Robert Stewart, backed up by telephoned death threats, and to the people he loved as well; its purpose, so he would drop the charges and release Giuseppe Castalone from prison. But Robert would not budge. And until the trial was over and they had a solid conviction on the Castalones, everyone had to stick by their guard. And more round-the-clock protection was initiated.

20

A surprise turns of events lopsided the Castalones faith in loyalty, even more so, when it became known that Renee had also accepted to testify against her father and brother, at Robert's request. And when they learnt that she was still lusting over Robert, even after what he was doing to her family, and the way Robert turned her against them, they took it as a gross betrayal and turned her out, without any money. Robert, knowing this, was prepared to offer her a sizeable amount of monetary compensation even, for her testimony. She accepted. But she wanted him in exchange.

The next day, Alfonse Lorenzo made personal contact with Robert inside his home. He had just learnt from his contact also in liaison with the Castalone emissaries, a messenger for both sides, that the Mob had put a special contract out on him, and had hired a professional hit man to do the job. His family and all witnesses to the trial were also feared in danger.

Robert understood that this Mob was still able to run their business from behind bars, especially with Rowan on the outside carrying out orders, he was still a threat. A threat that could only end once his trial led to a conviction, and he was thrown for life in a federal penitentiary; isolated from any contact with the outside world.

That evening, Robert saw Giuseppe in prison, and gave him a stern warning. One of the utmost of seriousness: "You send any of your hit man swine anywhere near me, my family, my friends, even casual acquaintances - I am going to forget that I am a police officer, and I am going to remove each and every one of you Castalones from the face of this earth, personally!" Robert then smiled, his famous ironical smile, "You can count on that!"

After his encounter with Giuseppe Castalone in prison, Robert went straight to his office to attempt his investigation into the most recent Mayor's and Commissioner Gordon's fatal assassinations.

Robert studied documents of the former Mayor's history and his suspected involvement in the Mafia. It was believed, that prior his assassination, he resigned his standing as leader in his next election, due to either being forced out, or turning his back from allegiance to the Mob, thus they made a threat on his life. Despite some opinions to the contrary, Robert was to pursue the lead that the former Mayor was under Mafia patronage, to the point that the Mafia backed his political campaigns, with the support of the local newspapers, and even fixed his elections. That perhaps, robbed his opponent of a well-deserved victory.

Robert questioned colleagues close to the deceased, but sensed evasive behaviour. And departed company, only thanking them for their time, and indicating his questions were all answered, and he would no longer require their assistance.

21

Robert returned moments later to City Hall, with a stream of police officers, and John McCallum. Only to find in the hands of the deceased Mayor's colleagues', boxes, of ballot papers that they presumed to destroy before a shredder, in a room opposite the former Mayor's office. The boxes contained ballot papers that were rigged, fixing the election. Upon the Mayor's death, and Robert's investigation into it, they planned on shredding, and then burning the ballot papers of evidence that proved Robert's hunch of a conspiracy made to fix the former Mayor's election was correct. When he returned he found men carrying boxes in an unusual frenzy from a storage room to a shredder. He noticed how desperate they were in dumping these boxes before a shredder being operated, and he felt something amiss was hidden inside there. The police confiscated the evidence and arrested the former Mayor's colleagues at City Hall, only moments before they were to destroy the evidence. Robert did not need a search warrant. Robert did not require a search warrant where people were destroying evidence, as he only assumed they would do so, by their behaviour of suspect and evasiveness to his line of questioning during his initial visit. That alone, had created more than ample reasonable suspicion. So he had thought of everything, thus arresting all co-conspirators involved. And, if the former Mayor was still alive, his title would have been revoked to his opponent.

In prison, members of the former Mayor's support group had received a visit from a high member of the Chess Player's regime, Chief Executive Officer, Kerry Gilbert. The very executive responsible in the Chess Player's buffer, whom such people as those he visited in prison, such as: District Attorneys, Mayors and police, with all their staff, all on family payroll had reported to. He acted as a go-between for the Chess Player, in an extensive buffer system that even separated him from the family's inner circle. For security forbid even Kerry Gilbert himself to know of his employer's true identity, other than that of the Chess Player. Anyhow, he came to remind those colleagues arrested that if they talked, they would be killed. That they were to serve out their full prison sentences cooperatively, and implicate no one else. The Chess Player would not help them. Since they were foolish enough to expose themselves with the evidence, and not destroy it sooner, they would in turn have to pay the consequences. The Chess Player wiped his hands completely from them. The Chess Player was to offer them no help at all. No one was going to risk the exposure of helping them out of prison. They were to serve their sentences in silence. And should they, so much as even mention the codename of the Chess Player in connection to any of this, their punishment would be a lot worse than that of a prison life confinement.

Police on the Mob payroll were also supposed to give protection to such members of Mafia allegiance, such as Politicians, Mayors and District Attorneys. And support them in upcoming elections. But when Robert witnessed the evidence of ballot papers, they were powerless to prevent such an action, as Robert did not apply for a search warrant. He gave no forewarning, so the police could not tip their political counterparts within the Mob payroll to destroy all of the evidence, before he had arrived.

Robert just went back to the station house office, rounded up the men available, and took them with him. Did not even tell them where he was going. They just followed him until they had arrived at the office of City Hall officials, where ballot papers were hidden. And in turn, they were forced to arrest their own co-conspirators they were otherwise paid to protect. Robert's way of handling investigations left very little loopholes for reaction by these criminal figures. His methods proved very successful in law-enforcement.

That was how he had escalated through the ranks of the police department so swiftly, to become Captain, armed with the highest-grading arrest and conviction rate ever.

Though no one talked of their alleged superiors, who were in fact bankrolling them, Robert suspected from this moment on, widespread corruption of Mafia involvement. Not only in the former late Mayor's cabinet, but throughout politics in general, and on all levels, just as Commissioner Gordon had only explained too well, prior his untimely demise. Perhaps, many other politicians had their elections fixed for allegiance to some unknown sinister power above them as well.

Following his findings, Robert returned to the station house to alert newly-appointed Chief Commissioner Jeffrey Baits, to reopen Commissioner Gordon's assassination case file, to further investigate alleged foul play.

Robert sensed something amiss, something more to the assassination than just a random drive-by shooting by punks who were recently arrested for the crime and the case closed thereon. That there was perhaps a vendetta against him and other members of the force, by powers higher up, than a simple case of delinquent random shootings. That his findings of fixed ballot papers linked the former Mayor's assassination to retaliation via supposed Mafia involvement. And Commissioner Gordon's assassination was instigated due to his findings as such. Hence, these powers removed him and any other police official not in allegiance to them.

The chief swayed his head, from side to side, and smirked at Robert's outspoken theory. Making it appear as though he really had nothing to go on. That it was as hard to believe as a fictitious novel. There really was no proof in his assessment of the situation. That it was only an illusion. He claimed his accusations showed deep holes in logic. As if his reasoning only stemmed from strange feelings that was best to have shaken out from his head.

Nonetheless, Robert insisted, "I want to reopen the case."

The commissioner lifted his head from a stack of reports on his desk, and said, "Now, my dear fellow. The assailants were captured, and are dead. The case is closed. We cannot waste manpower chasing up leads that simply do

23

not exist. Your findings of alleged ballot papers are also over. No one has talked of powers higher above dictating their illegal actions to some conspiracy. So, the case is closed. There's no linkage between the two crimes - finished."

Robert knew if it were Commissioner Gordon he had confronted right now, he would have jumped at the chance to pursue these valid theories. But Robert, for the first time in his career, realised that as a police officer of the law, his hands were tied. However, he still persisted, "Look, don't you find it strange that a bunch of hoodlums robbing the former Mayor's home on the night before his and Commissioner Gordon's assassination had managed to also kill as many other police officers that they could muster that very same day of their murders across the city's borough? These people were not robbers. They were not joint smokers. They are bloody assassins. It was obvious that they were more interested in killing police and the Mayor, than anything else, disguising the freak attacks or their motive, as a burglary gone wrong, perhaps. As if not to leave witnesses behind after the fact. All initiated by these powers unknown, setting up scapegoats to conceal a very sinister conspiracy lurking around us. Come on Chief. Aren't you concerned that there is a conspiracy against the police and the Mayor? That the Mayor was a target! After all, a call came into the station on the morning of the Mayor's public resignation, deliberately informing Chief Gordon of this. He attends City Hall to personally warn the Mayor himself, and outside he is killed and so is the Mayor. And seven other police officers, other good cops in the firing line also targeted in the city that day. Making it appear as burglaries and random killings by doped punks who were stoned out of their minds. So then the case is closed-"

The chief, appearing uninterested, said, "Now, what makes you say that?"

Robert replied, "Evidence at the scene. The morning of his assassination the call stated that the Mayor would be victim to a further burglary attack - so why kill him? Why kill the police? For burglars they seemed to act as paid assassins."

"Perhaps," the chief said casually.

Robert said, relieved, "I knew you would see it my way."

The chief interrupted. "Perhaps, they were in a desperate bid to get away and save their own necks. Perhaps, the Mayor knew their identities, and in a bid to avoid prison, they took the chance in shooting him in public. Even in broad daylight. And make a run for it."

Robert laughed at his careless reasoning. "Then, why would they, after the funeral, suddenly confess to the murder, and connected murders that followed, knowing full well what they planned to avoid, would result in at least a life prison sentence, maybe even the death penalty?"

The commissioner acted rather hectic in his reports, sprawled across his desk, and said, "I don't know Robert - maybe an attack of conscience. We both know the criminal element can work in mysterious ways."

Robert further debated. "Then why were they killed in self-defence by police officers after making such open admissions? If they were willing participants to turn themselves in, then why the need for police to react with revolvers in self-defence to kill them, as they were planted in the same prison lockup facility?"

"Robert, I admire your sense of dedication. But - I must say, no. Listen Robert, why pursue this? The conspired robbers are dead, finished. There is no need for an investigation. No need to chase ghosts."

Robert stared at him coldly in the eye, he was so angry he could spit. Robert shot up from his chair, he was enraged, the chief sensed that, and even began trembling. "I got to thinking - what about all those officers in the past year and previous years before that, which were killed in supposed freak accidents? There is only a certain amount of accidents that can take place, Chief. But when they take place too often, it becomes clear! It becomes obvious!"

The middle-aged chief's hands were shaking; he placed them beneath the desk to remain unseen. He felt as though Robert were accusing him. He coughed to relieve the shakiness from his voice, and then spoke, "Robert, my good man. I think that you are manufacturing a problem that simply does not exist!"

Robert snapped, "Well, I don't think so. I suspect a conspiracy here. That perhaps the robbery, all those past and present supposed police accidental deaths - such as twelve police officers dying in a gas explosion in a weapons laboratory last year; another mass group of police dying in a police transport bus accident from a blown tyre and sudden loss of brakes are a set up. I suspect by the Mob. That the Mob is clipping these good cops in their most vulnerable groups, by a leak in the system, a breach in the force, right here - a serious breach in security. That there were others involved!"

The white-haired, lean-featured chief, grunted, "Robert, this is impossible. It is far-fetched and exaggerated. You have insufficient or, lack of a better word, no evidence to back up or substantiate your theories. You have nothing to go on, but endless theories and speculation, with no foundation. Now, I order you to drop this. I would really hate to have a good cop reprimanded or suspended from the force for disobeying orders, and going off on his own to initiate an illegal investigation!" The Chief too rose from his chair and added, "Robert, you are the best police official we have on the force. I would hate to see this stand in the way of our mutual friendship. I hope you understand." He stretched his hand over to Robert, across the desk.

Robert lifted a sceptical eyebrow, now with an ironical smile; he shook his hand and said, "Of course Chief. Of course-" Before he showed himself out of the office.

25

Three months later, the Chief Commissioner Jeffrey Baits would make contact to a high-placed member of the Chess Player's payroll, from his office, in secluded privacy, using his secure untraceable private phone located inside his wall safe in strict secrecy. He picked up his receiver and dialled.

Chief Executive Officer, Kerry Gilbert, who served as his higher-up, though beneath a buffer system that separated himself from the chief council of the inner sanctums of the Chess Player family, answered.

"It's me!" Jeffrey Baits smiled. "I set up the trap and they took the bait. I set up the whole deal, covered my tracks, and in case anyone wishes to investigate the disappearance of the police, they will not find anything. The plane is set to blow once it reaches fifteen thousand feet, with a bomb of such magnitude that it would be beyond recognition. It will explode everything, so there is nothing left to identify, even by the most advanced scientific equipment at our disposal, nowadays. Everything destroyed to ashes. And it will be written off as a plane crash, an accident - another open-and-shut case." The police chief commissioner could hear the man on the other end of the phone laughing. "Yes, your plan was excellent. You were right, sir. There was a way we could have used this mission to our advantage, in order to kill the police, who will fly to Los Angeles to assist in the bust of the Santucci family drug cartel there, that has operated in our city. And because of this, I volunteered the names of certain police officers to fly to Los Angeles to assist FBI and local police officials in the city, in the bust, to further their career ambitions!" the commissioner chuckled.

Once he placed the receiver on the hook, he locked it away inside his safe, and then Commissioner Jeffrey Baits, using his desk phone had ranked for his new lieutenant to enter his office. He wanted him to lead an armed squadron of his men to Los Angeles to meet the police there, on that end. And aid them as back-up, concerning a large drug deal by the Santucci crime family. The local, state and federal authorities were involved as well. This was above the local police jurisdiction, but a federal case. "The government has finished investigating, and since our precinct was responsible for stopping many of the drugs in our city, by the targeted family, they request our professional assistance as back-up, on their ends as well. It is a serious case, and so I have assigned fifteen of our fellow officers to join you!" The chief held a file in his hand and handed it to the lieutenant, bearing those names he wanted assigned to the case.

The chief continued, "Now, I have already made arrangements to have a private plane ready and waiting at the airport, to have you and these men flown to your destination in Los Angeles, and meet the troop as scheduled - any questions?"

The mid-thirties aged, dark-haired lieutenant was clear on his orders, had no questions, and shook his head in gesture to that effect as he sat before him with a pad and pen dutifully taking notes. The police lieutenant would round the men to be assigned to the case - and they would leave immediately.

To plant the explosive device on the plane, the Chief Commissioner Jeffrey Baits debated whether to involve a second person as a careful measure. But basic reasoning prevented him from doing so. Nothing was certain. And should it be profitable for one man to testify in court over the chief's orders this day, it would not be as effective as having two accomplices. One against one meant an equal balance of simply one's word against the other. But a second member, posing as a further witness, would tip the balance unevenly. The results would be dangerous.

Two hours later, a non-commercial flight exploded, shortly after take-off, from the Brooklyn private air terminal, claiming the lives of sixteen police officers, with the pilot. The families to the dead were called in to the airport by police, to make the necessary identifications of flight reservations. There were no survivors. No one knew how the explosion happened. And from that moment after the investigation showed mystery cause, it was ruled an accident.

CHAPTER 3

Three days later marked the trial date commencement for the Castalone family. Robert had woken early that morning, four hours prior the courtroom battle commenced. And his son Ryan also joined his father at 6:00 a.m. in the morning, for their usual routine in their tracksuits of jogging around the block. Robert enjoyed exercising with his son of sixteen years. Sometimes he practised kung fu with his son, and his daughter Stephanie of fourteen years watched. Whenever she could wake up so early she too joined the Stewart ritual, as Robert enjoyed teaching his daughter some self-defence techniques, which may prove handy at one point or another. They always had good times together, and as a close family unit they shared everything. There was nothing too drastic they could not consult their father with. Nothing he could not advice them on. And much like his friends, his children too shared the same sentiment that life was never dull with Robert around, particularly as their loving father.

Having been unfortunate to raise his children most of his life as a single parent, for his wife, the mother to his children deceased of natural causes when they were at a very early age. So they never really knew their mother, though enjoyed the stories Robert would tell them of her, and cherished the family photo album of pictures of the goddess-looking lady who was their mother. Robert, in a bid to fulfil both the duties of a mother and a father in their life, always tried to do what he believed was best for his children on his own, despite missing his beloved wife terribly. Whenever the children's birthdays came up, he always threw big bashful parties with the help of his folks, who helped with the preparations of food and beverage, and of course his children were permitted to invite as many friends as possible. Though Robert always scrutinized them, and made sure their qualities of judgement were as sound as what he had taught them to follow. He always had long conversations with their friends, made them comfortable around him, and was impressed to see how his children's judgement of character was astounding for people at such an early age.

They were good kids, smart kids, always cleaned up after themselves. Stephanie took after her mother; blonde hair, big blue eyes, a warm smile and a face of an angel. Ryan inherited Robert's genes for being the charmer. Only a teenager and he could not keep all the girls away from him. Most nights the phone was ringing, and if not a friend, it was the many girlfriends from his class at school, who he always spent hours in conversation with them, making it very difficult for Robert to work from home. So he got his own private line in his study, in case of any important calls, personal or professional, of a police nature.

Above all, he could not ask for better children. And sometimes found himself after a rough day in the office, sitting alone in the lounge, sipping on some brandy or wine, preferably beer, when he arrived home late and his children were asleep, before he turned in himself. He relaxed on the sofa and turned the stereo hi-fi on, and played his favourite tunes, whilst his mind drifted away to happier thoughts, forgetting the savage brutality of the other side of the world he dealt with at the station house. For at home, his mind was conjured up by happy thoughts, and serene memories of his children and of their mother. But despite her unfortunate passing, he would always relax on the leather sofa, rest his head back on the cushion, holding a drink in one hand and allowing the pieces of music to bring out his emotions of personal satisfaction - as he thought how lucky he was to be blessed with such wonderful and beautiful and intelligent children. That he looked up to the ceiling and smiled, allowing the music to play happy thoughts on his mind, and forget the trauma of his police life for a moment as he thought: "The world is a beautiful place."

Robert began his family at the early age of twenty-one. He was now thirty-seven years old. Robert's children and his family were his inspiration. They were the reason he did everything he did. They became his motivation to work and struggle through life to make their inherited world a better and safer place for them to grow up in, in a much easier and peaceful environment, with more of the good influences and less of the bad around, as from experience he realised how the imbalances of that pendulum could make one's life very difficult.

Sometimes in the morning, Robert looked forward to waking up early and spending the quality time with his children, which sometimes were few and far between because of his busy police schedule. In the summer, he enjoyed swimming with them, taking them on the pier for some fishing and taking them to the family summer house. Teaching his son and even his daughter how to use an air gun in target practise - setting up beer cans metres away as a target, and letting the children rest the barrel onto his shoulder, as he knelt before them, as they took aim and fired. He enjoyed playing archery with them, kicking a football with them, helping them in soccer practise for school tournaments. And early in the morning he thrived on being with them before he faced the horrors of this world down at the station house precinct, which also helped him achieve perspective and much needed objectivity on the work front.

He loved talking to them and exercising with them, enjoyed jogging as well as teaching them martial arts. Where he often laughed at how Ryan gave Stephanie brotherly jokes of her ill imitation to the art form. And watched how her big brother corrected her and looked out for her. Robert could not help, but feel a sense of pride in how he brought them up, as his own father taught him when he was a child as well. One golden rule Robert always taught his children was to love your family first and foremost. And always be close, because when it boiled down to who was going to be there for them in the hard times, it was family more than anybody else, that special bond, that closeness that only a family could share.

And Robert felt impressed how quickly his children absorbed his teachings. How he admired them for being good kids, and how relieved he felt that they were brought up in a neighbourhood that was still much safer than during his time growing up, surrounded and threatened by the spreading and overcrowding of gangs and warfare on the street, that Robert fought as a child living with his parents on the waterfront. Their life was much simpler. They were luckier. Everything he wanted, everything he worked for in cleansing his neighbourhood was for his family, to make that dream come to reality.

His kids not only were good kids, but they always brought home above-satisfactory grades from school to show their father, who always helped them with their homework when he was home early. But, because of his unpredictable profession and its often enduring long hours, after his wife passed away, he hired a maid to help out with the children and treat them in a way that a mother would. Though she was of middle age group, Robert thought it would have been appropriate that the children have a female role member in the house to talk to and influence them. And even though she was a substitute, unable to fulfil the role to their real mother, she always acted the role of the substitute by helping them in ways a mother would.

She did the cooking, the cleaning, and the housework for the children as she had taken up residence in one of the spare guest bedrooms.

After they finished their morning ritual exercises of physical fitness, they each waited their turn to enter the shower, Ryan always telling his sister to hurry up and stop spending hours dollying herself up, and not to finish the hot water.

Then they each assembled and had breakfast that the maid had ready for them on the breakfast table, which comprised of cereal and orange juice for the children, or bacon and eggs, or their favourite; sometimes pancakes and jam, cream and honey, that Robert and sometimes the children enjoyed making.

After breakfast, Ryan and Stephanie would head off for school, as Robert usually had dropped them off on his way to the station house, or sometimes if he was on a stakeout that kept him away most of the night, or he had to leave very early in the morning, the maid would drop them off and pick them up after school finished. Or they would sometimes take the bus home.

Robert inside the car started the engine. He wore a formal suit and tie for this morning's courtroom proceedings. Waited for his son and daughter to jump in, Ryan and Stephanie always took turns as to who sat in the front passenger seat next to their father. And enjoyed the conversation on the way to his work that he had with his children, forgetting for a brief moment of the sheer toughness of the day that was bound to follow in that courtroom, when he became one of the star witnesses against the very members of this society that he could not understand how it could be so terrifying, and inside his car right now the atmosphere was so peaceful. How could life offer such extremes?

The Castalone trial was scheduled for the morning. And members of both sides of the defence and prosecution were scheduled to assemble inside the Brooklyn Supreme Courthouse, courtroom number 2, at 10:00 a.m., for the formal proceedings.

Robert pursued all avenues necessary to prevent the list of jurors from being bribed, by what he believed were a bunch of desperate Castalones, as he found bugs still planted inside his car.

Judge Ernie Bells ascended before his place in the courtroom. This morning Alfonse Lorenzo, the major key witness for the prosecution was scheduled to testify. Everyone took their rightful places inside the courtroom, except for Alfonse, who was absent as yet, and murmurs and crosstalk between Robert and Larry Circle, the District Attorney, was the result of bad vibes. Alfonse Lorenzo had police protection, round-the-clock; they should have brought him here by now. In fact, he should have been the first to arrive. Suddenly a policeman approached with some disturbing news to present to the District Attorney and Robert.

He reported the dead body of Alfonse Lorenzo being spotted inside his bedroom, a supposed overdose of sleeping pills. Robert knew that someone, perhaps a corrupt or bogus member of his security team had entered Lorenzo's room at night, and forced those pills down his mouth. The autopsy report was bound to prove this, but nonetheless, due to these events, the court was adjourned for tomorrow morning, until the prosecution, now in limbo, was able to reschedule its next witnesses, and prepare its next lines of questioning. This left smiling faces on Giuseppe and Rowan Castalone.

Judge Bells went to console with a stack of papers inside his Judge's chambers and conferred with counsellors to both parties; of the defence and prosecution attorneys, to examine what happened, and ensure that they still had witnesses for tomorrow.

The next morning, Robert called upon Renee Castalone, their greatest key witness next to Alfonse. After Alfonse's tragic demise, Robert had tripled security around himself, his family and the rest of the witnesses. Renee was scared to testify as she knew that her father would not tolerate anyone who betrayed him. No matter whom it was. He would kill his brother, his sister, even his own children; anyone, who betrayed him.

But until they entered the courtroom, Robert had to play this one very carefully, to prevent this witness from also being assassinated.

So leading a decoy witness through the Courthouse hallways; a policewoman disguised as Renee, wearing sunglasses and a wig, knowing taps were placed inside his car, Robert made the call from his car phone, so that the Castalone members would listen, and informed his police partner John McCallum that he would be leading Renee inside the courtroom. But behind the scenes, Robert had informed Renee of the set up put into place to spring out any assassins. He arranged for Renee to be brought inside the courtroom disguised as a police officer. Robert led the decoy through the hallways, posing as the Castalone daughter and key witness to this morning's courtroom proceeding, acting nervous, and trying to hide her face.

Suddenly a man, resembling an ordinary member of the press, prowling the hallway outside the courtroom, had quickly appeared before them, pointed a gun at the decoy woman, conceding it was Renee, ready to shoot, until Robert and other fellow police officials dressed as plainclothesmen, all in readiness, had pointed their guns at him. The gunman surrendered, and police immediately confiscated his weapon, then arrested him, and had taken him away.

Robert radioed a patrol car outside and said, "Bring her in."

Renee Castalone was then brought inside the courtroom surrounded by five policemen. She turned to her father, who looked shocked, and his defence attorney whispered to him, "But I thought she was supposed to be killed?" But Giuseppe ordered him to hush as she was led to the stand, to be sworn under oath by the bailiff and commence her testimony, following the District Attorney's line of questioning.

An interesting, though not so surprising turn of events had precipitated the morning's proceedings, to members of the prosecution, and Robert, when it was revealed that Rowan Castalone made no attempt to appear in this morning's proceedings. Thus, he chose to skip bail. Robert instructed that an immediate search be put out on him, and turned to John to coordinate a nationwide All Points Bulletin (APB), on the man.

Nonetheless, Rowan not showing up at the courthouse this morning was suspected because of Renee's involvement. That perhaps he would show once members of the family clan reported their other greatest threat was eliminated. But since a yet, very frightened Renee Castalone was still willing and able to testify, he chose the alternative of not showing. He, no doubt predicted the outcome to the trial's events as not favourable for him, considering, and chose to rather live life as a fugitive on the run, than live out his days in a federal penitentiary with his father.

Rowan's absence inside the courtroom today proved a further disadvantage to him and his father's case. As this serious breach of his bail conditions would be considered as a major first impression in the jury's minds: If he was not guilty he would not have anything to fear.

Old man Giuseppe's defence attorney knew now that with the remainder of the witnesses still unaccounted for, Giuseppe was finished. Perhaps he should have struck a deal with the District Attorney. Somehow by entering a plea of guilty, at least, he could have given his son a chance. Rowan may still not have gotten off scot-free, but, he may have only had to serve a minimal sentence, with early parole. And he could have been out on probation in only a few years, and saved the hassle of a long destructive trial. But now he faced a life sentence if captured, to join his father. Though not admitting to his face, his own attorney was disappointed in his padrone's failure to correct the situation, and thus feared his own future could be affected once Giuseppe was convicted. He would be out of employment. No income, especially with what little was left of the family business, now placed on the market for his competitors to swallow. Thus, it may leave himself, even as defence attorney and house-counsel to the Castalone family, without food on the table to feed his wife and children; as no one would hire a known corrupt attorney, who served under convicted heinous murderer, among other things, Giuseppe Castalone.

Though, either way, Giuseppe would have to serve a hefty prison sentence. At least, he could have saved his son Rowan's freedom, which perhaps, could have recuperated the family business to continue its line into the next generation. But instead, his choice left an inevitable result. He was about to lose everything: The family business, his freedom, his power, his heirs and his respect. And thinking in terms of selfish reasons, his counsellor knew that once his serving client of many years went down, he would send him and the rest of his people straight to hell with him. As far as he was concerned, the life he left for his son and the rest of his family, they all may as well be sent to join Giuseppe in rotting in prison. That he concluded at this very moment, prison would not be far worse than the life he left for them on the outside.

With the remaining witnesses unaccounted for, ready and willing to testify against Giuseppe, the Kingpin of the Castalone crime family was bound to prove lethal. And this day marked the end of the Castalone era, which had taken generations to build and years to amass its former glory. And today it was all dismantled as rapidly as if it had never existed.

At that moment Judge Bells entered the courtroom. The bailiff instructed the court's members to rise, and when the judge ascended in his place, he himself instructed the people to be seated. Everything appeared to be in order for today's second attempt to try Giuseppe Castalone for drug and arms deals and several counts of murder.

The prosecution introduced the case to the jury, the judge and the courtroom's members, prior to his line of questioning, and said: "You the jury, and the judge, and I, the prosecutor, and those members of the police force, who brought this disease here this day, are right now taking up roles as surgeons. Surgeons, that by the end of our examination, you-the jury will come to the same conclusion, how important it is to cut the Castalone malignant cancer from our society, and isolate this malignancy, so it cannot spread its diseased tentacles to those innocent people we cross paths with everyday on the street any longer. And you the jury must supply us with the tools we need to castrate that Castalone form of cancer!"

Along with Renee Castalone and Robert Stewart's damning testimonies, two Castalone witnesses on the Castalone drug bust also found on the pier, which were arrested at the same time as Rowan and Giuseppe Castalone, and summoned to court via plea bargains were pressured to become witnesses. They had testified how they were drug dealers for the Castalones illegally-imported white-powdered merchandise: How Giuseppe Castalone, with no buffers involved, had supplied them with drugs and arms and orders to kill people, as they served as his soldiers. And many more witnesses forming deals with police in exchange for lighter sentences spoke against Giuseppe and his son, in damning testimonies, proving the sheer brutality and ferocity of these people, which was enough to put nails in the coffins of both defendants, present and otherwise. And throughout the trial, the very absent Rowan Castalone was too proven to be in on his father's crimes, as an accessory, and ruthless aider in drugs and multiple counts of murder, sharing an equal amount of complicity as his father.

Renee Castalone would testify of her family history; her mother's findings and suspected disappearance; and how her home was constantly surrounded by shady characters in very tense situations and confronting stressful conversations.

Robert, as a member of the law and actively participating against the growing drug problem, a drug problem the Castalones had otherwise participated in its creation; found that it was no longer a problem, but an epidemic. He testified how Giuseppe, being a major supplier of drugs, had sold his merchandise even to kid drug dealers, who in turn had sold the drugs to their friends, and even their brothers and sisters to become addicts and potential customers. Stopping the Castalones would indeed help, though it was up to the jury to make the difference to their society.

The judge ruled a recess, to reconvene after fifty minutes.

In conclusion to weeks of trial and concrete testimony by the prosecution, given unstable testimony by the defence, today, in the court's final standing, each awaited the jury's deliberations for a verdict decision.

Everyone assembled in their places inside the courtroom, as the twelve jury members came to a decision. And the bailiff showed them inside from their jury deliberating room, following the judge's direction.

The foreman juror rose and answered the judge's question that indeed he had reached a verdict.

It was folded on a piece of paper, which was handed to the judge by the bailiff for inspection. The judge nodded approvingly, and the bailiff then returned the paper with the verdict again to the foreman juror.

The Judge instructed members of the defence to rise as the Foreman Juror would read the unanimous decision: "Verdict is GUILTY!" And the guilt stemmed to all counts!

Robert and the prosecuting District Attorney shook each other's hands for a job well done, and turned to the direction of the diminished Giuseppe Castalone, whose attorney appeared slumped and speechless in his chair, his demeanour, rather casual, not even consoling his padrone in regards to the jury decision. As if he expected it, all along.

Though - his counsellor eventually approached the judge for him to grant an appeal for a retrial. The motion for an appeal was denied.

The judge would also pass sentencing today, refusing to put off the sentencing date and delay his decision already reached. Giuseppe and his son Rowan Castalone, yet absent from the courtroom this day, nonetheless, the judge seemed unaffected that he was not in attendance, nor able to defend himself, and had passed sentencing as if he were present. And the judge had sentenced both the Castalones to life imprisonment, in the state's federal penitentiary; maximum security facility, with no possibility of parole, whatsoever.

Robert knew Rowan had not shown up, since perhaps he had forecasted what was to eventuate from his trial and its final verdict and sentencing decisions, and already he could be escaping the country with a phoney passport, fake name and identification. Regardless - the Judge passed sentencing immediately, without further ado. Meaning Giuseppe was going to prison and there was no way out. Giuseppe's attempts for lodging appeals to higher courts for even a lighter sentence were sure to be rejected.

Though following the conviction, with Rowan Castalone's whereabouts still a mystery, via local, state and federal authorities combing the entire country on the lookout for him, Robert had arranged to have Renee Castalone placed in a Witness Protection Relocation Program. Where, she would be sent to another country, with a different name and social security number, to make a new life for herself, until Rowan Castalone was captured. She had no friends to give up in New York, so it would make her protection program transition easier. Her only regret was leaving Robert.

Though before she was scheduled to leave, not wanting to leave the country or Robert, she still hoped her brother would be captured first.

Meanwhile, Giuseppe's counsellor was approached inside the courtroom by an outside contact keeping surveillance on Robert. He was called out of the courtroom for a moment. The contact murmured a few words to the counsellor in the hallway before he left. The counsellor disappeared for approximately fifteen minutes, leaving the comatose Giuseppe alone to dwell on his own fate, surrounded by short-distanced courtroom police guards, until he returned and seated himself beside the motionless Giuseppe Castalone, to brief him of the current news update. "Appeal or no appeal, our man had just intercepted Stewart making a phone call from a public phone booth to a man named Brock Stevens. It was a brief call, he asked for Brock concerning a case of the former Commissioner's and Mayor's death. Immediately I brought in our sources to investigate this Brock character. He is an English descent, mild-featured, dark-haired thirty-nine-year-old man. We have been monitoring Stewart's movements, and all his acquaintances as you requested, sir. This Brock fellow, you would not believe… He is SIA. He is a captain in the Specialised International Government Agency. This is what our associates say, our business partners, who have had a brief encounter with him in the past, once or twice."

Giuseppe regained control again, and shouted, "He's what? Why would Stewart have conversations with an SIA agent? Unless-"

The lawyer interrupted and said, "Well, they're not related or personally acquainted in any way, which leaves us to the only forgone conclusion. Stewart is SIA!"

The ageing Giuseppe Castalone murmured slowly in distress, "He's also a secret agent?"

The counsellor implied, "And given that, with the power and resources he could muster, you will never be given a fair chance of appeal. That's possibly how you have already been refused a retrial. He could use all his connections and make sure you never live out your prison sentence to even build a case for an appeal." He explained furthermore, "The SIA is one of the country's most resourceful government agencies, with branches and operatives all around the world; handling many of the most difficult and dangerous cases pertaining to public safety in general. They have networks with Interpol and the FBI – all national and international government departments and federal, state and local police groups' globally. And Robert Stewart is one of the agents that is responsible for the SIA's well-regarded arrest and conviction rate of many of its targets; even winning out, in many instances, over the other law enforcement agencies across the country."

Giuseppe shouted, now hating himself for ever trusting him, the very trust that marked his downfall. "Damn that man! Damn him!" He paused a moment, and said, lowering his voice, "He took my power. He made me suffer, and I must make him suffer. For help we must go to the Domenico Armando. He is the only one who can foil out a victory from Stewart and his government cronies. I want you to see him. I want you to arrange a meeting with him, and tell him what needs to be done!"

The counsellor replied, "Yes, sir. But this won't happen overnight!"

Giuseppe shouted, and turned purple in those enraged tantrums he was so famous for. "I will not die in prison. So help me, I'll murder you all!"

Before courtroom police grabbed him, placed cuffs on his hands to escort him at once out of the courtroom, he glanced at Robert talking to the District Attorney, Giuseppe began foaming at the mouth, and shouted, "I spit on you Stewart. I spit on you." As he tried to cause spittles on the floor, as hatred for the man responsible for his incarceration this day, and personally embarrassing and humiliating him to behaving in such a desperate nature, for a man of once, he believed himself to be, of noble attributes.

Following the loss of the Castalone family, it left the grand underworld in a bit of a bind; losing his influence and financial support, and left the underworld leery of more attacks on their turf. Though, the political wheel had been swinging in their favour despite a minor hitch. It was not long before prized District Attorney Larry Circle furthered his career into the United States Senate, winning his power as prime nominee for the Democratic Party, which left a vacancy for Mob-influenced Assistant District Attorney, Don Keaton, to take his place as the officially new reigning District Attorney of New York. The Mayor and District Attorney's offices were facing elections at the same time. Mob-influenced District Attorney, Don Keaton, won his election, securing the Mafia power on that end. But the former Mayor's death left the Mob in a bind, as they had no one to replace him in Mafia allegiance, as Mack Williams won his re-election to serve the state of New York for another four year term as Mayor, once sworn in upon his predecessor's death. Though fears in the underworld had escalated, as word in the rumour mill had it known that popular politician, Larry Circle, who entered the Senate, had ambitions for Presidency. Thus, his popularity posed an undying threat to the future of Mafia-influenced Republican Senator, Ron Bishop. And whether they were able to build and maintain a secure future for him as United States President, without ambitious and dedicated Senator Larry Circle to take his place, had developed concerns. The Mob ordered close scrutiny of the situation to secure its turf.

CHAPTER 4

Officer Johnson requested Captain Robert Stewart's return to the station house precinct the next evening, after clearing his calendar and his desk of all the paperwork of reports to be typed, and files to be sorted. As several needy people demanded the services of the only man they trusted, to help them with pressing concerns. Robert saw his first visitor waiting in line in the police hallway, which Officer Johnson showed inside his office.

Senator Larry Circle came to see Robert as well. The former District Attorney wanted Robert's help to make the city and country a safer place to live in. The violence that had suddenly flared into the city had stirred up a lot of thoughts in his mind. He had been working for the law trying to enforce it all his life, and now he had a chance to have an active say in the law, when he entered the Senate Seat, after having received a call from a friend in Washington, who had seriously considered him to be nominated as the front seat candidate for United States Senator in its election; in its leading Democratic Party opposing Republican, Ron Bishop. He wanted that post for a long time. And now that he had been considered, and filled the vacant seat of former retired Senator Woods in the party, he was grateful that since Robert was always supporting him with all his friends when he became District Attorney, that he had as well equally supported him when he came to Robert, once the opportunity arose for him inside the Senate.

He knew Robert was a much respected person, with ample clout. Whose word had carried a lot of weight, to even the business and political community, who many owed him their gratitude for previous services rendered. And having Robert's support, which immediately won him the support of many of his friends, had in fact won his place in the Senate, when the party in Washington made their decision to back Larry Circle as candidate. And they nominated him. And this day he came to thank Robert personally, for his support - and recognition, which he considered Robert was, perhaps, a large part responsible for his success.

Robert was delighted in his career objective hitting its fine path that would aid him also in minimising the crime in the city. Larry was a good, honest, hard worker, with lots of experience, and he considered, that they could not have found a better man for the job.

Before he left, he shook Robert's hand, and said, "With both of us working for the good of the community and its people, look out anyone who wants to commit a crime! A visitor will come to you shortly, as I have already made investigations into the mysterious police deaths which have occurred recently, and the alleged accidents that occurred in the past, and the former Commissioner and former Mayor's fatal shootings in this city. This is Mack

Williams, our Mayor of the state, who has agreed that we will light up havoc against these criminals!" Leaving a proud smile on Robert's face, as he left, one of even triumph, to have the political power to initiate the very investigation into a case that Commissioner Baits left closed.

Mayor of the State, Mack Williams, made a visit to Robert's office at the station house as well, as members of the precinct, in stunned whispers, stood across the hall's perimeters, from Robert's office, who envied Robert's popularity this day. For politicians, an assortment of other various members of the community, and everyone of the who's who of the business world, in many instances in the past, had stopped everything to see this man, to help them in their deepest troubles.

Mack Williams, also concerned about the police deaths in the plane recently, and other police murders as well, saw Robert, to inform him, that the government had ordered him as Mayor of the state, to head up a secret taskforce in the New York police department, code-named: 'The Break'. It was so named, to break the type of people who caused Commissioner Gordon's death - and to stop other serious crimes from being committed in the state. And they nominated Robert to head up the secret taskforce, and he was able to nominate those participants on the secret faction himself in which he wanted to become members of the taskforce. And write their names on a list, with the surprised approval of Commissioner Baits. Only to Robert, it had in fact raised a curious eyebrow, in suspect of this; for the commissioner's sudden turnaround in a matter he only recently wanted left buried. Though, it was moments as this, which Robert came to appreciate the friends he had amassed over the years, particularly now, Senator Larry Circle in politics. This meant that he could break the chain of obstacle in investigations, by outranking the otherwise close barriers, through veto higher above the very local influences, such as Commissioner Baits, whom only stood as roadblocks to them.

The Mayor of the state had informed Robert that previous to his briefing him, he spoke to Commissioner Baits, and him and Baits have formed the special taskforce to uncover the suspected conspiracy into police deaths in New York. And other taskforces of the like were being set up in other cities across the country, where the same peculiarity was occurring as well, which was considered more than just accidental coincidences. And they had all unanimously nominated Robert, as head of the taskforce, who would as such, be solely responsible in the decisions and handpicking of those inside his precinct, which he wanted to join the taskforce.

Robert, not in favour of the idea, asked, "Whose idea was this?"

The Mayor exclaimed, confused, "It was mine. But the commissioner is going along with it!"

The Mayor observed Robert's reservations, and said, "What's wrong?"

Robert replied simply, "What's wrong is that I wish someone had approached me about this, before making it public, to people such as the Commissioner!" The Mayor appeared interested, as Robert further elaborated, "We have been good friends for a long time you and I, ever since you first became a member of the Democratic Party. And what I say to you, I say in strict confidence. I personally approached the Commissioner concerning reopening the investigation into the death of Commissioner Gordon, and police deaths before that, and even those thereafter. Now, I bet he did not tell you that he refused my request. I also bet he did not try to talk you out of your idea, nor debate the taskforce concept, because now the government is involved, which would suss him out to what really is going on!"

The Mayor said, speechless, "You're not...You don't..."

Robert said, "There are few people in politics I trust. But you and Larry Circle are the only ones I would put my money on. Look, I am working on a theory that these police accidents are not the only conspiracies here. If an investigation is warranted, it is not via a taskforce, which tips off the Commissioner, whose actions are more than a little questionable. By letting him and his other confederates within the force know that we are onto him - and them. And what I explained to you, that he knocked back my plea to reopen the case, and he did not tell you about it, proves so. If anything, the government should not coordinate its efforts with the local police department, that is in fact losing some of its good members, because that alone, should raise questions to those initiating the investigations within these local departments that in fact have led to such numerous police fatalities. That since some of these officers are dying in the line of duty, assigned to such assignments, resulting in their fatalities, especially by the Commissioner himself, then, perhaps, the Senate Investigative Commission should coordinate secret investigations on their own. And these local police departments should be investigated through Internal Affairs, for corruption. You must understand, that in all probability, any suspected outside influence cannot dictate the life and death of a police officer on duty, without certain criminal moles running around within the walls of the precinct itself, which is what we all agree on, right - a conspiracy?"

The Mayor, in total understanding, said, "Your point is well taken," and nodded his head at Roberts's logic; the very logic that obviously escaped him, and surprisingly, even, Senator Larry Circle himself. Who had been an extremely successful prosecuting attorney for many years, with conviction rates outmatching all those before him across the nation. He should have been the first to pinpoint these theories, as valid concerns, and as a typical line of questioning, and enquiry, being the founder to the investigation. Perhaps, that was why Robert had so many of these powerful friends in his pocket, which came to him for help, instead of hiring their own army of private detectives. Since Robert seemed to have a knack for looking at all angles to a theory that many overlooked. Never to be taken by surprise, and always knowing who not to trust - and certainly never overlooking even the tiniest detail in investigations, which by many, were strongly missed.

As soon as possible, the Mayor would reiterate the theory to Larry Circle. And by the end of the day, the taskforce set up concept would be dropped in New York. And the idea to initiate similar taskforces in other cities across the nation was as well dismissed. The police chiefs in those areas, such as Commissioner Baits, would only be made to understand its irrelevance.

Commissioner Baits was then reported to have cancelled his stay at the office, for a celebration, that was induced by a sudden hyper-invigorated state to his demeanour. Which Robert concluded was relief for him, in himself, to being somewhat let off the hook. Robert thought, in his mind: You go and celebrate, but if you are messing with Chief Gordon's position, I will be right there to catch you!

Later on that evening, before Robert was ready to leave the station house precinct for home, Detective Grebe entered Robert's office. He was fresh out of traffic duty, and joined the Detective Division of the police force to serve beneath Robert's command, that he longed for achieving. And Robert became a great mentor also to him. He in fact came to inform his superior in command that he had one final visitor scheduled to see him this evening.

Robert received a final visitor - the unexpected presence of multi-billionaire and business-entrepreneur, Naples-born tycoon, Domenico Armando, who recently returned back to his Brooklyn residence from his childhood homeland Sicily. Who entered Robert's office by the officer announcing his turn, leaving his four formally-dressed, huge, burly-looking bodyguards waiting outside, after he closed the door to the office. After all, he had predicted that whilst in Robert's presence, his safety was assured, without the usual sidekicks acting as shadows. Otherwise, Domenico never left away from his side that frequently have had to use strong-arm tactics on crowds of fans who mobbed the popular powerhouse, whenever his appearance was made public: on the streets, in restaurants, and in business as well.

Robert was surprised, and indeed flattered that such a high-calibre man would drop everything to visit him. Robert cleared away his desk, smiled at the man in greeting, shook his hand in introduction, and asked him to sit down and tell him of what business he had to discuss. That brought him here to police headquarters, this evening.

Though introductions, prior to discussions to take place were somewhat formal, introductions really were not necessary; each knew the other from the press article clippings and tabloids, which had their popular faces plastered on at one time or the other. Nonetheless, Robert and Domenico merely knew each other only by reputation, rarely ever meeting face to face. But each was fascinated with the shining stories told of the other, and the great first impressions - and just knowing that, a mutual respect was already established.

Each one was aware of the clout and importance they played in people's lives, dominating a line of fans. And the fact that so many groups of individuals, rich and poor, owed their livelihood to the two, at one time or the other, and praised them so dearly, as two unique and rare type legends the world could not do without, was a symbol to their success. It was a treat for both of them, such formidable forces - to find themselves in the same room together. And enlist the cooperation of the other. To coordinate efforts together, in order to solve whatever the matter Domenico came to Robert's domain to discuss.

One thing Robert was sure of was that his visit here today, was more than just announcing in person his formal invitation to a party Domenico was hosting at his home in two days' time. As he extended Robert, then and there, an engraved invitation! Informing him, that the party was a sort of welcoming back home party, he thought of hosting, upon his return back to New York, after a long absence abroad. This also came as a surprise to Robert, being only his first official meeting, in person tonight, with the Great Domenico Armando, inside his police office. Judging by the look of seriousness posed by the great Domenico Armando, his visit was sure to also dominate a professional level as well.

Domenico, in his mid fifties, still remained a somewhat youthful appearance, vital and stocky. And his presence expelled power and authority, in a rather enigmatic way. Which, to many minds, lured the consensus, that wherever Domenico's feet passed, and whoever were crossing his paths, it was sure their lives would suddenly be lit up - in the sort of adventure one normally sought from Hollywood Box Office smash hit movies, and Oscar performance winners. And Robert was very anxious to learn of what could possibly have lured this intriguing vision of magic to his office this day. Indeed, the two forces working together, in the same room, would prove fascinating.

Domenico went straight to the point. He wanted Robert's help in finding a group of men responsible for the random theft of valuable merchandise, and even large sums of cash, from one of his wholesale-manufacturing companies, which dealt with the manufacture, and then its sale to consecutive retailers, of antiques, machinery and automobile parts. He explained the theft was occurring from one of his large warehouses down at the waterfront. That proved to be where a lot of crime was happening nowadays.

Robert took a break from the brutal impact of conversation Domenico imposed on him, and asked, "Would you like some coffee?" As he poured himself a cup full from the jug already sitting on his desk, of fresh brewed Nescafe, in a white paper cup.

Domenico said, in a deep Italian accent, and seeming change of face, from his prior hospitable demeanour, "No, my friend. I would rather we cut with the amities."

Robert nodded his head at the strangeness to the man's behaviour, and put on a serious face, after he seated himself behind his desk, and urged him on, as if that was what was expected of him, inviting him again to also be seated. But in all this, all the reputable bravado and glossy spreads he read about him in the papers, concerning his charitable workings in this country, and even third world countries, as a great benefactor, Robert had sensed something strange in this personal type meeting, face to face, as if it were all along planned for. Even calculated and staged. As some perhaps, inevitable, fateful meeting, that had to eventuate, and now, all of a sudden. As if even a facade for something, maybe even vaguely sinister. Yet, there was something powerful and ruthless about him. He had a compelling presence that spelled power, even danger. That his presence here, a man of his significant stature and power, coming to Robert, for his aid, as such, posing as a victim, may deter others from viewing him as some evil figure, otherwise immune to all the misfortunate wrongs which ordinary people had experienced. One thing Robert was convinced of was that this man was above and beyond ordinary. And, in light of his inconspicuous dissection, Domenico thought the same of Robert.

Domenico said, "I did not file a report because I did not want to deal with any of the little people in here. I wanted to deal with you directly. That way, I know I would get the results I desire." He said knowing Robert should feel somewhat even flattered for the compliment, coming from a virtual stranger, who knew him by reputation only. And, as if predicted the line of questioning Robert was to ask, Domenico answered them, before they were put forward, by saying, "I have suspects to the crime, someone behind the theft. Though, in short, there are a few men amongst my employ, who, shall I say, I suspect are performing disloyal and disreputable acts within my company. I want you to help me find out exactly who they are. It could also be an outsider. But, I also want you to investigate all possibilities that have eluded my security people as yet, stationed in my company. Yes, I can afford private investigators. But I would rather you handle it for obvious reasons. Perhaps, those members of my recruitment team are running their own business on the side; selling these stolen goods from my warehouse, then to interested buyers, friends. I have little pieces of goods missing, and cash also, at random, in small amounts. Compared to the gross I make. That possibly, the thieves expect I shall not miss it. Or, I even may not be fussed over a few thousand here and there, missing. Compared to the gross I make from the company. That is, well in excess of millions of dollars, annually. But, as all successful businessmen and wise entrepreneurs, I am fussed over each dollar

I make. And each dollar spent; in order to capitalise the most gains on my many returns."

Robert smiled, as if expected to be impressed, as well as flattered, and said, in a normal expression, "Because the theft was obviously done so cleverly, by eluding your security people, as you say, I believe as you, that it must be an inside job. That a few of your workers there are stealing behind your back. The way I will pursue this, is via an investigation. I will send someone, one of my reliable contacts, to work undercover at your company, as a new recruit of yours. This man will blend in with the thieves. And once he gains their trust and confidence, in order to figure out the next appointment scheduled for further stolen goods, which we must assume meanwhile, the thefts will continue, then, we'll be waiting on standby. And we will catch and arrest the perpetrators in the act. It is only a waiting game, for them to strike again. I must say, the undercover man is the best chance we have in catching the culprits responsible!"

Domenico replied, "Very good. Now, I will arrange for us two to hold a meeting soon at the complex one morning, to discuss the undercover man's choice, and various other details."

Robert hinted, "No, I don't think that we should be seen together down there. It could disturb our chances in catching the culprit or culprits."

Domenico raised his hand as if he missed the logic, to deter Robert from noticing that he was merely testing him, a point Robert caught on subtly, and Domenico grinned, "Very good point." Then in a serious tone he explained, "I have a hunch who is behind it. Perhaps, the same people after my daughter, to pursue relations with, the Santucci family, an old rival of mine. I know you are familiar with these people. I hope to see you at the party in my home. We can talk there. I know you are a busy man. I will give you all the details there."

Robert said, "I will look into it!" interested that he was only a further candidate, over the years, to make unsavoury allegations against the growing unpopularity of the Santucci family.

Robert, in all this, saw an aura of mystery about the great Domenico Armando that radiated power and danger. One that a glance at him was sure to send shivers down the backbones of ordinary people. But Robert would remain unintimidated. From the little he knew about him, however, one glance at him had illustrated a possible numerous rapid, vivid thoughts. Robert knew of him. Read about him. But these were casual observations. Only seeing this man, in person, was different.

Robert studied him; his eyes, his demeanour, rather inconspicuously. It all would normally be enough to fool anyone else. But without showing it, Robert had no idea that Domenico Armando was aware of his scrutinising of him. Not even looking at him, Domenico was able to always test his man, by giving them a chance to give themselves away - their true intentions.

Domenico knew exactly what Robert was thinking. Robert was going to check this man out. And for a brief moment, the vibes Robert had received from years of police work had developed instinctual reactions. And his hunch now told him that Domenico was going to do the same thing, and check him out as well, if he had not done so already.

Suddenly each had developed an air of weary about the other that they had never experienced with anyone else. As if each were dissecting the other. In an atmosphere that only these two were the only ones who could study the secret thoughts buried deep inside each of their minds, getting deep into the heart of their inner recesses of their very mind camp. And suddenly a feeling of nervousness was established on both sides, toward finally meeting a possible chink in their otherwise impenetrable armour. Possibly, even, a threat to their very existence, as each was able to see through any facade the other may impose on the community; and society as a whole. Both could spot a phoney a mile away, with their perception and excellent, rather instinctual judgement of character.

For it was then brought to their attention, that it would be best that the two remain allies and not opponents, for now. Though worthy of adversaries they may be, an understanding that each had suddenly met their match, in a few minutes throughout years of their life. It was as if the two great leaders of men had their minds in sink to the same thoughts, when each had conjured the very same instincts to suddenly end the obvious scrutiny of the other, and pass on as normal folk. At least, to each other's faces, they would drain all unscrupulous thoughts they may have had of the other. As if each could not conceal their thoughts, whilst in the same room together.

In understanding the other, and in order to appear, somewhat of neutral ground, Robert said, "Well, Mr. Armando, it was nice meeting you."

Domenico replied, "Oh, please Mr. Stewart; call me Domenico, now that we are personally acquainted. As I hope you extend me the privilege of also a first name basis?" Robert nodded; and Domenico continued, also oblivious to his irony, "Very good to meet you too my friend, Robert!"

They both rose from their chairs, extended their hands at one another. They shook each other's hands in gestures of final goodbyes, before Domenico opened the door, and left Robert's office, signalling his four awaiting bodyguards outside, to follow suit.

Robert yelled out for ranking of Officer Johnson. And when he walked into his office, startled, Robert said, "Call Sergeant McCallum in. We have three new cases. And I want him to assign our best men to handle them!"

But before being ranked, John McCallum had entered Robert's office, somewhat in a seeming comatose state. His eyes remained plastered on Domenico and his entourage, strolling down the hallway, towards the exit of the police precinct, until they disappeared. And he turned to Robert, and said, "Can you believe that – him seeing you as well? Who's next, the Queen of

England?" he exclaimed, also dazzled and captivated by the man's uplifting presence. "What do I dare ask does he want?"

Robert began scribbling a draft report for John to officially type up, of details pertaining to Domenico's visit. Once he finished, he had handed the slip of paper to his police partner, John McCallum, and said, "It's all here. As well as a statement concerning two other cases I want you to head up investigation for. And assign our reliable people to."

John read through the Armando report, and said, "Theft? Why? Surely, he can afford to buy out all the private detective firms in the country. And I know he owns his own firms of private detectives, as anyone knows who has read about his commodities, which is all public record. I mean, men like that look down at police as just lackeys - why you?"

Robert replied, as if refusing to admit any unconstitutional reservations he may have had against the subject, simply had only shrugged his shoulders for now, and said, "Maybe even all his money cannot buy loyalty. But one thing has peaked my curiosity-" Robert said, scratching his forehead. "Could you get me all the files we may have, anything you can get on Domenico Armando. Perhaps, run a background check on the man, just out of curiosity."

John chuckled, and then said, "Admit it, partner. I know you long enough to know when you don't trust someone. Come on."

Robert, denying John's allegations as false, said, "He's an interesting man. I just want to know who I am dealing with, since now we'll be working together on a case. I just feel it's best I get to know the man a bit better, that's all!"

John returned only momentarily, stating that Domenico's record was clean. He had never been accused, indicted, convicted or prosecuted of even a parking infringement. The police computer had nothing on him. Though, he did bring him a copy of the week's magazine, called, 'The Business Review Weekly'. It outlined Domenico as the richest number one businessman in the country.

It stated a financial insight to Domenico's current estimated net worth of money and assets was 12.27 billion dollars to the public eye. Though, how incredibly sizeable that amount was, Robert debated whether or not his assets exceeded even that. If possible, that was only a gross underestimate to the public. Perhaps, he may have had money in Swiss bank accounts, offshore accounts. All varied widespread locations, and perhaps, in different names, different countries: Stocks, bonds, real estate property, and bank accounts, all in different names. Nonetheless, Robert was fascinated by the report, when it concluded that his net worth did not include the money he left and set up for the rest of his family; his wife and four children. That must have meant that with the dollars he sprung out alone, he could afford to pay the country's national debt, twice over, perhaps. If not, cover that expense even in other countries as well. It also stated his father was a poverty-stricken farmer; a cattle-herder of poor descendants from Italy.

Robert thought, "How can a man rake all that money in one lifetime generation, unless...?"

BOOK 2

CHAPTER 5

Two nights later, Robert Stewart drove his jeep wearing formal attire, to attend the home of Domenico Armando. For the party held to commemorate Domenico, scheduled to commence at 8:00 p.m., for all invited guests; of friends and family of the Armando clan, prepared by Sam Cornelli.

The dark roads were easy to view as the New York City streets had been lit up by yellow glaring lights.

Though, the evening's celebration was simply a reunion of old friends and acquaintances, it soon had spanned into a double-celebration of sorts. As Robert's attendance was also a cause for celebration by the invited guests, for all his aid to them in the past, on a local police level.

At the gates, stood guards pointing direction at the stream of cars awaiting entrance to the Armando mansion. Domenico's residence was in Brooklyn Heights, on 5th Avenue, in the upscale market place. Robert lived in the western end of Long Island in Brooklyn, on 10th Avenue.

The iron fence to the Armando palace was barbed wired. And, as each car arrived and assembled outside the huge iron gates, the guard would press a button on the control panel in his post, opening the automatic gates, to allow the traffic of invited guests inside, and showed them the way to the parking lot ahead. They would pass the guard barrier, by showing their written invitations to the gate guards posted out front, and the guards would run their names through the checklist, and cross each name out as they arrived.

The guards were also seen running towards intruders, to scare them off, with the uninvited members of the press, who foolishly attempted to bluff their way passed the guards. The guards had jotted down number plates, and shooed them away.

Once inside, they were greeted by several menservants and butlers. Sam Cornelli, who prepared the Armando house, with all the decorations for the party had embraced Robert in greeting. He then showed him inside the mansion, through the huge rooms to the rear patio, and opened its huge glass doors to the pool and the garden that he had also decorated. He showed off his finest work to welcome him and Domenico this evening. The party was of course, for everyone, black suit and tie, formal attire, except for the women, who wore their most expensive outfits for the evening.

Robert smiled, and said, "It's a fine spread we have here."

Sam Cornelli was famous for his fine work and decorations of many a bashful party as this one. Even funerals, he helped to decorate with his family for the folk of the city and weddings for Domenico's children. The community appreciated Sam Cornelli, of middle-age, part Italian and Greek background, as a man with a big heart. He was owner to one of the finest nightclub-restaurants in the city. And sometimes, he brought in the poor, and gave them free meals, and still ran a very profitable business. For he could afford to do that, simply by the rich, upscale cliental, that smothered his establishment every night, and appreciated the entertainment, and its variety of singers, dancers and stage shows, which he sometimes had lured from Hollywood and Las Vegas.

Everyone assembled inside the living room of the Armando palace. The guest list he set up was very impressive. However, he had to obtain approval from Domenico himself, prior to issuing the invitations. All the wealthy and powerful, high society businessmen, in the New York City's legitimate community were invited. Each stood sipping on their champagne as the white-coated butler had floated silently in and out of the occupied room, where guests gathered around to talk. Who passed around to them as well, some hors d'oeuvres, and caviar, that Sam and his wife had prepared for the guests also. The deliveryman had arrived with the large cake, which Sam had ordered from the bakery. And he carried it to the table, in the middle of the living room, and placed it aside the cake Sam himself had his chefs at his restaurant bake also for the evening. The manservant went around handing watered-down wine to the children underaged, with some cheese, and fruit. He made it a point to say to the children, aloud, for Robert to ascertain: "We, at the Armando residence, make it a habit, not to serve those underaged, any liquor, without the parents' consent." Robert nodded his head at the manservant, as to show his appreciation to him, for noting such a valid point.

The party was in fact decorated to an environment of a 'Dynasty Rap Party'. The city's elite were in attendance, wearing formal attire. And specific members of the press were invited to meet their special guests, and guest of honour. After all, it was not everyday that they got to rub elbows with the country's 'mighty men'. It would indeed make grand headline news in their society columns, surely.

In the past, Domenico had it known of his crusade to turn the country's main city into tremendous growth and development, in a bid for creating more jobs. As gratitude to New York's contributors to his success, and his life-long Sicilian friend, Lawrence Bolermo, who had flown all the way from Sicily to be with his dear friend, and American counterpart. Lawrence and Domenico had close ties with one another, and Domenico used many of his businesses to launder bills through.

One member of the press, who had a little too much to drink, commented on how they could feed all the hungry in the entire country, perhaps, even in more than one country, with the splurge of 'mighty men' dollars in this room, this evening, just by the taxes alone, assuming they paid taxes. And he received snarls and disgusted glances by the conservative anti-humorous group among them. Though, in all realism, his sarcasm was quite possibly not far from complete truthfulness.

Everyone was situated within their own circles, talking to their own groups of families and friends they brought along with them. They would not mingle, until they found the man of the moment, to grace them with his presence; waiting anxiously, as their heads peered, side to side, to see where he was. As if they could not wait to see their charismatic host of hosts.

Their ears were burning, for at that very moment, Domenico Armando had descended down the staircase, inside the living room. He had appeared the vision of some Black Knight, with his family, whom followed him inside the living room, stationed perfectly behind him. Everyone suddenly turned their eyes to him, in a comically stunned, maybe, comatose state. They became mesmerised by his wondrous, so ever powerful appearance, and noble profile. Everyone had immediately applauded him, upon arrival. People had genuinely loved Domenico, and respected him undyingly. That gave a peculiar tilt to their friendship to him. He had a mystique about him. An enigma, he was. His entire vision, and magnanimously undefeated style, had generated an incredible hero worship by his many fans across the state of New York. His entire magical presence indeed resembled, as he was much labelled an: 'Eternal Leader'. He stood greeting at his guests with handshakes, smiles, and even kisses. His family smiled proudly in their corner as they received warm embraces also.

Domenico took a glass of champagne from the tray by the approaching butler, and raised it to Robert, in honouring his presence, delighted he attended his party this evening. And Robert returned the greeting, by also raising his glass at him.

But Robert also received the official red carpet treatment, by those all for the Castalone incarceration.

Though the house was fixed very posh and high society, with pure gold cutlery, and the most expensive crystal glassware, which everyone handled carefully, it was a comfortable environment.

Domenico was seen talking to his eldest, most favourite son, Domenico Armando Junior, named after his namesake. (Officially, on his birth certificate, his name was Domenico Armando the 2nd, but really never referred by anyone using that title.) He was sometimes called Domenico Junior, or D.J., for short, by his friends, even his family. He was thirty years old, and was known as a ladies' man, much like his father, very handsome. Though rumour had it known, he was nothing in measurement to his father, nor resembled his charisma in any way, shape or form. Certainly, he lacked possession of all his father's great qualities that made a strong leader of respect. He too lacked the strong, magnetic powerful presence, and stocky build, even the great intelligence, foresight and determination of his father's wrath. He was leaner, simpler, and not so recognised as brutally tough or ruthless in the business community, for he was not even aware of a large portion of his father's illegal business dealings. But he was the chosen one to be groomed as the sole heir to his father's fortune.

"Senator Ron Bishop is flying in from Washington tonight to join us, in a few hours, with some of his government colleagues to meet with me, for further support in his campaign. I want you to sit in with us for the meetings, and learn about the family business!" Domenico exclaimed.

His son smiled, and said, "I would like that father!"

Domenico's two high-prized executives were his Counsellor Rex Higgins and his Underboss, Domenico Junior.

Domenico Junior was made in charge of the Armando family construction company in New York, one of the largest in the world, and was running it for his father.

Despite his flaws, Domenico Junior was a brilliant straight A student, who went on to college to further his career in his father's dynasty. He majored a degree in Business Administration. And upon gaining a Master's Degree in the field, he went to work for his father's construction business, and was given great responsibility also in other facets of the Armando family corporation: The family's newspaper firms. He was put on the directors' board of the Armando Family Private Hospital. He would overlook the day-to-day operations of the Armando Empire's massive retail food chains, clothing and transportation industry. And its trucking company in the state. He was directly responsible for the promotion of political leader, Senator Ron Bishop, on the family payroll. And the family had bankrolled his campaigns from the onset. Sometimes, Domenico Junior also gave public speeches and wrote cheques to various politicians, before the press, and media, on behalf of the sponsoring Armando family.

And his long-serving Counsellor, Rex Higgins, had approached Domenico, holding at least, half a dozen gifts for him, saying, "These are from some of the judges, and Congressman Bob Murray. Two union officials and two Pentagon Staff General Officers who could not make it this evening, though insisted on paying their respects!" Domenico welcomed the gesture and asked his counsellor to take them to his study room office, when he so dutifully followed his instruction.

Domenico glanced at his other children; his second son Tom, known as the black sheep of the family, four years his brother's junior, at the age of twenty-six. He was very thinly built, and everyone complimented him on his thick, curly, dark hair, that was all he had in common to his father. He was chatting up some of the Armando maids, whilst pigging out on the hors d'oeuvres. Though he knew where to draw the line, and act in a manner in which an

51

Armando was brought up to follow. It was typical of Tom at these social functions to act accordingly, though it was not in the usual roam of behaviour for any Armando to be fraternising with the help.

Tom was not so intelligent in business. Yet, despite all of Domenico's children working for the family business, none of them had the unique attributes to carry on the family name, in the family tradition, their father had founded. Which became a great concern for Domenico, who intended on living a long, long time, though knew one day, it would be time for his children to carry on the empire he himself had built all his life. But still hoped one of his children, he counted on Domenico Junior, to head up his legacy. To rule the family operation with the same iron fist in which he had founded it.

One thing for certain, Tom was not the chosen heir. He was careless, in not only business matters, but family matters. He had even amassed himself a few police records behind the family's back, in the past, which his father managed to, wipe off from his record. He was always in trouble at school. Beginning from the time he attended secondary school. His year levels were marked with '0' grade levels. In fact, the only grades he earned on his report card were a large number of absences, which were described as a disgrace.

And Domenico had to bribe the teachers, and even the school principal, to grant him at least a respectable ninth grade report card. When he left school, he joined his father's business; where he was sent to Sicily for a brief period to manage the Armando affairs on that end, guided by Domenico's close friend, Lawrence Bolermo, who was only too glad to aid an Armando child. Who taught him the ropes to the family's import-export business, when he was placed in charge of the Armando family power there. The entire Sicily operation, where he learnt everything successfully, and the time away gave him at least some perspective to his interests. He later flew back to the United States to rejoin the family operation based in his father's home in New York.

Though efforts were made to transform the young Armando, he would never relinquish his casual liking and approach to business. Even to life itself. On many occasions, he said, "Life is a joke. You live you die."

He never maintained a steady relationship with any girl. He did not know how to respect family matters as he was taught; in the sense of the importance in family, the importance of having children, and the importance of putting a mark in this world, for others to follow, by example. He was more materialistic, more concerned with what his father's fortune offered him. Such as new clothes, jewellery, flashy cars and bimbo women on a one-night stand basis. Domenico was concerned about what he believed was his purpose in life, for he acted so casual-like in all matters of life, including matters of the heart. Nothing was sacred to him. There were no goals or career objectives, though no one planned on giving up on him yet.

Tom handled the Public Relations Department for many of his father's businesses, mainly for his nightclubs in the city, and construction companies.

Domenico's wife, Rita, was a good dedicated house wife, and the perfect mother to his children; she fulfilled her obligation in life as a caring wife and a good mother. However, through her observations of her husband, given some reservations concerning his business practises she suspected, she had still always kept to herself. She never debated him on particularly professional matters, that Domenico made it clear, at an early point in their marriage; she would hold no part in. So she respected his wishes, and never asked nor debated him. She was only to bear the responsibility of a full-time house wife, and mother. And she had accomplished both duties admirably.

Though none of his family members really knew Domenico's true, hidden, and rather sordid, secret life - some suspected, but chose not to believe words from the rumour mill, to the contrary, of their beliefs, that he was the greatest father any child could have. He spoiled them rotten. He surrounded them with the belief that whatever they wanted, they could have. And nothing was too big a request for his children, whether it was financially, or through support, or fatherly embrace. No matter how busy he was, or how far away he was on business, they were abreast with the knowledge that whatever their concerns may be, his children would always take priority over money and power. He taught them that family was first, foremost and bottom line. Family was everything. And all that he had derived from this life meant 'family'.

Domenico had also two daughters. His eldest daughter was called Monica. She was twenty-four years old. If anyone in his family was the closest in tune to his real ways, it was her. In fact, she was the only child he had, whom resembled her father in ways of obsession for possession. She would kill for power and money. And Domenico, having been aware of her abilities for years now, chose to confide in her. In things no one else in his family was informed. She was strong. She was stubborn. And she preyed on having her way, with the same brutality of that of her father. She was his only child he had on his lap, concerning the complete family matters. She had blonde hair, baby blue eyes and a face of a goddess princess. Though her heart was capable of being the very opposite to her face, should she be crossed. In fact, she even aided her father and offered to be part of his business in every way, which delighted him immensely. She would always be seen by her father's side, embracing him. Holding his hand proudly, and kissing his cheek as the favourite daughter to any man. And he proudly named her his, 'Golden Girl'.

Indeed, if there was someone that he would have preferred to be heir to his legacy it was her. She had all the forceful intelligence and charisma, and rare qualities of her father, to carry on his name in the family tradition. A trait marred, only by her female sex origin, and a pretty angelic face, that no one would take seriously in the business community of butchers, in which he dealt with. He knew they would eat her up and chew away at her bones, being a female. Nonetheless, she carried on her role as a further aid and support to her great father's wrath. And she also helped in the complex issues of the family business as well, as chairperson to the family's many committees', responsible for the disbursement of funds to aid its many charitable causes. Particularly in resurrecting their hometown Sicily, and in sizeable donations to many impoverished, third world countries. And she had also made many a public speeches on behalf of the Armando family, to commemorate its role as a great benefactor in society.

Even as Domenico's children had getaway holiday houses each around the country, and even the world itself - and even as they were now all considered mature of age, whether married or unmarried, yet chose to live with their father and their mother only, with their entire family together at the huge Armando family main home estate in New York. With intentions to also have their children (to be their father's grandchildren), also grow up in that very same house, with the rest of the entire Armando family together, as one sole entity! After all, even their father, Domenico himself, would not favour it any other way. Wanting all his family together with him, and in himself; against the dreaded strangers of the world!

His last child was Annemarie of twenty-two years of age. Now, Annemarie was the exact opposite to her older sister. And was the youngest in the family. She was his only child who he palavered incessantly over, who he kept an extra fatherly protective eye out for. She was naive. She was as sweet as a small child. If any of his children were made intentionally unaware of the family business, none were more than her. She merely could not cope with as much as the smallest horror that life had to offer. Her heart was as pure and innocent as her unique beauty, and high-pitched vocal.

However, Annemarie was also a good student in school. She obtained a diploma in teaching. And her father had opened up one of the finest educational institutions in the world, a private school that he made her Headmistress and teacher of, right here in Brooklyn. Despite her father's incessant assistance to her, even professionally, she decided to be a teacher, and was also a candidate whom prided herself in her independence; to pursue her interests using her own accord. And not seeking employment with the family business. Though, Domenico had still managed to turn this obstacle to his advantage. By opening up his own school, and he made sure that he himself, and no other individual outside the close family sanctums, had benefited from his children's, and his family's accomplishments and successes – no one, but himself. So, after all, his daughter did end up on the family payroll, anyway. And also, the money she made had benefited herself and her family only.

Despite her fine career path, she was the sort of girl who had seen the world through rose-coloured glasses. And had never seen bad in anything or anyone, which in the past, had led her to having been taken advantage of by many an unscrupulous hoods, who had thrived on molesting that rare form of innocence; she had been used, cheated and even entered into a failed marriage once before. And her father had helped her out of a marriage she thought all along was promising, only to learn the man was a con artist, after her money. And what concerned him the most was his daughter's blindness still to the world, and its deceitful practises by those unconstitutional persons, that led her to the doorstep to another would-be marriage, of an even more shady character. A man that he even insisted on Robert's aid, to cease her attempts to a second marriage of even worse disaster, now, to the evil Santucci family heir apparent son, and one of the family's horrendous future leaders, Con Santucci.

Domenico tried to warn her, tried to show her newspaper clippings of the outright convicted crime family. Even trumped up other forms of ill publicity of the family in his own newspapers, in which he had owned, through fronts, in order to convince her that he was terrible bad news: That, the Santucci family was a rival to his, for years; that, this marriage proposal was a farce; that they saw her as a weakness; a pawn. To use her to get to him, in a life long vendetta. But the enemy seduced her heart. Told her how much he loved her and spent money on her. Took her to expensive restaurants and bought her nice dresses. He was feeding her lines, and she was too vulnerable to see through the act of that grubby little parasite. He was taking advantage of her blindness to the treachery and deceit of the world; she, being a sucker for affection, and the old, tender, love and care - fell prey, once again, as a damsel in distress, to another black shark. Only to find, that she would not allow her father this time, to be her White Knight and Shining Armour, and rescue her from another broken heart.

She would not listen. She would not see the bad in anyone. Proof or no proof, she would not care. The world was as beautiful as the gardens she loved pruning for her father's estate so much, so she believed. She was his only child whom he worried about considerably, whom he would leave nothing to chance. And he would stop at nothing to pursue all eventualities to protect, though; his efforts seemed marred by her innocence that failed her, in protecting herself from the evils of this world, which had now, quite possibly, placed her life in extreme danger. Though unintentional it was; she would not open her eyes to the fact that any involvement with the Santucci family was playing with fire.

And he could not kill Con Santucci. He could not retaliate on this despicable assassin to his evil father's family. Or prevent his daughter from seeing him even, by force - and risk, in himself, breaking her heart, once again. And that was why he was forced to the doorstep of Robert Stewart's domain. To also aid him in this pressing matter, as the only man who could prevent such a tragedy from occurring. And so that was the reason he enlisted Robert Stewart's help, to also cease the marriage. And hopefully, open his daughter's eyes to a more objective reality - coming from an outsider, than that of an overprotective father; who smothered her all his life; in which her childlike innocence had prevented anyone close to her, to convince her that this marriage was all wrong.

Annemarie was the only child that he displayed overprotective traits to, and worried about dearly; simply because her innocence were qualities that none of his other children had possessed. She was his only child who could be conned and taken in as a fool by some bastards in this world. She was his only child he showed great affection, and the most concern for. And he had always insisted on giving her the most support, the best advice and aid, to help her without diminishing her white look on the world.

And from a distance, Domenico eyed the two together, enjoying their kisses. Enjoying their arms around each other whilst dancing to the music and sharing dessert spoons of cake. And he contemplated his next move, though nothing erratic, or too sudden. But, he would conjure up a scheme that was effective in its approach to rid this disease from penetrating his fortress and scarring his daughter's heart, wounding it permanently. For when Domenico was presented with the guest list Sam Cornelli had made up, and had seen his daughter wrote in her companion as a Santucci enemy son, that she insisted be included in on the guest list, Sam, understanding the history between the two families, had approached him, and said, "As great respect for you Domenico, I want nothing to do with him or his phoney family either. Should I cross out the name?"

Domenico replied, simply, "He is a man of no scruples. No morals. And absolutely no social value whatsoever. But I do not want to break my daughter's heart. So, invite him. Invite him into the lion's den." He chuckled triumphantly.

Meanwhile, the group of invited guests, comprising of friends, family and business acquaintances, and colleagues, had openly romanticised the popular Host of Hosts; so-called by those dear to him, who knew him personally.

Domenico was renowned famous for his aid to the homeless, and for his participation in many charitable events, and fund-raisers. He was also renowned for being a global benefactor, particularly, in aiding the third world countries through multimillion-dollar donations annually. Domenico also sat on the board of directors of certain overcrowded and understaffed public hospitals, whom, because of much needed budgetary cuts, were in need for men such as Domenico's charitable, financial contributions, to assist them in remaining afloat. And he wrote cheques even, this evening, to hand to the city's Hospital Chief of Staffs, whom had attended, and they issued him with a plaque that stated: 'Philanthropist of the Year' for his additional generous donations to them.

And quite grand into the charitable arena, Domenico even had opened up his own family controlled private hospital. In which he had operated profitably (despite offering many poor folk in the state free treatments), by incorporating sound management team structure, with highly-qualified doctors and surgeons, in which he had recruited from around the world, to help deal with the city's emergency situations, always flaring up.

Domenico called Robert by his side, as he signalled the attention of everyone, when he stated, "I hope that we can all work together to make New York a better state to live in. And due to my long absence from New York, I see before me, new faces invited to this celebration, of people I am told are new in this town. That I do not know personally. And I hope I can acquaint myself with each and all of you, as I see this as an opportunity for myself, to make acquaintance with all the leaders of the financial community!" There was a great applause sounded in conclusion to his introductory speech.

Both Domenico and Robert were viewed as heroes in New York, for ridding their territories and neighbourhoods of drug dealers and all forms of crime artists.

Members of the press stood in a circle, jotting down notes, and taking snapshots of everyone. New York City's newspaper press were invited, comprising of The Financial Times, New York Times, The Chronicle, The Spectator, and other anxious competitors, whom demanded a scoop of this, to what was described, as a royal gathering of the country's most influential people.

Rex Higgins, also of Sicilian descent, was present, and stood beside his superior's side, as any right-hand man, who held the key subordinate position in the family business. Rex Higgins, of middle age, held a degree in law and only serviced one client, Domenico, as the Armando family's Counsellor. In fact, he had arranged the meeting and called for the press. Though, they were only invited under the strict guidelines that they were not to participate in any forms of questioning and statements, both written and verbal, which was considered personally offensive to any member of the Armando family.

It was at that moment, when Rex Higgins looked up, relieved that someone else had entered the room, distracting the reporters. It was Senator Ron Bishop, whom entered with two colleagues. And Rex Higgins then quickly had showed him to the study room upstairs, away from the press, who were anxious to invade the jet-lagged politician.

Among the reporters was Sandra Armando, wife of two years to the eldest child of the Armando family, Domenico Junior. Sandra was a full-time journalist and reporter, working for the city's 'Chronicle'. And she also sat on the board of directors of the Armando family hospital as a secretary. Domenico Senior was concerned about his son marrying a reporter; who always pries into matters he otherwise wanted to remain uncovered. But she became useful in influencing other rival newspapers to the positive publicity for the family. Regardless, Domenico had remained ill at ease with a nosey reporter in the family.

She too prided herself on her independence, and never allowed her marriage into the rich, royal Armando family to present her with an, in herself, painstakingly uncomfortable spoilt life.

Initially, come the marriage between Sandra and olive-skinned and dark-eyed, astute businessman, Domenico Junior, she was his gofer for many years, then worked her way up to being his assistant. Taking all his calls for the Brooklyn family-owned newspaper firm, in which Domenico Junior also ran for his father, before he had funded her ambitions and explored her talents as a journalist. Refusing to work in the family-owned business at first, she established experience in a rival newspaper, the Armandos did not mind too much. When, she made it clear, that she would return back to the Armando family newspaper firm, in her usual domain, once she had achieved the level of experience in which she had felt had earned her the privilege to operate thereon, in her husband's controlled Newspaper Corporation. Refusing any form of appointing of favourites.

Robert Stewart's profession as a police officer had seemed to also further her journalistic career as a reporter, through his many cases solved, which had, on many occasions, granted her exclusive stories.

Aside from her journalism, she was the family's own decorator. In fact, she had spent several hours, prior to the party commencing, decorating the many acres of garden, and the house for the guests with Sam Cornelli. She volunteered her efforts in the garden, pruning the flowers and the roses, and had taken much pride in decorating the family mansion herself.

She replaced the regular table cloths, cutlery and glass vases with new, more decorative cloths, vases, and antiques that were displayed in the main living room for the party. And she arranged fresh flowers to be placed on each table and corner window of all the rooms inside the estate.

Domenico Junior was seen embracing his wife, and smothering her with affection, as they appeared on many occasions to still act in a manner perceived as yet newlyweds. But his father's counsellor appeared, and excused his interruption for a moment, to have a word to Domenico Junior, alone.

Sandra always made an effort not to pry into the Armando family's matters, uninvited. She quickly became accustomed to the important traditions of the rich, royal Armando family and its boundaries. A habit born once married into the family. And she was educated of her rightful role to unconditionally love, honour and obey her husband.

As a reporter, Sandra also understood not to write unsolicited articles on the family.

Rex whispered a few words in Domenico Junior's ear.

D.J. responded by saying, "There's no need for a further delay. I have taken care of all our books for inspection. The records are up to date and clean.

There is no need to give them the run-around and put them off. Set the meeting first thing in the morning!"

He returned to his wife once Rex had disappeared and embraced her as she asked, "Is everything all right?"

He responded, "Yes, it's just routine business. It has come to that time of year again. The IRS has just called a meeting with me, seeing as I am running many businesses for my father; they wanted to do an audit, that's all."

Robert Stewart, who was of part Irish-Swiss born descent, medium-build, with dark-brown curly hair and rugged-handsome strong features, was enjoying the company of many of the party guests this evening. Though everything around him seemed dreary for a moment, his attention was soon focused to some commotion by a man in a bikie jacket and jeans, who was being interrogated by one of the guards outside the living room to where the guests were situated, in what appeared to be uproar.

Robert, stunned by the man being manhandled by the burly-looking bodyguard, had realised that he had recognised him, and then quickly darted to his direction to adhere to the situation.

And overheard the guard saying: "No, your name is not on the guest list, so you have to leave, by force, if necessary!"

The uninvited guest replied, "I am Robert Stewart's brother. He's here. Ask him! I am Paul Stewart."

The guard forced both of his huge hands around Paul's shoulders and shook him violently saying, in sarcasm, "And I am his brother too!" Before another word was said, Paul had punched him in the face, and began beating into the sorry guard with his fists, until the guard was knocked to the ground, before he felt his arms pinned behind his back, pulling him away from the wounded bodyguard.

Paul Stewart, stunned by the man behind him, had struggled away from the clamping hold, forcing himself to turn around, to view the face of his further attacker?

He faced the man whilst panting and puffing, out of breath, with his fists covering his face, all ready for a further attack. And suddenly, they heard the heavy footsteps of Domenico Armando rushing over to the scene to see what had created such uproar in his party. And seeing the man was controlled by Robert, Domenico greeted a 'Hello' to Paul, without time for an official introduction; as he knelt down to tend to the wounded wails of one of his bodyguards.

Paul recognised the man releasing him as his brother Robert. And suddenly his angry face had immediately changed to a smile. And he lunged himself to his brother, hauling himself to him in a relieved, yet brotherly embrace, and said, "God, it is good to see you again, big brother, it has been a while."

Robert chuckled, also pleased with his presence and said, "Too long. I am glad you have not lost your touch. Danger still attracts you like a magnet, little brother."

Paul released his embrace and smiled as Domenico helped the minor wounded guard to his feet. Then he eyed his stare to the guard, in order for him to comprehend that he was telling him the truth, that yes, Robert Stewart was indeed his brother, before the bodyguard was taken away to have his bleeding face tended to.

Robert studied his brother's attire in jeans, a shirt, leather jacket and boots; half unshaven, typical of Paul's demeanour, and said, "Well, little brother, I am glad that you took the liberty in acquiring proper attire for this little getup!"

Paul, slightly embarrassed, as his eyes glanced ahead to all the other guests wearing their formal clothing and said, "Yes. Sorry about that. If I knew it was monkey suit night I would have put on my tux. I just got into town tonight, and I rang the station house for you to see where you were. And they told me you were here tonight, since you left them a number of where you could be reached, in case they needed you for some emergency or something. I guess I forgot to ask details of the dress code. I was just anxious to see my big brother again!"

Robert, still very much pleased of his younger brother's return to New York, now making his entire family accounted for and complete, had said, "It has been too long. It is good to see you as well. We missed you. I was really worried for you in the army. You did not write for months. I had to pull a lot of strings to see you discharged and tend to your well-being after you were shot in the shoulder on special assignment investigating treason within the country's army. It is good to have you back. I hope you are here back home where you belong, to stay for good, this time. We all missed you, especially mum and pop, and your sister. We have all been worried sick about you!"

Paul stated, "I am. I am here for good."

Robert concurred and said, "Well, come on into the party and join us!" And introductions were then made to stunned, curious members of the crowd, who complimented the two Stewart brothers' resemblance and similarities in certain aspects, which in fact was a dead giveaway that they were brothers. They were both men of action, perhaps Paul was the erratic tilt though to the equation.

On stage, Domenico Armando's daughter Monica was now given the limelight, and the attention of the audience that now became hers, in a well-rehearsed speech for the evening's agenda.

She would exchange a few choice words in a ceremony of people honouring the Armando family name, for their charitable works.

Domenico, as he stood aside her before the crowd, had announced to welcome his daughter, by saying: "My daughter Monica is put in charge of disbursing monies from the Armando Family Charitable Wing, to all worthy causes. Please welcome my bright and beautiful daughter, Monica Armando!"

All applauded and then she spoke. "Thank you ladies and gentlemen. The Armando Family Benefactor Wing, renowned for its global charitable works and grants, set up by my father, that I am put in charge of in running for him, is set up to help build new hospital wings, community centres, to help in people's education in our schools and universities. And to help the poor and homeless all over the world; and aids in pharmaceutical research for our medical community. We always make sure our donations are reached by all those who need it."

In her hand she had a cheque for one hundred and seventy million dollars to be donated to the city's Mayor, Mack Williams, who was there to accept the donation to assist in rebuilding the city's growth to create jobs. And also she handed a cheque to Senator Ron Bishop, to assist in his campaign running for future Presidency.

Domenico, having amassed the Senator in his debt would solely sponsor him. Domenico knew he was his ultimate candidate to enter politics when he had scrutinised him from the onset, at many a fund-raiser he had set up in the past for his candidacy, but Domenico with a rare eye out for talent became his sole benefactor.

And of course, all the cheques were made out in the name of Domenico Armando. And it was inconceivable that any of the receivers would spend the money unjustly.

After Monica's speech, all rose in applause to appreciate her performance, that was perceived as one as rich as her father's speeches, and Domenico embraced his beloved daughter and kissed her on the cheek, and said, "I am so proud of you my beautiful Golden Girl. Good on you!" And she blushed at her father's praise that she melted to.

Unlike her sister Annemarie, who was shy and introverted, Monica was the exact opposite. She was quite an aggressor. And despite that, she was also very beautiful, most men found that quality in her as attractive.

Monica was the product of an affair to a woman outside Domenico's marriage. His wife Rita had felt somewhat ill at ease about this; for despite their long marriage, she had still maintained her attempts to honour her marriage vows. Her real mother had died of breast cancer when Monica was only age three.

Monica was Domenico's favourite daughter in the aspect that she was his only child who understood him. Accepted his business unconditionally, and thus developed a special attachment; a special bond that was rare for a father to have with a child. To her, he could do no wrong. And she never debated or questioned his motives and actions, but insisted on participating with them.

Domenico could share everything with her, from his business to his personal life. It was never like that with any of his other children, there was a special bond.

She knew of his ways, all of them, and approved of them. And she was willing to stand as heir to his illegal enterprise, and she loved her father for everything he was. Domenico only could feel disappointed that it could never be like that with the remainder of his children.

Possibly, the similarities arose as their childhood was equal in tragic circumstances. Both Monica and her father were more alike than any of his other children through their upbringing, both having lost a parent or parents. And after having lost her mother, she was placed in the protection of Lawrence Bolermo in Sicily to protect her from the ongoing war against the Santucci family, whom targeted all his children in a vendetta to harm Domenico.

She was isolated from her family due to the complex circumstances. And for years, she was raised in a foreign country under the protection of her father's childhood friend and associate colleague, whom had to pose as her father for the most part. Thus, being in danger growing up, and facing much fear due to such precarious circumstances that surrounded her, she became driven and much accustomed to her father's ways.

In order to sway an attack, and in sworn vengeance against the enemy Santucci family whom prevented her from being with her much missed father, she once had committed murder on a man by fixing his car to drive over a cliff, who was endangering both her and her family. Domenico was not upset unlike any other father of a child who had just committed murder, though his only emotion was disappointment that she went about it alone. Thus jeopardising her safety, in order to attack a man he had just targeted himself, recently.

And since the enemy had no idea Monica was Domenico's daughter, as at the time Domenico's own family had not even been told of her yet, it was easy for her to use her feminine wiles to charm the target and get close to him in order to seduce him. She got close to him, and had established a trust, where she could set up his death. She proved herself to be as cunning and as relentless as her father. She was only seventeen when she killed her first man, and she could pass as a twenty year old. She was very mature for her age, both physically and mentally.

When he confronted her, she replied, "I am like you father. I overheard you on the phone with your man a month ago, when you put a contract out on him, and I did it for you. I want you to teach me the family business!" She was only seventeen years old. She insisted on leaving high school before college, to be taken in by her father, to teach her about the business, and life, and the streets, as her sole mentor, as Domenico too never finished school. And so she was educated to serve in her father's world, the very world that taught her the give and take attitude of society and success.

Sam Cornelli, the host of the party, had ascended on stage honouring the two guests of honours, Robert and Domenico, as his two dear and best friends. Robert was a city hero, and Domenico worshipped as philanthropist for his charitable work. "Here, I have invited all the top-notch gentlemen in the community to honour our fellow leader Domenico Armando back home. After all, he could not arrive back in New York after one year's absence without some kind of event to kick it off. And on behalf of everyone, I would like to recognise Robert Stewart. This great man invited here this evening has saved our city from one less problem after halting the existence of the Castalone era!"

Everyone applauded. And Domenico raised his hand in a salute type gesture at Robert, who smiled at him in response, and raised his glass at Domenico for appreciating the Castalone crucifixion. But, nonetheless, Domenico seemed the centre of attention here this evening. It was a usual display of attention he received from all his walks in life.

And through his ways Domenico was considered a very versatile man with many talents; a new-rich from a poverty-stricken family, whose parents were cattle grazing farmers. And from that, the Armando dynasty grew to become the most powerful and richest family in the world.

In fact, the press and journalists from television stations that Domenico controlled and owned shares in had wanted to do a series on the Armando dynasty for a week, covering everything, from Domenico's childhood to his current status as 'multibillionaire, business entrepreneur'. Of course, the rich always brought in the highest ratings. Domenico's story showed more interest now than most others being brought to their attention, at this very moment.

Domenico considered allowing the scoop of his family for the first time to become public record, for a brief moment, though given censorship, would be a must in noting his real detailed life's accomplishments. And that was why newspaper and media ownership became much sought for by him and all powerful commissions he thus controlled. For any outside communication concerning himself and all those around him became much under his power and veto.

In all this praise and idolisation of Domenico Armando by his fans, Robert Stewart watched from a distance inconspicuously studying the man, and had scrutinised his soaring to fame, and the peculiarity he sensed in it all; though people either showed him full blown affection or others appeared to be somewhat guarded and nervous around him.

Meanwhile, Paul Stewart was entertaining the Armando maids and the younger single ladies at the party. They ate spinach and feta cheese turnovers, and as a liquid refreshment for the occasion the girls chose martinis to become happy with. Though, Paul insisted on drinking his favourite beverage, beer.

The girls had placed their hands around his broad shoulders, and through his long black shoulder-length hair, as if checking him out from top to bottom, which he took no offence at, as they examined his masculine attributes; his huge forearms and strong build that bulged out of his leather jacket from the heavy slavery of his army career, had him confined to a daily routine of several hours hard labour. Though he was rough around the edges, they seemed to not stop hovering over him this evening. They recognised him as an army hero when his picture was printed in Life Magazine with a printout article of his heroism, and the medals he was rewarded for such deeds in helping the country against its many foreign enemies.

Despite the grief much received from his army days, he told stories that made them laugh. One was whilst he was in the army he remembered they put things in people's food, not his, as he was onto the whole set up and conspiracies, by hearing all the gossip and crosstalk whilst he served in the Special Operations Unit he was assigned to, having dealt with all the string pushers.

For, when the soldiers were in training and in the battlefront, and not performing as best without their female entourage left back home, they put something into their food so they would keep their mind on the battle and not on the opposite sex.

It was called 'Saltpetre'. Of course, there was no proof they did so, but rumour had it known that the army officers in charge were tampering with the soldiers' food when women were scarce for miles.

It was solely for the purpose of keeping a man's mind off women, by rendering him temporary helpless. It made them impotent. It was a drug type compound used to temporarily numb their sex drive. Though, he had noted, it was quite embarrassing when (finally) in the company of a female companion and wearing only bare essentials for the art of lovemaking, she wondered what happened to her otherwise partner's sex drive, when the sex organ, so to speak, had remained limp. Some stories were told of how women had even taken great offence to this. They stood there naked before their lover when the entire act to follow appeared as though it was more of a strain than one of nature's enjoyments. They all laughed.

And suddenly Paul found himself dancing to Lambada and Tango by Monica Armando, who swept his arm and motioned the family's private music band to play, luring him away from bumping the breasts to those young girls he seemed to flirt with. And Domenico looked at them in admiration, as guests whispered in his ear what a great couple they made on the dance floor. And all the guests were applauding their dance in the middle of the room, clapping their hands in time for the orchestra's wild strumming.

Meanwhile, Annemarie Armando and her date Con Santucci were dancing to the Italian music cheek to cheek, as her family and Robert Stewart could not help, but notice the anger in her father's eyes who was watching them from a short distance. After they finished, Con had tried to convince Annemarie to formalise their engagement here, and set a date for the wedding before everyone. And so he had.

Domenico was furious, but did not show it, though Robert sensed the tension. The sheltered Annemarie had no idea of her father's fury right now. She was young and naive. She always saw the good in everyone, even the bad. Annemarie turned to her mother whom smiled at her. And her brother Tom whose hair was braided for the party came to congratulate her, oblivious to the history the two families shared. But Domenico Junior and their half-sister Monica made no comment to the toast in which they considered was one of disastrous proportions, but convinced that the faith they had in their father would see it end.

But Annemarie turned to her mother Rita whom smiled at her. She was her favourite child. She was her only child who resembled her mother when she was her daughter's age, in fact blood ringers. Though it was rumoured some of his family were concerned about Monica's paternity by Domenico in an affair, no one dared confront him on such a delicate matter to his face, not even his wife. Domenico one day brought Monica home and everyone were taught to treat her as family. He simply said: "She is my beautiful daughter. Accept her." And so everyone indeed had.

And now in their private space in a corner of the room, Con Santucci whispered into Annemarie's ear, "Why don't we elope the wedding? We don't need a big wedding."

She protested. "I will not marry without my father and family present!"

He insisted on the idea of a small, private wedding ceremony with just a witness. "We can leave here tonight. Let's leave now without anyone noticing us. I can arrange for a justice of the peace or one of my own family's judges to perform the ceremony, and I'll bring a friend to both the bride and the groom to witness our blissful nuptials!"

But she placed her hands over her ears not wanting to hear. She did not want to do anything behind her father's back and without his blessing.

It was now Con Santucci realised the mistake he had made in formally announcing the engagement before everyone.

Con Santucci was a strong pillar in his father's family whom performed many of the actual hits ordered down by his father. Robert of course knew he was a crook and his father remained on the run and in hiding. Wanted by the police in a twenty-year manhunt and they knew his son was a killer and had killed people at the behest of his father, though they had to prove it.

At this moment Domenico wanted him dead. But it could not happen right now. He could not kill the enemy son right now. For Annemarie was bound to be suspicious as Con Santucci meanwhile was bound to fill her head with words of her father, saying that if he had died, Domenico was responsible. And that was why Domenico had much required the services of Robert Stewart or risked alienating his daughter.

As Domenico vanished from the circulation, his son Domenico Junior patted the enemy son on the shoulder, alerting his attention, excusing his sister for the intrusion of breaking up the chatter and small talk he was making to her, and said, "My father wants to see you to talk about giving you his blessing inside his private study!"

D.J. signalled two members of his father's entourage to escort Con Santucci to his father's study room office. And as he left the scene with the bodyguards showing him his way, D.J. had embraced his sister and signalled the musicians to continue the music, and everyone to dance, distracting their minds from the intense scene, as they witnessed the man being escorted through the living room, passed the guests, with two guards posted at his side, reminiscent to a prisoner.

D.J. then smoothed over to his curious wife Sandra to whom her jaw hung in astonishment. He soothed her panicked state of mind and smiled. "I deliberately sent him over there to get chewed up. My father would chew him up and spit him out, that stupid imbecile. How can he fantasise to put one over on a man like my father? His tact is as convincing as this farce of a marriage he proposed to my sister." He then had laughed jokingly, saying, "If this were a script in a movie there'd be a raise in handkerchiefs for the dehumanisation and degrading of a fellow human being named Con Santucci, that's occurrence is only, but brief moments away!"

His wife was even shocked at the pleasure he sought from this display that she could only describe as misery.

Inside the upstairs study room office, Con Santucci was escorted by the two bodyguards whom brought the nervous man standing before their Chief Master Padrone, Domenico Armando, and one of them said, "Yes boss, you sent for him."

Domenico replied, propped behind a huge desk, "Yes, close the door!" They stood behind Con Santucci, closing the door to the chambers, where Domenico was settled into a swivel leather armchair, puffing his Havana cigar, blowing smoke rings from it into his intruder's face and watched him cough.

Con entered the office in short nervous strides as he was brought before this man who now stood behind his huge desk. It became a classic picture of some petty thief that was brought before their Roman Emperor, who, anytime now, would lure him to the guillotine as punishment for his foolish charade. Now, whilst being abandoned from his family security, lured to enemy camp this way, he would have to modify what he said. Though to break the air of silence that Domenico imposed upon him via his malicious gaze and scrutiny of him for a long moment, Con had pledged his undying love and loyalty to his family.

Domenico laughed. He was no salesman. His act was so transparent, but Con lamely replied, "I am trying to work with you!"

Domenico stomped his foot onto the ground harshly and shouted, whilst hitting his right fist into the open palm of his left hand, not in the mood for small talk, "You fucking little mosquito, worm of the ground, bug!" Con looked at Domenico baffled, for he never heard his temper flare up as that before, and suddenly realised the situation was way out of his family's depth right now, having felt isolated from his protectors.

Domenico yet cursed. "To insult a man was low, but to insult a man in his own home was fatal. Didn't your father ever teach you that? Killing you would be merely a cut and dried chore. That's how easy it would be you stupid idiot. You are a fool, you know that!" There was pin-drop silence by the enemy son. Domenico made his point.

However, Con Santucci had summed up all his courage to talk. "All my family wants is your permission to grant us our right to invest in your project. No one wants to harm your daughter!" One of the bodyguards brought Domenico a suitcase that Con had stashed away inside his car. It was to be the first instalment in his project on behalf of his family. To form some sort of an unholy truce - and work together as allies. The contents of the suitcase contained ten million dollars that was laid out on top of his desk for Domenico to examine.

Domenico placed his finger to his head, and added, yet threateningly, "So that's what this is about!"

The lean-structured Con Santucci had insisted, "I love your daughter."

Domenico's face then changed, astonished at his ill-conceived veracity. For how had he even expected him to believe that rubbish? There was no force or conviction into his words. And Domenico only replied, by hinting, now with a small chuckle, "Brava." For a performance he much considered pathetic and weak. His eyes were the windows to his soul. Domenico could see his eyes gave him away. He did not love his daughter. He only used her to get to him. "The answer is, no. Your family will take no part in the commission I control!"

Con insisted, "I am here on behalf of my father. And he wants to help."

Domenico chuckled again. "How can he help me when he cannot even help himself? He is a fugitive!"

Con implied, "This decision makes me sad. What has happened between our two great families? It makes me sad!"

Domenico mimicked his comical words, "'you feel sad'. Don't be sad my son. You will be taken care of. I swear on the lives of my children, I will kill you before you talk to my daughter!"

The air seemed so hostile, though before the guests of the party they exchanged pleasantries in cold politeness, and then parted company. There was no clue to the guests of ill will between them. That base was covered well, at least for the most part.

Domenico was very demanding and inflexible - and Robert Stewart was the only individual inside the living room of invited guests who knew something was wrong, and was able to put his finger on Domenico's behaviour to Con and his daughter from the onset. They shook hands and parted on friendly terms, so it would have seemed to those strangers, as it appeared all fine and polite. But there was electricity of bad vibes in the air from Domenico's part that only Robert inside the very large room of the party's attendance knew of the mystery.

Domenico said, "What you are doing to my sweet innocent daughter is a dog's act. You are a fucking dog. You think you can play in my league, is that what your foolish father told you? He sent you here on a suicide mission. My resources can outrun you all one thousand times, you fool." He then clamped his hands together and shouted, again, "Brava!" For a performance well sunk. "Your eyes give you away my friend. But I insist in my life not to exert my efforts in grudges against scum, even those such as you. You see I simply murder them. Yes, you idiot. I will straighten you out. You fool!"

The now trembling Con Santucci pleaded his defence for life, and said, with no intention to be spiteful, "I want to marry your daughter. I only want your blessing."

The bodyguards forced the whimpering serpent to his chair when Domenico approached him, grabbed a fistful of his hair with one hand, and using his other hand, he beat his clenched fist once into his cheekbone, which had sent his nose bleeding.

Domenico then removed a handkerchief from the agonised Con Santucci's own front jacket pocket, and forced him to clean the blood off his own face, not wanting to draw any unnecessary attention to any unexpected visitor. Domenico then shouted, "You were always a dreamer Con. My daughter will think nothing of you by the time I am through with you. Just as your father, you were always weak. You were always getting personally involved in things. Your emotions always get in the way - just as your fucking father who I detest so much!" Domenico then raised his glass of cognac from his desk, in some futuristic vision of Don Santucci's presence, and smiled: "To a formidable rival, Santucci. May the best man win!"

68

Domenico would set his final piece. "You planned on marrying my daughter for convenience, a fantasy you and your cocky father entertained to try and penetrate my fortress. Once you married my daughter you would have tossed her aside, may never have even consummated the marriage. And then you would have bid to commence in your scheme to come and go in my house as you please, to get to me, hmm? Is that not it? Hey, you stupid idiot? Well, my friend, I send you and your father my regards. For another lost bid at success," he saluted to him a hand gesture and said, "You are trespassing on private property. I order you to leave!"

Though Con, now concerned about his family's investment of ten million dollars at this moment in which Domenico had forfeited him all rights to, had all of a sudden showed anger for the first time in all this, when Domenico placed the briefcase behind his desk, in a bid to keep the belongings of the Santucci group - as a price he must pay for his disrespect. Thus – terrifying the Santucci son to showing streak signs of defeat.

Domenico waved his hand at the two standover men. They were ordered to take him away. They grabbed him on and around either side of his shoulders, lifted him up off the ground, one placed his huge arm around his neck to silence him, but Annemarie barged inside the room, demanding to know what was detaining her fiancé.

The bodyguards turned to their superior for instruction. Domenico glanced at his men, nodded his head slightly in gesture, in order for them to release the mercenary. Then Con and his daughter disappeared back into the party. Moments later his daughter returned back to find her father now seated behind his desk with his feet propped onto the desk itself, puffing away at his cigar.

She asked, "Why did Con leave the mansion so abruptly? He made a hasty exit without saying a word to anyone!"

He glanced at his daughter sympathetically, extended his arms at her, when she went to embrace him in his invitation. He seated her on his lap, as he had since she was a small child, caressed her head and said, "Perhaps, my sweet daughter. Perhaps, it was fate. You must understand that your destiny has been formed so that whatever happens is only for your very own best interests. Trust me!" He said embracing her tightly.

Domenico Armando had returned to the party and commenced his preliminary discussions with Robert Stewart, who was fixing himself a drink at the bar. Domenico too fixed himself a shot of brandy and lit a cigarette. For a moment, he had endured his thoughts to Robert. Romanticising his abilities and works that indeed had made him famous to the man he himself was. And now recognised Robert as the only man he had come across who had created an impact in this world, which had certainly changed people's lives to the scope he himself had orchestrated. And he acknowledged the resemblance as a sheer phenomenon. He in fact took great pleasure in exposing the similarities. Though, Robert shrugged off any hint that they may be equals, as Domenico had possessed power and money. But Domenico insisted that Robert had family and dear friends, a wall of them; and those qualities were in fact very rare for individuals to also possess. That undying respect and loyalty by his fellow man Robert seemed to have acquired so easily without really much effort. And though they may have led two different lives, Domenico could not help, but point out the resemblance they both shared as equals in that regard. In qualities that really mattered: A good family, well-balanced children, friends - and being the sole benefactor to changing people's lives for the better.

Domenico smiled at the thought and said, "People like us do not exist anymore. If something should happen to us – to me, imagine the walls of lives that would collapse beneath the feet of my empire. There would be chaos. There would be thousands of lives left in shambles."

Robert smiled and raised a sceptical eyebrow to Domenico's love of control, the power he had over people's lives and behind all that he made himself an image of vulnerability, for just a brief moment. Knowing that as a whole, he really portrayed himself an image to a man who was completely impenetrable - an eternal leader. Robert had dealt with many a big shot in his life, and not one he found measured close to their supposed noble attributes behind such diplomatic facades they painted pictures of themselves in being. And not one of them was beyond reproach. And certainly, not impenetrable!

Domenico had showed Robert his special personal game on a small table across the bar in the room which he enjoyed challenging all his worthy opponents to. He revealed his real gold chessboard and smiled at Robert. "You are familiar with 'THE GAME OF KINGS', I hope?"

Robert too smiled and nodded. "It is one of my favourite pastimes."

Domenico hinted, "It is more than just a recreation to me. The game of chess is the game of life. And I believe it should be to everyone who masters it; one that I enjoy to indulge in on many occasions with worthy opponents, even vicious competitors and astute allies. The game of chess is, in short, the instruction manual to how empires are built and great fortunes amassed. Only those who are wise can really comprehend, even appreciate how such a game is played: The concept in overcoming all obstacles, the concept in turning all obstacles to your advantage - until you reach the desired goal of a checkmate victory, my friend!" He chuckled.

Robert, seeming impressed, had nodded his head in appreciation to such a valid point made out by the one game.

Domenico went on and said, "Though, I believe chess should always be played by candidates of equal rank. Perhaps, almost equal! And, perhaps, we should familiarise ourselves in a rare battle of the Game of Kings, one day soon, hmm? Though, I must warn you, I have never lost to even the most so-called astute, even ruthless member of the business community. I do believe, however, that you my friend should turn out to be an astute competitor by far!"

Robert replied rather modestly, "I cannot see why not. Soon, I shall take you up on that."

Domenico raised his hands in the air triumphantly, as if he had won himself some tremendous battle and said, "Wonderful. Yes, indeed. And judging by your fantastic efforts that put Giuseppe Castalone behind bars, exposing his comedy of errors to the world, you will make a greater competitor by far in the noble Game of Kings. You see, it is people as you and I who really can make a difference in this world." Domenico then raised his glass of brandy to Robert and celebrated him as his equal.

Robert raised a cynical eyebrow to all this. Though in a desire to end the small talk of what he considered meaningless empty flattery, Robert had abruptly changed the subject by motioning his eyes around Domenico's home, and noted how the food was high society; how his house had in fact resembled a fortune spent on an elaborate movie set: His walled estate was in fact a replica to the home of a Roman Emperor, even Kings and Queens. Its swimming pool, a pasture and stable for a herd of horses, massive grounds and a plantation. How his tour of the grounds by Sam Cornelli had shown him the garden to such a spectacular job of freshly mowed grass, frequent pruning of the hedges and flower beds. That his estate in New York had 36 rooms, and had many acres of land, 4 tennis courts, a stable and 25 horses; a gymnasium that he and his family practised on, a spa and a swimming pool the size of what worldwide champions had used in their international sporting competitions. Indeed, his house was something many here tonight in this room vowed they would die for. There were precious antiques collected from the days of Lois the 16th. There were paintings, statues and marble all along the floor. Indeed, Domenico had quite a history. And his children were brought up in the surroundings to accept the future generations to be established in the Armando royal family.

Domenico had also created a wine in his cellar and called it 'Monica', after his daughter. Having explained to him that she had survived a harsh life she was forced to endure as a child also as himself.

Domenico's home had also incorporated much security that was modern, advanced and state of the art. The electronic security and legion of security team vowed him and his family to be impenetrable and untouchable in their home. It was a fortress; everything airtight, no leaks. And on many occasions his house comprised of an assortment of guests: Police, politicians, judges – the world's richest business people, even royalty acquainted him at times as his guest.

Domenico explained, "Our house is a sacred place for both me and my family. Only our most valued friends are invited here." Domenico said

71

furthermore, whilst noticing the appreciative demeanour Robert had displayed in his remarkable decorated home and all its possessions, "I live well because I insist on it. And I insist that the future generations of my family continue the tradition of royalty that I have established for many years to come. It's not a question. It's a necessity!"

Domenico smiled and welcomed his son Tom, whom entered the conversation, breaking away from those maids he so loved entertaining. Domenico embraced his son and made sure that he was enjoying the party. Apparently, Domenico, even Robert suspected his son's abrupt approach was perhaps one in request of a favour. And Robert and Tom were introduced. Robert smiled with a nod in greeting to the member of the Armando clan.

They were right. Tom, not to give himself away too soon made some small talk about how he enjoyed all those rich guests and then he went on to explain the purpose of his interruption. He asked his father for some money as he had to leave right now to purchase a new sports car tonight, as someone else was bidding for it - and he did not want to lose the sale. As the seller would only put it on hold for him only for tonight. He put down a huge deposit and did not want to forfeit the cash he had already spent, or the car that he wanted urgently.

Tom explained, "Father, I ran out of cash. Can I borrow some?"

Domenico fetched in his blazer pocket and pulled out his wallet, but Tom interrupted and said, "Sorry father. I'm going to need a lot more than that."

Domenico casually, as if lending a nickel or dime for a child to blow the candy machine, said, "Ok. I'll give you one of my credit cards. I will speak to the bank and you can withdraw how much you like."

Tom, in all this, turned to Robert and apologised for the timing in asking for this in the middle of a big party. Domenico insisted, he slapped him on the back and said, "Never apologise Tommy. You are my son." Tom had the attitude of a big kid still. He was spoilt rotten as his brother and sisters were. He wanted to buy the flashiest, all popular latest model of the Fiat sports car. And his father smiled at him as he gave him one of his 'credit cards'. Following this, Tom ran out of the party happily. Domenico then raised his hand in ranking to his counsellor who was on the other side of the room courting his American wife Anita (who also both resided inside the Armando estate, in one of the guest bedrooms), and the Armando boss said to him, "The bank is closed at this late hour, but would you call the bank manager. Tell him I appreciate our good friendship and that I am sure in light of this he can arrange to meet my son Tom at the bank now, as he wants to make a purchase on a car. Being as it is my son, as with all my children, I need not ask any questions as I trust their judgement."

After the counsellor made himself scarce, Domenico turned to Robert and said, "I spoil my children rotten, just as you have, I am sure. Children should be spoiled because you never know what troubles they may succumb to later

72

on in life. Knowing some of your friends, you and I share the same trait. Both of us are family men who have spent our entire lives going through the turmoil we had as children, so as to prevent our own children from experiencing the same grief. Our fathers, I am sure, have tried their best to keep us safe. But you Robert became a police official and I have tried to amass great power, financial wealth and influence to have a say in these things. To clean up our world from the sort of people in which our own parents' witnessed us, as children, being threatened by. And, it brings me such great joy to see my own children with things that I have never possessed growing up. You see, to make your children happy, even any child happy, knowing that you were entirely responsible for making a tremendous difference to such precious lives makes a man's heart and his soul feel good."

Domenico and Robert spoke a lot of family. It appeared it was a subject that they had established great common ground with. Domenico spoke of his troubles he had with Tom, but despite his son's childlike crusades in material items, obsessed only with what money could buy him, he loved him no less than any of his other children, a love that was unconditional. Robert, vaguely mentioned the troubles he had with his brother Paul, whom inside was a good man, though always wound himself up in scrapes of trouble, through pub brawls and boozing and other forms of strife, ever since he was a child, and he always had to bail him out of something or the other.

Domenico, though not spiteful, took great pleasure in noting the similarities in each of their great families, sharing a supposed black sheep as one would quote.

Domenico in not too long of an acquaintance had admitted to Robert that he already regarded him as a brother, and treated him well because he was impressed with the similarities. He loved family and would lay his life down to preserve his family. Domenico further commented on how he had seen him with his family - anyone could tell how much he loved them and how they loved him. "It is a great feeling to know your family feels about you what you feel about them." Domenico further added, placing a hand on Robert's shoulder, "I like you Robert. I already consider you a friend. You are more open and down to earth than others. Why don't we spend more time together? I hope you feel the same way? Let's have dinner soon, here. Invite your entire family!"

Now it was time to dispense with the pleasantries and niceties and attend to the important heart of the matter at hand, the crux of the conversation: His daughter Annemarie and the cessation to the marriage of Con Santucci.

Domenico knew Robert was a man who liked to do things his own way. Not bound by a set of restrictive departmental rules. Robert's methods proved a great deal more effective in giving him expedient results.

In all this, Domenico could not help, but state, "What a formidable alliance we shall make, especially on this agenda."

For marking the downfall of the Santucci family was one they each had shared a mutual personal stake in as well, as the enemy family had affected both their families' lives. Though Robert only remained close-mouthed to the fact right now that the pooling of their resources against a mutual enemy had only established further common ground between them. But the misfortunes each had shared by the mutual target was really only made apparent when their histories were revealed in the open to the other at this moment. Robert hated the Santucci family as much as Domenico had, and wanted to bring them down as such. He was after the kingpin for years in a personal vendetta. Domenico knew Robert always preyed on his man, and vowed vengeance against the Santucci family for certain deaths they had caused on the Stewart clan as well.

The Kingpin, Don Santucci's freedom was lost, and his twenty-year manhunt on the run was made apparant by Robert's own Uncle, Fredrick Stewart. Who was a commander in the Brooklyn Police Department, 20th division precinct station house. He had destroyed his freedom; and in turn the Santucci family exacted their revenge by brutally murdering Fredrick Stewart and his six-year-old son, by sending a group of terrorists to bash the youth in a violent death, and murder the boy's father, Fredrick Stewart, with gunshots fired at him from a distance later at his promotion ceremony as Commander, for bringing the most notorious crime family leader in its day to justice. The slayings was committed by a man of no honour, no scruples, as a message to other law-enforcement officials not to cross him or participate in his manhunt.

Robert knew the Santucci Mob had endorsed the hit to execute his two family members, as well, as executing the murders to many innocent lives in the city. Robert was after this family with a personal stake to destroy their power ever since his joining the police force in a life-long vendetta as well.

Robert, aware of Domenico's daughter's involvement with the rival enemy family, had also displayed his concerns and knowledge of the family as dangerous men. That there was a twenty-year manhunt on Don Santucci, and his sons' were suspected of murder themselves.

Though they knew Con Santucci was as much of a criminal as his father, they yet had to prove it. All they had was circumstantial evidence. He also knew that his daughter Annemarie had some apparant blindfold where people as the Santuccis were concerned. Con had somewhat brainwashed her into thinking of him as an angel, disregarding the real truth. And Robert also understood the ploy made against his daughter. That he did not love his daughter, but was merely using her to get to Domenico. And these were the events which led her into accepting an ill-fated marriage proposal into the family.

Domenico too was worried that should she marry into the family they may kill her. That despite his warnings to her to stay away from him, it only persisted in driving a rift in a very solid father and daughter relationship - and seemed to draw her closer to the enemy family as a magnet attracted metal. The Santuccis were using his daughter to get to him. They wanted to destroy him, and Domenico's temper had suddenly shown as he said, "there is no way that I am going to allow it to happen."

Don Santucci was attempting to destroy him in a long family feud; a history which began with their forefathers. Domenico explained how since his parents and his entire family were rivals with the Santucci family; they were responsible for the death of his parents, leaving him an orphan at a very early age, to be taken in by Lawrence Bolermo, he added quite openly. He also made it a point to add how he would never reveal such a story to an ordinary police officer. For knowing Robert and his reputation, he felt he could trust him, a rare quality he found in this world. He quickly decided to make him privy to the entire story. And from then on, he and Don Santucci became old-time competitors; enemies in the business world.

Domenico pointed out, "He took my parents and now that family is out for my daughter."

Robert stated, "I know. I will keep close tabs on your daughter as you have done with your own resources available. I will also initiate close surveillance on the Santucci clan. In not too long a time, I guarantee before the wedding ever takes place, I will present the opportunity to prove to Annemarie what Con is really made out of."

Domenico, rather pleased with Robert's input already, had stated, "Wonderful." Then added, "Now, I have a document upstairs that I wish to show you, a copy I made for you. Such as names to their unscrupulous associates, a mapping of their territorial places and so forth which may assist you in your investigation!"

Immediately they had excused themselves passed the guests. Domenico saw his family all huddled together, though among all the guests he asked about his daughter Monica. Robert also peered around the room and could not notice his brother Paul anywhere among them either. They looked at each other questioningly and wondered, "They would not have left, would they?"

The thought remained inconceivable, though was shrugged off as perhaps they were out checking the grounds with their companions. Anyway, they walked up the stairs to Domenico's private office study to show him a copy of the dossier of files Domenico insisted he had made up of the Santucci family.

Their journey to the private study had them walk passed a room opposite the office. The door was open by a crack and they heard moaning and loud sounds of trampling inside. Their curiosity got the better of them. And opening the door they saw the room was occupied by a couple in the bedroom, their clothes removed all over the floor, as if desperate to endure themselves in the Satin sheets of the guest bedroom; all naked, making what

75

appeared mad passionate love. The man's face, though not yet recognisable as the back of his head was facing them was lopped on top of his female counterpart, their lips pasted together in ecstasy. And in one brief moment he placed his arms around her lower back, and turned her over so they were now holding each other lying on their sides in each other's arms, still unaware of their invasion of the utmost intimate personal privacy.

Though, to the amazement of those witnessing, they identified the couple as Paul Stewart and Monica Armando. Both Robert and Domenico turned to each other, as if to say, "Now, there's the answer to where our missing family members were."

Domenico, surprisingly chuckled at the intimate and sexual display between the two great family members, and seemingly approved of the acquaintanceship. Robert, too tried in effort not to show humour to the predicament, but broke out a smile. Though Robert smirked at Domenico's surprisingly calm reaction, for a man with his power and stature, not offended at the very least by his daughter's fallen easy prey into a mere stranger's arms. Domenico coughed to excuse himself, and let their presence known.

The two inside pulled apart, quickly fetching for the sheets to cover their exposed backs whilst gasping for air. Then they sat up in the bed. Monica, for a brief moment had covered her face under the sheets, not embarrassed, but to hide her laughter from Paul's reaction. He was coughing profusely in order to cover his embarrassment, and she knew that right now he felt lousy having been exposed by these two men before them. He even had feared that her father would attack him for catching him in bed with his daughter, making love to her this way. But to his surprise, the opposite was true. And using her feet, she hit him on the leg to ease his tension and relax him before she poked her face from out of the silk satin sheets.

Domenico, still finding amusement in the situation, if not conceded the entire union as something as sweet and wholesomely pure as the introduction of the two lovebirds settling into their love nest, at the beginning of Adam and Eve's saga which announced man and woman's first bond together. He turned to Robert and said, "Let me introduce you to my daughter Monica. I am sure you haven't formally met."

And Robert first gave his brother a grin, and shook his head in a "you can never stay out of trouble" glance, and introduced his brother Paul now formally as well. Paul was just merely back in town and he was already messing with the Armando daughter. He sure knew how to pick them. Even for Paul, he did not concede the notion that perhaps he was getting over his head, messing with that family of all families, Robert thought.

Paul, now feeling more at ease with the acceptance to such an exchange had said, rather cocky, "It's all right folks, no need to introduce me to Monica. We have formally been introduced."

76

Monica, too, in giggles at the scope, reacted by saying, "And in more ways than one," before she placed her tongue between her teeth not to laugh.

Paul also surprised at her show of bravado.

Robert, holding back his own laughter had said, "I think we can see that little brother."

Domenico, still amused himself, had stated, "Well kids, I hope you come down soon. I do not want you to miss the party."

Robert turned to Domenico and said, "I see your daughter and my brother have a lot in common, both free-spirited, troublesome people."

Domenico remarked to the two in bed, "Well children, enjoy yourselves, and take as long as you like. But I hope you join us later."

Domenico then closed the door, and said to Robert in a smile of approval, Robert understanding now his approval to the somewhat transaction of sorts between their two families, "My daughter, and your brother - a Stewart. It has a nice ring to it, I say. Let me show you those files."

Indeed, Domenico could not have been more pleased at what had just taken place between his daughter and her current lover. And it was not until now that Robert had realised why. He had a fascination with his family.

Domenico had handed his dossier file document to Robert on the Santucci family, and on his way down the hall leading downstairs to return to the party room, Rex Higgins and the man who was Godfather to all of Domenico's children, named Lawrence Bolermo, seated in the corridor, had smiled their greeting to the famous police captain.

Rex Higgins then turned to his Sicilian counterpart and said, "Now, I will arrange for you and Domenico to talk in private. I will tell him you are here, waiting. He is expecting you," he smiled at him thoughtfully. "He will be happy to see you privately. Domenico's own words, 'So much has to be planned. So much has to be discussed.'"

Lawrence Bolermo said, "As I will too be very happy to see him." He then added in Sicilian dialect, "I love and respect him!"

Rex Higgins disappeared for a moment inside Domenico's office and reappeared moments later to give his Sicilian friend right of way to enter as his padrone's agenda had been cleared for him this evening, his final and most special guest.

Lawrence rose from his chair abruptly and was ushered inside the office room, when the counsellor closed the door and also seated himself before a vacant seat in front of Domenico's desk, to be included in the discussions.

Domenico embraced his dear friend and they kissed each other on the cheek in greeting, as such old friends and colleagues were accustomed to do.

Lawrence Bolermo had loved and respected the man he considered a god. The man to whom broke off the strict partnership they formed in their youths in Sicily, and headed to the United States to claim a kingdom far greater than any before, with the distant influence and aid of his close association with the Bolermo family. That resulted in Domenico becoming the Boss of Bosses of the entire global underworld.

Where the Bolermo family fronts in Sicily had aided all the while in the Chess Player's fronting family with handpicked Italian immigrants to smuggle offshore into the United States slowly, but by the masses of thousands over the course of fifteen years, to strengthen many of its police and narcotics rackets across its widespread American soils.

Lawrence and Domenico had much considered themselves as brothers. Lawrence's father, the now Late Alberto Bolermo, was neighbours and friends to Domenico's parents. Once they had died, the father had taken Domenico in and Domenico formed his own family with Alberto, the Chief Mafioso of Sicily at the time as his teacher and sole mentor.

Now Lawrence and Domenico were in their mid-fifties. Lawrence was leaner in structure, where Domenico had a greatly imperious gaze and vastly stocky build. Lawrence was full-blooded Sicilian, where Domenico was born in Naples, and his parents moved to Sicily under the protection of the Bolermo family there, during a period of underworld strife headed by the menacing Santucci family, which claimed the Armando parents, leaving Domenico then growing up under the influence and mentorship of the Bolermo family.

Domenico of course, grateful to all he was worth and much indebted to the Bolermo family had said, "My friend, you honour my family's friendship. Time and time again we have won many a bloody battles together. Many wars we fought together. And I cannot help, but reminisce of those times when you have protected not only me, but even my children, especially Monica; you took her in under your wing in Sicily. And right now, we shall also defeat all our present competition for the future!"

Domenico motioned him to sit himself aside his counsellor and make himself comfortable.

And Lawrence Bolermo commended his padrone by saying, "You are a man who has sources that could find out things not even the United States President knows. I look forward to many prosperous years to come!"

Domenico nodded in appreciation. Lawrence continued. "We are heading for our goal - partnership with a cooperative, friendly government. With the government in our hip pocket we can achieve tremendous success. They will help our business. And with the 'Power Project', we will be protected. We can run our empires freely by controlling the police and all those government departments."

Domenico lifted his hands in appraisal and chuckled before he said in solemn agreement, "Yes. There will not be an individual power in this world that will not become vulnerable to us. We will be able to buy anyone and anything out: any institution, any person, no matter how big. For no one will be beyond our power and control. I will become the almighty King in this

Game of Kings. If I am not already! Even in our youths, possessing only limited power, we still had managed to expertly avoid the law. Imagine, where we are going to be in one year's time, when all our hard work in amassing our limitless infrastructures turns full circle and I become the law of all sectors!" He chuckled, then added, "Like the expert Chess Player that I am, I have planned, prepared and put myself in the position so that if any obstacle arose, such as the incarceration of the Castalone family, we could turn all such obstacles to our advantage and rise from the ashes as the Phoenix. You see, men like Castalone concede on luck. That is why he is where he is. And I am on the glorious outside. His luck meant that he was not in control; his men were running circles around him. And he had only hoped that his reputation as a madman would ensure loyalty and honour. Look what happened. I, me, on the other hand, will never be taken by surprise. I know everything and I see everything. My planning is faultless. I am prepared for even the most vicious of circumstances to eventuate. Yes, indeed. I am prepared. And I will win!" He ordered, clenching his fists authoritatively in the air.

Lawrence Bolermo was responsible for the Power Project operations in Sicily. The infiltrating of police departments on that end of the globe however was not to the advanced state as in the United States. The obvious reason was without the Lorenzo family's support, and now losing the Castalone family's support, the loss of investment and influence slowed down considerably the funnel of monies throughout such foreign regions.

The Bolermo family, much like the Armando family, was also not suspected of illegal activity, especially among the United States government regions. And also, the Bolermo family was responsible for the safekeeping of SIA and FBI hostages on its secure territory, extradited to serve as prisoners in the hidden underground fortress in Sicily. Though all hostages were made prisoners of war, those assigned to uncover the identity of the 'Chess Player' were snatched from right beneath their government's noses. And to this day were still marked as men 'missing in action'.

And of course, after one year of planning and business deliberations in Sicily, Domenico had worked closely with the Bolermo family, and when Domenico returned to the United States, given this evening's welcome home party initiated by friends, invitations had spanned all the way to Sicily. Lawrence had flown all the way to welcome and honour Domenico in his home.

Domenico had made introductions of him to all the guests; even politicians, union delegates, judges (who had attended) and Robert Stewart as well, for Lawrence had a clean record. The FBI had nothing on him. They suspected him of nothing unconstitutional; Domenico made it a habit never to publicly associate with anyone, especially in his own home, who was suspects to the Justice Department. That was a no go. As Domenico, Lawrence was neither a fool nor careless. And they had not amassed such great fortunes by being one or the other.

Anyway, Lawrence Bolermo would stay the night in Domenico's estate, though he would leave in the morning via his chauffeur and private plane back to Sicily.

Domenico said, "Our planning and partnership together will see us through a beautiful friendship. My friend, I insist that our plans for the future will make us the biggest powers since Germany invaded Poland in 1939! But, unlike Hitler, my vision is foolproof, and I will conquer control over the police and government in all the countries of my vested business interests. To then expand my goals and look to conquer the entire world; and control all its authorities; something nobody has ever been able to accomplish before. And anybody, any institution who puts their life against me will be wiped out completely; Non-existent. My plans will not stop until I takeover control of everybody and everything-everywhere, that otherwise serves against us!!!"

Lawrence, though, on behalf of all the families, summed his courage to discuss a matter close to each one's security, yet, on the subject of the Power Project had stated, "On behalf of all the families concerned, why are you preserving Robert Stewart? He is a man who always preys in getting his man and seeing justice be served - his particular brand of justice. He is one aggressive cop who has been known to do more damage to a man than the entire FBI. Look at what he has done to the Lorenzo and now the Castalone family. He is detrimental to our health, and yet you invite him to your party and declare him a friend?"

Domenico demanded, "With respect to you and your family's worth, I want to tell you just as I have told the rest of the commission. I want Robert Stewart handled with skill and restraint. I am the only few of the bosses who knows him to be a Secret Agent and Government Spy, an SIA Veteran. Suffice it to say, I have plans for Stewart I do not want affected. When the time is right, we will extract him from the picture."

Lawrence explained, "He is a famous cop. He was known to save certain Senators and even the life of the United States President once from an attack you ordered. Word is he can read people's minds just as expertly as a professional doctor can diagnose a particularly hard case just by looking at their face! He can find things that no one else can find. He can see things that no one else can see. Though, I must emphasise this as a point to be duly noted. He is an obstacle to the success of our Power Project. He once proved this by preventing our termination of the United States President whose ideas proved detrimental to our success. He is obsessed in cleaning house of all the Families, causing endless raids. We must keep our house in order."

Domenico rose from his chair and instructed his counterpart to do the same. He embraced him, kissed him on both cheeks and motioned him to a good night's rest and a safe return to Sicily, and said casually, "My good friend. You trust me and my judgement?" Lawrence Bolermo nodded. Domenico added, "Good. Now, what I will say is everything is going according to plan. Remember that. Those who do not coincide with the plan at the right time are removed from the picture. And Domenico Armando raises the final curtains to a grand finale. No one else! Suffice it to say, that for now with Robert Stewart close as a friend to me, his every secretly opposing thought will be clearly read by me; his every discovery, his every plan of attack. And he will be helping me to an extent. But the real beauty is that he will not know he is helping me. Yes. So, you see? Understand?" He chuckled victoriously.

His now happy ally returned the embrace in complete understanding that everything was under control, and was shown out to his resting quarters by the counsellor dutifully.

Following the departure of the two, Domenico was welcomed by the visit of his namesake, Domenico Junior. Who said, "Father, all the guests are missing you. Some need to leave, but won't until you see them off. Even Robert Stewart - that cop is asking about you, to confer some details concerning his reading of the file you gave him on my sister."

Domenico lopped his hands on his son's shoulders appreciatively and said, "He is now, hmm, my son. Well, we must not disappoint the good Captain Stewart and keep him waiting, hey!" He said as he escorted his son out of the room to make their way to the party downstairs.

His son could not help, but note, "Father, now that is a man that I would never like to have as an enemy!"

Domenico chuckled at the thought, paused for a moment in deliberation, and remarked to his son, serious-faced and mesmerised in sudden thought, "Yes, my son. Yes!"

CHAPTER 6

Robert Stewart, one week later, first thing, had made contact with Domenico Armando confirming a meeting scheduled that morning. He was given his private line telephone number and did not have to go through a secretary or channel of gofers. He spoke directly to him and Domenico insisted he would be awaiting his arrival. Robert, in fifteen minutes had arrived at the Domenico Armando mansion to finalise the business at hand, when Domenico had called him two days' earlier, concerning the finale to the ending of his daughter Annemarie's relationship with the troubled family son, Con Santucci. Domenico was in war with the Santucci family for years. The enemy family had spent a considerable investment of monies in security to hide and protect their father, Don Santucci, from his rival, and the authorities.

Robert had entered the mansion, escorted inside by the Armando butler and a bodyguard who peered at his direction from a distance, then turned back and whispered to his padrone, dutifully, "It's Robert sir. Robert Stewart!" As he was ushered to the lavishly decorated living room, where Domenico and his victimised daughter sat waiting, Domenico jumped with joy at his new found friend's arrival, and greeted him with a grand smile and a firm solemn handshake. Apparently, he was just wrapping up an early morning strategy political meeting with Senator Ron Bishop, some press, accompanied with his campaign manager, and a few reporters anxious to levy these events in the next morning edition of their respective newspapers. The Senator had again arrived in New York the previous evening after spending the last three days in Moscow with American correspondents, on the eve of a summit meeting.

The Senator was seen regularly with Domenico inside his plush estate. Not only was Domenico a sole supporter that funded his political campaigns, but they were in small businesses together. The Senator was also a wealthy man. He was a multimillionaire, despite his insistence that he would pose himself as a middle-class citizen to appeal to his constituent voters. He had owned businesses in hotels, had his own chauffeur, two interstate mansions, prestigious intown apartments - and led the lifestyle that of a privileged politician. But with his sound private businesses and shareholdings with many of the Armando enterprises and a multimillion dollar bank account, he led the life of a capitalist.

Though, despite his chosen lifestyle, in the latest opinion polls, a random selection of individuals whom judged candidates' professionalism before an upcoming election, were showing that Domenico's man was more popular than the opposition. The middle-aged, lean-structured, slightly grey-haired

Senator, with his sponsor, understood that the key to winning any election, of course, were sound policies and, most importantly, possess the talent to obtain popularity with the public.

The public viewed him as a friendly, down to earth, All-American fellow, which made him more popular and able to win an election even should the opposition's policies perceive more fruitful to the people. And the voters, seemingly, given the random selection of a small group of opinions would overshadow this. And mixing with Domenico on a regular basis, he imitated many of the actions of behaviour to his greatly charismatic sponsor, in order to attempt to pose himself off as a man of charisma, and somewhat charm himself, though he was not a natural born talent. Though the Senator considered that once he was long enough around Domenico's presence, some of his envied personality and character traits could not be helped, but rub off on him.

And of course, to put forward his new talent, the Senator would always be seen in public, in shopping malls; buying clothes, food - anything. And shaking cashiers' hands, and mingling and socialising with retail customers; kissing babies, and old ladies, and handing candy to their small grandchildren.

No matter how rich or poor, how black, white or yellow their skin colour was; or what culture and background their origin, he perceived to treat everyone as equal.

To Robert's surprise, Domenico had then placed one hand on his shoulder, and the reporters' present suddenly took an interest in the two newfound powerful allies. The reporters insisted that a photograph be taken of them, standing side by side as a formidable force together. Besides, Domenico was honoured to have a picture taken with such a reputed member of the community as Robert. It helped improve his, at times, tarnished image. Or, perhaps, tarnish Robert's highly acclaimed reputation. Whichever the reporters had thought, in themselves, but would not dare make public.

Once the limelight had changed to the Senator's direction, they turned their backs to the reporters and Domenico said to Robert, now privately, "I consider us good friends and I hope the feeling is mutual? I would like us to become professional partners. We work well together. You have the law skills and I have the funds necessary to help make the community a better and safer place. After all, we are both after the same goals - and with two brilliant minds working together to accomplish that, the results I see would be of a beautiful, harmonious and peaceful future for the good soul citizens of New York City."

One reporter who snuck up behind them and overheard the dedicated words, scribbling down notes on his pad in frenzy insisted, "When this gets out on the front page of tomorrow's edition, you guys will seem like super heroes. Two powerful forces uniting as one, working together to achieve the same goals, peace and prosperity. This is great!" He smiled, finishing up his notes.

Domenico, not the least offended at the career-struck reporter's eavesdropping, gave him an impressed look of, I could not have said it any better myself, and impressed with his words and speech manner, he stated, jokingly, "You should enter business!"

Robert realised his taking of no offence by the reporter's intrusion was his ulterior motive because he only hoped his speech would enter the minds and hearts of millions, to look favourably upon him, thus cancelling the otherwise slur on his name entirely - of suspicion and slander. Robert could not help but notice a false front in it all. That perhaps he was using him for some hidden purpose.

The interviews were brief, only pictures, a few snapshots here and there and one public interview of the Senator. However, Robert and Domenico refused private interviews as the reporters saw it as an opportunity for obtaining news-grabbing headlines, to boost the circulation of their newspapers.

Thus, the crux to the small press gallery invited to Domenico's home this morning would serve the purpose in not only improving Domenico's otherwise tainted reputation, but to further assist in the promotion of his Senator; and, in the process, however unintentional, it gave morale and a boost to Robert and the New York City Police Department.

To wrap up the meeting, following the reporters' departure from his home, Domenico gave the Senator a briefcase filled with large amounts of dollar notes for his campaign. And the Senator smiled at it, and said in whispers, his back turned towards Robert, as he quickly opened it, took a peek inside, then closed it again and staggered back at its contents, "You know something, I haven't seen that much money in one place since my days of attempting to bribe some very important public officials!"

Domenico smiled as his political man picked up his things and darted for the exit, extending goodbyes and many thanks to everyone present inside the living room, now trying to avoid the last minute rush of reporters, yet posted outside, and only begging for more feedback. He was shown to his awaiting limousine quickly when it drove away. It was not long after the reporters were too gestured to leave the Armando estate completely by the outside guards, so now the house was left in just the company of family and Robert Stewart to discuss the purpose of their own meeting.

Robert of course came to the meeting prepared with a briefcase containing the necessary information to convince the daughter Annemarie to back away from the enemy family, and end her association with them entirely.

Robert had shown her files on the Santucci family. Particularly Don Santucci - and the son she chose to wed. The documentation of evidence he provided her to open her eyes with had shown the crimes he committed. And also that Con had killed men as well for his father. And they suspected and knew he was a killer, a very diabolical man as well. A man much like his father, though the courts of law required the special evidence.

Yet, as she was shown the information, she became rather dumbstruck to the situation, and caught for words, in sudden shock, as any fiancée in her position forced to listen to such obscenities of a man she only moments before had devoured. But nonetheless, she listened to Robert being an outside objective influence, and considered his reinforcement to her father's claims all along. So she would accept what she was told by him wholeheartedly.

Everyone eyed her in silence and studied her reaction as she was given the files to absorb. There were SIA, FBI and local police files. The Justice Department Robert insisted had a warehouse filled with files on the family. And he admitted to her how the Santucci family was also responsible for the death of his uncle, a former commander in the city's police department. He noted that he was a very fine officer of the law, a man who was responsible for the evil family's leader being on the run as a fugitive from justice in a twenty-year manhunt.

Domenico was indeed impressed with Robert. Annemarie had then dropped the files as tears rolled from her eyes in a sudden outburst of emotion. She then rushed into her father's arms for comfort and moral support, saying, "Forgive me father for not listening to you. Please forgive me."

Domenico closed his eyes, held his sobbing daughter tightly in a fatherly embrace before she broke away and ran to her room calling out her mother's name to ease her in such a trying time.

All in all, Domenico could not thank Robert enough. And the wedding was called off. He shook Robert's hand, delighted at his efforts. In fact, he wished to embrace him as a comrade-type gesture of renowned friendship, and said, even chuckling to Robert, "You are a man after my own heart."

Robert solely had accomplished what he swore his solemn word to do. He kept his word. He proved they were bad news. That he knew them from the past and convinced his daughter to stay away from them. And of course, coming from a policeman whose golden reputation spoke for itself; she chose to believe what was said as gospel and true.

Domenico was overwhelmed in gratitude and said, "I am in your debt. If you need anything, please let me repay you. Don't hesitate to ask."

Robert nodded his head in understanding.

Domenico went on, "Now, to our other business at hand, my security problem. Your call earlier explained that you have made progress, and that you have assigned a professional detective to handle my case, someone local. Someone you recommend highly. His name, I believe is Des Horsecraft, owner of Des Horsecraft Investigations Detective Firm."

Robert nodded and handed him a slip of paper with the address and contact details. "Yes. I have come with information on the case. I have already informed him of your case. He will see you at your earliest convenience. He will give you the results you're after. He'll fix it up. This is after all a problem that requires the solemn workings of a good detective agency. He runs a small firm here in Brooklyn. But they do not come finer than him."

Domenico smiled in appreciation, placed the slip of paper cautiously inside his front blazer pocket and said, "I will instruct my secretary to arrange a personal appointment with this character."

Robert said, "Though he did raise similar concerns as to the location of your security breach as I have previously. I understand that the Farlev family territory is on the waterfront where your warehouse was apparently burgled on the pier?"

Domenico offered Robert a drink as his maid entered the room. Robert accepted to join him in a coffee, and then the Armando chief answered the question of sorts by replying, casually, "My business revolves around many people - sordid or otherwise. Perhaps, some of these people are of questionable character, but that cannot be helped. And in no way means that I handle my affairs or live my life as they do."

Robert raised his eyebrow, a familiar gesture of cynical scepticism he often wore, now studying him, aware that Domenico was conscious of his scrutiny. Robert then smiled, as if ironical, and said, "Yes."

In all this, Robert, in himself, had only debated whether or not Domenico's security breach was even a valid undertaking. Or perhaps, it was really only part of a secret agenda. Perhaps, the entire act was even staged. So when Robert was invited to investigate a matter on Armando territory he could possibly report back to police headquarters that Domenico, the seeming victim, and no way an instigator of any sordid activities was only running a very tight ship. And, Robert using his own influence that even had reached to governments' ears, Domenico would continue to sway authorities away from him – and Domenico's record would continue to remain clean and unhindered on all levels.

Following Robert's departure from his home, Domenico had arranged for a messenger via one of his bodyguards to send a telegraph to the new leader of the Farlev family, Niko Sasselli, a warning of sorts. Despite Domenico's engineering of the theft in his own waterfront-controlled warehouse, and its seemingly tight security yet left unhindered, it was no way a reflection to the ever growing crime rate of burglaries and thefts on the docks. The telegraph explained that too much crime was committed on Farlev territory on the waterfront, which Niko - as the new leader of the family, should be protecting. Niko Sasselli was warned to run a tighter ship on that area and put control on those freelancers threatening their businesses and livelihood, or else the Domenico Armando would move in and takeover his territory, by force, if necessary.

It was not long before a reply was sent by messenger from the Farlev family leader that extended his deepest friendship; insisting that he would drive all the crime away and make the rest of the families' parent companies around his territory completely safe.

Domenico, having received verification, now arranged for another messenger to send another telegraph this time to Con Santucci. And extend his immediate invitation to his house. To keep it silent - and to proclaim his invitation was a meeting of sorts concerning his ten million dollar investment left in his hands at his party. His father was otherwise expelled from all commission meetings, and forced to withdraw his family from participation in any and all underworld-shared projects. To serve as an example of what would happen should Domenico Armando's autonomy be questioned and toyed with. So when a peace resolution was hinted, any hint that Con Santucci may seek repossession to such a prize, crucial to his family's fortune-keeping; it would really only serve to sweeten the kitty just that little bit extra, thus luring him into the enemy camp, all so blindly, with a false sense of security.

Domenico was now seated inside his home private office room study with his counsellor and most prized and skilfully feared retainer, named Kong, nicknamed, the 'Bulldog Bodyguard' - for his ferocious slaughter of the Armando family's targets, posted by his side.

Domenico chuckled as he received confirmation to the Santucci son's arrival in just a moment. By literally pulling blinders over his eyes and summoning him over to his home in such a way, given the sweet temptation, Domenico clasped his hands together in one loud clap, and smiled to his two most trusted protégés: "The blind mouse is coming. The choice I gave him, after all, was no choice at all. What else could he do - but walk into my trap!" He laughed, and took great pleasure in his two favourite employees sharing the same enthusiasm, by breaking out a tiny smirk on their faces at their superior's flare for the dramatic.

It was not long before the bodyguards found the prompt arrival of Con Santucci, once Domenico's wife and children had vacated the house to run usual errands. Leaving the much required privacy as the Santucci son was waiting anxiously outside the front doorstep. And the well-behaved mercenary was shown inside to the den of the man in command. A tap on the door was sounded. The Bulldog Bodyguard invited the man inside. The two other bodyguards had closed the door behind them, and waited outside as previously instructed, enforcing secrecy and in order to scurry away any family members who may pose an intrusion to these crucial deliberations to take place.

Domenico was laid-back in his swivel armchair behind his desk. And Con Santucci was aware of his predicament that he was nobody in the kingdom of the great and influential Domenico Armando. And Con had suddenly felt the same isolation as his previous encounter not so long before - and this time he was enticed so favourably with a proposal, he believed, was sound and beneficial - which he felt safe to attend the meeting without family bodyguards present. Con, unaware of Domenico's thoughts, his Counsellor Rex Higgins, however, knew exactly what he was thinking now as his padrone chuckled: For Con Santucci really was a foolish descendant to a foolish family. And had a fool for a father - living a life as a fugitive from justice. His son was careless also, and had not learnt a vital lesson from his father's chronic mistakes in life. One was, never underestimate your opponent. And the other was, never second-guess a situation. One must be certain. He must plan out the very thoughts of those around him; forecast the possible scenarios that could eventuate - so that nothing takes him by surprise. Thus, Con having entered the lion's den unarmed, and with no aid, meant his father had not taught him anything of substance. He was a fool. His son was now as isolated as his father was from the commission. He indeed was a sorry excuse. And deserved to have end his course of life in a manner well-suited as a descendant and upbringing to a fool.

First, his family was refused all accommodations by his world. And then so viciously forced away from his daughter that he disregarded any attempt that his life may be summoned here for reasons of ulterior motives. As if oblivious for even a moment to the ferocity the Armando ruler commanded. He had just entered the office casually, and seated himself down when asked to. As if he actually thought all would be forgiven and forgotten. And then he may walk out with his ten million dollars - and all would be right with the world.

Experiencing the sudden fear of silence that was cast around him, Con had felt enemy eyes posted before and behind him. Con insisted on breaking the silence, and became the first to speak. At the same time Domenico thought: "No. There would be no mercy for this fool."

Con put forward words that were also on behalf of his father in hiding. He stated again that they wanted a peace, a truce: To form some sort of unholy alliance and work together, not against each other; to be included in his illicit plans and not be singled out of the commission, and, to forget the generations of hostility between the two families. And he brought forward a wrapped gift from his jacket pocket to hand to Domenico. The bodyguard named Kong had quickly grabbed it from his hands before he placed it on the desk. He lifted it to his ear, as he shook it, and listened. The bodyguard said to Domenico and the counsellor, "Our security people will check the package out for any explosives."

Con angrily shot up onto his feet, grabbed the package from the bodyguard and tore away the wrapping paper, then opened it to reveal inside a case of Havana cigars. And insisted to Domenico: "It's clean. It's a gift for you and your family from me and my family."

The bodyguard had placed two hands over his shoulders and forced him back onto his seat, and the gift was placed on the desk.

Domenico said simply, "My answer is no. No. You won't be handed your ten million dollars."

Con, now his mind working in sudden uncontrollable fury over his tormentor's actions. He suddenly became aware that this meeting was a set up. That any hint to a peace talks gathering was simply just a rouse to draw him into the lion's dungeon, just a hoax. He shouted, "Then I will continue to pursue relations with your daughter - and I will not stop until you return our family's money back."

Domenico chuckled, as if amused by such behaviour, and glanced at his protégés who stood at the door behind the man. They too gave Domenico a stare, as they shook their heads from side to side, astonished of how a man could make such a threat. And lack such tact. And show no regard for such words, as if he had actually, for even one second, thought he would get away with making an idle threat, as if to some high school bully. Those words were enough to have him sign his own death warrant. Now it was certain to happen.

Domenico had leaned forward still in his seat and said, "So, you are telling me that my daughter is your bargaining chip against me, hmm? That she is a simple pawn in your little game to be bought and sold as a business deal, with no regard for Domenico Armando, hmm?"

Con shouted, as if hysterical, "Yes. Yes. Yes." He said so freely, not counting on the fact that Domenico would kill him. He only felt safe by the notion that Domenico could not kill him as his daughter would surely know he was responsible. And, yet unaware that she knew of his true colours, still considered the notion that she still loved him. And this was what made him speak his mind and feel safe right now, feeling that the Armando daughter was still his ally.

Domenico's face had now changed to dead seriousness, his voice tone raised, that sobered the hysterical man to quivering dead silence as he spoke. "Don't you ever refer to my daughter with such words! I was once asked, would I kill by association? The answer is-" He paused briefly, as he signalled to his bodyguard Kong, with a nod of the head, a gesture he was well informed of, that meant he now knew what he must do. Domenico continued, "The answer is: It was your unfortunate destiny that you were born a Santucci. And your entire bloodline will be made to suffer for your father's actions. And suffer dearly you will - before I kill you all."

Con attempted to utter a word, but the bodyguard crept up behind him. And using his fist coming toward him, he smashed him a powerful blow in the larynx. The impact had suddenly caused his air passage to collapse, as he began to choke and gasp for air - depriving him of oxygen until he had collapsed off his chair and rolled onto the ground motionless, soon after.

The Counsellor Rex Higgins had checked for a pulse and confirmed that Con Santucci was now dead.

Domenico rose from his chair, clapped his hands together, as if the world would not miss such a fool with no tact, who could lower his guard so foolishly. Then, as he walked up to him, patted his bodyguard on the back, signifying a job well done, then turned to his counsellor, and said, "Let us send our friends of the remaining Santucci family their message, our reply to their invitation."

An hour later, the dead-bodied corpse of Con Santucci was delivered in a coffin to the Manhattan home of his two older brothers, Sebastian and Bruno Santucci, where they then tripled its security.

They buried the corpse in a small private funeral and the family had kept the death hidden from police to hide its embarrassment.

CHAPTER 7

Robert Stewart had been posted inside his home secret annex SIA installed communications room awaiting faxes pertaining to the Chess Player case.

His home communications room had been fitted with computers and wall maps; all state-of-the-art equipment, which had given him access to all highly classified government information, secrets pertaining to relevant cases, by tapping into the required access codes. His security was brilliant, yet advanced; ensuring no outside parties or intruders could break into the secure room and tap into the mainframe. As codes and passwords to databases were changed frequently, securing the event of infiltration by enemy factions.

The communications room enabled Robert to communicate with SIA headquarters, together with its widespread branches, accessing files all over the world.

Robert insisted, once assigned to the Chess Player case, that his security and communications room facility be updated to its peak, by initiating these passwords and access codes to databases and top secret government information. And also, he insisted that such codes be changed frequently, and only few people would be informed of the changes, only SIA Boss, Chief Lloyd McKenzie, Robert and his SIA contact, Brock Stevens.

Robert even kept a gun at his home for his and his family's protection against the danger this case was bound to create, and exercised his role to combat the danger.

Robert reviewed faxes sent to him pertaining to the Chess Player case. He read through the files of faxes from Anthony Lorenzo, who was their key informant. He also studied the list of possible suspects such as the Farlev family, and the main Five Families in the New York State region. All families, Robert had crossed paths with in the past, at one point or another, concerning crimes that ranged from illegal gambling, tax evasion, loan-sharking, and extortion – to money laundry, drugs and murder. Some, he had arrested on charges they fought and wormed their way out of, what was described as a technicality. Some ensured their freedom by buying out scapegoats in order to confess to the crimes they were otherwise accused of. Niko Sasselli was one such culprit. And now the biggest suspect in the Chess Player case. Once indicted for murder and drug trafficking charges, and promised another prison term, after serving, already, two terms in his life in prison - recently assured a third consecutive incarceration; he had set up a scapegoat to take the fall, the rap for him.

Niko Sasselli set up his own lawyer as his perfect 'fall guy' to go to prison for him, thus confess to all his crimes.

Despite authorities doubting his counsellor's intelligence to mastermind such crimes he was indicted for, he had simply confessed that his boss Niko was a victim in all this, of his own counsellor's will. And the counsellor confessed to being the head of such organisational rackets that were large and widespread, complex and diverse. Of course, everyone knew he was paid to take the rap for his boss. But conveying knowledge to such illegal enterprises and confessing in detail to it all, the jury had no choice but to convict him. And Niko Sasselli had escaped from serving a third term in prison, free to become the number one prime suspect to the Chess Player's identity.

Robert had studied the grand underworld commission's entire family tree hierarchical power structure. The Chess Player was the boss of bosses. And somewhere in those files was this enemy who controlled all of them.

And now matters were only made worse with the recently confirmed death of Anthony Lorenzo, in an apparent suicide. He had died overnight from an overdose of sleeping tablets. He even confessed himself, in his own handwriting, to the Chess Player charges. In a dossier he allowed the authorities to confiscate upon his death. No doubt, in a bid to spare his remaining targeted family from their real enemy. All along, he would inform on the Mob, but when it came to the crux of it all, the heart of the matter, the one big question - who was the Chess Player? He became nervous, agitated and began to sweat. He would not talk of it. Fear of his safety. Fear of his family's safety. He insisted the government could protect him from any other family, but if he crossed the Chess Player himself, personally, by revealing this pertinent and destructive piece of information to his true identity, thus, luring authorities to penetrate his evil cunning world, he knew all along that it would come back to haunt him. That word would get back that Lorenzo broke the silence, the omerta, and he would be made to suffer the consequences - and in such despicable fashion. He would be made to suffer dearly. No protective custody, no government or army they could muster to guard him, could protect him or his family from that man. Who could, and in fact had proven to much penetrate and in fact had infiltrated more institutions of power than one would care to boast of.

However, Anthony Lorenzo's death proved insight to his accusations against the Mob of how influential and cold-blooded they really were. Robert, aside from the sideshow of Lorenzo's death; how it all appeared on the surface, and unfolded altogether, knew the Chess Player, their real culprit was behind it, and had managed to get to him even from a secure FBI army barrack. Even from there. Thus, Lorenzo's fears were finally proven. But - at the cost of his dear life.

Robert was sent faxes of police deaths as far back as fifteen years, which were suspected to be by the Chess Player in the country's four main targeted cities. They showed gruesome images of past and recent corpses of police and politicians in the United States and even other countries' regions, such as Italy and South America. The Deaths incorporated by the alleged underworld's labelled 'Power Project'. So dubbed by the commission group that documented the so-called accidents of police in New York and at least three other cities that were backdated from fifteen years ago of patterns to the crimes. In 1973, he saw deaths of mass police. In 1975, he read of the death of the Governor in the state and two famous judges in Chicago, which made the biggest headlines in those years; and, in 1985, the attempted assassination of the United States President. It showed the deaths of Mayors and district attorneys and news reporters. Such deaths throughout the nation over the past fifteen years shattered homes of millions of Americans, whose horror to losing such good people were discussed in shock by all households for years. Some never stopped. Some of these deaths were still discussed and remembered by the nation to this day. The loss proved turmoil to many and a complete devastation. Some of these famous people would never be forgotten. Commissioner Gordon was among the noble men.

Robert went through more faxes and newspaper clippings of the past crimes that the agency collected and sent to him now. And he went through the backdated issues of national newspapers. Old wounds were reopened when he was struck by a word of his uncle in one of the articles who was a police officer, died too. And other police officers supposedly died in so-called accidents with hundreds and thousands of other police officials.

Once Robert concluded his perusal to such SIA highly classified government information, pertaining to such a case of top secrecy, he dispensed with the correct access codes, giving him access to retrieving such files, and done away with it carefully. And he stored the faxes of highly classified government secrets neatly in his secretly installed annex-type communications room. The secrets he contained in this room could be explosive if landed into the wrong hands; so security remained at its tightest.

Robert Stewart kept his appointment at the station house to see John McCallum inside his office an hour later. They immediately went through their files and background analysis of Domenico Armando.

John agreed. "It seems as though everywhere he walks the walls tremble with excitement and force. His wealth is not exactly a state secret."

Robert uttered, rather ironically, "No, possibly just how he really makes it. Although the figure to exactly how wealthy he really is I am sure is far from known and grossly understated, is well kept hidden."

But Robert came to realise that if Domenico was into anything illegal, he left nothing, but a microscopic trace. They had nothing on him. He was clean. He was into many diverse businesses. And they all seemed legitimate. Other businesses were a publishing and broadcasting empire. He also bought and sold companies for huge profits, particularly on the stock market. And he invested in land and real estate, pharmacy chains, mining, chemicals and hotel resorts. He used the profits, the sale of his Wall Street shares, such funds to invest in more property, real estate and hotel holiday resorts here and overseas. He also had investments in media assets, public hospitals and many diverse holdings: car, clothes and food manufacturing plants, all of which ran at a loss until he became part of them and took over ownership to such corporations. And he was a billionaire, with a net worth of an estimate of well over twelve billion dollars.

John asked, "Do you think he's what he makes himself out to be? What people think? Do you think he's clean?"

Robert shrugged his shoulders, yet uncertain, never condemning a man unless there was proof, beyond a shadow of a doubt. Though never ruled out any possibilities of suspicion either, when he replied, "If he is into anything illegal, that twelve billion dollar estimate of his net worth is only what he wants the public to know. My guess is - perhaps, he may have billions more stashed away in hidden assets offshore. And in Swiss bank accounts, all in different names. So far, he's got no police records of any sort - for any crime. All we have is suspicion of him, heightened also by the state of his wealth. Questions in how he really makes such a vast turnaround and so quickly. Which, I suppose makes him a candidate for public harassment, anyway, and, a possible scapegoat for crimes and investigations; in his case, maybe, then again, maybe not!"

John understood Robert and his hunches all too well. Being his most trusted friend and confidant and police partner for many years, he knew Robert was suspicious of Domenico Armando - and of most people. It was his suspicious nature that had him solve hundreds of supposedly unsolved crimes, and kept him alive all these years. After all, his suspicion of Domenico was believed to have merit. No one had acquired such wealth in the past, particularly in one lifetime generation, unless they bent and in fact broke many rules along the way, in the process; and was in fact involved in illegal activities. Robert found there was little, if any other relevant information printed on him. Even in social magazines. He kept a very low profile. It was all a bit suspect.

It was only then when the vision of Domenico Armando appeared in the hallway and entered Robert's office. John thought to himself, speak of the devil, and gave an innocent look, not to appear as though his was the topic of their discussion. Robert saw a line of bodyguards posted outside as he quickly fixed up the file report on him and hid it inside his desk drawer. Studying the legion of Armando guards posted outside for his defence, as if awaiting battle with an enemy army, for one moment, he was sure not even the United States President had so many guards posted around him in the most riotous of public rallies. What was that guy into to require that?

And Domenico replied, as if he had performed an instinctual reading of his mind, and quick assessment to his thoughts, "Excuse the guards Robert. I am

94

a wealthy man. And there are a lot of elements out there who we must guard against. Well, I just assume be prepared."

Robert, appearing to take it as it was given, entertained the notion, in himself: And this was the guy suspected of not even a traffic offence or anything illegitimate?

There were quick, polite smiles and nods of greeting between John and Domenico. Domenico was dressed in one of his expensive black pinstripe Italian suits. John then excused himself outside Robert's office and allowed them privacy as he closed the door after himself.

Robert insisted Domenico to take a seat and smiled, saying, "So what can I do for you Domenico?"

Domenico replied as he remained standing, "On the contrary, my dear friend. I came here to do something for you as wonderful as what you have done for me, just returning the compliment: For stopping my daughter entering a marriage of comical disasters and assisting with the theft business on my property. The man you referred to me, Des Horsecraft, that private detective, is doing a wonderful job, thank you Robert. Such talent as yours should be duly rewarded, I say."

Domenico pulled out from the side pocket of his expensive pinstripe blazer a small gift box. Inside it was money folded by a gold clip, a thick roll. Perhaps three inches in width of a thousand dollar notes, that was bound together by the solid real gold money clip with Robert's initial on it. That was engraved.

Robert lifted his hand as if to stop him with a grunt to its necessity, but Domenico insisted he accept the small gesture as a token of his gratitude.

Domenico grunted forcefully, in a tone as if he was issuing out an order, not a request. And interrupted by saying, "I know you have not billed me for your advice and services. And I don't have to pay you. But, I do not know many people in this life that I can trust like you Robert. And I do consider you a true friend. I do. After all, I admit that I am in your debt. I want to thank you for helping me in such a delicate matter - and your success in accomplishing the task. All the tasks I have assigned to you!"

Domenico insisted Robert open the palm of his hand to accept the gift. And as he had, Domenico added, "To a man who deserves to be called, 'Friend.'" And he also made it a point however to specify that the money he gave him was not from Armando enterprises. It was from his own personal account. "This gift is simply a gesture of friendship to you and your entire family. It is not business. This is personal."

After the 'great' man left his office, Robert was suddenly overwhelmed with the truth of realism. It was only at this very moment when Robert realised wholeheartedly, beyond any doubt, that Domenico really did not require his advice or help. The Armando family was so wealthy that Domenico knew many people on his payroll. Perhaps, it was some sort of ploy to intertwine himself with his entire family by getting them to work for him, to get close to him. Thus appear vulnerable to the police by posing as a victim of sorts, even, as an ordinary man requiring ordinary aid for ordinary services. That he was not what people rumoured at times - a generous philanthropist; that, in fact, he was powerful and dangerous to people.

Nonetheless, Robert pondered to himself the answer to a constantly nagging question. "What game are you playing, Armando?"

BOOK 3

CHAPTER 8

When Cassandra Smith had returned home to Brooklyn, Robert vowed it was the happiest day in his life. She surprised him with a visit in the morning at the station house precinct as he was on official police duty. As soon as her plane landed in the city, the first thing she did was have the cab drive her to the station from the airport to meet Robert. She looked at him and suddenly the tragedy of the day was controlled by each other's presence.

John, present inside the office, also had burst into happiness, and gave a chuckle in greeting at a long lost adored friend. Meanwhile, Robert had stared at this woman with such wonder in his eyes. He was seeing a vision. Robert dropped what he was doing and laid all files onto his desk when he and Cassandra both embraced in each other's arms, without any words being said at first. They gave each other a long kiss on the lips for moments. Then she wept in his embrace.

Her father was buried last week and she mourned for so long; dreading the loss. It was horrible. All she wanted to do was come home to New York and see Robert. She missed him for so long. She said, "I love you so much!"

Robert replied, "I have waited so long Casse. I love you too!"

Cassandra then gave the answer to a nagging question, which was, "I'm here to stay. I have closed up shop in Chicago and I am going to reinstate my partnership in my law practice here in New York, once again."

Robert stated, delighted, "It is going to be good to have you home, back into my house - our house. Ryan and Stephanie love you. They'll be so excited. They missed you so much!"

Cassandra smiled warmly. "I missed them too; I missed you, the children, the home. I bet nothing's changed."

Cassandra, to Robert and so many who knew her was a strong independent woman, yet caring and warm. She was very beautiful; slim, blonde hair, blue eyes. She was fresh, sincere and giving, a career woman. Even a mother to Robert's children for so long before she was forced to leave to tend to her father's health crisis in Chicago, ill from terminal cancer.

She was a defence lawyer who also valued family, and sacrificed her own happiness with Robert to be with her own troubled family in a time of need.

This very moment upon her return, John admitted, "It's going to be good to see my two best friends back together again. Just like the old days!"

Robert and Cassandra stared in each other's eyes and smiled simultaneously. Robert agreed. "Yes, the good old days - the old Robert and Casse!"

In the past, Cassandra had defended many of the clients, people Robert in fact recommended to her, who he believed had much required good defence. Who were otherwise taken advantage of by the justice system.

Cassandra had owned one of the most prestigious law firms in the country. Whilst in Chicago looking after her family, she also tried to help many troubled clients in the small firm that she worked from there, employed by a small Legal Aid Practice. And now she would resume her duty as normal in her Brooklyn Law Practice in the city, which was being maintained by her law partners in her absence.

Before she had arrived back in New York, she had recently wrapped up her last case there she was litigating, of two parents' suing a school for providing education ill-equipped to meet modern-day criteria standards. And thus passing students through each grade level who mostly, did not even know how to read or write and count. She won the case, and the State ordered them a compensation payout by the school, which had made the families considerably wealthier for their children's neglect. This was a large case that would help her re-establish herself once again in her law firm in New York, and even put her law practice on the map. Thus, opening the eyes to all those responsible to stop this sort of incidence from continuing. She was renowned also for her own heroism; not only for tackling such a case, and cases of national proportions, but through assisting the genuine needy; otherwise victims to the justice system. She had even offered clients, whom otherwise struggled with law expenses, very competitive and affordable rates. Even when necessary, she had defended clients for free. And clients were constantly referred to the honest and successful Law Attorney, Cassandra Smith, even recommended highly by the District's Clerk of Courts.

Robert took the rest of the day off work at the station house, following no immediate emergencies which warranted his personal attention, and went home with Cassandra. Later Robert had finalised Cassandra's packing of her belongings into their home, and the children were delighted. They talked a lot of old times. They had a lot of catching up to do.

Less than one week later, Ryan and Stephanie Stewart had spent the entire day preparing the house for their father's return, with the help of Cassandra, who was now settled in as part of the family again inside their home. They baked a cake, put a candle on it, and prepared the table for dinner upon his arrival. There was roast beef, baked potatoes, a large salad dish, and chilled champagne for the occasion.

Robert had spent a two day stakeout away from home again. When he had arrived home later on that evening he looked beat. Obviously, it was one of those bad cop days he refused to talk about.

Anyway, as he entered his home, the lights were off. That was odd, he thought to himself. It was not that late. Either everyone was out or they went to sleep already, a thought that disappointed him, for he had always looked forward to spending quality time with his family after work.

As he closed the door behind him and keyed the chain in the lock, as soon as he turned around suddenly the lights came on. And heads peered in from what appeared to be out of hiding behind furniture, and loud voices shouting, "Surprise!"

Robert lunged back astounded, as he studied the faces being his children, with Cassandra, his mum and pop, his younger sister Sue and his brother Paul, being the youngest of the Stewart siblings who was holding the birthday cake.

Robert never made a big deal of his birthday, but to his family it was. It was the day to recognise a great hero to so many people. His family had conspired together, in what appeared secrecy, to throw him a large party, and were waiting for him once he returned home. Then, they all let it be known that they called the station earlier which confirmed his arrival tonight. Thus, a surprise was waiting for him. Surprisingly, they all noticed that his own birthday had slipped his mind. And he thought his family would have forgotten. And had they, he would not have even mentioned such an error to them, anyhow.

Apparently, not a soul had forgotten. Nor would they allow this day to go on unannounced, as they appeared waiting. Cassandra embraced him. She was his soon-to-be bride, as shortly they announced their engagement to everyone. His entire family cheered in ecstatic cries. It would have appeared sudden, but not to Robert's family. They all knew her and of her. And understood all too well the fascination they had with each other in their past relationship for over two years, separated due to Cassandra's father's diagnosis of terminal cancer. And now that they were back together for good, the engagement was made official.

Robert's mum and pop embraced the two, and said, "You two belong together. We're so proud!" Followed by the simultaneous love and affection displayed by the rest of his family.

And Robert had even handed her a ring on this day. An engagement ring he bought for her this evening, prior his return home, from the twenty-four hour shopping mall jewellery store. She accepted the proposal in teary-eyed emotions of happiness, at a love that they considered was so powerful. And the actual wedding date would be set as soon as possible, prior mutual discussion. But it was promised that they would try not to let the engagement only drag on for too long a while. Though, once everyone recovered from the surprise of the moment, they had considered, but one strange paradox in it all. An irony they found comical. Even in laughter. That on his birthday, Robert had even planned on allowing it to remain forgotten, and as such, he was the one buying gifts on his birthday.

It was not going to be. For everyone stood in a line to congratulate him. Pulling out from behind their backs, their hands holding gift-wrapped presents they enthusiastically handed to him. His daughter, mum, sister and fiancée were the first to surprise him, and showered him with kisses and embraces. Then his father grabbed him in a huge bear-hug embrace, as his huge, stocky-built pop had actually lifted him off the ground. Robert felt his back being relocated, and coughed to such an embrace to be eased as his father said, "Happy birthday son. I am so proud of you." Then his son and his brother were the last to surprise him with gifts he would unwrap later.

Robert placed the gifts on the couch and glanced at his family in one of those sarcastic grins he was famous for. Then said, "Next year when you decide to do this again, can you please bring more presents!" He chuckled, as his sister and fiancée hit him in the stomach and attempted to tickle his ribs until he grovelled for help at his brother and father – to its unease.

Once they regained themselves, they all assembled at the dining room table to eat the dinner the family prepared. Which included a huge casserole of chowder that his father Carl, of Irish descent, and his mother Julie Stewart, of Swiss descent, had prepared for him at their waterfront owned fish market business earlier, to bring with them, as it was his favourite. Following the dinner, dessert was prepared almost an hour later, upon such a huge family meal being digested, leaving enough ease and comfort to ingest sweets.

After the meals Robert offered to help out with the dishes, but he would not hear the end to their refusal. In this family, no birthday boy undertook any work. They were only pampered silly, and no whim was left unattended to. He sat on the sofa and relaxed to the sounds of some music playing in the background, and thought to himself. Suddenly his bad day at work had ended in another of those heavenly family encounters. I must be the luckiest man on this earth to have such a family.

Robert began his family at an early age of twenty-one years of age, when he married his first wife – now long deceased of natural causes. In that year she conceived their first son Ryan, and two years later they were blessed with another child, their daughter Stephanie. And at ten years old, young Stephanie had realised her talent and abilities to sing; when she sang today at her father's birthday. A favourite song she rehearsed all day yesterday at the rehearsal hall inside Sam Cornelli's music studio, to have ready upon his arrival tonight. And of course, to surprise her father with such a special gift, which would become extra special, as he was not one to make a big deal of his own birthday; only other birthdays, particularly his children's.

From the onset, Robert had introduced his daughter to Sam Cornelli, a long-term friend, who had experience and friends in the music talent industry, to make his daughter a star and nurture the Great All-American Dream. For her, it was to sing more than anything. And to sing at her father's birthday was equally as important; not only because it was his birthday or simply because he was her father. But, also to thank him for all he was worth on behalf of herself and many others; as his wondrous contributions have aided them all with such astounding opportunities.

The Stewart family was one that was indeed envied by those close to them. And others too envied such a family's closeness and real-family bonding - described by many, as the perfect family; brains and spunk. Despite the struggling which became more apparent, when danger by those elements Robert had fought had entered into the very lives of all those he was, at the same time, attempting to preserve.

Once the party's attendance left for the night, Robert found Cassandra had adjourned to the master bedroom. As he entered once the children had nodded off to sleep, first thanking them for the surprise birthday celebration, he found Cassandra had slipped into a negligee. She sat at the dressing table brushing her long, thick blonde hair. Robert knelt down beside her, took the brush and assisted her.

As if instinctively, they both then rose from their seating positions. Perhaps, mixed with a tad bit of unease for a partnership and love that went unkindled for so many months, she motioned towards the bed.

They joined hands and they buried their lips together. And he worked his way down to the gentle-smooth flesh on her neck. At the same time his hands felt the familiar touch of her body: the shape of her hips, the firmness of her buttocks, and the gentle fullness of her breasts.

They glanced in each other's eyes, a look of simultaneous wanting. And she moaned, "Make love to me."

He was enticed too and gently pulled her on the bed, then fixed their positions so that they could remove each one's clothing when the breathing became more intense, as their excitement was aroused; his body vibrated on hers in arousal. They still had some clothing, but their lips would not part for now.

He removed the straps of her negligee from around her shoulders and lifted her body, then removed it entirely from beneath her. And she kicked it onto the floor as she unfastened the buttons on his shirt and removed it as well. And in moments they had removed the entire clothing of each one's bodies. He removed her panty's and laid it gently on the floor, studying the familiar beauty he had longed for, for so long. She reached her fingers to him, forcing his head to hers, fingers curling in the thickness of his curly hair. And his hands began its sensual motion along her body, again his mouth plunged along her neck, and then lowered to one nipple, his tongue tasted and sucked it gently as it became erect to the touch and then in circular motions moved to the other. His hands caressed her buttocks and moved across her legs as his mouth probed and tasted and excited her entire body in sheer eroticism.

He placed his fingers across her stomach, fingers moved below the navel, then lowered further for the clitoris, tickling the sensitive vaginal area. She gasped at the touch of the sensitive area and screamed at the point of climax, then begged for an encounter of his maleness, now enlarged and rigid. His fingers left her vagina and caressed the black mount of pubic hair, his hands again felt around her stomach then breasts. He then leaned his body over hers; she raised her hips to guide entrance of his organ between her legs. The violent pounding had both of them climaxed together, each gasping for breath.

She was still set on the bed lying on her back and he moved down on her again. As their lips met, she felt the tingling of her breasts as his hands felt them, and his hard maleness between her thighs, yet moving vigorously inside her wet swollen flesh. Her hands massaged over his back, fingernails coiling around his neck and back as their bodies joined together again, allowing no man or woman to separate them ever again, that would be the next worst thing to death. Eagerly she pulled at his back and lifted her pelvis to him by locking her silk-skinned legs around his hips as they fell in another orgasmic tremor.

Their lovemaking was as endless as its power of electricity. Only after many hours later, once it was over, and their familiarity with each other's souls was quenched, had they lay in bed in each other's arms, exhausted, gasping for air, smiling at the power of electricity they had just generated. Robert still caressed every inch of her perfect body that he admired as the most exquisite dessert; he could never have enough of. He was in awe of her completely. Those blue eyes, the dark-tanned skin, and her wild vaginal lust for passion were as great as his matrimonial avidity, and her body aroma that was a sweet enhancement to her powerful sex.

He sat up on one side of the bed as he fixed a stare at her naked body now sleeping peacefully on the other side, then rolling into his arms. She was an incredible woman; he vowed now to let no one ever come between them again.

One week later, Robert and Cassandra got married in a local Brooklyn family church. Close friends and family received invitations to the wedding. And John McCallum stood as Robert's best man.

Following the wedding reception, the chauffeur carried their luggage to the car and had driven them to the airport to catch the flight out to their honeymoon destination in Hawaii, scheduled to return in one week's time.

BOOK 4

CHAPTER 9

It was another week later when Robert arrived at the police station and met with John McCallum inside his office for a prearranged meeting deadline following his brief honeymoon departure.

John was temporarily assigned to some other minor police cases at present when Robert simply asked for this meeting with him, being his only trusted friend in the precinct and his confidant. And he requested a favour of him. That was to help him in secrecy on the Chess Player case - and not to tell anyone; John accepted very easily. He saw Robert was disturbed by the case, and being a life-long friend since childhood, as well as neighbours in their youth, he would do anything to assist him, thus the grounds were stipulated clearly. For no one must know of his participation. Confidentiality was imperative. Secrecy was a must, especially from the Commissioner. John understood.

John was also close-linked with the entire Stewart family as close friends' as well since even prior his joining the police force. He was a security guard before deciding to become a police officer in Robert's precinct. And now Robert was his best friend.

John understood the Chess Player case all too well. He and Robert discussed pertinent details in clashing conversations in the past. And John knew in secrecy that Robert was also a government agent when no one else publicly had been given the privilege to such information. John understood the Chess Player enemy had been responsible for the death of his uncle and was threatening his colleagues, friends and family's lives as well. Everyone was in danger, including himself and Robert from a threat that had in fact spanned its tentacles to the local police groups' as well. Robert, in himself, had to warn John - and each one agreed to keep a close watch for the others safety.

Robert confided in his friend his growing concerns for his welfare and safety by this enemy, particularly that of his family's. John nodded his head in agreement. Robert was being strong for all of them, never showing his anger or concern before his family. Though, at times, he hinted it. Nonetheless, he was their inspiration.

Robert made sure his calendar was cleared for this morning's briefing with John, given no interruptions. He went over the case list of suspects he considered, the first one being Niko Sasselli.

Niko Sasselli, due to Robert's past investigations into his criminal activities had recently concluded serving a ten year prison sentence in the state penitentiary for illegal gambling, possession of narcotics and stolen firearms and manslaughter. He was released on early parole for good behaviour after serving only three years. Nonetheless, he was forced to see a parole officer for seven years, once a week. He was doing fine so far, though the frequent reports to a parole officer was said to have put a cramp in his day-to-day business operations. Asked if he thought he was clean, Robert hinted, "He'd be back to his old tricks again."

Though, when Robert questioned him in relation to the Chess Player case, inside his very home in Brooklyn, Niko had strongly denied participation or knowledge, past and present to it all, and said, "Why would I risk my parole over any sordid criminal activity?"

Robert simply cast his eyes at him and smiled ironically. "Why exactly?"

Niko Sasselli, at his own defence had stated, "You cannot blame me for all the problems in the world. I just got out of prison. Surely, you cannot blame me for every crime that was committed since then?"

Robert nodded his head in sarcasm, then put his point across to him rather bluntly, stating, "There's an old saying Nik. 'He who tends to play in the mud becomes a filthy pig.'"

Niko Sasselli knew that from that moment his old arch-enemy Robert Stewart had placed him in the hot seat once again.

Right now John had exclaimed, "Nonetheless, we must not underestimate that man who became head of the Farlev family by shooting his way to the top; killing his predecessor that he served beneath, and got away with it by pleading guilty to manslaughter. Where, all the while he headed the Farlev family regime with his small army who took charge. That old man had a lot of gist."

Robert concurred. "Yes, our Mr. Sasselli has a very bad reputation. Not exactly a model citizen. He poses himself now as a law-abiding person, but that's rubbish. Anyway, he is my number one suspect for the Chess Player case. I have no proof right now as our search for the target's identity is frustrated by a bureaucratic hierarchical structure left unpenetrated. Right now I'm thinking one alternative, partner. That is for us to go off on our own like the old days. Perhaps, bend the rules a little. It has worked in the past."

John knew exactly what he was thinking and asked, "Well, do you have any other suspects, possibilities?"

Robert replied, simply. "One man I suspect who is basically the last person anyone seems to suspect next to the Pope is Domenico Armando. It's just a theory now. But, if he is the Chess Player, or whoever he is, he obviously has

104

his lackeys doing his dirty work for him. And he has kept his fingernails squeaky clean. That's why this guy is not even suspected of so much as jaywalking."

John remained speechless and listened to Robert's theories that were always proven beneficial in the past and urged him on, as Robert proclaimed, "This Chess Player never gets his hands dirty. Always gets other people to do his dirty work for him as he controls them whilst lurking from backstage."

John understood Robert had a personal stake in such a case, what with the death of his uncle, friends and police colleagues over the years. And the growing danger he himself and his family were in because of it all. And right now he was willing to suspect anyone and everyone with just cause. Robert had exhausted all possible leads. The Chess Player family was an elite group of professionals, certainly, not an average crime family. If such a profile, as 'average', in any Mob-related case had even existed.

Robert exclaimed, furthermore, "Look partner, in this line of work I always believe that no matter how cunning a man, there is always something he leaves behind. We just have to find it."

Nonetheless, Robert had a plan and he enlisted John to aid him in casting it into motion this evening. Some very dark thoughts had been entering his mind and he was certain that they were not the product of overwork. Right now, all he knew was that they had a list of suspects, some possibilities, some not. Robert would begin checking out the possibilities and ruling them out one by one whom no longer fitted the Chess Player bill; the entire profile. To hence, shorten the suspect list until they had obtained a fix on their man. Thus, by ruling out unnecessary suspects meanwhile, they had less to work with.

Now, one thing experience had taught him was that whenever he was struck by a crossroads and his path was not clear, to always listen to his instincts. His 'gut instincts' never failed him. And right now he was going to follow his natural inborn reflexes and accurate intuition in order to uncover the truth. He was going to set his man up to reveal himself; and force him to play his hand. He was going to put Niko Sasselli to the test.

Robert picked up his telephone and dialled. He arranged for a telegraph to be sent to Niko Sasselli by messenger this evening; the text to the telegraph stated that there was going to be a meeting at Brooklyn, Pier 19, at midnight, concerning the Power Project by the man in charge. But Robert left no signature.

Robert kept surveillance on Niko Sasselli all through the evening. And had even wired the targeted pier for sound in advance, with discreet listening devices which had transmitted to a miniature speaker receiver they held in their possession. As he and John hid out of sight, beneath a close-by stairwell, awaiting the arrival of Niko Sasselli, whose arrival was, prompt with one bodyguard.

Niko had waited himself almost fifteen minutes in anticipation, striding nervously along the pier decking, when they overheard his bodyguard saying: "Perhaps the Chess Player wants to set you up, sir?"

Niko replied, "Hardly. All his demands were met."

Robert, with his partner John, holding tight surveillance on the area had glanced at each other as their thoughts resulted in the same conclusion. They now knew that Niko Sasselli was not the Chess Player and ruled out the possibility when Niko said to his bodyguard, "Our associate won't show. Let's go. Perhaps you are right. This could be a set up."

So now Robert had one less suspect; one less suspect on his target list to work with. Niko Sasselli was immediately ruled out from the Chess Player suspect list.

BOOK 5

CHAPTER 10

Despite cold animosity Robert had felt for Domenico, a friendship nonetheless appeared to ensue. Domenico had constantly issued invitations to Robert and his family for dinner at the Armando mansion. And of course, Cassandra and the children were delighted to be invited, and dinner with the Armando clan had always turned out a fascinating evening. Domenico had openly declared his friendship and confidence in Robert before the two families present at such dinner occasions. The last was this evening. Robert never turned down an invitation by Domenico, or gave him or his family the opportunity to suspect his ill-feelings towards him. Robert realised that if Domenico was practising unconstitutional activities, the best method in gaining insight to them was to become close to him. And that could really only be accomplished by not exposing his suspicions or making public allegations against the man. But to play it calm and see where the supposed friendship had led him.

When Domenico first met Robert, there was something he sensed from this fascinating man, that as he got to know him even more so, he could not have had more respect and admiration for him if he were part of his own blood. For he detected an intelligence, smarts, courage, force and power in everything he said and did. And as he spent more time with him, and learnt more about the Great Robert Stewart, he found his love of family was as much an obsession for him as it was for himself. Each had spent his life fighting for what they believed in was just, sacrificing their own happiness only to benefit their families. And so they lived their entire lives through their families' eyes. And their children's joy became their joy. Knowing that they would have all their needs catered for. And they would not have to endure the hardship they themselves had only experienced at their early age, fighting only to survive and preserve their families. Robert, who had to fight the terror-ridden waterfront since the age of fourteen, in order to protect his family, and Domenico faced with the same horrendous predicament as a child, in a family feud with the Santucci family that cost him his parents.

So Domenico had felt a sort of closeness, a bond between Robert and himself, even much despite Robert being an officer of the law. Though apart from sharing similar family belief systems and ideals they had only lived two different lives. One fought for justice against criminality, and the other believed in creating a family business powerbase, thus amassing control over all the Don Santucci's of the world.

Robert was strong-willed, and Domenico knew he could never be converted into his world as he was not an ordinary man. For Robert stuck to his convictions. And this was a rare trait only the strongest of men could sustain. Domenico had realised, both he and Robert, though opposing in one certain ideal, had in fact shared numerous similarities. In himself, it was so refreshing to meet a man as Robert who could match his own strengths and beliefs as such, when no one else could. Domenico had finally met a man he considered equal to him in every way.

Domenico had even considered that his daughter Monica's marriage to Paul Stewart was a vital stepping stone into luring Robert into the picture as well. As a marriage would join the two families together and unite them as one.

As later that evening, following Robert, his wife and children's departure from his home, Domenico insisted to his Counsellor, Rex Higgins, in private, inside his study room den, "Yes. It would create an alliance between the Armando-Stewart families. And with the two greatest families joined together and bonded as allies and friends, there is nothing I cannot accomplish - as this alliance would mean friends and allies forever. Yes. Robert Stewart's fate is in my hands. I will control his destiny."

One week later Robert had stopped over at Domenico's home as Domenico requested his services furthermore in order to examine his security system this time as it was false-alarming. Robert also previously admitted to Domenico that he was much experienced with such a home-security field, as he had done much of the security even on his own home, admittedly, and for his family and friends. And Robert, in only a short time had diagnosed the security problem in the Armando estate, and then had corrected the loose wiring. Domenico, seeming in an urgent hurry at this moment had informed him that he needed to go out on an emergency meeting that was called at his Brooklyn head office. All the bodyguards were out of the house with his wife who was doing the shopping, and with the children who left earlier.

His Counsellor Rex Higgins had stated, "Sorry sir. I have sent them all with your family. I did not think you were going out right now."

Robert had seen Domenico for the first time raise his hands in the air in a bit of a bind. He never left the security of his home unprotected. So Robert offered to drive him where he needed to go, and he could rank his chauffeur and bodyguards to his office later on to pick him up.

Domenico slapped Robert on his back at an idea he saluted and said to his counsellor, "There's no need to rank our other reserve bodyguards. I'll be with Robert. He will be by my side every moment that I am out of the house. I'll be safe!" He smiled with tremendous confidence and faith in Robert's single-handed abilities, as if those abilities would outmatch his stream of bodyguards. He understood Robert was a good man and would guard him well. After all, Robert in his profession in the past at times had served as a bodyguard to many individuals, even high-profile persons. And with his keen eye and ready wit was known to guard a man even more effectively than a legion of trained bodyguards.

In not too long and with the Armando chief counsellor's blessing, Robert had driven Domenico inside his civilian car to outside the Armando Brooklyn head office. Domenico's office was situated on the greatest height floor of the 28th storey building he completely owned on 30th Avenue. Robert first had parked the car in a space across the road.

As the two had walked the street together, Robert taking Domenico safely to the office building's main entrance, all the passers-by; men, women and children, who recognised the two, what they described as much legends of New York City, seeing them together, had mobbed them. Ladies swarmed at the two and kissed them on the cheek. And men had shaken their hands extending much gratitude for all their good deeds in the past and present. Normally, Domenico was rushed passed the swarming fans broken away by his four bodyguards. One posted on either side of him. And one positioned behind; and the other in front of him. But he seemed just as carefree with just a singular aid this afternoon, because it was Robert acting as his bodyguard. After all, Robert posed as the sort of character man no one would mess with. To mess with the Great Robert Stewart was asking for trouble. And he would certainly make them plenty sorry for their ill-conceived attempts!

The people viewed them two together walking the street right this very moment as heroes saving them and their neighbourhoods in the past. And now being observed by each other's side, walking the street together, in what was seen as a fabulous alliance, had in fact overwhelmed the whole city of passers-by this very moment as something remarkable and powerful. To have two great equal forces working together in indeed a much considered partnership was tremendous, even inspiring to many.

But the two became alarmed by the sudden screams of departure by the mobbing crowd as they pointed ahead to alarm them, and warn them of the emerging danger. Only fifty meters ahead they spotted four assassins wearing sunglasses and a hat pulled over their heads and faces to prevent identification, wearing all heavy black-linen overcoats whilst holding huge machine guns. They rushed towards them to fire their machine guns at point-blank range. The ambush caught them unaware until now being warned off. When Robert quickly threw Domenico to the ground at the same time as he warned the close-by residents to run for cover and safety inside the local shops; the incident happened so quickly when an innocent elderly pensioner nearby was caught in the crossfire before he could exit the lines of fire as two other people were shot by the gunmen. Robert too dived for cover and rolled next to Domenico behind a nearby car on the sidewalk of the busy street across the mall of shopping centres, to avoid the spray of bullets that targeted the car they hid behind. And he noticed more innocent victim bystanders fell to the ground being struck by bullets, when Robert pulled out his revolver and quickly reacted.

Robert raised his revolver to the side of the car, peered an eye at the gunmen drawing closer and he fired at the gunmen, maybe eight shots until his chamber was empty. And when it was, the firing had ended. And it was safe to draw out now as a witness called out to them saying that all the gunmen have been hit and were dead on the ground. Only confirmed moments later by paramedics called at the scene to examine the wounded. And swarming police squad cars pulled up and approached their Captain. Robert gave them names of witnesses to question and he would return to the station house later on to file a report and issue an official statement concerning the freak assassinations.

Robert frustrated by their leaving him no choice but to fire at them in retaliation. If one assassin were alive, they could be questioned as to who had in fact ordered the hit. But Domenico insisted he needed no questioning. He already knew. It was his arch-enemy rival, the Santucci family who ordered the hit.

Domenico, whom moments earlier had raised himself onto his feet, seeming unaffected, and no nerves showing, had only cancelled his business meeting that afternoon when Robert in his car returned him back to the safety of the Armando family fortress in Brooklyn Heights on 5th Avenue. Escaping the now angry crowds of people, scorning at the evil dead men for even conceding of doing harm to this country's two men of considered, gospel sainthood.

It was now in the security of his own home when Domenico embraced Robert in a brotherly affection; extending deep gratitude for the recognition he placed upon his saving of his life this afternoon.

Domenico said with two large hands lopped on Robert's shoulders in deep emotion, "I owe you and your family my life. I will do anything to repay you. Robert, this very day I declare you like family. If there is anything you or your family needs, anything, I am in your debt."

His counsellor stood concerned for his padrone's safety as he overheard the news on the radio. He announced his family was on their way home as they too were concerned. They telephoned a short while ago startled by an attempt against their great father's life. Anyway, Rex Higgins was now equally stunned by the revelations and powerful words his master had presented before Robert. It was a gesture that signified his most noblest of respect for him as family. Robert too was astounded by the shock and the force in what was said.

But Domenico did not finish. He went on to say, "Robert, I would like to offer you a job as my personal bodyguard. If you leave the police force and come and work for me, the rewards will be something beyond your wildest dreams. You will not have to leave your family on trips. Your salary will be doubled, even tripled. You can have anything you want as an addition to the employment package." He said now confident that Robert was able to protect him more efficiently than his own paid bodyguards.

There was a moment's silence. Robert refused to comment. And Domenico and his counsellor eyed each other thinking the same thought. It seemed as though Domenico was not going to get Robert Stewart on his payroll just yet. He would not budge at the tremendous offer. Nonetheless, the offer would remain open for him to consider for as long as he required. And the gratitude was there all the same for him to collect.

Once Robert had left his home, Domenico turned to his counsellor in a changed face, a temper that became violent and rare, which he had never displayed to his counsellor before. But this very day Rex had disappointed him. And Domenico had demanded that in future he follow his orders with extra care to rectify the situation. He considered his sending of all the bodyguards from his home at one time without first calling the emergency standby employ was sheer carelessness on his part. He too blamed today's almost assassination on his head. And his failure to conduct crucial business was marred too by his counsellor's sudden carelessness. Domenico considered as simply out of character for a man he placed in such high regard, both personally and professionally. Where he went on to explain that if it were not for Robert, today he would be a dead man. That in itself was a staggering prospect for the counsellor to digest. And in fact Rex Higgins was allowed no utterance on his own behalf to establish a defence.

But Domenico still enraged, refused to notice the concern displayed by his closest protégé, and said, "Do not fail me again!" Domenico grabbed him forcefully with two hands clamped onto both of his shoulders and shook him almost violently. As if sternly warning him that if he were a lesser man in his organisation he surely would have ordered him dead right now. But realised his rank and importance only got him off with a simple warning this time when Domenico went on to say, "Do not fail me again for your sake as well as mine."

Domenico Junior and his dutifully-trained wife Sandra Armando too shared a great fondness and liking for Robert and Cassandra as Domenico had. They asked Robert and Cassandra to stand as Godparents to their seven-month-old son, Domenico's first grandchild, Domenico Armando the 3rd. They accepted the honoured gesture. It of course came with a great responsibility, and not only binding a close relationship and a religious bonding with the child, but with the Armando family as well. Robert as Godfather to his grandson meant that he was to ensure the security of Domenico's family and its heir for the future generations to his throne.

Robert and Cassandra, despite reservations were honoured to stand as Godparents at the Christening of little Domenico Armando the 3rd. They now became the second parents to the child to look out for him with his real parents as well.

Domenico, as he stood outside the Brooklyn Catholic Church where the ceremony had ended commemorating the boy's first communion and baptism, said to Robert, "We are family now." For in himself, now the child would certainly intertwine and link the Stewart family with the Armando family.

Domenico too had visions of his daughter Monica to forward a marriage with Paul Stewart, but that only turned out to be a fling. Nonetheless, with Robert as Godfather and Cassandra as Godmother to his grandson the families would be tied together as 'One' anyhow.

Domenico at home later that evening in a private celebration left the room of guests where Robert and his family attended too, and spoke to his counsellor in his private study, now oblivious to the mistake Rex Higgins had recently made, as Domenico enforced, "Now that Robert is Godfather to my grandson we are presented with an interesting paradox. Supposedly two enemies of each other's world are banded together in an area where we are admittedly the most vulnerable - Family. Both Robert and I are now presented with a blood bond, one that must never be broken. From here on out we are bonded together by family. Even despite my realising that my terribly suspicious new-found friend Robert Stewart became Godfather to my grandson even without much convincing. Perhaps, maybe, even for reasons of his own hidden agenda and purpose, as I, the excellent Gamesman that he is; much like myself! And he only persuaded his very lovely wife to also become Godmother. Though, of course, he would never ask her to get too directly involved in our game here, naturally, the devoted and extremely protective husband he is. Nonetheless, I have them all! Yes. For I wanted Robert Stewart on my side and all along I told you I would get him. Ahh, yes, you see, I told you. And I can see it in your now smiling eyes right here that you approve, yes? Ahh, perfect! And now I even have him in such a way in which is better than I had initially intended through only just a job offer. For now I have him not only as a friend, but I have him as an addition to my family. To me, that serves my purpose even better. Yes, indeed! And should his brother Paul wed my daughter - and with Robert and his wife's relationship with the Armando family, it will create a powerful link in itself with the Armando clan. And with Paul's linkage as well by a wedding, the Armando-Stewart family alliance will be bonded only eternally in a blood chain so powerful that nothing will break it. And they will learn soon to become allies in my world. And their families will follow the Armando spirit through and through."

Domenico hit his hand onto the shoulder of his now favourite protégé in a chuckle of triumph, reminiscent as a man to whose plans were going exactly as he proceeded. He smiled victoriously with his fists clenched together at the power thus wielded by two mighty forces joined as allies. He then said, "My consigliore, everything is going according to plan, everything."

It was only at that very moment when his daughter Monica entered the room weeping for her father. Monica Armando felt greatly ill at ease when she sought solace from her father as the man she loved was in love with another woman. And he left her without a word to marry this woman. Monica had shown her father photographs of his new wife named Amy Reed. She was brunette, gorgeous and in her mid twenties - an apparent childhood sweetheart of his from European middle class background. She told her father how Paul had even sought his own independence by seeking employment as a private investigator working for a man named Des Horsecraft. She showed him the pictures of Paul and his new wife Amy together, confirming that she had Paul followed to see if he really loved her as much as she loved him. And the truth dawned on her. Monica of course went to seek comfort from her father.

Domenico tried to ease her troubled mind by revealing, "The Stewarts are united strong. They have powerful personalities. They would in fact die for each other!"

Monica brushed the weeping tears from her face and said, "Paul is in love with another woman. He doesn't love me."

Domenico caressed the shoulders to his troubled daughter and reassured her by a simple fact. "He broke your heart, yes. But, it is my experience that you can force anyone to do anything. Even in matters of the heart. If you want Paul, you only have to ask and you shall have him. You can have your own nuptials with him anytime you choose. I will make him yours."

Monica exclaimed, "Yes. It would be easy to have Paul and get rid of his wife Amy, that obstacle. But would it suit my purpose? We can force a man to do things, but we cannot force him to feel things he does not feel. He can never love me like he loves her. It would only be a one-sided love. I cannot live like that."

Domenico understood now how his daughter truly loved him - and still had. She felt never for any man as she had of Paul Stewart. He said to his daughter, "It would be so perfect if you and Paul were united in marriage. It would bind the two strongest families completely, adding to the link Robert and his lovely Cassandra have bestowed upon us as Godparents to my little grandson. And I could beat any competition with any foreign power by pooling such powerful resources. My Golden Girl, all you have to do is ask. I will arrange for Amy to, how shall I put it, disentangle her marriage vows and her existence from his life entirely, and make the road clear for you. Always remember that. Remember, that if you want something bad enough you can have it, meaning Paul Stewart. And remember my daughter that what you wish is my command! You are my daughter and you can change your mind at any time. I shall refuse you nothing, whether your mind is fixed tomorrow or next year. All you need do is ask and I will fix all your problems for you. Never forget that."

Monica raced up to her room, put her head on her pillow and lay there on her bed for a moment in a sudden changed face. She even chuckled as she contemplated the thought that thrilled her body with shivers of electrical excitement. With a father like Domenico Armando she had the connections at the base of her fingers to change the course of a man's life to suit her purpose at any one time. She could either bring man happiness or take it away from him. The thought of any man's fate literally being changed by one heartbeat had her rolling on her bed in crazed laughter, tearing away beneath the flowers to a rose plant she snatched into her hands from her bedside table. She dropped each leaf on the ground, reminiscent to that of a Russian Roulette Prank, saying to herself as each leaf was dropped, "Should I-Should I not kill Amy?" And all the while giggling at the thought that her father, the great Domenico Armando, who was only a request away was willing to do just that, and perform such a deed for her as simply as robbing the local candy store. It was wicked!

BOOK 6

CHAPTER 11

Domenico Armando had spent the next ten days preparing for the battle ahead between his family and the Santucci clan. He had reshuffled and reassigned his soldiers and captains to patrol the territories in the city occupied by the enemy. And of course regrouping his power infrastructure and thus amassing certain allies in other families to aid in such a bloody battle most certain to arise. Though his family was the strongest, particularly in power structure to that of the enemy, Domenico insisted meanwhile on taking no chances and leaving no stone unturned to ensure his family's safety. Domenico winning such a battle against the Santucci family; even against any family across the nation was guaranteed. For the odds were much stacked into his favour. But to ensure the safety of his family and children, which were at the most vulnerable spot and line of attack by the enemy, double and triple precautions were legislated.

Preparing for battle, it was realised that the Armando family was indeed quite a powerhouse prepared to retaliate with a heavy blow, particularly, with its new alliance and the taking over of the demolished power of the Castalone era. Giuseppe Castalone, what with his incarceration in prison and his business having suffered the loss of most of its power, the repercussions were fatal to his infrastructure. Many raids by police had wiped a great percentage of the empire. And what was left of that family was taken over and incorporated into the Armando family operations by Domenico himself. And its people, soldiers, even his own son, Rowan, had offers cast at them by the Armando group in order to accept positions in a change of families. Otherwise most left without incomes and a source of family protection, naturally accepted.

Rowan, after all had an ulterior motive for pledging his undying loyalty to Domenico. For not only the power he himself could wield from such a friendship, but also in hopes that he may be able to secure a future for his father as well, since he would refuse to ever turn his back on him, despite his circumstances. And he had arranged a meeting with Domenico inside a secret abandoned warehouse in the outskirts of Brooklyn. A place where no witnesses were present and no one could see them speak together, as they left and entered the meeting room separately. And of course, the warehouse was checked prior to the conference for eyes and ears possibly in the roam.

Once they received the all clear by Domenico's standby bodyguards to proceed in the secret meeting in the dead quiet of the night, Rowan pleaded his case to Domenico. "Inmates are beating into him. I want a statement. I want another hearing going. I want him to be transferred to a minimum security prison. You can arrange anything. Perhaps arrange for credible witnesses to testify on his behalf. And then get him out of prison and out of the country with a fake passport, which we could smuggle to him in prison. And have him disappear somewhere to start a new life for himself. My father's health is deteriorating. He is developing a heart condition. I need your help to move him to another facility. He needs your help; the help of a patriotic friend in the public's eye: A statement of support testifying on his behalf in a court. Prison life may ultimately kill him. He won't survive on the inside. That bastard Robert Stewart will kill him and be the death of my father. You - I understand, cannot get mixed up openly in this. But, surely you can arrange someone to testify on my father's behalf; something – anything; my father always respected and supported you. He never refused you an accommodation to invest in your projects. He was your friend and as an ally helped influence others to support you as well. He had great faith in your business judgement and acumen. No rational person could question his support."

Domenico, concerned for his valued protégé's desperation had insisted he would not look the other way and ignore his plea. Though some thought would most certainly be required into the particulars of it all to eventuate in order to achieve such a goal of Giuseppe's safe departure from the country.

Domenico said, "I understand; though out of the same respect I insist on not permitting your father to walk out of prison empty-handed. And since the Castalone family is wiped out, non-existent in the eyes of the commission, with all its assets and money accounted for, I shall make sure to make a place for him in my family, now that his health is in trouble as well. I understand how accustomed a man of his stature was to his creature comforts and lavish lifestyle. He will be deprived of nothing. After all, the Castalone and Armando family had always established a close friendly alliance together. So he will be promised a position also when he leaves prison. And financially he will be looked after to tend to my other businesses - perhaps in Switzerland."

Rowan insisted, "We must not overlook anything. Nothing can go wrong."

Domenico nodded, "Of course. For his departure from the country we must arrange his false passport; all the necessary documentation to be waiting for him – and the necessary transportation to fly him by plane to his new country hideout on my secure territory. Only the most competent and trustworthy people will be assigned to the task for his escape of removing him out of prison and escorting him by plane out of the country safely to my foreign turf. Everything will be untraceable: the vehicles to transport him to the private plane, his change of clothing on that day, the private plane itself -

everything! And the licence plates on the vehicles to be used for his transfer out of prison will be all phoneys. Everything will be taken care of perfectly!"

Rowan said, "Robert Stewart, our mutual enemy must not stand in our way. He has blocked all legal paths to my father's freedom. He provided the courts with damning testimony and hard evidence against him. He is a very clever and dangerous enemy. He must not get in our way!"

Domenico agreed. "Yes. I assure you, I know how to cover my tracks. I have a plan already underway, though it would not happen overnight. After all, breaking someone out of prison is not a popular thing to do. And it does not matter what people think, so long as they cannot prove anything."

All in all, Domenico had agreed to aid his father on one condition - that once Giuseppe had escaped, he worked for him, and not for himself, for obvious reasons and an insistence not to lose a prized employee as Rowan, now serving the Armando family. The agreement was made and the process to get him out of the country safely was underway. After all, Domenico would also benefit from Giuseppe's escape because he had operations abroad in which he had required someone capable as Giuseppe to run them.

Though it was made evident that Giuseppe's legal way of escaping the harsh reality of prison life was a virtual no go. Especially with his son's history and the fact he fled the courtroom at his father's trial, and in all the eyes that mattered why would he run if he was not guilty. Rowan was skinny, but strong - with a reputation for being quick with a knife and gun. He was a convicted killer and drug peddler who aided his father as a ruthless strong-arm. To the authorities in general, he was a dangerous menace to society!

And of course Giuseppe's reputation was just the much gleaming. He was known to have killed his wife and his father and threatened the life of his daughter Renee in witness protection relocation program who refused him. He was a man who had changed in recent years to relentless savagery and barbarianism. A man who was also very much feared by his colleagues next to Domenico. Giuseppe was a man who could kill his own family. There was no telling his capabilities. All that was assured was that Rowan still persisted in faith in his father, particularly at this time, what with Giuseppe's deteriorating health crisis. However, the likeness in father and son became all the more evident. And it was believed that such closeness in their relationship had remained unchanged due to the fact they shared such similarities. The main being that Giuseppe Castalone and his son, the entire Castalone family were caught under Robert Stewart's wrath. At Giuseppe's arrest, the judge denied him bail, all things considered. His arrest led him open to shame and scalding by the rest of the Mafia commission. Even by Domenico himself, who made the highest bids for his territory. He had taken over the remaining bits and pieces of his empire that was left after Robert invited the government to procure endless police raids, seizures, confiscations and crackdowns on most of the Castalone family operations. Thus following the Castalone downfall and Giuseppe Castalone's incarceration, the famous old ritual was realised: His enemies had gotten richer by what he had left behind. And in not too long a period, the Castalone family empire was incorporated into the Armando family operations.

But despite such hopeful praises by his son all along in aid of support to his father, Giuseppe's health had been rapidly deteriorating. Following his arrest he had suffered a nervous breakdown and then heart problems. It was not long before Giuseppe Castalone's escape ambitions were brought to an abrupt end. Three nights later, he suffered a fatal heart attack inside his cell, two hours before his next meal was scheduled.

And following the death of Giuseppe Castalone, Renee Castalone's body had turned up dead, reported shot to death in the head three times in her hiding place in the Caribbean. And Robert Stewart knew it was another Mob hit and that Rowan Castalone had a hand in it. However, theories to deeper Mob involvement were linked, that they perceived her as a future threat to the organisation at an entirety. She was a traitor to the Mafia, and now that her father was dead she may feel safe to withdraw from hiding and capitalise the police efforts against the Mob. Despite ongoing speculation into the death, all that was confirmed was that a third party was surely involved and that Giuseppe Castalone was only the beginning to their underworld rivalry.

CHAPTER 12

Domenico Armando had prepared himself thoroughly for what was declared the unlosable battle against the Santucci family. With the entire commission as his ally fending for his corner, it seemed as though the Santucci family were headed for a fast-approaching defeat and its turmoil was made apparant.

It was almost sixteen years when Domenico had called on the national gathering of family bosses and its representatives to put forward his POWER PROJECT, as a preliminary discussion and introduction to the underworld commission. It was a secret meeting he hosted in a top secret plush establishment in the city; a plan that was given no choice but a united support front by all the bosses. It became a meeting that also officially recognised him as the Boss of Bosses - the Godfather of all Godfathers. And his role as power broker over the entire commission was thus sealed and accepted. Such a meeting had other motives and purposes as well.

A formal gathering of all the bosses with the exception of the Santucci group were invited. Such a strategy was made, thus to isolate the enemy family from the rest of his former friends and allies. And such a clever manoeuvre proved it's wiser to this day, now that such a battle had resurfaced once again, initiated by Domenico. Thus, to drive the family out of its established territories in the United States and settle a long term personal vendetta as well with the chief Don of the family - Don Mad Dog Santucci. Who had only recently been rumoured to have surfaced above his underground hiding place, since two decades, to meet Domenico Armando face to face in this personal vendetta, and square away his own retaliation for the murder of his son to wed the daughter Annemarie of his chief arch-enemy. And to wager an attack on the Armando group in order to prevent his entire family now from being driven out of its established United States front, with the support of the entire commission as Domenico's entourage against him.

Such a retribution attack by the Santucci family was indeed derived as desperate, if not foolish. For in all probability and calculation Don Santucci could never win a battle against the Armando family and especially outfight Domenico, with the entire commission in his pocket as well. What with being forced to fend off attack from the police and government variety that were also out for his blood at the same time, which in fact had proven such extreme danger to the Santucci group – on its own; and were perceived his greatest enemies beneath Domenico. Domenico, controlling such a panel of power from both sides of the law had it declared that the battle he was facing against the Santuccis was indeed the 'unlosable war'.

However, Domenico had simply refused underestimating such an enemy. And calculated such a move to come out of hiding and make his public appearance into New York at some point soon, was indeed the product of the ravings and insanity that of the 'Mad Dog' his bitter opponent in battle was so nicknamed, and dubbed by the commission to be.

Such action was indeed a desperate move. One made by a man who obviously understood he could never win a battle against Domenico, the most reputed and powerful family leader in the entire country, who controlled the main New York Five Families which were supreme power in itself. Though such a move was forecasted by the Mad Dog as coming from a deranged man who was really only trying to settle at the very least a personal score with the Armando chief.

Domenico was considered impenetrable. There was no way the enemy could get to him, through a layer after many layers of armed shadow security surrounding him by the minute. Though Domenico estimated his desperation had wagered to seek revenge against him by getting to his family.

So, Domenico had initiated house rules before his children in particular. They were not to leave his house at all, unless absolutely necessary, with at least ten bodyguards in two cars following each one of them; and, a team of bodyguards to sit on either side of them in the passenger vehicle to secure his children.

In crux, Domenico had foreseen his family being the targets of an immediate danger that the Santucci family would attack as the most vulnerable targets of all the Armando family empire. So, Domenico had forecasted the Mad Dog's strategy for retribution and avenging his son's death, thus by striking all of Domenico's children, in a reminiscent display to an eye for two eyes kind of perverted vengeance. And Domenico had sought to prepare himself against each and every one of such possible eventualities bound to take place; in careful strategy.

So security was tripled and tripled again where his children in particular were concerned. And of course such security teams were forewarned to impose much scrutiny over certain traps imposed by the enemy family, who may resort to pretence and trickery in an attempt to drive his children out of the house and into the open. To be made apparent targets for execution. Thus, to prevent such traps, Domenico had ordered his children to control their parts to his business from home, and not the outside office at Armando Towers in their high-rise building on the east side of Brooklyn.

And such emergencies that may suddenly flare up, supposedly to draw them out into the open would be handled by Domenico and his counsellor. Who would investigate the nature of its validity, and any and all such dilemmas would be handled by their people thereon beneath them. In short, Domenico, his children, his entire immediate family, including his grandchild little Domenico the 3rd and his son's wife Sandra were not permitted to leave the house. And guards were made privy of such strict orders and under no circumstances was his children or his wife or grandchild who would stay at his house leave until the battle and score against Santucci and the immediate danger was over. And such orders of release would only be carried out once the go-ahead came from the very top - only the Domenico Armando himself, personally.

There was no concern at such present time for his family's emotional dilemma to such confinement of 'remaining prisoners in their home', or being subjected to a form of even 'house arrest'. It did not matter what they called it. Their only priority was their safety and well-being. And strict orders and guidelines were insured to preserve their safety. Guards were posted around them, shadowing their moves inside and outside the Armando house constantly. For the Armando estate was recruited with a specially armed team of specialist soldiers, an army of them to ensure such family's safety. And all the houses along the Armando estate had been bought, owned and rented by the Armando family. As well as owning the entire street Domenico bought once his rise and soar to fame to claim his nefarious power as the Boss of Bosses was initiated. All houses had been refurnished with resting couches by the network of soldiers to rest in, given replacement guards in turn to guard and secure the Armando livelihood round-the-clock. And all expenses to the maintaining of the households' effects were billed to the internal captains of the Armando family.

Thus, close surveillance along both sides of the street and its entrances was plenty notice for their chief boss to react in case an enemy was spotted. And in the meanwhile his family and children were not to be deprived of anything. Whatever they required, Domenico or his counsellor would send a completely trustworthy employee to purchase and bring them whatever they wished.

Following Domenico's reign over the commission and his ultimate power over everyone that mattered, and his public exclusion and isolation of the Santucci family from ever being included in such commission meetings and commission discussions; such isolation went on for twenty years. And, years prior, since before Domenico's formal meeting of bosses to discuss the Power Project was initiated. And since Don Santucci was not invited, and thus singled out as an outsider, given no respect for the past two decades, he would never approach anywhere within the city limits near Domenico or the facets that he had occupied. Even if such families guaranteed his safety and pledged friendship then against their new leader, he would never fall for such a set up or an elaborate trap or hoax to spring him out into the open during his twenty years in underground hiding, whilst eluding the firing line as such. He knew Domenico was the master of cunning, very complex; a brilliant mind, and a genius. And had accomplished what no one else could. He had controlled all the families in his back pocket.

Though understood Domenico would never ask them to get involved in their personal vendetta and interfere in what was only between their two families, unless absolutely necessary; if Domenico passed down a referendum to legislate such a move. Or if in turn, the war had obstructed and threatened their livelihood which was a present concern. Apart from that, the Santucci-Armando family history had marked no bearing to them or the rest of the families' everyday conduct of business. It was not their concern unless invited.

Though among all the gossip in the rumour mill beneath the noble facades of the royal commission nationally, had suggested, not publicly or to anyone's face, that such an otherwise defeat of Domenico may in fact relieve a large chunk of anxiety from silent minds, eager to have his hold on them relinquished. So they could finance their own powers individually as the old days. And go their separate ways without the burden of an equivalent Gestapo dictator and communist leader otherwise pulling their strings. Were such thoughts of those, despite being closemouthed with a 'be silent and live longer' rational, yet had a knack of giving themselves away. Though in all actuality, a defeat against the source Domenico was out of the question.

All the families together, should suggestion be made to all line up against Domenico as well with the Santuccis could not outmatch his power, influence and manpower to outfight, defeat nor penetrate his thick impenetrable security. Even then, it was highly unlikely. However, such irony was considered humorous. With what nerve had the Santuccis, with the strength of one half of the least powerful of an individual family, and with what gusto, could they even consider aligning themselves against the Armando league?

Such a rejection imposed among the Santucci family had indeed been attempted in countermand by such a panic-stricken group. And indeed whose representative had passed a bill to emissaries owing allegiance to both sides via a somewhat negotiator. That had taken place before the vote was cast to succeed the Power Project in its first official meeting discussions - that indeed he wished to invest also in the project with the other families. Domenico realised the cash disbursement that was in fact then presented by the family through this negotiator had comprised of a large sum of the Santucci liquid powerbase. And Domenico also understood such an investment was necessary to keep the family in business. Domenico had accepted the money presented to him inside a black leather briefcase. He stated that he had never mixed business with personal reservations. He never refused business for personal reasons. That was in fact bad business altogether. So Domenico had accepted the money, with no return on his investment; only to split evenly the spoils among the rest of the families, thus reducing their initial investment. In consequence, the Santucci family was put in a stalemate scenario what with the loss of millions of dollars. And understood Domenico still planned to wipe them out when thereafter attempts were made to take over pieces

122

of the Santucci Empire. Then Don 'Mad Dog' Santucci had again dived underground that was the following to a commencing lifetime sentence in hiding. That only promised to end once the entire targeted enemy family was dead.

And history repeated itself by Con Santucci's brave performance and attempt to wed the Armando daughter, to try and get to the power boss Domenico - in order to free his father finally. Such actions had too failed, resulting in his demise and another loss of a huge investment of millions of dollars, used by the Santuccis once more, in an attempt of bribery to invest in the Power Project. It was an effort to worm their way into the Armando clan once again. The saga, as before had resulted in tragedy and the loss of further millions to the family yet again. The Santucci family, not only lost another huge fortune to the Armando group, but a son also.

And following such a Santucci travesty; and a second-time winning streak for Domenico, the Armando Boss spoke out famous words before his closest companions, ever proud of himself for preceding such a magnanimous defeat and capitalising twice on the Santucci family's ill-fated investment. That stipulated again, history repeating itself in a poetic form of justice. "There is only one Santucci family in this lifetime. And they were laid perfectly before my very feet."

Domenico's prime philosophy he practised was never would he reject or interfere business transactions on the basis of personal feelings. Though, being such an enemy as the Santuccis in fact were, having possessed qualities of no leadership, no regard or respect for their own employees, had in fact created mutiny within their own organisation. Where his own people had began conspiring against Don Santucci. He had no control on his people who had constantly made freelance moves without prior consent to their chief padrone. And insubordination by his very people was hence tolerated; and such ill-borne character dismissed. So all in all, it was alleged the principle of the case was the methods he, Don Santucci himself, had acquired were an injustice to all concerned - disloyalty breeding disloyalty. And such a man could not be recognised as an ally of sound business mind to capitalise from.

Don 'Mad Dog' Santucci in business and personal proved a liability to all those foolish enough to associate with him; even proved a detriment to his own children, whom he sent to do his own bidding for him against Domenico. And openly he left them unprotected that cost him one son's life already.

Now with Rowan Castalone's expertise in coordination with his superior's efforts against the enemy, the Armando conquer was well at ease in its battle. Rowan now had a high-ranking position in the Armando Empire. He was Chief Executive Officer operating via the inner circle coordinating the power of drugs and captains and soldiers; every power that dominated the war. And next to his counsellor, he became Domenico's right-hand man in the war effort.

And such a heavyweight commodity had indeed paid off in only a short space of time. Rowan not long after revealed a traitor cleverly botched up beneath the Armando employ, inside their very house as the hired help, a cook. Such a traitor he uncovered was sponsored by the Santucci family.

Domenico was sitting behind a huge desk humming to the opera lyrics from his music box inside his office study, picking fruit with his fork from the large bowl laid out before him, whilst his Bulldog Bodyguard and his new star recruit Rowan Castalone had escorted the double agent to him inside. The failure of a hired help was summoned to his executioner with his hands cuffed behind his back, accompanied with Domenico Junior who supervised the performance of bringing the hired help up for reprimand - to an Armando punishment. That was well approved by his father, as he welcomed his son's slow coming turnaround to accepting the Armando family traditions for all they were worth. And indeed showed an impressed look on his face to his son at the sight of his ever growing strength.

The story behind the traitor cook was unravelled by inconspicuous security moles that imposed surveillance upon the traitor in his bid to outfight the Armando family by snuffing them all out in one night; in fact, through slipping poison into their next meal. But what surprised Domenico Junior was that everyone else was astounded by the close proximity to such an assassination plot attempt that could have gone either way, except for his father. Domenico's reaction was merely one of amusement in it all. He chuckled, not the least surprised. As if he expected such a plot, a devious manoeuvre, so cunning in its approach by the enemy family - and planted so diabolically close to home.

D.J. was shocked for a split moment at the thought that his entire family; he, his wife and child could have been poisoned to death and at that moment the Santucci family would have won the unconquerable battle against the Armandos.

But D.J.'s mind had finally worked. His father, after all, had a talent for reading people's minds and spotting a phoney when no one else could. Nothing or no one ever took his father Domenico by surprise. And then Domenico Junior had smiled to himself. At the sudden realisation that for a split second he was worried for his father's safety as everyone else had, present inside the room, when Domenico himself was capable of outmanoeuvring the most genius of criminals. And cursed himself now. For how could he think anyone could take his father by surprise? He understood everything now.

Domenico had set the traitor up. He simply allowed him to slip passed security and continue his charade as a hired cook, knowing all along where his true loyalties lay. He set the trap until he was found with a bottle of arsenic to place into their food meal to be served to the entire Armando family and its guards. But Domenico and all his high-ranking staff bearing positions by his side all along were onto the phoney manifest. And until such time whilst monitoring his slip, the food was of course inspected; the alcohol bottles, the water, the fridges in case of tampering. For constant surveillance on the enemy left no breath he took undetected.

Domenico turned to his bodyguard Kong and Rowan and said, "You know what you must do with him. And quick before the rest of my family have a chance to see anything."

Rowan, of course was in disguise, so he could come and go inside the Armando home and take orders from his master Domenico personally. And now with two extra bodyguards, Rowan had dragged the screaming resistant enemy outside the office to meet with his capital punishment.

Domenico said to his son D.J., "You understand my son the police would not be able to help us. You know he must be killed."

D.J. in a sudden understanding for his father's philosophies and what they stood for had only now accepted the necessity to rule death with an iron fist. And condone his father's behaviour and actions as necessary. For it was his family's life or the enemy. D.J. nodded his head at his father to concur that now, only now, he came to the realisation and understood why his father's methods were really the only solution possible to deal with such an enemy. And now groomed as his father's heir to stand to inherit the Armando power he clearly understood what that meant: It meant more power than he ever imagined possible to possess.

Domenico smiled at his son's quick education and his sudden turnaround to accepting the methods of his true world. And the excited cold chilliness that his son had now experienced overwhelmed with the idea of what power meant. And what it could do.

And Domenico sunk in his chair to say, his most favourite phrase to emphasise his triumphant victories: "When it's good it is good."

Within an hour, Domenico received confirmation from his counsellor that his two professional hit men had successfully performed the execution against the Santucci spy.

Rowan Castalone was a professional when it came to handling a gun. And of course he used a gun that was untraceable to anyone and anything on the Santucci cook, several shots in the back of the head inside the car he was dragged to in the estate's parking lot.

Domenico's Bulldog Bodyguard disposed of the corpse on Santucci turf, making such an execution public and apparant to the enemy. And then Rowan and Kong arranged within the next hour for a cook of their own to be sent into the enemy family within the city, infiltrating its own army ranks. Who cut glass and placed it into the food and drinks of the house containing the two remaining Santucci son and heirs, to whom occupied it as their headquarters during the war effort; that had instantly killed their counsellor. Thus, warning them off from sharing the same fate as he was reported to have bled internally to death. That marked the death of the 'apparent' brains behind the Santucci family.

When Rowan returned to the Armando estate he was embraced by his padrone as a symbolic appraisal commending him on his first assignment's success; Rowan proved himself in battle already. Rowan had too been struck by a miraculous realisation. When he lost the power of his father's family he thought at first he lost everything, but now realised in Domenico's family there was room for greater success within the ranks and more power at his disposal than his father ever imagined of mustering.

For Domenico's family was the Greatest of the Great of all the Families to work for. No other family could compare with it. And now realised even if granted the power, he would not turn back time and change his serving of Domenico Armando's every whim. Rowan knew Domenico's was the far better family to work for. And respected other families' proposals and job offers prior to his acceptance into the Armando sanctioned power, but knew the only way to remain on top, above all powers who had bid to crucify him as they had his father, was to work for such a man who controlled those otherwise very demeaning powers as the Greatest Family Leader, Domenico - the Chess Player King.

Rowan understood with Domenico's determination he could never head up his own family and right now nor had he the ambition. And in not too long declared his undying love and respect for Domenico as his key retainer next to the Bulldog Bodyguard and Rex Higgins. And such devotion bore legendary as such a man he too prepared himself to devote his life entirely to Domenico Armando.

Meanwhile the war in the city had cost both sides enormously - not only financially, but economically. And all the while bloodshed and the body count were escalating. Though in the next few weeks the Santucci strike of attack had lessened and so had the Armando fire whom perceived the Santucci strategy for ceasing fire was not to make a bid for a peace talk resolution to end the war, but a clever attempt to have the Armando family lower their guard perceiving the worst of the danger was over. Domenico smelling a rat understood the ploy to lower his guard. And as he ceased fire to attempt to play into the enemy's hands for a short period, in one day he ordered all his captains and soldiers to declare a full-scale massacre against the enemy who had not forecasted the Armando halt on their attack was to also have them too lower their guard. Which fatally they had; and cost them the lives of over a hundred muscle soldiers weakening their manpower for attack, altogether.

126

Though Domenico had realised the cease in fire was also one to attempt as a rouse perhaps, to lessen the necessity of Armando soldiers patrolling Santucci territory, thus enabling the safe smuggling of their Chief Padrone, Don 'Mad Dog' Santucci, into their New York based hideout in the city. To, no doubt, prepare to meet with Domenico.

Nonetheless, as the war continued there was still everyday business to conduct. That could not proceed as usual. For pending the complications of a surrounding all-out war, the Armando family as its enemies on their ends could not go about business as before. The Armando family operations had to be run and its crew had to be commanded solely from the Armando estate, which created a lessening of many revenues on both sides.

But it was not until now, during the Armando war when the traitor cook was ordered and in fact executed that D.J. broke out a lesser powerful chuckle, but reminiscent to his father in sharing the same enthusiasm of triumph in it all. Of how great - how bloody great the Armando family really was. For even committing a murder in public, though it was somewhat self-defence, they had succeeded in executing another of a Santucci family raw talent and in fact got away with it. It was greater than money. Then, in a sudden realisation to his out of character behaviour, his face had changed to seriousness. As if ashamed by the joy he felt for bloodshed in a mind lapse to his ordinary conscionable state, which startled him for a moment. For that instant he feared he was becoming a man like his father.

He spent many months learning his father's business. Domenico Junior had spent hours by his father's side with Rex Higgins as teachers of all aspects to the family's heritage. He learnt of its people as the 'Bulldog Bodyguard' so named; and Rowan Castalone. And why it was necessary to acquire such talent.

He began to understand his father's methods and philosophies. Domenico constantly had criticised those whose sole ambition in life served strangers instead of their families. He hated government people who risked their lives for their country; and such people who in turn criticised the close link of Mafia family as: 'The down side of life'. "Family was everything – those strangers were nothing," he often preached.

How he criticised those who would sell their own blood for money. Though that was what made the world such a target for control. Everyone's weakness was money; police, politicians, traitors - all of the like. And D.J. understood what his father's power meant. When you had enough of it - you could get anyone to do anything at your very whim. Greed was every man's motive for all his actions. It was what corrupted his very soul to be condemned to the fires of hell for all eternity. Such a classic example was a quick educative outlook on life: Women becoming ordained as priests; priests stealing money from the parish. Greed had overpowered everyone's soul. Nothing was sacred anymore.

D.J. was forced to understand the masquerade and hypocrisy of such people. The common folk; whom posed themselves as honest and decent Americans wearing formal attire and expensive silk suits, though understood such hypocrisy was what even politicians such as Senator Ron Bishop was part of. It was all phoney.

And in the battle ahead he was taught the necessity of power to secure what was most important, Family, and the money and wisdom to acquire men such as the Bulldog Bodyguard to secure the Family's turf.

The Bulldog Bodyguard was Domenico's most feared and devoted retainer. He was a soldier of unique strength, fighting ability, obedience and loyalty to only Domenico. No man was known to worship and obey his master as he. Domenico indeed preyed on such men who fought for, respected and obeyed him unconditionally - to inevitably prepare themselves to 'die for him'. With such quality, highly-devoted team within his ranks, Domenico could outfight anyone and defeat any army. And with Kong and Rowan Castalone serving him in such a way, D.J. knew that his father had constructed an army that was unbeatable.

Such a man named Kong in such a war never left Domenico's sight. He was a man known to have killed six men single-handedly with his bare hands. No weapons. He was head of all security for the family controlled hotels in New York; and Domenico had given to him a portable mobile phone that put him on call twenty-four hours a day in case of emergency.

His Bulldog Bodyguard was almost seven feet tall and 150 kilograms. There was a known legend about him that his hands had in fact revolutionised the field of army. He was once known to kill a man with his bare hands in such bizarre fashion, by placing them around his head much like a vice and squeezing so hard that he crushed his skull. Such a target to his wrath was an Armando traitor; and such an execution bore example to others of what he had done with traitors. In such a crisis period, Domenico found it imperative never to leave home without him. Took him everywhere he went, to act as his very shadow. He alone had been the driving force behind many a successful transactions for Domenico. All he need do was show his face and with him and Domenico together in the same room, no man alive was ever known to ever debate an issue with them let alone refuse a recommendation. They became quivering jellies.

Such a human commodity indeed proved beneficial and frightened the opposition into strict obedience. Such skill and ferocity by the Bulldog Bodyguard was indeed suspected at times by authorities though he was never charged. His professionalism expertise won him a clean slate and sheet by authorities and notoriety as his superior's most well-organised retainer. And in executions where a weapon was used; he always used the same gun. It never mattered if it were untraceable or not. For his unique fashion of murder had eluded not only authorities in general, but the entire national underworld all the same. When he killed a victim he first ensured the victim never touched him, not to leave the slightest evidence behind; or hint of evidence left via a struggle: whether it be a hair on his head or a button of his jacket. And he never wore jewellery in an execution that was an easy giveaway.

And when he shot his victims to death, the reason for his escaping suspicion altogether was indeed a revolutionised method of enforcement. After he shot the victims, he removed and eradicated the bullets from the dead corpses leaving only a large bloody hole. And after that, when necessary, even he took the body with him and had it disappear. It became virtually impossible for the police to trace the gun or the killer; having accounted for all possible events via removing the bullet from the dead target's corpse.

And that was why Domenico held such a man in the highest of his graces for exacting such unique attributes. He believed to run a successful empire it was crucial to have astute individuals serving beneath him: To seek their input, advice and extract such a man's rare talent to suit his purpose. Just as any large business required a solid foundation, a decisive board of directors and advisers; who were talented and inclined to make such a supreme power chief's plans succeed with the utmost of efficiency. And so Domenico Junior learned that that was why his father thrived on employing such rare talent who would serve him until their death.

Meanwhile, the history and reason for such an Armando-Santucci feud between the two families went back two generations of conflict beginning with their forefathers. And once they died it was continued by the son and heirs; now Domenico and Don Santucci.

Domenico was Italian-American. His parents were born in Naples, but because of the enemy family feud they fled for cover in exile to Sicily after Domenico was born. And Domenico's childhood revolved around the protection of the Bolermo family to whom Domenico's parents pleaded for their only son's safety being close friends with Lawrence Bolermo's father, who was only too glad to take young Domenico in at the time under their wing in their protection against the Santucci family; who wanted to eradicate the line of Armandos. And Domenico's parents thereafter went back to their hometown in Naples in order to offer peace, but the Santucci family took advantage of the situation and killed the Armando parents and then a war now between Domenico and Don Santucci was sworn to continue in vengeance to this very day.

And until today, a bloody war was waged in a bid to end the enemy threat; claiming hundreds of lives from both sides. The Armando family in a bid to preserve its strong recruits had its own family surgeon operating underground in the city. He was a doctor who secretly operated on soldiers who were injured in the line of duty.

During the war attritions, the Santucci family turned up the highest body count and many of its emissaries had then vowed to change their allegiance to the Chess Player family.

The Chess Player had put the word out on the street that he would triple the reward for Don Santucci's capture; dead or alive. He also had put the word out that even though the reward was quite hefty; the culprits guilty of hiding the wanted fugitive from him would be made to suffer in equal great measure! The Chess Player soldiers were combing the entire vicinity of New York in hunt for the Mad Dog kingpin of the Santucci clan.

Domenico said confidently to his counsellor, "If we can kill the President in any country we'll get to him no matter what - sooner or later."

The war between the two families was not about power or territorial disputes. It was purely about revenge. But getting revenge had meant stripping the opposition of its power and income to make them vulnerable, by invading its territory in order to gain control of its turf. And both sides interceded strongly in the war effort. And the Armando factions all along had its men muscling in on the opposition's territories in a bid to take over its captains in command to the bloody battle; who controlled drug rings in the city.

The news coverage of the war was phenomenal. The Santucci family had received the most of the heat and flack. The Armando family's name was never mentioned. Only scapegoats were established.

Santucci history was relived at the time of the Kingpin Don's almost arrest when he left the country with a fake passport, identification and elaborate disguise to elude customs officials and airport police, now two decades ago.

All the while, attempts to incorporate spies in the Armando family went unsuccessful. Such traitors were spotted, as existing Armando family personnel were each given a family password not to reveal to anyone. Those individuals among them, such as the traitor cook who did not know their security codes, became automatic known traitors to the family. And all along Chess Player captains slaughtered the infiltrators.

The war went on day and night invading all enemy turfs in New York City. In the last hour, three Armando gunmen burst into a Santucci Italian family restaurant and cut down three of the family's lieutenants. As they burst out to safety, they met with half a dozen compatriot soldiers on the far west side of Brooklyn on the Chess Player's territorial borderline, who hit the ground and crawled rapidly back into cover of the vegetation behind a small hill embankment, dodging bullets coming towards them by the enemy firing at them.

The Chess Player's captains in a bid to end the war quickly were used to muster over a thousand more men just in New York. The captains had recruited over a thousand soldiers to invade enemy territories; to eradicate all the enemy's influenced powers including corrupt police officials owing them allegiance against the Chess Player group.

The captains in the Chess Player Mob headed their own regimes fighting in different territories of the city owned and dominated by the Santucci family, in order to drive them out of their established land.

And such an attempt on the Kingpin's whereabouts were yet unknown. Don Santucci was rumoured to be underground somewhere, even close to the city limits. But, perhaps he was not in New York as yet. And for years no one could get to him.

Domenico could not afford to ever lose a war. He was known to be the most powerful crime boss and head of the toughest, most effective, well-structured family unit that served under his thumb. The loss of even one war would tarnish his reputation and otherwise notoriety established over many years. His enemy associates whom fear the Armando family may look at it as a sign of weakness; and their fears may go astray and so too their high respect for the Armando family. And when that happened an all-out era of wars targeted against the Armando family may flare up with all the families lining up against him; its purpose to remove his hold on them as Boss of Bosses.

However, Domenico proved all along to have the strongest and most undefeated war fighting army of them all. And with his daughter Monica by his side all along, he groomed his eldest son to aid him in battle, spending hours with him convincing and educating him of the family history; its heritage, and the necessity of bloodshed.

He revealed to his son his childhood. How as a boy he experienced his parents' cold executions by the Santucci family. They were sent to their knees and had blindfolds placed covering over their eyes when the Santucci assailants had fired a gun to their heads, a bullet apiece. And now his anger for the attempts on his daughter Annemarie, D.J. was coming around.

Domenico explained furthermore, "The only way to deal with the Santuccis and what they did is to eliminate them - to destroy them completely."

D.J. only now, recently having the idea that his father was responsible for killing someone, even many men, understood the necessity in it all, having experienced the same deep emotional pain and loss of his grandparents he never met. D.J. was forced to agree. For the first time he spoke with the same anger and temperament of his father and said, "Yes father. If anyone deserves to die, it's Don Santucci."

Though since the time of the Santucci clash with government authorities whom cracked down on its operations; and when Don Santucci lost his freedom, having fled the country in exile for long periods to avoid the police and growing attack from the Armando group - they were too under siege when a war was declared by the Armando family who also had involved using their police connections against them on top of it all.

Currently in New York bodies turned up dead, totalling almost one hundred weekly. The death toll stood at its peak for the first time in ten years by such an escalated war of the two families in feud. And all along investigative reporters who interfered were killed for their investigations on the mob.

And throughout the course of the war, business suffered on both sides as key operatives were assassinated in the crossfire.

For two decades the Armando hunt for Don Santucci had failed to murder the enemy because a loot of money and time by his children, his heirs had been spent to hide the kingpin underground.

Domenico sought to eliminate their power and wait for the right opportunity for the chief to show himself from hiding. When Domenico snuffed ten million dollars from the enemy's son Con Santucci after his daughter, which was a down payment for his family to enter into the Power Project and commission's good graces, Domenico knew such money was needed by the enemy family by a certain time frame or else their entire operation would sink. And by keeping the money long enough whilst cracking down on their operations, and draining its liquid and money-making ventures and revenues throughout the city; and taking over bits and pieces of the rival empire all at the same time was in order to eventually wipe them out - the entire Santucci family powerbase and its heirs. And, it would surely help wield a growing vengeance that would resurface Don Santucci out into the open, finally.

The growing unpopularity of the Santuccis became apparent to police, to the commission and to society as a whole. They had no regard for humanity and made no ambition to conceal their foolish activities to all. Such an even most recent public breach of misconduct was caused by the family's controlling of industrial waste lots across the city. The Santucci group controlled a lot which was next to a school and allowed toxic waste to be dumped onto their lot for huge sums of money. They were considered as men with no honour. Such waste was swept into the local school by rain and had entered rusty water pipes which entered the school's water supply poisoning many children. One of the children was the daughter to a popular family boss who died from the contaminated poisoning. And when word was known that Santucci owned the lot next to the school, the rest of the state's commission interceded and volunteered their efforts to aid Domenico in battle against the enemy crime lord. Thus - voted against him ever rising up in the commission.

The Santuccis too ran their neighbourhoods much like a disaster. Drugs were out of control, sold to children and schools. The rest of the commission had to step foot in and drive the enemy out in order to clean and preserve the neighbourhoods which was their livelihood - and thus Don Santucci was cut off from the action, his poor business judgement was a detriment. He had no control over his empire or its people whatsoever.

For the past several months that the Chess Player had waged war against the Santucci clan which got the main five families of New York in line against the enemy as well, the carnage had filled the newspapers.

Many men on both sides had been killed; though publicity of Domenico was never mentioned. Such New York families' involvement created these local-based families and its representatives to unmistakably take the flack as scapegoats as responsible for the war's effort, otherwise clearing Domenico from suspicion and police questioning altogether.

And following the entire New York underworld all lined up against the Santucci family as well, emissaries from the enemy family had finally requested the Chess Player to halt conflict - in order to propose a peace, a truce and ceasefire of all ongoing hostilities, now with their power diminished and Don Santucci still in hiding underground somewhere.

After the cease in fire was initiated, Domenico informed his counsellor to tell his captains to hold its people in reserve, but have them nosing around the city for word on Don Santucci's whereabouts. The internal captains were to move the bulk of their people back to their residences on the street of the Armando family and its underground hideout hospital facility. The counsellor had commenced negotiation over the phone and by messenger with the enemy family emissaries over some kind of a deal. All the while Rex Higgins had ordered two of his captains to continue pressuring Santucci men ready to change allegiance to find out if they knew where the hell Don Santucci was.

Since the Armando family had now halted gunfire and ordered the rest of the city's family chieftains involved to issue as well a complete ceasefire accordingly to its troops, the Armandos still wanted to kill Don Santucci. So they planted spies around different Santucci owned territories on the payroll of the enemy family coordinating as double agents.

It was a week later when no word of Don Santucci's whereabouts was heard so Domenico ordered a contingency plan to be put forward. Domenico immediately ordered his people to find out all the businesses of the enemy family around the city and muscle in on all of them - and all his territories. He then informed his Bulldog Bodyguard to bring him the son and civilian of the Santucci family, Bruno Santucci.

Bruno Santucci was somewhat the black sheep of the family who was not directly involved in the family business. He was a civilian. He was an outsider whom had spent his time under protection with his brother Sebastian; and now moved to the local family hotel in the Manhattan borough with lesser security, easier to penetrate. And of course the Armando bodyguard, upon the target's pickup, was instructed to drive in circles to the acquired destination so he was not followed.

Within an hour a car skidded to a screaming halt before the Armando front-owned warehouse located in the Bronx Borough Waterfront. After the car was parked a blindfolded Bruno in the dead quiet of the night led by the Bulldog Bodyguard was taken to the front door to the main entrance doorstep of the otherwise abandoned premises. And Armando security, guarding every door and every window, then opened the warehouse main door upon their presence being known. Kong had still knocked on the door to alert all those inside, when Rex and several other security officials approached them and Rex said to the nerve-stricken Bruno, now with a blindfold and rope hand restraints removed, "Mr. Santucci, we have been expecting you. Please come in and do not be alarmed."

Hesitant at first, Rex assured him, "If we wanted to kill you we would not have brought you all the way here from your Manhattan residence. We could get to you anytime! So don't worry."

He entered the building and was escorted to Domenico's private domain where only he and his counsellor and bodyguard were permitted to sit in for the meeting.

Bruno began to recall the stories of what his family told him about this man, Domenico Armando. How Domenico preyed on his victims like a crocodile in the mud. How he claimed his victims from all walks of life – and no one was able to stop him. He trotted silently across the earth's crust; no one could hear him approaching as he viciously targeted his victims – and then like a vampire he sought after his next target, never stopping. He could do whatever he wanted to anybody – and nobody could get in his way; or slow him down. No one could get to him.

Domenico made his moves against his targets so silently, catching them off guard; that nobody could hear anything, just as he kidnapped him this evening. He snatched him from right under his family's noses and no one saw anything. Domenico must be a ghost or something. He must walk through walls. And his appearance in black attire and white scarf he observed now the sight of those emperors with swords concealed in their gowns, prepared for the attack.

There were hundreds of aspects concerning this dangerous man Domenico that terrified Bruno, especially now, summoned all alone in his domain like that. And one of them was the fact that Domenico, with a click of his fingers, as expertly as a magician could unfold a miraculous trick from his very hands – had the power to literally change the destiny to any man's life; whilst his life constantly remained unchanged by any force on the earth. He believed Domenico Armando was completely indestructible!

Though, after his mind had coiled such thoughts; in a sudden fit of terror, he had blanked his mind to silence: From all bad words; from all bad

Armando thoughts, even from fear. As if the enemy himself, even telepathically, by purely just evil, uncanny sense alone, even in the darkness, may read his mind somehow and may become drawn to the correct conclusion; and grow instantly onto him, just by his ill thoughts alone even of him. And even minus any unconstitutional actions on his part against his otherwise conditioning debriefs he was surely to receive this evening, Bruno Santucci suddenly feared his life was hanging by a thread, the devil himself he indeed believed right this very moment Domenico Armando to be!

Domenico sat on a swivel leather armchair behind an old wooden desk. Aside it was a small buffet cabinet, he gestured his counsellor to fix Bruno a drink, and the discussion went straight to the point without sidetrack. Domenico said in a normal tone, his deep Italian voice yet sending shivers of terror raining into Bruno's entire being, "I called for this meeting to simply make a proposition to you."

Bruno pleaded as if to open up to Domenico, yet extremely nervous, "Please sir. I am not involved in any of this. My father and I do not get along. He calls me a weak loser; that I am not his son. And as such he has condemned and punished me for this. Please – don't hurt me."

Rex brought him a shot glass of brandy. Domenico ordered, "Drink up the brandy to settle your nerves."

Once Domenico focused his attention briefly on the appearing manservant who brought them some drinks, Bruno eased his posture on the wooden chair he was seated on in front of his new master, and showed a more relaxed demeanour; as if he had nothing to fear.

After the alcoholic drinks were brought forward, Domenico then insisted to proceed with the subject at hand. Domenico would immediately speak his piece. "First point, I want you to understand that I know you disapprove of your father's actions. But I want you to understand you did not fail your father. He failed you. Friend, I know you better than you know yourself. Men like your father find it very difficult to find loyal employees and why should you support him, an outsider to his business - because you're related, hmm? Not where it counts. Firstly, I have accounted for such a family. That masquerade your brother Con played with my daughter. He broke her heart, and look where he ended up. You don't want to end like that do you?" Bruno shook his head profusely. Domenico went on. "Good. I called you here to present a deal. I set the deal. It will comprise of the one thing that a mercenary fellow as yourself values the most; your life, for your cooperation."

Suddenly the white-faced quivering Bruno, who was rather ordinarily dark-skinned, with jet-black shoulder-length straight hair parted at one side, his features frail-looking at the age of thirty-three, with a leaner build opposed to his older brother Sebastian's muscular build, thick wavy dark-brown hair and tough-looking features at age thirty-six, had astonished the faces around him in his coming remarks. "Sir, I will help you." Bruno said.

135

Domenico turned to the astounded faces present before him at such a cowering remark and chuckled. Then his eyes focused again to his target and demanded, "So are you loyal?"

Bruno nodded. Domenico said, serious-faced, "Don't double-cross me." Domenico knew such a man's character. He was weak, a coward, and could be manoeuvred to perform as putty in his hand. And with the right manoeuvre he could be formed into the necessary shape needed. So that was why Domenico arranged for the weakest blood link in the Santucci clan to be kidnapped for one hour and to be driven to an abandoned Armando warehouse on the waterfront in the dead of night where Domenico was waiting for him.

Domenico said, "You know I can and will kill your family and become the winner. You know no one can beat me. But when your family is wiped out, which it will be, make no mistake you can come out of it with your life. How? - By meanwhile accepting to join forces with me by spying on your family for me. But, if you want to join forces with me you will have to pass a loyalty test, first, hmm. Now, I want to see how far you can go against your family, your stronger older brother Sebastian."

Bruno astounded by the order, said, "What do you want me to do?"

Domenico said simply and plainly, "I want you to destroy your family."

Bruno lowered his eyes to the floor and thought it was a disgusting, sick and disloyal proposal. Then when he saw an envelope Domenico's bodyguard held before his eyes, purposely waving the open side to him - exposing the contents of a two-inch thick roll of hundred dollar bills, he no longer considered the plan dishonourable. And said, first clearing his throat, "What do you want me to do?"

Domenico now motioned himself to a seat aside Bruno, patted him on the back and replied, "Wonderful."

His counsellor gave an impressed smile. Domenico had him exactly where he wanted him, obviously money talking. Domenico was a man who by his own right of power and money could make a man forget even loyalty to family. And his powerful convincing presence always had people quivering in strict obedience. What better way for Domenico to prove himself than to turn the son of his worst enemy to an ally. It was the perfect plan.

Rex also knew the weakest of the Santucci children forced before them right now named Bruno, would be pleased with the money. His father never included him in family affairs or took proper care of him, reason being; he was considered weak and stupid and a detriment to the family's security. Very naive, always unintentionally siding with the wrong people who were out to cause wrong doing to his family. And since there was no love loss between him and his father, Domenico perceived an opportunity to be prevailed upon by exacting another obstacle to his advantage.

Bruno was his father's obstacle. Only this time Domenico would turn his worst enemy's obstacle to his own advantage. And Domenico realised that in time he would be considered his family.

Domenico handed Bruno a piece of paper from his counsellor's hand and said, "Read it. These are your instructions. I want you here and now to read it. Study it and memorise it clearly in your head."

Rex knew exactly what the letter had written on it. After all, he wrote it himself as it was dictated to him by his boss. In essence, the letter revealed a party that Bruno's family would attend; the date, the time and the place. Something that Bruno much considered an outsider to his family had not been informed of as yet.

Bruno was to act as a chauffeur to his brother when he was to leave the party and escort him to a street in Manhattan. The letter contained a small map showing the route he would take. Nothing else was said. Nothing revealing what would happen once they had arrived to the street. Once the letter was read it was given to the bodyguard whom destroyed it by placing it in an ashtray he lit with a match to burn to ashes, so no evidence could be obtained that a meeting took place between them.

After it was agreed, Bruno would serve Domenico as a double agent against his family. Bruno Santucci was escorted again to his destination, wearing a blindfold; the car drove in circles all the while, but dropped him only ten minutes walking distance from the Santucci occupied boundaries. And the goings and comings to the meeting had airtight security, so no one would find out that Bruno was consorting with the enemy.

Domenico, prior to his departure as well, turned to his counsellor - Domenico had euphoria and satisfaction on his face, when he stated, "That Santucci puppet will do my bidding. Prepare him to enter the family payroll for now, as my pawn. Then I will take care of him once he has outlived his usefulness to me."

The counsellor nodded, "You mean – you're going to kill him as well?"

Domenico chuckled before he stated, "He's a dead duck - a lost cause. He's indeed a loose brick in the foundation of his family."

Rex understood. Domenico was one who always killed by association. No matter if Bruno was only a civilian, not involved in the family business. Domenico was more futuristic. A possibility always existed that once his family was finished that he may be in the business and out for revenge. He must die. Domenico made it a habit never to underestimate the enemy or its weak foolish character flaws. And prepared himself for every possible eventuality to take effect. It was best to always overestimate a person – and never be taken by surprise. To think as your enemies thought. And premeditate their every possible movement even before it was made. It was called 'chess'. In its entire worldly version.

Even Rex Higgins had considered that such a man as Bruno Santucci who could so easily be forced to change allegiance was a person who could sell his own mother and never be trusted or included in usual business of any sort. A character like that deserved to be used and discarded. Perhaps it was the only agreeably wise perception his father ever made, not to include such a son in business; a man who could sell his own family's soul for money - to betray them; was one who could never be taken seriously.

And Rex Higgins once again complimented his boss on a first-rate performance understanding the real gist behind his game plan with the Santucci family. His tact was genius and his strategy served in order to divide and conquer the enemy family. And the key was Bruno Santucci. By turning him against his family; and creating the necessary highly-botched kink in his father's security may be all that was required to pinpoint the location of Don Santucci; to finally flush him out of hiding. And by the execution of Bruno's brother Sebastian, Domenico had soon revealed his motives by adding, "It is my experience that the best way to punish an enemy is to harm the ones he loves."

The evening of the Santucci party which contained the main Santucci crew, minus the presence of Don Santucci was hosted by Sebastian, in order to celebrate the now 21st year anniversary of his father, Don Santucci's freedom from government authorities' apprehension, held in their main hideout in the borders of Manhattan. Bruno had volunteered to drive his brother Sebastian for the evening. His usual chauffeur-bodyguard had been given the night off. So Bruno offered to drive his brother, a feared Mafia underboss home after the party.

It was a ten minute drive from the Santucci hangout to 22nd Street in Manhattan. Bruno stopped in the isolated street in front of his former, now abandoned family home in the borough and silently pressed the button to lower the rear window where Sebastian was sitting. At that moment from the shadows outside in the dead quiet of the night a man stepped forward and fired several shots through the open window. Bruno offered to drive with no witnesses. And he wore gloves. Initially, Sebastian asked, "why wear gloves Bruno? The weather is not freezing outside. It's quite warm!" But he did not want to leave his fingerprints on the car. Bruno screamed in shock as his brother was massacred.

Bruno said to his agonised brother who was still conscious, but unable to utter a word, he cowered toward him and cried, "Sorry my brother for having to do this." And he saw the final bullet fired to his head to finish him off.

The gunman then disappeared and a car pulled up seconds later and two men hopped out and dragged the weeping Bruno into their car; then quickly wiped the car with his brother's dead body clean of any fingerprints. Glancing around, making sure there were no witnesses lurking around anywhere they then entered their vehicle again escaping the distant sounds of the ambulance and police sirens that made its way.

It was a short drive, where Bruno was again blindfolded and tied down during the car ride and taken to see Domenico with his counsellor and bodyguard at the same isolated warehouse spot. Where once greeted inside, after Bruno's restraints were removed, Rex said, "You did good. Domenico would like to meet with you."

When they entered the private small office room in the back of the warehouse, they saw Domenico orchestrating with his baton overtures to some powerful symphony; and singing also - his eyes closed, contemplating the beauty to the emotional piece playing in the background. As he heard Bruno, Domenico lowered the music via a remote control on his desk and walked over to embrace him and ordered his men to give him a strong drink from the setup buffet cabinet inside to settle his nerves. The choice of drink he left to their judgement. Domenico kissed his both cheeks and welcomed him as a comrade whom was suddenly initiated into his family once passing the test-of-all-tests, murder, and said, "We're family now."

Domenico knew what he was thinking. Obviously he had no idea there would be a hit. But Domenico seemed sympathetic; convinced him by stating, "It was the best thing to do for business. Your brother, may his soul rest in peace, would have understood it was business for him. Not personal. But you are now here with me. So now I can look after you. Your family never had. You were cut off from the action; turned loose with no money, no power, no position, and no future. With me and what you have accomplished tonight made sure your future was secure."

Bruno gullibly seemed to display sudden relief, even happiness at the thought. Domenico persuaded him furthermore, "Yes. I will take care of you."

Bruno still understood Domenico's vendetta was a personal nature against his family. Domenico, however said, "I salute you my friend. And yes, continue making yourself indispensable!" He smiled ironically with hypocrisy in his eyes as he added, "You do still have a job."

Domenico turned to his counsellor and said in a tone where Bruno could overhear, "He has passed the test by killing his brother. I think he can be useful to us again."

Rex, in an utter state of dumbfounded shock grunted, knowing that Domenico wanted him to kill his own father, the head of the enemy family, Don Santucci now. Not in so many words, but in rather subtle approaches, though in a language that even Bruno Santucci understood. Bruno bowed his head down and when he raised it he said, almost in a stutter, "You mean... you're asking the big... big one?" He understood that he was asked to commit murder on his father. Bruno debated the issue in killing his father, saying, "People have their limits."

Domenico said seriously, "Of course, many other people have limited abilities, yes, I know – but, not you. Never lose faith in your capabilities. I will teach you how to draw upon your own strengths and talents. You must learn to trust me. Friend, as I said before, I know you better than you know yourself. I am going to give you a chance in my family that your father has never given you in his. You accomplish this and you will be a pillar in my organisation and you will succeed beyond your wildest dreams."

Robert Stewart and John McCallum had headed-up the homicide investigation into the ambush of Sebastian Santucci that evening. At the murder scene two officers approached them after examining the car of the deceased and one of them said to Robert, "Sir, this car has been wiped clean. Not even the sign of the owner's set of fingerprints."

Robert turned to his partner John and said, "Somebody has done a very thorough job here. Ok, let's go over this place with a fine-tooth comb for witnesses, anything."

Robert had an idea, though questioning the suspect would get him nowhere. For the past several months Robert investigated the Mafia War in the city and his precinct was swamped in reports to the masses of murders incorporated daily against Santucci family members written in the obituary; of execution style murders by the state's Mafia Bosses' killing spree. Though a war between the Santucci family and the Five Main New York Families was said to be the apparant reason, Robert understood the nature of the crime was more personal on Sebastian; four bullets to the chest and one fatal bullet to the head was more of a personal nature. Robert suspected immediately Domenico Armando. After all, he was a known rival of the Santuccis - and for many years. And revenge was a powerful motive.

Though Robert understood when a Mob crime was committed, a little money came flooding into the police precincts and all crooked cops had kept it quiet and remained much close-mouthed to its details. The subject basically was kept shrouded.

Aside from how the murder appeared to be set up as an execution by the Mob, Robert suspected Domenico as responsible, though had no proof as yet. So when Robert wanted to find something out he would simply approach the accused. Face to face. He knew Domenico would not tell him what he needed to know, but after years of working as a professional police officer he knew that he could learn as much from what a man did not say as what he had. It was mere perception and reading between the lines. In fact, learning the truth this way, as a professional law-enforcement official became his art form. He as well taught many of his police colleagues to think this way. It indeed revolutionised the whole field of policing.

Later that evening when Robert questioned Domenico in his home on his participation or possible involvement in the execution-style murder of

Sebastian Santucci, Robert knew Domenico's denials were a complete falsehood; outright lies. Domenico was acting friendly and extended pleasantries as usual, now only more so. Though when Robert had informed him of the crime before it was broadcasted on any news bulletin, Domenico did not seem surprised. At that moment Domenico Armando became his number one suspect.

Not long after, Domenico Armando had received confirmation word from a source that Don Santucci had vacated his city hideout in Miami and was making his way in a private plane to New York and prepared to meet with his enemy, Domenico. Domenico had received this verification in his Brooklyn estate the next evening at 7:00 p.m. And had spoken to a source on his private office secure phone and silently he whispered to his bodyguard Kong as he halted his secret conversation on the phone for a moment, "Close the doors behind you and make sure no one is standing in the foyer."

Domenico had changed his plan. He was going to get his target at a meeting sooner. At the first sign of his plane hitting New York he was going to trap him. Right now Domenico was going to arrange that security around himself and his family be tripled again. All in all Don Santucci took a risk coming to New York City where his destruction was made apparent by the hands of Robert Stewart's uncle who took away his freedom.

But after he received word that he left Miami by plane, Domenico had a hunch that he was heading for his main New York estate in Long Island. Domenico also ordered that the private airstrip there be watched and the Armando Jet be made ready in case Don Santucci changed his itinerary.

Domenico had international sources that could find out things that even the United States President could not. He was the only one with knowledge of Don Santucci's arrival. Not even the government knew. Domenico had hundreds of soldiers out on the street twenty-four hours a day setting up command in secret flats across the entire city and state of New York ready for a possible counterattack.

Domenico was also aware the enemy understood that there was constant close surveillance cast right now on even both their activities by police since after the war. Thus, he felt assured of his safety that Domenico must halt in an attempt on his life whilst the meeting took place.

Meanwhile, Domenico was handed a telegraph letter from his bodyguard. The letter was hand-delivered by messenger courier confirming details of the neutral negotiator to both sides who then called him on his private line in his den insisting that Don Santucci wanted a meeting.

Domenico read through it. It was an invitation from Don Santucci. The handwritten letter stated that he wanted to meet Domenico at midnight tonight for the final hand in their war to be reasoned out. Don Santucci left his number to his cellular phone below the letter as he was eager for Domenico's response. The prize to be offered was peace.

Rex Higgins was occupied for the next two hours discussing crucial details with the mediator satisfactory to both Families so that the meeting could be set up with Don Santucci and his padrone. Of course the meeting was scheduled on a neutral territory where security on both sides was assured by their own people.

Domenico chuckled. "Yes, this is very interesting. I would not miss this game for anything."

The Santucci family emissaries proposed an investment into the Power Project with no equal partnership this time – just a token to end the hostilities. Domenico, only in himself, had refused.

Once driven to the meeting's dim-lit warehouse, having arrived early before midnight to the official meeting place held in an isolated part of town in the Northern end of Brooklyn, Domenico all the while had taken precautions as he instructed his chauffeur-bodyguard to take extra care not to be followed. That no one must know they had this meeting; or be seen together with the enemy. That was imperative.

Once inside, both family chieftains were surrounded by bodyguards. Domenico had seen the fatigue of emotional scars imbedded on the ageing, grey-faced, heavy-set Don Santucci who was wanted by the police and government in a now twenty-one-year manhunt from both the proper authorities and the global underworld commission.

It had been now two decades since Domenico had stood in the same room as his rival arch-enemy. And the outcome to the recent full-scale war; the fact that Don Santucci had himself lost two of his strongest and favourite sons took its toll on him. But without further delay, Don handed Domenico a briefcase. It was stuffed with one hundred million dollars to resolve a feud that would ensure his departure from the meeting safely.

Domenico accepted the gesture, though his counsellor and Bulldog Bodyguard present with him this evening had to attribute credit among themselves to Don Santucci for the nerve displayed in showing his face in New York like that after all these years.

Though Don Santucci right now had received permission to speak of his proposal and indeed it appeared sincere. "I have lost both my sons. Revenge will not bring them back. If you wish, I will forget about vengeance for my boys and right now end this ridiculous feud between us. I surrender in defeat. I have one son left. I do not want the next generation of our grandchildren to suffer for the feud between us and our forefathers. It must end. I am here to make a deal. The only threat to one another is each other. You can destroy me and I can destroy you. You have my two sons' souls accounted for. You have most of my money I handed to you right now as a peace offering. Yes, I am sincere. You can kill me-I can kill you. There is no point in it. You had double-crossed me by taking my money from Con and said I could invest and be part of your project. But, I am here to give you more money to forget about these troubles. Our only threat is each other; if we eliminate that threat then comes freedom; freedom for me to carry on my family into the next generation by such a truce. Allowing the last son and heir I have left to survive without the worry of ever stumbling across some unexpected fatal accident."

Domenico listened in silence without passing judgement and allowed him to continue. Don Santucci added, "Look Domenico, I want to reopen a base of operations here in New York that the war has forced me to close down. The deal is - you don't interfere in my operation and I won't interfere in yours. Before you turn me down my deal will be beneficial to not only myself, but for you as well; in terms of power and wealth."

Domenico replied simply, "My friend, you are free to do what you wish. I will not stand in your way. After all, all I need to do is call the police and have them arrest you. But, I am glad you trusted me enough not to do that by arranging this meeting. Let me make something clear, I do not trust you. I never will. So, I will be watching you closely."

Don replied also casually, "And I will be watching you."

Their conversation was interrupted abruptly by the Bulldog Bodyguard who whispered a few serious words into Domenico's ear after he called the Brooklyn estate for word on the meeting's security status in remaining undetected.

After his man had finished, Domenico turned to Don Santucci and chuckled. "Well, well, guess who wants to see me and left a message at my estate for a scheduled appointment this evening?" There was a moment's pause. Domenico continued. "Robert Stewart is waiting at my house for me. And I wonder what he would do if he found out you were here? The man he hates more than anything in this world; the man responsible for the death of his uncle and his uncle's son. Robert's cousin!" He grinned. "It seems as though our mutual friend Stewart's instincts must suspect that something was in the air tonight. I bet you he does."

Don Santucci left the meeting with the usual security that Domenico had - ensuring each one's safety to their secure estate destinations.

Once Domenico had arrived at his home within the hour, he saw Robert waiting and seated for his arrival inside his living room that indeed confirmed Domenico's insinuations.

Robert's instincts had indeed informed him that Domenico was up to something tonight. He could not quite put a finger on it, though he had no hesitation pointing out, "Domenico, I feel the game is just beginning. I don't know what my feelings are yet, but I guarantee you that I am going to find out - and when I do I will confront you again." And before Robert left, as he shot to his feet and darted to the door of the room, he turned back to Domenico and said, "Oh, by the way Domenico, my instincts are always right."

After he left, Domenico was seemingly impressed with the superior being vibes of such a man who must have felt the impact that indeed such an enemy as Don Santucci was nearby and closer than anticipated. Though before his two finest protégés Rex and his Bulldog Bodyguard whom overheard the conversation in silence outside the room had entered to greet their padrone - Domenico, who showed the least sign of concern over, in himself, Robert's inconsequential 'instincts', had only shoved them aside in his mind as a meaningless threat for now. However, he wished to embark on a celebration of sorts and an important point to elaborate on. "What irony my friends, Don Santucci has made my wealth wealthier and sacrificed everything for his last remaining son, Bruno - the very son that will snuff him out from existence once and for all." Domenico chuckled before he went on. "If only he knew I had spared his life tonight for the ultimate revenge - of surprise and shock; only to see his face when he learns his son is working for me preparing for his demise, excellent. Wonderful." Domenico chuckled in loud roaring laughters that his men too grinned at the humorous scope of it all in amusement.

The two men embraced Domenico, their supreme leader - who they considered their one true 'godly' master, extending him much praise with great admiration as old friends and comrades were allowed to do - and said almost simultaneously, "Congratulations sir!"

However, Kong went on to further say in an almost robotically-sounding deep voice, "Yes. Congratulations sir, for defeating the Santucci family and bringing that enemy bastard to his knees. Congratulations."

Domenico stretched out his arms high above his head, clenched his fists and said in the air of magnificent triumph and victory, "Yes. When it's good it is good."

BOOK 7

CHAPTER 13

Robert Stewart had spent the next week devoting his time to investigating the death of Sebastian Santucci. Not only had the New York Mafia War opened up importance to solving such a murder, but it also led police to cracking down on a major crux of the Chess Player's and other Mafia operations throughout the state, leading to dozens of arrests.

The salient nature to solving the murder was to establish and determine whether Domenico Armando was involved in his death and the hundreds of executions on the Santucci front in the major family war over the past six months. That had involved all the main five families in the state of New York, costing not only hundreds of lives on either side of each family, but a large chunk of innocent lives. Civilians whom were also left slaughtered in the street in broad daylight and throughout the evening as a result of the gunfire. Such human lives having been caught in the crossfire and public scorn on police mounted pressure on them to bring those responsible for their families' loss of loved ones to an unmerciful sort of justice. To in fact incorporate a capital punishment penalty against all those culprits - that as a result of the bloodshed widowed and orphaned many individuals throughout the entire state of New York.

Such case; despite much speculation, and lacking concrete evidence to the masterminded involvement behind the feud, Robert nonetheless, could pinpoint the alleged involvement of Domenico Armando in the death of Sebastian Santucci. Hence, such an investigation may open doors to the Chess Player case as well, perhaps. And revealing the mysterious and notorious identity to the code name was priority; that in fact such a target had otherwise overshadowed all obstacles by remaining faceless for so long to all parties searching for the face behind the mask, so to speak.

Meanwhile, such a case had much spanned out of hand. Drugs in the city were at its worst, and the prisons were even powerless to stop such drug criminals to whose Mafia regimes dominated extensive police and prison system patronage. Such officials assisting them in their illegal operations and vendettas created vast complications and difficulties for those genuine police officers who sought their police vows solemnly – 'To Protect and Serve', whilst in their quest of chasing such men, in order to stop them. All in all, the genuine police officers were losing their battle - and such crusades even had lives in the police force claimed by such criminal elements that waged their retaliation on those police officials opposing them. Who were placed on the proverbial Mafia-described, 'Death List'. And utilising such diabolical cunning, the criminal organisations had in fact established scapegoats to supposedly take the heat; such blame and fall for them.

Such reckless, if not shameful carelessness by police resulted in Robert being notified of a successful escape attempt by one of the Chess Player's key drug administrators. He was one of the heavyweight drug dealers whom operated under the Chess Player regime that provided more revenue for the family, with his incessant and relentlessly unforgiving nature to which he pressured buyers to purchase his drugs. Now, he procured his chance to escape a hefty prison sentence confinement to which Robert Stewart was responsible for his arrest almost one year ago. The dealer went by such a familiar code name: Dragon. And now he was back on the street to sell drugs again. Such an escape, Robert understood, would not have been made possible in a maximum security prison facility without extensive police and prison officials' support. As understandably, the Chess Player had controlled.

And since the Dragon turned out the greatest dollars for the criminal regime, as a major drug dealer operating beneath the family structure, it was understood the motives for allowing his escape. Such an arrest of course by such a major revenue-making thug would indeed cost the family a large chunk in its profits. Which in turn, police and prison officials were not keen on the idea of having their cut by the Mob reduced. So, of course, they would participate in such an escape - though his chances of operating in the city as normal were slim. Robert suspected he may be allowed permission by the Mob and much protection to serve them in another city. Hence, Robert's job was to find him before he left the city.

The Dragon's prison escape naturally became widespread news throughout the nation to the public via all the newspapers. And such news had Paul Stewart weary in concern over the threat such a man posed on his niece and nephew, Robert's children. For he knew it was due to Ryan's positively identifying the Dragon as being a dealer who sold drugs to the school that he and Stephanie attended, and fingering him to their father Robert, that led to his arrest to begin with.

And naturally, Paul, immediately following the news, landed himself in his brother's office offering his services and assistance to him. Robert cleared his hands of all the paperwork, files he contained on the Chess Player case of recent drug dealer arrests affecting the criminal empire, overwhelmed in anger over the escape. He lifted his head to greet his brother in reply to his offer for help. "Paul, the answer is no. I will not have you risking your life over that scum. You're hot-tempered; and I don't want that to cloud your judgement in this instance. It could get you killed."

Paul closed the door to allow privacy and raised his voice equally as angry and responded. "Stop treating me like a kid brother, some boy. Look big brother, I know you are worried about me, but don't forget I can handle scum like that. I can help you. You know it. I know it. Besides, from what I hear, you need a man like me. I am not some dummy who is wet behind the ears. I have served in the army. I know how such organisations that control the Dragon operate. I know he could not have escaped unless the police, your supposed buddies were helping him out. The very men you are supposed to trust and depend on."

Robert lowered his head, appalled at the revelation, though could not deny the truth to it all. Paul went on. "If you cannot count on your own people - the supposed good guys, who are helping the bad guys, it's your life you should be worried about. Not mine. So come on bro, I want to help you on this. Besides, I have a personal stake in this. That scum affected my family too. Everyone is in danger, including our wives! And when someone screws with my family I will screw with them. No debating the issue. So, if you don't let me help you, I will work on finding this guy on my own."

Robert shook his head from side to side understanding where he was coming from, though yet his concerns remained, unhelped. "You see little brother that is exactly the hot temperament, the pig-headed stubbornness I am worried about, that may cloud your judgement to making some rash, hasty decisions that you simply cannot afford to make with such a target operating beneath the Chess Player's family. Such a family took an awful risk in exposure planning the Dragon's escape, and they would not undertake such a risk for just any recruit or associate. That alone should speak volumes for itself as to the ferocity and cunning this Dragon character exacts. They simply felt such a talent was worth the risk. One they did not want to do without. A talent, I must add, that any slip up, any mistake on your part - well, let's put it this way little brother, you simply cannot afford to make. I don't want you to let that get in the way and get yourself killed. All right, you promise me?"

Paul broke out a smile, reminiscent to a child whose parent allowed him a special privilege, excited to work under his older brother's wing and said, "I promise you bro, I'll be careful. I just want to be in on this." His face now grew as solemn as his brother's. "I know who this guy works for, the Chess Player. And knowing that, alone, no one is safe, including you and the rest of the family. Besides, stubbornness and pig-headedness is something you're guilty of as well, and so is pop. I guess we both inherited it from him, hey? It runs in the family."

Robert lowered his voice in acceptance to his brother's participation. "Yes, I guess it must. Look, you're in. I agree with what you said. You are right about one thing. Only you and John are really the only two people I can turn to and trust. The rest of the cops' loyalties around here are questionable at best. I cannot tell the bad from the good — who they are as yet. All I know is that the only people I trust my family's lives with are you and John, whom I will involve in my efforts against the Dragon, that will further our efforts in nailing the kingpin behind the family he fronts for: The Chess Player."

Paul, delighted, said, patting his brother on the back, "Well, I guess we'll be working together on this. Besides, we make a good partnership. You, John and I will make a good reliable team."

Robert nodded in agreement. Though clenched his right hand around the back of his brother's neck, in brotherly concern for his safety, such worries had not been alleviated from his mind as yet, and said, "I want you to be careful and exercise extreme caution. I do not want you to forget who we are dealing with for even one moment in all this. And if you think the Dragon is dangerous and a sworn killer, who I must add, is likely to kill again, well – he's a sweetheart only compared to the Chess Player he works for. And where our real enemy in all this is concerned, there is no need to spell out what he does to enemies and people in general who cross him. This Dragon guy is the toughest drug leader serving beneath the most evil and monstrous drug supplier of them all, we have tracked him to - the Chess Player."

Paul shook his head, his usual cocky attitude, debated the issue, as if for a moment suggesting an impossibility for such a man to outmatch all their cunning combined, and snapped out, "Let's do it. Just tell me my part in this?"

It was not long after John returned to the station, informing Robert that they had just received word that the Dragon set up camp at a downtown apartment building in the Bronx, that was abandoned, and they now knew his exact whereabouts and location. And apparently, their target was preparing himself to reclaim his livelihood and pick up where he left off in his little drug dealing operation. Robert thought otherwise. If he was still operating in the city, he took an awful chance. And Robert suspected that perhaps the Mob may have other plans, plans that even the Dragon himself was not fully aware of. All in all, to allow him to operate this close to home made little sense, though Robert halted on picking him up and arresting him.

Robert instead ordered that he did not want him picked up as yet; he wanted him free to roam around under inconspicuous police surveillance to see where he leads them. That was Paul's job. And immediately Paul was briefed on his exact role of his assignment for his brother.

Robert asked his brother to follow the Dragon and keep a twenty-four-hour watch over him, to swap shifts even with John, to see where he went. Who he saw and where he obtained his drugs from; and from whom, his supplier. He needed names and places, everything.

Paul thought of infiltrating the gang. It should not be too difficult for him to blend in with his hip looks and whatnot. That way, he could immediately set himself up as a small buyer even - and obtain all the information he required on the entire crew; but Robert debated the issue. He knew it was too long a procedure to set up a buy-bust operation as such. By the time he won their trust, New York could become another hell on earth. But his way, through just keeping surveillance, all he needed to know was where the Dragon had obtained his drugs from. And once they had located the supplier, then it opened up a new ball game for them by having them working another link higher up, serving beneath the Chess Player. And before long, he could begin raining on their parade.

Paul left the office and began weeks of surveillance work. He and Robert were not in touch until two weeks later when Paul met his brother secretly inside his office, arranging another private meeting. Paul informed him that the Dragon had mainly frequented an electrical goods retail outlet. He made massive purchases, and sometimes took with him ten large boxes. This surveillance was conducted everyday. And everyday he was spotted frequenting the same retail outlet; he seemed rather chummy with the owner. Robert sensed something fishy, but as yet he could not put a finger on it.

Then the next day, Paul followed the Dragon through a Bronx alleyway where he got into a fight with perhaps another drug dealer. Paul planted on a hill embankment overlooking the alley had witnessed everything. He watched the Dragon beat senseless the life from this apparent dealer. A squad car went by, and a police official had stepped out and approached the scene. He did not even arrest the Dragon. He, instead, acted as his friend. Paul could not exactly hear what the police officer was saying to him, but he got the impression that they were friends, and he was warning him off somehow - to be careful. And before the Dragon left the scene on foot, he kicked the semi-conscious drug rival who was on the ground, a killer blow to the head and then laughed. The cop then seemed rather angry, looking around over his shoulder and making sure no one witnessed this before he left in the opposite direction, towards his squad car.

Once they had vacated the scene entirely, Paul went to see Robert again, but first made an anonymous call to the ambulance, which turned up momentarily. But the victim who lay on the ground was obviously dead. And that police officer, also at the scene, having witnessed the entire act, was corrupt. A crook much like all those dealers he was apparently protecting.

Paul asked his brother, "Do you think he's in it with them?"

Robert replied, "No. I think he's involved higher up in the chain of command, with the supplier - the Mob. Can you give me a description of the cop?"

Paul gave him better than that. He handed him instant-developed camera snapshots of both the police official and the assailant dealer. And he pointed out, that he practically had wasted an entire roll of film picturing the entire incident, as he removed the envelope of fully-developed pictures to hand to Robert from his coat pocket.

"Excellent." Robert hinted. Paul had already proved himself an excellent detective for the job. And since he could not trust anyone else, especially on the force, he was really glad he could turn to his brother in confidence for such a task. He could not have come at a better time. Robert was proud of him. Paul acting as a true brother made Robert forget about all the turmoil and terror their past relationship had endured, especially when he abandoned his family and left for the army, and, his involvement in the wrong crowd, with bad influences, always winding up in scrapes of trouble, and Robert rescuing him each time. They made quite a team. And no matter how stormy their relationship was in the past, it did not stop the fact that they were prepared to give their lives for each other. After all, the Stewart blood was thicker than all.

Studying the pictures, Robert was very familiar with the faces in the clear snapshots and was able to make a positive identification of the police officer. "He's working right here in this precinct under my command. Lieutenant Steven Folds. He's known to beat up prisoners, only the wimpy thugs and sleaze on the girls. When Commissioner Gordon was around he fixed him with so many reprimands, charges of misconduct in his file report, and suspended him off the force one time for bad-mouthing him. Once the chief died, such charges and complaints seemed to die with him, his report now clean. You see, when Chief Gordon was around, our precinct was run more effectively. Now with the new chief, it's deteriorated since. And when the police department's performance is rejected, the Mayor gets pissed off because he's in charge. So the Mayor tells off the commissioner, and the commissioner tells off the police in charge of the cases; such complaints were made against - whether such a case was poorly handled or simply lagging too long unsolved. When Gordon was alive, we never heard complaints of lagging discipline. But now, everyone is running around doing their own thing. The new chief in command is turning a good precinct into the pits."

Paul asked, "Are you going to arrest the cop?"

Robert said, "Now we are learning more about the Dragon's history. But if we arrest that dirty bastard cop he is in cahoots with right now, it could ruin our chances; such an arrest may tip-off all the other dirty cops. And we could lose sight of their operation permanently. He may be our only lead to solving this case. He could lead us to his other crooked colleagues, the bad cops on the force. And more importantly, he can lead us to the top dog. I want to see who he works under in the hierarchical chain. Who pays him in the Mob? Then, when that happens, we can have every piece of evidence to arrest such a cop - and work on the next man higher up in the ranks."

That moment Robert began his investigation into the Mob by using the lieutenant. And moments after that, Robert was given a call from a series of police officers. It seemed as though another gang war had erupted in the city

150

in broad daylight, in the Bronx. And by the time they got there, they found twelve dead bodies lying on the ground in the middle of a busy street. All of them were suspected drug dealers. One of them was the dealer Paul took the pictures of, the Dragon. Robert smiled at the accuracy of his instincts once again. He understood the Mob would keep him alive long enough to bid for them, and then relinquish their protection on him. And justice had caught up with him.

Robert left the scene showing no emotion. Only instructing his men to take care of the necessary procedures; to clean the street and write up their necessary reports.

Once Robert uncovered that Lieutenant Steven Folds was a corrupt police official and seen with unsavoury characters as well as known to have a hand in drugs, he enlisted the SIA's help to secretly use their connections in the telephone company. And they tracked down all incoming and outgoing phone calls he made and received from his office at the station house even. It seemed as though for months now, he was receiving calls from a street phone booth in a Mafia neighbourhood. Robert knew it was going to be an all-out war. Because going against one crooked police officer was such a dangerous territory, that he knew not only would he have this corrupt police official after him, but all the others in the New York Police Department as well. And especially the Mob they were working for. Robert had long suspected corruption in his precinct, and, arranging with his telephone company friend, so that he could obtain a list of all the telephone calls the lieutenant made and received in the past several months, had confirmed his suspicions.

Robert instructed his brother to be prepared in case he required his services once again. To wait for instructions on standby now that the Dragon was dead. Robert understood the most effective weapon was cutting off drugs at the source. He turned to Paul a tad concerned, and said, concerned for his life and the lives of his entire family that may be affected by opening up such an investigation. "Our war against drugs has just begun."

So far they had a lot to go on. One corrupt cop link and the link the Dragon had given with the retail outlet he frequented before he died. The electrical retail outlet owner was called Dino Martello. He was a heavy-set forty-eight-year-old Italian businessman. He operated on 38th Avenue in Brooklyn. Robert hooked up with an old SIA colleague and called him. He was the SIA Computer Operations Specialist, and asked him to find out if the SIA had anything suspicious on Dino - the retail proprietor owner, in any of their files on their computer system. Robert instructed him, "Use the access code and call me back on my private line when you find out anything," before both receivers clicked.

Robert waited inside his office with his brother for almost thirty minutes before his SIA friend had called him back. Apparently, he told him that Dino's couriers had been putting large amounts of cash through banks, investment houses, both local and offshore - and investment institutions of the like. Robert understood. "Thanks old friend, I'll be in touch." Robert turned to his brother. "My first instinct was that I was suspicious of that place for attracting a regular hangout for drug dealers such as the Dragon. And now my suspicions are confirmed. I bet you this owner Dino is in on a piece of the action. Selling televisions and video recorders does not turnover the kind of revenue he is making. He must be involved in drugs somehow to make such large amounts of money like that. They're covering their tracks well until now."

Over the next four weeks Paul maintained surveillance on Dino's enterprise. He wore elaborate disguises provided by his brother Robert, and frequently purchased electrical items from the retail joint, waiting for occasions to slip bugs in and around the counter area and the seating positions under frames of tables. The bugs were as small as microdots. They fitted in screw holes all conveniently issued by Robert, supplied by the SIA.

Through the company's bugging, security was not as tight and slipping bugs into a bug detection circuit free-zone was easy. The transmissions were recorded and transmitted to a local tape recorder worn by Paul, as he sat inside his vehicle for hours a day, two street blocks away in close proximity to the retail outlet, to ensure clear transmission.

Such bugging turned up important information. Robert had intercepted an emergency meeting being scheduled of all the New York State's franchised electrical retail outlet proprietors and a few of its street dealers, all influenced by the Chess Player. And also the manager of the New York retail chain and the city's narcotics affairs would host the meeting. His name was Kerry Gilbert. He was in charge and made head of the organisation's narcotics division that included the overseeing of the proper conduct of the narcotics and retail divisions in the city. The nature of the meeting was a result of concern of all the arrests made so far; and murders of their drug pushers.

Such a meeting was forewarned and it took place on the Brooklyn dock on the waterfront, Pier 27, inside a warehouse in the dead of night. Robert intercepted the meeting in plenty of time for him and his brother to bug it and plant a hidden mini-camera that recorded the entire actual event.

Kerry Gilbert, a medium-built, middle-aged man with stoic features headed the meeting and was heard discussing its nature to his audience seated in rows and columns evenly before him. "If any one of you is arrested and talk, we will find you in your jail cell and we will kill you. Jail will not ensure your safety. And you should know what we can accomplish. Remember your friend who talked inside his cell was shot to death inside his cell. Also remember Andrew Morgan or the Dragon as we know him by, also talked once to a cop who pressured him. And he was also arranged to be killed last month. We will do the same to any one of you. Also, the purpose of this meeting is to discuss some of you dealers. Some of you - who are all clients, have held back a few debts. There were four. Three were just twelve hours from drawing the deadline, but one of you is twelve hours' overdue. Such a client knows who he is sitting inside this room. He owes me and the family $1,000. Now, I advice - I insist, you never sell our products, our drugs, by just handing them over to prospective customers without demanding full payment first - because, things like this happen. We do not care how you decide to sell the drugs. Whether you give free samples or trust your cliental enough to ask for payment later, so long as you meet the deadline to us. Because - if you do not meet the deadline to pay us, this is what we do."

At that moment, one of Dino's couriers had appeared in silent tip-toes behind the seated dealer in question, held a baseball bat in his hands, raised it, and sent it down in five consecutive powerful blows, smashing down at the head of the dealer. Large cracking sounds were heard by the impact of the powerful blows, with a gore of blood forming onto the ground before all of them. Everyone inside the room had staggered back in fright and horror at the brutal sight which merely served as an example to displays of misconduct.

The body collapsed to the floor to be removed by two more couriers from the room set up for the meeting.

Kerry Gilbert coolly showed no remorse as he said, "You punks think you are tough on the street, but when you mess with us we become tougher and meaner. You hold back on a debt, all our arses are on the line from the big boss when he looks at the monthly fax report and sees a debt payment is missing. And we do not like it when our arses are on the line. Whilst you punks go out and party, the retail proprietors maintain the books. No figures can be missing." He raised his voice now to emphasise a point. "We know what to expect and the expected balance must be met; on time!"

The nature of the meeting was forwarded with plenty of notice given to both dealers and retail proprietors. It reinforced its codes of conduct. And discipline was strict for these people. Workers, such as the retail business owners who made mistakes from alcoholism or drugs or plain negligence found their accounts were debited when they made such errors. Also, when a dealer held back on a debt to his supplier, it was up to the manager, Kerry Gilbert to oversee why. And if payment was late, the manager then debited the fee missing from the accounts of the retail workers. And it was up to these retail workers-the proprietors to maintain strict discipline. And of course, when a dealer held back on a debt it was them who suffered when they had to pay the family from their own pockets - the same for the dealer to the customer. It operated as links in a chain. If one link in that chain fouled up, it was up to the key of that chain, the retail proprietors, to correct the errors of each link leading to the impropriety - no matter who suffered. So long as the family was credited.

153

Also, the rules of conduct were strict. Their entire lives were controlled by the Chess Player. They were to wear unidentifiable clothing; they were to drive nothing flashy - only simple, very ordinary nondescript cars. And they were to live in normal apartment buildings. They were not allowed to draw attention to themselves in any way, shape or form: no getting high on their own merchandise, no drunk and disorderly behaviour and no riotous parties that disturbed the peace in their neighbourhoods - nothing that would draw the proper authorities to them. Breaches of the Mob's rules were reported; and the culprits, without failure, excuses and second chances were all executed. This unmerciful system founded by the Chess Player produced few shortcomings. The penalty for any member of the cartel that deviated from the Family's strict rules was death - not only for the drug operators, but also for their families back home.

At the same time the meeting took place on the pier, Robert and Paul Stewart had seized their opportunity to begin their search once knowing the retail company was cleared for the evening. Found it as a perfect opportunity whilst the waterfront meeting was in progress to break into Dino's enterprise and begin searching for files. Upon picking locks and temporarily dismantling alarms and disabling the premises entire security system, the coast was clear for them to proceed; once inside, it was ten minutes later when they discovered a file inside a cabinet in one of the back offices, filed under the name, 'Retailcotics'. They took snapshots of the entire file, and then they left everything inside the way they found it, resetting the alarms and reactivating the building's entire security system of surveillance cameras installed everywhere within the interior of the retail company's perimeters, then returned to the waterfront warehouse after the meeting was over and everyone had vacated the premises.

Paul waited as an emergency lookout in the car outside, in direct radio contact with his brother, as Robert entered inside the warehouse and removed the mini-surveillance camera planted on top of a large Wall Unit in a corner of the building overlooking everywhere inside with several bugs scattered around the vicinity, plastered in different areas: from chairs, tables and pot plants. The bugs transmitted to a pocket-sized voice recorder he hid in one of the pot plants, the camera filmed everyone inside who were dressed casually, only the manager was dressed in an expensive Italian suit. Though when Robert had arrived, he found the place was immaculate, spotless - the blood to the murder (that was entirely filmed by the camera), was cleaned off everywhere inside the warehouse. And they even dusted off their fingerprints from the entire premises and took the body with them, giving no clues as to where they would take it. And dispose of it.

All Robert understood was that after many years of experience in Mob-related killings, they were going to take that body to a place where no one

154

would find it again. They would probably throw it in a river in pieces; parts scattered in different areas, or chop it up and throw it in some sort of acid concentration; or dispose of the remains under some construction house foundation in the ground. Maybe even just cremate the body and bury the ashes. They would never know.

From the meeting, further salient, pertinent information was uncovered into their Chess Player crusade. They uncovered another name, a further step up the buffer ranks higher than the dealers and the retail chain owners: The Manager, Kerry Gilbert. And that the retail chains were somehow used as a rouse for their drug operation in the city.

Robert immediately ordered a complete and thorough background check on Kerry Gilbert using the SIA's in-depth resources, apart from his local police files that established Kerry Gilbert only having a very clean rap sheet. Bank account records for the past five years found he was worth ten million dollars. He owned a car manufacturing warehouse, though the SIA suspected it was placed in his name, that he was fronting for the Chess Player as such a car company was in fact suspected as another rouse for smuggling drugs into the country and city. That his accountant had deposited two percent of the car manufacturing company's profits and the electrical retail outlets' profits into his own personal account in the bank. And the rest was credited into the one business account, minus the overheads, such as salaries and electricity and various other business purchases.

The business was filthy rich as the Retailcotics file had indicated, having taken snapshots of through microfilm. Similar transactions occurred in two separate entities. Large amounts of money were deposited into the business account, but they did not know where it went after that. He never made any outstanding purchases. He did not have anything to hide. The tax department was not after him and he was running a legitimate business, so it seemed - all allegedly. For once the money was deposited into the business account, it was lost somewhere. He did not incur any sizeable debts. It was as if the money was transferred to someone else's hands, they did not know who. And if that was the case, it was lost somewhere. Kerry Gilbert was not using the money for purchasing shares or anything. And collating entries missing from the business account to possible similar deposits made into family members' accounts such as his wife and children did not match either. Obviously, there was a third party involved.

Robert immediately held off also on Kerry Gilbert's arrest, and placed the damning evidence they had already compiled against him via the bug and the hidden camera recordings in a safe place, to meanwhile use him as well to lead them to the next man higher up the Chess Player's ranks - that he reports to.

Robert immediately contacted SIA Boss, Chief Lloyd McKenzie and instructed a twenty-four-hour tail be placed on Kerry Gilbert by the SIA's most professional trailer, again, he trusted no one from the police department. For weeks nothing turned up. Then they followed him out of the main branch bank in Brooklyn on 49th Street, carrying a briefcase with a large sum of money that they found out he withdrew from an SIA undercover operative who stood from a short distance aside him inside the bank, radioing a local SIA surveillance van outside. Kerry Gilbert had walked to a local parking lot to an awaiting limousine; he entered the back left hand side and exited the right, without the briefcase. Obviously someone else was inside the limousine, possibly his superior above him - another person higher up the Chess Player's hierarchical family structure. And following the tinted-windowed limousine, they found a man disguised with a hat and sunglasses. The SIA followed him using unmarked vehicles whilst changing to different vehicles; also, their target had changed vehicles at all times so he was not followed. He entered an underground parking lot in the borough after travelling several miles from the initial bank point, then the limousine had stopped and their mysterious person then got into another vehicle, this time an awaiting Mercedes Benz. The driver had also vacated the limousine into the same vehicle as his passenger. Then, the limousine left with another driver, so if he was followed, they follow the limousine that became a decoy, a diversion, the wrong car thinking he was yet inside.

After this, surveillance on Kerry Gilbert and the unidentified person inside the limousine reached a dead end. Kerry Gilbert did not meet with him again. Nonetheless, Robert insisted surveillance on Gilbert still be maintained for the next meeting that they could only hope would eventually take place once more, not to lose sight of their mysterious target again. Robert had checked the number plates of both the limousine and the Mercedes Benz that exited the scene at the same time, eluding them, but, they were registered under names that did not exist; professionals. The man inside the limousine, they could not tell who he was, but when he vacated the vehicle, he lost his pursuers. They could only wait for their next meeting and chance encounter to catch both Gilbert and this mystery man together, again. Rumour had it; it may take months for such another close encounter to eventuate.

Meanwhile, the months of investigation led Robert using his SIA contacts to keep close tabs on the main parties connected, including Dino, and through such surveillance they learned about the drug cartel headed by the Retail Drug Front. They found Dino's couriers were using a certain public phone constantly and it was ordered bugged as well. And immediately Paul Stewart volunteered to pose as a street hot dog vendor in the Mafia neighbourhood in the city where the phone was used. And the bugging identified such a public telephone was being used by gangsters of the Retail Outlet to call drug sources in Sicily concerning heroin shipments, specific orders from the Chess Player. When the phone was immediately tapped, it provided large evidence against United States and Sicilian Mobsters, all on the Chess Player's payroll. Paul had inconspicuously taken pictures of everyone there with a mini-camera that Robert had supplied him from the SIA that he placed on his jacket, sowed on the front, just above his stomach, that resembled a button. The camera was small, but accurate, that enabled him to take snapshots of everyone and everything just by the touch of a button located on top of the camera, as he posed as a hot dog vendor. Such recorded conversations proved no one knew who the Chess Player was. No one met his face. They were dealing with a complex buffer of middlemen left unpenetrated as yet by authorities to only Kerry Gilbert.

Robert knew the mystery man who met Gilbert outside the bank was either the middleman or one of the links; perhaps, higher up in the buffer chain and such a man could lead him to the other buffers, until they worked their way to the Chess Player himself. But such a target man had disappeared; his whereabouts were never discussed even by Gilbert over the telephone, and this target remained in clever hiding. Such buffer system would have the Chess Player himself pass down private instructions and orders to various operatives, until Kerry Gilbert received word. And once it reached Gilbert, the operational man, he would give direct word to the police officials on the take, the retail workers, and then they would give word directly to the dealers. So no one could trace the Chess Player's identity - another example of the Chess Player's genius.

Such wiretaps revealed the existence of a retail drug front that was about heroin smuggling between United States and Sicilian Mobsters that existed in New York, and also dominated among at least three other cities: Los Angeles, Chicago and San Francisco; so that explained why Paul found the Dragon frequenting Dino's electrical business because it was used as a drug market for these drug dealers. The retail drug front bugging illustrated the drug trade for Robert to hand down to authorities as soon as he learnt the Chess Player's identity. However, arrests and seizures would be held off meanwhile, not to tip his enemy's hand prior. And already, one name of a corrupt police official, Lieutenant Steven Folds on the take assisting them had also been uncovered.

The Chess Player had contacts where the poppy was grown, owned plants for heroin in Sicily and Japan, and ran cocaine from Colombia. This outlined an international connection. And from Sicily and the other regions of the world, he shipped to the United States, where distribution was made to different ports, all around New York, Los Angeles, Chicago and San Francisco where the drugs were begged for.

It gave light to the faction headed by the Chess Player family. Through the bugging of the payphone, Robert overheard gangster couriers telling sources in Sicily about heroin shipments through the retail outlet. The bugging confirmed evidence to SIA officials that couriers for Dino's retail business were transferring enormous amounts of money through diverse financial institutions, investment houses and banks in New York, Bahamas, Italy and Switzerland.

And for every drug deal, the gangsters on the payphone telephoned the proprietor of the retail outlet, and informed him to have his drug couriers made ready on the docks to meet the goods coming in, where they would take the merchandise in bulk to a Mafia-owned warehouse, where drugs would be removed. Then the couriers, whilst one was transporting the drugs to another secure warehouse, others would transfer their legal goods to which the drugs were smuggled inside to their appropriate destinations. Clothes were distributed to Mafia-controlled wholesale companies - then to retail clothes outlets and so on.

Court-approved wiretaps in Dino's retail enterprise turned up other names, including the three other cities of the United States retail chain owners. Dino's group made contact to these other retail outlets, its owners in those cities, informing them when drugs were going to be distributed there also, in their areas, via small planes or boats, avoiding customs. And the retail couriers of these other cities were instructed to meet the shipment coming in on the docks for transportation then to their secure destinations, prior distribution – where the arrangements would be made for purchase by its customers; following the same procedure as in New York. These electrical retail outlets were owned by fellow Mobsters and served one distinct purpose: It was a cover; a front that was controlling the drug trade in the Chess Player's regimes in the United States. And Robert immediately planned to arrest all participants in all the four cities after the major drug deal entered New York. All the main retail outlets in those four cities were all connected to the Chess Player; then they distributed all over their cities where drugs were sought after. The case had now reached a major breakthrough.

Robert instructed federal authorities of the SIA variety planted in those three other cities and New York to release an indictment charging the four retail proprietors with conspiracy to violate drug laws, but to hold off on any arrests until they received more information. For any arrests now could result in the enemy being tipped off prematurely; jeopardising their chances in finding out who the Chess Player was; and, possible leads to drug warehouses.

In a short space of time, the number under U.S. indictment had grown into several hundred. According to the bugging, the members of what was clearly dubbed the 'Retail Drug Front' had smuggled some 2,950 lbs. of heroin with an estimated street value of 2.95 billion dollars into the United States from its principal source in Sicily during the past year, then laundered the profits. The arrests would shock the entire country, especially those in New York.

And street dealers who purchased from the Chess Player's drug cartel, acquired delivery in very brief and precisely-timed meetings from middlemen (electrical retail owners), and, the street dealers in turn sold their drugs to customers and some small-time drug dealers. By just the bugging alone, Robert could make a clear picture of how the Chess Player ran his vast narcotics empire by listening to the players involved whom mentioned another quarterly arranged major drug shipment was coming through in three months. Explaining the intricate details of a drug deal and its smuggling methods scheduled to take place in three months. In the ship that was to dock in New York, it would contain legal cargo on it, where drugs would elude customs officials as it would be concealed inside these legal goods. Now, the legal cargo to come in comprised of cars, food, clothes, construction company supplies and jewellery.

Once the ship docked at the New York harbour on the preselected port protected by the Farlev family whom vastly controlled the waterfront, the retail couriers would unload the shipment of cars and so forth on a huge towing truck on a trailer. They would transport the entire shipment to a main warehouse in the city. Then when the cargo was sorted out, the clothes couriers would transport the clothes to clothes wholesaler stores; and food couriers would transport the food to food wholesaler stores and so on. Then, when the drugs were removed, they would be stashed in electrical retail supply boxes labelled: televisions, video recorders, music stereo systems, computer monitors. And the retail (drug) couriers would then deliver them to a store room in the retail outlet. They would deliver enough to the company to supply all the orders made by drug street dealers and the rest of the drugs would be stored in another warehouse waiting to be sold.

When making an order, the drug dealers would first call the retail owner, give them an identification number or a code number consisting of numbers and letters; each code contained ten digits, similar to that of a social security identification number. Then the dealer would order so many kilos. And when they go and pick it up, the owner would say, "Here's your order." And he gave him the drugs in an ordinarily-marked retail box, for instance, a video recorder box; sometimes he may give out several boxes depending on the size of the order. And so customers may not become suspicious, the buyer paid him the amount of what they would be worth if they were the items marked on the box. For three boxes he may pay $600 as very small collateral for the real price owing. This method of drugs was only to pass the drugs from supplier to buyer, and the buyer may have an account with which he secretly pays by a certain deadline due date that must be met. He would pay the money to the retail owner where then the couriers would take this money and deposit it through banks all around the country and other countries as well - in different names, so such money could not be traced to the one person, particularly, to the Chess Player. The Chess Player had used his legal businesses to run his entire illegal operations.

All the while, drug plants were protected by bribed policemen. And should the few genuine police officials find out about the dirty cop and speak out, not only would they be made target by the Mob, but all the bad cops would also come after them in order to protect their own livelihood. These corrupt police officials had kept the drug plants secret and under their protection. They protected the dealers under their regimes, in their operating districts. They protected their Mafia employer and informed the family if police were warding too close to home. Of course, if a genuine police officer had intervened, the obvious reason why the corrupt police officials would react and react brutally, striking viciously at such possible threats, was not only in favour to their boss, but because they were accustomed to such wealth their secret employer had presented them with. It was a dessert in themselves with which they did not want to part with, mixed with their many drug money privileges. There were so many good cops who turned bad, it was no mystery why they were frustrated when they risked their lives everyday in a job with which entailed long hours and the reward was measly and salaries turned out pittance. So when they were offered a chance to broaden their lifestyle, when one corrupt police officer noticed the frustration of a prospective ally cop, and approached him with such words and said, "You want $50,000 or one million dollars a year?"

Of course, the temptation proved too great to refuse and turn a blind eye to, by so many who chose to accept the million dollar bribe and work for the Mob, instead of against them - and protect their illegal rackets and assist them in the drug trade. For providing themselves and their families with financial security and freedom to send their children to college; and to take the occasional overseas vacation, and spend one night a week dining in a fancy restaurant, all proved luxuries irresistible to pass up - by so many, who considered money their one true god.

Robert had approached SIA Boss, Chief Lloyd McKenzie, now set up in a secret SIA safe house, established in Brooklyn. He arranged a meeting with him, issued him a tape and files with new information concerning Sicily's involvement, to prepare themselves for the twelve weeks opportunity they spent, seemingly, so long waiting for. "We are also investigating the Sicilian connection and drug ring, sources of the Chess Player." Robert pointed out. "This is the tape recording of the phone booth that illustrates the Sicilian connection that operates outside established American Mafia organisations, to supply much of the heroin that enters the United States. So you can notify your other operatives in that country. I have the names of everyone connected to the drug trade on this tape and files here. Everything is explained here in full detail because they have arranged another drug deal.

160

Only this time, the deal is the biggest in U.S. history. One so great, that they planned it months in advance. We know the time, the place, and the source locations. We must prepare for the biggest bust of our careers. Only you and I must know of its details, for now. We cannot give the enemy the opportunity to be tipped off and change his drug routes, and miss out on this chance. Sicilian authorities must be notified, only last minute, as well as the remaining authorities in the United States's three main cities targeted as well for the deal. Everything must be kept hush, hush until then. And we must hold off on all arrests until the drugs enter here in the United States!" Robert exclaimed.

McKenzie, the fifty-nine-year-old, bald-headed, stocky-featured man of English descent had nodded his head in agreement. "I will notify all parties of how imperative it is that such a secret be kept closemouthed for now. I just want to say Robert, you have done an excellent job here. Your involvement has been invaluable. In the short time you were assigned to the case, you have uncovered information that has eluded any other operative we have previously assigned to the Chess Player agenda. You are by far our number one, most prized operative!" He said gratefully shaking his hand. "Within three months, once and for all we may put an end to the Chess Player's entire illegal drug operation and then spring him out into the open and uncover the identity finally of this dirty beast to whom we are dealing with. We are talking about thousands of arrests here, never has the SIA struck it so lucky. This will be the government's greatest jackpot."

Robert shared the same enthusiasm and smiled before saying, "Yes. Now, when that ship would enter the country and this city on that pier, it will be the biggest ship and most significant drug deal in recorded history by any Mob organisation, estimated street value, a cool 5.5 billion dollars. Some other Mafia families may finance their own shares in on this deal with a minor percentage in it. And in three months, once those people would get off that boat, we'll be there waiting to seize and confiscate and arrest all parties in all those cities and the two countries before they pipeline those drugs to their underground warehouse channels for sale and distribution."

Robert and McKenzie's faces lit up in smiles in thought to what would in fact amount to 'the mother of all triumphs', grabbed and clenched each other's shoulders in such force, yet overwhelmed, and said, simultaneously, words they were prized of in comparatively smaller great winnings in the past, "This will be the greatest victory of them all. Three months, on September the 12th of this Great year 1988."

CHAPTER 14

The Chess Player had solved his problems by murder. Negotiations - backed by murder. And the Mob had always calculated what it would gain or lose in a spectacular murder of a famous man. Most deaths of such men declaring personal vendettas against the Mafia in personal crusades were killed as a symbol, not just to the United States government, or to its people to back off, but to authorities abroad, that the organisation was indestructible and terrifying. And so the United States government would think twice before sending in thousands of assisting peacekeeping forces of its own soldiers and those from allies abroad, in their war against organised crime.

In the weeks that followed the deaths kept mounting. First, the New York City Mayor, Mack Williams, was assassinated outside his home in the morning as he walked towards his car. A supposedly sniper attack who shot him dead then disappeared leaving the State of New York and his family and friends, now devastated at the loss.

Two days later the former President of the United States who resigned from office not so long ago, in fear for his life, died from a possible heart attack. And such expert doctors of the SIA variety that were called in to examine the death and run an extensive autopsy on suspicious grounds, found no traces of suspected food poisoning in his system. It was written-off as natural causes. But Robert's hunches could not shake the eerie feeling that the state Mayor and the former country's President whom initiated, prior to their deaths, that a total and complete crackdown on Mafia crimes be made forthcoming and its vastly destructive activities across the nation be given a similar zero tolerance, in fact died from questionable circumstances. As a result to receiving certain death threats, the former President had resigned to work independently with a Senate Investigative Committee, to live out his vow of 'cleaning house' of the country's tyrannical syndicates. His mission was top secret following his resignation. He died before he could commence his planned proceedings. And the autopsy ruled that there was no evidence of foul play or murder involved in the death. Robert could not avoid the nagging suspicions. In Robert's mind, only one man had the answers. "I must find this Chess Player bastard!"

Niko Sasselli, in his mid sixties, of full Italian descent, born in Palermo, who adopted a Jewish son because of a sterile condition, emigrated from Palermo as a child; he lived in San Francisco until early adulthood and moved to New York as opposed to his rival Domenico, who grew up in Sicily, then moved to Brooklyn. Niko grew up on the waterfront, and thus claimed the waterfront his livelihood and sole business powerbase, and grown to manhood there. He was employed by the United States Farlev family syndicate who controlled unions and gambling; who controlled politicians and tough policemen. His predecessor was caught off-guard when he was overthrown by such a novice immigrant as Niko. And he was also caught off-guard by his ambitious aggression, and his loyal compatriots would not counter it, because in their minds, fighting against Niko's undesired goal was not worth the carnage it would leave behind. Niko was the second most powerful New York family Mafioso beneath Domenico. It was believed that if the friendly alliance between the two most powerful families in the country had broken, it would be disastrous for everyone, as a war between them would hurt the other families severely. And the entire United States underworld commission's involvement would become necessary in a war that would only initially affect the New York families. But surely develop all over the country. And each primary family could muster such all-round families' support to fight for them; where the remaining affected families occupying outside territories to such primary families' flow of business activities would be forced to choose which side was more rewarding and beneficial to fight for – depending also, on who they thought would win. Though it was far wiser to stick with the winner in which they estimated.

Such a war to ensue by the two most powerful leaders may in fact order the rest of the families' support on either side. Following any refusals, it was bound to affect their businesses that would suffer from the war, caught in the crossfire, particularly, economically, such mainstream families who drew their livelihoods from the power of the elite New York families. So they would have to become involved to find a more effective remedy for resolution to such a war, as each family's support would surely result in the opponent enemy drawing a step closer to its detriment; its end.

Niko was one of the smarter leaders, never showing his opponent emotion or cause to guard against an attack he would wager silently. And if a war broke out, Niko would never allow Domenico to know he was behind it. And Domenico knew his sly cunning manoeuvre in the past that attempted to attack his notoriety as Boss of Bosses, thus, Niko's short-lived bid to replace his otherwise competitor with such a prized notoriety as head of the entire national commission. Following Niko's failure to win over national support in such a far-sighted goal, the Armando-Sasselli business relationship had proceeded since then with much weary and tension. However, it had not affected their relationship in pooling resources for a common goal, until now. When Niko, so affected by almost losing his unnatural son in the crossfire of the Santucci war, had he come forward to Domenico with no course for pretence and trickery, to confront him on his anger for a war he knew he initiated for his own politically and more personally motivated selfish reasons; a war that almost cost him his only son. Niko even threatened to withdraw his allegiance and funding into the Power Project, which would leave

Domenico in a somewhat bind, with the loss of his great investment and share. Domenico, without further ado, proved he was a man that in fact no one threatened.

Rowan Castalone, in another of his infamous elaborate disguises, was immediately sent to portray the task of a double agent in enemy camp. Before long, he infiltrated the army to the Sasselli family, and arranged for security to be at its most vulnerable. When at night he snuck inside Niko's brother's room, his underboss asleep with his wife, he taped their mouths with black tape and their hands and legs were also taped, together taping their bodies to the mattress single-handedly. And kerosene was poured onto the bed over their screaming bodies, and a match lit them on fire burning them alive, until they were reported dead. The murder was a unique Armando murder, used as an example to outline how serious things would become if anyone made the Armando family their enemy. And by killing the brother of his nemesis inside his home, defying his security as such, showed it was more of a personal nature. The murder was committed against the brother, his sole adviser on the subject, who influenced Niko's decision of pulling out the investment to Domenico's project. A mistake duly warned never to be repeated again!

The American underworld commission had not approved of Domenico's ideology that he forced them to participate in and support him in, but he was untouchable. No one could get to him. And they knew he had eyes and ears, such informants in each of their families cleverly deployed in high places, untraceable. Listening in on their top-secret meetings and reporting any hint of rebellion to their one true master. The families had attempted to employ spies of their own on their people, especially those serving directly under the inner circle, given direct orders from respective leaders, even their own counsellors and advisers became prime suspects. The families' leaders even had become frightened, had they uncovered the traitor that removing him by the ultimate punishment marked their names as a breach on Domenico's terms. Because if they were paid by Domenico, such employees serving as double agents for Domenico, killing them, may in fact have Domenico retaliate. He would become their enemy. It was outrageous. And paranoia had developed across the entire nation's underworld.

Such bosses at times developed leery in leaving their homes, even, whilst armed with a legion of bodyguards, paranoid that they may have unintentionally displeased their respective boss of bosses. Had heads driven in panic to some Armando gunman camouflaged outside their homes, ready to do away with them, should they have slipped in some ethical deed and made an enemy out of the Chess Player, somehow?

Domenico had a tremendous shield over their families that prevented them from running their own empires democratically as they wanted to, without

Domenico's permission to be granted first in every significant move they had undertaken.

Domenico's Power Project, nonetheless, after a massive commission-endorsed split share investment had guaranteed to save him and the rest of the families billions of dollars annually from seizures and other losses. Domenico's project and escalated hierarchy as Chief Godfather had provided him with a distinctive power from both sides of the surface, the police-political law and the entire grand underworld.

And such rumours by the American underworld commission had it known, that Domenico, once his man became United States President, his family would be strengthened financially as well, after all, the treasury would invite his hands into the pie of taxpayers' money. Billions and billions of dollars that would go for the taking to Domenico, with records rigged and hidden transactions passed, eluding the country as a whole and the media, everyone. His plan would enhance his stature to more criminal proportions far beyond that of the most powerful and richest man in the world. And if he succeeded, which he never was known to have failed, no one could stop him.

Some, in their own minds, only debated such similarities between 'Domenico' and 'Hitler', and that such 'monster-beings' should indeed have been stopped at the beginning of their evil reign of terror and power. Eluding such a crucial escape to becoming hostages of their own power had, at this moment, rendered them sunk to Domenico Armando's infinitive power, infamous wrath and tyrannical control.

BOOK 8

CHAPTER 15

On September the 12ᵗʰ 1988, the drug deal was scheduled for the day's evening, the crew was due. Robert and the SIA were in complete readiness. Standby agents were assigned within close inconspicuous proximity of the now confirmed 'seven' main targeted United States Cities; waiting for instructions to go-ahead and conduct the necessary arrests of all the Chess Player police officials and dealers in those affected cities. Robert and John and his SIA contact, Brock Stevens, with various other SIA confederates immediately planted its own SIA spies to keep an eye out on Brooklyn Dock 32, posing as couriers, mingling with the crowd. To catch much of the heated gossip where the action was planned for months to take place on this deal, which was the greatest in Mob Recorded History. Worth an estimated street value of 5.5 billion dollars, that had minute shares also from other New York and national Mafiosos. Though, the major investment, the one to hold the greatest burden in it all, would be the Chess Player, who would lose the most by his estimated 90% net share of the deal. And also, Robert had assigned other agents to standby and keep surveillance on the targeted corrupt police officials and dealers who would be arrested also in New York, to ensure in the meantime they had not escaped.

And following the arrests, it was rumoured to have the prisons by the end of the night overflowing in the seven main United States cities, and all those targeted abroad, arrangements were immediately underway to execute their arrest warrants as well with the cooperation of the foreign local governments. To have them all extradited to New York to stand trial for what was assured to be a lifetime behind prison bars.

And to prevent any such Mob loophole in this once in a lifetime opportunity, Robert and Brock had conceded to cover every such loophole that the Mob would concede to foil their attempts, via being tipped off and escape what was destined to happen to them this evening. Robert and Brock had immediately first thing that morning, arranged for the SIA to capture and detain Mob suspected District Attorney, Don Keaton, outside his home before he attended work early that morning. Keeping close watch on his home all night, and close surveillance to ensure no midnight business calls would have him escape his detainment prematurely. His doorbell to his house was sounded, and once he opened the front door, several SIA agents stood to greet him, and then had taken him away to a local safe house compound, until such time the drug bust was completed. And he too would be added to the official arrest sheets as well, and hauled down to the local police lockup facility to be charged, tried, convicted and sentenced also for his participation in Mob crimes.

And other United States Attorneys and Judges in such now bugging confirmed, 'seven' targeted cities of the country, suspected as well, had the same circumstances plunged on them too. Conceding evidence to Mob payroll with their police compatriots through planted wiretaps, they too were detained and held in, for now, unofficial government custody in local SIA safe houses established throughout the country, to have them replaced with proper officials.

This unofficial detainment process for now was incorporated so they could not procure hitches in the proper law enforcers' attempts of arresting every party in question, right to the lowest common denominator. And so meanwhile they could not warn their Mob confederates and perform any leaks.

And hours prior the drug deal was scheduled, Robert had those known crooked offending police officers, their names obtained from the retail drug front bugging, also throughout the country's targeted cities with New York detained much the same way, so they could not cause any interference with all the arrests planned. They were held also in secret SIA safe houses established across the country's targeted cities.

Following the bugging war, it uncovered the evidence of widespread police corruption in New York, Los Angeles, Las Vegas, Florida, San Francisco, Atlantic City and Chicago. Where further raids of Jeffrey Baits's personal files and walled safe had uncovered his secret private phone he used for his untraceable conversations with the Chess Player people; as well as ledgers, upon deciphering cracked codes, they found contained the names of all the corrupt police officials, corroborating even stronger evidence that operated in all the targeted cities of the United States. The files had thusly contained the secret sheet money from the Mob dispersed to dummy front accounts, collating the same records they located in Kerry Gilbert's top secret files. That included the street dealers' names aside each bent police officials' names on the ledger lists thusly appointed jurisdiction over on their beat, headed by Chief Baits and his superior, Kerry Gilbert – everything. All the incriminating evidence was there. And cross-filing it with the list of names of his own, Robert began marking off those already detained, to those yet unapprehended on Chief Baits's list, until they accounted for every single dirty police officer in the seven cities of the country serving beneath the Chess Player.

Steven Folds and Jeffrey Baits were the final of the corrupt police officials to be picked up and detained at their homes. Kerry Gilbert, their direct higher-up in the Mob was the final link in the chain that remained loose for now.

From the bugging alone, Robert had as well intercepted the Mob's national and international drug plants, and already attempts were made from both ends of the globe, and also, further standby agents briefed to scour such areas both around the country and abroad, to seize them and its operators after the historical drug bust was completed. Each government operative was in direct radio contact with the other across the country's main targeted areas together with those abroad awaiting such signal and order to commence in the official arrests from Robert Stewart himself.

Each agent assigned to the case had totalled over a thousand and the carnage of bloodshed massacres from both sides was expected in retaliation.

From the bugging alone, Robert, with the aid of SIA moles into the heroin drug trafficking in Sicily had revealed the inventory contents to the ship. Already Robert knew exactly what time the ship was scheduled, which dock it was to arrive at and he knew exactly what the ship's contents were that the drugs were hidden inside. He also knew the ship departing from Sicily was going to make a detoured stop first to Mexico before entry into the United States, to pick up manufactured goods from the wholesaler for a construction company. And inside those goods, more additional drugs that were stashed in warehouses there were going to be shipped into the United States, cocaine from that depot. Of course, once the ship left Mexico, those in Mexico also would be arrested as well, given no opportunity to local calls or any attempts to warn their American counterparts, as similar measures obtained in Sicily. Thus, every possible eventuality and precautionary measure on that end was taken. It was beautiful.

But since the greatest drug deal in the United States Mafia recorded history was in progress to dock in the country, arrests on that end in the United States were held off until the drugs consecutively entered the United States. Why? Because if the Mob became aware that war was waged on them, they may create a diversion and establish another route for entering the drugs unmonitored into the country by the proper authorities. And the seizure to confiscate the shipment may be lost to only hit the streets successfully again and injected into the veins of more junkies as well as the merchandise in the preselected warehouses may be moved. And Mob policemen and drug operators connected may turn to exile the country in fear, evading government arrests.

It was a full moonlit night in Brooklyn, Dock 32, a night filled with the cold, noisy wind that had blown in across the ocean fronts, moaning through the city's streets and driving its inhabitants indoors. The huge ship had docked on the port at midnight, where police from their hiding distances had observed the actual smuggling taking place in numerous ways. All corrupt police officials accounted for would not interrupt their chores this evening.

Robert and dozens of SIA agents had been on the longest, most nerve-infuriating stakeout ever, hiding their stakeout-surveillance vans and keeping their presence secret, as they waited and watched with night vision binoculars at a safe distance from behind dump masters - and planted behind reams of construction waste on the dock, watching at the huge ship that had just parked aside the waterfront wooden platform, that had suddenly become swarmed with known gangsters and mobsters. To whom some had their reputations known as legitimate retail couriers; they studied the entire operation from mobsters unloading the shipment to delivery vans to be transported to drug warehouses by retail couriers. The ship contained merchandise to the contents of cars, clothing, jewellery, prepacked food and ceramic tiles. From much of the information supplied by agent officials abroad, concerning the inventory, the cars came from a manufacturer overseas loaded at the Italian docks, and the jewellery, clothing and prepacked foods from Sicily. They examined a load of ceramic tiles being shipped from a company over the Mexican border to embark into the New York dock, where the government agents would then locate its actual address to be transported to its warehouse in the city.

Robert disguised himself as one of the workers and couriers on the dock unloading the shipment, all last minute, to avoid his credentials being checked in advance, by simply blending into the crowd. In order to follow the major delivery truck inside that contained the contents of the then loaded major shipment, to its main warehouse storage destination before distribution to its dealers. And of course, standby back-up were in hiding and in direct radio contact with Robert, who wore a transmitted microphone in case of emergency. Robert realised that infiltrating the gang during their unloading of the shipment with cranes and heavy machinery through the scurry was, perhaps, a more reliable option than closely tailing them later and risk being detected at any turn.

Robert, in direct radio contact with the SIA, and inside the delivery truck, once they had reached their final destination, without arousing suspicion he had secretly notified his back-up to the warehouse destination during a casual conversation with the truck driver. That perhaps was not even necessary, since Robert had discreetly placed a tracking device onto the tail of the truck prior its departure. And once the army of government reinforcements had arrived, the arrests began.

The shipment came from Sicily where it made also its rendezvous stop at Mexico to pick up its load of tiles before resumed its sail into the United States. The United States and Italian authorities in a united front had long suspected the existence of the Sicilian connection, though only now were they able to prove it and bring a stop to it. At inspection stops at the U.S. port, the forewarned city's border patrol customs officials had looked inside the hollowed-out beams of the wooden pallets that held the tiles and they found a fraction under a billion dollars worth of cocaine. And inside the remaining cargo of cars, food, clothing and jewellery packaging combined, they found billions of dollars worth of heroin. Replacing some of the heroin and cocaine with a look-alike substance, unable to totally have stripped off both engine and body of the vehicles in a short space of time - together with the other cargo of the like, and replace such an incredible large amount of illegal merchandise prematurely, they allowed the shipment to proceed to its final New York port. And once the cargo was loaded onto the delivery trucks in the state, the SIA had followed the target vehicles to its final destination holding search and arrest warrants for the numerous parties of people connected.

When they raided the address of the warehouse where it was sent in Brooklyn, they found an additional 1,100 lbs of heroin, plus handguns, automatic and semi-automatic military style combat weapons, jewellery, a pallet that contained a load of electrical goods for their retail drug front business (shipped into the country separately), and 150 million dollars in cash.

The city's outer was mostly deserted at this late hour. And what small number of local residents appeared had not noticed as squads of armoured cars raced through the streets with gun-carrying officers who swept through the city into three sections: The dock, the electrical retail outlets and the homes of other Mob workers ready and waiting for the word to spring out their arrests and seizures and closing down the illegally operated premises', all in radio contact with the very man who orchestrated the grandest sting operation in its history, Robert Stewart.

Only the street cleaners, who had just began their rounds, witnessed the armed lawmen kicking down doors and awakening the mobsters out of their beds and hauling off to jail the men whose names appeared on a single, shockingly long arrest warrant. The authorities had conducted the biggest crackdown on the Mafia in its history.

Supplied with numerous copies of the warrant for the arrest of 1,200 Mafia members, 950 of whom in the United States were already in jail from New York and the seven total cities of the country, closing down premises' there as well in raids that had not included the hundreds arrested in Sicily and Mexico. With intense ferocity and extreme force, the government police had rounded up the rest of the 250.

As soon as the crack of dawn raised, the jails that had been set up for the operation in all seven cities and the now confirmed 'three' countries were overflowing. Carrying the dazed Mafiosi to prisons in Southern Italy and the seven cities of the United States and Mexico, not only to officially charge them, but to keep them from warning their confederates that Italy and the

United States had finally declared full-scale war on the organised criminal 'Mafia' commission!

The raid directed by Robert Stewart had tremendous stakes in the United States. The Palermo city crackdown was only tiny in comparison to those on the American soil. The American authorities had ordered the arrests of at least three times that of those arrested in Sicily and Mexico, in the total of arrests made. And the Italian and Mexican authorities began the necessary procedures to extradite them to the United States for trial.

From the Retailcotics file and ledgers confiscated in consecutive raids on Mafia operatives and their hangouts, Robert found that the Chess Player was into every business there was to smuggle drugs into the country: From clothing, food, cars, jewellery, industrial building equipment to retail outlets. He was an import-export trader and supplier to many car dealerships and freelance operations in America and other countries, and he brought drugs in with each import. Now, in its final docking port in New York, the cargo was all stripped and the illegal merchandise all confiscated.

Following the cargos final warehouse destination being established in Brooklyn-New York, everyone was arrested on sight, both at the warehouse address and the waterfront pier: including longshoremen dock workers who helped unload the ship, customs crew officials on the take, additional police spotted on the scene, transport drivers, couriers and the entire ship's crew. Some gunfire on the dock was open, but the drug people all found themselves surrounded and outnumbered by the government agents doubling the criminal men that resulted in a lesser carnage than expected for what was at stake and lost. The outnumbering had little resisting arrest and culprits dropped their weapons almost immediately. That resulted in few lives massacred by machine gun barricades as they were forced to surrender their guns and hauled in bearing handcuffs around their wrists, arms pulled behind their backs and frisked at the same time, as Robert Stewart had led his government army in confiscating their machinery weapons simultaneously before all hurled to a legion of huge arresting getaway vans.

In correspondence to this drug raid, massive drug raids began forming; seizing billions of dollars worth of drugs and drug money which began in the state of New York. After the official drug bust in Brooklyn, Robert in direct radio contact gave the SIA Captain Brock Stevens the command to the SIA agents staking out the buildings of all the New York Mafiosi to arrest them, it was now time. Drug people, retail outlet middlemen workers and couriers and many other known corrupt police too were arrested. The electrical retail store buildings were raided and seized. Also, hidden inside a bolted safe on the floor of the drug store room inside these retail outlets authorities blew open with sticks of small dynamite, they found record books, files with a ledger balance sheet, names and financial transactions under the file heading 'Retailcotics'. A dummy name that made millions each week according to the file, that contained the names of all those drug street dealers who conducted business with them in the now marked 'seven' United States cities in mention - those who paid their debts and those who still owed the cartel money.

And had revealed much information of those participants abroad, with documented evidence to have the international drug cartel crash to a standstill before their record files of evidence of them could be destroyed, such files were now confiscated from the retail operators. That supplied authorities with more names, more places and further arrests that overflowed the local prison cells on all ends. The raid had led to more and more arrests crippling the Chess Player's narcotics empire at an entirety.

This procedure was also happening in the country's other connected cities at exactly the same time. Prison house facilities suddenly became chock-a-block with prisoners. And also from the bugging and the raid of the Brooklyn warehouse of drugs and legal goods being stashed, they uncovered the names through hidden files of other warehouses and seized billions of dollars more of drugs, arms and dirty blood money.

In conjunction to the massive drug raids that seized billions of dollars worth of drugs and drug money and illegal assets in the United States, Mexico and Sicily, the drug processing plants of heroin and manufacturing wholesalers in Sicily and cocaine in Colombia, the sources to such drugs were also destroyed. Everyone from street dealers, to drug middlemen of retail operatives and proprietors, to drug processing plants, police and political officials owing the Mob allegiance were accounted for. Everyone, except the source, the Chess Player, yet, who remained a mystery, who controlled such a faction and factions, headed the family behind it all, who recruited all such men – remained invisible for now. And Kerry Gilbert was the sole remaining operative in the link allowed to roam the streets for now, to serve as their primary lead to tracking the evil dictator and uncovering his identity, once and for all, to finally lure him to justice for all the deaths and suffering he had caused!

Though, out of all the masses of arrests made, it was important to mention that no one who was questioned, even those placed higher up, such as corrupt police and political officials knew of the Chess Player's identity. And what was even more important was that no one would speak against their anonymous family chief who they only knew as the Chess Player. When Robert and his confederates questioned them, in general, of their family leader known as the Chess Player, they suddenly all developed, no exceptions to the rule, a common Mafia-frightened illness called 'amnesia', upholding its century old law code omerta, by remaining silent and close-mouthed. Not revealing anything, as they solemnly believed that not even the government could protect them from their master ruler's yet existing influence and retaliation. The power of his retaliation!

Meanwhile, the United States and Sicilian arrests were two sides of the same coin, as was the Mexican connection. They were prosecuting the same organisation, Mafia chiefs from such foreign terrains worked hand in hand with each other.

After the trial, unbribed jurors had established over 2,000 convictions with overwhelming evidence from tape recordings, ledgers and record-keeping files confiscated in street dealer and electrical retail outlet hangouts. That outlined many corrupt police and political figures in allegiance, had protected them. The evidence led the government to solving finally many other unsolved crimes such as the mass murders of police and judiciary authorities and politicians on each level, in each country in a united front, committed for almost two decades, and other United States murders. Following the extradition of the international Mafiosi to all stand trial together in the United States with their American counterparts, upon their convictions, many were to be deported back to their own countries to serve out their issued life sentences. The three countries' governments were in cooperation and agreement with their new extradition treaty and deportation policies formed in relation to the Chess Player case which affected all their countries combined, creating an 'international incident'.

Though, throughout all the arrests and convictions made, no one, even the phoney police, District attorneys, and even Judges prosecuted with such overwhelming evidence that established precedence to succumb them to lie detector tests, knew who the Chess Player was. No one of them had ever met his face. The bridge was formed and ended with Kerry Gilbert. Though not even Kerry Gilbert's name was mentioned in the trial. Robert understood that had really only worked to their advantage in keeping him on the street for now, under tight-watch.

And Robert knew that Kerry Gilbert was also a middleman who reported to someone else, higher ranked in the Chess Player's organisation. For it was understood that not even Kerry Gilbert had known of the Chess Player's identity, nor had he also ever met his face! He was employed by the family as an 'external' operative. But he served as a lead to another higher up, and this higher up was, perhaps, their passport inside the home to the Chess Player himself!

Following what was dubbed the 'historical drug raid', Robert refused to publicly acknowledge the credit for all such mass arrests and convictions of such Mafiosi people, where only the SIA became known as the party responsible. Robert's involvement with them was not public knowledge. And his name was completely unmentioned in those arrests to the newspapers, as he remained the secret party behind it all, who masterminded the downfall of the Chess Player's drug cartel. Why? To protect himself and his family from any possible retaliation should such information become publicly exposed. And also, not to blow his cover meanwhile in his further attempts to unlock the doors to the Chess Player's domain.

Robert Stewart, through his sheer tactical brilliance, unyielding tenacity, courage and bravery proved a master of bringing down crime leaders and their criminal organisations. By his hand alone, he had cut down drugs in society by a greatly significant proportionate chunk. And, what with the destruction of the Chess Player's infamous Power Project – now brought to an abrupt end too, it contributed to a vast weakening of the Chess Player's empire, both economically and influentially; reducing his major power on all ends considerably.

Though the price for such a success proved bitter-sweet as well with serious repercussions brought forward by their anonymous enemy in it all. And all were made to witness first-hand the cold-blooded retaliation of the enemy who proved the force of his brutal hand once again by exacting his revenge.

That moment a bomb exploded under a parked car outside the United States Embassy in Rome, killing a woman and her two children. And when the embassy was backed up by telephoned death threats, it had caused twenty United States officials and their families to exile the country.

In Sicily, twenty-nine members of the United States sponsored SIA agents ordered to eradicate the pushers established there were killed, sixteen of them the State Department had been informed after being tortured. Robert had suspected that the Italian syndicates had incorporated the murders as the drug raids in fact hurt them back home in Sicily where it reached as well as their United States smuggling operations in both countries.

Furthermore, intelligence agents discovered that Mexican and United States and Sicilian traffickers had paid a gunman $500,000 to murder a United States Ambassador in Colombia. The Ambassador was executed inside his home before they could ward off the brutal gunshot massacre against him.

The violence by such arrests was rumoured to stop, but the criminal Mobs' inner circles had mounted violence to continue as the U.S. and Italian Drug Kings had sworn to kill seven Americans for every compatriot extradited to the United States in the future, by forming legions with secret terrorist forces. They had even placed another $500,000 bounty on the heads of several U.S. government agents and two Chiefs, McKenzie and DEA Chief, wanted dead or alive. To ward off the attack by such tough and ferociously mean group of men, the DEA Chief had resigned his authoritative power post and position that moment and lived in exile with his family. Ten of his former agents joined him in exile.

SIA Chief Lloyd McKenzie had immediately ordered an army of private guards to surround him and his wife round-the-clock at all times, even when in the security of his head office in Washington, D.C., SIA headquarters, once he had arrived there by private plane only yesterday. He would not leave the protection of his Washington safe house, and would conduct business from indoors from now on until the Chess Player and those around him were incarcerated.

CHAPTER 16

Three weeks of further increased surveillance on Kerry Gilbert proved very forthcoming as predicted by Robert. The additional surveillance was ordered on Gilbert as it was forecasted that the crash and destruction of their major source of income via the collapse of their drug kingdom may call upon last minute meetings to be arranged by more edgy Mob men now, more irrational, more inclined to slip up as a result of their anger. And in turn, such anger would have them risk the exposure in calling unplanned last minute meetings, contradicting their usually cautious family policy laws.

Robert's hunches proved accurate once again. Kerry Gilbert, the bagman that afternoon, was finally found entering the same downtown city bank, carrying a large canvas bag this time, larger than usual, clearing all the money for his higher-up. The Chess Player required the funds to recoup losses and invest furthermore, as police suspected he would. Seeing as Gilbert was in charge, the middleman who had passed down the funds to retail workers, and at the same time, he had passed to buffers higher up - the profits from drugs to the direct family's inner circle underlings, as he controlled and also was in charge of withdrawing and depositing such funds in the banks and parts of its investment.

From their inconspicuous distances, Robert, John and his SIA contact Brock Stevens in one van in direct radio contact to an army of SIA men locally placed in car patrol on standby, ready for pursuit, and covering all the major streets in the city within the vicinity of Brooklyn, and the entire state of New York itself, had presumed to follow the Gilbert's reporting upper link once the brief meeting was concluded and their target had left the scene. As they were all prepped and ready to keep surveillance in unmarked civilian cars ready for Robert's go-ahead to tail their route.

Robert gave out his instructions to his team inside the van. "We're putting an extensive array of tails on him this time. Now, anybody can lose a tail when they really want to, which is the first thing our MR. X. will check out for, but - this time, we have a car established on every road within the vicinity of Brooklyn. We have used every SIA man available and we will bring in extra men if necessary. And we will be changing vehicles at all times as they do, not to be followed - so the target will not know we are following him in different unmarked vehicles. With each car equipped with radios in direct contact with us. I have plainclothesmen everywhere. No one will notice the agents. They'll look like ordinary people. Even should someone notice the licence plates on the cars, it will be registered in phoney names, so we have covered all bases here."

176

Gilbert again had entered the bank and left after twenty minutes, having withdrawn a larger sum of monies this time as the agent posted inside the bank reported, wired with a microphone that transmitted to Robert's surveillance van loudspeaker, that the money was quickly transferred by the bank manager into a briefcase once again. Same SIA contact keeping close watch reported back from the bank in his inconspicuous seated post, gaining a clear view of everything, and understanding only this time the assailant withdrew all the money in an emergency - closing all such accounts, having received official authorisation from the bank manager to do so. And the undercover SIA plant inside the bank radioed Robert's surveillance van, alerting him to get ready and silently begin his vehicle's engine, and alert all other surveillance vehicles planted across the entire city on standby, via secured frequency, and plainclothes agents on foot patrol scouring the entire area outside the bank, to keep their eyes out for once Gilbert had made contact with the target vehicle.

Given strict instructions to follow Gilbert outside the bank, he again had walked across the busy street to the same covered parking lot as the previous time to meet a similar make and model, black-coloured limousine. It could not be determined whether it was the same limousine as previously or not. It was suspected different, not to leave traces or patterns, as the number plates were different again.

From the parking lot, Gilbert walked to the limousine, agents in the car park reported he entered the rear left side as usual and exited again from the right, without the briefcase. Obviously, someone else, his higher-up was inside that vehicle again, perhaps, the superior. And following the tinted-windowed limousine, they found a man seated inside the rear seat, the same man disguised with a hat and sunglasses covering his face, and they could not make out his identity once again, the agents labelled Mr. X., and followed him changing also to different vehicles as before.

Their dubbed Mr. X., using similar modus operandi had changed vehicles again, when he was seen entering another covered parking lot on 72nd Street, only a different parking lot to the previous instance; when he still vacated the limousine as the last time and entered into an awaiting Mercedes Benz, also with different registration plates. Then, the limousine left with another driver, so if he was followed they follow the limousine that became a decoy immediately thereafter, a diversion. Only agents planted and much scattered all across the vicinity of the city, taking no chances this time, had only foreseen their final break as Gilbert's days were numbered. Conceding to no expense this time, they reported to Robert of this occurrence in direct radio contact, revealing the number plates and make and model of the vehicle that they sought to now surveillance on, that again the limousine was a decoy.

This time Robert planned a very elaborate surveillance operation so they would not end up following any decoy vehicle to a dead end. This time

Robert had assigned SIA men on foot patrol in plainclothes also, using the entire agency's manpower to patrol every street and street corner within the vicinity and underground car park; to cover every lead, every street within the vicinity of a fifty-mile radius - of each agent assigned from the initial bank commencement point. Such men were equipped with radio devices, the open frequencies removed to only transmit to direct secure radio contact with that of Robert's surveillance van.

And the method Robert had procured for their professional target to be followed was by dispatching many dozens of SIA vehicles, civilian cars scattered all across the area, which only after a short while each agent was relieved from tailing their MR. X., so the target's driver would not grow suspicious of the same vehicle and driver behind him for long periods of time. And in direct radio contact they would alert the next car assigned at various close intervals at alternate posts citywide, all arranged via secret premeditated discussions beforehand, of their relief to take over, so the same tails were never on their target's vehicle for more than one minute each. And no same vehicle made a turn into another street in pursuit of their target. Always a replacement vehicle planted on each street corner within the vicinity on standby would be made ready to emerge. Another SIA unmarked car of different make and model, to take over in relieving their former compatriot planted tail, leaving no patterns and nothing to chance this time.

Different agents followed the target going east, then west with its many attempts to elude trailers that agents accounted for. The target vehicle travelled through the highways of the city in different directions, in zigzag motions, and the car spiralled over the bridge approach slabs of the Brooklyn borough's border, seemingly exiting the city of New York completely - but only taking detours of its final destination into the city.

Throughout its route, the target was found changing to several different late models Mercedes Benz vehicles, different colours, via various underground car parks all across the borough; and SIA agents staked out everywhere had spotted each vehicle transfer.

Finally, the last to take over was Robert who had a change of clothing inside the van as well not to be recognised by the target searching lanes of vehicles and drivers that may be trailing him throughout his route as his vehicle had emerged on its final course. And Robert followed the last Mercedes Benz all the way with John and Brock in the front seats aside him until the short trip had ended its journey in Brooklyn Heights on 5th Avenue into a mansion entering through gates. Where the familiar owner was now revealed as the Chess Player, who until now kept his identity a secret by the extensive chain of order he had initiated within his organisation.

The Mercedes Benz was followed to the home and residence of Domenico Armando. Where the guards outside had opened the gates to allow the car entrance inside. Robert, with binoculars parked metres away on the other side of the street next to a line of parked cars to remain inconspicuous, had seen Domenico step out from his house and greeted the exposed passenger with gestures to that of an embrace by an emperor to his underling, and all smiles holding the briefcase their initial target handed to him. The man removed his hat and sunglasses for a brief moment to greet his superior accordingly, kissing him on both cheeks and his hand.

They now knew it was true. Domenico Armando was the Chess Player. Though their MR. X.'s back was towards them, Robert impatiently at that instant, grunted, "Come on, damn it, turn around before you put those glasses and that hat on!"

And he turned sideways prior entering the front door to the Armando mansion before he placed his hat and sunglasses on, giving Robert and his confederate partners enough time that were all armed with binoculars to make out the positive identification of their categorised MR. X. assailant, who was Rowan Castalone, now under the employ of the Chess Player, Domenico Armando.

Then Rowan left the Armando house without the briefcase perhaps only three minutes later to disappear through the rear exit-entrance, and left the scene again inside the Mercedes Benz through the front gates. By now all surveillance agents were called off, so they lost sight of the secondary man to deal with the shock of discovering who the Chess Player was. Brock and John inside the surveillance van looked surprised, but Robert appeared more composed than surprised. Perhaps numbness was his initial reaction.

Once they recovered from the shock of the day, and as soon as Rowan left the Armando mansion, as the others remained in the van, Robert had made an excuse to invite himself into the home of Domenico Armando, passed the guards at the gate, whom just opened then closed the gate again at his calling. The excuse was to see his Godson, D.J. the 3rd.

The butler informed him as he entered the front door inside the foyer, once invited to do so, "Mr. Armando is in a meeting with his Vice President and one of his Chief Executive Officers, Captain Stewart. I apologise, he cannot be disturbed, sir."

Before Robert had departed the estate, he walked into Domenico's small empty private study room office left open upstairs, as Domenico was locked away somewhere downstairs, no guards in sight, on his long route through the house to his godson's room, where he saw a fax on Domenico's desk under the name 'Retailcotics', before a shredder. The name that signified his Retail-Narcotics joined organisations. And he now knew - and it was confirmed that Domenico Armando was the Chess Player himself, and now he had to prove it.

Immediately the number plates of both the limousine and the four Mercedes Benz vehicles used were checked. But they were registered under names that did not exist, all phoneys - professionals. And when Rowan left the Armando estate, he had lost his pursuers. And following their instincts, Robert, once he had returned to the van with Brock and John, they all agreed to let things go on as before. Not to tip-off Domenico or tell anyone that they were onto him. And they would not arrest Rowan Castalone until after such time Domenico Armando was placed behind bars. Things had to be played extra carefully from now on or else all hell would most certainly break loose. And many more innocent lives would be lost in the crossfire – or, as a price.

Robert and John had finished their long day's work when they burst inside Kerry Gilbert's house on the west end of Brooklyn, Robert kicked the door open and led the way inside as his police partner followed with Brock as back-up, holding an arrest warrant. Kerry Gilbert understood what was to happen. He was also found packing his bags and presumed to leave after he was informed by his higher-up that the incarcerations also of Baits and Folds confirmed the police were closing in. So he naturally feared for his life, that his demise was near, as all those under him were accounted for. His autonomy was now shattered with no manpower that otherwise consisted of street dealers, police and politicians he thusly controlled in the country's seven main cities, that served him - as they were either dead or in prison. And he presumed to make a final attempt for departure from the country at the earliest possible convenience.

After all, if all his men were arrested and convicted in a court of law with solid evidence, then that really only meant that it was not long until police had connected his name to all of them - and behind it as well.

Robert and his men found him packing clothes in huge suitcases inside his main room holding his flight itinerary to a destination unknown; they caught him off guard as well. Gilbert knew he was next, though never thought it would happen so soon.

He pulled out his gun quickly and Robert, John and Brock with revolvers drawn had immediately opened fire, and he was massacred in a riddle of bullets instantly as he had done so murdered and ordered murdered many an honest man. Robert's justice on Gilbert and all those he controlled was now finished, leaving the Armando family in a state of financial ruin and turmoil over its vast extraordinary drug cartel collapse. And all-round losses incurred. It was now complete. As called in police picked up the body in a body bag to deliver the dead corpse to the city's morgue - at the same time, Robert with his two confederates remained behind for a moment to contemplate what was next ahead for them. Now that they knew the Chess Player was Domenico, they had a far greater fish to fry than Kerry Gilbert. It had just dawned on them that their war had not ended by the death of Gilbert, but had only begun by the life of Domenico Armando.

180

Robert, still numb from the shock of the confirmed revelation, though it came as no real great surprise to him in itself as he long before had suspected the possibility. Though now as the reality to it all stepped in he realised from here on out beyond anyone's control that all hell would ultimately break loose. And after they parted company, Robert returned home to his wife and children later that evening, the burden that he could not tell them the cold truth only to protect them proved much to take, as he always confided in them. That the man who they believed was a great benefactor, only to shake off suspicion from himself through donating millions yearly to charities and even anti-drug programs was in actuality Chief to the country's vast illegal drug cartel - and turned out a hero. Everyone idolised him. Robert had only scorned at the thought of his number one enemy's two-faced persona; what a brilliant tactical move. And what was even more genius was he proved a friend by even insisting that he and the Stewart family become intertwined when Domenico asked or arranged for him and his wife to become Godparents to his grandson, by getting close to him, his enemy, so he could monitor his movements whilst undermining and scheming to prohibit him from uncovering the truth against him - the Chess Player.

Robert's mind had worked very well, knowing everything now. Knowing how Domenico tried to earn the entire Stewart family's trust so he could sway their focus off his real activities and onto somebody else, a scapegoat Domenico himself would set up to take the fall for all the crimes he himself had only committed. Similar to his war with the Santucci family, when every other Mobster in the city had fingers pointed at their direction in blame – everyone, except for Domenico himself who masterminded the entire bloodbath that struck New York City for months, resulting in hundreds of deaths - and many civilian lives killed as well!

Robert planned to deal with him very shortly. His noble colleagues suffered so wrongfully; the massacres that Domenico orchestrated against good honest individual police officers and in bloody masses as well - slaughtering them, and the hypocrisy in which he portrayed himself and his wealth as a patriotic law-abiding citizen. His status as a benefactor of the poor and the needy was as phoney as hell!

Though, all in all, Robert was not really surprised, though the confirmation to it dawned on him. On the other hand he should have known, after all, all the classic signs and symptoms were there: His outstanding wealth as the richest man in the world, his obsession for power, his tyranny and shrewd cunning in business and his known rivalry and link with the criminal crime family, the Santucci family, that killed his parents and in turn drove him to achieve such infinite powers that had him become a certifiably obsessed madman - a monster. And Robert was Godfather to his grandson who stood to inherit a legacy of insanity handed down by Domenico and his heir apparent son D.J. to that criminal throne. In himself, he had to stop his godson equally from being corrupted by such evil.

And it was now that Robert found out that the Chess Player was behind his uncle's death, where the Santucci family pulled the trigger for reasons not only for themselves, but by an authority with far greater political reasons than their own. Robert's joining the SIA having succumbed to such a decision through his ambition to achieve a greater scope in law enforcement had now realised the Chess Player was behind his uncle's calculated death, as he was killing the police in a series of sordid criminal conspiracies. The Santucci family carried out the actual order of his uncle's assassination but not until after the Chess Player himself approved the go-ahead for such a cold-blooded execution to take place.

A maniac Domenico indeed was to mastermind such a conspiracy to kill police and politicians by the great masses throughout the country – and even other countries, by invading such rival powers, overthrowing the old by having them massacred and bringing in his own men - his new people. To take over even the judicial law which was simply the work of a madman. He and Hitler could shake hands on such a twisted ideology. It was uncanny what that maniac had pulled off that secured his identity as crystal clear for so long as all those around him that he controlled including the underworld had met destructions at one point, though only he had survived such extraordinary odds that only until now had revealed his identity. Such atrocities by such an inhumane being had to be stopped and abolished. He was indeed one of the worst menaces of society that had ever existed next to Hitler, perhaps his sworn reincarnation.

Though the one thing Robert had considered in which he himself had to his advantage now that in itself, in his mind, placed him one step ahead of the enemy was not only the knowledge of his notoriety, but also convinced of the fact that the enemy had not known that his security was thus penetrated and breached so fatally against him. That such incriminating highly-secured secret maintained since the founding to the prime of his existence, a secret locked away for over twenty years finally was leaked out and uncovered by his greatest enemy, Robert Stewart.

And it was a long time before Robert went to sleep that night. And he only could because his body was exhausted and he had not slept in over three days.

In that evening, Domenico Armando was at home long before his wife had arrived, and Domenico was with his wife's younger sister with the doors locked inside his upstairs master bedroom, having intercourse with her, and all the children were out of the house handling the day's previous given engagements, most of the guards were called elsewhere so they had the house to themselves.

182

Inside the bedroom, shacked up with his wife's younger sister Maria, Domenico heard his wife coming towards the door of the locked bedroom, dangling keys, Rita's mind in such emotional turmoil preoccupied by her husband's turning her into an errand maid that day, to run chores for the family outside the estate, had not thought why the door was locked. And she had not bothered knocking; as if oblivious that it was locked because someone could be inside. The woman he just made love to was his wife's sister. She was in the middle of saying before hearing her sister's intrusion outside, "Now that I am divorced I have to admit that I was never a virgin before marriage, but I cannot let my sister see me here. What time will she return?" Before she was startled by the surprised and abrupt presence of her sister outside her husband's locked bedroom, they were still quite close, and the prospect that her sister would find her in such a compromising position with her husband inside their bed, naked together, had her give out a small grunt. After all, her sister would never forgive her if she found out.

Domenico placed a quick hand around her mouth, a gesture of abundant silence. They had been sneaking around to see each other, sleeping together, Domenico had been giving her money and bought her a secret nice condominium apartment in Manhattan, and had purchased expensive gifts of jewellery for her behind his wife's back for years now - and bound now not to let their private affair be found out.

Domenico, bearing no clothes, even no time for any attempts to snatch his favourite robe in the closet, had quickly shot up and jumped from the bed, abandoning his terrified mistress, before grabbing the robe attached on the nearby dresser. He, in silent footsteps, darted to the door as he heard keys grate in the lock, and with both hands grabbed the handle of the door in tight grips so it could not be turned, and forcefully leaned his body weight against it, with absolute silence. And made a gesture with his finger at his mouth to his wife's sister now sitting upright in the bed to be silent, so as his wife attempted to open the door outside, she could not, thinking it was jammed. And when his wife could not get inside with most of the hired help nowhere to be seen, and no bodyguards in sight, all called away, she gave in. And with no intention to yell for even the kitchen help or the maid to open the door, he heard footsteps trotting away down the stairs.

As his wife left, Domenico and her sister inside the bedroom quickly fetched for their clothes, got dressed, and he embraced her with a small kiss on the mouth complimenting her first, after he quickly got rid of the empty champagne bottle in the frozen ice box on the bedside table and the two glasses, he placed in her purse to take with her and dispose of. Dissolving of all the evidence, so his official wife could not see when she returned to her room. And he also straightened out the creased sheets himself on the bed and sprayed his aftershave in the room quickly to dissolve too the scent of Maria's own familiar perfume that masked her being here. As Rita, no doubt, would recognise and suspect everything - particularly, if she sniffed her own sister's perfume in her "husband's" bedroom. He did not do this for his own personal benefit, but for the sake in not creating bad blood between the two sisters if Rita ever found out of her sister's ultimate betrayal to her!

Domenico kissed her on the lips again in compliment. "Yes. You are beautiful, but we'll talk after." He said, before signalling her to leave the back way as he would go downstairs to distract Rita and keep his wife preoccupied. So it would be safe for her to sneak out through the rear exit of the house and leave without being seen. And he would have a trusted driver waiting for her up the road to drive her back home in the Borough of Manhattan.

Domenico gave her one last kiss on the mouth and said, "Fear not my beautiful lady; this will be a secret between us that we shall take to the grave. No one will ever know the secrets of I-me, Domenico Armando, the Great!"

BOOK 9

CHAPTER 17

Robert Stewart, the day he found out Domenico Armando was the Chess Player he returned home not telling his wife or family, even Paul with his famous temper as it would put them all in danger. All along he was anxious to tell someone, and when he could not, that horrible night he took a cold shower to settle his anger and nerves, to relieve the tension as he was too keyed up to sleep. And inside his bedroom, he saw the figure of his wife in bed, already asleep; he went downstairs inside the communications room to speak further to SIA Chief McKenzie who also could not sleep when he heard the news. And they talked for hours of their plans to nail the Black Knight. The investigation had come to a head after so many years. They reached a crucial breakthrough.

The Chess Player case had been hounding Robert for years, and only now had he known, without any doubt, the Chess Player was Domenico. It affected everyone. Everyone was in danger, including himself and his family and colleagues, Brock, and even Chief McKenzie. Robert, despite his making tremendous inroads in the world's priority case at hand, realised the walls were closing in. He discovered real fear - for himself, and for his family's well-being and safety. After all, when all hell broke loose, Domenico knew where his family lived and breathed. They could run, but nobody could hide. On the second night he made love to Cassandra to forget his fear of the nightmare just for one brief moment.

From then on, Domenico had invaded Robert's mind even when he was asleep. He began having nightmares about the Chess Player, the man, now weeks before he discovered as Domenico. And every morning from then on he woke up in a cold sweat and Cassandra each time wondering why?

It dawned on him. Domenico killed so many people, and now, finally, the house of cards was starting to fall in around him. Robert, the day he found out the truth, when he spoke to McKenzie to inform him of the important breakthrough they had discovered, Robert had another purpose for contacting his chief. He immediately had arranged to put twenty-four-hour plainclothes guards on all members of his family; his wife and children, even the rest of his family and their homes. And insisted they not leave home. The children were on school holidays, so it was all right to send them out of the country for a while to live with a close retired police friend Robert had called and arranged to have them spend the holidays with him and his family for a while - no questions asked, not even from his children. Then, when they would return, they were to stay at home and not leave, despite the discomfort it caused being placed in the situation of 'house arrest'.

All in all, Robert had no proof that his immediate family were in danger or he himself was for that matter, but he did not want to take the chance that Domenico was onto him and was simply not letting on. Fear was backed by paranoia; which stemmed from the unknown.

Questions were raised; Cassandra would not stop nagging Robert for answers of what was wrong. After all, she had a legal practice to attend to and a firm to run which Robert forbid her to attend and leave the home, which she had to postpone her job and her seeing her clients. And even, if possible, arranged that any urgent business she had she run it from home. She had the phone and a messenger assigned to her to bring her any urgent paperwork - the entire bases were covered. If his children were to see friends, such friends would visit them, security clearances issued; they were not to leave the house. And once their schooling had resumed, should the danger surrounding them not be neutralised at that time, their education would be conducted through private tuition. It placed a chill on everyone.

But Robert knew he could not delay telling his family any longer. And an important family meeting was scheduled. Paul was contacted and invited in on the meeting. They ate dinner, and then afterward Robert broke the news to them concerning the monster in their neighbourhood which had disrupted the lives of his considered 'perfect family'. Naturally, they were shocked.

Following the revelation to his family, Robert assured them that he had his house dusted for listening devices and surveillance equipment early that morning. Nothing so far was detected.

His brother Paul took the news that Domenico was the Chess Player and his family's greatest threat against them as predicted by Robert. He took the news rather badly and Paul's immediate response was, "I am going to kill him!"

That was exactly what Robert was afraid of. Robert pointed his finger at him authoritatively and said, "That is exactly what I do not want you to do. That's why it took me so long to tell you, Paul, that's why I waited. Continue playing it cool for now. If you bump into him, act as though you know nothing, ok. Remember that. Let's play along with him and see what he is really planning." Robert, then in a changed face added, "Let's make that bastard think that he has the upper hand."

Paul had a sudden recollection, a fading glimpse to a memory of what Robert had done to Giuseppe Castalone not long ago, and knowing that nobody else had been able to break old moneybags, perhaps, now, the man he was looking at, was as well Domenico's match, his heroic brother, Robert Stewart.

Robert went on breaking Paul's thought. "I want Domenico brought up on more than a murder charge to some cheap criminal. I want to burn what's under his fingernails. I want to uncover all the skeletons in his closet and bring them all out into the open."

Paul responded between clenching his teeth. "He's just a pinch of garbage that disguises himself in French perfume by his supposed concern for the needy, a complete bullshit artist, that you bro - even never bought it. You were right all along to suspect him from the beginning. No matter what, Robert, my money is on you. In the end I know you will bring him to justice just as all the others, you will outmatch and outwit that sick and evil son of a bitch!"

Despite Paul's optimistic confidence in his brother's single-handed abilities against such an enemy, Robert's wife, unhelped, had only displayed a very worried demeanour for her husband's safety. Cassandra jumped onto her feet at the revelation. "My God Robert, this changes everything. If he is the Chess Player and so close with our family, then all of us are in danger, including the children. I think of them like mine too. Domenico is so respectable. No one thinks of him as a Mafia Hood."

Robert assured her. "That's what makes him so dangerous. And we must play his game with our rules. He must not know we are onto him. He must be given no signs. It must seem like nothing has changed."

Cassandra ran into Robert's embrace and wept. "Everyday I read in the newspaper or hear on the radio the deaths of police and government people in their quest against the Mob and I do not know if you're going to be next. Do you have any idea what hell I am going through? Finally when we get our lives together and get married, this mess comes out of the woodwork and hits us in the face. I know that everyone needs you to solve this case, but I need you too. I cannot lose you."

He embraced her. "Hey - hey Casse - you are not going to lose me-"

She broke out, feeling overwrought. "Can you guarantee that? Can you guarantee that one day they are not going to be carrying you in a stretcher with tubes running all over you?"

Robert looked down in melancholy and she said, "I am sorry Robert. I did not mean that. This is just so frustrating. I am saying crazy things. I love you."

Robert responded, "I know. I love you too."

Before long, Robert immediately ordered Chief McKenzie to bump up the manpower of plainclothes guards around his family, though inconspicuous, not to scare them for now until he let them know slowly and they understood. It was the next best thing to them leaving the country. And in the meantime, Robert appointed himself guardian to his wife Cassandra.

That night Cassandra had two consecutive nightmares. The first was a crazy dream. She did not understand it. It all happened so fast. She heard Robert arguing with a man outside their house and she ran to see what it was when she heard a gun go off. She saw Robert lying on the ground and Domenico was standing over him holding a gun, he turned to her and raised his head chuckling in roaring laughter.

When her exhausted body almost three hours later, after recovering from the first nightmare went to sleep again, she only proclaimed another nightmare. That she and Robert were walking through the foggy night and then suddenly Robert collapsed to the ground and she did not know why. She did not hear anything. Then she glanced ahead and saw Domenico holding a gun again dressed in black, reminiscent to a Roman Emperor or black Royal Knight, looking at her and laughing.

BOOK 10

CHAPTER 18

Domenico Armando was not surprised the least by the escalating war his staunchest enemy and most cunning nemesis Robert Stewart waged against him – and, as such, planned a counterattack to undermine his adversary's efforts. He understood that the one place not tampered with by police surveillance was a yacht he purchased at the harbour for his back-up plan to escape a life of confinement. And under elaborate disguise he managed to avoid detection, elude his trailers and mysteriously disappear from their sight for a few hours after his rendezvous with Senator Ron Bishop in his home earlier for a political function - and he used an unmarked car. His driver bodyguard drove him to his yacht where he would finalise his plans for the future that late evening.

He arranged for his man secretly to smuggle his daughter Annemarie's newly-wedded husband, Colin McMurphy over to him in a separate car to meet his yacht at the harbour, without arousing suspicion of his sudden breakaway from his new wife in the middle of the night. The six-feet-tall, well-presented and well-groomed forty-year-old Colin McMurphy was taken also under disguise to descend on Domenico's yacht to meet him in person. Domenico embraced him in greeting upon his arrival and filled him in on the urgency in their meeting - and the nature to the secrecy of it all. Colin seemed startled for a moment. He thought he was being lured over to Domenico in the dead quiet of the night to be executed somehow also by its urgency and secrecy in it all, that he was not permitted to tell his daughter, who was asleep anyway.

Domenico read his mind well and responded. "You have been a dutiful husband to my daughter so far, how you can think I would make my daughter a widow without just cause!" Domenico went on to explain the real purpose to the meeting, handing him a shot glass of whisky, a strong drink to settle his ragged nerves all of a sudden, as if he was taken alone to be condemned in hell by the master devil himself. Domenico had a job for his new son-in-law; he wanted it used as a testing ground for him. In short, he talked of his plans to use Colin to help him kill Robert Stewart. Domenico had complimented Colin on the glowing reports he admitted having received of him by his people since his marriage to his daughter so far, very impressive. He had been placed under the direct scrutiny of his counsellor who assigned one captain in the city and three detectives under his regime's control to the McMurphy watch, and twenty-four hours a day supervision - to which a report was sent to Domenico everyday. Domenico was impressed, and now had come up with the perfect plan that would enable Colin to be transformed into the man he wanted him to become - a man of strength and good character, to aid him in his pursuit against the enemy.

After all, Domenico knew Colin was a man who loved money. And Domenico always planned to transform Colin McMurphy's weakness of his shady, scheming past; which comprised of white-collar crimes such as fraud, embezzlement and forgery into strengths - and to use such strengths in the right way. Domenico allowed the marriage to his daughter to proceed because she fell in love with him upon their meeting at his private hospital, in which he sat on the board of directors as a minority shareholder; so her heart would not be broken. Thus, Domenico had stipulated from the onset, that his marriage to his daughter assured him no inheritance to her fortune.

They talked for hours. Domenico wanted Colin to kill Robert Stewart for him as a loyalty test tomorrow evening. He would supply him with an untraceable gun right here and now for his task to do away with his target. Domenico explained his orders precisely. "We will also have drugs planted inside his home - and his fingerprints will be planted in certain murders to make him look like the very killer he was always accusing the people in my world of being!" Once they finished the meeting, they parted company separately from the yacht. Domenico's man returned Colin safely to his wife's bed in the Armando mansion.

Once Domenico had returned home to the Armando estate and entered the downstairs study room to brief his counsellor of all his current plans, he was thusly questioned by his curious counsellor also working late for his padrone that evening, finalising aspects of his future plans. "I thought you did not want Robert dead?"

Domenico replied simply, "I never wanted him dead. But, should he die - well, I guess then he is not the competition I thought he was."

The counsellor, though detected his boss's too close to home intrusion by the enemy all of a sudden on the Armando security he had so successfully penetrated, raised his eyebrows, eyes wide open to his padrone and said, "So it's only a test?"

Domenico laughed. "Yes!"

Domenico then confided to his Counsellor Rex Higgins of his not so distant future plans. Domenico lit a cigarette and took two drags before he paced himself to the small bar set up inside his private den and fixed himself a shot of cognac. After he skulled his drink, as if quenching his emotions, otherwise, now drunk with rage, he revealed to his counsellor who seated before him his current agenda. "I will never go to prison. They will never catch me. I can do so much to them, but they will never find me when I disappear." Domenico exclaimed in bitterness.

Domenico took another drag on his cigarette before he went on, yet standing. "I fed the poor. I cured the sick with my hospital that contained the world's greatest doctors. I provided shelter for the homeless. And the middle class was provided with employment by me. They all drank my most expensive wine, ate my most expensive food, and indulged here in my estate as privileged guests. I turned this city into something exciting. I lit a fire under its otherwise dull exterior. People threw themselves at my feet – and, now this country has sought to turn everybody against the Armandos. They have destroyed my empire and now I want revenge!" Domenico raised his voice to a shout as he struck his desk brutally with the side of his clenched hand and demanded, "REVENGE!"

His voice now lowered as he further revealed his plans and the motivation behind them. Domenico placed his burning cigarette in the ashtray, then, he clenched his fists and waved them in the air forcefully, his face deadly serious when he further articulated his point across. "Tonight, I will leave the country. And my two sons Tom and D.J. will join me in my endeavours; to be groomed completely to serve my world. I have plans with my foreign allies against my enemies. My pilot has informed me that my private jet is all ready and fuelled. Everything is in complete readiness. My revenge will first commence on the entire United States underworld commission who have proven disloyal to me. Not one of them is going to survive. And, after I have finalised my plans abroad, by the time I return to transfer my belongings far away, I will then unleash my revenge on the rest of my enemies in this country. All the police, the government, and, society as a whole, who have destroyed in one day, my entire empire - that has taken me a lifetime to build. They are all going to suffer! I am going to bring hell to their lives like no one on this earth has ever experienced before; and nobody is going to be able to stop me. They are all going to pay with their very lives for what they have done to me. I do not care how many thousands the number of them are, not one of them will live." Domenico enforced. "Yes. After today, I will return only once to remove my belongings from this country, and by the time I disappear for good out of this nation, my nuclear attacks will proceed. And every one of my bitter enemies will be destroyed! But before I leave, there is something I need to do... I am going to have my very first confrontation with my staunchest enemy...!"

Domenico Armando planned one final encounter with his most worthy adversary in their life and death chess game war before he fled the country tonight; to be their very first confrontation together. Within that hour, Domenico had his driver take him to the abandoned, Armando family owned prestigious concert hall in Manhattan.

Inside the backstage section of the large hall's arena, he stood before his target now tied to a chair before him, physically unable to move. His prisoner was Robert Stewart.

Robert Stewart received an anonymous call from his car phone after work, explaining the location he was to drive to, concerning information about the Chess Player.

Robert had informed his police partner John McCallum of the meeting he was to attend to at this late evening. John was to meet him at the address provided, but he never showed up.

And once Robert had arrived at the hall, after parking his car across the road, having walked to the concert hall's front doors, he never made it inside on his own volition. By the time his hand grabbed the handle to the front door, he was struck by the butt of a gun on the back of his head, when he fell to the ground unconscious.

When he woke up, he found John McCallum tied and gagged onto the floor, lying next to him, before his feet. Robert was tied onto a chair, greeted by his enemy who arranged the set-up meeting, to now confront him in a new light; a hostile confrontation for the first time in their secret battle against each other. Now, the meeting between them, as sworn enemies would expose finally their true motivations against the other, to each other's faces, concealing nothing.

Domenico stood before Robert, serious-faced, as two of his men, Kong and Rowan Castalone, posted on either side of him, had guns trained at their prisoner. Domenico always warned his men to never underestimate Robert Stewart. Even now, as he was surrounded, outnumbered, and was forced with ropes to a chair before them; isolated from his own people. For his cunning and cleverness was a very distinct threat to their world, no matter the circumstance. Robert Stewart's resourcefulness was always a far-reaching danger.

Domenico grabbed Robert by his shoulders, forcefully, and shook him violently, as he raised his voice to say: "No matter what, you will never defeat me and my world. No matter how hard you try, my friend! I have more people, power and resources than you and your beloved government colleagues could ever muster against me! I am going to wipe the lot of you out. Not the other way around. Remember that, until your last breath is drawn, Robert Stewart!"

Domenico then stepped back and motioned Robert's eyes to his left side. Robert saw Rowan Castalone, holding the gun directly at him; to his heart.

Domenico then explained, "You think you would still be alive today if it wasn't for me? After what you did to his family, his father- I was the only one who stopped him from killing you, just as I was the only one who stopped the rest of my associates from coming after you!"

Robert gave a sarcastic laugh. Then he too raised his voice to say, "Yes, I know, because you wanted to pump me for information. To see how close we were getting to uncovering you as the Chess Player, right?"

Domenico made no attempt for denials. And in complete disclosures he added, "Yes. But don't get me wrong, I always considered you a friend. And our, how shall I put it; battle of wits against the other was very entertaining. I knew you always enjoyed to challenge me as much as I enjoyed to challenge you, my friend! And shortly, it will become a real war – even similar to WORLD WAR 1 and 2. You see, I will unleash my revenge on society as a whole for what YOU did to me!" His eyes lit up as if consumed with fire right now as he insisted: "I will use bombs, I will use guns. I will use every resource at my disposal to send every single person in this country straight to hell!" Domenico then raised his voice and pointed his finger to him; he became extremely exasperated. "Because, of what you did!"

Robert raised his voice in anger of his own: "You're crazy! You want to kill everyone for one person. Why don't you just come after me? I'm here!" Robert shouted. "Kill me! What the hell are you waiting for?"

Domenico gave a small chuckle before he said, "Because eliminating you will be too easy. You will die-yes. But you will be the last to die! - For you are going to witness first-hand the deaths and destructions of your friends, of your colleagues. Both the police and the government! And society as a whole! Thousands and thousands of them who will be massacred! And you will suffer! And I will enjoy watching you suffer! Yes, as you witness the mass slayings of all your beloved police and government colleagues. And all the good people, beginning in New York – and then spreading throughout every other city in this country. Similar to the entire architectural structure and concept of the POWER PROJECT, you are so familiar with, hey-"

Robert, had desperately attempted to loosen the ropes from his hands, tied behind his chair. To free himself, with wild visions to pounce on Domenico and his mob men – and do away with them right here and right now; to free society once and for all from this evil dictator and mass slaughterer. When he stated: "Damn you Domenico! If you want to get anyone - get me! Don't involve any innocent lives! Get me...!"

Domenico raised his voice now and shouted: "There is nobody in this world that is innocent! No! No! No! No! I am going to make them all suffer! They are going to wish they had never been born! I will have my revenge on all those who stood by like cowards, doing nothing, when my empire was being attacked!"

Robert snapped, "Well, perhaps they didn't know you were the Chess Player!"

Domenico went on, not hearing his words. "After everything I have done for the people in this country, they stood back and did nothing when you and your people declared war on me! So, now it is my turn. They will be forced to pay it all back. Everything I did for them. And they will pay with their very lives! They will all be massacred to death, horrendously!"

Domenico raised his voice now to even greater heights as he declared: "I want you all to stand around me in a circle - I am going to make you all hunger for my blood as I hunger for yours; the pack of you!" His face, his eyes lit up in complete insane rage as he grabbed Robert with one hand placed firmly across his jaw and roared in terror, "Nobody crosses the Armandos and lives to tell of it. You hear me. Nobody! You are all going to be destroyed before I am through!" He proclaimed: "THE LOT OF YOU!"

Domenico's sudden split personality transformation, never displayed as this before, had even startled, if not absolutely frightened and terrified his own people, such strong-arms, as they understood their master was capable of committing anything, any unspeakable horrendous act at this very moment!

Domenico released his hand from Robert's jaw as he shouted his final statement and declaration to him, that became enough to force his adversary loose from his restraints, to begin his attack. And Domenico's final words to Robert were: "You will also witness your family's: your wife and children's massacres to death as well. Then, depending on whether or not you live after tomorrow – I will finish my revenge on the likes of you!"

Robert Stewart, using every ounce of strength he could muster, fought away through the knots of his rope restraints until he freed himself, finally. He had no concern for the men holding weapons before him, ready to shoot him, as he bolted to his feet.

In almost lightning-quick paces and using his fists, Robert began attacking the army of men, who suddenly appeared in swarms before him, wanting to overpower and restrain him once more. He began fighting them. And they fought him. Men began dropping onto the ground, as more men entered the room and began brawling against Robert. It did not end until Robert was overpowered and knocked to the ground. He was forced onto the cold-concrete floor aside his friend and police partner, John McCallum, who was still tied and gagged onto the floor, struggling himself to break free.

Moments later, when Robert recovered from the haze – the excruciating after-effects to the brawl with Domenico's men, he quickly untied his friend John McCallum and they rose to their feet. Robert wanted to end it right then and there with Domenico. But, by the time he regained himself and freed his friend, his ambition was cut short. He turned around, and raced around the entire hall's perimeters, but found Domenico and his people had disappeared...!

Domenico had intentionally kidnapped him this evening; to in fact reveal his plans to him... Even gloat of them. Its purpose: because he simply wanted Robert to know what he was planning. And Domenico would take great pleasure in such revelations made to his adversary, of his final plans.

Knowing Robert could not stop them... Knowing Robert could not stop him...!

It was moments later, when Robert and John finished searching the entire abandoned concert hall's perimeters, when they found no trace of Domenico. He had simply disappeared...!

And Robert thought to himself: If I don't find him... If I don't kill him... He will unleash his next insane plans that will claim even more innocent lives than his atrocious POWER PROJECT... Everyone in the entire United States is in danger. Domenico wants to kill EVERYBODY! I cannot let that happen!

CHAPTER 19

The next evening Domenico Armando arrived at his secret underground Caribbean Island hideout with his two sons, who accompanied him in the plane ride unmonitored by authorities.

Domenico was posted inside the luxurious office den of his new headquarters, standing before his two new prisoners: Niko Sasselli and his Jewish adopted son, Marco.

D.J. and Tom stood on either side of their father.

Niko Sasselli and his son were both chained at the ankles and wrists, surrounded by the Armando strong-arms, who extracted the two from their home in New York the previous evening, only twenty-four hours earlier, then extradited them to meet with their Chief Master Domenico on his secret foreign turf under hostile circumstances. Domenico much labelled this forced meeting an 'extradition' — considering himself the one true authority and government with the real power to initiate such an action, overruling all previous statutes.

Domenico held his maestro baton in his right hand as he tapped it repetitively into the open palm of his left hand in deliberation. He was preparing himself to physically accost his new target summoned to his domain like this - lured as a common thug.

Niko Sasselli was once a man of stature. Domenico was intent to correct that, what he classified, a grossly-perceived error. Domenico instantly reduced him to no more of a man - no more of a human being, than a simple punk on the street.

Domenico intentionally revealed his true power to this, in himself, so-called 'patriarch' forced before him. Domenico showed Niko Sasselli that he was very mistaken to ever think for one cold moment that he could compete against the great and almighty Chess Player.

Domenico eyed his target coldly. His face resembled stone; a gruesome and frightening sight he became. His face was stern, tense and terrifyingly cast with manic eyes, unchanged, upon his current victim. And Niko began to sense his fate. He knew what was in store for him; and his dear son.

Niko Sasselli's legs began to tremble. He could not control the shaking. He became frightened senseless by this ruthless bully standing before him. Niko knew that he was powerless against his captor. He understood everything now. Domenico was able to arrange for his kidnapping and his extradition from right under his own family's security, so swiftly, simply because his own guards — the men he trusted were unknowingly employed as Armando double agents and spies from the very beginning.

196

Niko almost collapsed from shock at the revelation. He finally understood that all his high-ranking trusted personnel for many years - were really only ever loyal to the man he despised and feared more than anybody else in this world: Domenico Armando. Not him... But Domenico!

Niko knew his fate was bleak. He was going to die. His captor was also going to annihilate his son. But Niko's mind smoked in terror at this moment as he only could wonder why then had this brutal dictator with an aura of demonic hell painted across his evil face - why had he arranged for his kidnapping - both his and his son's? Why first had he resorted to this, if death was the single most purpose he had in mind for the two of them inscribed in his hideous agenda?

Domenico wished to keep him in suspense no longer. He yet tapped his very baton into his hand - the very instrument he used on many occasions to orchestrate to his powerful symphonies in perfect rhythm. Now there was no music playing in the background. No sound; but this heart-wrenching tapping noise, as if he was preparing his mind for his battles ahead; masterminding his diabolical plans and premeditating his precise movements in careful strategy.

He lashed his baton up and down onto his hand contemplating his next plans of madness. The sound of each strike of the instrument upon flesh made Niko blink his eyelids constantly in fright; his heartbeat began racing ferociously.

Domenico began to speak. His voice developed a horrible tone. The darkness of its sound became chilling to everyone present inside the room. Not only to his captives. But the very words that were spoken from his mouth were even a more gruesome colour; much darker, terrifying and demonic.

Niko indeed felt himself paralysed at this moment. He felt he was being confronted by the very 'Bogeyman'-the very 'Hitler Equivalent' the world spoke about now in reference to all his hideous crimes as the Chess Player.

Domenico took great fanatic and much bizarre joy to his current victim's fright of him. But he would not break out in laughters this time over it. No. His face remained the deadly-framed picture of stern cold stone.

Domenico's entire appearance remained taut, tense and catastrophically demented in its dire features as he spoke the words: "I want you to confess to all my crimes!"

Niko's jaw immediately hung loose in a comical fear. The rhythmic motion of his captor's baton was suddenly only a little over an inch from touching his face; swaying up and down quicker at this time.

Niko cowered at the thought that Domenico was going to strike him with it anytime now. Niko became frozen in his spot, speechless. He could not utter a single sound.

Domenico went on. He quickly confirmed Niko's suspicions. "You think I don't know what you and our illustrious-but corrupt and bogus SIA Chief

McKenzie were planning behind my back? You were recently meeting secretly together inside churches in Brooklyn and Washington. The two of you were smoking cigars inside the deserted churches on weekdays. McKenzie called you and offered you a deal. You met him on several occasions inside the houses of worship and decided to join forces with him, in exchange for a period of amnesty he would grant you from ongoing investigations by his agency. He wanted the two of you to join forces in order to 'neutralise' me – if I recall the words correctly, right?"

Niko Sasselli could not believe his bad luck right now. Domenico knew everything. Niko could not speak. Domenico spoke for him. He added, "Yes. You and that greatly deceptive SIA Chief thought you could amalgamate your empires to defeat me. Then enjoy the fruits of my labours following my death and destruction, hmm? And after your atrocious discussions and, hence, plans for my murder in such biblical places, you had the audacity to enter the confessionals, both in New York and Washington, and reveal your sins to not one, but two different priests, in two different churches, hey! You even paid, or should I say, bribed such priests with large sums of money to supposedly offer you absolution from your atrocities. You really think that would work? After each crime you pay a priest one million dollars to supposedly forgive you and save your horrible soul? Is that what you truly believe is possible? To be absolved after showing pretentious contrition." Domenico scorned in irony. "You are really stupid! Worse than stupid! You know that?"

Domenico wished to set his target straight right now by assuming the role of the world's most brutal taskmaster. And the earth's most unmerciful. He spoke furthermore with hostile ferocity. "You call yourself a boss?" His voice tone rose horrifically at this very moment as each word proceeded. "You are a mouse of a man; an insect, a bug. You are a worm of the ground who foolishly thought he could ever equal the powers of I-me Domenico Armando! You are nothing compared to me, NOTHING. You are weak and stupid. You could never accomplish what I had. You simply are not strong enough. You are not wise enough. You only need to read a glimpse of any newspaper at any time to see what sort of a world we live in – and those misinformed police want to persecute me? And a stupid foolish man as you thought he could imitate me? You think you can be Domenico Armando, hmm? NEVER!" he shouted. "I am going to end it all, my friend, Niko Sasselli. For all of you! I will do whatever it takes to fulfil my ultimate plans for Revenge!" he cursed savagely. "I will destroy all my enemies in this world who tried to destroy me. All those who took my generosity for granted. All those who tried to steal what I have, my notoriety; meaning you; beginning with you, little man; a parasite who attempted to steal my title and position as Boss of Bosses!"

Niko would never be able to speak again. He was stunned by the most horrendous shock a man could be subjected to. He was forced to listen in silence to the ravings of this lunatic posted before him. And Domenico would now reveal his entire 'master plan' to him, without delay. His inane ravings kept rolling on. "Now, you listen carefully, you silly little man. You have no power, no intelligence and no hope to escape me and my bitter wrath. You will do exactly as I say. Because once I have annihilated all my enemies in this entire world – you will come forward to exonerate me. You will in fact take liability for everything that I have ever been accused of committing; and everything that I will continue to be accused of. Meaning the complete and total destruction of My World of Bitter Enemies! You hear me? You will remain here as my prisoner; both you and your son. I will provide you with files, with tapes - everything you need to study and recite perfectly by heart, every relevant detail concerning my life. And I will assess your performance constantly; until I am convinced you know it all.

"I want you to learn and recite everything before me and my people, as if I am a judge and my men are your jury of peers. If you can convince a hard taskmaster as myself – then you will have no trouble convincing any fool judge and jury of it all – who have a precedent of sending innocent men to prison and many guilty home free! You will confess your guilt, your complicity in all the crimes and charges they will otherwise throw in my direction!" Domenico motioned his baton even closer to his eyes. "This baton I have here as well as my own heavy shoe will become your incentive. Should you fumble on any detail I provide to you, I will strike you so hard with these new weapons of mine here, until you fumble no more. I will make you black and blue, until you learn everything, PERFECTLY!

"Now, you ask, why have I brought your son here as well? After all, what possible use does this Jew here have in our agenda?" he said, viciously stooping to using mocking racial slurs for the first time throughout this. "Well, let me enlighten your uncomprehending mind. Your son is simply a tool; a pawn to be used to keep you cooperating and in line with my demands. Should you ever go astray – if you ever so much as even think to double-cross me, I will immediately have my people here send him to the room next door. Each time you prove either careless or disobedient in my plans for you, your son will be sent to that electric chair. And the more you anger me, the greater his punishment will be! I will increase the voltage of his electric shock treatment each time you prove erroneous, hmm. You understand? Believe me. You will confess and confess convincingly – and in great detail – to every crime I am and will be accused of. You will learn it all.

"You will also confess to creating Domenico Armando look-alikes to attempt to frame me! The SIA and FBI government hostages have been relocated recently to my secret underground compound here. I have instructed my doctors to proceed at once with their surgeries. I have carefully selected each of the prisoners for a unique purpose in mind. All those resembling my exact height and build are kept alive to fulfil a unique purpose for me. Their faces are currently being altered by my specialist doctors flown in from France. Following their expert reconstructive plastic surgeries, and once their metamorphoses is complete in the weeks that follow, and they are fully unmasked, their bandages able to be removed – they will in fact resemble me in every way; apart from my fingerprints and voice, of course. But that does not matter; because no one will ever be able to get close enough to them in order to figure anything out.

"You see, they will be used meanwhile as decoys to draw the proper authorities who are out, hunting for my blood, away from my precise whereabouts. They will be brainwashed to follow my command – and mine alone! They will be planted in different regions, different countries around the world. Once my 'revenge' begins - every opposing power, every government and every army this world has to offer will be assigned to the task to find me. They will all be hunting for my blood. Hence, these decoys will simply serve the purpose in eluding my pursuers from ever finding me! Particularly as I float from region to region, instructing my troop to proceed in my Revenge Plans in one city and state after the other... And one country after the other...! Ordering my armies of people and networks of personnel stationed everywhere globally on their precise instructions.

"Now listen carefully. Once my revenge is complete, you will be released from my custody and escorted to New York to confess to it all. The police will find evidence to the creation of the impostors on your territory; picture and film evidence. That will open the doors for your confession. You will appear in those pictures with your family's doctors – taken in your laboratory, on your turf. You will swear that you created them to frame me, for YOUR crimes – and you killed them all; disposing of the corpses without a trace, including the doctors who performed the transformations, to cover your tracks. All I need is confirmation to their existences and the world's knowledge that you were behind it. You were an old rival of mine who wanted to take what I had, so you used such impostors to commit crimes and speak fouls in my name, in order to make me look bad. And sound evil in front of everyone; thus, forcing me on the run. No one will ever know when it was me or one of your creations they saw acting peculiar in recent times. How can they prove anything? My plans for freedom will also be realised!

"In any case, your son will remain here until you are found guilty. Then his fate will be realised – as yours. Make no mistake; the fate of both you and your son is sealed. But it is up to you how it will all unfold; whether swiftly in prison by another inmate, or here now in an unbearably gruesome manner! No one will be able to save you from me. Not even my very tenacious friend, Robert Stewart!"

By this time – it was only Domenico's henchmen who kept Niko standing on his feet. Domenico's entire lunacy and his plans of madness had Niko Sasselli paralysed from fear and shock, unable to move his legs for now. Two men planted on either side of him held him by his arms in a firmly upright position. His legs collapsed from fright. He could not stand on his own.

Domenico ordered his men to take Niko and his son to their single dungeon room quarters. They would only be fed bread and water, as all his other hostages. Domenico ordered Niko to rest well for four hours. Because once that time elapsed, his reconditioning sessions and consecutive debriefs would proceed with no delay. And there would be no more rest for him – for days, weeks and the months it took for him to learn everything he had to – word for word, concerning the life of the devil himself: Domenico Armando!

It was only three hours later when the Armando henchmen reported to their chief, the confirmed deaths of both Niko Sasselli and his son Marco together inside their dungeon room. Niko and his son hanged themselves to death using their prison clothes they were given as a loop. They each used their clothes as a noose around their necks from one end, wrapped in knots around a large heavy chandelier dangling from the ceiling at the other end.

Their bodies were completely naked, found dangling together in their locked room, feet suspended off the ground, from the large chandelier inside.

Following this reported thwart into his plans, Domenico had immediately collapsed onto the hard parquetry floor inside the private den of his underground palace.

In the days that followed, the Armando doctors ran test after test, double and triple checking results, concerning their master's prognosis. And once the diagnosis was confirmed, without error or doubt, they could not delay disclosing the information to him.

Domenico was diagnosed with an inoperable brain tumour. There was no mistake in the results of the exhaustive tests undertaken. The conclusion was indisputable; the evidence undeniable. Their master Domenico Armando was dying. He only had six months to live, according to the many expert physicians' prognosis he had positioned by his side.

Domenico took the news remarkably well that night as he was seated inside his office, talking to his two sons; teaching them the 'true' Armando family traditions. Even the doctors surrounding him were impressed by their master's brave face displayed in all this.

Domenico lifted his hands in the air, as if showing no surprise – no remorse – and said, "Then I guess I must finalise my Revenge Plans quicker than I had initially anticipated. The bombs must be positioned perfectly in all the targeted places by New Year's Eve, beginning with my concert hall in Manhattan. It will be hired by Maestro Rodolfo Giovanna that evening. Ten thousand guests from around America and many from various parts abroad will attend this gala event, to enjoy the glamour and unique entertainment provided by our famous Italian conductor. But before the clock strikes midnight, it will all be over. At that very exact moment, it will all end as well for all the targeted police precincts. My family's private hospital will also cease to exist before the New Year. No one out there will profit from my legacies ever again!" Domenico clenched his fists together, proving to his family and his people his yet true strength of character. He vowed: "I will not die before my revenge against all my enemies is complete!"

Suddenly the truth of his own mortality began crushing his spirit. The myth of his own 'immortality' he had created his entire life – to himself, to his family and to his many people who literally worshipped the ground he walked on – the truth now that he was as mortal as any other man had gravely haunted him. Domenico's head staggered back almost in shock, as he was seated in his leather armchair, addressing all the people he loved; all those who were loyal to him.

Domenico realised now that his powers were really only limited. He could not fight 'mortality'. He could not fight that cold-calculated horrible word called 'nature!' Its fate and destiny bestowed upon man unexpectedly – always catching him off guard. He could own the entire world. He could defeat any army. He could create any bloodbath anywhere in order to wipe out his entire opposition. But nature could always intervene much like a catastrophic earthquake and take it all away. Domenico hated the idea that he could not fight the invisible powers surrounding him - surrounding them all; the horrendous powers of nature that picks and chooses which man to strike at next - with no warning, no mercy. Domenico realised that no matter what – no man alive was even capable of being as ruthless as a natural disaster: whether sickness or a devastating earthquake, flood and tornado. Domenico's emotions fell amok right now, as he understood that nature could destroy him - destroy everyone - the entire world and everybody in it, a whole hell of a lot more swiftly, than any man ever dreamed in cleaning out his opposition. How can anyone compete against that? He was forced to ask himself: How? The myth that he often spoke out – the belief that Domenico Armando could never lose-Domenico Armando could never die was only an illusion. Domenico suddenly felt hollow inside. For the first time in his life he felt empty and outmanoeuvred.

Once his children adjourned to their rooms to turn in for the night, Domenico ranked for his primary enforcer Kong inside his private den and now spoke to him alone. He instructed him – without question – to order his guards to round up all the government hostages and terminate them at once. He considered that he no longer needed them now that Niko Sasselli and his son were dead. He now realised that his plans for FREEDOM REDEMPTION, his hopes to restore his former glory into the outside world was only a fantasy. He finally accepted that he could never relive the days of his former glory. He could never return to the outside a free man again! And he could never look into the eyes of his now disillusioned sweet daughter Annemarie in New York, and talk his way out of any doubts she currently had concerning her once loved and respected father.

He realised that he would never be able to hold his daughter 'Annie' into his arms again - and this time tell her that, 'He was set up'. That – 'It was all a lie – a trick. Something sinister his enemies in the world played on him'. He knew he would enter the grave with his sweet daughter doubting him.

Domenico's face suddenly screwed up in anger at the thought. He summed up all his energies that were rapidly subsiding due to his health crisis – to vow himself a promise: 'If I can never be reunited with my family in New York ever again, then I will live out my plans for revenge against all my World of Bitter Enemies! I swear it! Then I will have my final confrontation with my bitterest enemy of them all – Robert Stewart. I will force him finally to admit that he could never outmatch me, Domenico Armando. Then I can die in peace knowing that!' he said to himself.

Once the news concerning the twelve SIA/FBI hostages' reported deaths had spread to the entire occupants inside the secret Caribbean compound, D.J. stormed inside his father's private den the next evening to confront him.

The twelve Domenico Armando look-alikes were ordered executed inside the compound's gas chamber facility the night before. Their corpses were then disposed of by Armando guards inside another room that contained a specially-fitted human incinerator. Naturally, D.J. was shocked.

He found his father inside his den all alone, holding a glass of water in one hand, whilst quickly plunging a handful of pills, prescribed drug medications into his mouth with his other hand. He drank his water to flush down the many tablets; then massaged his head from the excruciating pain that began erupting in his brain.

Domenico rapidly placed the glass onto his desk and fetched for a burning cigarette that lay in the ashtray aside it. He took two drags, when he began humming to the composition of his favourite powerful symphony, playing from speakers in the background of his office, at medium volume.

D.J. approached his father now standing before him in the middle of the room; whether D.J.'s concern stemmed from the dozen dead victims or the ill-timing of it all, could not be ascertained by his father as yet.

D.J. broke out. "Father - why did you order the deaths of the twelve prisoners? Wasn't that a bit hasty? I mean, you still could have used them as decoys to elude all your police and government trailers. Now they can find you more easily without them! Even wearing a disguise, you cannot shake them away from discovering your exact whereabouts as expertly as you could have – had the prisoners remained in circulation for the time being!"

His father eyed him with a blank expression on his face. Domenico accidentally dropped his cigarette onto the ground in shock. He quickly extinguished the burning flame that fell onto a small rug with his shoe. Then, unbelievably, he struck his forehead with the flat of his right hand, almost ashamed at himself and his out-of-character mind lapse, developed so unexpectedly; its repercussions drawn much fatally against him and his current plans.

Domenico could not believe he made such a terrible error of judgement; for not conceding such a valid point. Domenico shook his head in disbelief at his own deteriorated logic. His brain cancer was rapidly showing terrible signs. His disease was swiftly transforming him into a mental vegetable. He could not think straight anymore. His mind turned to fog all of a sudden. His thought processes were rapidly becoming shattered; his focus and necessary concentration was marred. Domenico then eyed his son in confusion.

D.J. was shocked. He never saw his great father appear so desperate. The once 'genius' and 'indestructible' Domenico Armando was suddenly reduced to delinquency. His impervious mindset was no more.

Domenico cried, "My God; my God, my son. What have I done?" Domenico then approached and embraced his favourite son and terribly grieved furthermore. "My son; my wonderful son D.J. - I don't know what is happening to me? How can such a thought have escaped me, my mind?"

Domenico then pulled away his embrace. He placed his hands onto his son's shoulders firmly. He looked at him dead in the eye and pleaded profusely. His face masked in desperation. "My son; you have to help me. I cannot live out my goals without you… Please… I need you now more than ever…!"

BOOK 11

CHAPTER 20

Robert Stewart spent the next few days and nights coordinating the intensive search party for Domenico Armando. He did not sleep at all during the past seventy-two hours. Robert had ordered his army of policemen to scour the entire city in search for the enemy. He had gathered the files of all the enemy's known local, interstate and global properties, his possible hideouts. Robert ordered the SIA and the FBI to search thoroughly all the known Armando interstate and abroad hideouts as he and his police comrades turned the local areas upside down for any clues to Domenico's whereabouts.

Robert instructed all his police and government colleagues to double and triple check each site. Then he ordered them to check the places over again. Robert also instructed his people to search the hideouts of all of Domenico's known underlings. Perhaps the enemy was using one of their hideouts to disappear in for now. He could be using any place on this earth to vanish inside which could be owned by any number of fronts. So all of Domenico's known associates and henchmen were also placed under scrutiny. Anyone who had even a remote association with the devil himself was targeted as possible leads to that demented evil man's location. Robert left no stone unturned.

In a short space of time, Robert became a changed man. He became more driven, more obsessed, even more crazed in the idea in 'getting his man at whatever cost' than any other time in his history of policing. Where Domenico Armando was concerned, Robert was now capable of anything. Robert did not just want to find Domenico. He wanted to in fact make him pay for all the people he had harmed and killed throughout his miserable existence on this earth. In his mind, Domenico deserved to suffer! Robert wanted to see him succumb to the very depths of misery he had inflicted on so many masses of individuals throughout his severely destructive days in circulation.

Robert knew he himself had changed in recent times. He could not help his thoughts. He could not help his feelings right now. He felt hatred for another human being as never before. A part of him wanted to see Domenico dead. But another part of him thought that that prospect was even far too easy. He felt Domenico would be let off the hook far too simply because of it. He wanted to see Domenico brought to justice for the first time in his life. He wanted to be the man who had finally finagled all the proper strings to operate. He wanted to make the law work against the enemy for the first time.

Robert wanted to finally hear the judge sentence Domenico to the death penalty. He wanted to visit that horrible man in prison, pending his day of judgement. He wanted to see the look on his face when he was forced into a prison cell situated on death row. Robert wanted to study his sick and demented eyes, when the enemy was finally forced to concede the very truth that the law he had so strived to mock and control, had in short finally worked against him.

Domenico tried to control every law and local, state and federal government in the United States. He wanted to control the proper powers across the entire world. What sweet poetic justice it would be to watch that man be swept to his end by the failure of all his plans, Robert thought. That was justice. That would be beautiful. Domenico killed many good police and government colleagues in his insane quest for 'total control'. Robert wanted to watch that horrible man be crushed by the very law, the very power he tried to destroy throughout his crazy existence!

Robert could not help his emotions. He gradually changed from a humble happy man to the very determined terror his enemy was proclaimed to be. Robert, in himself, could not help but feel justified in his emotions in wanting to see that dictator suffer a slow torturous end. Domenico made many people suffer. He tortured so many. Why should Robert feel guilty in wanting the same torments inflicted on that very man who practically reinvented the word: suffering?

Robert would never feel guilty. In fact, he felt very much alive. Whether his emotions were in the right or wrong - he could not help but fall in love with the idea of hating Domenico Armando. He thrived on it. He felt powerful because of it. He relished in the challenge of this true to life 'cat-and-mouse' game. Robert now understood how Domenico felt every time he had created one of his grand plans. Domenico felt the same power. But Robert's motivations were in direct contrast to his enemy's. Robert understood, but could never condone that despicable man's actions. No. Never! But Robert felt now the same way Domenico felt all his life. He felt the same life running into his veins, but via the prospect of destroying Domenico Armando!

Throughout his life, no matter who he battled, Robert could still find much objectivity in his crusades against his numerous targets. But this time, things were different. Where Domenico Armando was concerned, the war was immensely personal. Because Domenico had sought to personally attack his family. That was how his enemy operated; his modus operandi. Domenico never only attacked his single targets. No. He also involved his victims' families; their loved ones. That was the sickness in how he operated. He was never satisfied until he not only destroyed his enemies, but he also wanted to destroy all those around them; meaning their friends and families; their colleagues and casual associates. Domenico wanted to destroy all the Stewarts. So this war was personal. It was bloody personal!

And so Robert felt much compelled in the idea in wanting to see Domenico suffer before his day of judgement came. He wanted to see him brought to his knees and bark like the very dog he was before he was executed by the law. The very law he tried to eliminate, then take over! Robert could not wait to get his hands on that bastard! He wanted to rip him to a million shreds as he deserved to be torn to pieces, the mad animal Domenico Armando indeed was!

Robert's obsession slowly came to the day he found out Domenico Armando was the Chess Player. And now his obsession had turned into a sleepless one the day that horrible man threatened to kill his whole family with the entire world around them! Robert's course of action was unchangeable. His destiny as a warrior and a hunter was set in stone.

Robert was partly camped inside his office at the 25th division precinct station house day and night for the past 72 hours. If he was not at the precinct waiting for any news, he rapidly hit the streets either working alongside his men, or covering single areas on his own. Searching for clues others may have overlooked. He worked with his army of people scouring the streets everywhere across New York City - and waited for word on any latest developments during the search for Domenico Armando. He waited in anticipation for any updates to his enemy's location.

Robert had now returned to his office long ago. All four walls inside was covered with maps and blueprints of the target's known international and local properties. He placed markers on all the areas his people had covered thoroughly. Close-by government and local police officials had contacted him by radio on their updates. International and interstate police and government agents had faxed him their reports regularly. Robert commanded his troop relentlessly. He studied the maps of such properties. He looked for any underground hideouts, bomb shelters that could have been recently fixed by the enemy. He and his men questioned local tenants and neighbours if any activity was ever spotted in such locations. Robert wanted to know whether builders or maintenance men were seen, any activity taking place in the vicinities of such areas - which could signify Domenico possibly having installed and renovated a new facility, such as secret underground hideouts in the buildings to hide inside.

After all, Domenico was a Chess Player. He must have forecasted his current dilemma taking place; his freedom being snatched from him. He must have suspected the possibility – and in turn looked to twist that obstacle to his advantage. As he always was known to turn all such dilemmas into his favour. Robert covered all bases. And he instructed his entire national and international troops to also exercise complete thoroughness in their search; leaving nothing to chance; and overlooking no detail. That was imperative!

It was 9:00 p.m. that evening. Sergeant John McCallum entered his Captain's office with the very update Robert was waiting for. His police partner reported that Annemarie Armando had just been rushed to the Armando Family Hospital.

Robert's mind ran in a frenzied state. His mind jumbled a dozen thoughts in a split second before his best friend could finish his report. At first Robert suspected it was a marital problem. Robert authorised complete surveillance on the Armando estate. He knew D.J., Tom and Monica Armando had disappeared around the same time with their father. They also were not seen since, for weeks now. Robert also had initiated discreet surveillance on all the members of the remaining Armando clan that remained here in New York.

Robert was familiar with the comings and goings of all the remaining Armandos. Rita, the children's mother, and Annemarie were never seen leaving the house in weeks. The paid servants brought them whatever they needed. But Colin McMurphy, Annemarie's husband, was a different matter. He was also under police surveillance. He was seen constantly leaving the Armando estate at all hours of the day, even overnight to book rooms in various hotels across the city. Hotel register books were checked upon his arrival by undercover plainclothes police. They knew his room number. Many times during the past few weeks, female officers dressed as hotel maids entered the room where Colin McMurphy was situated. They knocked on the door also claiming to be janitors and cleaners, and once McMurphy invited them inside, such officers found it as a perfect opportunity to plant listening devices inside.

What they uncovered was obviously the very thing McMurphy was attempting to conceal from his wife, especially her brutal tyrant father. But since Domenico's freedom was in tatters, Colin obviously felt his father-in-law had more important things on his mind right now than keeping his eye on the newest member of his family. Such as keeping his butt out of the line of fire from all those police officials who wanted to plug him with bullets and end his life, via a shoot-to-kill order that was now being directed against him by the New York Police Chief Commissioner himself; so given that, Colin felt safe to cheat behind his wife's back.

Police reported to Robert that Colin McMurphy was apparently sneaking outside the Armando estate to have sexual relations with many other women without Annemarie's knowledge. He constantly booked such hotel rooms in advance, and once he had arrived, he indulged in all his sordid erotic fantasies, one after the other. He was tape-recorded inside the hotel rooms contacting the city's most expensive escort agencies, in a desire to entertain and fulfil his many vivid sexual tastes. Sometimes he booked one expensive female prostitute, other times two or three at the same time. He certainly decided to live it up right now since his threatening father-in-law was no longer around to tell him what to do – or how to do it – in regards to his daughter Annemarie. No doubt, Domenico would have had Colin work his arse off trying to please his daughter, the vicious dictator the Chess Player indeed was. But now that Domenico was in hiding, Colin felt safe to do as he pleased with his life. And conduct himself as he saw fit. And he certainly had with mostly prostitutes and his professional business lawyer, named, Samantha Emery.

From the audio recordings via the many listening devices planted inside McMurphy's hotel rooms, it was his secret meetings inside these places with his lawyer mistress that turned out the most fascinating of information for the authorities.

It seemed as though McMurphy confided to this mistress his every sordid thoughts and actions. He hinted how he married Annemarie only for her money. He admitted how he wanted to become Domenico's heir, to one day inherit the entire Armando fortune. Samantha Emery rebuked the idea. She would tell him how that could never happen. She would insist that his scheme was unrealistic because Domenico had four children and a grandson who would always come first and foremost to him, in his eyes. They would always take priority above all else.

And Colin revealed his most heinous ambitions, come that. "What if the old man dies? Domenico might think he is immortal, but he will die one day. Just like the rest of us. We can only hope. All I have to do is play my cards right and pretend to be the dutiful husband he wants. And when he is caught and in prison, he could still hand me the reins of power as gratitude for keeping his daughter happy and fucking her properly as one of his frigging conditions. In prison, he might be knocked down to size, to reality. You know? He might be humbled. He might think more generously. Then everything he has could become mine. He'll give it to me. The very key to what is left of his kingdom. And bang – I've hit the jackpot! Excellent; what do you think? We'll both strike it rich! Is it a good idea or not?"

Samantha Emery could only rebuke the idea again. She explained, "Even if Domenico is caught… after everything I have read about him in the papers… I mean he makes Hitler look like an amateur. He makes Saddam Hussein look like a wimp. Will prison humble him? Fuck, no. God, Colin, how can you even think that? The only person who can humble Domenico Armando is God himself, when he sends that evil ratbag tyrant into a fiery hell where he belongs, where he deserves to go. As to handing you anything: The answer is, definitely, unconditionally, NOT. He would never do that! He would always favour his children. And he would never look to an outsider to carry on his legacy. He would never look to you-"

Colin interrupted, yet in eagerness. "But what if he dies in prison?"

209

His mistress snapped. "What? Do you mean what if another prisoner knocks him off?" Colin smiled. Samantha Emery refused to even entertain the notion as she continued. "Look it. Domenico is liable to kill all the prisoners just through the sight of him. He is liable to scare them all to death before anyone would even consider blowing him away. Before anyone could even get close enough to do it! That is how he operates. I mean, any man who could scare the entire Underworld of ruthless Mafia Bosses to do his bidding for him, to conceal his real identity as the Chess Player from public knowledge for almost twenty years does not scare at all. He is the one who makes the entire world afraid of him; including the most hardened criminals who are rotting in prison, for some of the worst atrocities. Who are there destined to die in prison as we speak. So, in response to your suggestion: forget about it! Dreams are good. But that one is completely fictitious. I mean, even where Robert Stewart plans to send him, in one of those maximum security prison facilities interstate... to rot his days in complete isolation; to sleep on a concrete bed, with all his phone calls tapped; with all his mail running through numerous scanners, being checked and opened; with Domenico himself being denied any visitors or any contact with the outside world. Even then, Domenico Armando would never crack. He would never be humbled; you cannot defeat a man like that. He is the devil incarnate, just as the newspapers say. He is the devil himself. And Colin, the rest of us are ants compared to him. So, please, do yourself a favour and get that horrible idea out of your mind before it kills you. Don't even think about it. You never know. Domenico may even be able to sense what you are thinking from even thousands of miles away. Where he is concerned, anything is possible. He is very scary. You should also be scared of him, more than anyone. Especially if he finds out that you are plotting behind his daughter's back. He will tear your bones apart! He will make you scream in the worst agony before he lets you die! Then he will attack your soul!"

Colin became impatient. "What are you trying to do? Scare me into a heart attack, here, love? I'm already getting heart palpitations!"

She snapped. "So you should. Maybe then, fear might keep you alive a bit longer. It might keep me alive too. After all, Domenico is a man who does not stop at killing his victims. He kills his victims' families, their colleagues, their friends; their mistresses; meaning me, sunshine. I don't know about you, but I have an aversion to gruesome torturous antics before I am allowed to die. And since I am sleeping with the husband of his daughter, then I am sure he would kill us both all the more brutally compared to others! The ruthless man he is."

But Colin either had an ambitious streak or a death wish. Samantha Emery could not tell right now. Anyhow, Colin McMurphy still persisted, ignoring his fears for now. "Look, what if I bide my time. Wait until he is either captured or killed. Then I may con his daughter to put me in her will; the very will her father took my name out off – and made no provisions for. What then, if I join a rival mob family, someone who obviously hated being under Domenico's thumb as much as I. What if I plant the idea in their minds that his children could one day become the very thing they loathed and also were frightened by? As someone planted inside the Armando estate, I can always say that I know what they are planning. And if I mention that they are in fact rehearsing Domenico's sick old ways… to relive his sick old days… well? Fear might also drive his detractors' actions. I can arrange for them to move in on the rest of the Armandos and rid the world of them ALL! Then I can inherit everything. I will be the boss. All I have to do is bide my time. Just wait… Anyhow, it's an idea. But nothing can come of it as long as the evil darkness remains in circulation. Because, I agree with you, darling, even in prison… no matter what Robert Stewart thinks he can do to him… I know that Armando would be calling the shots! As long as that evil spirit of satanic proportions is alive, only he and he alone would be running everything; no one else."

But he stopped talking suddenly. He felt himself unable to continue. He became almost mute at this point. Colin, as if by some unexplained reason, was instantly struck by a realism of fear and dread as reality hit him. "Shit. I just got the strangest feeling that he could be in tune with my thoughts right now, just as you said before. He may be able to read my mind. And if that is the case, then we are both fucked! I'm sorry, sweetheart, but I don't think we better fool around right now. I need to clear my head. I've just got this strangest sensation throughout me. My muscles are feeling cramped. I better get home-"

Colin McMurphy quickly raised himself off the couch then ran to the front door of his hotel room and opened it. He ran outside towards the elevator and within minutes he exited the entire hotel building without another word's utterance.

Based on all the information he already gathered on Colin McMurphy so far, Robert knew that Annemarie's husband was human garbage. He was scum. He was the filth of the planet. So naturally, Robert suspected that perhaps Annemarie suddenly discovered the truth about her husband. She confronted him. They had an altercation. Maybe even Colin struck her. And that was the reason for her being rushed to hospital this evening. Robert only suspected that, because where a man like McMurphy was concerned, even fear of Domenico may not stop him. After all, fear did not stop him from screwing behind his wife's back. Fear may also not stop him from physically assaulting poor Annemarie. Not even the consequences for his actions. Robert knew, no matter what: If Colin struck Annemarie; Domenico would literally amputate his hands. If he knew his son-in-law was cheating on his daughter, Domenico would also castrate him. He would want to hear him in painful unimaginable torment for many moments before he allowed him the dignity of death itself; the privilege of dying.

Robert's mind began to work properly now. His mind focused more clearly out of the haze of emotional fog he had been feeling for so long. He realised that it would not be true. Colin would not dare strike Annemarie. He may cheat on her. But, surely, no one would be stupid enough to physically assault that nice girl, especially whilst Domenico was still alive, breathing somewhere within the vicinity of this world.

Besides, if McMurphy did strike her, Robert would have been notified before the call came that alerted them all of her ambulance ride to the hospital. The surveillance agents who had in fact bugged the entire Armando estate would be the first to have known about it.

In the meantime, Robert was in a dilemma with the McMurphy situation. He wanted to help Annemarie out of that marriage of disaster she was in right now. He wanted to expose that bum she was married to, and force him out of her life. Then he wanted to maintain the police surveillance on him – until they could catch McMurphy conspire to put his ideas into actions – and before he would – then Robert could nail that son of a bitch also. He could throw him behind bars.

Though the dilemma Robert faced was, that if he exposed McMurphy right now to Annemarie, before her father was captured, Domenico would retaliate. He would murder him. Robert could not do anything that endangered another life; no matter how horrendous the target's life may be; meaning Colin McMurphy. So Robert had to keep McMurphy's adulterous behaviour-his infidelity under wraps for now. He could not expose the truth to Annemarie until such time as Domenico was first captured or killed.

Anyhow, pending Domenico's fate being realised and justice being served, Robert would keep his people plastered on Colin McMurphy as well. Any hint that Annemarie's life became endangered by him, Robert would then move in for McMurphy's arrest. For now, he had no choice but to play another waiting game where the real enemy's son-in-law was concerned as well!

So, at this moment, Robert allowed his police partner to finish his report.

John confirmed that the agents keeping an eye on Annemarie Armando uncovered, following her being admitted to hospital, that the reason for her being checked in was 'depression'. She was suffering severe anxiety for many weeks now. The cause was not because of her knowing about her husband's actions behind her back. The reason went far deeper than that.

Robert's mind clicked. His eyes opened wide in deep thought. His face became serious. Then he snapped in excitement: "That's it! That's the break we've been waiting for!"

John asked, confused. "What? Annemarie's depression?"

Robert immediately corrected him. "No. Of course not. No matter what I think of her father, I have always thought highly of her. In fact, the irony in all this is – that I truly care for her. Once we get Domenico, I will do everything within my power to free her from that scumbag husband of hers. But what I am talking about now is something else!"

John wanted to jump up and down for the answer. He eagerly insisted Robert tell him what he was thinking.

Robert gave the answer rapidly. "It's Domenico. I'm willing to bet my entire month's salary that Domenico will show up at the hospital. Look it. No matter what Domenico is, his only redeeming quality is his undying love for his family. If anything happened to any one of them, it would not matter what his circumstances are. He would move heaven and earth to be with them!"

John debated the issue. "That's crazy, Robert. Surely he wouldn't risk the exposure to come out of hiding like that and be seen in public. Not with everyone out gunning after him. I mean, the commissioner literally ordered our men to shoot him on sight if they see him!"

Robert argued his point furthermore. "Crazy, maybe; but we cannot underestimate the man we are dealing with for even one second here. You have to believe me, partner. He will show. He will risk the exposure. He is both cunning and shrewd enough for it. Whether there is one hundred or one million people on his tail, makes no difference to our man here. His determination and willingness knows no bounds. We have to get there right now. Tell our people to meet us at the Armando Family Hospital immediately. Tell them to check anyone unfamiliar to them who enter that hospital room. He could be in a disguise. He could be dressed as an old woman on a wheelchair, for all we know. We have to cover all ground on this one. All I know is, that one way or another, he will attend his daughter's hospital room. We cannot forget for one second who we are dealing with-what he stands for. To the entire world, that man is a danger. He would kill anyone. But for his family, no force on earth would drive him away from being with them in a time of need!"

John first smiled in thought: "You mean like you Robert. You would do anything for your family as well. You are also renowned for your outstanding undercover abilities. Talking about the enemy's disguises; it is as if you are describing your own abilities. Many times you went undercover disguised even as an old man, and even an old housemaid in order to infiltrate certain enemies' camps. It seems that you and Domenico, sorry to say, have that unique clever trait in common!"

Robert ignored any comments that may attribute his having anything in common with that monster, despite them being referenced without insult. But he ordered: "Let's go. Let's get to that hospital. We'll call for back-up using the car's radio!"

But they were quickly interrupted by an officer who entered Robert's office holding a package that was just mailed anonymously to the station house, addressed to Robert.

Robert took hold of the package from the officer's hands and suspiciously asked, sensing something foul in all this, "Did you check it out? Did you run it for prints?"

The officer nodded. "We already anticipated you on that, Captain. But there were no fingerprints. The package is not dangerous. We unwrapped it, and put it into this grey box here. It's a videotape by Domenico. There is also enclosed a handwritten letter by him as well, but no prints."

Robert shook his head side to side in amazement. "He deliberately sends us a harmless package, wanting us to know he's the sender. But he decides to wipe his prints off it!"

The officer explained as Robert placed the videotape into his video player connected to his office television screen, "Sir, it confirms that Domenico has recently disembarked back into town. In fact, we know where he is!"

Before reading the letter and whilst the videotape was loading its images onscreen, Robert snapped, "He's at the Armando Family Hospital here in Brooklyn!"

The officer nodded in correctness to his superior's assessment.

Robert understood everything perfectly. The bluecoat officer remained silent for now, as Robert read the letter just as he viewed the now playing videotape at the same time, before he would say anything about the contents.

Domenico confirmed to everyone Robert's initial suspicions. But Domenico revealed he would attend the hospital without disguise. He would just march on in-inside with his henchmen who would cover every floor and every window of the premises. He explained on the videotape that if anyone tried to interfere with his visit to see his daughter this evening that he would turn the entire hospital into a bloodbath. And everyone inside would be killed. He also revealed footage of two extra hostages he had tied together in one single room on two chairs, back-to-back in one of the guarded rooms on the same floor as his daughter, inside the hospital.

Domenico startled Robert by his revelation: "As you can see Robert, I have your brother Paul with your Honest SIA Chief McKenzie locked up in that room together, guarded by my people. If you interfere and try to stop me from visiting my daughter this evening, they WILL ALSO DIE! I only want to see my daughter. You can come and visit me; but only you; alone, and unarmed. My men will check you for weapons at the door, prior your entrance. I will see my daughter, Robert. Relay that message to your people – and the consequences of what will happen should anyone try to stop me. Hundreds of innocent men, women and children in that place will be wiped out. So will your boss and most importantly, your brother Paul. I can get to anyone at any time. I can find anyone. I can enter into anyone's house and poison their water supply. I can poison their food. I can spike and pollute their alcohol bottles, without anyone being the wiser. I can extract anyone anywhere. That is how my people were able to snatch them so easily. So, I give you my word: LET ME SEE MY DAUGHTER IN PEACE. THEN LET ME LEAVE THE HOSPITAL IN PEACE. AND ONCE I AM SAFELY AWAY, MY PEOPLE WILL BE CALLED OFF AND THE DANGER TO ALL THE OCCUPANTS INSIDE THE HOSPITAL WILL BE REMOVED. AND YOUR SIA BOSS AS WELL AS YOUR BROTHER WILL BE LET GO SAFE AND SOUND. THEY WILL BE RELEASED WITHOUT HARM! DO NOT DO ANYTHING THAT WILL BE THE DEATH OF THEM ALL TONIGHT, MY FRIEND, STEWART. OR ELSE THEIR DEATHS – ALL OF THEM – WILL BE ON YOUR HEAD – BOTH YOURS AND YOUR PEOPLE - NOT MINE! BECAUSE IF I DIE TONIGHT, YOU WILL ALL DIE WITH ME!"

Robert also read through the letter which confirmed Domenico's sole invitation to him this evening; for them to meet inside his daughter's hospital room. It read: 'The rest of my family will be called away during our meeting alone together. Only six of my men will be stationed inside the room, as an army of my troop will be stationed everywhere else. Do not try anything foolish, Robert – for all our sakes!'

Robert screwed up his face in anger, and then shouted: "Damn you Domenico!"

John questioned him, concerned for his best friend's safety. "He's got us all over a barrel again. What are you going to do, Robert?"

Robert responded solemnly. "I'm going there alone. But I want you and the remainder of the officers in this station house to attend, but wait outside for my command." Robert removed his revolver from his shoulder holster and handed it to John. "Mind this for me, for now. I've got a portable police radio in the car; I'll be taking with me inside the hospital. Domenico said I cannot have a weapon on me. He never said I can not carry a police radio; so I want you all to leave in your own vehicles. I want you to cover the inside and outside of the entire hospital area in case Domenico plays some sort of double-cross against us; but that aside, as much as it kills me to say it. I must. For the sake of all the lives in that hospital who will be attacked - and my brother – DO NOTHING ELSE. Just stand there, assuming your designated posts. Let Domenico enter. Let him leave." Robert's face became sterner, but he assured them: "Only for now. He won't escape us for long. It's just temporary. Our main concern right now is to ensure that there are no casualties. So do not make any rash movements; because we do not know where Domenico's people could be hidden. They could also be disguised as doctors, nurses, even patients. So, if Domenico plays ball - just do nothing, but station yourselves on every floor and on guard at every exit and entrance, door and window of that entire hospital building – inside and out - as lookouts. Pass the word to the rest of the officers. And alert the FBI, giving them 'only' the same instructions: Keep in sight, but make no moves unless I order you otherwise. And if Domenico ensures I cannot – and if our enemy starts opening fire for no apparent reason – then and only then – open fire! SHOOT TO KILL!" Robert ordered: "Ok. Let's go!"

Robert Stewart arrived at the Brooklyn Armando Family Private Hospital in ten minutes. He had the police sirens blazing from his civilian car so he could rush passed all the roads' red lights and arrive at his destination in record time. The traffic was not too hectic at this late hour. Once he parked his vehicle in a vacant parking space outside, he saw his army of men arrive in official police cars. They were all abreast of their instructions. The FBI and SIA reinforcements were on their way. But no choppers were to be called in as yet. Domenico would spot them.

But if anything went wrong, all the arrangements were in place. In short, all hell would be unleashed upon Domenico Armando. Before he could finish his mass assassinations, he himself would be struck down by numerous police and government cavalry. Robert would make sure that bastard would not walk out of that building alive! That was a given.

Robert stormed inside the front door. He already knew the floor and the hospital room number Annemarie was admitted inside. Robert became paranoid. So he avoided the possible death trap elevator. This time he preferred running all the way up the stairwell to the fifth floor. Once inside, the nurse at the nurses' station approached him. She was in a state of panic. She recognised Robert instantly. She cried in terror: "He's here. The devil... I mean, Domenico... Domenico Armando!"

Robert quickly placed a comforting hand on her right shoulder and nodded. "I know. Just remain here and keep calm. Tell everybody else to stay put. Keep right away from Annemarie's room until I tell you it's safe, ok?"

She nodded; admiring the courage of this one good police captain she too took enjoyment in reading about his recent exploits in various newspapers. She was only one of many citizens across the entire country who admired Robert – for all the good he had done for the United States and for countless people in the country.

Robert darted to the room in question, number 23. There were several guards posted out front. He knew they all belonged to Armando. Robert allowed them to frisk him. He was clean.

They opened the door to allow him access inside, then closed it and remained outside upon his entrance.

Robert saw six other burly-looking men scattered around the large room, eyeing him suspiciously, ready to pounce on him if he dared even consider making a wrong move against their master.

Robert understood quite clearly what the stakes were. He had to psyche himself to complete cool and calmness right now. Robert approached the centre of the room where he saw Annemarie lying in bed, in what appeared to be a drugged sleep.

Robert saw Domenico seated on a chair aside his daughter. He was weeping intensely whilst caressing her head with his hands. Then he turned to Robert and diabolically attempted to disarm, even further, his greatest enemy in the world, by turning to his direction and said in a deadly tone: "Look what you did to my daughter!"

Robert instantly became enraged at the comment, the brutal insinuation. He cursed: "What the hell are you talking about, Armando? I didn't do anything to her!"

Domenico quickly rose from his chair and stormed towards him. He confronted Robert. "No? You think? The doctor gave her a strong drug to put her to sleep, so she can rest and relax. Fortunately, she can't hear us! She is in this hospital because she is suffering from chronic stress and anxiety. She is depressed. Why? Because of what you have done to me!" he shouted, pointing his finger directly at Robert.

Robert turned to Annemarie. He truly was concerned for her health. He then turned to Domenico and asked, "So what else did the doctor say? Will she be all right?"

Domenico was still plenty mad. "Isn't that rich coming from the man who destroyed my whole family!"

Robert felt numb by the repercussions of their war affecting a wonderful girl as Annemarie. He even felt heartbroken as a result of her suffering. But he rapidly corrected Domenico's false accusations by insisting, "Look Domenico, no matter what, I did not want her to be caught in our war. I am deeply sorry for what she is going through. But you have some nerve to blame this on me. Your actions as a killer of innocent men, women and children were responsible for your situation right now. Annemarie is only another innocent party caught in the middle. That - I am deeply sorry for. But don't you dare blame me for this! Blame yourself; your life of crime; your brutal ruthless life of drugs, murder and insane desire to control everything and everyone At Whatever Cost!"

Domenico too became disarmed suddenly by the truth. As much as he blamed Robert for his daughter's depressive state right now, Domenico still could not deny the truth. He was mostly responsible for his daughter falling ill this evening. He could not bring himself to deny the repercussions of his life's actions – and how it impacted on all his children. He knew he had to shoulder some of the blame.

But Domenico could not admit this truth to his worst enemy on earth. No. He could only admit the truth in silence within himself. And so Domenico quickly changed the subject. He approached his daughter again, kissed her forehead and wept: "Rest well my beautiful daughter. You must rest and recover!"

Domenico pulled out a silk white-coloured handkerchief from the front of his expensive Italian blazer pocket. He wiped the tears from his eyes. He glanced at his daughter again. Then he walked over to Robert once more.

Robert became the first to speak now as he said: "You have a lot of nerve coming here like this Domenico, wearing no disguise. Just walking inside the building passed all the police and security with your henchmen, as if you own the entire world!"

Domenico gave a small grin. "Well, my friend. Courage and cleverness and a love for family are what we both share in common – is it not?"

Robert nodded. "It is indeed!"

Domenico exclaimed: "Yes. And you should know that freedom or no freedom - not even the forces of hell could stop me from seeing any of my children-my daughter if she or they are in trouble. You see, to hell with your rules; to hell with your world, Robert; and to hell with all those pestering police and government agents of yours. They are no match for me. If I want to get something done – then I-me-Domenico Armando gets it done! It's simple as that!"

Robert too gave out a smile, but ironical. "Yes. Domenico. You certainly do. No matter what you have to do. I know. I know how you operate. But no matter what, your day will come Domenico. All your money and all your henchmen will not be able to save you from your day of justice!"

Domenico gave an almost disgusted look. But he also became alarmingly forthright. "Justice you say? It has already struck me!"

Robert turned to Annemarie then added, "She is not what I am talking about!"

Domenico insisted: "Neither am I!"

Robert eyed him questioningly.

Domenico stated, "Justice has hit me in a very peculiar way, Robert. And that even has nothing to do with you!"

Robert asked, "Then what?"

Domenico replied, "I am talking about nature! How do I look to you?"

Robert humoured a man he would always regard as insane, no matter the circumstance. He replied, "You look the same as you always have. Why do you ask?"

Domenico lowered his eyes to the floor in despondency for a moment. Then he raised his eyes at Robert and insisted: "You have answered that question only with hatred, Robert. Your lagging objectivity in this instance has made you blind for the first time in your life. You have looked into my eyes, but you have failed to see the truth-this time. You hear my words, but for the first time in your life you also fail to listen to what is said between the lines! Can you figure out what I am telling you?"

Robert considered this as one of Domenico's elaborate mind games he chose not to entertain. However, he added, almost with humour. "You mean you want to turn yourself in and tell us everything we want to know about your life of crime!"

Domenico could not help but find hilarity to such a comment. He briefly chuckled, but his face grew serious very rapidly. He shocked Robert with the truth. "I have an inoperable brain tumour, Robert. The doctors have told me that I do not have much longer to live!" Domenico studied Robert's reaction. Robert clenched and unclenched his jaw as he listened. He appeared surprisingly emotionless to Domenico's supposed revelation. Domenico could only wonder why? But Robert was one enemy who was not predictable in his thought processes as others were to him. Domenico maintained his truthful streak for now. "Let me guess. You don't believe me? You think I am tricking you? Perhaps as a rouse to make the world believe I am dead when I am not? So I can resume my freedom without police and government intervention?"

Robert gave another ironical smile in reaction. "The thought has crossed my mind!"

Domenico remarked. "Of course; of course that is what you would think. After all, I would think the same thing if I was in your position. You see, we are two brilliant minds. Two master game players. But the problem is, that we are so good at it – the game – that our; even what could be described as paranoia, at times, may even rob us from uncovering the real truth. The truth that could indeed be much simpler than what our complicated and overly intelligent creative minds may in fact otherwise interpret such facts to be!"

Robert calmly said, "You could be right, Domenico!"

Domenico then added, "In any case, look at us right now, Robert. What a breath of fresh air, isn't it? Despite my circumstances, I am here-out into the open talking to you like this, in a much civilised fashion. Who would have imagined such a thing was possible?"

Robert snapped. "Well, let's not forget, Domenico, that you are holding an entire hospital as hostages at gunpoint to accomplish that. Not to mention my brother!"

Domenico said, "And of course your SIA Chief. And let's not also forget that I own this hospital!"

Robert snapped, "But that does not give you the right to kill those people! How is my brother and McKenzie?"

Domenico insisted: "They are fine. You will see them shortly." He studied Robert's eyes. "My, my, such doubts you have. But, I am a man of his word, Robert. As I said in my message earlier to you: If I leave this hospital safely – they will leave my custody – also quite safely. But for now, let us enjoy this talk. Let us savour the moment!"

Robert curiously asked, "So, Domenico. Is that brain tumour story true or false?"

Domenico clapped his hands in laughter now. "Bravo, Robert. At least you have an open mind. You are not dismissing what I am saying, simply because we are sworn bitter enemies."

Robert interrupted, "Well – so what's the answer, Domenico?"

Domenico insisted, "Yes. That is the answer. You want to know if the world is going to finally be rid of the big, bad Domenico Armando, soon, hmm? The answer is, yes. Well, according to the doctors anyway. But how accurate are their assessments-usually?" He went on. "In any case, I feel the truth, Robert. I feel death is inside me. So why do I tell you this? - Because I know you very well. In fact, I know you would not take pleasure in anyone's suffering – no matter how much of an enemy he is! That is why I feel comfortable telling you this. And I am going to tell you something else. It concerns your boss McKenzie. Perhaps it's even startling!"

Robert nodded his head and gave a, 'well, let the games begin', type of glance and urged his enemy on impatiently. "I'm still listening, Domenico!"

Domenico quickly ordered one of his bodyguards present inside the room to go and untie SIA Boss McKenzie and bring him here to this room, to join them in their talk. "And if you see the police, just walk passed them. Ignore them!" Domenico then turned to Robert once his man left the room to carry out his orders. "My next series of daunting revelations includes your SIA Boss. I have ordered him to come here so that he can clarify what I will tell you. Just in case you choose not to believe me! But please… In the meantime, do not worry. Your brother is safe and will remain that way. I am sure your government chief will confirm that for you!"

It was only momentarily when SIA Boss Chief Lloyd McKenzie was ushered into the room to join them by the Armando henchman. McKenzie quickly greeted and embraced his most honourable fellow agent, Robert. McKenzie confirmed Paul's welfare and safety for now.

Domenico would divulge everything at this very moment. "All my life I considered myself wise and lucky. But it seemed as though my luck had taken a drastic turn for the worse since I personally became acquainted with you Robert, especially in recent times. During the past few weeks since I found out about my untimely illness, I worked fervently in search for a cure. I know there is no cure in Western medicine. The irony is: the government has sought to condemn me for distributing heroin and cocaine, but they legalise pharmaceutical drugs which kills people a lot faster via its very lethal side effects. What irony. The entire world is warped. Our churches are run by money and satanic forces and this government-you Robert have taken it upon yourself to bring me to destruction."

Robert's impatience grew at an alarming rate at this moment. "Get to the point, Domenico!"

Domenico willingly chose to oblige. "I looked for avenues other than Western techniques in hope for a cure. I researched alternative medicine. I came across Professor Mark Jenkins. He came up with a technique which involved altering certain genes that promote ageing and cancer in humans; to reprogram a healthy life; to extend the life span in humans at least twofold. So we did not have to die prematurely. He was an expert in genetics and cell biology. A scientist and a herbalist. His work involved experiments in drastically prolonging life. To reverse disease and repair damaged cells. Similar to a sort of Fountain of Youth discovery; he could make a human live much longer than they usually do. He came up with the solution; now to my streak of bad luck. I had my people approach him as he lay stationed in Chicago. At the mere mentioning of my name, he dropped dead from a heart attack, then and there. No one could save him! He was only fifty years old."

Robert was familiar with the name and his work. "Well, now we know how he died. And also all his research and findings were soon after destroyed by his own colleagues following his death."

Domenico appeared startled at the thought. "Yes. To prevent me from accessing this vital piece of information that could have halted the progression of this ridiculous illness of mine, they destroyed it. So I even looked to other avenues; again in Eastern medicine; acupuncture and herbs and so forth. What was so annoying to me was that out of all the sixteen practitioners I had selected, based on their expertise, from countries all across the world, they would rather die than help me. They would rather watch their families die beforehand; each of them; one at a time."

Robert became rapidly angry. He was familiar with the recent disappearances of such men with their families. Now the case was solved. It seemed as though Domenico was behind every disaster which had befallen the entire world. "So you killed them all!"

Domenico first warned Robert, before declaring his open admission. "Remember Robert, keep calm. Yes. I killed them. Even when I threatened to cut off their arms and legs they still would not budge. But if truth be told - it does not do a man's heart any good to know that the world hates him so much to want to see him dead; to not care if he dies slowly and in excruciating agony which this disease of mine would indeed eventually cause me, very soon."

Robert and McKenzie eyed each other shaking their heads in simultaneous thoughts concerning this menace before them.

Domenico went on. "And this is why I brought your chief here. You see, I even requested his advice into any possible solutions for my illness. I was hoping that for a price, he may be able to recommend someone highly-regarded to me. Perhaps, even convince this practitioner to work with me instead of choosing suicide as all the other fools and wimps before him. And you know who he recommended? Professor Wu Yang!"

221

Robert turned to McKenzie in outrage over the merest mentioning of the name. Robert knew the name well. In fact, Domenico even knew of his adversary's knowledge. After all, Robert was also assigned to investigate this doctor for fraud and negligence which resulted in the chronic harm and the calculated murder of many of his patients.

Domenico stated: "This so-called noble government chief of yours here recommended to me the worst of the worst; an absolute walking disaster area; a complete and utter moron; a practitioner who never cured anyone. In fact, everyone who entered his clinic, were eventually destroyed. An acupuncturist who was a thief, who overcharged his clients; a charlatan who did not know what the hell he was doing. He was someone who was so negligent that most of his patients resulted in deaths in either weeks or months after commencing treatment with him. Because they were all killed via acupuncture, its effects took place outside the professor's clinic. So naturally, it became harder to prove. But the government was aware of all the complaints and coincidences, when most of his patients fell more ill than the original complaint reported - and hence, shortly fell into their graves like dominoes. They died one after the other – and often in mass heaps.

"Our health system in both Western and Eastern medicine is just another faction of our society that is grossly warped in horrendous corruption, that is only motivated by too many corrupt medical practitioners' inclinations to make large sums of money at the expense of their patients' health and wellbeing! His desire to open up a clinic here in the United States came with much forethought and planning. It was a calculated conspiracy to make money via fraud. For Wu Yang calculated the risks versus the laws in this Western country. To achieve his reward: money. For in America, should something happen to his patients, following his treatments, in whatever individual time frame the side effects of his treatments took place, whether it was days or weeks, Wu Yang's response was: 'the patients signed a contract indicating the treatment methods by me!'

"After all, in his mind, such a contract he requested his patients sign prior obtaining treatment from him was his one ticket to escape prosecution. In China, that man would have been hanged by his testicles. But in this country, as in all Western countries, no one was the wiser to his evil scheme until it was all too late! That was why that five-feet-five-inches tall evil fifty-seven-year-old Chinese so-called practitioner immigrated into this country over thirty years ago from China to begin his practice of deception.

"Where following the signature of such a contract, the patients had resumed with the treatments. Following his treatments, they got up off the treatment couch and walked out of his clinic fine. They went back to his clinic for further treatments. Until the real effect of what he was doing started to show severe physical side effects. Before long, they found it difficult to get up in the morning. They felt fatigued. Their muscles lost their elasticity and became cramped. Their stomachs were feeling nauseous and acidic from all the tension that suddenly formed. They were developing intolerances to foods and beverages such as a cup of tea they never had before, which only fed the acid; and further cramped the oesophagus - which was the beginning of something not quite right happening. But whatever it was, Wu Yang's cliché was, 'He left my clinic happy!'

"The patients ascertained that Wu Yang made them feel this way, he must know how to pass it out; and so it became the money-grabbing hook for Wu Yang: treating the symptoms, worsening the problem through his particular brand of acupuncture. Where Wu Yang, through his acupuncture treatments, made someone who appeared very normal suddenly appear as one who had every infectious disease known to man. They lost extreme amounts of weight. Their muscles became paralysed. Blood circulation became so poor and constricted that their skin became a humiliating yellow. And they lost the ability to even speak properly due to the extreme damage he also rendered to his patients' nervous systems. This was in fact an atrocity of torture committed to masses of his patients who first entered his clinic with mostly, 'extremely curable' problems, particularly by Eastern medicine.

"The patients were so weak they could not even fight him or take action against him. But, there was no scientific proof in these Western countries that acupuncture even worked - or created any side effects for anyone. So the patients were left to suffer in humiliation due to their mental and physical deterioration. Until the cramping became so severe, that his patients could not survive for long periods of time under those excruciating, suffocating and greatly stressful conditions caused by such abnormal symptoms of tension; such extremely uncomfortable muscle cramping of the entire body! Those brutal symptoms caused by constriction of the body's Circulatory System - was the side effect to Wu Yang's treatments that his patients'-signed contract was intended to cover him from such liability against thereafter!

"He lured his patients into his clinic via his deceitful conman advertising, claiming to be something he was not: A world-renowned alternative medicine practitioner - in order to sucker all the sick into his web. And like a bloodsucker, he stole their money, their health and finally their very lives!

"Of course you know all this Robert. You have a file on the man. SO DO I. I checked him out upon his referral to me by your SIA Chief here. That man was a true evil piece of shit! He was a little sewer rat, arsehole cunt! A real barbaric scar on the face of this earth! McKenzie knew this. And that was the scum he recommended to me. So that I would hopefully die the same way from the side effects of a piece of garbage like that doctor whose ill-knowledgeable work resulted in countless fatalities of almost every single person who went to see him. He was someone who was only into the business of making money and chose acupuncture because any consequences of ill treatments by him in that regard would really not be understood. And any actions against him would not be able to be fully prosecuted by such Western countries, yet very much ignorant in that field of medicine; we know works, but lacks scientific evidence, as they say. McKenzie wanted him to also kill me!"

Robert turned to McKenzie and asked, "Why would Domenico come to you for help? Were we not working together to bring him down? Explain what was going on between the two of you!"

Domenico quickly relished the idea in creating mutiny and division between two former allies. Domenico did not allow McKenzie to respond with possible half-truths. So Domenico answered the question for Robert. But beforehand warned him again to keep his temper under wraps, no matter what he learned. "McKenzie was working against me. But he was working also in competition with others for my kingdom. What I am saying Robert is that he was a 'player' in my game. He wanted a piece of the unholy pie. He wanted to control the world as I had. He wanted to take over my notoriety as Boss of Bosses. You see, after our confrontation in my concert hall, Robert-before long I secretly contacted your chief here. I wanted to use him to help me set you up as a vigilante killer. After all, the world knows about your hatred for criminals in general. It would not be that far of a stretch to the imagination if it came known that your hatred in fact became an obsession. Perhaps after all your years chasing scum, the pressure of it all got to you in the end. You self-destructed. You became the very culprit you were slaving your whole life away to lock up. Any scenario where proper government witnesses could testify against you-seeing you commit these atrocities would work to my advantage. That was why I enlisted McKenzie's cooperation. I also wanted him to arrange for narcotics to be planted inside your home. My motivation in that matter was clear-cut. The drugs were simply for comedy's sake. Anyhow, upon search warrants being issued, once you became a suspect for the labelled, 'vigilante murders', of targets you were otherwise investigating – it would be your very own colleagues who would have located the evidence inside your home and arrested you."

Robert turned to McKenzie, enraged. "Is that true?"

McKenzie first coughed nervously, and then replied. "Yes." Nonetheless, he rapidly attempted to calm his still considered friend from now attacking him. "It is true Robert that I wanted to take over the Armando operations, but not to run it the same way as him-Domenico. I wanted the power he had only to do better things. It is also true that Domenico approached me to have you set up as a killer, with drugs planted in your home. But what Domenico failed to reveal, was that I fought him tooth and nail against his crazy scheme. I did not want to participate."

Robert studied his government superior's eyes. He knew he was telling the truth, though was disappointed immensely in him, much the same. "Why did you not come to me about this?"

224

McKenzie replied, "And say what, Robert? Domenico would have ordered the two of us dead. I simply was using stalling tactics. That was why I tried to refer that corrupt doctor Wu Yang to him; to free us all from his evil clutches. But Domenico-the devil he is; he knows everything. He kidnapped the doctor. He tortured him relentlessly. Wu Yang eventually died. And he blew up his Brooklyn clinic two weeks ago. It was Domenico behind it!"

Robert asked, "And Yang's family?"

McKenzie answered: "All dead. Domenico was behind their deaths. As all the other practitioners and their relatives - they did not just disappear. He murdered them!"

Domenico became invigorated. "Trouble in paradise I see."

Robert snapped: "Shut up, you snake!"

Domenico hinted: "Why are you so mad at me, Robert? I did what you could never do. I solved your case for you. Professor Wu Yang was an unconscionable corrupt doctor of monumental proportions, who escaped justice simply because of the loopholes in your justice system's key laws; its very weak laws. I simply gave you an easy way out. I did you a favour by eliminating him. If left to the courts, he could have escaped justice again, just as he had always done before!"

Robert became plenty mad angry at this point. "Yes. But you won't, Domenico. I promise you, you won't escape justice. Not this time."

Domenico chuckled at this point. "We shall see, Robert. We shall see. However, there is only one more point I wish to raise with you; something that was always bothering me since my freedom was taken away!"

Robert eyed him, now with a deadly serious facial expression. He raised one eyebrow in scrutiny, studying his subject, and then remarked, "What would that be, Domenico? Or should I guess the answer?"

Domenico found amusement with his greatest adversary in the world at present. He could not help, but highlight that point. "How I will miss our challenge, Robert. I often conduct to my powerful symphonies, either in private or before an audience comprising of my family and my army of people; my, how the inspirational pieces inspire me. And you know what is the predominant image I always get in my head every time I listen to my classical music? It is of our battle, Robert. I dreamed many dreams about my victory and my revenge against you. It is as if I have something to prove to myself. The images I get in my head, every time I conduct to my beautiful music are so vivid, so real, so lifelike to me! You Robert — and you alone — have managed to consume my every painful memory of the recent past. And you — and you alone — have managed to be my very driving force that is keeping me alive right now. Because, no illness, no disease will stop me until all my plans are realised! I swear it!" His eyes lit up briefly in a demented rage. "I swear it! And you know what else I think about when I close my eyes listening to my motivational compositions?

"I think of everybody on this entire earth who has betrayed me! Sometimes I get so mad at all of them... that I want to blow up this entire world and send every despicable treacherous person in it, straight to hell! All those people who lie, who cheat and steal from others, from all walks of life; all those who are hypocrites – those who would sell their friends and their mothers' souls for money. How they make me sick! My daughter Annemarie never could hurt a fly – and she is being inflicted by sickness. When it really should be all those creeps and scumbags surrounding us who should be in hospital, in bitter misery at this very moment! THAT WOULD BE JUSTICE! I look at my daughter lying here, suffering like that – and I want RETRIBUTION on everyone, Robert! All those motherfuckers out there!

"You know, I often conduct to my classical music in thought of such people that has consumed this earth, and you know what I say to myself? What I imagine? I imagine that I am posted standing on the World Stage with all of them as my audience, and I am confronting them all before I will destroy them. And I rehearse my speech to them. I say: 'You are all vermin; dead in spirit, boring bums! You are nothing compared to Domenico Armando, nothing! Only I can manage to bring excitement in every corner of the earth I choose to walk on!' That is what I imagine saying to all of those horrible people.

"But at least you are different to all of them, Robert. You are like me. Always loyal to your people and your world! You are indeed a rare breed of animal. You always knew how to defend yourself where I was concerned. All the others, including your very weak boss here, never could. They were always brought to their knees by Domenico Armando; but never you, my friend. No. Whether you care to admit it or not, you and I are very much alike; both of us are not scared of anyone. We would kill anyone to protect ourselves, especially where our families are concerned. For that, I must admit something: I do admire you. But, I want you to tell me Robert, what is really bothering me right now. What is the one thing that is really irritating me? And yes, you can hazard a guess, if you wish!"

Robert, unimpressed, by the deranged sort of flattery that his enemy directed towards him, stated, "Is it concerning your ego, Domenico?"

Domenico surprised everyone with his reaction at this moment. He raised his chin in the air and began echoing laughers of irrational hysteria for some time yet. He clapped his hands together and shouted: "Bravo. Yes, bravo again, to you, Captain Stewart. I salute you. Ego was exactly the point I wanted to raise. It was the one thing that was bothering me! Yes, indeed!"

Robert understood everything. He read Domenico's mind well. He knew exactly what his enemy was thinking; what he wanted to achieve. Domenico wanted him to admit before him that he was not of a greater calibre, or more superior than he-Domenico himself was, in their battle against the other.

226

Domenico studied Robert's eyes. He yet saluted his adversary's brilliance. Only Robert could come to the correct conclusion and decipher what he was talking about. Domenico then insisted: "So, Robert – can you sum up the ultimate courage right now to finally admit that you could never defeat me in our very lengthy war?"

Robert broke out in laughter of his own at this point. But his face quickly changed to seriousness once again, as he turned the question around-over to his enemy this time - and repeated the same question to Domenico, in which he had asked of him. "What about you, Domenico? Can you find the necessary courage in yourself to admit that it is you, who is in fact the lesser man? Can you ever admit that you lost in this, little game, as you call it, in the end? Can you also admit that it was you – and you alone – who destroyed your entire world – and all those around it, including your family?"

Before long, Domenico had given his yet sleeping daughter a very warm goodbye, and then he extended an abrupt gracious, parting of the ways, for now, towards Robert, before Domenico had finally left the hospital completely with his large number of henchmen, unscathed.

Robert was reunited with his brother shortly after. He untied his many rope restraints and the rest of the hospital staff members were also safe for now. The Armando gunmen, who had recently forbidden anyone from leaving the hospital, were now called off, upon their master's safe departure and consecutive, successful disappearance.

After making sure Paul was all right, and instructing a nearby police officer to safely drive him home, Robert questioned McKenzie alone now inside the hospital's cafeteria.

McKenzie denied nothing. He was frank in his statements, corroborating his version of events he told Robert in Annemarie Armando's hospital room.

McKenzie though seemed worried. "What are you going to do, Robert?"

Robert replied gently, "You mean am I going to arrest you? Am I going to force you to resign from the SIA as Chief by turning you in to your government superiors in Washington, D.C.? That does sound tempting. But I did not hear Domenico mention your culpability in any crimes or murders. If there were any, he would have bragged about it, the snake he is. Divide and Rule were his style and trademark. But, Domenico's efforts in this instance in trying to turn us against the other did not work. Let's work in getting him through the proper channels – then we'll see what will happen!"

McKenzie shook Robert's hand and nodded in gratitude.

Within the next forty minutes, Robert interrupted his conversation with his SIA Chief, when he contacted John McCallum using his portable police radio he carried with him, and consecutively radioed two FBI contacts thereafter, concerning updates to their enemy's whereabouts.

They each reported that Domenico's private jet had escaped their radar. They could not trace his whereabouts – FOR NOW."

Robert insisted it was only temporary.

Once he finished his radio communications, McKenzie asked him an important question, perhaps in a desire to satisfy his own personal curiosity about a certain pertinent matter. "If Domenico attempted to set you up as a killer, what would you have done to stop it?"

Robert responded very naturally, without any pause for thought. "Well, I would have initially had to avoid being arrested, at whatever cost. Because I would not be able to uncover the truth of my set up or prove my innocence from behind bars. Then, I would have faked my death in order to stop the killings. If the world thought I was no longer alive, Domenico could not continue with such a diabolical plan. He could not continue killing anyone in that regard. I would have had to work from hiding myself in order to smoke him out, the culprit responsible – and prove my innocence at the same time! It would also be easier to accomplish all this once the police pressure was removed. Hence, if no one knew I was alive!"

McKenzie smiled. He was extremely impressed. Robert was truly the smartest operative he had ever encountered inside his agency. He was quick-witted and brilliant as always.

McKenzie made one more revelation. He confirmed to Robert that Domenico had also been responsible for the deaths of Niko Sasselli and his twenty-nine-year-old adopted Jewish son, Marco; also divulging the enemy's culpability behind the murders of all the SIA and FBI government hostages.

Robert shook his head from side to side in utter contempt. "It just doesn't stop with that tyrant. It just doesn't stop. He kills and kills and keeps killing. But I promise you, Chief – I am going to destroy Domenico Armando. One way or another, I will get that maniac. I will finally rid the world of him!" Robert then gave his Chief a cold stare when he further added, "You are wrong about one thing, McKenzie: Domenico does not know everything. He only pretends he does. He certainly had no idea about the true extent of his son-in-law's deception against him. Or else he, too, would not be around today. In any event – where Armando is concerned - I do not want to wait for nature to take its course. Cancer or no cancer - I want to get Domenico using the law. I want him brought to justice the right way. Him dying a natural death just does not seem fair after all the misery and suffering, deaths and destructions that bastard has been responsible for!"

McKenzie agreed. They shook hands and joined their forces once again – only this time it became a pact against their primary target; a mutual enemy he certainly was. They formed at this moment what exactly resembled a 'blood oath'.

BOOK 12

CHAPTER 21

Robert Stewart was stationed inside his unmarked tinted-windowed vehicle that evening, parked discreetly outside the Armando Estate in Brooklyn Heights, two blocks away. But still close enough. His police partner, John McCallum, was seated aside him in the front passenger seat. They kept close watch on the Armandos and listened for any clues-anything that may hint even a remote lead to the sadistic Domenico's location. The discreet listening devices planted inside the target's mansion picked up a perfectly clear signal.

It was now exactly one week after Domenico's fiasco he created in the city. One week after his visit inside his private hospital to see his daughter Annemarie – and the consequences of such a visit. Forcing himself back into everyone's lives in New York City using every dirty trick and bloodthirsty tactic he could muster in order to achieve such a well-organised return.

Annemarie was now released from the hospital and returned back to the Armando mansion under doctors' supervision. Robert knew that it was Domenico who arranged for the many private doctors and nurses to watch over his daughter, following her release from hospital. She was still reported in a very fragile emotional state. But she was considered well enough to return home.

Robert was posted inside his car for two hours now, waiting and listening for some sort of word. Robert chose to personally takeover the surveillance detail this evening because they also received word only yesterday that Domenico Junior had recently returned into the city as well. He was back in New York. In fact, he was right here, inside his father's estate. Robert considered this to be a very salient turn of events. He suspected immediately, following his re-entry into the city after many weeks of disappearing with Domenico, that D.J. was obviously back in order to carry out orders for his father.

D.J. had no reason to conceal his return as yet. His freedom was not in tatters, unlike his father. So D.J. could come and go right now as he pleased. Nonetheless, this was a very crucial turn of events for Robert. Obviously, whether D.J. would care to admit it or not, Robert knew that he was hiding with his father all this time. He was planted in some land of anonymity, no doubt being corrupted by his father's evil ways.

Robert was sure, beyond any doubt, that D.J. would turn corrupt much like his father. It was only time before that happened; if it had not happened already. Obviously Domenico would have used these past many weeks in isolation with his three children, to no doubt brainwash each and every one of them to do his bidding. To become the evil sadistic nightmare that he-himself was to the entire world; similar to a sort of reincarnation of him. And no doubt, D.J., being Domenico's eldest of his children would be mostly targeted by his father to in fact take his place once his days on this earth had abruptly ceased to exist.

Domenico would most definitely want his legacy to continue after he was gone. And his eldest son D.J. fit the bill to some extent (not as the most perfect), but as the more favoured candidate to carry out his father's nasty profile, in Domenico's eyes. Of course Robert knew that compared to his father, D.J. was very wet behind the ears. He was indeed small potatoes. He was rather squeamish when it came to bloodshed and even committing murder. Robert understood that D.J. never really participated in the dark aspects of his father's business. Not until now... Obviously, with all things considered, following Domenico's most recent change in fortunes, he would have used this time in isolation with his children to convince, specifically, his rather 'inexperienced', if not 'naive' son to follow in his footsteps; to become a man like him. That, it was time his son grew up – and popped his cherry, so to speak.

After all, the Armando family was under attack by the very powers opposing them. His father would have convinced his son that the only way to combat defeat was to resort to his ways of retaliation, bloodshed and unmerciful execution-style mass murder! Robert could sense Domenico's brainwashing tactics imposed on his children, namely, JUNIOR. Robert understood perfectly how Domenico thought. How he spoke. How he would act. He could sense his rather hypnotic and convincing personality being imposed onto all his children, specifically D.J. – until they and he had succumbed to their father's spell – and fell prey in a trancelike state to Domenico's, soon to become, irresistible wicked ways, delivered through a type of pretentiously charismatic, yet evil charm. A hypnotic charm it surely was, much likened to many past dictators almost matching Domenico's scope, who could convince people, armies and even entire countries as a whole, to listen, to believe and become manipulated to see black as white and vice versa! To swiftly follow such a man into the depths of hell – where once inside that very factual pit – THERE WAS NO WAY OUT – FOR ANYONE – EVER!

And now as he listened in silence to the happenings inside that mansion, much haunted by 'Domenico's Ghost', Robert could see the rapid transformation of a once meek man; suddenly take a turn to the more wicked.

Domenico only had some weeks with his son, in complete isolation. But in that short time he actually was able to finagle his greatest achievement to date. To hypnotise, perhaps even somewhat effectively brainwash his son to CHANGE!

Robert overheard D.J. inside his father's private den. He was all alone inside the downstairs office study room of the mansion, speaking to one of his henchmen over the telephone, giving irate instructions in a tone as if they were really delivered by Domenico himself.

Robert turned to his police partner John in amazement. Robert saw John was also in a state of astonishment. As they listened to D.J.'s tirade over the telephone, they became convinced that Domenico was truly a 'master manipulator'.

John even hinted to Robert: "This does not sound like the D.J. we once knew. The transformation in such a short time frame is incredible!"

Robert nodded. The transformation was indeed, PROOF POSITIVE. It was now confirmed. "That son of a bitch Domenico really did it this time. He finally got to his son. He corrupted him into the very same maniac he is!"

They overheard D.J. shouting from the top of his lungs to one of his family's henchmen situated on the other end of the phone: "My family is under attack by all those goddamn fucking police and pain in the arse government officials! My father's health is deteriorating rapidly every single day. He has had another seizure because of his brain condition. He is now recovering from his brief coma. He cannot move right now. So you better listen to me very carefully. I am taking over in the running of this family's affairs whilst my father is temporarily immobile. So I am going to give the orders now. And this is what I want carried out... And I want my instructions fulfilled immediately. I want Robert Stewart DEAD! He was behind all this craziness that has turned my father's life upside down as we speak. As long as Robert Stewart is alive, my father will not have a moment's peace. I want you to gather our people right now and find this family's primary enemy, Stewart! I know what my father said. But my father, may he recover rapidly, is not thinking straight! Robert Stewart is too dangerous to be left breathing any longer! He cannot be the last to die! HE MUST BE THE FIRST TO DIE! All right, you understand?"

Following a cough in the affirmative delivered from the other end of the phone, D.J. continued his rant: "Good. You get Robert Stewart tonight. It is 11:00 p.m. right now. I want him dead before midnight. Then you go and kill all those guards surrounding his family! You execute them first. Then you finish the rest of those bloody Stewarts! Put several bullets in the brains of his wife, his two children, his brother, his sister and those damn parents of his responsible for conceiving such a menace named Robert Stewart. You kill his parents too, you understand. They were after all responsible for bringing this threat against us into this godforsaken world we live in! I want bombs planted

231

in all the Stewart family's homes. I want all such buildings and horrendous memories removed from this world. Once my father awakens, I want to be the first to put his mind at ease. I will tell him that the man responsible for his current misfortunes has been removed from this earth in bloody fashion. I am going to make my father proud of me! You understand? And any other fucking ape rat bastard that puts his life against my family's will also be removed once our greatest threat is gone! Any insignificant pest who crosses us ever in the future will become written on my shit list! I am going to rescue this family from all its threats! I am going to eliminate all my father's enemies. They are all going to burn alive for even thinking of doing this family harm – all those damn cretins and halfwits! So you go and carry out your instructions right now! And do not call me back until you have this good news to report to me! Because I feel my father's anger! I understand him completely at this moment for the first time in my life! I have listened to him – and I agree with his words: 'For us to succeed – we must ensure that the entire world fails in its endeavours! For the Armandos to be preserved – we must destroy everyone in the entire world!' At the end of the day, there is no other choice! They must all die! All right! Go do your job! Go bring me the news of Robert Stewart's murder! Both him and his family! I want to smell their blood. I want to mock them on each of their tombstones! I will engrave the words of my victory against them on all their gravesites. The words will be engraved with their own blood. And such words will be written with the finger of my great father! So, GO! Go! Go! Go! Go kill and destroy my father's principal targets. For I cannot wait until he awakens! I will personally gladden his heart. I will personally lift his spirits with such long-awaited news – yes, my hero of a father who I idolise with all my heart and soul – just as you have idolised us- your children all your life. Now, I will become the son you want! I will become you, oh father! I will make you proud and victorious…"

D.J. cradled the phone in his right hand, but he could not finish his words. He felt his body flung to one side. Robert Stewart stormed the house in a hurry, grabbed the phone from him, placed it onto the desk, yet connected. He quickly grabbed D.J. with one hand clamped around his throat, in a choke hold, and with his other clenched fist, he sent one powerful blow into D.J.'s face. D.J. fell onto the ground in shock. Robert lunged towards him onto the tile floor and with two hands clenched onto the collar of his jacket; he quickly hauled him onto his feet and began beating into his face, ribs and stomach. Robert became furious. He was uncontrollable. He shouted to his enemy as he consciously beat him: "I will kill you, you son of a bitch! I will kill you and your demented father!" Robert cursed as his fists uncontrollably struck his target with such speed and ferocity that he surely intended on having him removed from his sight into the hands of a mortician at this moment.

Robert quickly felt his arms pinned behind his back and a familiar voice shouted, "Stop it Robert! Stop it! He is not worth it! Think of your family!"

Robert was uncontrollably mad right now. He shouted at John, who held him back now from yet proceeding to grab Junior and finish him off: "My family is all I am thinking about right now! Just let me at him! Let me kill him right now!"

John yet pinned his arms behind his back firmly and insisted: "No! I cannot let you do that! Calm down! Just calm down! I won't release you until you settle yourself, ok!"

Robert quickly took many deep breaths. He was still very angry, but he could not find it in himself to fight his best friend in order to outlive his much anticipated objective right now: killing D.J.! Robert felt himself settle down somewhat at the soothing sound of his friend's voice.

John soon after released his grip, then stood between Robert and his target who had now again fallen onto the floor in agony, his face all bruised and bloody!

John then raised the struggling D.J. onto his feet and shouted: "You are under arrest Domenico Junior Armando for conspiracy to commit murder on a police officer and his family! Robert is my best friend! I am going to make sure that you never see the outside of your awaiting prison cell for as long as you're alive! And soon your father will join you there!"

Robert felt an urge of utter death precede every fibre of his being at the sight of D.J., but the phone's receiver yet lying on the desk distracted his mind for now. Robert saw his police partner place handcuffs around Junior's wrists, and then he heard him reading him his arrest orders. Robert quickly picked up the phone's receiver and spoke into it, "You're still there! Well, are you?"

Robert overheard a police officer on the other end of the phone say, "It's Officer Harrison, Captain. We traced the call here as you requested in your car moments earlier. We've arrested the Armando henchman D.J. was talking to. We're just about to place him in the squad car to take him to the station house now. We're at a public phone booth on 74th Avenue!"

Robert replied, "Good job!" Robert then turned to D.J. briefly; his eyes lit up in pure hatred as if consumed in flames by the sight of him. Robert looked away for now to focus his attention clearly onto the officer on the other end of the phone. "Soon Armando's son will join him. And with any luck, before much longer, so will Domenico himself! All right! I'll see you down at police headquarters shortly. I cannot wait to write up tonight's arrest reports on these two subjects in question!"

The officer replied, "Got you, Captain!" before both ends clicked.

Robert instructed John to escort D.J. downtown, have him fingerprinted, his mugshot taken and placed inside his awaiting lock-up jail cell. Robert hinted he would be down there in a little while to help him write up the necessary arrest reports. Right now he had something else, equally as important to take

233

care of. He only mentioned that it had something to do with his plans to also 'capture the big fish'.

It was two and a half hours later before Robert returned to the station house. It was past 1:30 a.m. in the morning. He made a stop first at the prison lock-up facility to witness D.J. inside his isolated cell. Robert was content. D.J. was lying on his bed wearing his prison blue uniform. He was contemplating his foolish actions only hours ago which resulted in his present confinement only hours after. He was also attempting to rest his wounds from the altercation with his family's biggest threat against them, Robert Stewart!

Robert studied his demeanour thoroughly. Robert could not help but smile in reaction to all this. Watching that pissant in prison was such a refreshing sight for him. Prison was made for such scoundrels as D.J. – that was for sure!

Robert's face became stern now as he pointed out to the overwhelmed Armando heir apparent, "Don't worry, D.J. – you won't be alone inside your cell for long. Your father will soon join you here!"

Robert soon after returned to his office situated on the other end of the premises. He briefed John concerning the reasons behind his delayed arrival this early morning. Now that D.J. and his henchman were locked up in different cells, Robert went straight to the heart of the matter to his police partner who waited for him.

Robert explained, "The reason for my delay was because I arranged for additional security to be placed on all members of my family. I also alerted the remaining Armandos, specifically Sandra Armando, of D.J.'s arrest. It seems that whilst we arrested D.J. who was alone inside his father's former office room, that the rest of the house guards and the family were upstairs with Annemarie. So I informed them of what happened earlier so they would not be surprised once the newspapers and television media broadcasts the arrest to the entire world."

John asked curiously, "How did they take the news?"

Robert hinted. "Not too good. This is to be expected. Anyway, I tried to contain the situation. But I also asked to speak to D.J.'s wife Sandra in private. I wanted her to pack her belongings, of both hers and her son's, and accept my offer for Protective Custody which I offered her!"

John was shocked. "What? I'm not following you. Why-how did you offer that?"

Robert eyed his friend and police partner with a sparkle of cunning illuminating his eyes. He explained everything. "John, unfortunately, we're going to have to play dirty on this one; whatever it takes to also finagle putting Domenico right here to join his son in prison. Anyhow, at first

Sandra was not keen on the idea of leaving her job, her home or her life here in New York. It took a bit of convincing..."

John asked, yet curious, "So what did you do to convince her to leave the country under Protective Custody?"

Robert stated bluntly, "I played her the tape recording of D.J. threatening me and my family, in order to show her the man she was really married to. So she could see once and for all what sort of a man he really is!"

John asked, "Then what? How did she react?"

Robert stated, "She was shocked, bewildered, disillusioned – you name it, she experienced it; all manner of confused emotions. In crux, I basically told her that for the sake of her son's welfare and her own, she really had no choice but to take me up on my offer – and get as far away from her husband as possible. From listening to the tape she was able to decipher what it all meant for both her and her son. D.J. was no longer the same person. He had changed swiftly into a cold-blooded sadistic killer as his father. Sandra was made aware that D.J. may even attack her with the same vengeance if she ever so much as disappointed or refused him, even unintentionally. She was too made aware that if she stayed and did not get away from this evil Armando family, that her son may too one day become corrupted into the same monster her husband had become. She was not too keen in raising a child who was at risk of growing up into another terrorist of sorts; endangering and destroying people's lives! She was also made to understand that if she ever unearthed D.J.'s sordid ways on her own, her disapproval would most certainly result in her separation, or forced separation from her son. D.J. would take him away from her. He may also threaten her life with violence if he ever felt she knew too much – especially since she is a fairly decent reporter. So you can connect the dots to see what happened next!"

John questioned Robert further. "So where is she now?"

Robert replied, "She is on a plane with her new FBI bodyguards, being transported to a secret location overseas. I did tell her that it was only temporary. As soon as we can nail Domenico to the wall, she could return, once that danger to hers and her son's life was removed!"

John's eyes lit up in query. "So what did you mean by saying we may have to play dirty on this one? There was more to Sandra's and her son's forced departure than meets the eye, isn't there?"

Robert nodded. "Yes. With D.J. in prison and now with his grandson, D.J.'s son taken away - Domenico will try to do everything within his power to get them back. And that, partner, is the trap we have set in motion to finally spring Domenico out into the open so we can finally get him, with his guard down, at its lowest point. And especially with his physical and mental health going downhill rapidly, this is the most perfect time to strike at him. It is a certainty that Domenico is not at the top of his game right now. We can strike. We can get him. And he won't know what hit him!"

John asked, "What do you have in mind?"

Robert explained everything. "Domenico will know that I am the only one who knows where his grandson is. So, what am I planning? I am going to set myself up as bait. I want Domenico to come after me. I want him to find me. I want him to take me to his hiding spot for a supposed further confrontation – or interrogation concerning the whereabouts of his grandson. Then once he gets me, we can get him!"

John asked, "How?"

Robert explained, "I am going to make it easy for Domenico to find me! It'll be done at night in the park, three blocks away from my house. Meanwhile, I have arranged for my family to also temporarily disappear from my home, so Domenico cannot use them for any sort of blackmail in exchange for his grandson. I will have a miniature tracking device planted inside my watch. The signal will be transmitted to your portable computer. So as soon as Domenico picks me up, you follow him whilst radioing for back-up, until we get to the final destination. But only use parallel surveillance in your unmarked vehicles. We don't want Domenico's people spotting anyone!"

John shook his head in dismay, much concerned. "I don't know, Robert. This plan of yours sounds awfully risky. Things could go horribly wrong. You'll be risking your life. He could kill you. This is too dangerous. It's suicide!"

Robert ordered, "Look partner. This is a risk we are going to have to take! Besides, Domenico will not kill me quickly. He will want or need me alive as long as he thinks that I am the only lead to his grandson's whereabouts. So what do you say? Are you in?"

John nodded, but yet airing his reluctance. "Yes. I'm in. But for the record, I do not like these sort of heroics."

Robert understood. "I know. But sometimes it's necessary to stop people like Domenico. At the end of the day, do we really have much choice? Just make sure you stay close, but not too close to me once I am picked up. And get back-up to bust into the place where Armando takes me, as quickly as possible. That way Domenico won't have enough time to do anything he has planned. We'll get him before he can do anything. Ok, partner?"

John nodded. "Ok!"

Robert enforced: "No matter what we have to do – we must get this bastard off the streets at whatever cost; because even if he's on his last legs, and his heart is still beating – EVERYONE-EVERYWHERE IS IN GRAVE DANGER!"

CHAPTER 22

Robert Stewart's plan worked with the precision of a well-oiled clock. Two nights later, the enemy took the bait! Domenico summoned his strengths to return back into the city once more. His men located Robert in the isolated Brooklyn Park at midnight. Robert was all alone. No guards in sight. He was seen sitting on a park bench reading the newspaper beneath one of the dimly-lit public garden lights. Robert wore his bullet-proof vest. But he still feared the enemy was going to attempt to shoot him in the face if he intended to kill him.

Robert felt his intruders approaching. But he signalled no reaction. He felt silent footsteps creep towards him from behind. He heard the faint sounds of leaves crackling on the grass ground. Robert felt nervous all of a sudden. He felt the rhythm of his heart beat faster. But Robert psyched himself to total strength. He convinced himself not to panic. He thought of his family, his friends, everyone in this world who opposed his enemy. Robert did this for all of them. He proudly and bravely risked his life to save every single person in this world who opposed Domenico Armando. He considered all such people who were aligned with him against the enemy as potential targets. He must do whatever necessary to rid that threat from their lives. So once he convinced himself of the necessity for his dangerous actions right now, particularly in regards to preserving his family, Robert's emotions were restored to complete strength. And if there was any further doubts that entered his mind, Robert had no more time to concede them.

The enemy's henchmen rapidly crept up behind him and one of them lifted the butt of his gun high above his head and sent it smashing down on the back of his skull. Robert immediately collapsed onto the ground, losing consciousness thereafter as rapidly as a dying light.

One of the hugely-built henchmen lifted him with both hands and swirled his unconscious body over his shoulder, then carried him to a nearby parked car situated meters away alongside the curb of the deserted road. Two extra men operating as lookouts were waiting posted on foot directly outside the unregistered vehicle. Another opened the rear boot and Robert was shoved inside; quickly and instantly all the henchmen entered the large late model brown-coloured station wagon vehicle. The driver began the engine and the car drove off that moment, disappearing into the next street corner within seconds...!

Robert Stewart woke up by force that early morning. Domenico Armando's looming presence was felt in brutal fashion. The tyrant emerged rapidly. Robert felt himself being beaten by strong hands. Domenico's fists hammered into his face several times. He then grabbed him by his hair and cursed at him wilfully, "You horrible pig! You first destroyed my empire. Now you arrest my son and hide my grandson from me! I am going to make you bleed to death. I am going to hurt you like no man has ever been hurt before! I am going to make you scream in terror! I am going to blow you out of this world, you fool. You think you are mightier than Domenico Armando, hmm? You stupid man… Yes. I have reduced you to the definition of stupid. Why? - Because by your recent actions, you have signed your own death warrant. You may as well have put your own gun to your head and pulled the trigger. It would have saved you the agony that you will now bear at my hands, you contemptible man! You will suffer dearly for what you have done; both you and every other idiot who chooses to put their life against mine!"

Robert Stewart gasped for air from his wounds. He felt a mixture of hatred, but fear and isolation at this moment. He was tied onto a wooden chair in some isolated warehouse spot, perhaps in the Bronx. He could not tell right now. The warehouse was also faintly lit. But he had no time to study his surroundings as Domenico continued to terrorise him physically and emotionally, with the intention of wilful breaking point!

Robert's mind felt confused. His eyes became blurry from the beatings to his head. But he did notice that Domenico had a gun in one hand right now. He pointed it at his forehead and shouted: "Where is my grandson, you bastard? Where is he? Tell me – or I will kill you right now!"

Robert coughed in agony. He felt his hands weakened behind his back. He could barely move right now. He took deeper breaths to attempt to restore strength into his body to fight through his rope restraints as before. But he felt tired and weaker for some reason. He could not tell – but he felt as if Domenico injected him with something before he woke up; something that would make him more obedient to his interrogator's demands. Robert felt groggy. But despite his body feeling weak, his mind would not budge. He felt mentally confused, but Robert's emotions were still in control.

He felt as though Domenico gave him something to weaken his senses, because that was the only way he figured he would talk. Because even with a gun pointed to his brain, with Domenico ranting and raving like a lunatic, with his henchmen planted all across the room – Robert would still resist communicating to him the very answers to the questions he wanted to know at this very moment.

Domenico grabbed him more firmly now by his hair with one hand. He pointed his gun to his face with the other hand as he began yelling threateningly: "You think you can hide my grandson from me? You think you will remain silent here forever, hmm? Believe me, my friend. You will talk. One way or another, I will make you talk. I will make you tell me what I need to know - because right now my hatred for you has restored my mind and body to its former strengths. What will kill others can only invigorate me. It

238

can only make me stronger-more powerful. So, you listen to me, Stewart – and listen carefully. The rules of the game have now changed… I am only going to ask you once more. And you had better tell me the very answers I seek – or else I am going to start shooting ligaments off your body. I am going to start physically cutting you to pieces. And I will weaken you to the point of complete mental deterioration! Then I will decapitate you!"

Robert yet felt somewhat disorientated. But he could still ascertain and much process what Domenico was telling him. He felt he may die right now. He also could comprehend the effects of Domenico's confirmed illness on the enemy's constantly declining mental state. Domenico was rapidly losing perspective. He was losing all sense of reality. Domenico was certainly born mad. But his brain tumour was compounding such madness in very insane ways. Domenico was becoming more of a lunatic; more out of touch with reality every day. Robert could comprehend that perfectly.

Robert summed up all his strengths right now to remain mute. He prepared himself for the end - for death. Because no matter what Domenico planned for him, Robert would NEVER talk. Not ever! If Domenico did not realise that – then he was surely slipping – and slipping with much ferocity with every passing moment!

But Robert felt his tongue loosen only to say, "Go ahead… Go ahead and shoot, Domenico!" But it was not necessary for him to even speak such words.

Before Domenico could utter another word, the armed police cavalry entered the warehouse and instantly overpowered Domenico's henchmen. The police ambushed them before they attempted to take aim and fire in retaliation. Domenico felt a gun pointed in his back. It was John McCallum who shouted, "Drop your weapon Armando. Drop it now or I will shoot!"

Domenico observed the dead corpses of his small army of men sprawled across the concrete floor of the building. He then surrendered himself without showing emotion. The police quickly untied Robert – who regained himself onto his feet in a rapid manner. John placed the handcuffs around Domenico's wrists. Robert approached Domenico and grabbed him by the collar of his expensive suit jacket and shouted: "I am going to see to it that you rot behind bars Armando until your day of execution! And it is going to be you who will talk to me… You are going to answer all my questions, you understand that? You are going to tell me everything I want to know!"

Domenico suddenly revealed emotion. He smiled in reaction, attempting to mock Robert's abilities against him furthermore by stating: "And by what miracle do you think you can pull that off with?"

Robert became overcome with rage once again, now with Domenico as he had demonstrated to his son most recently. Robert grabbed him now more fiercely with both hands clenched firmly around the collar of his blazer and shook him violently, shouting: "I will do it Domenico! You will see!"

John intervened once again, removing Robert's hold from the enemy, insisting, "He will get what's coming to him!"

Robert shoved the flat open palm of his hand into Domenico's shoulder, tripping him up slightly, his feet became briefly off balance, gaining his attention for now as he insisted: "I haven't even started with you yet, Armando!" Robert then ordered his men: "Take him to prison right now, before I kill him!"

Domenico gave Robert a vicious stare, now his face became as solemn as Robert's; at the same time the police whisked him outside into their squad car – to take him away!

To any onlooker who watched these two men at this very moment, the conclusion was obvious. The Grand Finale in this bloody battle between them certainly, and with absolute undeniable surety – without question – would not end until one of them was DEAD!

CHAPTER 23

Robert Stewart received the highest accolade any police officer could attain at this moment for accomplishing such a spectacular, if not, historically great feat. Putting Domenico Armando behind bars had in fact won him much acclaim, applause, appreciation and commendation by his peers and superiors.

At 2:00 a.m. in the morning, following the enemy's transportation downtown to police headquarters to join his son in the local lock-up facility, Robert became widely popular throughout the entire state of New York. He also received personal visits and phone calls from various important people in the country. The New York City Mayor, the Governor of the State of New York, the District Attorney, the Police Commissioner and many others wanted to extend much tribute to this great hero in their eyes known as Robert Stewart. He instantly that moment was regarded as one of the country's true heroes. He was their human saviour! He was saluted and recognised as one hell of a tremendously successful enforcer of the American Justice System!

He made large threats to their prized nation obsolete! He made such big men as Domenico Armando crumble in defeat. He made them small. He brought Domenico to his knees. He knocked that hideous tyrant down to size. He made him fall flat on his face – and Robert intended that Domenico Armando was not going to rise from the ashes again, so to speak! The enemy's days of widespread torture, terrorising and mayhem were finally over! He was going to wallow in his misery until the day of his much anticipated EXECUTION! That day would truly mark the workings and success of the Almighty American Justice System. A system that could work! A system that could prove fair to the soul citizens of the county! A system that was not as weak and ineffective as men such as Domenico Armando believed – and thrived on the idea of indeed mocking its judicial processes every time, in barbaric fashion!

Robert Stewart proved that with hard, dedicated effort the law had strength. It had muscle. It had legs to stand firmly against the insidious corruption of such evil bearers as the Armandos - who indeed threatened to crush and wreak havoc and eventually destroy all aspects of their society!

Robert was a man considered godly and just at this very moment! A man who outwitted and outmatched one of the most heinous terrors the country had ever seen in its period!

Domenico was no longer laughing. In fact, that despicable atrocious human being was reduced to crying bloody tears! He was reduced to dust. His days of living were numbered. His justice was now considered a certainty! He was not going to last long enough for his terminal illness to put him in his grave. No! NEVER!

Robert Stewart made one final stop that early morning to his two enemies' shared prison cell. Robert witnessed Domenico and his son huddled together in attempted secret conversation. They were both stripped of their expensive clothing, their high-society gourmet meals, their million dollar jewellery, their high-priced mansions, servants, maids, hit men and all their creature comforts! They were both reduced to prison blue rags situated in a very uncomfortable drafty cell. Robert could not help but feel pleased at this great result he had achieved this morning. Watching his two foremost enemies reduced to wearing 'shit clothes' – both removed from the public – and forced into isolation together could not help but bring out a reaction of immense happiness to Robert. This was indeed 'poetic justice' in its finest form! Robert could not help but agree with the Police Commissioner, the Mayor, the District Attorney, the Governor of the State and various other officials. The wheels of justice in America can work! All it takes is for 'one man' within the proper sanctions of the law to give a damn to do his job properly! To speak up with vigour and tell the powers that be what needs to be done! That was it! No excuses! Everything else was a smokescreen – a cover-up! An act of cowardice! The law was surely stronger than these criminals! Watching these two fiends stripped of their freedom was a prime testament to that fact! It was tremendous.

Robert could not help but smile and smile again and continue smiling at this very sight before him. A comical display it became! Indeed, he was not ashamed to gloat right now!

Domenico recognised the visit by his greatest adversary and he wished to even congratulate him.

Robert was in no mood for games. So he broke the long silence by insisting: "Domenico – don't even think of attempting to bribe any guards in order to secure your freedom, because I have them under close watch. Their bank account records are being monitored closely at this time. Any financial transactions changing hands into any possible secret safety deposit boxes are also being scrutinised! You and all the guards in this local prison facility are being monitored twenty-four hours of the day! Even if any of you sneezes, we will know about it! I have taken it upon myself to undertake all possible safety precautions during your stay here as my prisoner – until your preliminary hearing tomorrow morning when the judge finds enough evidence to warrant a trial. Then you're going to be sentenced to a maximum security prison interstate, both you Domenico and the son you ordered to kill for you, sitting next to you on that lower bunk. Where the two of you will await what you both so richly deserve: the death penalty!"

Domenico smiled himself at the thought. He raised himself from his seated position aside his son and approached the door to his cell. He placed two firm hands around the steel bars and congratulated Robert once more, much sarcastically before he added, "Very clever Robert. It is also very clever putting both me and my son in a cell together. But your tactic is clearly obvious to me! You want to see and hear what I have planned next. Perhaps maybe I might slip out something unconsciously to my son concerning any planned escape ambitions - is that it? Perhaps it might also slip my mind somewhat, even for a short period of time during these discussions, that you have wired this cell for sound, with cameras watching and listening to us also twenty-four hours of the day! Maybe I might tell you something that you want - or need to hear, is that it?"

Robert replied vaguely. "Domenico, you can interpret that in any way you so choose. In fact, you can rot in hell first before I tell you anything! But just remember one thing: after that courtroom hearing tomorrow – it will be the beginning of your end! I am going to see to it personally, that every good life you took, who is turning in their graves right now – turning, waiting for the wheels of justice to turn on you – FINALLY GET THEIR WISH GRANTED! For the record – it is no great secret that I am very much looking forward to it! I said my piece! Have a good rest, Domenico! You're going to need it!"

Domenico and his son were now isolated in their prison cell. Robert had departed from the scene. Domenico glanced at his son's bruised face with concern and anger. He seated himself aside him again on the lower bunk.

D.J. confirmed, "That son of a bitch Robert Stewart has given me some scars to remember him by!"

Domenico remarked in a soothing tone before his son, whispering into his ear, hoping their police intruders could not hear him. "My son, I promise you. It is nothing compared to the scars I am going to give Robert Stewart! You will see!"

D.J. eyed his father confused, as if his father's illness was yet causing him to delude himself. "Father, look where we are; look at the shit clothes we are wearing. The scent of mothballs is eating into my flesh and making my skin itch like crazy! Our $800,000 custom made suits are worth more than what those miserable hopeless cases who call themselves police earn in a lifetime! Those heinous police could not wait to strip us down from all our riches and glory – and replace them with these wretchedly grotesque rags we are now forced to cover our backs with! We have lost everything! Robert Stewart has won! We are stripped from all our power and money; all our manpower too. There is no escape from here. We are doomed. How can you still find it in yourself to talk REVENGE, from here? How? The only place we are headed is into our graves!"

243

Domenico gave out an amused smile at his son's yet considered naivety. He again whispered in his ear. "My son; how is it that after all this time you still do not know me as well as you should? Do you seriously think we are going to stay here? Look into my eyes! Do I resemble one of this world's many mediocre delinquents to you, hmm? Do I look like someone who accepts defeat – no matter the circumstance, hmm? Please, my son. Answer truthfully - or better yet, let me answer that for you. All my life have I not provided for you everything your heart's desire, for both you and all my children? Of course I have! I have treasured all of you-my wonderful children! I gave you all riches! I gave you all protection and nurturing! I gave you all the freedom and influence to overpower all your obstacles! In fact, I brought you all up with the knowledge-the very truth that I am a man who can do anything! Despite what all those horrible journalists have been saying about me in recent times. Calling me crazy and whatnot… Saying that I will be remembered as a madman; the truth is that I will be remembered as a man who loved his family to such extremes that I was willing to destroy the entire world in order to protect you all! That is me-Domenico Armando!

"Not this crap that we are seated in right now. You know this is not me! You know I don't belong here! So how do you doubt that? How do you doubt me? How is it possible that you have suddenly lost faith in your father's unlimited abilities? I have cherished all my children since the day you were all born. And in return, why do you see fit to mock me-your father, hmm?"

D.J. also spoke in a low tone of voice: "Please forgive me father. It is not my intention. You are the best father anyone could ever have! You never yelled at us! You never cursed at us! You never struck us like all the other people's fathers out there. You provided for us in every way! We never had to take shit jobs with embarrassingly insufficient salaries working for fools in order to pay our bills and survive… unlike all those other men who call themselves fathers… who brought their children up to struggle in poverty and take the crap from society; such children being forced to grow up as misfortunate puppets and slaves to the entire world, struggling for everything – even human essentials such as food and clothing. You had the wisdom to strike it rich first before you raised a family. That is why we were so much better off for it. We were not puppets. We were leaders. We didn't have to answer to anyone! We could only thrive, with the whole world at our fingertips…!"

Domenico was so proud and pleased by his son's words-such high recognition he gave him. Domenico placed his hands gently around the sides of his son's head and kissed his two cheeks in gratitude for such high praise. "My son, if only you could understand how those words affect me right now! I feel so good hearing that from you. Thank you, my son! Thank you, indeed!" he said kissing his cheeks once again.

244

D.J. went on. "But father, what I am saying is that I am scared. I know the word 'fear' is something you are ashamed of. But as my father, I have to tell you the truth… everything we built… everything we achieved is past tense. It has been for nothing. Whatever we had cannot get us out of the mess we are in right now. It cannot extract us from this miserable hellhole we are now forced to call our home until… until they kill us!" he cried.

Domenico placed a comforting hand on his son's shoulder. "I know how you feel. But don't be afraid my son. As you know, I have always protected you in the past – and I shall continue to do so now in the present and the future! And to offset any doubts you may have… that time will come… right about now!" he chuckled triumphantly, no longer in whispers. He rose to his feet once again and outstretched his arms; his clenched fists now raised high above his head towards the ceiling and shouted at the grand heights of his powerful voice, for the world's camera to see: "I have awakened from my coma in record time to show you all my true powers! I have plans that will shock the world! Domenico Armando will return you idiots! You hear me? Domenico Armando will make a comeback! So you had better all get ready! Because I am going to make you all shake at the sound of my voice! I am going to make you all tremble at the very sight of me! I am going to cause an epidemic of disasters and catastrophes such as you won't believe, for all of you out there, in this dreary existence you call a world, you pack of fools!"

D.J. had no time to display utter surprise and shock at his father's dramatic display before the cameras and hidden microphones planted inside their cell. At that moment a guard appeared before the door to their confinement. He held a set of keys. He placed one key inside the door's lock. He turned the key and opened the door to the cell.

Domenico leaped towards him. The guard quickly filled him in on the latest developments.

Domenico turned to his son, walked towards him again and smiled: "Let us go, my wonderful son. Let us return to the world and show them all how it's done!"

D.J. felt his legs frozen; he was utterly bewitched by what he saw. He was cast in a spell like no human being had ever experienced before. He could not believe his eyes right now. He could not comprehend what he was seeing. He surely thought he and his father were certified dead men, but now it came to pass – that in fact the truth was an entire different reality altogether.

D.J. recovered from his temporary spell and suddenly laughed as well as the guard had shown them the way out of their cell – to a much unexpected freedom – unanticipated by him, anyway.

Domenico placed his arm around his son's shoulder and hinted: "It's all right. It's not a dream, my son. This is real! This is a true testament to your father's supremacy! Let me show you the way to freedom. Let me show you how to defeat all the so-called authorities in this world! Come on!" he said as he ushered his son outside the prison door and into the corridor to the doors of freedom.

D.J. was still experiencing more shocks by what he witnessed on his way out, walking alongside his father through the corridor. He saw a long line of dead bodies sprawled to one side of the long hallway.

Domenico smiled as he followed the guard to the gates of freedom, embracing his right arm around his son's shoulder. "These dead people are all the guards removed from the picture in order to secure our grand departure from these dreary premises! They were struck down at this early hour once word was received that Robert Stewart had left the building with his police partner John McCallum in order to preside over an important meeting with the director of the FBI, who also entered the city to congratulate our aspiring friend Robert Stewart's success in supposedly bringing me to my death! But what a surprise Captain Stewart will get when he returns and finds that all the guards who were assigned to my watch, who belonged to him, has been eliminated. All two dozen of them! You see, what Stewart did not know was that out of all the guards watching me, every second one of them was on my payroll from the very beginning. And that was how they were able to overpower the remainder of them so easily! They arranged for an untraceable vehicle to be waiting for us outside to take us to our private plane. We will disappear forever, my son. I will only reappear on the eve of my master plans for the good people of this country! Yes. I cannot wait to get them all!

"Don't they realise by now how dreary and boring the world would become without Domenico Armando around to spice things up! How does the world put up with such idiots? You tell me, my son - if anyone can answer that question. Within one hour Robert Stewart will know that there is not one prison house facility on this entire earth strong enough to hold Domenico Armando in it! And once he sees the deaths of all his precious prison guards here, with their names written in their own blood onto the wall with the finger of Domenico Armando – the entire world will also know that I am unstoppable! I WILL NEVER BE DEFEATED, NEVER. NEVER!" he chuckled, another of his favourite clichés, until he and his son were shown to their awaiting vehicle outside, which instantly transported them to freedom into the land of ANONYMITY!

246

BOOK 13

CHAPTER 24

Robert Stewart vowed Domenico Armando's Reign Of Terror would end. The enemy was not going to win this time. His days of terrorising the people in this world and vanishing each and every time as the Chameleon would cease.

Robert knew Domenico was now a man in great turmoil. His freedom was snatched from him without warning. He was a man on the run from every authority in the United States, including many other countries' armies all searching for him. Domenico was now angry and desperate. And his desperation was going to be his downfall. For the first time in his life he was going to slip up. And when that day happened, Robert planned to be there! Robert swore to himself that he was going to be the death of that public menace number one. Whatever it took... In whatever measure he had to incorporate in order to accomplish that great feat... And in whatever time frame required! He would turn this world upside down-inside out if necessary. Robert would never stop hunting him down until Domenico was found and his demise was forced henceforth - for good this time – and immutably.

Robert undertook many steps; he went to great lengths to see his goal reach fruition. He had every global authority out looking for Domenico; covering all his known hangouts and territories – both local and abroad. The United States President had every local, state and federal police and government power assigned to the Armando manhunt! Even the country's Army, Navy and Air Force units were instructed to have its people combing the entire nation and others, absolutely deployed on the enemy's lookout. Every intelligence component available was being utilised. And other countries' governments were alerted to coordinate the very same determined actions on their ends – should the enemy have fled to any one of their countries abroad in the meantime.

The hunt for the madman Chess Player became worldwide news. His capture was labelled: TOP PRIORITY. But in the meantime, pending his apprehension and arrest, the death toll kept rising.

Domenico's political power was shattered once word broke out in inner government departmental walls that he was the Chess Player. Domenico's political links such as Ron Bishop resigned their political posts and dived underground for cover in fear that their sponsor was the mass murdering monster who masterminded the worst atrocities in history, equal to Hitler's Holocaust.

Forty-eight hours later, Senator Ron Bishop was located inside his New York mansion in Queens. Police cordoned his main room where he was found tied and gagged onto his bed, infested with deadly arachnids.

Forensics officers wearing protective clothing had fumigated the room the Senator was found inside of the deadly spiders. The police then collected the dead man's stung-ridden corpse for analysis, prior its final delivery to the city's mortuary.

The coroner's autopsy report confirmed that Senator Ron Bishop had died after being attacked and poisoned by a swarm of black widow spiders, planted inside his bedroom the night before.

Following his lack of inclination and persistence to continue in his new employer's bidding, Bruno Santucci's dead body was found by police in Long Island, shot in the head three times, his body was dumped in the open street in the dead quiet of the night.

The dead body of Don Santucci was also found in a hideout in Brooklyn. He was killed in his bedroom with a local prostitute, massacred to death in a riddle of machine gun bullets.

In that same period, following the failure of his test to assassinate Robert Stewart, having cowered from proceeding in the entire order altogether, Colin McMurphy and his lawyer mistress, Samantha Emery, were found shot dead in a Brooklyn hotel to which they had been frequenting recently following a secret romantic liaison together.

In conclusion to his investigation, Robert Stewart understood that Domenico Armando was also responsible for the double murder of his son-in-law and his mistress.

In one fell swoop, a National Mafia Bloody War was ended with the deaths of all the country's Family Chiefs and their heirs and their kinsfolk in bloody fashion, by snipers being sent countrywide to target all of the entire Mafioso leaders in all different sectors of the nation and all at the same time. The Mob Bosses were killed in their houses, in hotel rooms and inside their office buildings with machine guns and bombs - all 57 of them, all dead.

Following his investigation into the mass slaughters, Robert Stewart again concluded that Domenico Armando was behind the exercising of his bloody wrath, then targeted against the growing disloyalty of the national underworld commission; their bloodlines now completely deceased.

The final of the murders was that instant when a bomb was delivered to the Washington home of SIA Boss, Chief Lloyd McKenzie, thrown into his local state's house via a passing car - claiming his life together with his wife, and that of Brock Stevens, at visit to his residence at that time. And, further ending Chief Lloyd McKenzie's secret reign to claim power as The Boss in the Power Game, leaving Domenico Armando as the sole remaining identified-public competitor!

Furthermore, Robert Stewart ascertained Domenico Armando's blueprint in the triple homicide – and now, the active search party continued its fervent efforts for Domenico Armando and his mass murdering co-conspirators.

And following that period, no more underworld strife was reported for a record 10 weeks straight. The police and many international governments combined, operating in a united front during the manhunt, all affected by the notorious Chess Player and his mass murderous conspiracies, had accepted this somewhat reprieve as little, if any serenity for what was still at stake – and at much risk for their countries' people in the future. The threat of many more masses of lives to be lost at some point by the very existence of such a bitter enemy was a grave concern. He was still circulating the streets freely to re-enter their countries at some point unknown. The Chess Player was still out there somewhere; scheming and plotting meanwhile his further plans and agenda! And it was an absolute certainty that their number one sworn target, the homicidal maniac he was, would - without warning; show himself to the world, only on the eve of his next sinister and diabolical plans for mass reprisals. He would begin his insane acts in the country that he first swore to attack in solemn vengeance: The United States of America.

And Robert Stewart knew that was only the beginning. If they did not find their enemy first before he planned to reappear into the country to personally instruct the go-ahead to his next acts of widespread carnages, then it could be too late to stop the countless masses of further lives their target vowed to be claimed as a result of his unequalled wrath!

At that very moment, the international authorities had declared a full-scale 'bugging war' on the entire global underworld; all their hangouts: their homes, their cars, their businesses – even the local churches they attended in each country were ordered scrutinized. In an attempt to cover every lead, and acquire every piece of information via listening in on the Mafia Bosses' secret conferences, until the Armando compatriots revealed the precise whereabouts to their target. And they uncovered where their number one enemy was hidden! It was at that very moment the Chess Player was 'marked for termination!'

Within four weeks, an international crime stopping taskforce led by Robert Stewart intercepted a foreign syndicate secret underworld meeting in a secluded villa in Rome, Italy - hosted by the Armando family's Kingpin, Boss of Bosses, Domenico Armando, of all the foreign Mafia syndicate leaders owing allegiance to the Chess Player family. Vowing revenge against all elements that crippled their American power holds. Including the proper authorities' police surveillance agents intercepted. The international underworld had at that very moment placed a hefty bounty on the heads of six American government officials, one New York judge and Robert Stewart - All of whom were the actual participants in their crucifixion!

Domenico had included his two sons Tom and D.J., and his daughter Monica for the meeting, bringing with him his Counsellor Rex Higgins for assistance with his two primary enforcers, Kong and Rowan Castalone.

Global bosses from areas such as Australia, the Bolermo family from Sicily and associates from Japan, China, Colombia and Mexico were in attendance to adhere to their host, Domenico Armando - all his foreign allies whom participated in his former 'Power Project' – to secure their United States operations.

Upon Robert Stewart leading the army of taskforce officials inside the spotted secret meeting place, heading an multinational arrest, Mob representatives' bodyguards raised concealed weapons from inside their attire to open fire, but were immediately cut down in a barrage of gunfire that immediately erupted by retaliating taskforce police. Whom such cavalry opened fire immediately on the syndicate leaders and their cohort men at that same time as two officers physically forced Robert Stewart onto the ground out of the line of fire, before Robert Stewart concluded reading them all their official arrest orders!

That - at such time - resulted in not only the absolute removal of the Armando family, but also at such time the complete and total wipe out of all its global terror-driven links and support systems and followers!

Four days before the New Year of 1990 emerged, Robert Stewart and his government cohorts tracked the Chess Player's secret island fortress in the Caribbean – through files confiscated following the government raid on the Mafia in Rome, Italy. The proper authorities instantly overpowered the network of guards stationed inside the heavily secure compound in a bloody gunfire battle.

The government operatives located the Late Domenico Armando's various torture chambers he used to torment his prisoners inside. The government men soon located his hidden files and uncovered the Chess Player's entire global network operations he controlled from the foreign fortress in the Caribbean.

Before the day ended, the taskforce police took possession of the extensive secret files inside labelled: 'The Revenge Project'. That contained a shocking number of targets with pointers in the form of large asterisks aside names and large groups of people to be claimed. Furthermore, they dismantled and smashed the Mob's entire communications network of global operations – and ordered the remainder of their people, scattered across the entire United States to move in on the rest of the Late Dead Chess Player's yet existing personnel.

The government agents scouring the waterfront docks and the commercial and private airport terminals of the fifty U.S. States targeted for attack, had discreetly followed the henchmen carrying concealed explosives to various destinations across the entire nation's perimeters; for final delivery to numerous police stations throughout, and the Armando Family Concert Hall, also, the Armando Family Private Hospital in New York.

The henchmen were all dressed as tradespeople and maintenance men with falsified credentials in the form of plumbers, electricians, carpenters, cleaners or building inspectors; also with manufactured reasons for their impromptu arrivals to such vast number of establishments.

The Chess Player was quite specific in his previous instructions to his people. They would carefully plant the bombs early and have them all detonate by remote control in each state at exactly the same time – all synchronised; only minutes before the New Year arrived, New York time.

At the exact moment the hundreds of total goons entered the premises', the police made their move. They shoved them to one side, frisked them, confiscated their heavy bags armed with a staggering number of powerful explosives-weapons of mass destruction, then arrested the underworld perpetrators across the entire country - before they had a chance to plant their bombs in the multitudinous targeted buildings set to go off, on New Year's Eve. In only four days' time!

The Chess Player had planned one spectacular Doomsday Operation for the United States of America, to take place in the final hour of 1989, on New Year's Eve. The Chess Player and his plans – had not lived to see that evening.

It was only two days later when Robert Stewart returned to his family in Brooklyn. Robert could not wait to see his wife, his children and his entire family and inform them of the news that the danger was over. The police guards could be removed from them.

For Robert had saved everyone's life in the state of New York, and the country as a whole, that New Year; and his family's lives were now saved as well. It was in fact an after Christmas Miracle in itself!

MADNESS TAKES ITS TOLL

BOOK 1

CHAPTER 1

Robert Stewart's mind was on fire. His piercing eyes stared at the masses of blood-soaked bodies inside his prison lockup facility at the 25th Division Precinct Station House of Brooklyn, New York.

The police cordoned the entire area. The coroner examined the two-dozen dead corpses. They were all killed with knives to the throat, mixed with several gunshots to the head and body. It was a mockery of justice like no other. The devil in hell was locked up inside such a facility only but some hours ago. Now he vanished into thin air, like some sadistic magician. He disappeared without a trace, so incredibly. And he took his bloodline with him; his evil heir apparent son to his much criminal throne. No trace of either one of them.

Robert's mind still smoked in terror. Such a thing had never happened like this before. No one could ever escape from such a secure prison facility. No one would ever have the ambition, wit or resources to pull off what was indeed pulled off this horrid evening! It was unimaginable! It was cruel beyond words. It was sick! It was a true disaster!

Robert was so angry he remained mute for some time. He knew his emotions would eventually take over again, and he would shout bloody murder from the top of his lungs at the gory sight of all this. The injustice! The unfairness! The bloody cruel hoax of it all! It was pure unimaginable! What the hell sort of an enemy was this, who could surprise them all in such a way? What sort of a creature was this bastard who could astonish them all with such a terrible turn of events? Not only had he escaped from their custody, but he left another carnage of dead bodies behind! This man was beyond anything the world had faced before. No criminal mastermind, no

252

mobster or Nazi figure had managed to accomplish what this irredeemably evil monster had only managed to finagle some hours before!

It was unthinkable! Robert watched the coroner's officers place body after body, corpse after corpse inside one body bag after the other. They lifted each dead man onto a gurney and wheeled him out, to deliver to the local morgue! What a sight! It was the picture of something so horrendous it would even drive a perfect angel into insanity!

But what drove Robert even more crazy right this very moment, was that just as they were grieving the repercussions to all of this, the loss of good officers of the law, mixed with their loss to one of the most wanted men on earth at present; Robert at the same time knew that their enemy was laughing at them right now. That son of a bitch was most surely laughing, gloating and celebrating such a spectacular victory this horrible day!

The enemy managed to escape their custody so expertly, so astonishingly, with indescribable cunning, never witnessed before. He escaped without leaving one lead, not one solid clue to his whereabouts! He vacated a very secure, much guarded and bug-and-camera-recorded jail cell, leaving no trace to his location! Where did he disappear to? Any place on earth was the answer! Only God knows! It was utterly unspeakable!

Robert could sense his enemy's demeanour right now! He knew that walking atrocity was thinking of him. His thoughts, as if telepathic, were reaching him somehow, taunting him, attempting to mock him and his side of the law, serving the proverbial, common good!

The enemy was surely trying to drive him crazy with such thoughts at this very moment! He was laughing at the police! He was laughing at the government! He was surely laughing at their so-called steel bars and concrete walls they called a jail. Domenico Armando, as if portraying himself as some sort of evil spirit, something inhuman; which could even float through walls was surely thinking very foul and offensive thoughts at this moment! He was chuckling very diabolical comments against them and much in favour of himself and his spectacular triumph and victory this day.

And undeniably it was a victory! Domenico Armando had pulled off what no one else had been able to do in the history of criminality! No mobster, no Nazi had ever escaped prison like this! NEVER! Only Domenico had managed to accomplish it, the impossible. So of course he would be laughing! Of course he would be celebrating! And of course he would most certainly continue planning his next carnage and series of mass carnages for the world which would make this spectacle of deaths here this evening resemble a simple carnival of horrors in comparison!

Robert's fury at present was only compounded furthermore, because anyone who could provide him with information as to the location of their enemy had also disappeared with him. All the police, all the corrupt police guards, obviously on Armando's payroll had too vanished! There was no one to question!

Robert ordered a thorough ballistics report to be made out on all the dead bodies. The preliminary autopsy report only confirmed Robert's suspicions. That the bullets taken out from the deceased corpses and examined matched those fired from a police standard-issue revolver! It was police who killed police. It was corrupt officers of the law who massacred and slaughtered those honest rivals of theirs, only, but to secure the freedom of the one man who they vowed to swear allegiance to: the devil of all devils: Domenico Armando!

Even the henchman arrested with Domenico Junior, who planned to orchestrate a hit on all the Stewarts, was found too vacated from his cell. Domenico covered all bases. He left no stone unturned! No remote solid clue behind for anyone to use in order to pinpoint his whereabouts right now!

Robert only needed one man left behind. Robert would have interrogated the hell out of that culprit. He would have redefined the word, third degree in his line of questioning to be delivered to such a thug. He would have put him through hell. He would have made his life miserable! He would have broken every law he swore to defend in his much anticipated efforts to obtain the information that would surely assist him in tracking down Domenico Armando and ending it right then and there, in the only course of action, the only solution deemed appropriate right now!

Robert needed just one person on Armando's payroll to have remained behind. But it was not to eventuate! Every Armando strong-arm and paid thug had vanished right along with their master. And all that was left behind was a carnage of dead bodies throughout the entire police station in order to secure such a nefarious release of this irredeemably evil criminal.

Robert could only wish, much painfully, for circumstances to have resulted in something to the contrary! He only could dream that there was someone he could punish right now and royally so, in order to extract every piece of information he needed concerning the presence of this hideous devil who was their enemy. And once he found this heinous and deadly beast, Robert would not be considering locking him up next time! No! Robert was a man who never repeated a failed course of action! That was for sure. No! This time Robert would end it in the manner it should have been ended long ago! Robert's mind smoked with hideous visions of killing Armando with his gun, with his bare hands and with his much justified rage, anger and fury he felt at this very moment! Because where Domenico Armando was concerned, nothing else would work!

Domenico was not any common criminal. This son of a bitch was extraordinary to the fiercest of extremes. He was one of a kind! He was ferocious! He was sly! He was beyond courts of law! But in Robert's mind and his much-darkened heart right now, Domenico was not beyond a bullet or a bomb or his strong hands planted firmly across his neck and squeezing so hard that Domenico would certainly not be able to continue breathing for long – and he surely would soon die thereafter! That is what Robert wanted to do to him right now! He wanted to find him! He wanted to kill him! There was no other choice! That bastard had to die! Prison could not stop him! Concrete walls and steel bars could not even slow him down! No! Only a bullet, a bomb or Robert's very firm grasp along his neck and squeezing and breaking it was the only logical solution to ridding the world of this monster, this maniac, this horribly evil devil, who was STRAIGHT OUT OF HELL!

Robert's mind was only further preoccupied by the repercussions in all this. With all his enemies vanished from sight, blending back into the world's fold and mixing into the earth's circulation had really only spelled disaster for both him and his family right now! They were all in extreme danger! After all, Domenico's now confirmed lunatic son had only recently plotted to kill both him and his entire family. And D.J. and the henchman he commanded to perform the diabolical hits were also on the loose with Domenico himself. This meant big trouble for all of them! All the Stewart family with society as a whole were in terrible danger at this very moment!

Robert had to work on his chessman strategy to not only flush the enemy out from hiding but at the same time he had to figure out a way to also protect his family, himself, his friends and society holistically who were all facing death at any moment as they now lived and breathed!

Robert had to distract his mind from his thoughts of haze and fog, the product of his fury right now, and he had to come up with a solution to save his family first and foremost before he could attempt to continue his search for Domenico himself: this time to not only locate him, but to accomplish, once and for all, the only viable solution that meant freedom for himself, his family and the entire world. That was: killing Domenico! It was the only way! Nothing else would work! No other recourse! Because the system stank! The law was pathetically weak against people as Domenico. Robert was now forced to concede that! Domenico could not be brought to justice, because the Justice System in America was ineffective against him! This bloodbath inside this so-called secure prison facility only confirmed that! Robert was a police officer! He had a badge and a gun! He had to use that gun now to defend himself and everyone who was at risk from this enemy's life merely remaining a part of their society, currently! Robert had to end it right now! It was the only forgone conclusion! It was the only choice! That would be justice! That would be justifiable homicide! No one would question it! Even the most rotten scoundrel of judges would have to congratulate and celebrate such a result.

If such a judge had anything between his ears worth salvaging, no man could possibly be punished or questioned for ending the life of this despicable creature, and inhumane beast known as Domenico Armando!

Robert returned to his station house office with his police partner John McCallum, his SIA Boss Chief Lloyd McKenzie and the middle-aged, grey-haired, stern-faced FBI director, all present with him right this very moment.

First thing was first. Robert spoke to his SIA superior concerning the safety of his family. McKenzie assured him: "Your family are safely hiding in the secure SIA safe house in the state. They are under constant guard twenty-four hours of the day. I have increased the manpower of guards around them. Even your parents, your brother and his wife, your sister are stationed safely together in that secret location with your wife and children. Armando will not find them. I can promise you that!"

Robert snapped: "That's not enough!"

McKenzie looked confused. "What do you mean old boy? What more do you think needs to be done?"

Robert demanded: "It does not matter where they are hidden. As long as Armando knows they are hiding, he will eventually find them!"

McKenzie's white-skinned very pale English complexion suddenly became purple in bemusement. "I don't follow you Robert. What do you mean by this?"

Robert insisted: "The only way to protect them is if Domenico no longer thinks we are around to kill!"

McKenzie was shocked as all the others present inside the room with them. The SIA Boss questioned Robert further: "What the devil does that mean? What do you have in mind?"

Robert stated plain and simply: "I'm going to need your help to make it all appear as if my family and I have resulted in some unexplained, sudden, tragic, fatal accident!"

McKenzie stuttered, "You don't mean what I think you mean?"

Robert nodded, reading his thoughts now much in sink with his own. "That is exactly what I'm talking about! Domenico cannot attack what he does not know is there! I am going to orchestrate it so that by this time tomorrow the whole world, including Domenico Armando will believe that the entire Stewart family has deceased! And I need the SIA to spare a decoy plane for me!"

McKenzie would not dare argue with such a brilliant plan. "You mean you want two planes?"

Robert nodded. "Yes. One of them will be thought to carry my family on it. It will be rigged to explode by remote control at 20,000 feet. Your pilot will be groomed when to bail out by parachute and set the bomb to explode the plane to pieces. And I want you to use your connections with the media to make everyone believe that my entire family with me were on that plane when it exploded. Make it look like a sabotage. Not an accident. I want to throw Domenico off-balance. I want him to start second-guessing his own people. He will wonder who killed me, perhaps someone employed by him. It'll confuse and baffle him some…"

"And the second plane?" McKenzie interrupted.

Robert replied, "The second plane will be the real plane that takes my family safely out of the country for now!"

"And what about you?" McKenzie asked curiously, yet concerned.

"I'm going to remain behind," Robert stated. "I'm going to work undercover to find Domenico and put an end to him once and for all! And I'm going to need more supplies from you in order to do it!"

McKenzie asked with fear now more than curiosity. "And what might that be?"

Robert said, "I'm going to need some human paint. You know, face and body black make-up, a black wig and fake identification and credentials matching that of a professional psychiatrist!"

McKenzie laughed as if it were some joke. He quickly regained his icy cold demeanour, but with added warmth in his eyes as he insisted, "What the devil are you planning Robert?"

Robert quickly responded. "By what happened here tonight, every person who could help us locate Armando and his son has been either killed or removed from the picture with Domenico. So after tomorrow when that plane blows up and the entire world thinks that I and my whole family are dead, I am going to assume the identity of a made-up doctor with falsified credentials; a psychiatrist, and then I am going to use that in order to infiltrate the Armando camp, until we can finally pinpoint Domenico's exact hiding place and then I'm going to get him, my way!"

McKenzie stated, "How?"

Robert kept him in suspense no longer. "I am going to become Annemarie Armando's newly-appointed psychiatrist. You see, wherever Domenico is, you can bet your last penny that he has his people watching over his family in New York and constantly reporting back to him. So once they report that I am helping his daughter, this may open doors to an invitation into his inner sanctums. And who knows, I may even get to shake hands with the devil himself. And when I am shaking his hand that is the golden opportunity I will have to do this world a long-awaited favour. That McKenzie is when Domenico's days on this earth will come to a screeching halt. I will make sure he will never hurt anyone ever again! Are we all in agreement?" Robert asked, as he glanced to all the faces in the room.

McKenzie was the first to nod his head, followed by the same simultaneous gestures delivered by his police partner John and the FBI director all present and willing co-conspirators in the grand plot to smoke out the devil himself!

Robert explained further. "This plan will enable me to kill two birds with one stone! Through my disguise I will be able to help Annemarie at the same time as using that situation to bring me face to face with Domenico himself, finally; Once and for all!"

They all nodded in agreement. It was the perfect plan. And hence, complimented Robert's superior skills, his creativity, if not, all-out genius in coming up with such a spectacularly perfect plan, which in their minds, had the possibility and high probability of succeeding if carried out carefully!

The next evening Robert Stewart's plan was put into effect with perfect timing and success. Once reaching 20,000 feet the United States of America was shocked by a spectacle of the decoy plane exploding to smithereens. A spectacle of fire, smoke, ash and flames consumed the night sky, witnessed by many.

Within the hour, the entire world was informed that America's heroic Master Detective Captain Robert Stewart had died by that bomb blast inside that plane. His entire family were also reported dead with him.

The deaths sent shock waves throughout the globe. The citizens in America, Robert's greatest fans mourned and grieved the loss terribly.

Robert was soon planted inside a Brooklyn top secret SIA safe house with his SIA superior once he kissed his whole family goodbye, and they were all driven to the Borough's private airstrip and taken, also under assumed identities safely onto another plane surreptitiously into the safety of another territory and country entirely.

Robert now was free to move onto the next phase of his plan; the burden of not worrying about his family being in danger any longer helped him think more clearly of his next equally-as-important goal at present: finding Domenico.

McKenzie supplied him with his disguise as requested. And Robert went into another room with a very large mirror so he could expertly cover his entire face and body into the disguise of a black man; gluing his black wig onto his head; given credentials, that of a psychiatrist assuming the name Frank Northgate. It was to become his perfect alias whilst undergoing his undercover assignment against the Armandos; using such falsified psychiatric qualifications for cover.

Once wearing his disguise, abandoning all his old habits, mannerisms and clothing, and replacing them with his new title, Robert came out from his locked room and showed himself proudly to his superior.

McKenzie was indeed overwhelmed in shock, much proud himself. If he had not known of the plan, he certainly would never have recognised Robert. No one would have. He indeed wished to compliment him. "Well, you certainly have earned yourself the reputation of Master of Disguise, my good man, Robert. This is incredible. No one would ever be able to tell it is really you. Not even the canny eye of our very cunning and dangerous enemy himself!"

Robert wanted to test his own skills even further when he disguised his voice perfectly. Making his speech sound deeper, more unrecognisable to his true identity as he spoke the words: "Are you sure about that?" testing his boss's reaction.

McKenzie broke out in laughter, which he usually had never done before as a man born with a peculiar strait-laced cold English descent. But McKenzie could not help himself. He was amused beyond words. And he could not hold back from dishing out further compliments to his best operative. "My goodness. Well done, man. Well done, indeed. You have honed your skill for disguise in every way imaginable. It is as if you have been rehearsing the role for months, maybe even years. No one could ever have performed such an acting role so quickly. I love it. Domenico will never be able to recognise that it is really you!"

Robert laughed himself, but tried not to blush at the compliments; although seeing his superior succumb to laughter at his unique performance indeed made him feel good for the first time in a very long time now. It distracted his mind some from the real horrible reality they faced. But just as his mind recalled the hideous thoughts of that real world truth, his feel-good state had suddenly diminished – as he began to understand the real gist of what he was to embark upon from this moment forward. It was most certainly no laughing matter! It was a very serious drastic measure that would have equally great implications connected to it! That was unmistakable. Once that fact sunk in, Robert clenched and unclenched his jaw several times in concern, mixed with emotions of despondency. His family had just departed only moments ago tonight, and he already missed them. He knew in his mind that he must accomplish his task rapidly, but with fine-tuned precision much targeted for success if he was ever to be reunited with his family again as normal, inside their New York home.

Robert knew there was no room for any slip ups in this one. Because failure meant that both he and his family's lives would pay the ultimate price as a result. In himself, he would never let that happen! He vowed that Domenico was his man to the death! He vowed Domenico would not survive this one! No! He simply could not! The stakes were too high! But the risks right now were even higher. Though Robert knew he had no choice! There was no turning back from the course of events fate and destiny had bestowed upon him!

Robert Stewart's train of thought was suddenly distracted when his boss's cellular phone had rung. McKenzie quickly answered it. It was SIA operative Brock Stevens who had some rather distressing, if not very surprising news to report, but disturbing nonetheless.

McKenzie's face became extremely pale all of a sudden. His speech was slurred. The conversation was brief. Robert eyed him curiously as to the reason for his sudden droopy and despondent demeanour.

As soon as he ended the call, his hands began to tremble and he accidentally dropped his portable phone onto the tile floor. Robert was puzzled. He quickly urged him on to tell him exactly what had happened.

McKenzie took some time to regain his ability to speak. He was still very shaken up by the news bulletin his second top operative had just directed to him from his close proximity within the city limits, much aware of their secret plans.

McKenzie coughed. He took several extra deep breaths in order to compose himself and then he stated to the also panic-struck Robert, who was concerned whether anything may have happened which could place even a slight damper on his plans and progress to cast them successfully forward at this point in time.

But what McKenzie had to say was indeed the very news Robert suspected. It was the very tragedy he did not want to hear, which would surely put their plans against Domenico Armando to a crushing standstill – if not, all-round defeat!

Robert insisted: "Tell me, man. Come on, spit it out!"

McKenzie stated: "I've got the most horrible news to report. There's been a tragic death at the Armando house. You won't believe who died. We must abort our plans. We must instead prepare to run for cover. Once Domenico hears about this there will be a rage such as the world has never seen before. We are all in big trouble! We are all dead! Not just me and you... but... but the entire world is going to suffer because of what has happened... We must think how to get out of this mess. This tragedy I'm afraid is far greater than any of us could ever imagine! It is far bigger than any one power can handle! As soon as Domenico hears about this, THE WORLD AS WE KNOW IT WILL NEVER BE THE SAME AGAIN...!"

BOOK 2

CHAPTER 2

Domenico Armando had murder and genocide imbedded into his heart, his soul and his mind as he constructed his extremely large DEATH LIST. His list comprised of all his considered WORLD OF BITTER ENEMIES. And he vowed that not one of them would survive the aftermath to his bitter onslaught against them all!

Domenico had returned quickly and much undetected to his secret underground Caribbean Island hideout. A palace of a large compound it was. He returned with his son D.J. and all his henchmen who aided and abetted him following his spectacular prison breakout only hours before. He escaped Robert's custody leaving a trail of dead bodies behind.

Domenico kept his celebrations to that effect brief. Now he went straight to the business at hand inside his private den, plotting and planning with just his Counsellor Rex Higgins by his side.

Domenico sat behind his huge wooden desk onto his swivel leather armchair. His face was buried in a ream of paperwork. The journal he filed was titled, 'The Revenge Project'. And the writings on it contained individual names and large groups of them he planned to target in his wholesale massacre scheme; names compiled of people he planned to target in areas all over the world. But his first order of business was to attack the country that started their war against him: the United States of America!

It was the good old USA in Domenico's mind who destroyed his world as he once knew it. And the rest of the world would have to succumb to his bitter payback plan as a consequence for such actions against him.

Domenico felt victorious right now. He accomplished the impossible. Escaping from a supposed secure prison facility and returning back to freedom once again. But he quickly considered his success in such a grand scheme of things as really only bitter-sweet; because he escaped one prison only to return to another. Yes. His island compound was made up to resemble the surroundings fit for a King and Queen. But he was still not free to come and go as he pleased. And for that he wanted sweet revenge! He wanted all his world of enemies to be destroyed so that he could one day resume his life as he once knew it inside his fabulous home in New York with the rest of his family.

Domenico would not rest until that day happened! And as he wrote his numerous list of targets himself, in his own handwriting with his counsellor by his side as his key accomplice, he could only find satisfaction with more and more masses of targets he needed little to no excuse to add their names onto it. The journal of targets marked for death was in fact a replicated large novel in size. That was how many people Domenico planned to kill from all countries across the world.

And as he jotted such names he constantly thought of his most deserving though worthy enemy at that, Robert Stewart. His thoughts scattered back and forth from his large journal to Robert. And he would think to himself: 'Yes, Robert. Are you feeling angry right now? Are you mad? Are you irritated? Because my friend your anger has only begun. I haven't even commenced my plot of vengeance against you yet! Yes. I have thrown your prison clothes into the flames and now I am wearing my expensive black silk robe as I construct the list of targets from your world to massacre to death!

'Yes, Robert Stewart! They will all be massacred! They will all die! But they will all first feel my anger and rage against them as a consequence for what you have done to me! I am going to destroy everyone in your world, Robert! And I am going to enjoy seeing you watch them crumble onto their knees and fall into their graves, one by one – and in large masses and groups. And you will not be able to do a thing about it! No! Never! You will never be able to stop me! You will never be able to slow me down! And you will never catch me!

'Because once I have destroyed all my enemies... all those people who are allies to you, meaning the entire world, minus a few... all that will be left is you and I, Robert Stewart! I am going to witness the look of defeat in your eyes! I am going to also enjoy watching you crumble to your knees. And you will finally admit that you were a complete and utter fool to ever think for one cold moment that you could win this war between us, my friend!

'Ahh, what beautiful victory that will be; I cannot wait! Yes! I cannot wait, indeed! Because you are going to pay for what you have done to my world, Stewart! You are going to suffer dearly! You are going to curse the day that you ever took up your oath as a police officer, vowing to serve any law apart from mine – and mine alone! Yes. You will see!

'You will experience a fear like never felt by any man before! You will experience isolation when I wipe out all your world of allies, friends and bloodlines! You will be all alone, Robert Stewart! You will be placed in a new world, controlled by me – and me alone. And there will be no one you could turn to for defence, or retreat or any form of comfort whatsoever; because the entire world will soon only be ruled and controlled by one man and one man alone. That is me-Domenico Armando! No one else!

'Indeed! There will not be one sole entity and individual left to pledge allegiance to you! Because they will all be wiped out. Finished! Dead! And it will be just you and me! You will become my prisoner! Then you will have no choice but to finally concede defeat and surrender your will to me! And finally you will become the one thing that I have always wanted to achieve Robert Stewart! And that is my pawn! You will finally be forced to serve me and my world. And you will do as you are told! You will do what I tell you to do! And all your strengths and all your skills and smarts will serve my world! And mine alone! And there is not a damn thing you will be able to do about it! Because in the end, your will, will become mine! I will control your mind, your thoughts and all your actions! You will have no say in anything you do or say or think! Because I-me-Domenico Armando will control you completely! You will become my servant! You will become my soldier! And indeed, you will do everything that you are told to do as everyone else in this world!

'How do you like that Robert, hmm? Can you hear me Robert? Can you hear my words ringing in your ears like bellows from a nightmare you will never awaken from? Can you sense my plans against you? Can you envisage your fate and destiny being controlled by me? Do you know you will never defeat me? Are you aware Robert of all of this? Come on, my very good friend! Give me a response! Give me a frightened reply! I want to see the look of fear in your eyes! I want to hear the sound of your voice trembling in my ears, even telepathically!

'I want to sense it! I want to hear and see your panic-stricken demeanour as you witness masses of deaths around you – and there is nothing you can do to stop it! The murders will never cease! The screams and shouts around you will never stop! You will collapse from fright! You will sink to your weakened knees as you realise just how powerless you truly are against me! And your mind will implode as you come to your senses finally to understand what a grave mistake it was to ever challenge the unbeatable and indestructible all-powerful genius that is Domenico Armando! You will see, Robert. But you will witness it all when it is much too late! And then you will be forced into the new world controlled by your new master, that is me – and only me alone! Yes. You will not be able to do a thing about it, just as your foolish allies will not be able to do a thing about it, but scream and suffer and eventually fall dead into their graves one by one and in masses of groups together.

'Yes. Thousands and thousands, tens and hundreds of thousands will be wiped out… and millions and millions more! That is the price you will pay Robert Stewart for ever tempting fate and trying my patience one too many times! I will never stop with you! I will never cease in my attacks against you! I will enjoy tormenting you until the day you crack as well! I want to see you crack! I want to see you beg for a mercy to which I will never give you! You will never have a moment's rest! You will never experience peace of mind ever again!

'Indeed. Because everyone in your world who otherwise serves you and provides you with comfort will be removed! And from that moment on, your life as you know it will transform into an unending misery such as your imagination could never ascertain or concede, but only when it is all too late. So, prepare for the end of your life, Robert Stewart! Because very soon the old Robert Stewart will be dead! And a new better Robert Stewart will be born! One who is more obedient. A man who will never be foolish enough to think he could ever fight me! No! No! No! Because you will transform finally into something which you never thought possible! But I will make it happen! Yes, indeed! I will control every thought, every action and every part of your destiny, Robert Stewart! So enjoy yourself with your lovely wife for the little time you have left! Because very shortly all your friends, all your family, all your colleagues will be struck down by my bitter wrath. And they will all fall into their graves, dead! And when that happens, a new world will be born and the new Robert Stewart will be forced to emerge to serve the only man you should have voluntarily surrendered your will to, from the very beginning. And that is ME, Robert Stewart - and only me!'

Domenico Armando was on a momentous high via the product of his thoughts and vivid dreams right now. He planned to destroy the entire world's population, but leaving only all those who were his allies and blood, with Robert Stewart!

Domenico swore vengeance against Robert Stewart, but unlike all his other targets, he only wished to dish out his bitter revenge on Robert in a different way as he continued the product of his powerful mind camp: 'Yes, Stewart. You are a special enemy! You see, you will not get the privilege of dying! No! No! No! That would be too easy! That would be letting you off the hook far too simply! But instead what I have in mind for you is an ultimate victory for me, which will fulfil my need for emotional satisfaction that your death quite simply could never provide me with! For what irony it will be, when you realise that you will be groomed to serve my world finally – the very world you always swore to destroy! Yes. That would serve me with the appropriate revenge where you are concerned Robert Stewart. That and nothing else will suffice where you are concerned! You will see! But first I am going to turn your world upside down! I am going to toy with you! I am going to weaken you both mentally and physically. Then once your will is completely broken and shattered into hell itself, your conditioning and transformation into my world will be made all the more simpler and effective! Yes. I cannot wait for it all to unfold!

'So right now, I must focus on my plans on all those in this world you swore to defend. I must destroy everyone who also swore allegiance to you! And once you witness these mass slayings and come to realise just how powerless you really are against the almighty King Master Domenico Armando, then you will be weakened. And finally, you will become mine! So let me finish my Death List! Let me put all my targets in line like ducks in a row. And let me finalise my plans for their complete and utter annihilation and total wipe out, then you and I will meet face to face once again Robert Stewart. But we will meet under very different circumstances! Hostile, indeed, it will be! But once you realise you have nowhere else to turn, then I will possess your mind and your will – and you will become what I have always wanted you to become! My soldier! A killing machine which only serves me and my world! No more police. No more government or foreign army to me! They will all be gone! Because in the end, it will be just you and me and my world! Ahh, what a beautiful plan! What a poetic thought! What sweet, sweet revenge it will be! Oh, I cannot wait! Very soon, my friend! Very soon we will meet again!'

Domenico Armando had soon relished and much savoured the notion in finalising his extensive Death List. All his targets were jotted down; and his plans for their deaths by bombings, by machine guns and small planes and helicopters dropping mustard gas on towns, on villages, cities, states and countries at an entirety around the world was now heading completion. All his men and soldiers he assigned for the tasks to do away with his World of Bitter Enemies were also wrapped up. His thorough plans and plots for mass executions of his victims were headed for a monumental completion.

Domenico now sat back in his chair, tilting his head against the wall behind him with a cigarette in one hand and a glass of his favourite alcoholic beverage, cognac in the other contemplating the grand success of his work. The hard laborious task of his mass reprisals was now complete. And soon he planned to put such a hideous scheme into practice. And once it was, he vowed: "The world will not believe it even when they witness it! The mass executions of the entire world which serves against me will be dumbstruck and shaken like no Nazi or Iraqi Leader could even dream of accomplishing. What glorious spectacle it will be! And once it starts, no one on this earth will be able to stop it; Fantastic; Marvellous; truly wonderful. We will remain here in this highly secure fortress of a palace, safely underground until my people give me the good news that the entire world has been wiped out, then, and only then, will I return to claim my new world onto the outside, where no one will be able to get in my way ever again! Then Robert Stewart will finally be forced here into my world, to serve me as his new master. His only master! That is a sight I cannot wait for! Yes, indeed! Victory will be mine - AT LAST! At last!" he then chuckled triumphantly.

Domenico's counsellor who was seated by his side could not help but find humour and much magic and entertainment being derived from his master's madness, his plans that would no doubt not only shock, but in fact consecutively wipe out the entire world's population as it stood right now. But at the same time, Rex Higgins was still a human being! And he could not help but become shocked himself at his master's drastic actions and complete

268

and utter insane measures he thusly conjured the plans for to soon put into practice.

Rex Higgins could not help but relay his concerns before his boss. "I cannot believe that you are planning to wipe out more than 99% of the world's population. Isn't that a bit too much, a bit excessive on the extreme side of things?"

Domenico's eyes suddenly turned to a manic episode; his temperament became much apparent, now developing a very solemn demeanour as he forwarded his head, glancing at his protégé with perhaps concern mixed with anger painted across his face as he told off his counsellor now: "What? Are you suddenly becoming soft on me? What? Are you suddenly trying to preach morality to me? What is that garbage you are spouting before me-your king?"

The counsellor lowered his eyes to the floor as he then sat across the other side of the desk facing his master. He lowered his head in submission, in order to dodge the painfully uncomfortable gaze of his boss now imposed upon him. Rex said in a soft-spoken voice, "I was just saying…"

But Domenico cut him short. "Please, Rex, don't say anything, all right. If what you say does not please me, I do not want to hear about it! Besides, I have chosen you to be my counsellor. Meaning, you are to advise and assist me in carrying out all my plans. I am not paying you to question me, all right?"

Rex Higgins nodded his head dutifully.

Domenico continued. "Good. Because no one questions me! They only follow my orders as I insist my instructions be carried out. There will be no questioning or debating anything I say or do, do you hear me?"

Rex Higgins nodded again in strict silence.

Domenico went on, "Very good, excellent. My plans will be carried out very soon. Because as long as they-those people who are opposed to me remain in this world, we will ALL remain prisoners on this island for life. Is that what you want to happen to you and to me and for our families living with us here?"

Rex only now dared to speak, "Of course not!"

Domenico ordered: "So then what makes you think that we really have any choice in the matter? Because we do not! It is either all of them or it is us! I choose us! And you?"

Rex insisted, "I also choose us!"

Domenico now smiled, easing his intimidating glance away from his key subordinate as he further spoke his mind. "Very good; we are finally in agreement here! Because I will destroy all those in this world who have destroyed me! And I will destroy the world of all those who have destroyed mine! Hence, those people comprise of EVERYONE who are not connected to me as a patron in any way, shape or form. You understand? Then it will be me and Robert alone in this, what will become a cleaner, simpler existence onto the outside, once all the heinous people who serve against us have been removed!

"And it does not matter what others say or think. What applies to others is only an exception where Domenico Armando is concerned. Regardless of what those sissy fag doctors say about my prognosis and so-called short time they think I have left in this world! I am Domenico Armando! I am tougher than everyone! I am smarter! I am made of spring steel! I will never die! Everyone in this world will see and know it, before I massacre all of them! I will beat this ridiculous illness of mine through sheer willpower. I do not need drugs or herbs or any other form of bullshit medication! I will simply cure myself through the power of Domenico Armando's positive thinking. And I am sure that keeping busy on my plans for revenge will not only lift my spirits enormously, but that alone should help diminish any form of illness raining inside of me! You follow?"

Rex Higgins now smiled, much more relaxed and entertained by his master's pure magical demeanour. He considered Domenico born to rule the world and suddenly came to the realisation how mistaken he was to even think for one split second that Domenico's plans to wipe out all his enemies from the entire world was excessive at all.

After all, these people did not see the visionary genius and charisma that he had the privilege to witness in his master Domenico. And since such people chose to side against his master, Rex clearly understood right this minute the necessity to put into effect all of his boss's plans, expertly, and successfully, if only to spare such a true royal king in to existence. And considering all the great leaders of the world in history, Rex Higgins had to admit that no one was far more superior and greater than this man he was privileged to know and serve dutifully and loyally for decades – that man was the Great Domenico Armando!

Domenico continued: "You see, you of all people should know how it enrages me very much to know that I am being judged by the very people in this world who are truly immoral, unethical, corrupt hypocrites!

"How many doctors have refused to treat me? - Many. So I had to kill them. The fuckers have taken an oath to cure the sick and not play games or prejudice pranks on anyone. But they broke their oath and solemn vow to help 'all' the sick when they refused to treat me! So naturally, they deserved to die!

"And how many doctors in this world are in fact taking advantage of their patients; cheating and stealing from them; giving them false diagnoses and incorrect medications only to line their pockets for repeat business and never curing the sick? Practically all of them! Psychiatrists manufacturing problems and false diagnoses as well so people can see them only to give them money.

"Priests causing the most heinous sexual acts behind the public's back and teaching the entire world false beliefs and religious-deceptive lies only so the church can gather its large client base – in order for such clients to donate to them large sums of money – to feed the greed of all those church workers! Those man made priests residing in those man made churches have been brainwashing the gullible in this world for centuries – and they say that I am the bad guy? Utter nonsense! I have been a saviour, a rescuer for decades to the poor and impoverished. I donated to all those who could not fend for themselves! I did more for the needy than what any hypocritical wolf in sheep's clothing could ever pretend to do! All those wolves had really only tricked the world that it cared for anyone. But instead they really took the money from the rich and kept it only to line their own pockets and do what only served them. They had no one but their own interests in mind.

"So how can I possibly be questioned by anyone in regards to my course of actions? How? I simply cannot! The whole world is corrupt, filled with hypocrites and heinous spiritual destroyers. So naturally, I am much compelled in my rightful plans of attack! I believe that all such people who are in fact damaging the world - and everyone in it - through false teachings, false beliefs and anti-spiritual laws must be condemned! They must all die! I am not the bad guy! I am the good guy! I am simply ridding the world of all those who are corrupt! If that comprises of more than 99% of the world's population, as you put it – then so be it!

"If I do not destroy them, they will simply continue to destroy the world and everyone in it, including themselves! You see what I mean?"

Rex Higgins nodded his head in total agreement.

Domenico stated: "Everyone lies! Everyone deceives! Everyone steals and kills and does all manner of perversions – so who exactly am I ridding the world of? I am simply cleaning or wiping out all those who eventually would only cause deaths in others! Whether mentally through false teachings or physically through rape and all other forms of perverse acts that such a world filled with wolves in sheep's clothing would no doubt undertake!

"And the gall of such scoundrel bastards to think or pretend that they are better than me; to pretend that they have a right to judge me makes me so angry right now! That is why it was so easy for me to prepare that large list of targets to be added to my vast plans for revenge! It came with little consideration, little debate and empathy without a shred of mercy!

"You think I am going to remain a prisoner whilst such scoundrels in this world who truly belong behind bars are walking free? No, my friend! That will not happen! All those fiendish priests and psychiatrists and corrupt politicians and so on who are taking it upon themselves to incorrectly judge me publicly are all going to pay with their miserable lives! Every lie they say will cost them dearly! I am going to rip out their fucking tongues so they can never speak another bullshit word again! I am going to make them turn in their graves in bitter agony as a price they will ALL pay for their lives much filled with shameful HYPOCRICY!

"You see, my good friend, Rex. I hate such people! I detest them beyond words! And they are all going to pay dearly for every atrocious false word and immoral action they have undertaken throughout the course of their very destructive lives!" Domenico said with renewed manic eyes; his spirit filled with absolute conviction for his words delivered at such time. His fists now clenched, waving in the air in such bitter thoughts as he insisted: "Vengeance will be mine! And all those who want to bring me to my grave will be the first to enter their own tombs! They are all going to die! And I-me-Domenico Armando is going to thrive! I will survive! I will outlive all my critics! And by the time my last bullet is fired… the last bomb is detonated… and the final poison gas is dropped from plane height below – Domenico Armando will return to the world and every single day I will walk over the graves of all those former enemies of mine – and I will celebrate their ends and destructions! And I will celebrate my immortality!"

BOOK 3

CHAPTER 3

Domenico Armando supervised the special brainwashing serum drug potion (his scientists had finished creating) being intravenously administered by injection into his next target, Bruno Santucci.

Bruno Santucci was ordered kidnapped and delivered to Domenico's secret underground Caribbean hideout only hours after he had arrived, following his grand prison escape from New York.

Bruno was quickly summoned into the highly secure compound facility wearing a blindfold. Now he was tied onto a chair inside one of the prison dungeon rooms. His blindfold was removed. He was isolated with only just Domenico's people.

Domenico witnessed the brainwashing methods imposed onto him by his special doctors. Bruno was struck by electric current into his brain and he had the five nails of his left hand removed. And following that, salt and vinegar were applied onto the open wounds as a reconditioning treatment method designed to transform the chosen soldier from weakness into strength.

Domenico always believed he was a man who could perform the impossible. Even where a considered 'hopeless case' as his current victim was thus labelled; he still planned on working the impossible; turning flab into muscle; transforming a lack of intellect into much desired street smarts. And that was the plan Domenico had in store for this weakling of a Santucci son right now.

Bruno was kidnapped from his New York hideout only, but hours before. He was taken right from under his father's nose, unseen by his eyes, defying his family's security as such. And now Bruno was escorted to a secret location to be fully groomed to serve his new master on foreign terrain. The purpose: Domenico wanted him to destroy his father first and foremost. Domenico had many plans for certain select individuals in New York City prior casting out his grand orders to wipe out all his world's enemies. But before he had performed his wholesale massacre of the large masses, Domenico wanted to embark on the personal satisfaction to see certain appointed 'special enemies' being raked over the coals. And one of those chosen enemies was the Santucci family, specifically, Don Santucci, Bruno's father.

Domenico wanted to derive much pleasure from the enemy's final son he had left in the world to accomplish such a sordid job for him. Domenico wanted his own son Bruno to betray his father as such. He wanted him to kill him!

Bruno of course hated the idea. He was against such a treacherous plan. But Domenico was persistent with his agenda concerning Don Santucci. And he was equally determined in how such a plan was to be carried out. He demanded that this enemy was to meet his fate via his own son. No other way! Domenico knew that killing Don Santucci any other way was a too easy task. It was far too boring. But having the pleasure in witnessing his eyes as he was betrayed by his own son before his death was something Domenico insisted he would not be deprived and robbed from.

Bruno Santucci was previously groomed in undertaking such a task. But he was not a willing participant in fulfilling his new master's requirements in that regard. So that was why Domenico had arranged for him to be brought here this way and he would force him to comply, since Bruno was not a cooperative individual in his chosen assignment.

Domenico ordered the typical torturing tactics to be imposed onto his current prisoner, the same way as his previous prisoners.

Domenico wanted the nails of his left hand removed, one by one. He wanted salt and vinegar applied to the open bloody wounds to serve his purpose to that effect. Domenico previously ordered his men not to cause damage to his right hand. Bruno Santucci after all was right-handed. He wanted that part of his body working efficiently. Why? Because Domenico insisted that it was with his right hand that he would perform such a delicate task of doing away with his chosen target, Don Santucci.

Domenico insisted to his henchmen performing the mental transformation of their target: "He will use his right hand to fire the gun I will provide to him – with bullets striking his father's heart and between his eyes! And I insist that Don Santucci must die no other way, but with the treacherous hand of his own son! That will satisfy me perfectly!"

And so what Domenico wished, his men were only too willing to carry out such instructions ever dutifully, to perfection, as always. This was no exception.

Domenico's transformation tactics onto the helpless young Santucci prisoner were also to be delivered unmercifully and much swiftly. He was going to learn how to endure pain and torture, by force. Since he was not a willing participant to act on his new master's orders willingly, then he had to be groomed, as Domenico saw fit to describe, in the 'hard way!'

Domenico's men who were performing such brutal torturous antics, mixed with the brainwashing tactics, in themselves were concerned about going too far! After all, who could withstand such fierce brutal torments! But Domenico's orders were strict and understood. No one ever debated Domenico to his face or otherwise!

They all knew that Domenico was hardly concerned about going too far! Perhaps his anger clouded his judgement. Because he had not thought for one moment that perhaps Bruno was not strong enough to endure what was given to him. After all, even the strongest of men had crumbled to far less. But Domenico said, "That man is weak. He must be toughened up some, before he can be released again back into New York to accomplish his task for me: the death of his father, Don Santucci!"

So whatever Domenico ordered, Domenico was not to be denied, according to his ever faithful, and perhaps much fearful employ.

But their fears were shortly realised in brutal fashion. Reality hit them gruesomely. Following such torture being inflicted, Bruno screamed in terror for moments before he rapidly lost consciousness. They all understood that such brainwashing tactics could not work on a man who was in fact both mentally and physically weak. How could it?

But Domenico insisted: "Keep going. Eventually he will wake up! And when he does he will become my new soldier. A man transformed into strength to do my bidding. He will obey only, but one master. And that is me-Domenico Armando! I will not be denied the satisfaction of seeing my handiwork in making an unwilling man do things what he normally would never contemplate. Such as killing his own father as he was coerced into doing the same thing to his brother Sebastian recently! He must comply! He must obey! He will follow my orders or so help me, I will make him die trying! No one refuses Domenico Armando! No! No! No!

"No one denies Domenico Armando, no matter how stupid and worthless he may very well be! Bruno Santucci has lived a life of failure since the day he was born. Eventually he will come to realise what a favour I am giving him by this unique opportunity to become a man for the first time in his silly lifespan! He will become a man! He will transform from a little boy at heart to my robot! He will become another of my soldiers, destined to obey me and me alone!

"And he who tries to defy me will suffer dearly! They will experience the very same tortures of the damned that are all cast into boiling hell! Their screams will never halt! Their tears will never stop oozing out of their weeping eyes! Their minds will never be quenched from such horrors I will bestow upon them! And I will never stop until they surrender their entire lives to serving me and my orders!"

Domenico witnessed the head-sunken sight of Bruno Santucci who lost consciousness for over fifteen minutes now. Domenico was rapidly losing patience.

He approached his comatose prisoner instantly. Domenico's men stepped aside to allow their master free terrain. Domenico quickly became irate. He grabbed Bruno Santucci from the scruff of his neck and shook his unconscious brain many times, insisting that he no longer disappoint him as he shouted before his closed eyes: "Wake up, you useless man! Wake up! You will do my bidding for me! It is too late for you! No one will save you from me! So you had better regain consciousness right now or else when you finally do, I am going to make sure that you lose more than just your nails on one of your hands! Because I am going to make sure that you lose your hands, your feet, your arms and your legs if you so much as even think of failing me – or disappointing me any further. YOU HEAR ME?

"You have a job to do! And so help me, you are going to do it! You will accomplish it the way I want it accomplished! I don't want your father to die in any other way, but through you! I want him to remember me when he is in hell! I want him to know that it was because of me that he was sent there! That it was his son who killed him at the behest of his worst nightmare imaginable: me-Domenico Armando!" he cursed, now holding a chunk of his hair in his hand and using it to brutally shake the man's yet unconscious brain to reality. But no matter what, his eyes remained closed. Bruno Santucci refused to regain consciousness for now.

Domenico was rapidly losing patience. He cursed and screamed at his tormented target, even whilst in Bruno's deep sleep, he still attacked his soul!

One of Domenico's white-coated doctors stepped forward and checked the prisoner's vital signs. Both his pulse and his heartbeat, and confirmed to his master that he was still very much alive.

Domenico then began attacking his doctor, accusing him of much deliberate incompetence and negligence in carrying out his orders effectively! Domenico grabbed the six-foot-tall doctor with two firm hands planted onto the collar of his white coat and began shaking him now insisting: "Then if he is alive why the hell he is still unconscious, you fool? What have you done to him? I need him awake! He is no use to me like this! He has become a vegetable, you incompetent derelict; you foolish imbecile!"

The doctor stuttered out a defence, now much frightened for his own life. He insisted: "Sir, maybe Bruno was not strong enough to tolerate and withstand the methods of brainwashing we imposed upon him! Some people may successfully transform, others may just collapse from exhaustion and the impact of it all! Bruno simply could not handle it, sir! Please, I beg you… Please, I assure you, we have done nothing wrong! We followed your orders with expert precision. We administered the brainwashing serum intravenously into the veins of his arms at all the correct doses! Even the electric current into his brain was not delivered excessively! You must believe me! I would never do anything to displease you…"

Domenico waved his hands in the air, yet furious and cut the doctor's pitiful display of cowardice to an abrupt halt, insisting: "I don't want to hear it! Just shut your mouth for a second! I am getting a headache here, all right. I need to think! I need time to turn this fiasco into my favour as I had always been able to do before in similar situations!"

Domenico quickly placed his hands onto the sides of his head, massaging his own excruciating pains he usually experienced during times of great stress. He now knew that no matter what, his own mortality may or may not be able to be dealt with by just sheer will alone. He may need medication.

But Domenico stepped aside into his own corner for now. He did not want the doctors then focusing their attention onto him. Nor had he wanted them to try and convince him to take drugs to settle his own pain.

Domenico insisted that he needed to remain focussed and alert without the crap mental side effects to be delivered to him, via the prescription of pain-killing medications, which may affect his own state of mind and thinking abilities!

Domenico insisted that he would endure the pain from his own recently-confirmed mortality, at the sake of having a clear head, until his prisoner here had woken up and satisfied his need for justice against one of his bitterest enemies in the world, named Don Santucci!

Domenico now approached again his yet unconscious prisoner plunged onto that chair and still cursed at him: "You will do my bidding for me, you hear me? You will do exactly as you are told to do! You will follow your instructions to the letter! I am your master. You will obey me without question; so wake up you fool. I need you to kill your pathetic father for me! Wake up now – or I will force you to wake up in more bitter agony than you could possibly imagine, you silly good-for-nothing worthless little rat!"

But it was useless. No matter what would be done, Domenico suddenly could comprehend in his own shattered foggy mindset that his prisoner here was surely subjected to a little too much. He was neither strong enough nor smart enough to withstand such extreme torture and excessive brainwashing methods!

Domenico now lost all patience with his current victim. And he lost all patience with his people at this moment that performed the failed deed. He faced them all with his demented eyes, usually displayed during flare-ups of his anger and he ordered them: "All right. This was obviously a failed experiment. Untie him and get him out of here… Get him out of my sight! Tell our pilot to bundle him back onto the plane and deliver him back into New York. I don't want him dead yet. No. That would surely be a testament to failure today. Keep him alive for now! Who knows? Perhaps one day this disappointing human being will learn to follow orders correctly and not fall apart like some weakling that he is! After all, what can we expect from a Santucci heir apparent! Of course he is weak! Of course he is a disappointment to both me and my plans! Yes. He is pathetic!

"But I have come to realise that no matter my good intentions today, sometimes there are those rarities when certain people will just disappoint me and let me down! It is not insurmountable! He will be dealt with accordingly once he has outlived his usefulness to me. Because make no mistake; Don

Santucci's fate will be realised by the hand of his son. One way or another, sooner or later, it will be done!"

Domenico now turned to his doctors fiercely and ordered them in a tone of voice resembling a shout, which startled them to heartache: "What the hell are you waiting for? Get him the hell out of here! And the rest of you can get out of my sight as well! You have all let me down this day! You are all lucky that I haven't ordered your executions to take place too for this stuff-up of yours! But who knows, maybe I might! So get out of here! Get out of my sight! I don't want to look at your stupid faces for a very long time! You understand? You hear me?"

Domenico's insanity was clearly understood. His frightened personnel quickly carried the yet comatose and much unconscious Santucci son out of the room, to make instant arrangements for his transportation back to New York City!

Just as the last one of them vanished out the door of the dreary-looking dungeon room, Domenico cursed some more: "Don't forget to get someone to clean the shit mess of blood and crap that you caused in this room!" Domenico now shook his head in dismay and said to himself in a lower tone of voice: "Yes, you idiots. Clean this room! Who knows, maybe I might need to use it to lock you sorry fools up inside here. Maybe… maybe I might just do that! We shall see!"

CHAPTER 4

Domenico Armando had stomped his foot firmly onto the ground at the sight of his next prisoner. He was Colin McMurphy, husband to his daughter Annemarie, delivered to him into this secret compound surreptitiously as well. Colin McMurphy was kidnapped from his own bed, aside his sleeping daughter in New York much unexpectedly and forced onto a plane to meet his master on foreign soil. He was also tied onto a chair, placed into another dungeon room at the same time the Santucci son was previously being dealt with; Colin too was forced to await his brutal assault to be delivered by his padrone, Domenico Armando.

Domenico now stood before him with bloodshot eyes which steamed with bitter rage and fury at the mere look of him.

Colin knew Domenico, for whatever reason wanted to do him irreversible damage. He wanted to hurt him unmercifully for whatever slight it was that Domenico considered was made wrong against him by this McMurphy fellow.

Colin suspected the reason as he waited in anticipation for Domenico to break the long gaze of silence he cast upon him. The very uncomfortable gaze made him tremble in unbearable fear right now! Colin could only hope that Domenico did not suspect the truth concerning all his transgressions made against him, especially to his daughter. That would mean instant death to be delivered upon him at this very instant.

Domenico kept staring at him. His mind was fuming in rage at every thought he now conjured against him. He wanted to watch him suffer. He wanted to hear him in grave pain. Then he felt like doing away with him completely.

Colin knew what he was thinking. His fierce evil eyes gave his thoughts away. But just as Domenico kept him waiting for his speech delivery, Colin too would not communicate. He couldn't. He was too scared to utter a simple word from his mouth. He knew that would amount to disrespect in this perverted captor's mind. And whatever the reason for his kidnapping and being forced onto a plane at this late evening, delivered into foreign land to be confronted by this demon, face to face like this; well, Colin McMurphy did not want to compound the situation any further by giving this horrible man any further excuses to display his black-hearted fury against him!

Domenico finally spoke. His eyes yet remained the picture of a ferocious beast ready to attack his prey; ready to kill at any given time now, with only the slightest whiff of provocation. Domenico said: "You are a treacherous little insect. You understand that? You have betrayed me, you little shit! And for that I want to teach you a lesson right now you will never soon forget!"

Colin coughed in fear for his life. His vocal chords were so shaky he could not utter a single word.

But it was not necessary. Domenico spoke instead as he stood before him wearing his black robe, resembling a terrifying Roman Emperor type executioner, as he maintained his deadly-cold stare into his eyes, not even blinking once. Domenico's arms were crossed arrogantly as he delivered his vicious assault before this, much considered in his own mind, to be a petty little man. Domenico continued his vicious onslaught: "You think you would get away with double-crossing me, huh? I told you from the onset to always be loyal to me and my daughter, without question. And before the first month's marriage anniversary to my daughter you have already created treachery and deceit against me and my precious Annemarie, you little bug!"

Colin felt his bowels and bladder lose slight control. But he feared further humiliation. So he clenched his inner thighs to stop any possible leakage.

Domenico would not stop his ferocious words right now. "I commanded you to kill Robert Stewart and you could not even do that, you despicable son of a bitch. Why? Because you are a coward! Because you are a useless traitor of a man! Do you seriously think that I would let you get away with defying my orders this way, huh? Of course not! But you should know something: my daughter is your only ally! If she was not in such a terribly fragile state right now, I would have surely ordered you dead long ago, you stupid man! You failed me! And now I want to tell you exactly how it is and how it will be!

"As soon as my daughter recovers, I will remove you from her life by force! I will remove you from the face of this earth in the only fashion that you deserve! And I seriously want you to know that! But don't you dare die from fright right now! No! No! No! No! Because the reality is, that my daughter unfortunately still needs you. If not, you would not be walking out of here alive!

"But, very soon, my friend, McMurphy - I will give you exactly what you deserve! I will teach you a really painful lesson in what happens when a fool such as yourself fails me and disappoints me. You get that? You will pay one day very soon! But unfortunately it won't be today! Because you will leave here unharmed only to tend to my daughter's every want and need! And you will do it perfectly! You understand me? You will satisfy her every desire! You will spoil her rotten. You will spend every last penny you have in making her happy and pleasing my beautiful Annemarie! Do you comprehend what I am telling you, my clumsy friend?

"And once my daughter recovers from her fragile emotional state right now, then I will make my move against you! I will remove you not only from her life, but from this world, you despicable little nobody! But do not die on me right now. No! Because you have to go back home and help make my daughter well again! Then I will surface – and after what I do to you, you will surely die from a combination of multiple strokes and heart attacks by the very fear of the unbearable physical agony I will cast upon you, you wretched little creep!

"Because I know what you are! And don't even think of running! Because no matter where you go, I will find you! You see, I have eyes and ears watching all my enemies everywhere around the entire world! I want to assure you of that fact! And I also want to assure you of the truth that no matter what, justice will prevail against you as it will against every horrible insect like you that swarms the earth, polluting its existence! You follow me?"

Domenico studied his terror-ridden eyes. Colin McMurphy surely could comprehend the enormity of his master's words. Domenico was on part satisfied at that. "Good. Very good, indeed! I know you understand me. And you will understand something else. Just because you may not be able to see me around New York, don't ever think for one minute that that means that I do not know what you are doing every second of every day. Because I do! I also know what you are thinking! I also know what you are planning! You see, that is why I want you dead!

"And you know how I am going to do it? Let me tell you. That day when it comes, I will force you to crawl on your hands and knees onto the muddy ground of a deserted cemetery. I will force a shovel into your hands. And I will command you to dig a very deep hole into the ground. Then once you are finished, I will throw you inside that hole and I will bury you alive! That is

283

how I will destroy you, little man, for ever thinking that you could get away with betraying me! So get ready for your end as everyone else must get ready for theirs. Because the world will never be rid of Domenico Armando!

"No one will ever be free from my wrath! Understand that, you fool. And never forget it! But for now, I will give you your current orders. And this time you will follow them all to the letter, without exception. That I can assure you, you tiny baboon!

"You will be transported back to New York the same way you were brought here to me; wearing chains around your wrists and ankles and wool covering your eyes. And every cent you have in the bank, you will withdraw and spend it on my daughter. Every day you will take her to a fancy restaurant. Every day you will buy her a new dress. You will give her the most expensive bouquet of flowers! You will buy her the most expensive perfume. You will shower her with gifts and all forms of what an imbecile like you defines as displays of love and affection! Because you are going to help cure my daughter from her very distressed mindset! You are going to bring my daughter back to me the way she always was! You had better! I tell you!

"You will do everything imaginable to make her forget about her present stresses and disappointments of life itself! You will buy her expensive rings! You will take her to the most romantic movies! You are going to work your sick arse until you croak from the hard slave labour of it all! I am going to make you move heaven and earth to please her! I am going to watch you gasp for air. And there will not be enough to keep you going. But you will continue. Believe me you will! I will make sure that you do not suffocate… you do not surrender… you do not collapse into your grave until every demand and order of mine is met!

"Yes, indeed, you fool! This time you will carry out your orders for me to the letter. And most perfectly! This time I will be watching you like a hawk! I will make you sweat blood, you miserable man! You are going to rue the day you ever crossed me! You are going to curse its existence! You are going to wish that you never entered this world. Because by entering it, you have fallen into my trap! You see, I will control you! I will work you like a dog! And just as others would think you've had enough I will keep the pressure on! I will make you sweat it out more and more! You will see!

"This will be an example of what happens to anyone who dares defy Domenico Armando! It is a mistake no one would ever repeat again! I'm sure you understand that right now! But it is too late for you, Mr. McMurphy. Yes. It is much too late for you! You see, there are no second chances here. There is no wiggle room! There is no reprieve! Nothing left for you, but pain and anguish! And I will enjoy tormenting you, you see! So you go back to New York and make sure that my daughter is happy every second of every day!

"Because if she is not I will blame you! And if that happens, your end will only be blacker than what I have already planned for it to be! You understand me? As I stand here all alone with you in this room, I cannot put it to you any plainer than that!

"And before I release you, I will set out some very explicit ground rules and conditions you had better bear in mind. And don't forget any of them, for even one moment. Because your pain will only become more intense! Your existence on this earth will only become more unbearable! And much so at my hands!

"So listen carefully. And absorb every word I will tell you; because I will not be repeating myself. You hear me? These are your conditions: If you ever so much as think of stealing so much as one cent from my daughter's purse or any member of my family, I will personally tear you apart! If you ever defy me ever again in terms of not following my orders precisely, you will wish for a hole on this earth clever enough to hide inside far away from me! If you make my daughter grieve for even one second EVER I will find you and I will end it all for you right then and there in the most painful fashion! So you go and follow your orders very carefully, because I will be my daughter's eyes and ears. I will be her guardian angel watching over her ready to punish any fool who dares cost her even a brief moment's happiness! And peace of mind! So go and get the hell out of my sight!"

Domenico quickly called for his guard waiting outside and once he opened the door and entered the dim-lit frighteningly setup stone-walled dungeon room, he ordered his man: "Take him back to New York into my daughter's arms at once! I am sure he will not disappoint me again!"

Following the guard's instructions being carried out, Domenico adjourned back to his private den where he found his daughter Monica there waiting for him.

Domenico embraced her, then seated himself aside her on the sofa and insisted: "That McMurphy has been taken care of. He foolishly betrayed my

285

daughter, but he had better not ever try that again, if he knows what is good for him. And soon I will also take care of all the rest of my children's needs! Meaning Paul Stewart! He betrayed you as well, my daughter by running off and marrying another woman! But do not worry; his fate is sealed just as McMurphy's! I will get them all, my daughter. Every single person who ever crossed us Armandos is going to pay dearly! Yes! No one will get away this time! No one! Especially my very old and dear friend, Robert Stewart!"

Monica quickly urged him on. She was all ears when it came to his master plans!

Domenico would oblige his daughter instantly. "Robert has no idea what my plans for him are! But he will very soon. Suffice it to say, that I am going to blacken his name. I am going to tarnish his reputation in such a way in which no one could question the sincerity of it all. No one will be able to dispute it! By the time my immediate plans for him are cast into motion it will appear as though Robert Stewart was the very sole individual who was behind my escape from prison. It will seem as though it was him and him alone who gave the guard in question the keys to open my cell door and release me! And with what I have planned, even his own wife and his entire family would not be able to help, but question Robert Stewart's innocence in this instance!" he chuckled victoriously.

Monica asked, "Why? What do you have planned father?"

Domenico replied, "I have put in motion a plot against Robert for weeks now. You see, he has been a thorn in my side for much too long a period. And now I am going to stick those thorns into him. What I have planned is something so deliciously brilliant and unique that is going to send his world crashing downhill so rapidly, that he will wonder whether what has happened to him is reality or one of those very bad dreams, every time he wakes up and sees my angry face before him!

"My daughter, I have created something so ingenious, so original - that by the time it is revealed to the world - everyone is going to question Robert Stewart's morality. Everyone will wonder whether or not they had ever really known him. They are going to become confused about this man! They are going to soon concede that Robert Stewart was not the good and holy hero who rescued them each time from the travesties of our world!

"But instead they are going to see him in a new light. They are going to think of him as something different! They are going to be blown away, if you will, once their minds are transformed to another truth which identifies Robert as nothing more than what the world now identifies me myself as being: one crazy monster!"

Monica seemed blown-away herself by her father's mysterious revelations. She could not help but urge him on furthermore.

Domenico said: "I have created a Robert Stewart impostor; a most perfect impersonation and look-alike of our number one enemy. And shortly this man will be unleashed into the world to take Robert's place. He will begin to perform such heinous acts in Robert's name, until the whole world starts believing that Robert was really only a criminal from the very beginning hiding behind his noble facade since he became a police officer. And in the process, once Robert is removed from the picture by force in this way (whether it be via his being arrested and imprisoned or locked away in some mental institution) it will also serve me in such a perfect way by means of not only framing Robert, but also discrediting the New York City Police Department all at the same time, to look like one mob of very sick-minded lunatics!" he chuckled triumphantly. "You see, everything they threw at me – every charge and accusation – I will now throw right back into their faces. And by destroying Robert's reputation, it will also strike every law-enforcement official in the United States of America right between the eyes and into their hearts!"

BOOK 4

CHAPTER 5

Domenico Armando revealed his closely-guarded secret to his son D.J. that evening. His son was ushered inside his private den by his father and introduced to a new recruit of the family business.

At the sight of this man he recognised painfully clear - for a moment, D.J. became startled. He staggered back in fright and stuttered, "No! It cannot be! This is our enemy! He hates me! He wants us dead!"

Domenico placed a comforting hand on his son's shoulder and reassured him. "No, my son; this is not who you think he is! This is merely one of my cleverly-plotted creations I designed to make him look like the man you think he is! He is merely an impostor; our newly-appointed killing machine to do my bidding for me!"

D.J. broke out, "But how? He looks exactly like Robert Stewart. No one can tell them apart!"

Domenico smiled: "Clever isn't it? I had my team of reconstructive plastic surgeons work on this plan for a while now! And not only does he look like Robert, he also sounds like Robert!" Domenico turned to his impostor and ordered him to greet his son.

The impostor did as he was told. He extended a hand before D.J., shook it and uttered a hello.

D.J. was shocked. "My God, I don't believe it. He really does sound like Robert. This is incredible, father. What exactly do you have planned for this man? How is he going to fit into our plans here?"

Domenico flicked his hand into the air in gesture and revealed his plans rather triumphantly before his son. "Ahh, now that is something no one in the world could possibly imagine is possible. You see, I have been working on this for weeks now. Our impostor friend here has been given every piece of information he needs to learn; everything, every detail and every part of Robert's history to, in short, take over his life and wreak havoc upon everyone else's, commencing in New York! He will be used to make our hero of a friend, how shall I put it no longer resemble the hero everyone idolises him to be! This man here will be used to tarnish Robert's image, his reputation… He will also be used to turn all his friends into enemies; his allies into his persecutors. Even his family will instantly become disillusioned and begin to doubt him once they are forced to see what this man here commits in Robert Stewart's name!"

D.J. questioned his father eagerly, "But what about Robert Stewart? I mean the real Robert Stewart. What are you going to do about him? Surely you cannot have two Robert Stewart's roaming around New York. Everyone will know something is wrong. They will put two-and-two together!"

Domenico remarked, "Exactly, my son. You are precisely right. So what I have planned is to simply arrange for our friend here to not only take over Robert's life in order to fulfil my purpose, but he will also replace Robert entirely!"

D.J. asked, "How, father? How?"

Domenico first chuckled victoriously ever proud of himself before he replied. "The answer to that, my son is part of my very large plans where Robert is concerned. You see, I will arrange for Robert's elaborate kidnapping. His capture will be performed in a time and place that does not arouse any suspicion to our involvement! And it will be performed in a private place without witnesses! Then as soon as Robert is snatched from the world and secretly held in my custody, then this impostor will step in and take over Robert's life. And the events which unfold thereafter will truly send New York and the entire United States into unbelievable chaos and much upheaval! They will not believe what they witness once they witness it! They will not believe their eyes! They will not believe their ears! His friends will practically die from the shock of it all! His family will be completely mortified once such actions begin to unfold!"

D.J. was truly amazed, astonished and blown away. He still could not believe what he was seeing himself; though he did manage to rapidly regain his senses to stutter his next question, "And what about the real Robert? What are you going to do with him? Are you going to kill him?"

Domenico responded, yet smiling, "No, my son! Not yet! Robert Stewart will be brought here and held as my prisoner. He will be informed of everything that is taking place in New York. And he will be informed of who is taking over his life in his hometown! And I will enjoy every minute of it! I will relish it! I will savour it! And it will give me such pleasure to look into his eyes as he is shown what is happening many miles away, but being powerless to do anything about it!

"You see, my son; I have arranged for my technicians to place surveillance cameras all over New York, particularly around all the parts that Robert and his family share together. Like their home! And such images are transmitted to my own personal computer screen by satellite. So I can see and hear everything that takes place in the heart of all my enemies' habitats! And you know something: So will Robert Stewart! He will be shown all of this and the look in his enraged eyes will not help but bring out a reaction in me which is extremely pleasing to my senses! I will toy with him! I will mock him! And he will be tied and bound in one place, with gunmen surrounding him, training their weapons on him at all times. And my very good friend Robert Stewart will be forced to endure every bit of pain and suffering he has forced upon me! And that my son is only the beginning of the plans of revenge I have against Robert Stewart!"

D.J. asked curiously, "What else are you planning father?"

Domenico responded immediately with delight in his eyes. "My impostor friend here will take over Robert's world very soon. He will assume his identity and once that happens, my plans of attacks will begin. You see, this impostor will be ordered to kill in Robert's name, in front of witnesses! He will be ordered to steal in Robert's name, in front of witnesses! And he will be ordered to commit all manner of perversions with Robert's face in front of many witnesses. And he will disappear expertly each time!

"And once that plan has been finalised and Robert's name has been blackened to the extremes, then and only then, will I release the real Robert Stewart – and have him transported back to New York to face the wrath of his own system and the punishment to be delivered to him by his own people – who will ferociously come after him! Robert Stewart will be charged by his own police colleagues! He will be arrested by his own police partner! He will be brought before a courtroom and put on trial by his good friend the illustrious New York City District Attorney – and for all goes well, then he will be brought to the death penalty by his own friendly judge! And even his allies such as the Governor of the state of New York City and the President of the United States will fall short of ever offering him a reprieve – and certainly not a pardon from his, to be many handed down convictions for such numerous committed atrocities!" Domenico clapped his hands together three times in great vigour and insisted: "And that is a beautiful revenge I am looking forward to!"

"Then what, father? What happens next? After Robert is dead, what then...?" his son asked curiously.

Domenico instantly said, "Ahh, my son. But he won't be dead! You see, this whole setup of his is part of a bigger, much grander plot of mine! You see, after he is convicted and put in prison awaiting execution, then I-me-Domenico Armando will step in and arrange for his release or escape if you will!"

D.J.'s eyes lit up as if stunned by the greatest of surprise: "What? Why? How?"

Domenico took much pleasure from his son's eagerness as he chose to oblige. "The whys, hows and whats will now be revealed to you as well! You see, Robert dead does not suit my purpose. It will ruin my plans. Because everything I will do concerning my plans against all of my enemies in this world revolves and much centres on Robert! It all hinges with him! It is designed to bring him the very same grief and misery he simply wanted to inflict upon me!

"So if he dies, then I lose. You understand? But if he's alive, well, then I have much leverage, much power at my disposal to use against him and the society he created against mine!"

D.J. seemed confused. "I don't understand father. Please explain whatever it is you mean!"

Domenico nodded his head willingly and said, "Of course, my son; of course! You see, what I have planned is simply to do to Robert what he has done to me! I will simply put him in the same position he has currently put me in! He tried to destroy my world, I will destroy his! He took away my freedom, I will take away his! He has separated me from my family, now I will make sure that he never sees his! You follow?

"So once that happens, I will arrange another meeting or confrontation between me and my very good friend Robert Stewart and then the real negotiations will begin!"

D.J. asked, "Negotiations?"

Domenico insisted, "Yes, my son, negotiations! Robert Stewart will be placed in the same stalemate situation that he has placed me in, in regards to his freedom on the outside becoming swiftly removed. So what am I planning? Robert Stewart will be forced to work with me so that we can both come out of it with our normal lives restored!"

D.J. snapped, "But father, surely he would not agree to that. You must know that! He would never help you regain your freedom!"

Domenico seemed more confident as he explained himself, "My son. When a man is pushed to the limits and brought to the brink of desperation, I seriously doubt there is not much he would not agree to! Even the strongest of men such as Robert Stewart would succumb to any pressure brought against them, if it served their purpose. And Robert's soon-to-become bleak situation would most certainly force him to comply with my demands. Because if he does not, he will simply never be able to see his beloved family again! Robert is just like me on that score. He loves family more than his own life! He would do anything for them as I would mine! And also like me, it would destroy him if he were put in a position that dictated such harsh terms to him, forcing his indefinite or even permanent separation from such a family! So given that, do you seriously think he would refuse me for long? I do not think so! It will only be a matter of time before he agrees to my terms and strict conditions!"

D.J. asked, "And they are?"

Domenico replied, "They are that in exchange for my help in exonerating him and proving to the world that he was setup and framed by a manufactured scapegoat, he must also prove to the world beyond a shadow of a doubt that I was also the victim to some cunning plot made against me. So that all the past and pending charges to be brought against us at that time will be removed – and we can return to our lives back in New York as normal!"

D.J. was still not convinced that such a fantastic scheme was even probable. He yet insisted, "I don't know father. I know Robert just as well as you do, and he is like a bloodhound. Once he gets the scent of his man which he targets for death, he never stops coming after him and he certainly never changes his mind!"

Domenico simply agreed. "I know that my son. I know. But what you don't seem to realise is that his circumstances will dictate his actions in this instance. His desperation will surrender his will to agree with me and my terms. After all, we will both come out of it as winners. He would be a fool not to agree with me in the end! And let me assure you of one thing my son. Robert Stewart is a lot of things, but a fool, he is surely not! Besides, I will sweeten the kitty for him in such a way, that my offer will be much too lucrative for him to pass up!"

"Whatever do you mean father?" D.J. asked.

Domenico insisted. "I will make an offer to Robert of peace!"

D.J. laughed for a moment. "Peace?"

Domenico too smiled in humour. "Yes, my son. Peace. You see, I have just decided that there may be an alternative to in fact have everyone escape my brutal onslaught I have planned for the world. And my proposition to Robert will simply be one that he will have to ultimately choose between two options: war or peace!"

D.J. was shocked. "You cannot be serious, father. After all the lives he knows you were responsible for claiming, he would never make peace with you!"

Domenico flicked his hand in the air triumphantly again, and broke out a cunning smile on his face. "Ahh, my son, but he will! Robert is a practical man. He was someone who served his world and his family faithfully and honourably. And he will simply be forced to come to terms with the truth of the matter and its very dire consequences, given any refusals on his part! You see, Robert would move heaven and earth in order to protect his family and his society! He surely knows he cannot do that if he and I remain connected as sworn bitter enemies. So I will simply present to him one true OUT! He will be given the opportunity to in fact preserve his family and his friends' lives with the society he chose to protect all his life. You see, I will offer him the chance of a lifetime to fulfil his obligation as a law-enforcement agent by partnering up with me! Yes, my son. I will even offer to assist Robert financially with my own resources to help clean up our world from the filth that currently pollutes it! And I will offer him a lot more than that! After all, it is in my interests too to remove such people which also endanger my family's lives!"

D.J. was fascinated. He could not wait to hear more.

Domenico read his mind perfectly at present as he continued his very magical and fascinating revelations. "I will simply explain to Robert that it is time we end the war between us for the common good! That it is time we stop trying to harm the other. That it is time we stop trying to hurt the other.

That it is time we stop threatening each other. And stop trying to kill the other.

"I will also insist that I want to work with him. We can become a team. I will help him make his job easier. I will assist him in solving quite effectively all his outstanding police cases, yet remaining to be solved. I will do whatever it takes to remove every rapist, every serial killer and scam artist from the streets and into his jail cell. You know the one that we both visited only recently, my son!"

D.J. broke out in laughter at his father's successful attempt at humour.

Domenico went on. "Robert will become bewitched at my offer. And I will convince him that I am genuine in everything I say, in that regard. But not only that will I offer, but I will give him a lot more, even!"

D.J. was bewildered, but with much delight. He gave his father a 'what else' type glance.

And Domenico was simply only too obliging, eager himself to comply. "What else?" he replied, reading his son's thoughts. "I will offer the world a large chunk of money. And I will work with Robert to in fact change it FOREVER!"

D.J. appeared concerned.

Domenico studied his eyes, but immediately put his mind to rest. "My son; I mean it all in goodwill and good faith! How can Robert refuse my further offer of peace and prosperity and goodwill to the world when I tell him, quite sincerely, that I will ensure that no one who is hungry in the world will remain that way? When I tell him that I will provide food for all the hungry, water for all the thirsty and shelter for every homeless person who resides not only in the United States of America, but who are situated across the entire world! Do you think that is enough, my son? Because I am far from finished, yet!

"I will also tell him that I will invest my money in medicine. And I will effectively help the world cure itself of every disease that plagues every human being across the world. I will come up with serums to cure cancer, to cure AIDS, to cure Parkinson's disease; to cure every single currently labelled 'incurable' disease known to mankind! I will do it. And I will cure myself whilst at the same time replacing all those money-hungry frauds that currently occupy every facet of our medical community – and replace them with genuine honest doctors who indeed are ambitious enough to want to obtain cures for diseases. Not just temporary fixes which mask symptoms and create a backdrop of repeat business for them by keeping their patients sick so they can only return with deeper and newer problems caused by their incorrectly prescribed drugs only so those fiendish doctors can make more money from their unknowing victim patients!

"No! No! No! That will all change, my son. I swear it on the lives of all those who I love – that if Robert Stewart accepts my offer, things in our society, everywhere around the world, will change for the better, for everyone. And yes, I am most certainly sincere about the lot of it! I mean every word of it! The rest is up to Robert! It is all in his hands, what he wants for himself and for those in the world he made a vow to protect and serve! Yes! And that will also provide me with an out. Indeed! Once those filthbags who call themselves doctors are replaced with good-honest practitioners, I too will become closer to my dream, my goal! For then, I too can get cured! I can live for a very long time as I had always intended. And I can return to my family in New York and live with all my family together once again, happily ever after! But it is all up to Robert! Whatever will happen, will be in his hands! For the world's safety, success, prosperity and transformation for the better will make history! It has never been done before! None of this world's single-minded and self-serving greedy thinkers had ever come up with such a wonderful goal! All we need to fulfil that dream and pull it all off, is the green light from Robert Stewart!"

BOOK 5

CHAPTER 6

Domenico Armando had certainly overwhelmed his son, now serving as his audience at the revelation to his grand plans! They were fantastic! They were magnificent! They were magical and spellbinding! And D.J. was sure of the fact that his father was wholeheartedly sincere. After all, Domenico's own plans to beat his growing mortality depended on its success!

But the Robert Stewart impostor, present with them inside his master's den right now, was much eager to proceed with his role.

He was given extensive files, tape recordings and transcripts to learn off by heart, every relevant detail he was ordered to ascertain concerning the life of Robert Stewart. He studied all the important names, dates, places and amounts, word for word. And Domenico tested him constantly during his private sessions here in his compound until he was satisfied that his newly-appointed impostor could pass as the original Robert Stewart, perfectly. Domenico was pleased. His chosen man had memorised everything he needed to know and ahead of schedule. He was now ready to commence in his role for the job of impersonating Robert Stewart. He would be sent to New York as soon as Robert Stewart was located and safely taken away to be locked-up securely and inconspicuously in Armando foreign terrain, far away from anyone, particularly in New York who could ever come into contact with him.

According to Domenico, things had to be played perfectly from now on! And the timing of it all had to be PRECISE! No mistakes! No slip-ups on anyone's part! That was imperative! It was essential for the success in all his not-so-distant grand plans!

The Robert Stewart impostor was given a copy of Robert Stewart's file to read over constantly from time to time and ensure his mind kept fresh on all the many details he had to know perfectly.

Domenico insisted that it was important that he knew the entire history of Robert Stewart like human nature. Including his mannerisms, his soldier-like

walk, his facial expressions, the way he talked and smiled and laughed –
EVERYTHING!

But once the impostor was to be released from Domenico's island and once the time had come for him to enter New York and commence in his role of impersonating Robert, all the evidence would be left behind. The files he was given to memorise, photographs, tapes, journals, diaries, everything. No one on the outside, especially Robert's wife and children, his family, his friends and colleagues could ever see him with such incriminating evidence. There could be no clues left for anyone to ever piece together the truth and come to the correct conclusion! Domenico was adamant about that! His instructions were clear and concise and straight to the point. He insisted that nothing must ever go wrong. Because his entire life and everything he wanted to achieve, including his hopes and dreams for obtaining a complete cure for his terminal illness hinged on it!

So the impostor was whipped into shape and warned accordingly to ensure that he followed his end of the plan perfectly without deviating from any relevant detail – or else anyone from Robert's former life (the original would be forced to temporarily leave behind) may surely piece the puzzle together – and Domenico warned: 'If that ever happens, heads will roll!'

So the Robert Stewart impostor was much trained in the relevance of his procedures and how he was to conduct himself once in the company of all those acquainted to Robert in every way, shape and form. And he was also made aware of his master's temper and the consequences of what would happen to him should Domenico ever become disappointed in his performance also in any way, shape or form!

Domenico made it quite clear to him that he would never want to experience his Armando rage! Because he would simply make him disappear, FOR GOOD!

So naturally, the impostor became rapidly fearful for his life. He became rapidly fearful from Domenico and much fearful in ever disappointing his new master! All the ground rules were set.

Though part of the impostor's key determination in commencing with his role instantly was due to the fact that whilst he studied the file of Robert, he could not help but feel much drawn, if not attracted to the pictures supplied of Robert's wife Cassandra. He considered her beauty was addictive. And in himself, he could not wait to get acquainted with her. He instantly became obsessed with her; though he tried to keep that fascination a secret for now. He knew that was deviating from his role. He knew that falling in love with Robert's wife was not part of the plan he was given by Domenico! So naturally, he kept his emotions in check whilst in his master's presence. He surely did not want to displease Domenico or certainly experience his wrath. He knew Domenico had a violent temper only demonstrated to those not related to him by blood. And he certainly knew what the consequences were if he or anyone provoked that wrath of his against them! It was lethal! It was fatal! But before all that, it was unbearably and much unimaginably painful! He certainly did not want to ever experience it!

So the impostor behaved himself. He did everything he was told. He read what he was told to read. He memorised everything he was told to memorise. And he kept his mind constantly fresh on all the extensive details by rereading the file material over and over again! He rehearsed before Domenico everything he was demanded to recite – and quite perfectly. So far he pleased his master! And he did not want that to change. Also Domenico paid him much handsomely for his efforts. And his master further insisted that if he pulled off his charade as instructed – and well – that there was going to be a hefty bonus also added to his remuneration package. He was also made to understand what would happen to him should he fail in anything-any task Domenico had assigned to him. He would surely die; and not just that. Domenico did hint more than a few times to him that if he was ever targeted by him to be eliminated, that he would first make him scream in torment for a very long time before allowing him to close his eyes into eternity!

But despite his attempts to the contrary, the impostor had already underestimated his new master's profound genius. As he held the Robert Stewart file in his hand, flicking through the pages as instructed in order to keep his mind fresh on every pertinent detail he had to know prior his journey into New York to begin his role there, his eyes kept flickering to a photograph of Robert's wife Cassandra. It was taken somehow by the Armando henchmen and quite secretly when Robert and his wife were at the beach one weekend, not so long ago. It was a picture of her in her bikini. She wore a two-piece bikini; one that covered her breasts and the other covering the lower part of her body below the waist.

The impostor could not help his thoughts right now: 'My, oh, my. Geez, holy shit, look at that. Talk about perfect breasts and arse. Man that is one sexy, juicy and tasty dame. I cannot wait to get my hooks into that! Fuck, yeah!' he thought to himself.

But the detrimental mistake he made right now was assuming that his thoughts would not be read by Domenico himself. Domenico was talking to his son, as they stood only one metre away from the impostor.

The Robert Stewart look-alike had tried to hold the file upright away from Domenico's glance, but Domenico quickly had sneaked his eyes over to the file to see which part of it he was still going over, as if instinctively he sensed his much polluted thoughts. And then the scalding began.

Domenico had removed the file from his hands by force after witnessing this, slammed it harshly onto a small glass table next to him and began to physically accost his new recruit in front of his son.

Domenico's temper flared up rapidly. He grabbed the impostor by his ear harshly using his thumb and two fingers pressed on the piece of loose flesh savagely, then his hand moved to the top of his head and grabbed a fistful of his hair, he almost ripped from the roots of his skull, before he whacked him a firm hand across his left cheek. Then he sent the same hand, now the back part of it striking firmly into the man's right cheek.

The impostor gasped for air in agony, quickly raising his hands to massage the brutal pains which had rapidly erupted across both sides of his face.

Domenico then grabbed him by the collar with two firm hands and shook him violently as his eyes gave him a menacing stare as he now began to put this fiendish impostor into his place. Domenico shouted in a terrifying manner that sent his target now cowering in the worst fear imaginable: "You stupid idiot! You cretin! You rascal! You bloody scoundrel! You ratbag fool! When did I ever say that you could develop any such feelings for Cassandra Stewart, hmm?"

The impostor remained fearfully mute.

Domenico continued his attack: "You ingrate! You moron! I specifically told you your instructions. And they did not include allowing you to develop any such perverted sexual fantasies over Robert's wife that would get in the way of your mission here! You are not to act out your delusions of any flight of fancy on her, you understand that? Because if Robert-the real Robert ever finds out that you made a move on his wife, he will blame me. And all bets are off. My plans for freedom and achieving immortality will be shattered. And if that happens, there will not be a rock on this earth you will be able to hide inside from me! Because I will find you and I will tear you apart. I will break every bone in your body before I destroy you. Do you understand me?"

"Yes!" the impostor stuttered in physical agony and mental anguish.

Domenico yet raised his voice, cold as death at him. "Good. Because I suggest that you never forget my words and my warnings to you. Do you understand me? Your encounter with Robert's family will only be brief. I do not want you getting too personal with them. Your stay in New York will only be a very short one, in order to fulfil your duty. Then you will be removed the hell out of there so that the real Robert Stewart can return and fulfil the remainder of my plans. You hear me?

"Because if you so much as even think to deviate from my plans even slightly, I will make you disappear, not only from New York, but from planet earth entirely! Do not forget that, my friend! Or it will cost you very dearly! You will suffer the most serious consequences! All right! You are here to follow my orders, perfectly! You are here to do only as you are told! And you will even think what I want you to think! Nothing else! Do I make myself clear?

"I had better! Because if you ever think such dirty thoughts about Robert's wife ever again, I will castrate that stupid cock of yours! If it will get in the way of you accomplishing your duty to me, then you will have it removed, painfully. And the surgery will be performed without any anaesthesia. The pain will set you aright. Do you understand me? Do not be stupid again! Do you hear me?"

The impostor coughed. "Yes, Master. I hear you. I will do as I am told! I will obey you and only you alone! I will not think anything that you don't want me to think. But please, don't cut off any of my organs! I will do anything you say!"

Domenico released his firm grasp of him and said in a more composed demeanour, "Good. I suggest you do that. Or you and your friend below are no longer going to be an item! And a man without balls is a man no more! If you ever disappoint me again, I will hurt you with that ultimate punishment. Remember that! Now, you get the hell out of my sight!"

Domenico picked up the Robert Stewart file with his hand off the table aside him and returned it to the impostor with final clear instructions. "You take that file and study it all over again. But I urge you to glance only briefly at any and all pictures of Robert's wife in there. Because whatever you do, whatever you think, wherever you are – I will know about it. Keep that in mind my friend and never forget who you are!

"You are a man I located from the gutter. You are a failed stockbroker. You lost everything. Your money, your family, your friends, even your self-respect! You conned and cheated everyone very foolishly until you were caught, charged, arrested and released on bail. You faced prison. I could still send you there, if you so much as fail me in anything I tell you to do!

"I took you in from the streets, a desperate man. I gave you an opportunity to escape the dismal fate you left for yourself back in Chicago. I gave you a very good living. You now have food to eat, and water to drink! I rescued you from the brink of disaster! Everything you have now is because of me. I can quite easily take it all away, including your manhood-you know that silly thing of yours down there which makes you think stupid thoughts and do stupid things.

"So get in line and whip yourself back into shape – or believe me you are going to lose a lot more than what you initially had before I brought you here into my fold! You are going to be left with pieces of your body missing as well if you so much as cross me, even slightly. Now return to your room and start reading over that lengthy file. And keep reading it over and over again until it is your bedtime. I want your mind to be fresh and alert, without distractions. And if you find that you have any trouble controlling that thing you have in your head called a brain, I suggest you also keep thinking about my warnings to you! And don't forget them! Because only recalling my words in your head over and over again as well will surely keep you in line, out of harm's way! You know what I mean!"

BOOK 6

CHAPTER 7

Domenico Armando considered himself prepared for every eventuality to take effect. He much considered himself always able to turn all obstacles to his advantage; to premeditate his opponents' movements at all times – and hence implement his own counterattack agenda in crushing the enemy and enemies in defeat; by exploding their defences and rendering their attempts against him a complete failure. Domenico was known as the Chess Player. And like an expert in the theoretical as well as the practical aspects of the game of chance on a board and in life – Domenico trained himself to always win. No matter what, he always planned to come out a victor and smoke his enemies into oblivion.

But Domenico Armando was not prepared for the terrible series of bad news he was to receive this evening inside the private den of his secret underground palace he resided in at this time! He was not prepared for the stalemate scenario he was about to be hand-delivered to him by his own Counsellor Rex Higgins this evening after his late supper with his son. Domenico never expected to be given any piece of information that he could not turn around and create a successful result from an otherwise checkmate failure. No.

Domenico, for the first time in his life was going to receive two bits of bad news that he was forced to concede his absolute lack of power to overturn, or make disappear as if it had never occurred. Domenico, for the first time in his life would be forced to now concede defeat! He had suddenly struck losing ground! And there was no way out of it. Not even for the great Domenico Armando and all his powers and what seemed to the world as, supernatural prowess. Domenico could not do a single thing to change fate and destiny. He could not lift a finger as always in the past and as if by magic, make it all turn around back into his favour. No! This time, it was impossible. Domenico was also forced to concede the truth right now that the word 'impossible' mixed with his name had unfortunately blended together — as it had for everyone else in the world, without exception.

Domenico looked at his accomplishments to date. They were many! They were spectacular! They were incredibly fantastic and unequalled! No one could match him or beat him at his own game. Domenico had secured his power, his position and outstanding, not-so-secret wealth as the richest man in the world, especially the underworld. He had survived tremendous obstacles which were known to kill many others! He had entered a well-protected Private Hospital (owned by him) but covered with numerous powers such as police and federal agents opposing him - and he still managed to get out in one piece, defying the odds; cheating death.

And his greatest victory of them all was the day he was arrested by the hero of all American heroes, Robert Stewart — and before the signatures of his arrest could be finalised by all the relevant powers serving against him, Domenico had managed to escape from the dungeon prison cell of concrete and steel bars and re-enter the world a free man, taking his son and all his accomplice aiding and abetting tentacles and support systems with him; simply vanishing into thin air without a trace.

As soon as Domenico accomplished such a sensational prison breakout, once he had disembarked off his plane into the Caribbean, he could not help but throw a celebration for his freedom with his large army of men. A willing troop they were quite enthusiastic in joining their celebrated master to toast such a momentous occasion.

Domenico stood inside his private den as he had been right now at present. But, he stood before his large army of henchmen, waited for the applause to finish after the drinks of champagne and high-society servings of food was delivered to them all by his many maids and servants, in compliments to him, then Domenico began his memorable, and oh-so-powerful speech. The opening introduction of his words was considered magical — and the remainder of his speech had dazzled and bewitched even his toughest strong-arms he had planted by his side, who all could not help but feel much moved, much inspired and much appreciative to be surrounded and joined in the presence of a man they considered more than a king, more than royalty... But they considered him their god! They worshipped the ground he walked on. They kissed his hands, his cheeks; they embraced him whenever they were invited, in the highest esteem and respect possible. This man before them was completely superior to everyone else. He was magical. He was Prime Ministerial! He was considered their President. Their King! Their one true Leader! - An Eternal Leader. But most of all they considered him their one true god. Someone ever-so powerful, even in a spiritual sense, much blasphemously, they considered him to be a man who could withstand anything. A man who could survive anything! A man who could never age! And certainly, no matter what his prognosis – he was considered as a man who could never die!

And following his safe return to his island fortress, Domenico delivered his speech before his great crowd with much enthusiasm, much aura, power and sheer magical and forceful presence.

He spoke the words: 'I am Domenico Armando! And no one had better forget that! I want everyone here to remember this day for as long as you live! I want you all to celebrate this day yearly as an anniversary of my victory! And yes indeed, it was a spectacular win for me and for us all. I had proven that no man can compete with me! No man can defeat me! No man can outfight me or outsmart me! I also confirmed to the entire world that no steel bars and concrete walls could ever stop Domenico Armando. No prison made from the sturdiest stuff could even ever slow me down! I showed the world this glorious day that I am invincible! I am indestructible! I am tougher than all my enemies out there in this world combined! I showed them all what tough-stuff Domenico Armando is made of!

'Could Hitler survive his enemies? No. He committed suicide, taking what he envisaged the easy way out. He was a pretender. He was a man with a plethora of insecurities and phobias. He only acted strong! But neither he nor any other man could ever accomplish what I had this evening! No one could defeat their enemies and escape such a confinement unharmed and unhindered as I had done so this day! No one can do what Domenico Armando can do! And there has never been a man like me before – and there will never be another man like me again!'

Domenico could only thrive at the huge echoes of claps and cheers and idolising praises of adulation he thusly received at this moment. Domenico thrived on his audience, his fan-base worshipping him. And Domenico was certainly not ashamed in applauding himself and joining them in celebrating his own, in himself, considered spectacular magnificence at this very moment.

304

He yet had to finish his speech – and as they saw him ready to continue, the applause and cheers quietened down to make his splendour heard!

Domenico concluded his speech by adding: 'Every leader this world has ever seen was a phoney compared to I-me-Domenico Armando! They were all try-hards! I on the other hand am the real thing! I am the real deal! I am completely natural and 100% confident in a world of actors, pretenders and weaklings who can only do and say the wrong thing. Only Domenico Armando knows the true definition of great oratory speeches before masses of men. The rest have no idea how to deliver two words together coherently and honestly! Only I have the courage to speak the truth even when the truth is not to everyone else's liking. I never portray myself as a politician or a Hitler – telling people to their face what they want to hear and behind the backs of their people doing the exact opposite thing. Even their own men, women and children, such so-called leaders betray!

'It is good to be back here again! It is good to hear your applause and chants and unending cheers! And I will treasure this moment and all my loyal armies of men forever and ever!'

The applause continued, without end for a long period of time after that.

So, all in all, Domenico considered himself able to accomplish anything – and overturn any obstacle until this very evening when fate and destiny intervened yet again and forced him to alter his opinion, rethink his life's direction and make drastic changes to his grand future plans once his Counsellor Rex Higgins delivered to him the late edition newspaper of an occurrence which truly sent his world crashing downhill that instant!

Domenico read the front page headlines of the New York City press gallery which stated: **HEROIC COP ROBERT STEWART DEAD!**

And the subheading read: Nation mourns.

Domenico glanced through the article below it reporting the apparent mysterious deaths of Robert and his entire family via a plane explosion. They died that instant. The article had numerous theories as to the cause of such an explosion. But authorities had suspected that it was either accidental (of course) or murder via an act of sabotage. And the name to a suspected culprit was revealed as no other, but Domenico Armando.

Domenico screwed up the newspaper in shock and fury as he had never experienced before and cursed angrily: "What-how? This cannot be! No! No!

305

No! How can he be dead? Who had committed such an action? It certainly was not me! Those stupid police and reporters are accusing me of everything. But I am innocent! I did not order this! I am not responsible!" he cursed. "But whoever is responsible will be found. I want you Rex to have our moles in the New York City Police Department investigate this – and I want some answers given to me at once. I want to know how it happened and why it happened! And I want the culprit son of a bitch brought to me here, delivered at my feet! I am going to bury that bastard alive! He is going to be crushed to very small pieces with my bare hands! He is going to suffer! Yes. What irony - I will be avenging the death of the one man who I swore to destroy! And I will avenge it because this culprit has destroyed me too by committing such a murder of Robert and his family! Now my plans are shattered straight into hell! Everything I wanted to accomplish-all my plans for the immediate future have been destroyed by this tragic unfortunate occurrence.

"The scoundrel behind these deaths has robbed me too of my chance for redemption; to achieve a second chance at life. To be reunited with my family in New York! They have cheated me too! Robert was also the one and only remaining lead to my grandson's whereabouts! Besides, Robert dying like this is far too easy. He has been let off the hook far too simply! Now all my plans are shattered! My whole world has just crumbled before my very eyes! For that I will unleash all hell upon the culprit and culprits responsible. I want you to find out his name! And I want you to deliver that scum to me – and anyone else who helped him commit this death of my plans I want also brought to me! Because now that my plans are dead – so too will they all die right along with Robert and his family!

"I don't care what the remainder of the police conclude. I don't care about their reports of a stumbling block into their investigation hitting numerous roadblocks! Because if truth be told, without Robert Stewart the rest of the police could not solve even the simplest of crimes even if their stupid lives depended on it! So have no regard for what the police say. Because they are so dumb that I would also be surprised if that wretched newspaper article stated that they had any true definite clues besides the simple untruths of my name being fabricated so ignorantly in connection to this nonsense!

"So you gather our expert personnel and you bring me all the answers I need. Because I will not rest until the culprits responsible for the death of all my plans, including my goals for accomplishing my much-coveted and long-awaited cherished immortality are dealt with in the severest fashion imaginable!"

Rex Higgins nodded his head dutifully and left the room immediately to carry out his orders and make some phone calls and instruct the necessary Armando spies to investigate the matter thoroughly as Domenico demanded to know everything-every answer to all his questions!

Domenico had summoned his son to one of his dungeon rooms that moment. He wanted him to witness another Armando execution he had just ordered. The target was the Robert Stewart impostor!

The look-alike was immediately tied to a chair. He was surrounded by four burly-looking strongmen who wore brass knuckles. They were ordered to beat the impostor to death! Since Robert Stewart was dead, he was no longer needed. And Domenico was always a very thorough man who never left any clues behind!

Domenico said to his son as they witnessed the bloody beating: "That sleazebag punk was a nitwit anyway. His death will be painful. But just before his end, he will be forced to realise what a favour I am giving him by ending his miserable pathetic existence!"

So Domenico and his son watched the brutal bloody bashing of the impostor to a gruesome unrecognisable pulp! The strongmen struck him ferociously in turn and all together all over his head and body, piercing large pieces of the target's flesh to very open bloody wounds. And it only ended once one of the strongmen had struck him a fatal blow on top of his head with a clenched hammer fist!

Once the confirmation was made that his short-lived impostor was pronounced dead, Domenico was now satisfied. His men began untying the corpse preparing to dispose of it accordingly and clean up any human residue which remained inside the room after the fact!

Domenico took the murder well. But he was concerned in his son's reaction to it all. He watched his son cringe at the sight of every powerful blow that was delivered to the target. D.J. shook his head in much fright to it all. Domenico was truly worried. Even his own son was starting to lose his mettle, his edge after Domenico spent a long time now trying to build up his strength of character.

But D.J. was bothered by his current circumstances. Domenico knew this. But despite his trying to extend much moral support to his son, he was forced to watch D.J. crumble more and more into his own personal hell!

CHAPTER 8

Domenico and his son adjourned back to the private office den. Domenico was truly concerned for his son's emotional welfare, his apparent growing depression. But he still had another serious matter to discuss with him. And the nature of that was his wife, Sandra!

Domenico insisted, "Look my son. I know you may not be in the best spirits right now and we will deal with that together in due course. But right now we have something equally as important to talk about! And the product of that topic is treachery: meaning your wife's betrayal to you, to me and your son-my grandson!"

D.J.'s eyes became wide open and alert right now; mixed with much concern for what his father was getting at; what he was hinting.

But Domenico would explain everything that instant. "Look it, my son. I always warned you about marrying a foolishly stupid reporter."

D.J. became angry at his father for the first time in his life and raised his voice at him to say, "This is my wife you are talking about!"

Domenico snapped, "Wife?" he yelled. "How dare you argue with your father! You know I know best! Look my son. She betrayed us! That means she is not your wife any longer. She is a whore-faced tramp of a slut. That woman is a bitch! She is guilty of treachery. And that cannot be tolerated! She must be dealt with accordingly! We need to find your son-my grandson and then get rid of her! Robert Stewart whispered a few unsweet some things in her ear and then she left you so easily without a word or an utterance. She left taking your son with her!" he insisted.

D.J. showed his courage against his father in argument to this point. "Has it ever occurred to you father that she left probably because she was scared out of her mind? She left because I had transformed into something I have now grown ashamed to have become! What do you expect? I ordered a hit on Robert and his family. After she learnt of it, don't you think she had cause for alarm? Because to tell you the truth I am feeling very alarmed by what I had become! I am feeling bloody alarmed by what I had almost been responsible for committing!

"I cannot believe what I did or tried to do! I tried to kill a man! I tried to order the deaths of his family! I feel sick because of it! I should not be in this

309

position! I should be free to come and go! I was happy with my wife and my son before I let myself be suckered in by you and your insane ways! I should never have gotten involved in this craziness! I should have bailed out! When you first started to groom me into your world, I should have taken my wife and child and ran away. I should have left the country far away from you and your evil corrupt ways!"

Domenico took several deep breaths and spoke to his son meekly. "Look D.J., I know you are not happy with everything that has happened in our lives recently, but you must be patient because I am working to rectify the situation so we can all be free again. We won't have to hide like this forever. Just be patient a little while longer. I will take care of everything. Besides, it pains me to see you feeling any sort of remorse for a man who beat you to a pulp, with intent to kill you. He arrested you. So please, don't feel guilty about anything!"

D.J.'s depression had now transformed to aggression. "Father, what did you expect Robert to do? I tried to have him and his family killed! What do you think – that he should have just stood back and take it all right up the arse and do nothing to defend himself from my brief possession by your insanity?

"And father; how do you expect to rectify the situation? I have seen that horrendously huge Death List you have constructed sitting inside your desk drawer over there on the other side of this room. I have seen it and you know what my reaction to all of it is? I wish I was dead, that is how horrible I feel to be a part of this madness! I would rather be one of your intended victims than the culprit responsible for putting all of those people in their graves.

"Here you are saying that they are all guilty; that they are all worthy of death. But that is not true, father! You have included innocent women and children and sweet little old ladies in that heinous list of yours. You have marked them all for death; and for what? So we can return to the big world and live amongst ourselves, all alone with no one else in it? Can't you see what you are planning is insane? Do you want to include little old ladies and defenceless people on your horrible list as well? So we can call ourselves Big Men? Let's kill helpless people so we can feel like real tough and scary Armandos, is that what you think will happen, father?

"It is ludicrous! This is worse than insane! It simply cannot be allowed to happen! I don't want to hear your words that those people may or may not be descendants of anyone who is your enemy which warrants them necessary to

310

be marked for death… because to tell you the truth father… they are not our enemies. We are theirs. That is the truth.

"Since we got back here after our prison escape, I swiftly came back to my senses from all your corrupt tactics you imposed upon me! We have escaped from one prison only to enter another one! It redefines the word madness. And the only solution you have for us to save our wretched arses is to perform an equivalent Noah's Ark type destruction upon the free world; so that we are the only ones left ready to take up your blasphemous orders of repopulating the earth with only Armandos. Father, how can you not see what we have become? We are not warriors, we are scoundrels! We are not heroes, we are scumbags! We are bloody savage animals, barbarians - shitheads!

"If you were not so obsessed and consumed in feeding your giant ego in order to prove your awesome power to everyone and everything in this world, you would be able to see the truth more clearly! That, in fact, Robert Stewart should never have been our enemy! We should always have been working together on his side from the very beginning. But now, it is all too late. That poor man is dead! All he tried to do was stop fiendish scum like us. Why? Because we were killing his people! So he had every right to retaliate against us! It was the right thing to do! What else did you expect him to do?

"Instead of working with him, we worked against him. Instead of earning the world's respect, we made them all afraid of us! Instead of helping people, we began destroying them! And don't give me the cliché crap father that such people are unworthy of help because they were not strong or wise enough. If we were normal people, with any form of rational logic between our ears, we would have realised that we could have been society's guide-its teacher. We could have been an example for others to follow. But instead, what did we do, father? We chose to enter the wrong path and do everything that is immoral, oblivious to the fact that eventually we were going to be caught, imprisoned and forced to live out the remainder of our days like this. In some underground depressing mausoleum! Forced into complete isolation! This place gives me the shits! I do not care for its decorations in marble, silver and gold. It is still very depressing to me! Without my wife, I am even more depressed! Does that sound like we are winners, father? Because what we really are, is something horrendous and hideous, to all that is contrary of winning! I cannot stress that enough to you father. Now I am tired. I am not feeling well. I am going to go to my room and sleep! And with any luck I hope I will never wake up again! Because every day I wake up, I know that no matter how much I fight it, you have drawn me in so deep into your world, that I have no choice right now, but to participate in it and your horrible plans – no matter how much I detest every single one of them!"

CHAPTER 9

Domenico Armando was forced to endure the worst pain imaginable when events took a drastic turn for the worse and now he was made to attend the funeral home of his own beloved daughter Annemarie in Brooklyn, New York. He attended the horrible event in a disguise. He wore a white-coloured wig and made himself resemble an old man on a wheelchair, with a helper by his side and many safety precautions taken everywhere else around him in such a public and much floral-wreath decorated procession.

For security reasons, the remainder of Domenico's children could not attend their sister's funeral. It was decided that it would draw too much attention from the wrong people. Domenico would pass on any information necessary on all the current occurrences and happenings!

Domenico had taken an enormous risk attending his daughter's funeral in New York. He took a grave chance entering the city of his hometown once again. It was obvious that the police would stake out the funeral home, even wearing plainclothes, unrecognisable to anyone who attended, only to mingle with the crowd of mourners hoping to stumble across the deceased's father, should he have the audacity to make himself present.

But in himself, Domenico's risks this day were only much necessary! He certainly would never allow one of his children to leave this world surrounded by strangers and people he regarded, who really did not care for her or her father.

Domenico would allow nothing and no one to stop him from attending the funeral procession of his much loved daughter. And he vowed to fight anyone who dared try to stop him. And he vowed to fight them all to the death.

Domenico would arm himself with gun for gun against his enemies. Bullet for bullet! He would attend in anger and desperation only to say goodbye to his precious Annemarie. It was surely a death which struck him with much surprise and unexpectedly! In himself, he could not believe his bad luck which had rained upon him all of a sudden.

First his son D.J. was struck by the same disease his now deceased daughter Annemarie suffered for many weeks prior her death. D.J. was chronically depressed in personal misery. The look in his eyes was horrifying. Domenico was mortified. He knew his son was driven so far into the depths of mental hell that he also did not care to live right now. And his son Tom also with them in the Caribbean would hardly speak. He too became a quivering jelly. His other daughter Monica constantly mourned the loss of a man she once loved: Paul Stewart. And now the worst nightmare imaginable had become reality: His second daughter Annemarie had died without a word, with no warning.

The police investigators, mixed with Domenico's own spies in the local police force confirmed the tragic cause of her death. It was suicide. She overdosed one day on her anti-depression medications as she was alone inside her bedroom – until she went to sleep and never woke up again. The autopsy concluded that she died from a massive heart attack.

When Domenico was given the news by his counsellor inside his private den of his Caribbean island confirming this; showing him another newspaper article, now concerning his daughter's suicide, Domenico became frozen in a comatose state for a moment. Then he staggered back in fright for the first time in his life. He collapsed onto his knees and incredibly, much childlike he grabbed his counsellor's legs at the knees, wrapping both arms around them as he rested his head onto Rex's legs and mourned like a child who lost his mother.

Domenico wept and he cursed out loud: "My beautiful Annemarie dead! No. It cannot be. She was so young my precious Annemarie! She had everything to live for! She had every opportunity I provided to her! Why did she do it? Why did she kill herself?" he cried in agony.

Domenico's face then changed into fury as he moved himself and sat onto the floor, now his back against the wall of his private den. He became furious in thought; enraged at how she died. He suddenly clenched his fists in the air and looked at the apologetic eyes of his loyal compatriot, Rex Higgins and insisted: "No, my friend, it is not you who will be sorry. It is all those responsible for her death who will be sorry. I want them brought here delivered before me on their knees. I am going to massacre each and every one of them to death! But first they are going to suffer dearly. They are going to beg me for a death which I will not give them quickly. No, no, no! They will not die until their screams of bitter torture have quenched the fire boiling inside of me now, my counsellor! I am so angry, so enraged that my beautiful

Annemarie has died from a heart attack in her twenties. She was only in her twenties!" he suddenly wept into his hands, "Only in her twenties!"

Domenico's face and his emotions had constantly fluctuated between bitter tears and profound rage. "No child should ever die before their parents!" he said furthermore. "No child should ever die before they are privileged to experience all of life's opportunities! It is their right. It was my daughter's right to live to a ripe old age. She was such a good person. She did not deserve this!" Domenico's temper suddenly flared as he waved his right clenched fist into the air ready to take on the entire world right this very moment: "It should have been me! It should have been me who died, not her! Not my sweet Annemarie!" he mourned. "I tried to do everything possible to protect her-to save her from her emotional trauma she endured these last several weeks. But fate and destiny had prevented me from being with my daughter. That fucking nature had made me fail my own flesh and blood – and for that I WANT REVENGE! You hear me? REVENGE!" he shouted in terror.

Domenico now ordered his counsellor to perform his next duty for him – and at once. "I do not care what the newspapers say. I do not care what the police or anyone else says concerning the cause of her death! I know the real cause of her death! It was not suicide! It was murder! And the people responsible for killing her are those fucking scum doctors and nurses I hired to help her. But they took my money and they did not perform their duties correctly. They left her unsupervised knowing full well that she was unstable and suicidal. She overdosed on medicine they had prescribed to her, such deadly drugs; which means that it was deliberate murder! There is no other way to look at this! It was cold-and-calculated murder! So you instruct our people to put chains and shackles around the wrists and ankles of all those doctors and nurses who failed my daughter – and you put them on a plane and bring them here to me; because I am going to unleash my bitter anger of hell upon them. I am going to make them suffer the tortures of the damned for what they have done to my daughter!

"I am going to watch them scream and shout in bitter torment before they die. I want to hear them in agony! It is the only way my fury can be quenched even a little bit. And then they will die! And not only will they die! But the entire world who failed me and my daughter will also pay the ultimate

315

penalty! Because I blame them all for what happened. Everyone in the entire world is to blame for what happened to my sweet Annemarie!

"So you go at once and you bring me those doctors, because I first want to take care of them personally. After all, what they did to my daughter is personal. Then once I have taken care of them – then my plans for the world will be unleashed! Yes, Rex. There will be no way out from that this time! My plans for the ultimate revenge will proceed immediately following my daughter's funeral. Yes. I want you also to make all the arrangements for the expenses of her funeral. And have the pilot fuel the jet and make it ready because I will be attending that funeral in New York. Let anyone try to stop me! Let any police or government agent try to interfere with me attending my daughter's funeral and I can promise you one thing: that there will be a long line of consecutive funerals planned thereafter. Because they too will end up in a pine box quicker than what my Annemarie was put inside of one! That I can promise you! And I can promise you something else: EVERYONE IS GOING TO PAY FOR THIS!"

It was 3:00 a.m. in the morning on the eve of his daughter's funeral when all the doctors and nurses hired to ensure the emotional wellbeing of his daughter were delivered in chains to Domenico's secret underground foreign hideout in the Caribbean. They were all taken together lined up inside one huge grim-looking, stone-walled, dim-lit, concrete-floored dungeon room.

The doctors were all bound in a line next to each other on single wooden chairs. The nurses were individually chained left lying on their backs and sides onto the floor.

Domenico ordered five executioners to do away at the same time each of the five doctors. And the same procedure was cast forward upon the nurses. Five more executioners assigned to assassinate the five nurses.

Domenico instantly ordered his men to begin the massacres, but first against the female nurses. His five executioners each held a sharp wire garrotte in both hands and placed each garrotte simultaneously around the necks of all the screaming nurses. The garrottes bore a very sharp wire, so really there was little effort required to achieve the desired result. Each garrotte had sliced expertly across the blood-gorged throats of each of the targets. They died instantly and rather quickly.

316

Domenico in himself wanted all the nurses to die! But he left the real work of torture to be unleashed upon the five male doctors he lined up; now their anxieties taking over their bodies as the worst fear had consumed them.

Domenico first confronted them at the same time as he stood before them all who were seated in one neat row of chairs, in one given line. He said: "My daughter. My daughter… You took my money… You stole from me and for that, you will first lose your hands. Because your hands tempted you to steal from me and rob my daughter, you pack of filth and swine!"

The five henchmen were each armed with an axe. The five doctors had their hands chained before them resting onto the arms of the wooden chairs, quite visibly. The henchmen lifted their axes promptly and immediately sent the large heavy blades raised up and down in two consecutive manoeuvres across the two exposed wrists of each of the doctors severing their hands at the wrists in perfect aim!

The screams of torturous pain were gruesomely loud. But Domenico's powerful voice was raised at them, amazingly overpowering their screams all combined as he wanted to feel much compelled in their suffering right now. He thought of his daughter and every glimpse of her memory enraged him more. And the more enraged he became the more he needed to feel satisfied in his brutal vendettas thus cast upon his deemed culprits responsible for it all. So he wanted to hear his targets scream for many moments to come before he ordered his men to finish them off.

Domenico's henchmen became slightly mortified and shaken from the screams. It was as if they were cast into hell itself surrounded by the damned all screaming in bitter torments as many eel-like creatures were forced to eat into their spiritual flesh, wearing huge teeth and munching away and away forever and ever at the spirit that kept growing back again and again for these creatures (worms) cast upon each soul in swarms on every part of them inside and out, to never stop tormenting them.

And such unending screams for now had surely terrified the henchmen. In themselves, they wanted the voices to stop. They could not tolerate the bellows of loud voices any longer. The pain of their victims unhelped had made them sick right now. But they could only remain as they were until the go-ahead came from their master to end it all. And when the order arrived, the henchmen all considered it, not soon enough.

Domenico was satisfied. He nodded to his henchmen who all glanced at him waiting in eagerness for the word to be given and once it had, the executioners then each pulled out revolvers from the inside of their jacket pockets, armed their hands with the weapons, aimed them perfectly at the foreheads of the five doctors at point-blank range and fired two shots apiece until the screams had finally ceased. And the heads of all the deceased bowed forward. The gunshot wounds from their heads trickled down masses of blood dripping onto the ground, meeting amputated hands that also were dropped onto the concrete floor prior that.

Soon the ten corpses were all disposed of into another room which contained the human incinerator; which became the usual course of action chosen by them, in order to get rid of all of its dead corpses.

Following this, Domenico placed a small picture of his daughter Annemarie he held in one hand, then pressed at his chest against his heart and spoke the words: 'Rest in peace, my beautiful daughter! You can rest now for all of eternity! Because I have avenged your death! And very soon all our enemies in this world will also join those grubby doctors and nurses into the flames!'

And now at the funeral home in New York, Domenico Armando ordered his henchman to wheel him to the open coffin to see his daughter lying inside. He wept again. Domenico had spotted his wife Rita among the crowd of mourners, but he kept his presence a secret even from her. Domenico was haunted by the reaction of his son D.J. much blaming him for his current misfortunes, Domenico simply did not want to hear any words of doom and gloom from his wife warranting the same blame to him now over their daughter's death.

So Domenico kept to himself and spoke to no one. He even mourned to himself as he now witnessed the closed eyes of the white-faced corpse of his daughter. Domenico felt the tears trickling down his cheeks. He still could not come to terms with the loss. The Great Domenico Armando was taken by surprise for the first, second and third time in his life at present. And this was a surprise he could not utilise any of his otherwise vast powers in order to overturn.

No. This time he could do nothing about it or say nothing to bring his daughter back from the dead! The Great Domenico Armando who could escape from a room made of concrete and steel bars could not fight death itself. No. Domenico felt vulnerable at this moment. He hated it! He thrived on always feeling ever so powerful, but now this situation had truly brought him to his knees. He was helpless. He was defenceless. He was powerless to do anything about it! His daughter was dead and he had to endure it. He was forced to suffer the bitter torment of losing one of his children as he now recalled costing many others such offspring.

Domenico came to realise what his targets must have endured even by his actions. His mind unhelped became focused on all his targets he also had widowed and orphaned and ashamed of the sudden emotional weakness he was overcome by. He killed without mercy, without compassion, without any thought or feeling about it! He always slept well at night after the fact. But now, he could not comprehend what was happening to his mind. He could not control his thoughts at this moment.

He shook his head many times to attempt to have such thoughts pass away from his mind. He closed his eyes briefly in hopes that once he opened them his mind would not be so clear in that horrible picture of how his many countless victims felt after each successful slaughter of their loved ones. What the hell is happening to me? I don't like these thoughts! I never had them before! Go away! Go away! I don't want to think about such things! I am Domenico Armando! I am strong in mind and body and spirit! This should not be happening to me! To everyone else, yes! But not to me! Get out of my head! I don't want to see their faces! Get lost! Go to hell whoever is doing this to me! I cannot bear such weakness in my mind! No! I should not have such thoughts! I have to somehow get rid of this! Maybe if I make myself get angry again! Perhaps this funeral has disrupted my mind's normal functioning! I must get angry now again! I have to stop crying! Anger will fix me! It will cure my mind, I'm sure of it! That way my stupid feelings of sudden all-consuming guilt by such recurring thoughts will be overpowered by my feeling compelled to have done what I had done!

But Domenico found it difficult to control his mind's thoughts and the mysterious product to such thoughts. He tried to psyche himself and his emotions to feeling anger again, but he seemed too emotionally weak right now to change or restore his mind to its usual power. But before he could, Domenico was surprised yet again in much consecutive ill-fated streaks of bad fortune striking his life much like lightning just as he sat posted aside his daughter's coffin. He was surprised terribly now again, three times, in such a short space of time!

Domenico's mind playing tricks on him at present had caught him off-guard when he was struck by a man before him holding a gun, pointed directly at his heart!

Domenico did not recognise the man holding the weapon before him as his eyes made a sweep across the funeral home's perimeters and he noticed the sight of many uniformed police closing in on his identified men scattered all across the large room. Even an officer stood behind him, a gun now trained onto his helper who was moving his wheelchair around the premises for him, as he was seated inside it.

This was the classic picture of a perfect standoff. Domenico's men and the police had guns trained on the other. And everyone was fearful in firing a shot in case the other was killed.

The man holding a weapon directly in front of Domenico resembled a black-skinned officer Domenico could not recall ever meeting before in his life. But his attacker now wished to jog Domenico's memory and his recollection to his true identity when he forced the words in an abrupt and strong tone of voice: "Freeze, Domenico!"

Domenico staggered back in much surprise once again. He immediately recognised the voice even though he could not recognise his confronter's face. But the man did not wish to trick him any further. No. The games were over! And so were Domenico's days as a tyrant! "Your little games are over Domenico! You will not get away this time!"

Domenico instantly put two and two together. He suddenly felt his mind restored to its original focus, no longer distracted and maintained his brave front as he spoke to his adversary now quite firmly, though much surprised to see that he was alive. But his confronter's so-called death was obviously a trick, a hoax, a set up. One done very deliberately and cleverly in order to catch him-Domenico Armando off-guard, no doubt to bring forth his much-planned demise. But Domenico wished not to give his enemy, now much brought back from the dead, any sort of satisfaction by acting taken aback and showing any form of astonishment or sudden bewilderment at the very sight of him. "So it is you, Robert Stewart, my old friend. Or should I say my most worthy adversary in the world!" He then murmured the following words in much scorn, "I should have known!"

Robert held the gun firmly in his hand, pointing it at an incredibly constant steady direction, not wavering so much as an inch away from Domenico's heart. Robert now revealed himself, his motives and his clever movements all this time undercover, much under the radar and behind the scenes. Robert said, wearing his elaborate disguise as Frank Northgate, but without any necessity to reveal any credentials to that effect. "I knew you would show up here Armando. And I was waiting for you all this time! I was scrutinising with the crowd of mourners, checking them out inconspicuously, to see which one could possibly be you showing up here in disguise. I studied all of the suitable physical profiles whilst cross-filing their names and histories with our police records, until I found the odd man out; a too mysterious profile with an obviously trumped-up identity. And that is you. I knew who you were underneath that elaborate disguise of your own. You see, you came here under the assumed identity as your daughter's distant uncle. But I knew your family history! I studied it carefully. You see that disguise of yours does not match the physical profile and attributes of any of your children's distant uncles or relatives whatsoever, because they never had any distant uncles from your side, Domenico. You had no siblings, especially brothers. And your wife only has one sister. And she was married only for a brief period. Your children showed little to no interest in ever becoming acquainted with such a man. So, you made it too easy for me to zero in on you once I knew you would eventually show up at your daughter's funeral. And my men and I were also zeroing in on your henchmen, one by one all at the same time; all those who are planted around the walls of this building!"

Domenico was still in a state of grief and he struggled to gain the momentum of his usual anger demonstrated before his rival. But he did respond in a sober tone of voice. "So what do you want Robert? Would you like me to congratulate you? Is that it? Because forgive me if I choose not to. You see, my daughter just died. And I am sure you could guess that yes, when a man's daughter dies there isn't anything he would not do to bid her farewell from this world filled with treachery and hardship and many disappointments – particularly by all those out there who never gave a damn whether she lived or not! So I am here! And I have said my goodbyes! And I am grateful for that! I have also avenged her death with all those directly responsible for her apparent suicide-I choose to call murder!"

Robert only wished to correct his most wanted target right now. "You see, that's where you are wrong, Domenico! Whilst undercover, I was also investigating the real cause of Annemarie's death, as tragic and unfortunate as that death was... and I uncovered the real reason why she committed suicide! It was due to the evil of your ways: it corrupted her sanity. She couldn't cope with the truth. So she overdosed on her anti-depressant and anti-anxiety medications... until she had a heart attack! No one knows that more than your wife Rita. She lived through the hell that Annemarie was going through. The doctors and nurses, in actual fact, tried to do everything within their power to help her. But sometimes people choose not to be helped. You blamed the doctors. Yes, Domenico, many doctors are corrupt. But your judgement was not out when you handpicked those specific doctors and nurses to look after your daughter. You see, the truth is, they had actually prolonged her life. But they could not save her, because Annemarie did not want to be saved! She could not bring herself to forget about the reality of her existence and the reality of who her father really was and is! That is what killed her, no one else! So don't go around blaming anyone else Domenico; because if you want someone to blame, you only need to look as far as a mirror." Robert said angrily. "Your days of blaming people-everyone else for all the trails of deaths and destructions you leave behind are also over! It's over for you, Armando! You're finished! You're not going to get away this time!"

Domenico's hands were concealed on his lap beneath a large scarf covering them both. Domenico quickly lifted his right hand from beneath the scarf and produced a hidden pistol he also rapidly pointed at Robert.

And that was all it took at that moment to set off a chain reaction that would predict the deaths of the two of them right this instant.

The shots began to fire on both sides. Domenico fired his first shot. Robert fired his next shot. And together they fired three extra shots each into the other. Robert struck Domenico four times in the chest whilst Domenico fired four shots in Robert's abdomen.

That instant they both rolled onto the carpet floor before Annemarie's coffin, lying side by side next to the other, each with four bullets inside their bodies.

To the crowd of mourners gathered around them, this incident signified a double-and-triple tragedy. Annemarie was suspected not to become the only fatality which they would grieve for this afternoon!

BOOK 7

CHAPTER 10

Robert Stewart had awakened from his coma seven days later; his coma induced as a result of his gunshot injuries. After he was shot, he was taken to the secret SIA safe house in Brooklyn under armed guard. One of the rooms was turned into a private hospital facility. Special practising government doctors, surgeons and nurses were brought in to perform the operation and hopefully bring to life their beloved Robert Stewart.

Once the bullets were all successfully removed from his abdomen, the doctors were proud to report that the surgery was a success – and Robert was expected to make a full recovery. He had slipped into a coma for a brief period as a result of the trauma he had sustained from his injuries mixed with severe blood loss. But his father present inside the facility, with a perfect blood-type match had made himself available for all the necessary blood transfusions his son had required.

Once Robert had returned to consciousness, he was still rather groggy from all the sedative and pain-killing medications he was given. But his senses were alert enough to recognise all those present in the room who surrounded the bed he lay upon with medical tubes hanging all over his face and body. Robert was able to speak, but he only could slowly for some time yet.

Anyhow, he was first greeted by his SIA Boss Chief Lloyd McKenzie who sat on a chair aside him, patting his shoulder, welcoming his return as he said, "Good to have you back old boy. I made all the arrangements with our agency to tend to your every need to ensure your full recovery!"

Robert nodded his head slightly in recognition and much gratitude for everything his good friend and government superior had done for him. But that was not all.

McKenzie had a great surprise for Robert. Behind him stood his entire family present inside the room; all instantly had shown themselves and embraced Robert upon his return to consciousness.

McKenzie further added, "I took the liberty to have them all brought back here to New York safely to stay with you for moral support and help you in the healing process. The doctors and nurses insisted that having your family by your side was necessary to benefit you in returning to full recovery. So I made all the arrangements!"

Robert smiled at his chief much thoughtfully. His eyes became filled with warmth as he coughed, much struggling to speak. But he managed to say, quite lucidly and coherently, "Thank you, chief. That is much appreciated. Having my family close by my side is definitely what I need right now. Thank you!"

Robert then swerved his eyes across the room as he glanced at his entire family present with much happiness returning to his demeanour at the sight of them. His parents, his wife, his children, his brother and his sister were all present. Also his best friend John McCallum made an appearance and insisted: "It's good to have you back partner. You gave us all one hell of a scare!"

Robert's mind suddenly remembered thoughts he wished he did not have to recall right now. But he had to ask. He had to know the answer to his nagging question right now. "Domenico… Did you get him…? Is he dead…?" Robert asked curiously. After all, his family's lives depended on the answer to such a question.

John hesitated to answer. He briefly glanced at Robert's family, then his SIA Chief, whom all lowered their eyes in despondency. But John could not delay telling Robert the truth any longer. He knew that he would find out sooner or later. And Robert was as tough as nails. He was stubborn. He was too strong-willed to allow Domenico to get the better of him, in any situation; even now as he lay recuperating inside his private hospital bed.

John knew Robert could take the news, even if it was bad. It would not affect his recovery. Perhaps it may even assist him. In a strange way, it may speed his recovery when it became confirmed that he still had a very serious task yet to accomplish. The determination to do just that may be all that was needed to get him back onto his feet again in no time.

So John answered the question then and there truthfully, leaving no detail or salient point unaccounted for. "The truth is that we don't know what happened to Domenico, Robert. After you shot him, he too was seen unconscious. He could be dead or he could still be alive. We were in a stalemate to stop his men from removing his body from the funeral home of his daughter and taking it with them. He had just as many armed guards surrounding him as we had officers planted against his men. There were many innocent civilians inside that building. We did not want to risk their lives by opening fire and going all-out bloody on this. Because those civilians would have surely got in the way, and would have been killed in the crossfire by Domenico's many planted trigger-happy snipers hanging around all over the place – and the rest of us. We knew an ambush of this sort would not have been in our best interests. It would not have been very effective police work, even though our desperate goal was to neutralise Domenico and all his men at the scene. But, unfortunately, partner, given what we were faced with, such precarious circumstances, we had to let them go. We had to let them take Domenico's unconscious body with them. Two of his men carried him out and they shortly disappeared. No sign of any of them. Our police tails had followed them. Even choppers called at the scene lost them through various tunnels and what we believe was an elaborate change of vehicles."

Robert shook his head in dismay. "So during the past week while I was out of it, no one heard anything from anyone connected to him? No clues, nothing that may give us a hint what became of him?"

John replied, "Unfortunately not! The fact of the matter is that we don't know whether he is alive or not! I mean you gave him just as good as he gave you in that shootout. Maybe his injuries were worse, we don't know!"

Robert felt some pain emerge in his stomach region, and he wiggled his waist around slightly to ease the pain at the same time he used all his strengths to speak. "Then, we must assume that he is still alive. And it's business as usual. Without a body to confirm his death, we must assume that the enemy is not dead! And as soon as I am well enough I am going back out there onto the streets out looking for him! One way or another, we will find out the truth. And if he is alive, which meanwhile, we must assume that he is, then we will get him. I can promise you that. If he is still alive, it is only a matter of time before he shows his face again. But before that happens, I want to find him! I want to get him! I want to stop that maniac dead in his tracks!"

McKenzie insisted. "He is surely evil. I am sorry, but I am inclined to agree with you Robert. We must continue our search for the enemy under the presumption that he is still alive and kicking somewhere out there! Because

326

this could be a rouse – another one of the enemy's schemes to have us think he is dead. He could be lying low, playing the dead rat at the same time as he is plotting and planning his next insane agendas. Maybe he wants to catch us off-guard!"

Robert hinted. "Exactly, exactly; But he is not going to get away with it. He isn't going to be able to trick us into thinking anything that is not true! He will not fool us into a false sense of security via his manipulative tactics and false information directed toward us through his silence for now! I am surely convinced that our enemy is still out there – and I am going to get out of this bed as soon as possible. It just makes me so mad that Annemarie Armando suffered the ultimate price because of her father's insane and deranged wickedness! And it equally galls me that he tries to blame everyone else for his own shortcomings – everyone, but himself. Because he and he alone was responsible for his daughter dying! And I will not stop until he pays for everything that he has done!" Robert said now, as his old form was returning. His solid unyielding determination would certainly speed up the healing process of his injuries. And Robert's final words at this time to that effect were: "I am going to find him! And I am going to kill him!"

MANIAC SURROUNDED

BOOK 1

CHAPTER 1

Robert Stewart and Domenico Armando began shooting at each other with intent to cripple the opposition; to wipe out, to eliminate, harm, murder, kill and finally completely destroy the other.

Robert Stewart finally tracked the enemy down. He pinpointed his exact whereabouts. Robert was tipped off so to speak by someone, surprisingly, botched high up in the enemy camp, an unlikely source who told him, quite frankly and desperately the exact location of this madman. The unlikely source basically gave Robert and his confederates a literal roadmap to his new secret location. Domenico had secret hideouts all over the world. He now chose a seemingly peaceful, if not sleepy little town to hide inside at present. The location was in the heart of the Northern Territory in Australia. The premises was underground a 50-mile radius block of land. Domenico owned the entire 50-mile radius piece of land that surrounded the mansion and the underground fortress that was situated beneath it via a secret trap door.

Domenico owned the entire property via another array of elaborate fronts. Nothing of this magnitude of top secrecy was ever divulged publicly with his name in connection to it. Domenico was virtually situated in the middle of nowhere inside his new secret quarters. According to the source which tipped-off Robert, Domenico moved here to this foreign country and land because of medical reasons; divulging nothing else in detail. Just medical reasons, he said in general terms. The premises was equipped with all the necessary equipment and medical specialists to tend to his much-needed and urgent care. But Domenico was indeed confirmed alive; painfully very much alive to all those whom opposed him.

And upon such details being given, Robert hence gave a red alert to all his local, state and federal troops - and within 24 hours the Northern Territory in Australia was swarmed with US local, state and federal armies of police, FBI and SIA officials, the United States Army with the additional support of the Australian Army all combed the area, surrounding it entirely until the order was given to finally OPEN FIRE upon the enemy.

There were guns, handguns, machine guns, rifles of all makes and models and calibres. They were armed with hand grenades, dynamite explosives and other forms of bombs to be hammered upon the enemy. They even brought in huge bullet-proof tanks and choppers combing the entire 50-mile radius of the target's house. Basically, in short, all hell was going to erupt at this point.

Robert was armed with a police loud speaker and he ordered Armando to surrender. And the countdown to his time frame given to walk out of the premises with his hands above his head was given as 30 seconds. The enemy showed no likelihood of surrendering to their orders. Then the firing began on both sides.

Domenico's men were situated camouflaged outside above-and-behind trees and lying in the grass and inside trenches.

The government people also quickly dug out on all sides of the target's block of land very huge and deep trenches themselves to hide inside as the firing commenced; to attempt to protect themselves by dodging bullets fired at them by the enemy as they raised their weapons discreetly higher than the dirt ground above the trench they kneeled inside and fired away their extensive assortment of weapons.

Within minutes, that piece of property in the Northern Territory resembled a complete and utter war zone. Shots fired and bombs sent off everywhere left, right and centre erupted flames and fire and ash mixed with deafening ammunition-erupting sounds in broad daylight. The thirty-degree weather outside became hotter by the erupting fireballs that were triggered everywhere as a result of the gunshots and detonated bombs sent to go off at the enemy's people.

Robert was inside one of the trenches with his government partner Brock Stevens and his police partner John McCallum. All of them armed with guns firing at the enemy. US and Australian army soldiers crawled on to their hands and knees outside the trenches wearing their army greens, camouflaged in the same colour as the brown-and-green wilderness attempting to surprise the enemy's people scattered everywhere outside. But just as the enemy's soldiers were shot down so too were the government people in masses of numbers. Many men were being lost on both sides. Dozens soon spanned to hundreds and within hours the death toll on both sides was over a thousand, destined to become thousands more in bloody retaliation and calculated attritions of both the oppositions' resistances.

Robert Stewart, as he was planted inside one of the trenches made an attempt to crawl out, but Brock and John and the surprised arrival of his brother Paul pulled him back down.

His brother was the first to warn him: "Look it big brother, don't you dare go out there. We almost lost you once. We're not going to risk losing you again!"

Robert spoke with his usual strong-commanding voice, "Look little brother, I have to get that maniac! He is out there! He has to be stopped!"

329

Paul insisted, "And I came here to make sure that you don't end up killing yourself in the process of trying to kill him, all right! There is gunshots being fired everywhere around us; the noise here is bloody deafening too. People are dying all around us from both sides. I'm sorry Robert, but I'm not letting you go out there. It's been three weeks since you were released from hospital with serious gunshot injuries fired into you by that maniac. I'm not going to allow you to get shot again. This time it could be fatal. So, just stay here. Because the only way you are leaving this trench is over my dead body!"

Robert became impatient if not irate. "Damn it Paul. I am not too happy that you snuck on that plane ride here with me to enter into this danger. I did not want you here! You should have stayed back home!"

Paul suddenly lost his temper. He became irate himself, even uncontrollable as he grabbed his brother at the collar of his jacket with two clenched hands and began shaking him profusely. "I am sick and tired of you treating me like a kid. I don't need you or anyone looking out for me. I can take care of myself. And I am also sick and tired of your attitude towards me. I know the real reason you didn't want me to tag along with you here and that has nothing to do with my protection. You always thought you were a better man than me didn't you? You always thought I was an amateur compared to you, huh!" he said, his voice now resembling a shout in order to make himself heard above all the horrible gunfire noise being sounded all around them.

Before Robert could respond, John McCallum quickly intervened. He removed Paul's hold off Robert and interrupted them abruptly shouting: "What the hell is going on here between the two of you? We're in the middle of a war zone here. Do you brothers think it's the right time? Do you think this is an appropriate place to have a fistfight here? This is not the time to get your dukes up at each other in the middle of this lethal-and-dangerous battlefield, you hear me?"

Paul moved away for now in order to duck John's attack on them. Robert and John were now crouched side by side in their little place in the trench.

John now peaceably questioned Robert. "What the hell was that about between you and Paul?"

Robert replied coolly, "History, partner, just history. Something I thought was water under the bridge. But apparently my little brother is taking everything I say to him personally, even twisting my words around and upside down, just distorting everything. I didn't want him here for a different reason than he thinks. Just excuse me for a moment!"

Robert now crawled several meters to his brother inside the dusty-soil-brown trench and wanted to set things right at once between him and his sibling. Robert insisted, "Look Paul, I did not want you here because I think in any way that I am better than you. No. That is not the reason. I simply wanted you to stay back home to look after the rest of the family. Who else can I better trust for that job than you, huh? That is it, nothing more. So please don't read anything into this, ok!"

Paul nodded his head now more composed and more emotionally in control. "Got you; but I also came here because I didn't want to have to look at the faces of the family should they have anyone report to them that something happened to you, understand? That is why I came! To watch your back and make sure that this time we return home in one piece and most importantly, alive! That's my reason!"

Robert tapped his brother gently onto the shoulder with his hand and nodded his head, leaving it at that. Arguments over this incident would not solve anything right now. After all, what was done was done. Nothing could change that. It was not long before their argument was soon forgotten as they both raised their weapons and began aiming and firing at spotted enemies camouflaged in the embankment from a visible distance some thirty-or-so meters away above the trenches.

SIA Chief Lloyd McKenzie soon crawled over to the scene. What a surprise it was. What an inspiration it was to all the SIA personnel to see their chief volunteer quite enthusiastically to join them in the bloody battle against the enemy. Truly inspiring it was considered to see their superior - Mr. Suit and Tie, Mr. Office Boy, Mr. Clean-Shaven Bureaucrat to abandon his office formal clothing, formal disposition and mannerisms to join them in the trenches wearing too his Army Greens, with a rifle strapped to his shoulder pacing left and right in order to confer, order and counsel, even support his fellow SIA troop in battle. Now he tapped Robert onto his shoulder as he too ducked into the trenches on his hands and knees to also offer the same support to his two-greatest operatives, Robert and Brock.

Robert and Brock were delighted of his presence, though a tad concerned for the Head of the SIA risking his life like that by entering out into the battlefront facing the enemy and his bullets like this, as if without the slightest concern for his own safety.

But that aside McKenzie said, "This is going to drag out all night and possibly all day tomorrow – and possibly the next day and the day after that at this rate. Many men have been lost on both sides I'm afraid to report. But we have our objectives. We must do what we must do in order to win this one. Because as long as the enemy is alive our great country is at risk as well as any and all other countries the enemy chooses to enter, like this one, Australia! He must be stopped and hard!"

Robert nodded in complete agreement. "And in order to do that, we have to outfight and overpower all of Armando's people! We have to also destroy his entire communications systems all at the same time with our ammunition to ensure he cannot call out and bring in any further reinforcements which will only mean more lives to be lost and more time it will take to get Armando into our hands here, out into the open!"

McKenzie too nodded. "Precisely; you are exactly right, Robert!" McKenzie took a moment to respond to his portable radio he held in his right hand as one of his distant agents checked in to brief his superior on updates to their progress in this war zone; a usual progress report.

After his man had finished outlining his progress report, McKenzie relayed the message over to Robert and Brock. "It seems that some progress is being made, but it is very slow and very painful. Our man has just reported that our allies stationed here have now made a dent closer to that house in the centre of this fifty-mile stretch of land. They are now overpowering many of Armando's people and able to move closer in to the location of that house."

Robert smiled briefly. "So that's the goal. We have to overpower all of Armando's people in order to be able to enter that house and locate Armando inside there, and then... then..."

McKenzie interrupted, "Then hopefully he can be exterminated once and for all! Yes, my good man, Robert. That is the goal. That is most definitely our mission here!"

They all quickly ducked their heads as a spray of bullets towered over them from the enemy firing at their direction.

BOOK 2

CHAPTER 2

Robert Stewart had a very hectic police schedule prior his departure from New York, to arrive in Australia to face the enemy head-on in military combat fashion.

Within the last 48-hour period before he entered the SIA plane in the private airstrip in Brooklyn much tricky procedures had to be wrapped up first. And certain new developments had popped up from all directions as if to intentionally surprise him. They too had to be dealt with right away.

Firstly, Robert was handed the morning edition newspaper by his police partner John McCallum which reported a very salient turn of events.

The headlines read: **DOMENICO ARMANDO REPORTED DEAD!**

And the article below it stated the following words:

Domenico Armando was reported dead this morning by his daughter Monica Armando who returned to the borough of Brooklyn following the cremation and burial of her father; his ashes scattered at sea. (Which sea and where, she would not divulge.) She also claimed that he was fighting for his life from very serious gunshot injuries sustained as a result of the bloody shootout between him and Robert Stewart at his second daughter Annemarie's funeral. After three weeks of struggling from serious complications to vital organs he finally toppled over from his chair and fell to the ground into a coma and shortly died thereafter before his nearby physicians' could attempt to revive him.

And that was that…!

Robert Stewart read the article without showing any emotion. No surprise, no shock, nothing. He placed the newspaper onto his desk and leaned onto the edge of his desk in much preoccupied thought.

But his train of thought was quickly broken when his brother Paul stormed into his office holding the very same newspaper article his brother had just finished reading. But Paul's reaction was in direct contrast to his brother's. Paul's reaction was one of immense pleasure. He entered his brother's office smiling, laughing and did a crazy hop, skip and a jump gesture in a type of celebration over the fact.

Then he tapped his hand onto his brother's shoulder and said, "Hallelujah!" he repeated again. "Hallelujah! The son of a bitch is finally dead! Can you believe that? You did it bro! The world is now a much better place to live in! AND MUCH SAFER! How about that! Let's break out the champagne and party! What are we waiting for some kind of fucking written down invitation?

That scumbag bastard is gone forever! What is this, a funeral? Fuck him! Let's party!" He studied his brother's serious face and became confused himself as to why his brother did not share his same sentiment of an all-round 'highly good spirit' over the news. Paul had to know what the hell was going on. Why was his brother so serious about it? Why was he not too laughing his head off? The man he hated more than any other enemy he had ever faced in his entire life was gone. What was going on here? Paul had to know. He approached his brother and showed him again the front-page newspaper headlines concerning the enemy's demise right before his eyes and insisted: "Look at that, bro! Why the long face? What the hell is wrong with you?"

Robert scratched his forehead still in preoccupied thought. He would not answer as yet. Paul rapidly became concerned. He insisted again, still waving the newspaper before his brother's eyes, "Robert, don't tell me you're unhappy about this!"

Robert finally spoke. He eyed his brother; now deciding to open up to him exactly what was on his mind, what he was thinking. Robert said, serious-faced, but calmly, "That's exactly what I'm telling you, Paul. I am very unhappy about this."

Paul became baffled as hell. He was more than confused. He was surprised beyond words. He was shocked beyond description. "What the hell is that bullshit?" he cursed. "What the hell is wrong with you? After all the crap that son of a bitch has done to so many people's lives; the threats against our whole family; his close assassination of you – and you're telling me that you're all steamed up about that lunatic's reported death? What is going on here, Robert? Please, tell me. You're scaring the shit out of me here. Your reaction is making my skin itch. Why?" he insisted. "WHY?"

Robert would quickly explain everything to his brother before he succumbed to a nervous breakdown right in the middle of his station house office. Robert stated, "That's the key word that is making me steamed up as you put it. The word 'reported'".

Paul was confused. "I'm not following you!"

Robert replied. "I don't like the word reported blindly like that by an outside source. By someone in fact connected and much related to the deceased; saying that he is dead without any evidence to prove it. Where is the dead body? The article states that Domenico's wishes were to have his body cremated and the ashes scattered at sea!" Robert now raised his voice to a shout: "How convenient! How convenient that sob story is to have Armando say he is dead without a shred of proof to that effect; just his daughter's say-so!"

Paul was shocked at his brother's insinuation. "My God, Robert, you're not saying what I think you are?"

Robert nodded his head and insisted, "That is exactly what I am saying!" reading his brother's panicked thoughts.

Paul was indeed taken aback by this. He said, "All right, I understand his daughter is also some Dragon Lady, very evil like her father, but why would she go to all these lengths to make up a story like that? What's the purpose in that? Please, Robert, I've got to know!"

Robert quickly responded, much concerned for his brother's mental state growing rapidly perturbed right now. Robert replied, "To set a trap for us! This is all Domenico's doing. He is using his daughter to report his death so he can set a trap for us."

Paul shook his head from side-to-side strangely and blurted out, also his voice raised as a shout: "A trap? What bloody trap? What the hell are you talking about?"

Robert pointed his finger at his brother much disappointed at his naivety, his gullibility and stated, "Look little brother. Don't always believe what you read in the papers as gospel truth. There are many sensationalist journalists out there who get paid to write any sordid story, no matter how untruthful just to sell their newspapers and make a quick buck. Domenico of all people knows that. He uses such immoral twerps as the press to do his dirty work for him. He feeds them this crap story via his daughter. And who among the press gallery would not fall all over themselves to print such a very high profile, very important piece of information, no matter how untrue it is? Saying that Domenico Armando is dead would sell more papers than any other crap story being broadcasted to them this day! That was all that Monica had to say, that he was dead! But where was his ashes scattered? She would not say! And the suckers everywhere would listen and believe it! Domenico wins his next conquest of making everyone think he is dead in order to put his next crazy plans into effect. No doubt to be delivered in a time and place when we all least expect it! And voila! Another fine group of human beings is claimed at his behest; and claimed with his greatest ace up his sleeve. That is called surprise and speed. He would gather many people together in one place they would least suspect to be executed and he would indeed have them executed with the greatest speed such a massacre could be delivered. Do you understand?"

Paul became more shocked as he listened to his brother. But he finally came to agree with him. He was forced to it. Then he had another important question he had to ask. "All right, so if he is planning a trap… if he is alive… if this whole story of his death is in fact a setup, then the question I have to ask is where the hell is he? Where is he hiding?"

Robert looked at his brother square in the eye, cold as death as he demanded, "That's what we're going to find out!"

"We're?" Paul asked still confused.

"Yes, little brother. We're going to find out!"

"How?" Paul asked.

Robert insisted. "Monica has disembarked back into town. You two share a history together. It was brief, but it is still a history nonetheless."

Paul became offended at his brother's suspected insinuation. "Robert, we had a fling. Remember the one that you and her twisted old man walked in on at that party!"

Robert nodded, "Exactly!"

Paul insisted, "Well, unless you've forgotten I am now a happily married man just as you are. What the hell do you want me to do with Monica Armando?"

Robert shook his head slightly cross at his brother's incorrect thinking. "Paul, you think I am trying to reignite some sort of romantic connection between the two of you? Let me correct you. Definitely not! What I am suggesting is something completely different, but effective!"

"What would that be?" Paul asked.

Robert replied, "Offer her a shoulder to lean on or cry on. Get friendly with her. Get her to open up. Maybe she might slip out something we need, anything-any clue to confirm the truth of my suspicions and possibly even a lead to Armando's current hiding place!"

Paul explained, "Come on Robert. I haven't even seen Monica for ages. And I'm willing to bet that she's mighty sore at me, holding a mile-long grudge for marrying someone else. What the hell do you think? Do you think that once she sees me she'll give me some big friendly hug and tell me: 'Oh, Paul, I made up that whole story about my father's death because it is what Domenico wanted me to do and say. He wants everyone, especially your brother Robert who he hates more than anyone to think he is dead! The truth is, he is very much alive and making everyone think he is dead only so he can trap all his enemies in one place with automatic locks on all the doors and all the windows and everything booby-trapped from inside as well so no one can escape and booby-trapped from outside too so no police can enter and interfere with his sick plans for the final detonation of all the powerful bombs he has planted inside to blow everyone up to kingdom come. And by the way, I'll tell you where he is hiding too. His exact address...' Is that what you think she'll tell me, Robert?"

Robert was slightly entertained by his brother's sarcasm. But on a serious note, he stated, "Not exactly like that, but perhaps something along those lines. Look, we have two options here! Either you can needle her to emotionally slip up and reveal something or you can act like the sympathetic old friend and give her a shoulder to cry on, supposedly. Get what I mean?"

"And then what?" Paul asked.

Robert said, "I'm going to have you personally fitted up with an inconspicuous wire. It will be very small but highly effective. She'll never be able to spot it or feel it when you two embrace!" Robert smiled jokingly.

"Very funny Robert!" Paul too smiled. "Ok. So when do you want us to start?"

Robert ordered: "As soon as possible, tonight. She's back in town for now. And I want to make sure that she does not leave until we get all the information from her that we need. Because if Armando is alive, I can promise you one thing little brother: He ain't going to succeed with his sick plans. And he ain't going to escape from my clutches this time! So you go and do whatever it is you have planned for today. And meet me and John here at 6:00 p.m. sharp. We'll have some dinner and then you'll be set up to reacquaint yourself with the devil's daughter, Monica Armando! Now just in case you're wondering. If her father is not dead, Monica may very well not be in the mood for much crying. But just 'play the game' as they say. I need you to put on your finest acting performance as the concerned friend. Try to pump her for answers to very subtle questions. Do not be too obvious. Do not push it. Be natural and seemingly disinterested in details. You know, ignorant to any suspicious motives of her. Ok. Just play it cool or she'll just clam up. Meanwhile, John and I will be in close inconspicuous proximity to your whereabouts at all times to ensure things run smoothly and to run back-up in case Domenico's heavies may be at close bay!"

Paul now unintentionally mimicked his brother's initial reaction when he first entered his office. He lowered his eyes in much preoccupied thought, and then said, "And with any luck, we can find out everything we need to know."

Robert insisted, "And make sure that we foil the enemy's plans for that TRAP I suspect he has very much in the works for us all!"

CHAPTER 3

Robert Stewart had a lot of work to take care of between now and his meeting with his brother later that evening. He was seated inside his office reading over the surveillance reports compiled by their men of further important pieces of information gathered concerning new developments into their Armando case.

Robert conferred with his police partner John.

The pieces of information gathered related to the names of both Colin McMurphy, former husband to deceased Annemarie Armando and also Bruno Santucci.

Surveillance was heavily maintained on the two of them for quite some time now. Colin McMurphy was no longer considered a threat to his wife as she was dead. But some weeks back he was reported missing for a brief period of time; slipped right through the fingers of the police watching him and shortly thereafter upon returning back to his hotel suite in Brooklyn, tape recordings via the discreet police surveillance devices planted around him confirmed that he was in fact kidnapped by Domenico and threatened quite severely. Colin shortly thereafter complained to his lawyer mistress Samantha Emery (over the phone) not seen with her in person for now, that his accumulated funds were suddenly disappearing from his main branch Swiss bank account to which they were deposited. This was money he accumulated or liberated from his life of petty crime, not from any Armando inheritance he claimed Armando did not leave him. He would curse and scream and shout in panic that his money was being withdrawn by some mysterious source from his foreign, supposedly secure bank account. Again, Robert knew that Domenico was behind it even before Colin could put his finger on the culprit. But eventually he did with the help of his lawyer friend. He eventually came to the correct conclusion.

But this was not enough to corroborate Robert's hunch that Domenico was alive. Because this incident occurred much before Monica Armando came to town and reported the sudden death and burial of her father.

In any event, Colin McMurphy was being run into the ground and quite deliberately he was being made penniless, driven to bankruptcy. This was enough to send him over the deep end and now he was admitted to a Brooklyn based psychiatric ward for intense mental evaluation. In a nutshell, Domenico had driven him to lose the plot. Armando's actions against his former son-in-law was successful in driving Colin McMurphy to quite effectively lose his mind, his sanity and be admitted, even voluntarily to a local mental hospital.

The next series of news Robert received was concerning Bruno Santucci. He was also under constant surveillance for a longer time than McMurphy had been. Reason being; he was Robert's main lead to his wanted father's whereabouts - Don Santucci also being hunted down by the police and government just as Domenico had been.

But also, Bruno Santucci had slipped the police net at about the same time Colin McMurphy was reported missing. But similar to McMurphy's fate, though still quite different, Bruno was only admitted to hospital straight away, following his immediate return to the borough of Brooklyn in the state of New York. Only Bruno was admitted to the Brooklyn General Hospital for very serious chronic inflicted physical injuries as well as mental injuries sustained by the very same culprit responsible for McMurphy's mental breakdown: Domenico Armando.

Robert planned to visit the two of them. He needed to question them immediately. John volunteered to tag along. Maybe they could be made to talk, at least to tell them where they were both taken by Armando so that Robert could plan his trip and finally prove his hunch correct by finding Armando in that very same location. To prove that he was alive and nail him to the cross all at the same time, quite literally!

Robert Stewart and his police partner John McCallum arrived at the main Brooklyn Psychiatric Hospital on 92nd Street in twenty minutes flash. They were quickly posted inside the third floor psychiatric room with the newly-admitted patient Colin McMurphy who was under sedation and being supervised by a panel of doctors trained to deal with severe mental problems in which Colin was now diagnosed with.

Colin was conscious, but the doctor confirmed to Robert that he needed to be sedated because he was extremely hysterical and they believed more of a danger to himself than to any other person in the world at present.

Robert questioned the white-coated doctor, "Is he able to talk? I have some questions I need to ask!"

The middle-aged, distinguished-looking doctor with salt-and-pepper coloured hair had replied whilst jotting updates on his patient's medical chart he held in his hand, "We've managed to settle him down somewhat. He's not talking much to us. But hopefully he might say more to you. There is nothing stopping him from any ability to communicate, so you are more than welcome to try. But I insist on being present in case he gets in one of those fits again which may raise his blood pressure to dangerous levels. That is one thing that concerns me!"

Robert nodded. "That's fine!" He then approached Colin McMurphy who was lying on his back onto his bed wearing his admitted patient clothes. Colin lay still. His eyes open, but only staring at the white-coloured ceiling. His eyes maintained a sight of profound distress and fear; the product of his fate which landed him inside this clinic.

Robert began his line of questioning quite bluntly. "Colin. Colin. Can you hear me? It's Captain Robert Stewart! You have nothing to be afraid of. No one is going to harm you here! I just have some questions I need to ask you. It's very important that you try to talk to me. I want to find out what happened to you and who did this to you. It's my job to stop this culprit. So I need you to try and answer my questions as clearly and concisely as you possibly can. Do you hear me, Colin? Can you understand what I am telling you?"

Colin did not move. He did not utter a sound for now. But his eyes became more intense. His look of fear grew more apparent right now. Robert saw this quite clearly but he still attempted to reassure the panic-stricken subject as he insisted and reaffirmed his position. "Colin, there is nothing to be afraid of. All I want to know is who did this to you? Give me his name!"

Colin still was too shaken to speak. But he did cough. That was a positive sign for Robert. If he coughed, if he moved an inch, if he breathed, then eventually he should talk.

Robert yet persisted as his police partner John was posted by his side. Robert said, "All right. I'll make it easy for you; if talking is too much of a strain, then how about we try another tactic. How about you respond to my questions by blinking your eyes for now? How about you blink once for yes and twice for no? Does that sound easier for you?" Robert did not wait for a verbal response. He went straight to the point. Robert asked, "Colin, I suspect I know who did this to you. Now please I need you to calmly blink the right answer for me to my question. Was it Domenico Armando who drove you to this state? Remember blink once for yes or twice for no!"

Robert waited for a response. For a moment there was no answer. Robert turned to his partner almost giving up hope. But before he finally had, Colin jumped up off the couch-type bed, landed on his feet and shouted, "Yes. Yes. Yes. It was that fucking crazy bastard who did this to me. He stole all my money and he plans to kill me. Please, help me, Captain. Don't let him kill me. Please…"

Robert showed his usual compassion. "Ok. No problem. I will arrange for a police guard to be planted outside your door here at all times whilst you undertake your medical treatment. But I only have one last question for you. Please try to answer it for me. It is most important that you do. Here goes. Where exactly did Domenico take you? We know he took you somewhere approximately four weeks ago. Can you remember where exactly that was?"

Colin was pacing nervously up and down the floor of his room, barefoot and struggling to recall such details. He was mumbling ums and ahs in response for a moment. Then he stopped at the other end of the room. He briefly faced the wall then he turned around scratching the top of his head desperately and faced Robert. He replied, "Oh, boy. Where was it? I'm trying to think. But I know why I can't remember - because I don't know. I don't remember because I never knew!"

Robert asked curiously, "What do you mean? Didn't you see the place during your transportation there?"

Colin was still fumbling to respond. He stuttered, "No. I had a blindfold over my eyes during the ride. I remember several men grabbed me outside my living quarters here in Brooklyn, they shoved me into the back of a car, and then they placed a blindfold over my eyes. And my hands and legs were tied."

Robert nodded in understanding. "Ok. But what else can you tell me? Did you hear voices? Any clue, anything? Did any of his people say anything that may hint where you were taken? Did you see anything just before the blindfold was put over your eyes? - Flight itinerary? Brochures, maps possibly highlighting a route they would take - anything? Any lead, any clue? Think, Colin. Just try!"

Colin shook his head in anticipation, but nothing came to mind. He responded. "I don't know. I don't know. Damn it. The blindfold was placed on me as soon as I was put into the car in Brooklyn and remained on me all through the plane ride until I was taken to see the devil himself. Yes!" His eyes now grew demented in panic. "Yes. That horrible, horrible man locked me up in some damp, cold, very frightening, concrete, dark dungeon room and threatened me. He threatened me to treat his daughter like a princess then he planned to kill me. Yes. That is it. Please, Robert. Don't let him kill me. You have to help me!"

Robert nodded calmly. "Don't worry; you'll have immediate police protection arranged for you. He won't be able to hurt you again!"

Colin's eyes stared at him now resembling a mixture of fear and paranoia. He shouted in panic. "Are you sure about that Robert? Are you sure? He is evil! He is the devil! No one can stop him! When he wants to kill someone, he just kills them. He is a horrible, horrible human being. No. He is not a human being. He is a beast. He is a horribly grotesque mean-looking beast. He is evil!" He shouted in panic. "He is evil!"

Robert attempted to calm him down by insisting, "We know all that. But you will have constant protection. So please try to calm down. Now, when you left his hideout, can you remember seeing anything, any clues, hearing anything that may indicate the location to where you were taken? It does not matter how apparently insignificant even silly it might seem. Even the tiniest detail you can give us may be all that is needed to pinpoint his main hideout! Were there any pictures on the walls, any writing on the walls? Did the guards speak in some foreign accent or foreign language? Did any of his people say or do anything unusual? Did they mention the name of a foreign country? Were there statues, paintings that stick to your mind, anything? Please, think!"

Colin shook his head constantly in thought, but he could not identify with anything too specific. He did not recall anything. He replied. "No, nothing; I had a blindfold placed over my eyes before I arrived and after I was removed from his dungeon wherever that was. There was nothing on the walls. I cannot recall anything specific that I can tell you. And the guards were normal-sounding, just normal. Some were American, some perhaps Italian, some perhaps another foreign identity; just mixed. But I don't know anything more. If I could help, I would. But I just don't know!" he said racking his brain desperately, and then repeated again, "He is evil! That is why he left no clues. He is evil! He is cunning! He probably can float through walls. Oh, boy. What if he can hear me? What if he blames me for what happened to his daughter? What if he tries to kill me? Oh, I am scared. I am so bloody scared. Please, Robert… Please, Captain… Don't let him near me. He is evil! He is evil! He is sadistic! He is sick! He is a monster! He has no conscience, no mercy, and no compassion. Please, oh, please-"

Robert made tracks shortly after. Inside his unmarked police car, he informed his police partner to immediately arrange a 24-hour police guard to be posted outside Colin McMurphy's psychiatric room. Robert did hint with compassion, "The police guard will be placed on his room indefinitely." Robert however added with a sharp recollection to McMurphy's shady character, "Which by the way is more than he deserves!"

CHAPTER 4

Robert Stewart was placed in a very unusual position for the first time in his history and years of policing. He was forced to feel even greater compassion for a man who in fact was the offspring to one of his worst enemies, Don Santucci.

Robert was momentarily posted inside the hospital room of his next subject, Bruno Santucci. Again, there were many doctors tending to his care. Bruno was lying on his hospital bed with bandages covering his head and his left hand, with a nurse giving him a strong dose of morphine to dull his excruciating physical agony subjected at the hands of the world's most brutally sadistic monstrous madmen in existence.

Robert also first approached the doctor. His police partner John McCallum again stood by his side. The doctor insisted, "Whoever did this to him did one hell of a job. He's been in our care for some weeks now. His injuries sustained by his ordeal of torture fall under the category of brutal and cruel to say the least."

Robert clenched his jaw in anger for a moment and shook his head from side to side in bitter hatred for the bastard who inflicted this heinous form of torture against the victim subject.

John McCallum was also shocked at the sight of Bruno Santucci. John watched the patient struggle to breathe with heavy gasps for air from constricted lungs. Bruno groaned in agony with tubes all over his face and body connected to machines at the side of his bed. John also could not help but show emotion, mostly anger as he said to Robert, "No human should be treated like this! I hate that Armando as much as you do!"

Robert turned to his police partner with cold eyes also struck with rage at the subject's tormentor and said, "Believe me John, no one can hate him as much as I do, no matter how much you may try!" Anyhow, Robert further questioned the doctor. "Please doctor; give me the brief rundown of the injuries sustained!"

The thirty-five-year-old, jet-black-haired doctor replied, "He has been tortured gruesomely. He cannot walk. He can barely talk. You see his left hand with all the bandages around it?"

Robert nodded.

The doctor explained, "His hand had all his fingernails removed and the flesh underneath was burned with substances such as salt and vinegar solutions!"

Robert felt furious. "And the bandages over his head?" he asked.

The doctor replied, "He has been electrocuted; the sides of his head at the temple, the skin is severely burnt!"

"And what is the state of his mind?" Robert asked.

"He's lost! He's gone! We did a complete blood workout on him. He has been injected with some form of a rare drug compound we are still trying to familiarise ourselves with. But this compound in short acts as some form of mind-altering drug. In crux, he has been brainwashed as well as tortured!"

"You mean something along the lines of the work of the Nazis?" Robert asked curiously.

The doctor shrugged his shoulders. "Perhaps not a replica, though what was subjected upon Bruno was different, but you can say it is similar in the structure of inflicting intense bodily harm upon a subject. After all, he was tortured as the Nazis tortured its victims, just differently in Bruno's case. But the end result was no doubt similar in causing a well able man to become in simple medical terms, a lost cause; a vegetable who can no longer look after himself."

Robert further asked, "You talked about him being brainwashed. Was it successful? Can he remember anything? If I question him about his circumstances, such as who did this to him, will he be able to tell me, especially where all this torture took place such as the location and so forth?"

The doctor shook his head in dismay. "No. Highly unlikely; the truth is, he does not even know his own name! He does not know who he is, his age or where he came from!"

Robert said, "Are his injuries permanent or temporary? Will he ever regain his memory?"

The doctor looked at him with depressed even sad eyes. "No. I really doubt it. His brain has been damaged severely. His memory has been completely wiped out. His entire central nervous system has been shot down beyond repair. What we are talking about here is nothing short of a miracle. Unfortunately, our medical expertise is not yet advanced to the point to be able to help such a case of misfortunate brutality!"

And that was that. Robert would never be able to have his questions answered by Bruno Santucci.

Robert turned to his police partner and said, "I want police guards posted here outside Bruno's hospital room at all times as well!"

John nodded.

Robert then screwed up his face in solemn thought, "That son of a bitch Armando is still alive. I can feel it in my bones!"

John understood Robert's desire to want his worst enemy alive. Robert wanted Domenico Armando to die no other way but by him – and in front of him. Any other way was a perversion of justice. Robert wanted to see that sick and demented heinous maniac collapsing onto his knees in front of him. Robert wanted to see him feel great physical pain first for a very, very long time before he closed his eyes in death. Robert wanted to watch him suffer and scream and shout much worse than that enemy had ever inflicted such suffering upon anyone else throughout his very sick existence. Anything else

344

was a mockery of justice. Anything else was cheating him-Robert himself from a much-desired need – an emotional requirement - to see that man succumb to worse pain and misery than any and all his victims combined had succumbed to at that sick bastard's monstrous hands!

John concurred with Robert. "Look at all the misery that son of a bitch Domenico has inflicted on all these people. I am afraid that I am forced to agree with you Robert. I cannot believe that someone as sadistic and brutally monstrous as that can possibly be dead so easily. I think where he is concerned it's impossible. That gruesome maniac is still out there. He is out there hiding, waiting for us!"

Robert insisted, "I want him to wait. I want him to feel and know what's coming for him. And I tell you something partner, when that day happens, I will be there. No force alive or invisible power anywhere will stop me from being there when I witness his final end, the final nail in his coffin!"

Robert approached Bruno who lay on his hospital bed. The patient opened his eyes briefly. Bruno looked at Robert's direction but gave out a blank stare. He could no longer recognise him. His eyes closed then opened again as he also suffered immense bouts of fatigue and through his pain and anguish he could only stutter the words: "Who am I?"

CHAPTER 5

Robert Stewart and John McCallum headed up the surveillance detail operation again parked discreetly outside the Armando estate that evening.

Robert and his brother attended the target's house in separate unmarked civilian cars not to arouse any unnecessary suspicions.

Paul Stewart was invited inside the Armando mansion into the main living room area and quickly sat on the sofa immersed in conversation with the devil's Dragon Lady Daughter, Monica Armando.

Monica appeared pleased to see him after all this time, though somewhat surprised. However she was quite vocal in her disappointment over the fact that he left her without a word only to marry another woman. But the conversation was directed quickly to her father. She spoke of him quite openly and eagerly.

"My father was so heartbroken over many things before he died!" she said rather straight-faced. "He had so many plans, so many visions that were unfulfilled due to his sudden demise!"

"I bet he did!" Paul replied sarcastically.

She ignored the sarcasm and kept talking. "He suffered much onslaught during his final days and weeks on earth before his death after that tragic and violent bloody confrontation between himself and Robert. As he lay on his deathbed, we spoke for hours. He had so much sadness in his eyes. His face looked vulnerable for the first time in his life. His energy had slipped away. But at least I am grateful that I was there with him until the day he died. You know I held his hand during those final hours when he closed his eyes finally into eternity. It was heart-wrenching!" she stated, though surprisingly without shedding so much as a single tear from her eyes.

Paul stated, "Then you buried him?"

Monica replied. "Yes. I buried my beloved great father at sea. It was his final wish and last request to have his corpse cremated and the ashes scattered at sea. He loved the ocean. He always said that the sound of the waves and the chirping birds above in the sky helped him think and plot and plan greater and greater ambitions for his empire. It helped him think!" she smiled as if preoccupied in much thought. "He loved the sea and he loved his operas. And he loved us, his children!"

Paul could not help himself with his next comment. It just came out as he hinted, "But he also loved himself even more, wouldn't you say?"

She replied, "Well, think about it this way. If a father does not love himself how can he love his own children? What would anyone rather have? A father like mine who treated his family like gold or someone, one of those many bad fathers in the world who did not like themselves and went home every night and treated their kids badly and beat them up constantly? My father explained

346

that to me once. He said, 'My Golden Girl' that's what he called me. He said: 'My Golden Girl, I admire my kids because I have always admired myself! You are all a part of me! So you are winners! If a man loves himself, then his kids will grow up also much loved!' That is what he once told me. He was a great man. He was a great father. I love him. I miss him so much!" she said, still straight-faced.

Paul said, "His burial must have been hard for you! I wish you had called me wherever you were. You know I could have still visited!"

She suddenly became guarded, feeling that Paul was trying to have her slip out something along the lines of the location to her father's secret hiding place. So she said as a means to throw away any idea of his he may have in order to pump her of the name to the country hideout. "My father had many hideouts. We moved a lot constantly. You could say we were like nomads. But what choice did we have? Your brother was hunting him down like an animal. He was relentless in his search for my poor father. I cannot believe the brutality of Robert to shoot him like that, so ruthlessly and cold-heartedly!"

Paul could not help but lose his cool for now as he put her bluntly in her place, the nerve of this hideous bitch he thought to himself. "Who the hell do you think you are to make that monster bastard father of yours into some sort of victim, huh? My brother is a hero. Your father is the scum of the earth. My brother is idolised, loved and respected by everyone. He's the best good guy that exists. He has a conscience. He cares for people. Your father was hated by the world. He was loathed. He was sick and evil. He deserved what he got. My brother did this world a big favour by blowing him away. And just for the record, you sick and twisted person, your crazy insane father shot him first. My brother then shot him in self-defence. And even if it was not in self-defence, your father would deserve whatever bad was done to him. After all the lives that son of a bitch has been responsible for torturing and killing and destroying, I hope the motherfucker is burning in hell for all the sick things he's ever done! You got that!!!"

As they were planted discreetly inside the one unmarked vehicle, Robert Stewart and John McCallum listened to the voices being sent out by Paul's microphone, broadcasted onto their computer speakers his concealed wire had transmitted to, with the reception of all the voices sounding quite clear. John said, "Well, he's just given the game away!"

Robert had a different take on things. "Maybe not partner. You see needling her may also be just as effective as offering her his ear. She may become angry enough to tell us something!"

John suddenly agreed, but then said with a smile, "You must be touched that your brother thinks as high of you as the rest of us!"

Robert was modest. He remained close-mouthed to that comment and just kept listening to the conversation between his brother and Monica Armando.

Monica Armando's reaction to Paul's abusive insults of her father was quite surprising. She kept cool. And she kept talking as if she did not hear or absorb his words.

She said, "One of my father's dreams was for us to get married. It hurt him when we never were. My father nonetheless always had a great respect for your brother Robert. It was a type of respect that no one else in the whole world except your brother himself could possibly understand. He always used to say even when he lost his freedom because of Robert that he always regarded himself and Robert as 'equals'. He said that they were both enemies, but at the same time they shared much in common. They were courageous, clever, resourceful and two men of profound action. And often one served as the action whilst the other became the reaction and vice versa. One made a move, and then the other made a move. Like chess, his favourite pastime.

"You know my father even began writing a book once he was confined to a chair after that shootout with Robert wearing terrible injuries and scars. I was so excited that I wanted to read it right away. But he told me to wait until it was finished. And I told him that he should market it, but he seemed not keen on the idea.

"He said sometimes a man must do things for himself. The passion of his pastimes and his deeds outweighs the unnecessary ranking of his work by a world filled mostly with people whose overestimated and underestimated opinions really do not matter. He considered marketing his work similar to human degradation; like begging people to buy his books; something demeaning, immoral and evil. The prospect of holding his finished product into his hands was more valuable. Then he made me laugh with his last comment about the subject. He said: 'Besides, with the horrible taste this world has in books, do you seriously think I care what anyone would think about mine?' Then I told him that I might market it for him somehow!"

Paul became more composed. He asked, "What was the book about? Do you have a copy?"

She replied, "No, I don't have a copy unfortunately. I had the book cremated with my father's corpse, all at the same time. It was what he wanted. Oh, how he suffered during his last days. But anyway, the book was about power and his ambitions to conquer the world. It was also about the magnificent battle of courage and daring between him and Robert. It was really inspirational when he told me about its synopsis in brief detail. You know something else?"

"I guess I'll find out in a minute!" Paul said arrogantly.

She went on. "My father was very bitter when the world accused and much blamed him over Robert's death – or the hoax of a death it was. He considered it an insult to his name and memory, even his reputation. He would say: 'This world is really filled with many stupid people. Complete idiots. No one ever understood the battle between Robert and I; it was not

348

about hatred or killing the other; such meaningless and useless emotions and actions. The battle was about conquest. It was about WAR. It was about Winning. It was about CHALLENGE!' That is what he always would say. It was like, something reminiscent to a game of chess. It was beautiful and inspirational. To you too, I imagine!"

Paul revealed his tactless side once again, "Oh, yes. It was really inspirational when my brother slapped the cuffs around his wrists and hauled his sick arse off to jail. That was bloody inspirational!"

Monica's reaction was not what was expected. She even joked about that incident. "And for me too; it was highly inspirational when he escaped whilst kicking the arses of all those who tried to keep him there!"

Paul became silent at the comment by this snake. She intentionally wanted to twist the needle and wipe the arrogance off his face. She had succeeded for a short time at that.

Paul then changed the subject. "You said your father had plans to conquer the world, how so?"

Monica smiled in thought as she tilted her head back onto the sofa in proud thought. "Simply by mounting an extensive campaign of his troops against Robert's - and defeating them all in one final bloody battle. Then he wanted to try and coerce Robert to join him upon his defeat. He would offer Robert a chance of a lifetime to work for him or with him, noting the distinction between the two choices!"

Paul shook his head in disgust at the thought of both her and her father's twisted insanity; the prospect of even contemplating such a foolish idea was indeed a true testament to their insane delusional lunacy. How could they possibly think that would ever happen, those two crazy dumb fucks? Paul thought to himself, quite sickly at that. "Your father was completely not from this world. He really had a warped sense of reality. I seriously doubt that he had ever had even the slightest touch with reality!"

Monica now teased him, "Oh, bite your tongue you bad boy. You are what my father would describe as an 'ordinary man'. You could never understand or appreciate his extraordinary visions; no one in the world could except for your brother of course. Maybe you should ask him. I'm sure he'll tell you!"

Paul replied, "You're right about that. My brother would tell me how much he hated his evil guts. He would tell me that there was nothing he wouldn't do to rid the world of the likes of a maniac like that. And you know something, he never gave up. My brother beat him each time. And he still would have. Your father was a maniac that is why he never could succeed with his 'vision' as you put it. My brother succeeded against men like him because he is the strong good guy. And he's a hell of a lot smarter too! That's the difference between the two of them. Don't ever forget that. Your father might have admired Robert, but Robert hated his guts!"

Monica lifted her hands in the air in a quick casual gesture and simply said, "So what? What does that matter? My father explained to me that there is a very fine line between love and hate. They are both powerful emotions. They are two sides of the same coin. You simply have to feel something to experience either one of those powerful entities, or the two of them at the same time." She then smiled in thought. "My father always likened his battle with Robert as something of a great bullfight, something no common person could ever comprehend – no one that is, except of course for him and Robert!"

Her face now drifted into seriousness as she exclaimed, "My father was very bitter against the world towards the end of his life. He did not accept how people were so foolish and gullible to listen to men and women who claim to be priests and Popes and Kings and Queens simply because they were born with a silver spoon in their mouths! He loathed the gullibility of the human race to worship false gods, false idols and false prophets. He claimed these people they were worshipping were simply just human beings. After all, did such people have power, any real power to cure disease; to feed the hungry; to provide solid secure sustainable jobs for all the unemployed? The answer to all those questions was absolutely and definitely NOT! 'Then why the hell is anyone listening to those people? Why are they worshipping them? Why are they so blind?' My father would comment in disgust. Part of my father's vision was to rule via actions far outweighing the words of all those 'false prophets' as he called it. False gods who simply ranted and raved false words and empty promises to an entire world foolish enough to listen to such nonsense and accepting what they say without ever any real tangible results of actions provided and much delivered to match such words which were nothing short of complete and utter lies.

"That is where my father differed. But he was not given a chance. The world is filled with so many cowards. The weak always band together to bring down the strong; the strong men like my father. My great and wonderful brilliant-minded father! My father had visions and dreams to change the world. Once he became sick he actually empathised with all those in the world who also were dying with similar conditions such as cancer. My father wanted to help himself, but at the same time his inventions and creations; such cures he planned to manufacture for a vast assortment of diseases would also help everyone else in the entire world. And that is what my father wanted to accomplish! He wanted his actions to outweigh the world's false promises. He wanted to prove that for every problem there was a solution and for every solution there was a problem. That is what my great father wanted to do.

"He could have come up with cures for all diseases, food for all the starving, jobs for all the middle class and entertainment for all those depressed and despondent lost souls of the world who are bored with the humdrum; all those longing for one man, one voice, one magician to turn their emptiness and hollowness and days and nights of walking dead into LIFE! That is the great vision of my father. But he was not given a chance to fulfil his great dreams. His life was cut short like one of those great Ancient Warriors, who had the souls and spirits to fight the good fight but lost their lives all so tragically at early ages. My father was like that. He was one of those men.

"But just imagine what could have been. Think, in a perfect world, what could have transpired on that great day when my father met your brother, the place where they first met inside his police station office... Think, if after that meeting they remained friends for life, such great men, and such a great force they could have been. Both of them could have changed the world to greatness if only they could have been friends forever. Oh, what a thought. My father was so robbed of his dream. My poor, poor, wonderful brilliant genius of a father had his life cut short so prematurely. It breaks my heart! Oh, what could have been...!" she said, but still without shedding a single tear from her eyes.

Later that evening Robert returned to the 25th division precinct and teamed up inside his station house office with Paul and John.

Paul apologised profusely to his brother, "I'm sorry I could not get you the address and location of Domenico's hideout!"

But Robert seemed more cheerful, in fact the least concerned about it all. He stated, "You gave me plenty, Paul!"

Paul was confused, "Oh, how so?"

Robert said, "What did you notice about Monica's demeanour throughout your entire conversation with her?"

Paul replied, "Well, she ranted on and on about her father in pointless conversation, but she seemed normal!"

Robert nodded his head. "Exactly; a little too normal, don't you think? She had confirmed what I had always suspected. She confirmed my hunch was right. And I always trust my hunch, my instincts! Monica showed no emotion throughout your conversation with her concerning her father's so-called death. Which means Domenico Armando is not dead. He is very much alive!"

Their conversation was interrupted for now as the office phone rang. Robert answered it. It was his wife Cassandra calling him. She sounded greatly distressed.

"Yes, what is it, beautiful?" Robert asked.

Her voice was strained as she replied, "There are two prowlers outside the house. One of them is a young man in his late twenties and the other is a middle-aged woman. The man is hysterical. He keeps shouting that you killed his father, DOMENICO! He's holding a newspaper article standing outside our house demanding to see you!"

Robert darted to action promptly, "Ok. Don't worry. The guards are still there. Just don't walk outside the house. Don't step foot outside at all. I'll be right down!"

Robert quickly placed the phone's receiver on the hook, jumped onto his feet, darted to the door, grabbed his jacket hanging on the door, placed it over his back, fetched inside one of the pockets and grabbed his car keys at the same time as he alerted his brother and police partner that he had to leave right away, "Cassandra is in trouble!"

John hammered, "I'm coming with you!"

"And me too!" Paul insisted.

CHAPTER 6

Robert Stewart's car skidded onto his driveway rapidly thereafter at his home on 10th Avenue in Brooklyn. Meanwhile his children were staying at their grandparents (Robert's parents' house) also under heavy guard. Robert raced outside his unmarked vehicle and John and Paul who travelled inside the car with him also instantly jumped outside to assist him with the sight of the commotion they observed on his front lawn, just before the front door.

At the sight of his presence, Cassandra who was watching from the living room window ran outside the house into Robert's arms.

Robert then quickly approached the two strangers and gestured his wife to stand safely behind him with his arms outstretched in a backward motion holding her securely.

Robert's voice became authoritatively strong as he ordered the strange man to tell him what his business was standing here like this outside his house in the foggy cold evening like that, beneath the sight of a full moon shining brightly this night. "Who are you? What's going on? What do you want?"

The man insisted, "You, Captain. You!" he said angrily waving the front-page newspaper article he held in his hand, waving it before Robert's eyes.

Robert was familiar with the article. It contained a picture of Domenico. He had already read the article.

Robert stated, "Ok. You've made your point. Now tell me what does this have to do with you?"

The dark-haired, Italian-looking, rugged-featured man insisted, "You see this man here?" he said pointing at the picture of the front of the newspaper in question. "He is my father. He was my father! And you killed him!" He became hysterical at this point, "YOU KILLED HIM!"

Robert could hear the commotion of voices all around him. He heard his brother saying, "What the hell is he talking about? Domenico is his father?"

Robert then said to the strange man. "He's your father, huh, since when? Domenico never mentioned you and he was quite vocal about his family tree!"

The man insisted, "He didn't know I was his son! And that's the problem. He died before I could tell him. He will never know the truth now because of you!" he shouted angrily.

Robert saw the man was hysterical, but for some reason he did not feel threatened by him. He was unarmed. His hands only contained the newspaper in them. The man looked emotional, and the woman who identified herself as his mother standing next to him was trying to control her son and calm him down crying, "Please Donnie, please... Just forget I told you anything. Please, just forget about all this business about Domenico

353

being your father and all that. Let's just go. I don't want you to get into any trouble!"

Robert appeared sympathetic. "All right, I'll tell you what; how about I invite you both inside my house. Sit down inside the living room. We can have something to drink and I can get you something to eat and we'll talk about everything that's on your mind, ok Donnie? Ok, madam?" he said then glancing at the man's mother.

"My name is Francesca!" she said.

"Ok, Francesca and Donnie just come inside!" he ushered them shortly into the living room of his home and gave them both some tea and chocolate cake his wife had just finished baking only earlier this evening.

Robert then began his subtle line of questioning to the two strangers he invited inside his house. Robert excused the guards from their presence and motioned them to wait in the next room. "Everything is under control. I'll be fine," he ordered to them. He wanted his two guests to feel as comfortable as possible.

Robert asked once he was seated in front of them, "Ok, please tell me what's on your mind, both of you? What's troubling you?"

The man first addressed his mother with his dilemma, placing the newspaper he held in his hand gently onto the glass coffee table in front of them. He spoke to his mother now as they sat on the same sofa on either side. "Why mother, why did you keep the knowledge of my father's identity from me all my life? Why? Why did you wait until he died to tell me the truth? Why now? Why only today did you decide to tell me?"

His mother wept. Cassandra who was seated aside her husband Robert on another sofa opposite them rose quickly and entered another room and quickly returned holding a box of tissues she handed to Francesca, who removed one single tissue from the box and wiped her eyes before she spoke. Cassandra seated herself aside Robert again as Paul and John were seated on chairs either side of them.

Francesca now turned to her son; more composed and answered his question, at least attempting to be as forthright as possible. "I don't know, my son. I was scared. I was confused!"

"Scared and confused about what?" Donnie asked.

His mother replied after taking small sips from her cup of tea, "I was scared of the repercussions. I knew your father briefly. We met only for one night many, many years ago. He was married. He had children or just his first child I think from his official wife at that time. I was just an affair. As I said, I knew him only for a brief period, but I also knew what sort of man he was. There were stories, a lot of rumours about him. He was rich and powerful, with many resources and connections. He was also known to be quite ruthless and shrewd with those not connected to him by blood. So I was scared about many things. That is why I never told him that I was pregnant

354

with his child nor you that he was your father after you were born and old enough to understand!"

His son was still confused. "But mother, look at us. It was just you and me growing up. We spent our whole lives in poverty. Had you told him, he could have provided to us… we could have had a better life. He could have raised me and also looked after you. We would not have had to struggle all our lives even to feed ourselves. Why, mother? Why? I was robbed of a father and you were robbed from having a better life. We both deserved better than that. If he got you pregnant it was his responsibility to have looked after us both. You should not have denied him of his chance; you should not have denied us of our chance that we could have had for a better life!"

His European mother wept once more, and then she turned to Robert and Cassandra and decided to explain everything to them. "You see, Domenico and I met in France many years ago. I was a call girl, a hooker or prostitute as you may call it," she said quite frankly.

Donnie tried to hush her to silence, "Please, mother. Don't say that about yourself; stop lower-rating yourself!"

Francesca continued, "I was always honest to my son about everything, including the mistakes of my past and my youth - what I did for a living back then. We never had secrets between us. I only just kept one secret, and that was the identity of his father from him and the reason for that was solely out of fear for him and for me. You see, I told my son about my past. There was no shame, disgrace or embarrassment. He was a good son, always helping me with my bills. He did odd jobs like me. We did menial work, whatever we could find in order to survive. He wanted to go to college and further his education, but I could not afford to send him there. It was just him and me growing up. We were all alone. And I'll tell you the reasons why I never told him about his father.

"Like I said," she explained to Robert and Cassandra. "I knew Domenico was ruthless to everyone who was not connected to him by blood. I feared that had I told Domenico that I was pregnant with his son, he would have eventually taken him away from me. And he may have separated me from him because Domenico was married. But Domenico had his affairs and mistresses with many women all over the world. My son was all I had. I did not want to take the chance in his father ever separating us! So I kept it a secret. I did what I had to do. I lived each day with that lie!"

Donnie was still steamed up over the issue. "But mother, I would have made sure that he never would have singled you out. I would have made sure that he never would have separated us. Can't you see how we suffered endlessly and unnecessarily for no reason? Had Domenico Armando known that I was his son think of how much better our lives would have been today."

"Or worse!" Cassandra broke out in a solemn attempt to correct Donnie's perhaps false assumptions of the matter at hand.

"What do you mean worse? Please, explain?" Donnie begged.

Cassandra insisted, "I don't know what your full knowledge about your father is, but in brief he has a habit of destroying everyone he says he even loves. I don't know if you are aware of this, but one of his daughters had recently committed suicide once she uncovered the truth about him; the knowledge of his true evil ways; the knowledge of the true wickedness inside that man. Also, his first son, D.J., who is slightly older than you, was corrupted by his father. He became the sole personification of his father's evil. He tried to have us all killed, Robert and his whole family executed most recently. That was the cause of his arrest and living the life on the run with his father. So I am most certainly not viewing your ignorance in regards to the knowledge of your father's identity as a curse as you have been. In fact, I am seeing the whole situation as more of a blessing in disguise than anything else. You had it tough all your life due to your financial handicaps. It can certainly be appreciated why you longed for a better life. But please understand you would NEVER have obtained that better lifestyle had you been raised by that man you now call your father. In fact, you would have been corrupted and eventually destroyed like all his other children have been corrupted by him, living on the run like him and facing complete ruin by his very sick and twisted, greatly evil actions!"

Donnie lowered his eyes to the floor at the confirmed truth about the man who he suddenly found out was his father. The reality of this truth suddenly hit him hard. He shook his head from side to side and cursed out loud, "Oh, my God! Oh, my God! I cannot believe what I am hearing. I cannot believe this horrible destiny of my life to be faced with two horrible options: either live the rest of my life in poverty or face the truth of my demons and become a criminal like that man who I now am forced to call 'father'. What a horrendous choice that is!"

Cassandra went on, "No matter what, do not be angry with your mother's decision to keep the true identity of your father away from you all your life. Because the truth is, your mother did you a favour by keeping you away from him. She was protecting you! Domenico is a horrible, wicked, evil, repulsive, vile man. For a child as yourself growing up under that influence would have only been to your detriment. Nothing good would have ever come from it."

CHAPTER 7

Robert Stewart was immersed in police work for the next few hours that night as soon as his house was empty of all outside guests.

Robert entered the top secret high-tech government-installed SIA communications annex room facility inside his residence and was shortly on the phone with his SIA Chief Lloyd McKenzie whom had resumed his duties at SIA headquarters in Washington, D.C. at present.

Robert touched base concerning any new developments in their Armando case. Robert alerted his government superior that he was positive Domenico Armando was still alive. He explained that he questioned Colin McMurphy who was not much help. And he visited Bruno Santucci also admitted in hospital in the borough who would never be the same again.

McKenzie outlined his concerns for all parties who suffered the ultimate price by their apparent failure to terminate the enemy as yet. "It is an unfortunate act of fate and circumstance that has prevented us from neutralising this beast from circulation. But I must admit Domenico Armando is either the cleverest or the luckiest enemy we have ever faced; perhaps a mixture of both!"

Robert insisted, "He is not immortal. He is not superhuman. He is human like everyone else, chief. He will be found. He will be stopped. We will do whatever necessary to get him off the streets and bury that bastard once and for all!"

McKenzie opened up surprisingly displaying a side of him which was even a tad sentimental as he explained, "Robert, sometimes I wonder if he really is human or something superhuman as you put it. I have to admit that I've had many sleepless nights with thoughts of this deadly, deadly man still out there endangering us all! It is not easy dealing with the consequences we face everyday at our government's failure in stopping him. Every victim he claims as a result of that crushes my spirit. We are the United States government. We are a supreme powerhouse of a nation well equipped to deal with the likes of such terrorists. We have endless resources and modern technology at our disposal; satellites, special infrared-detecting equipment, high-tech surveillance and some of the best trained military men in the world – and with all that our enemy keeps slipping through our fingers time and time again. He keeps killing, terrorising, torturing, blowing things up; buildings as well as people and we have failed to do a damn thing about it. We have failed to bring that madman to his end after all this time! I am sorry, but how can I be expected to keep a strong cold face after all that? I face endless paperwork and frustration in explaining such things to the White House staff, even the United States President who wants Armando caught more than he wants to have breakfast every morning. It is just not easy dealing with all this. Wishing that Armando was never born and being able to finagle it are still two very different eggs in our basket." McKenzie paused for a moment. "Forgive me, Robert. As head of the SIA I know I should not be getting emotional, but I just feel angry and I feel comfortable at the same time expressing or confiding that anger with you!"

Robert was flattered and indeed proud that his superior held him in such high regard enough to feel safe to confide in him this way above all others. Robert said, "I know how you feel, chief. But we all are feeling the immense pressure and stress of it all."

McKenzie's voice seemed somewhat distraught as he said, "It is just so uncanny, so damn unnatural how Domenico has managed to defy our country's forces time and time again. He has been confronted by numerous obstacles over and over again and he manages to survive each and every one of them, with his horrible life and identity intact. Here he floats into our hands one minute and then the next he slips through our fingers like petroleum jelly. It is just really and truly remarkable how he has succeeded to pull that off. He has made a mockery of our Justice System far too many times, that even thinking about it makes my skin crawl. This is just so bloody frustrating. It is even beyond frustrating. It is maddening!

"We have him surrounded numerous times such as inside his private hospital, inside a secure prison cell and at his daughter's funeral and each time he slips the net. He escapes our custody. This is uncanny. It is incredible. It is gut-wrenching and the product of the implications each time spells disaster for all of us and everyone in our country who suffer the repercussions of this failure in putting an end-a stop to Armando finally."

Robert listened in silence for now as he allowed his chief to get his frustrations off his chest.

McKenzie went on further, "I'm sure you have seen our President on various news networks giving public press conferences all the time concerning this Armando situation we are all faced with. He appears cool, calm and collected before the press even as he has to explain why the United States government has failed to apprehend Armando, but behind the scenes he is a literal nervous wreck. I have visited him in person numerous times in recent weeks inside his office at the White House away from the press... I have been on the phone with him countless times over this horrible matter and let me tell you he is virtually pulling his hair out in worry over this too. He is simply running out of excuses-we all are when we have to explain why Domenico Armando is still out there in our society able to slip our forces and at the same time keep getting away with murder, mass murder, torture and the terrorisation of countless people in our society he manages to hand-pick in either a premeditated fashion or at random. I am sick of him turning all these obstacles we throw at him to his advantage like some expert wizard, some demented evil Chess Player that he is! Ahh, it is insane."

358

Robert understood quite perfectly his chief's bitterness at the prospect. Robert felt the same anger and resentment eating away at him. But just as his chief was apparently falling apart at the seams, Robert kept a brave front in all this as he explained, "Look it chief, this is a war. It is a WAR. It is us against the enemy, HIM! Just like that fought with the Nazis, Vietnam and Iraq. It's no different. Unfortunately, we have to just accept that these things take time to wrap-up. It takes time for us to dance our victorious tune. But we are in America. We don't stop until we win our wars against all terrorists! And we will win this one with Armando! I guarantee you that! We will get him! We will beat Domenico Armando at his own sick game! Domenico started his games in the wrong region of the world. Now it is war! And it is a war that he will lose in the end. Just like all the others who put their heinous lives against us. He will be caught. He will be dealt with. He will eventually be removed from our society. We must not give up, EVER! We cannot allow our emotions to get the better of us. We must only feel anger. Anger must drive our motives in this one. Anger will be our strength and driving force to finally getting this enemy and overpowering him as we can and will do. He will lose. He is not going to win this, I promise you. Let me repeat: We will get him. Domenico Armando does not have any future in our country, our society and he will lose. We will crush him! We will bury him! That is most certainly a promise! His end is near. His end is coming! And I only get more determined by every passing moment to see the sight of his dead corpse in front of us. We will not be deprived of that. I will make his living body into a corpse; don't worry about that, chief! Domenico Armando is a dead man!"

Robert's cellular phone began ringing. He fetched inside his jacket pocket and interrupted his landline call with his chief by saying, "Hang on a second here, chief, my cell's ringing." Robert placed his receiver with the chief's call onto his desk as he placed his mobile phone to his ear answering the call, saying, "Robert Stewart!"

The caller quickly identified himself. "It's John McCallum, Robert. I'm down at the Armando estate; I need you to get down here quick. There's been another death just reported here. And this time the cause is not suicide. This time it's MURDER!"

Robert quickly hung up the call ready to make tracks to his destination in Brooklyn Heights on 5th Avenue. He quickly extended his hand for the phone's receiver lying on his desk and alerted his government superior, "Chief, I've got to go. That was my police partner John. He just informed me that there has been another death at the Armando house. The victim was killed this time!"

He heard his chief give out a frustrated groan saying, "Oh, when does it all end? All right, Robert. You get down there and keep me posted on all the new developments!"

"All right!" Robert said as he placed the receiver on the hook, ready to make tracks immediately to the enemy's local fortress.

Robert was posted inside the Armando mansion within twenty minutes that evening. He saw an army of police stationed inside. He approached his police partner standing before the dead corpse that lay sprawled onto the carpet floor of the main living room with blood pouring all over the ground out from her head, a blood pool formed all around the corpse onto the floor. The coroner's officers were all over the dead body, examining the cause of death.

One of them darted to Robert after making a quick and brief determination. "The victim this time is Rita Armando, Domenico's wife. She was apparently killed with three bullets fired to the back of her head. From the point of impact of the injuries and the angle, it seems as though she was struck or surprised from behind as she was walking inside the main living room area – and the assailant shot her three times with a pistol at point-blank range!"

Robert turned to John and asked, "What else have you got for me? Was it a break-in or a robbery gone wrong? Is there any signs of forced entry?"

John replied, "According to the preliminary police investigation, there are no signs of a break-in. No doors jemmied and no windows broken. And nothing is missing. Rita had all her money and wallet and possessions in her pocket!"

Robert nodded in quick understanding. "Which explains why no one has seen anything - no police surveillance; this was obviously an inside job. What about the weapon used? Did the assailant leave it behind? Are there any fingerprints found anywhere near the dead body? Has forensics uncovered any hair follicles, anything that can positively reveal the identity of the killer?"

John answered his captain rapidly, "There was no weapon found, no gun left behind and nothing else uncovered so far. The killer has taken the weapon with him-"

"Or her!" Robert snapped. "Have you questioned the Armando guards? Has anyone seen anything? Where is everyone?"

John replied, "They're all gone!"

"And Monica Armando?" Robert asked.

"She's vanished too. We've searched the entire house both inside and the garden outside, there is not a trace of anyone!" John replied. "No Armando bodyguards, even the servants have all disappeared. It was the police who discovered the body after a routine inspection inside once they saw all the traffic exiting the house. They got suspicious when all these cars left with everyone all at the same time. So they checked the house, found her body lying shot like this inside here and then reported the murder to headquarters!"

Robert now knew all the answers to his questions. He knew exactly who the killer was. And he knew also who the person was who pushed the button for the killer to strike Rita Armando like this.

John studied Robert's preoccupied mindset and insisted, "You know who did this, don't you? So tell me!"

Robert replied, "This is like déjà vu. Remember the day Domenico escaped from his prison cell and everyone there on his payroll vanished from sight with him. Domenico doesn't like leaving any clues behind or any person hanging around for us to question. I don't need any forensic officer to tell me anything in order to determine who was behind this! I know exactly who was behind this and I also know why she was murdered tonight!"

John insisted to hear Robert divulge this information to him.

Robert said with his eyes cold as death, the tone of his voice became volcanic in rage, "Domenico. That bastard Domenico strikes again!"

"What do you mean?" John asked curiously.

Robert stated now in a calmer tone of voice. "It was Monica Armando who killed her mother-in-law, Rita!!"

"WHAT?" John said in shock.

Robert insisted, "It was Monica responsible for Rita's death. She was the only one who could get close enough, because she was already inside the building. She had the most perfect excuse to be here. She was living inside this house. No forced entry. She could go and come as she pleased without arousing any suspicion to our police surveillance men planted around here. The police surveillance operatives would never suspect her. And after Rita is killed-after she kills her personally, she leaves also taking all her belongings with her!"

"How do you know that? I was just about to tell you that her room was cleaned out!" John insisted.

Robert stated, "Let's just chalk it up to a good guess. Obviously, she did it, she killed Rita for her father, at his request – or should I say, order!"

John seemed much puzzled and confused at the notion. "Why would Domenico want to kill his wife? Why would Domenico order his own wife executed like this – and by his very own daughter?"

Robert gave an unsurprised facial gesture. "Where Domenico Armando is concerned asking why he wants anyone killed is because he is sick and twisted enough to kill anyone who opposes him. Anyone he deems as a threat to him!"

"So why would he see his own wife as a threat? She certainly has never been in contact with us-the police! This whole thing really makes little sense!" John exclaimed.

But Robert nodded his head at the exact opposite conclusion to his police partner's slight objection to the theory; a scenario that Robert found very obvious in himself. Robert insisted, "Domenico was behind this murder. I know it. I can feel it. Domenico ordered this killing as surely as we live and breathe. This is not a usual Mafia-style contract killing of a subject. No. Domenico ordered the death of his own wife I figure because perhaps she blamed him for their daughter Annemarie's death. And perhaps she attempted to try and pump one of the Armando guards here as to where Domenico was located so she could report it to the police-to me. The guards told him and then he ordered her dead. Monica was placed conveniently in the house at the time so she volunteers for the job to prove her worth to her deranged father and that's pretty much the story in a nutshell! That's what happened."

"Which also tells us something else," John stated quite alarmed at the revelation. "If Domenico is responsible for even killing his own wife, then that man is most certainly capable of killing anyone, which makes him a whole hell of a lot more dangerous than we have ever suspected from the beginning of this whole Domenico/Chess Player ordeal!"

Robert nodded his head in complete agreement. "Exactly; you're dead right about that, partner!"

Robert immediately ordered a statewide APB to be put out on Monica Armando. He wanted every exit around the entire city and state of New York blocked, everything covered by their police troops. He wanted roadblocks set up on all the major roads and highways leaving the city. He wanted the bus, train and private and commercial airstrips covered; all outgoing planes to be delayed from takeoff at this moment whilst Monica Armando's presence was being searched for. He wanted her picked up and arrested on sight. He wanted her hauled into police headquarters for questioning. He wanted the entire city ripped apart in search for her. Every possible avenue there was to apprehend her taken.

But it was hopeless. The seconds turned to minutes and the minutes soon turned to hours and all police radio checks by officers posted around the entire vicinity of New York reported no sight of her, including police helicopters combing the entire area. She somehow managed to vanish out of the city safely to disembark into foreign land, obviously to be reunited with her father again.

Which left Robert with the one final conclusion and that was: "We have to find Domenico. Once we do, all our problems will be solved!"

Robert remained inside the Armando house searching for clues with his other detectives until 1.00 AM; approximately three hours after the murder took place, according to the coroner's preliminary autopsy report indicating the estimated time of death.

No clue to Monica or her father's hideout was ever found. Nothing written down, no map or diary and so forth was discovered inside the huge mansion. But Robert's search came to a halt when he received another phone call on his portable cell mobile. Again, more bad news was reported.

It was the FBI director who called Robert on his mobile phone at this late hour. He had also returned to Washington. He had some more startling news to report. "Robert, it concerns Sandra Armando. Apparently, she's pulled a fast one on the FBI guards who were watching over her in her foreign hideout. She was reported escaping their custody, just some hours ago. She figured the reports of Domenico's death everywhere made her feel safe. So she escaped through a window of the bathroom. This happened over ten hours ago. The FBI agents searched all over the vicinity for her, but could not find her. I'm sorry, but it seems as though they all fucked up here. All those men under my employ assigned to her watch have messed up, big time! At their own defence, they claimed they did not see it as appropriate to follow her inside the bathroom when the likelihood of her entering was only to relieve herself. No one thought she entered behind everyone's back with the sole intention to escape!"

Robert shook his head from side to side in fury over this revelation. "That's all we need right now. What the hell was she thinking? Where is her head? I'm standing here in Armando's house investigating the murder of his wife! I've come to the conclusion that Domenico was behind his wife's death and now she leaves without clearing it with me? I always told her that I would give her the go-ahead when I felt it was safe for her to return and resume her old life in the city. Why the hell didn't she think to ask for my permission? Domenico is not dead! I never confirmed that he ever was dead! I never said that there was any truth in those reports of his demise to her! Where is her brain for crying out loud? If Domenico has killed his own wife, then she is in the gravest danger imaginable. Domenico will most likely do worse to her even than what he's ordered against his wife here this evening. Look, sir, we have to find her before Domenico does or else she is a dead woman! Another dead woman this day right along with Rita Armando! What about the boy, her son? Don't tell me, that she took him with her?"

"No, she did not!" confirmed the FBI director. "Thank God she did not. He is still safely in our custody in Protective Custody!"

"Well, at least she had the good sense not to put his life in danger next to her own by taking him with her! Ok; thank you sir for reporting this to me. I trust you will do whatever necessary to find her before Armando's people do. But I have a hunch I know where she is heading!"

"Where?"

"Right here in Brooklyn!" Robert confirmed. "Obviously she has not heard any reports of Rita Armando's murder, so she felt safe to return to New York once again. No reports of the murder committed here tonight were broadcasted because the police have not alerted the media as yet. But it will be broadcasted shortly in due course after we've wrapped up our thorough investigation here! We're not too keen on having reporters bounce around murder scenes prematurely, only resulting in trampling feet contaminating and possibly destroying evidence, even by accident!"

"Please keep me informed if you hear from her before our people find her, ok Robert!"

"You bet!" Robert confirmed before he ended the call to the FBI director.

But just as he ended the call, his phone rang again.

Robert quickly answered it hoping it was some news concerning Sandra Armando's whereabouts being located and hence meaning her safe return back into Protective Custody.

"Captain Robert Stewart!" Robert shouted.

"Robert!" whispered a woman's voice. Then she spoke louder. "Robert, it's me! It's Sandra! You know, Sandra Armando. God, I have missed you! How are you? How is New York City's greatest hero? I heard about Domenico's death and I have just arrived at the JFK International Airport. I'm on my way to see you. I just couldn't wait to hug you and thank you for saving us all from his evil clutches! I know it's late, but please tell me you're still at the station house. I'll catch a cab down there!"

Robert was overwhelmed in negative emotion. But as much as he was disappointed in her slipping her safety net, he was equally relieved to hear from her, that she was very much alive and well. "Sandra!" Robert said gratefully. "Look it, as much as I feel like telling you off right now, there is no time! Look, in brief. I want you to stay put. Don't catch a cab. Just stay where you are at the airport. I'll come right now to pick you up and take you to a safe place!"

Sandra began to panic. "I don't like the bad vibes I'm picking up here from your voice. Please, tell me… what's wrong? Domenico is dead! So what is wrong?"

Robert broke in quickly, "Sandra, I want you to listen carefully to every word I have to say, all right? Are you paying attention?"

"Yes," she insisted. "Yes. Please, tell me what's wrong?"

Robert said, "Look around you discreetly. Is the airport busy right now? Is it hectic? Is there a lot of people around?"

"Yes!" she replied.

"Excellent. That is what I want to hear!" Robert said now more sober. "Look, just stay there and I want you to hang around the crowd of people where you should be safe until I get down there. Don't go anywhere. When I get there, I'll find you. Just be on the lookout. Hang around the crowd, but don't get friendly with anyone, all right? Don't trust anyone down there!"

"Robert, you're scaring me! What in God's name is going on? Am I in danger? Is someone after me? What? What is going on?"

Robert snapped, "Damn it, woman! I wish you did not leave your protection. I did not give you the go-ahead for that. You are in a hell of a lot of danger. You understand that? Everything you heard being reported about

Domenico was garbage. It was a trap for everyone, including you. And you have fallen for it! You were a good reporter Sandra, but you have fallen for the obvious. So, just stay put. I'm coming right down to pick you up. Don't worry, I'll locate where you are!" he ordered before both ends clicked.

CHAPTER 8

Robert Stewart spent another sleepless night at the station house. He finished going over the reports now filed concerning the 'two' reported murders which took place almost back to back and all reports to that effect officially typed up at this late hour of the evening. The first was Rita Armando and the second was Sandra Armando.

When Robert arrived at the airport in a hurry, it was still too late. Robert located Sandra Armando's dead body inside the ladies' room of the airport terminal. She was stabbed in the heart. The bloody knife was found sticking inside her from one end and the handle lay popped out from the other end, whilst her body was lying on its back onto the tile floor, blood everywhere. The police also found no trace of the murderer. The murder weapon was left exposed inside the victim this time, but no fingerprints, no possible witnesses questioned seeing anything, no killer identity established by investigating police, no clues left behind at the murder scene, nothing! But again, Robert did not need any forensic evidence to determine who as well was behind this second death committed this evening. It was most certainly Domenico Armando who ordered the death of his daughter-in-law as surely as he ordered the death of his wife only hours before!

Robert was furious once he returned to police headquarters. He kept yelling and cursing inside his office. John was present. But Robert was angry at another life that was claimed this day, another victim that should have been spared. Robert was fuming as he shouted in rage: "Why the hell did she leave her protection? What the hell was she thinking? Obviously she was not thinking! This should not have happened! How the hell are we supposed to protect anyone like that if they go off and do something as stupid as what she did this night, how?"

The desk sergeant entered Robert's office that moment telling him he had a caller wanting to talk to him on his office phone. He claimed, "The caller does not want to leave his name. He only says that it's urgent he speak to you. Should I trace the call?"

Robert nodded, "Yes. Trace it! And record the conversation!"

"It's line 4!" the desk sergeant stated giving his captain privacy, leaving Robert's office, closing the door after himself. John was the only one present inside his office.

Robert pressed the correct numeric extension on his phone at the same time as he picked up the receiver and spoke into it. "This is Captain Robert Stewart, who am I talking to?"

"Please listen carefully. Just listen. I call to give you important news concerning the location of Domenico Armando!" the anonymous voice replied.

Robert's eyes became wide open as he listened in anticipation. "Who is this?"

The caller replied, "Please, just trust what I will tell you. I know where Domenico is. I cannot talk for long. I am with him inside his hideout in a country foreign to the United States. I have to give you the location and address of this wretched madman. He must be stopped. You are the only one who can do it. You must do it!" the voice stuttered desperately.

Robert listened carefully, "I'm all ears!"

The caller replied, "Once I tell you the location, gather all your forces and all your personnel and government allies and get down there quickly bringing with you as much ammunition as possible. Domenico has thousands of men guarding him. You need to bring in thousands more to overpower them. I know where he is staying because I am one of his high-ranked officials; higher than anyone else inside his organisation. I have dealings with him daily. I talk to him. So I am in the right position to give you all the information you need to blow him up sky-high. You must kill him once and for all. You hear me? He has destroyed three of my family members. He has been responsible for the deaths of three of them. Now, it's payback. I will betray him for justice's sake. He has to be stopped. He went too far with what he has done to my family members. He went too far! I want you to find him! I want you to get all your people down there with all your guns and all your ammunition - everything it takes – to finally destroy that monstrous bastard. I have to be quick. I am talking from another room inside his secret compound. It's underground. When you get there you will find a very huge stretch of land; fifty miles in radius all around the house. But the above ground house is a setup. He is actually located underneath that, underground. The floors above ground inside that house have a trap door leading to it. But to get inside there you must muster all the manpower you possible can sustain to overpower and destroy his soldiers, then once you do that, you can enter the house where you will find a basement inside the kitchen underneath the fridge inside there. Just swing it or pull it out the way, and open the trap door, you will see it. There is a metal lever attached to it. Once you open the trap door by pulling it up towards you via the lever you can get to him by climbing down the long stairway ladder which leads to the underground facility where he is living right now. Just go in there with as much men and weapons, filled with enough ammunition to blow up his entire world and all his people stationed down there in all the rooms with him and keep shooting inside every room until you get to where he is.

"I must hurry up and tell you everything quickly and silently. I am safe for now in another room, but I must hurry. I know you cannot understand my voice. I know you will not be able to positively identify me through the sound of my voice you hear from your phone. But it is not my intention to trick you or any of you. This is Domenico's doing. All the phones inside his house are equipped with some type of sound-control technology which makes voice recognition by callers from this phone impossible to detect via any of the receivers such as you. And there are scrambling devices inbuilt inside our phones stationed at Domenico's hideout. So, your tracking phone tracers will not be able to trace this call. The scramblers will only give your tracking devices multiple locations to my whereabouts. But pay no attention to it. This is all Domenico's idea to thwart his enemies from uncovering his location whilst he can call people and play games with them by frightening them. But he must be stopped. He has to be! You, Robert, must stop that bastard. He has destroyed my family. I want that bastard to finally pay. He must pay. Please, just listen. I will tell you everything you need to know. I will tell you everything-the whole truth. Because I hate him as much as you do! And I too want to see him dead for all the evil he has done to so many countless people!

"So just get him! Just kill him! Just kill him once and for all! It is what the Gods in Heaven would want! But you have to do it! Kill him before he kills more good people! And damages more families! Like he has done to ours! I have to hang up now, but before I do, this is the address: He has recently moved location to Australia. He is in the country of Australia in the Northern Territory. He is hiding there right now for 'medical reasons'.

"Much like all his secret houses around the world, he also named the street at his Australian hideout himself where he is currently living. He calls it: No. 4 Great Land Road. It should be listed in the current updated maps of the area. Then you should find the exact location and coordinates. The house is owned via fronts. It is not in his name. It never was. But please, get there quickly with all your men. Bring in thousands of them, including helicopters because that is where he is. The house is a white colonial mansion.

"But like I said before, he is hiding underneath that building in a secure fortress. And please trust that I am telling you the truth. I am not leading you or your people to some sort of ambush as I know you are clever enough to suspect that. But the truth is we were enemies once. But right now that has all changed. I am now your ally. Just get down there as soon as you can. He does not know I have called you and I must get off this phone now. You have everything you need to destroy him-all the relevant pertinent information. Robert, just do it! Just destroy him once and for all! Ok. I have to go now. Goodbye for now!" both phones clicked.

The caller spoke the truth when he said they would not be able to trace the call. The desk sergeant entered Robert's office at that moment saying that the call was most certainly scrambled. The location of the caller kept changing to different countries and regions all across the world.

The desk sergeant set up speakers inside Robert's office and they played the tape-recorded machine of the entire conversation.

After it was finished John said, "What do you make of that? Was this caller sincere or was he planning an ambush like he mentioned you might suspect by having you and all our men enter into that place and walk into a trap?"

Robert was preoccupied for a moment in thought. His mind went in circles trying to determine for certain the identity of the caller. On the surface the caller seemed genuine, if not desperate to help them neutralise Domenico, perhaps even for his own reasons. But was the caller sincere? Or was it a hoax-indeed a trap?

"What are your instincts telling you Robert? You know I've learnt to trust your instincts as well. I've also come to depend on them!" John admitted.

Robert exclaimed, "Look. If we can determine who that caller was then we will be able to decipher the true nature of that call — true or trap; to our benefit or to our detriment?"

John asked, "So who do you think that caller was? The voice was unrecognisable. And obviously the caller did not want to leave any clues to his identity. Maybe he's scared."

Robert nodded in agreement. "But he did say that Domenico was responsible for the death of three of his family members!"

"I wonder who it could be." John stated in deep thought.

Robert was also preoccupied in deep thought himself for a moment, and then he blurted out a name in conclusion to his mental findings, "D.J. Armando!"

John quickly replied, "But the caller said that Domenico was responsible for the death of three of his family members. Where D.J. is concerned, Domenico was responsible for two: Rita and Sandra!"

Robert insisted, "But counting Annemarie, it makes '**three!**'"

John said, "So you think the call was genuine?"

Robert stated, "Do you seriously think D.J. would ok the death of his own mother? - His wife maybe, but not his own mother. Honestly, I don't believe it. Domenico obviously went too far orchestrating that death. He didn't think things over in his head too clearly. Because his mental state has grown so deteriorated he is basically on the verge of total self-destruction. I believe his son would hate every fibre of his father's being for orchestrating the death of his mother, no doubt orchestrated behind his back. And when D.J. found out about it, he obviously flipped. He has now turned against his father. So in answer to your question, it is a resounding 'yes!' I believe that caller was D.J. and I also believe that everything he told us was the truth! And what is next for us is a DECLARATION OF WAR against the enemy!"

John hinted in anticipation, "But if that caller was D.J., his keeping his identity a secret from us does pose another problem. By not alerting us that it was him who in fact tipped us off, our people may actually shoot him down

369

in the process. Why did he not think about that? Why did he not give us that crucial piece of information that could spare his life?"

Robert could only come to one conclusion. The thought of Annemarie's suicide quickly sprang to mind. "Maybe he does not want to survive the aftermath, all things considered. Maybe he cannot live with the prospect of having betrayed his father to us and also the fate that is left for him once it's all dead and done with!"

Robert immediately picked up his phone and made two consecutive phone calls. One was to his SIA Chief and the other was to the FBI director, in order to keep them informed as they requested and he promised he would.

The news was explained to them concerning Domenico's location - the enemy's hiding place suddenly being established. And the order was quite clear-cut after that. Robert insisted to them both in separate consecutive conversations: "Let's get this nation's forces all lined up because we are going to have to declare all-out war on the enemy and the location is in the Northern Territory in Australia! There will be no holds barred. Carte Blanche is the order we must give to all the powers in this country to join us and bombard the enemy with the world's most powerful ammunition we must fire at his direction and not stop until we destroy him once and for all!" The order was understood and instructions would be carried out immediately. Private plane rides would be arranged for all of them within two hours. They would all have to go home and pack their bags and get ready to depart the United States of America. The destination was, Australia!

Within the hour Robert had his bags packed all ready waiting downstairs inside the living room of his house, waiting for his SIA car ride to arrive to take him to the Brooklyn private airstrip to meet the plane with his troop on board who would join him in his long trip to Australia.

His wife now stood before him with a sombre face, much concerned for his safety. Cassandra embraced him, weeping in worry.

"Did you remember to take many change of clothing?" she asked, distressed.

Robert nodded. "Everything is set!"

She then tried to relax her worries by commenting, "I hear the weather is warm down there, especially this time of year. It's almost Spring down there!"

Robert also attempted to ease the tension by teasing her gently, "I also hear in the Northern Territory the climate is especially good this time of year and a lot of women like to swim in the lake all topless, naked and sexy-looking!"

Cassandra was humoured. "I can see how a single man would want to live a life in surroundings like that!"

Robert grunted in a sarcastic gesture, "But then again there is the loyal, faithful, happily married kind of man-"

Cassandra smiled, "You mean just like my wonderful, brave, handsome husband, you!"

Robert motioned his hands gently on her waist and pressed her close to him, gave her a long kiss on the lips then said, "And don't you forget that young lady!"

Cassandra became suddenly bothered. She broke out, "Robert, why do you have to go? I am worried that something is going to happen to you! Domenico shot you once. He almost killed you before. I am afraid that this time your confrontation with him could end up much more tragically. I am worried you are going to die! Why do you have to go? You don't have to go!"

Robert paced the room in anticipation at the same time as he said, "No, Cassandra, I don't have to go. I can stay here and we can worry ourselves to death wondering what Domenico will do next to us-what he has planned next for our entire family. Is that how you want us to live the rest of our lives in fear, not knowing when he is going to strike at us? Because, believe me, he will strike. And I will kill him first before he gets anywhere near any of you, my family. That is my promise to you!"

Robert's parents, his children and his brother and his sister also entered the room next all together much extending their best wishes to Robert. His mother and his father then embraced Robert wishing him good luck.

"God bless you son!" his parents said simultaneously.

Robert tried to alleviate many troubled minds around him by insisting, "Just try not to worry. Christmas is just around the corner in a few months. Just think of me returning with handfuls of gifts for all of you!"

Robert's father's reply was uncontrollable. He snapped, "All I want is Domenico dead for Christmas so our family can be restored to safety once again and we can spend the holidays all together this year as we have every other year!"

Robert's car ride had arrived momentarily. His wife and his whole family embraced him once again, and as soon as he left through the front door, glancing back at them sympathetically one last time he felt his heart filled with emptiness.

Paul quickly disappeared from the circulation. He had his own secret agenda planned to ensure the security of his brother and his safe return to them hopefully in the not too distant future.

As soon as Robert disappeared outside the front door of the house, his family now huddled together, were left to wonder in much fear and worry whether they would ever see their beloved Robert again. Would he ever return home alive to them? The thought had killed them inside!

371

BOOK 3

CHAPTER 9

The whole world wanted Domenico Armando dead. They wanted him to be crushed and led into a humiliating defeat. But Domenico Armando exploded in outrage in one of his infamous temper tantrums and vowed, 'You will never have your wish granted, you fools!'

Then he swore to himself to make extinct once and for all the one man who turned his world upside down as it stood today and caused the entire world to despise him: 'I will march my armies against you and your allies Robert Stewart and I will crush you all! I will cripple you! I will smash you all to pieces and I will then conquer the entire world! I will reclaim my empire into the outside world by mounting my deadly vicious campaign against you and I will never stop until you are lying dead at my feet!

'This is the final battle to be unleashed in our war! This is it, Robert Stewart! Now it is time for your end! Yes. It is time for me to cripple your world, to strip you of your resources and to make your allies-your government penniless. Then you will all be dead meat!

'My power is too iconic, too strong for you all! This is not my darkest hour. No. This is the new beginning. This is my resurrection; my new reign of terror against you all.

'You will never rip my empire from me, Robert. No. I will outlive my goals. I will have the entire world at my feet. You will see. YOU WILL SEE!

'As you Robert have tried to terrorise me, I will become your terror. I will become what you most fear in the world. I will paralyse you, my friend. I will stop your heartbeat dead in its tracks. I will blind you. I will poison your eyes as you have poisoned my mind! I will attack you like a floating spirit. I will descend upon you and destroy all of you!

'You will experience the humiliation of defeat at my hands! Then the world will be mine at last! I will see my ambition come to fruition. Once you are crushed Robert, the crown will be placed on my head and I will become King of the World. So be prepared Robert. And beware of me. Your future is grim! Your future will be very short-lived! My friend, you will not have any future. I will see to it. Yes, I will see, I will see.

'So stop trying to entertain any foolish ideas that you will win this bloody gun battle this day which has erupted between us, because you will never defeat me. No, never.

'You should have left me alone, Robert Stewart. You should have left me alone! From the beginning you should have never come after me - because

372

today me and my indestructible impenetrable resources will become your untimely end. Your demise is today Robert Stewart. Yes, today!

'You think you will storm the gates of my palace and win against me? YOU ARE A FOOL! You will be condemned!

'Today I will terrorise and much haunt you with my retaliation – my bitter revolution against you! My conquest will be reached! My ambitions will be realised! I will seek victory in the blaze of glory in this battlefield between us!

'Like you, I have recovered from the bullets fired between us. Domenico Armando will make his comeback. He will put his final mark of victory on all your bitter graves. And the signatures will be made out with my strong hand, written in your own blood, Robert Stewart! Yes, with your blood I will sign your tombstone for the whole world to witness your very grim defeat against me! Yes. You will see! Yes. You will see indeed! My legacy will live on!

'As I sit here in my current hideout in the Northern Territory in Australia, in very posh and plush surroundings in my very secure underground establishment, I am the ruler of the world! I cannot be overthrown. No. It will never be over! It will never end! I am determined of that, my friend!

'Yes. You will beg me to kill you quickly. After what I do to you this day, you will indeed sink to your knees and beg me for mercy. But you gambled your life away the day you crossed me, Robert Stewart! You are finished! Not me! But you!

'I am too strong of a tiger to be caged. I am too ferocious of a lion to be shut up and kept quiet. Yes. Yes. Yes, indeed. You and your allies cannot stop me!

'Today in this final battle between us in the trenches, my men will bring me victory by destroying you all!

'I am too big of a character to ever fit inside your stupid little jail cell! I am too clever to ever be smoked out by you! Yes, indeed. You will see. You will see with your own eyes before I blind you all with poison!

'I am too much of a dangerous force to be stopped by your bullets, Robert! Yes, I have survived as you have! But today in this final battle between us, our war will reach a climax. And there can only be one winner! And that is me! And only me!

'You have made a big mistake coming here, Robert! You have entered into very hostile land! You will be crushed! Yes, indeed! You will be humiliated!'

But aside from his show of bravado at this moment before his armies of men, Domenico Armando realised that Robert Stewart and his police and government allied forces had despised him like no one else had they despised in their entire histories. They hated the Chess Player's guts!

He also was made to realise just how dangerous such an angry mob of people could be as they smashed into his secure foreign land and began the next global war against him. They began attacking his soldiers and large army and huge array of armies and networks with 'extreme force' – such government forces holding powerful weapons and firing their ammunition at his men who tried to get in their way, standing between them and their master; attempting to block the government agents' paths for now in a forward movement towards their Chess Player Master! – The proper authorities' target!

But despite Domenico's men being slaughtered in the hundreds and thousands in the bloody battleground, Domenico remained optimistic that he would become the victor in the end!

The United States government with the cooperation of the Australian government and many other international governments all combined against the Chess Player in a multinational effort which resulted in an International Incident against Domenico at present, wanted to all overthrow his communistic rule over the world and put a final stop against his endless slaughter of many of their countries' people in a united front – and they wanted to replace their society from his autocratic mob rule with democracy once again!

Despite his displays of cocky attitudes and shows of ceaseless arrogance inside his hidden underground quarters at this moment where he stood, Domenico was forced to watch Robert's allies slaughter his guards and fire tirelessly their heavy artillery, tearing their corpses to pieces, mowing his men down with extreme force!

Robert intended to scar Domenico with such a prospect of defeat. Just as Domenico killed so many innocent people throughout the course of his destructive days, Robert intended on creating an equal-and-greater carnage against his enemy's forces.

Robert wanted to become his terror, his horror. He wanted to make the very man who shook the world with death and violence, equally shake in his boots!

The bloodshed against Domenico was motivated by contempt against him. It was indeed a revolution mounted to overthrow his dictatorial hold on the world at large!

Robert indeed led his thousands of armed police, government and military forces in the march into the battlefield against the evil tyrannical Armandos.

And many of the government soldiers even resorted to firing Cannons and Bazookas against Domenico's people in order to strike a greater number of his men, and more expediently.

Very soon the Northern Territory area had been filled with blood and death everywhere in a giant carnage. It was many hours of combat so far, non-stop slaughter of men on both sides. Masses of men lay dead on the ground. It was only to be a snapshot of the horrors to come in this estimated FINAL CONFRONTATION between Robert Stewart and Domenico Armando!

The Grand Finale would result in one of them conquering and the other dying! This was the battle of their lives! Whoever would survive in its aftermath would first have to amass an army almost twice the size of the enemy opposition!

And that was Robert's main priority in the bloodletting epic saga dished out this day. He and his allies had to destroy Domenico's entire communications network so the enemy could no longer communicate to anyone in the outside world in order to drive more forces into this battleground against them. So phone lines and cellular phone networks were already being located in order to be destroyed until the enemy was crushed dead in defeat!

The catastrophic fate to be unleashed upon Domenico was endless. Robert was going to force Domenico to agonise in his final hours left on earth, until his mob people were all mowed down and the government allies would then move in for Domenico's final assassination!

Robert Stewart vowed this day to do Domenico Armando all the harm he could! And at the same time bring glory to his world, for all those who opposed Domenico with him!

Robert wanted to toast in his defeat! It was a plot, a scheme that would result in a bloody battle that would not end until one of them was buried into the ground!

But Domenico Armando vowed that no police or government army – even all of them combined globally – were still no match for the powerful force and charisma of the Chess Player!

'It is destiny!' he-Domenico Armando vowed to himself. 'I will make you all shake! I will be triumphant! I will be victorious! My legend will be re-established by the end of this day!

'You will lose Robert Stewart in your foolishly endless campaign against me. I will drive you to madness! I will make you berserk! You and all your allies will perish! Then I will launch my battle to the rest of the world!

'Yes. I will conquer the entire world once I conquer you today, Robert Stewart! It's over for you! This is the last straw! YOU HAVE TO DIE TODAY! And I will plot that death to eventuate with the element of speed and surprise before you can cause me any further damage! Yes, indeed!

'You came close to destroying me before, Robert Stewart, very close, but now it is my turn. By the end of this day I will be the one to destroy you! I will then applaud your destruction. I will salute your demise at my hands! Yes. I will rule the entire world! My quest will be realised!

'I will destroy all my enemies by cutting off their supplies for food, for water, for medicine and ammunition against me! I will become your nightmare Robert. I will conquer you! I will certainly make you all penniless! I will starve you all to death!

375

'You penetrated my fortress hideaway thinking it will result in your triumph! No! No! No! Your presence here will only result in a TRAP! You will not win this coup you have mounted against me! You will not overthrow this dictator! No. Never! You will feel my harsh justice delivered to you this day! I declare you and your allies to become dead meat by the end of this final battle between us! And I will win the war, finally! FINALLY!

'You will all sink in punishment as a lesson for ever challenging me! My influence is limitless. My power has no boundaries! My aura is spellbinding! My final onslaught against you will make history!

'Your defeat will keep my men worshipping the very ground I walk on forever and ever! It will inspire even more loyalty to me! My people will die for me willingly and without regret or remorse as no other leader could ever accomplish among their troop!!!

'Your government allies you have all united against me are no match for me, Robert Stewart! I will slaughter you all this day!

'I have resurrected from the dead in a quest to take on the entire world and reclaim my kingdom onto the outside once again! I will rebuild my empire that you have destroyed my friend to even greater heights of power and prestige than ever established before!

'I will plot your downfall Robert Stewart at the same time as proving my immortality to everyone in the entire world! And all your allies will be smashed to pieces, Robert! Then the world will be mine!

'I will invade every other country on this earth by marching my armies in a spectacular military coup of my own and the Armando Dynasty will be cast! Then the Armando Power Machine will be the one true ruler of the globe overthrowing all other pretentious leaders! I will order all those who are not for me to be shot down on sight after you are cut down this very day Robert Stewart!'

Domenico Armando had beaten the odds before. But now he faced a more resilient enemy than any other time in history!

Domenico never considered himself able to lose in any battle or challenge thrown his way! He considered himself impregnable, immune to any force against him!

But Robert Stewart was equally as determined to win this final war between them. And he vowed to crush the enemy and send his entire world tumbling down as a house of cards! He ordered his men to kill Domenico Armando on sight!

Domenico Armando thrived on dominating everyone. He thrived on outfoxing his opposition time and time again! But this time Robert Stewart vowed to outman and outgun the enemy's ill-fated authority and bring to reality his tragic destiny in one final crushing checkmate defeat! To destroy his empire forever! To destroy him and his army entirely in an epic battle that would be remembered in history forever!

Robert's troop had surrounded the enemy's hideout entirely on all sides. And with every Armando soldier cut down the government men were able to gradually march forward and advance closer and closer to the underground compound facility where Domenico was hiding inside! In an effort to give their final deathblow to the tyrant himself! And finally force the enemy to admit that, what he would never concede in his life – and that was, DEFEAT!

CHAPTER 10

Domenico Armando was brought to the brink of further outrage and fury when his computer monitor screen was shut down, no longer bringing him surveillance on all the activities going on outside. Robert's allies had shot down the surveillance cameras outside in the crossfire of the bloody act of full-scale military warfare operations which flared above ground from his hideout.

Domenico sat on his leather armchair behind his wooden desk inside his plush office angry that he was blinded to all the activities going on aboveground all around him. Now he did not know how long it would take for his enemies to enter his compound. Or how close they were to him! He also feared that his telephone networks would also be destroyed in due course. But before that happened, Domenico was eager to make a call to the very man who now made him truly edgy and much irritated by his extremely and unanticipated powerful onslaught delivered against him.

Domenico opened the middle desk drawer before him and pulled out his tiny leather-bound phone book. He searched the appropriate surname listed alphabetically under the letter 'S'.

Once he found it he sighed in relief, 'Thank Goodness I still have it. Yes. I have to call him right now. By the tone of his voice I will know exactly where I stand at this moment. I cannot rely on my men outside for communications any longer. Their cell phones may be shut down from me before much longer. So, I must make the call. I must find out everything that is going on out there straight from the horse's mouth. He will give me the answers with more accuracy than any of my soldiers, lieutenants and captains could possibly muster. My people unfortunately can only give me guessing games. But the one man I will call will most certainly help me understand exactly where I stand right now. Yes. I must call him!' he then smiled to himself. 'But, won't he be surprised when I do call him!' he then chuckled. 'Yes, indeed, he will most certainly be surprised. He will never expect it!'

Domenico noted the number. He picked up his phone's receiver sitting on his desk and heard a dial tone. He first gave another sigh of relief. 'Thank God it is still working!'

Domenico then quickly dialled the number to the man's cellular phone. He gave another gesture of relief. It rang. And before long it answered.

"Hello!" the voice on the other end of the phone said in a tone of a shout so he could be heard from all the gunshots being fired outside the Armando compound, with an earphone piece plugged into his phone on one end, the earpiece extended into his ear for clearer transmission of sound at the other.

Domenico gave out a chuckle of delight that he was able to make the call. Then he composed himself in much anticipation, almost feeling the electricity

378

of excitement rushing through every fibre of his being and all his bones at the sound of the voice of his most worthy adversary in the world. Domenico could not help but smile and smile and laugh and laugh over and over in the thrill of it all he experienced at this moment in time.

The voice on the other end shouted his hello again as Domenico was too overcome by a mysterious force overpowering him for now in his ability to speak straight away. But he eventually would. But for now he needed to savour the notion, to contemplate the thought and indeed gather all his words in the proper context quite quickly and within seconds before he would introduce himself to his greatest enemy in the world who wanted to do him in at this very moment – and indeed the feelings were mutual.

For Domenico wanted to see his blood splattered upon his shoes all the same, but before that happened he felt a strange force racing inside of him; his mind was equally racing very quickly in a type of obsessive compulsive type scenario where he needed to have one final discussion with such a man before they did the other final justice into the grave this day!

Domenico had to talk to him. He had to become immersed in conversation with the one man he loved to hate more than any single enemy he had ever faced in his entire lifetime. Domenico had to hear his voice. He had to talk to him. He had to picture his face, his desperation, and his thoughts just via the sound of his voice. Yes, indeed. Just through the sound of his voice Domenico could conclude a thousand and more mighty thoughts at this moment – and perhaps a thousand more.

So he quickly tried to compose his racing excited mind and he tried to settle his thoughts to finally bring himself to speak clearly and concisely to the one man who was destined to make history this day with the death of his caller or perhaps it was vice versa.

But anyway Domenico summoned his thoughts to silence right now. 'Enough of this nonsense', he thought to himself. 'I must speak. Yes. I must speak to my enemy one last time. And yes, it will be the conversation to end all conversations in the history of communicating such powerhouse of words', he dramatised such scenarios into his very powerfully twisted mind.

So Domenico quickly and rather suddenly just jumped right on in and his words came out as he rapidly identified himself as if he were making a call to a good friend or an ally associate. Domenico laughed still experiencing the tingling sensations in his bones of electricity at the prospect of talking to the one man who changed the course of his life as it were today whilst at the same time no one else in the world could ever manage so much as a dent against him.

But that was it. Domenico bit his tongue figuratively and identified himself quite forthrightly into his handset as he spoke the words: "This is Domenico Armando calling my very good friend Robert Stewart – the one who wants me dead this day!"

Robert entrenched inside the trenches aside his comrades in the frontlines of the gun battle erupting outside also surprised Domenico with his reply. Robert too experienced the same feelings of mysterious electric impulses rushing into his entire being. It was so uncanny how these two men hated each other, but unhelped still enjoyed having conversations with the other – and even thrived on the idea of the word 'challenge' every time they fought the other. It was perhaps crazy on both counts, but that was the true emotions felt at such time and Robert could not help but feel the same way.

Robert in fact was quite pleased at this call. Perhaps, in a strange way, it was a welcome distraction from the monotony of blood and death and displays of horrendous carnage which transpired all around him. The type of images Domenico was now blinded to. Anyhow, Robert ducked his head into the trenches alerting with a hand gesture to his brother, his police partner, Brock Stevens and Chief Lloyd McKenzie posted all around him to the identity of the caller. They all became stunned.

Then to hell with it, Robert too forced himself to settle his racing mind in the chilliness he suddenly felt permeate from his head to his foot at the prospect of coming almost face to face with his enemy right now who also was responsible for changing the course of his life – which no doubt was the product to his electrified thoughts and feelings currently at the prospect too of communicating with this heinous villain in another of those pretentious mind games Domenico was so famous for or infamous at delivering so readily.

But games or no games the call was still a welcome distraction even if it was from the likes of the one man he still loathed, despised and hated more than anyone else he had ever encountered in the world. But Robert also had to fight his strange feelings of thriving to hate Domenico; such electrical impulses he too vowed would or could not get in the way of having still a civil conversation with him, even though what was going on behind the scenes right now via their power plays was nothing short of the opposite. It was not civilised in any description of the word. What it was in fact was quite the opposite. It was the result of this horrid bloodbath displayed here today in what became a battlefield. A war!

But Robert too fought his own racing mind and also quite rapidly answered the call as all his allies around him could not wait to hear what the enemy wanted calling him this way - and right now in the middle of a war that was mostly his fault (Domenico's) than anyone else bestowed among them this day.

So Robert's words bounced off his tongue as he said, "Domenico Armando. This is Robert Stewart. How pleasant to hear from you!" he then said from a sarcastic to a deadly serious tone.

Domenico now spoke freely. "Why, Robert? Why have you and your people destroyed my surveillance cameras outside? Now I am blinded to the battle between us! Is that fair? You are fighting dirty my friend! You are playing rough! After all, I always liked to view such an enemy I am pointing my weapons to. I do not want to hear about my victory through second-hand information. I want to witness it first-hand with my own two eyes!"

Robert also spoke freely as well. "Domenico, you are delusional if you think that what will transpire here today will result in your victory. It won't. But if you want some advice, I'll give it to you; how about you end this insanity by just giving up and surrendering right now. Enough lives have been lost here on both sides. Just give it up, you maniac. Give it up. Walk out of your hole and climb to the surface and surrender. So we can end this whole sordid business in a civilised fashion!"

Domenico let him finish his words before he chuckled in laughter then said, "Surrender? Surrender, I-me-Domenico Armando surrendering? My goodness Robert that is one of the reasons why I always liked you my friend, it is because of your hilarious sense of humour. Me, surrendering?" he laughed.

But Robert was not laughing. "Look Domenico, who says I'm joking? Just give up right now and let's end this. Because I can guarantee you that you are going to lose. We are not going to stop until we wipe out all your people and then get inside your underground compound. And then we're going to get you the same way! So give up peaceably. Surrender and it will all be over. We're not going to stop until you are either captured or dead. Which is it? You should surrender!"

Domenico laughed again in another of his diabolically-sounding evil chuckles that roared on and on for moments and when he finally reduced his laughter to a mere smile he said quite fervently, "You think I would surrender? Are you crazy? Are you insane? Are you mad? Perhaps you are. Perhaps you have become just like me, Robert. Maybe we should both surrender together and see a psychiatrist, what do you say? Because my friend you are the one who is delusional if you think Domenico Armando would ever surrender!"

Robert broke in. "I never said that I thought you would surrender. I only suggested something for the sake of conversation. But do me the honour of answering me a curious question of mine!"

"I will if it's possible!" Domenico said.

Robert stated, "I thought you always said that you were a man who loved family more than anything else. So why did you order the death of your wife Rita? Don't deny it. I know it was you. You were always forthright with me before, keep it up again this time and answer my question honestly!"

And forthright Domenico indeed became. "She betrayed me, Robert. That is why. That is the simple answer and all that I care to divulge of the truth in this matter which you quite possibly already know anyhow. And besides - wives, girlfriends and mistresses do not count as family. Only blood does -

children. Now it is your turn to be forthright with me. I also have a question for you! How did you find out about this place? How were you able to track me down here in this fashion which has now resulted in this misfortunate gun battle between us? I obviously know it was an inside traitor in my organisation. But who was it?"

Robert exclaimed, "I cannot answer that question Domenico, simply because it is my job to prevent you from killing any further lives, even if that someone may be connected to you in your criminal activities!"

Domenico took in a deep breath. "You see, just as I thought. You are not playing fair these days Robert. You are playing most foul. I answered a question honestly to you, but you have refused to extend to me the same courtesy; so, what now?"

Robert appeared shocked, but he wasn't. He was simply playing Armando's game when he answered the enemy's obvious trick question quite bluntly. "Well, Domenico, either we keep shooting at each other or you surrender!"

Domenico gave out a slight disappointed vocal gesture. "My, my; you expect me to give out all the compromises. But you give nothing in return. Well, I have another suggestion. How about you surrender yourself to me? Then we can end this gun battle the same way! So, how about it? Are you ready to come and join my side? Come work for me! We'll put all this nonsense of the past behind us. After all, it does not matter really how many of each other's men we were responsible for killing on both sides. At the end of the day that does not matter. But what does matter is that WE are still alive! We have survived such bitter onslaught between us. We have even survived the bullets we recently fired into the other. But let us put all that rubbish aside. We'll bury the past and you can come and join forces with me! We can be like two compatriots. Forget the nonsense that you are the good guy and I am the bad guy. The truth is we are both a mixture of good and bad. There is not much difference between us. So let's stop the stupid guns and the firing and we'll call it quits. All I want in return is a high-prized soldier like you on my side - To join my team!"

Robert suddenly displayed anger. "Look it, you sick maniac. This is not a game here! Just give up! Just give it up and do the right thing or you, your people and even your family who may get caught in the middle of the crossfire will all DIE!" Robert shouted, but he did not realise that his words were not heard by Domenico this instance. The enemy's phone lines had just been destroyed as well, cutting off their communications entirely and ending the call prematurely.

As soon as Robert relayed the nature of Domenico's words to his allies next to him, Chief Lloyd McKenzie also kneeling in the trenches beside him yelled out to his armed troop of soldiers planted at a distance from them out in the

382

battlefield, indicating a deliberate order against the enemy: "Shoot! Destroy! Kill him!"

Everyone who heard the words were greatly inspired beyond description.

BOOK 4

CHAPTER 11

Domenico Armando got into a fit of rage when his eyes glanced at his blank computer screen sitting on his desk. It could no longer transmit the images of the war taking place outside between his army and Robert Stewart's.

Domenico Armando picked up his computer monitor with both hands, raised it high above his head, and then sent it smashing in one corner of the office den on the marble floor. It smashed and splattered in pieces everywhere; the glass made a mess all over the corner of his room.

Domenico was angry. He was bitter and he began to panic. He could not stand being blind to the happenings outside. His communications system was shut down. His electricity supply was being run by his installed generators. The mains power source also carried from outside was as well neutralised by the enemy. Domenico now began to panic immensely.

He walked to the closed door of his office, opened it and yelled into the corridor. He shouted for his special doctor Master Fu Zheng. The five-feet-seven-inches tall forty-six-year-old mean-faced Asian entered his den. He ran a chemist here in the Northern Territory. In fact, he was working on a cure for Domenico's terminal cancer. That was why Domenico chose to enter this country for refuge after his gunshot injuries. After the surgery, Master Zheng helped him recover from his bullet wounds with a concoction of herbal remedies.

Now Domenico enlisted his services to work on a cure for his cancer. Domenico wanted to use all his talents and all his skills to cure him as he stated, "Unlike all the others, you have medical expertise and the good sense to want to help me. After all, you also like money. And if you cure me, you will become a millionaire many times over."

Master Zheng was indeed a man with cleverness in medical research for chronic human diseases. But he was also unscrupulous enough to love money equally in the same fashion as his joy for medical research work in both pharmaceutical as well as herbal therapies. He would work fervently to help Domenico.

In fact, Domenico had a laboratory facility compartment specially installed inside his current Australian hideout, so Master Zheng could continue his research whilst in hiding with Domenico. And part of his willingness to help Domenico was due to Domenico's forthcoming assistance to his seventy-year-old Asian father, who was being hunted by the Australian Federal Police for acts of terrorism.

384

Domenico had also provided his father with permanent refuge inside one of his secret hideouts abroad, far away from the Australian authorities who were out for his blood.

So in exchange for his assistance to his family, Master Zheng was also quite keen to aid Domenico – and continue his research for him in these underground surroundings until he came up with the correct medical procedure and one real solution to cure his rapidly growing excruciatingly-painful brain tumour. Master Zheng also injected Domenico constantly with morphine to help him deal with the horrible pains of his illness.

Domenico asked him with much anticipation, "How is your research going?" He then added impatiently, "Time is running out for me, doctor. TIME IS RUNNING OUT! And I am not just talking about my health, but my enemies are moving in on me. They could break in here anytime now! I need to be fixed. A cure must be established quickly. Then I must escape these miserable quarters, what has transformed into a hellhole outside by all those who want to see me dead! But sometimes I still am left to wonder who and what will kill me first. Will it be Robert Stewart or this natural disaster burning inside of me?"

Master Zheng replied rather casually, "I am working on a few things to at least help stop the cancerous tumour growing and spreading. But I'm afraid a cure will take much time!"

Domenico nodded in understanding, much casually himself. He did not lose his temper surprisingly. Perhaps the sounds of gunshots outside had preoccupied his mind on other things at this point. So he waved his hand in gesture, granting the doctor permission to exit his office den and resume his work inside the laboratory, saying, "Thank you very much. You can go and carry on with your work!"

The doctor bowed his head dutifully and disappeared out of the room around a labyrinth of corridors and hallways, until he entered his quite modern and high-tech scientific laboratory.

Meanwhile, Domenico Armando felt death closing in all around him from all sides. And he no longer could tolerate being on his own and experiencing any further solitude. He shouted into the corridor outside for another name whilst posted at the door of his den. He ranked for his trusted adviser Counsellor Rex Higgins to join him inside his office room. And his daughter Monica he embraced glad she was able to return to him safely from New York also sat in for the meeting.

His counsellor would give him a brief rundown of the latest developments concerning the disastrous acts of war which transpired outside above their heads – a declaration of hell indeed it was being unleashed and much orchestrated against him by his staunchest enemy, Robert Stewart!

Anyhow, the counsellor reported that the news was bleak! "With our communications systems down, talks with our captains, lieutenants and soldiers outside have ceased. All cellular phone devices are no longer operable! We are finding it difficult to be able to communicate with them. We cannot reach our offshore contacts to help bring in further squads of reinforcements, simply because our radios and our phones no longer are operable. Nothing is working any more. Our guards inside have long-range, long-distance night-vision binoculars and telescopes they can use, but from what they can see indeed spells disaster for us all. We are losing our men to our enemies. And from what can be ascertained, Robert and his people are now moving closer and closer to us with every passing hour. It is night time now but our portable technology can still view what is happening outside. And our guards here have estimated that Robert and his people will be penetrating the house located just above our heads within a matter of hours now. Then he will find the trap door that leads underground here and he will move in to take us all out! - Meaning to kill us with his heavy artillery!"

Domenico shook his head from side to side and shouted in extreme rage and furious anger: "Damn it! Damn it! Damn him! Damn that Robert Stewart. And damn the traitor who leaked out our location to him. Robert Stewart has been tipped off. I want you to locate him-this bastard traitor. Find out who he is and dispose of him IMMEDIATELY. You hear me? I want to know who he is first, and then he must be dealt with accordingly and much harshly!"

"We're already working on it, Domenico. We're trying to establish what phones may have been used to call Robert. But with our communications systems down, we cannot call any of our local connections in the phone company who can tell us which of our phones was being used in order to identify the culprit responsible!"

Domenico struck the side of his clenched right fist onto his desk forcefully. "This occurrence here today is a true act of disaster. We are now surrounded by mayhem all around us, but I will NOT accept defeat, you understand that, Rex? I don't care how it looks outside. I will not accept anything-any estimation that our people say that may be to our detriment. You follow? Because one way or another, we have to turn this around. I must plan an OUT for us all, so we can escape this bloody turmoil which has erupted outside! I need to think here! I need to plan." Domenico now faced his real gold-coloured chessboard on his desk. He picked up one of the chess king pieces in solemn thought and said, "You see Rex. What is happening outside is no different to what is happening when two players are consumed in this very special game I have sitting on my desk. Winning a war is like playing a game of chess. You have to forecast all the scenarios that would take place with every move you make. So we must think and plan carefully before we act.

"But we must come to our conclusions rather quickly. And we must make our final move very soon. But before we make that move we must think what positives and negatives – what chess game scenarios will we impose upon ourselves. Will it grant us with a checkmate victory or will our movements render us into a further stalemate. And worse than that – a godforsaken checkmate defeat!

"So plans must be made right now and our move must be put into motion as soon as possible. Because if we do not, Robert Stewart and his lunatic Yankee allies will be bursting inside here whilst we are sitting in these miserable quarters ill-equipped to deal with a rampage of thousands of bloodthirsty government Bull Terriers! And if that happens my friend, you know the outcome, don't you!"

Rex lowered his eyes to the floor experiencing himself a flood of overwhelming emotions at this moment – which became a mixture of great remorse and fear as he replied, "Yes. I'm afraid I do. We are all dead men!"

So a period of intense brainstorming sessions was in order. And the discussions commenced right away.

CHAPTER 12

Domenico Armando studied the hand-drawn map his counsellor made-up of the entire radius of the surrounding land around and above their heads.

Domenico's counsellor was seated directly opposite his master's desk face to face with him whilst marking out all the areas their enemies had encircled.

Domenico became angry. "So what? Is this news you are telling me, you think, huh? I already know Robert's people have closed in on all perimeters of the outside land, covering every entrance-and-exit area within a now five-mile radius. From fifty miles they are now forty-five miles closer.

"The problem is we cannot contact our Middle East suppliers of Arms. If we could, we would be able to smuggle in enough explosive devices slipped in here to blow them all up sky-high to kingdom come! Now, that's the problem we face. We are trapped here like fucking rats in a hole!

"If we poke our heads out, well, we know what is going to happen... Our people are being put down into the ground every second. Our men are being dropped like masses of dominoes by the enemies' heavy artillery weapons. So the question is what is our strategy? What are we to do now? How do we extricate ourselves from this mess?"

Domenico's entire demeanour turned into a giant fit of terror as he exploded inside his office den all of a sudden: "Damn the traitor in my family who has betrayed me to Robert! Damn him! He tipped-off Robert to our location here. This culprit has destroyed me this day!

"You see, my island headquarters in the Caribbean is anonymously located on uncharted waters – it has never been recorded on any map. That is why I was never worried about Robert finding me there! Unfortunately, this location here in Australia has been found by Robert via a traitor in my family! I will find out who that person is and take care of him appropriately!"

Domenico hinted as his face yet resembled a time bomb ready to detonate any moment now: "No one betrays me. No one! My family was always immune to any forms of treason! Why? Because I commanded authority and my men had no recourse but to respect me. I was the wealthiest and most powerful leader of all other leaders in this entire world. I could always afford to pay my men extra - a lot more than what others could muster! There was no reason for anyone to ever betray me.

"I always looked after my people. I treated them and their families well. Yes. I looked after their families too. So the question is who the hell betrayed me this day? And the bigger question is why?

"Robert's allies have destroyed all the phone lines and all the portable communications cell phone towers connected to this address. What fucking bad luck has befallen upon us this day!"

Domenico picked up his cellular phone sitting on his desk in front of him and shouted in fury, "You see, there is no network coverage, no connection now thanks to Robert!" he yelled with a lion's roar, also throwing his $2,000 mobile phone at the wall on the other side of the room also watching it break in pieces.

Domenico could feel the walls of his compound shaking from the powerful blasts being fired outside. He kept shouting, "What the hell is this? What the hell is going on? And most importantly, who has done this to me?

"I can hear the gunfire. I can feel the gunfire all around me. I can sense my enemies moving closer and closer to my very location. And the only report you can give me is negative bad news. That we are running out of manpower. And our men are running out of bullets and ammunition as well at the same time as our enemies are always replenishing their reserves of both men and guns against us." His eyes lit up now resembling something greatly demented; a demented beast as he roared further, "This is a disgrace! This is an unexplainable disgrace!

"DOMENICO ARMANDO DOES NOT LOSE! But now fate and circumstance has put me into a situation usually reserved, constructed and concocted for both failures and losers! What a bloody mess we are in right now!

"This traitor here among us will be destroyed when I find out his name. That bastard will wish he was never born!

"The gunfire around us is no longer long-range. Our enemies are so close to us they can see the look of shit splattered on our faces! That is what is happening to us now. We have been thrown into the brink of humiliation and embarrassment.

"From unbeatable we are suddenly facing a crushing defeat! What a tragic turn of events! What a horrible act of fate that is!

"Our enemies are only a hair's-breadth away from us, maybe even much closer than we think. That fucking traitor is going to be hanged by his toes that little bastard shit for what he has done to me! THIS IS OUTRAGEOUS! This is a fucking calamity!" Domenico shouted in a bid to give the final rant of his life.

He vowed that he would shake the world this time, not with bullets (as he had none) but with ferocious words delivered via a very powerful tongue. "That fucking traitor is going to bring us all down with him – after I make him first bark like a dog before he enters his grave!

"I WILL NOT DIE HERE! You hear me, my counsellor? I refuse to die here trapped like a rat or a caged animal with no hope, no escape! No! No! No! There is a way out! We will find it! You understand?

"So tell me. Have you instructed all our people and my three children inside here to pack their things and get ready to leave?"

The counsellor replied, "Yes, Domenico. I have already anticipated you on that!"

Domenico nodded. "Good; because there is a way out, don't worry about that. We will be long gone before that damn American government storms these walls and starts blasting away like a pack of crazies!"

Rex Higgins asked nervously, "You have a plan?"

Domenico insisted, "Of course I have a plan. We just have to ensure first that our enemies have not blocked it as well! I have to make damn sure that when we leave here, they will not be standing anywhere near the escape route, waiting for us! But we have no choice. With our communications systems down, we will have to take the chance in choosing a route and playing what the ignorantly weak do: 'let's wish for the best'.

"Meanwhile right now all the standard exits are blocked. Our food and water supply is also running low. Those enemy fiends outside have fired their bullets into our water tank; gallons of drinking water has been lost. They want us to collapse onto our knees from starvation and thirst. So we have to make our move very soon. Like within the hour once we are all packed and ready. But before we do, I must learn the identity of this traitor. I know it is not you, my counsellor! But it is someone close to me, stationed right here with me within the walls of this underground compound facility.

"We must learn his identity, because there is no point escaping one entrapment like this here if this traitor is going to alert and tip-off Robert again of our new hideout location in order to have another TRAP there set up waiting for us! I must find out this heinous person's identity and first deal with him accordingly and painfully! Then and only then can we depart from here through one of our secret tunnels leading to what I hope is a deserted piece of land, where a car is stationed there at all times, to drive us to our plane and fly us the hell out of here to safety into my secret Caribbean Island quarters!

"Well, we will find out in due course if it is still a secret or if this wretched act of treason perpetuated among my staff has also alerted Robert of this crucial piece of information. But no matter what, we will be prepared this time. We will not enter another ambush of bomb-and-gun raids being fired at us, my counsellor. That, I promise you!

"Then once we leave here and disembark back into our safe territory and all our creature comforts are restored, I will plan an almighty FINAL ASSAULT against all our enemies! They are going to see many millions more deaths around them than the amount of blood they spilled against us this day!

"Here the enemy outnumbers us 10 to 1. But once we leave and I re-establish myself with my foreign allies the odds will be shifted back into our favour in a sweeping victory! And I will hit them all from all sides with a relentless series of death blows to be unleashed – even much larger than what they have struck me and my people with this day! And the corpse of this traitor who is nothing but a career opportunist, who wants to play both ends against the middle, will be sent to the very White House in a coffin. How does that sound? Good, hmm! It certainly does sound like music to my ears!"

The counsellor nodded in agreement to his padrone's words, though he himself wondered who could have betrayed his Master.

Domenico yet continued his volcanic rant as he insisted, "In order to find out his identity, we cannot use anyone else stationed here for assistance. We have to figure it out ourselves, because this traitor could be anyone. We cannot even accept food or drink from any of our staff, maids and servants here with us. Who knows, maybe the traitor might have a great reward waiting for him in exchange for poisoning me! Only you and my children will I trust to deliver me anything to consume! Indeed. This traitor could be anyone!

"But just as my enemies have waged war against me, I will hold the final piece of artillery that makes them all perish! You will see! No one will ever win victory against Domenico Armando! All those who tried to destroy me this day will all be exterminated in the end! They are going to be the fallen ones.

"As they have surrounded me this day, I will encircle them the same way with my vicious assault against them. I will strike them all from the front and from behind covering all sides. And I will be standing posted in the frontlines in my battle against them. I will witness their crushing defeat! I will celebrate in the glory of their dead bodies exposed before my very eyes!

"I will be very ruthless with my enemies! It will be a rude awakening for them! And Robert Stewart will feel my extreme ruthlessness firsthand for his oppressive resistance to my throne!

"And that person here who betrayed me will be buried in the same cemetery as all my enemies and Robert Stewart! Who does that fucking traitor think he is to betray me like that to my enemies? Hmm. Does he know he has signed his death warrant? Does he not realise what I will do to him once I find out who he is?

"He is a contemptible, disloyal son of a bitch; a treacherous little coward. He is the scum of the Armando family! He is a scum and a failure to think the government will be able to protect him from me! He does not have a shred of honour or backbone to betray a man like me who conquered all and everyone with my two hands time and time again! I will make him pay very dearly! I will open up his veins and I will make him bleed to death! He will die drowning in his own blood!"

Domenico Armando had no idea that the man he was talking about was his own son D.J. – His most favourite son! Named after him personally: Domenico!

D.J. Armando entered his father's private den and quickly closed the door. It was midnight. The gunfire sounds outside were terrifyingly loud now. His father's enemies were moments from their task of storming the underground fortress.

Anyhow, D.J. witnessed his father collapsed onto the ground. And all the guards, servants and maids with his counsellor and brother and sister around him were also onto the ground, but knocked unconscious onto the floor.

D.J. had just finished drugging all of them into a temporary unconscious state when he moved in for the kill. The target was his once loved father Domenico. He once loved, respected and worshipped his father before he knew the depths of his wickedness. Before he knew of the true extent of the evil inside that man once labelled, The Great Domenico Armando.

D.J. had entered his father's office den only moments before and gave its entire occupants, including his two siblings present and his father what seemed a large tray filled with evening refreshments; herbal teas for them all.

But he laced the drinks given to everyone else with tranquilisers he liberated from Master Zheng's laboratory – once he entered inside putting small vials of such liquid narcotics into his pocket, but confiscated a special article for his father. He did not know what it contained. But the small vial had a handwritten label attached onto the finger-sized glass bottle that read: **poison!** He saved that surprise for his father's drink.

So just as he laced the rest of the compound occupants' drinks with tranquilisers to prevent them from interfering in his plans – he doused his father's drink with a heavy dose of some mysterious poison; and after he served the beverages of apparent 'soothing teas' to everyone – the effects took place instantly.

All the maids, servants and guards, with the counsellor, and including his siblings Monica and his brother Tom (but with the exception of the missing doctor Master Zheng) fell onto their knees, rolling off chairs and couches and then their bodies collapsed entirely onto the floor.

But his father experienced a different reaction, a different kind of fate in store against him. Domenico collapsed onto the floor, now crawling onto his hands and knees in bitter agony. His body colliding into a legion of many unconscious bodies splattered all around him. His stomach ached like nothing he could ever imagine before. The pain was a mixture of fire and wild thumping aches that had his lungs gasping for air. He felt winded, barely able to breathe. His eyes became blurry. His vision strained. His mind became disorientated as he slowly crawled onto the floor groaning in horrendously excruciating agony as he began vomiting everywhere around him at the same time as his suddenly formed helpless-looking eyes stared up between fits of great lashes of vomiting baths forming liquid masses all around him – his strained eyes glanced in an equal mass of confusion at his unhelpful son who now confronted what he described as a son of a bitch of a father.

392

D.J. then spoke to his agonised father. His words were filled with utter contempt and profuse hatred as he said: "You deserve to die father! You deserve to die! You killed my mother! You killed my wife! And now I will kill you, you horrible bastard! Your reign of terror ends tonight! You will never become the puppeteer to anyone again! You will never control anyone again! No one! You will never harm anyone again! I spiked your drink father. I will do to you now what should have been done to you a long time ago! I am going to kill you!"

Domenico now stopped dead in his tracks. He was still planted on his hands and knees. Despite the physical and mental torments he experienced at present he could yet comprehend his son's words to him and the manner he confronted him, now filled with feelings of complete and utter contempt! His son felt for him the same hostile emotion as his swarming enemies outside above their heads felt for him. They all wanted Domenico DEAD! His favourite son included shared in the exact same sentiment of wanting to see his father's corpse lying motionless and inoperable now – and PERMANENTLY!

D.J. had rapidly considered Domenico's terminal illness as Divine Intervention – and his poisoning of his father as sweet revenge! But now D.J. wanted to speed the whole process of his father's demise with his own justifiable intention against him and his evil!

And between groans of unbelievably excruciating abdominal pains, Domenico's much-strained-blurry eyes stared up at his son, trying to achieve some focus at the picture of D.J.'s face, and he stuttered out in a reduced much-less-powerful voice, as if begging for a mercy no one in the world at present, his eldest son included, considered that he deserved: "My son... My son... Why? Why have you done this to me? I am suffering here. Please... Please help me!"

But D.J.'s face became cold as stone. He now almost resembled his father's old forceful powerhouse of a character. And D.J. did not answer. He only stared at his weakened father in icy-cold silence with what he concluded as justifiable malice as the only help he wanted to give his father right now was a powerful push and a mighty shove into his much-anticipated GRAVE!

BOOK 5

CHAPTER 13

Domenico Armando contemplated his fate only moments before. He considered himself to be a certified dead man. He much thought in dismay that once the poison had taken full hold he would finally close his eyes forever only never to wake up again. He thought he was finished. He considered his life over, collapsed, LOST FOREVER! - Hopelessly lost. Gone!

Domenico surely did not expect that once his eyes in fact had closed, losing consciousness, that he would reawaken hours later onto a plane being driven to safety with his son D.J.'s head lying onto his chest weeping for his father's life. Domenico never anticipated that would ever happen during his final gasps of mental and physical anguish he experienced before his consciousness died onto the marble floor of his office den most recently.

But it seemed as though once the tranquilisers had worn off and the rest of the compound's drugged occupants had regained consciousness thereafter, they helped their Master with the surprised assistance of the man responsible for almost putting him into his grave, D.J. – and they took their motor car rides awaiting them inside the secret concrete tunnels. They drove the 80-mile length of the faintly-lit tunnel to the end (far beyond the length of land that of Domenico's compound) where one of the guards climbed the wall's stairway ladder, pushed forward the trap door after unlocking the metal lever; which brought them to a deserted wilderness above outside, no life in sight, only darkness at this early AM hour after midnight – and then they lifted Domenico's body into safety above ground where a car was parked camouflaged beneath a line of huge gum trees concealing its view from any passing helicopters of the police and government variety. Such cars were discreetly planted outside the entire compound's tunnel escape routes prepared much in advance in case they were ever needed for such urgent getaway emergencies.

The driver stepped out of his vehicle with his torch and helped them carry Domenico's unconscious body inside the car and at the same time as Domenico, his counsellor, his daughter, with Tom and also D.J. who were all safely taken away inside that one awaiting vehicle, instant arrangements were made for the pick up of the rest of Domenico's people to have them also transported by car and flown to safety to all meet separately in the Armando headquarters in the Caribbean.

As Domenico lay recovering on his bed inside the plane he then showed no surprise to find his son seated beside his bed, even much concerned for his father's well-being.

D.J. explained to his yet slightly-groggy father, "The guards took your unconscious body to safety. We took a gamble at one of the escape routes through one of the mazes of spiralling tunnels and a car was waiting for us to take us all to this local plane where we are now being flown to safety far away from the hell in Australia!"

Domenico was still aware that his son had tried to kill him earlier. But apparently the heavy dose of poison he gave his father was still not fatal to him as he intended it to be. Domenico would not die from it.

Domenico now understood as well that it was his SON who betrayed him to Robert and told him where he was located. The culprit was his own son!

Now that his father was awake, his son wept again as they were situated on the plane in privacy for now. D.J. mourned at his own character or lack thereof when he cried, "Why is it that I wanted you dead before – and now that you are awake I want to see you back on your feet again, father? Why?" he asked confused at his warped sense of thinking, unable to control his mind's patterns of behaviour. But all he knew was that no matter what happened between them and whoever his father had killed throughout his life, Domenico Armando could and would never EVER harm one of his own children in any way, shape or form. That was why D.J. felt safe. Anyone else who even thought about killing him would have been surely dead the second he woke up. But forgiving his son was as mysteriously simple as his son forgiving his father for his heinous acts at this point.

Domenico's reaction to his son was amazing. He had empathy in his eyes and much forgiveness imbedded into his heart and soul for him. He now had the energy to respond to his son's question. "We are blood, my son, which is why! No matter how much you have tried to fight it or deny it, we are the same you and I. We are the same!"

D.J. asked his father another question out of curiosity, "What happened to Master Zheng? He has mysteriously disappeared!"

Domenico would respond even humoured at this point at his son's interesting question. The answer was quite a fascinating one indeed. He said, "Before you poisoned me, Master Zheng met with his untimely demise! He no longer wanted to continue his important work for me. What can I say? In crux, the whole story of that matter was another act of fate playing a comedy of errors against me.

"You see, Zheng's father apparently deserted the hideout I provided for him like a fool. Interpol caught up with him. He resisted arrest by trying to shoot his way to freedom. But instead, the police shot him to death. Master Zheng heard about it. Then he refused to continue his research for me. So as a consequence, I was forced to have my people shoot him dead as well."

Domenico then shook his head from side to side in dismay at his next statement which marked a deadly truth he found too much to bear. "Perhaps, it's fate's way of saying that it's good night for me, I'm afraid! Just as my enemies have failed to bring me to destruction, nature has stepped forward and succeeded!"

Domenico also groaned in disbelief at his next revelation. The nature of that was also mixed with a plethora of sordid misfortunes as well. "At around the same time as Zheng's inevitable end was realised, some further disappointing news concerning my business affairs was also broadcasted on the public radio. That other fool, Senator Ron Bishop said publicly he was going to resign his candidacy for the United States Presidency! He is running scared, in his own words: 'After he found out how dangerous his sponsor was!' Meaning me, my son!

"Once I heard that too on top of everything else thrown our way I was bloody angry as hell! I wanted that fool to be established in the United States government as President so that I could use him for political power whenever I needed to. But all that money and time I spent on him – what a waste!"

Domenico now was forced to prepare for the end of everything: the end of his enemies, their world, including the death of all his hopes and dreams - mixed with his much-anticipated MORTALITY.

Domenico now knew his death was also inevitable. That prospect was confirmed by the death in all his much-cherished grand goals. All that was left – the only product that stemmed into his thoughts right now was that of Death and Destruction! Domenico could feel death at hand inside of him. But he also wanted to plan the deaths of all those in the world he targeted — for them all to enter the grave together; both him and his enemies.

Domenico spoke to his son his final plans prior his own death and burial: "The time has come. It is now the end! I want Senator Ron Bishop dead! I want Bruno and Don Santucci dead! I want Colin McMurphy dead! I want the entire United States underworld commission dead! I want SIA Chief Lloyd McKenzie dead! I want to arrange a meeting with my global associates to be held in our usual meeting place in Rome, Italy. Then we will plan the deaths of the entire world of our enemies. I want them all dead! Yes, my son. I want all my enemies sent into their graves! They are all dead men in this End Game! And most importantly, my nemesis Robert Stewart's fate will finally be realised! Robert Stewart will also be terminated, FINALLY!!!"

Domenico said scornfully, "I had such great plans – such great dreams which hinged on that idiot Senator getting into government by winning the Presidency! You know, I could have gotten a Pardon that was had that happened.

"I could have then returned to New York and continued to resume my life as normal. I could have slaughtered all my enemies at the same time and the President would be in my pocket, my ally. He could even vouch for me!

"I would have rubbed it right into Robert's face. I would have entered his police station again and forced him to be civil with me. I would have entered his house in broad daylight and my men would have taken hold of his wife and his entire family. Robert would be present. My men would hold him back whilst I instructed my people to fire their machine guns at his entire family and showed him MY TRUE POWER! Then I would have him put in prison on charges of defying the crowned King Domenico Armando!

"The United States and every other country would be run by me! And everyone who opposes me would be executed! But Robert would spend his days behind bars! He would then be executed behind bars! That my son was my dream! But that bastard Senator ruined everything by running scared at the last minute. Well, so be it! They all have to be dealt with my son. I want Senator Ron Bishop and ALL my enemies in the entire world DEAD!!!"

And that was when Criminal Chief Mastermind Domenico Armando orchestrated the deaths of all his previous mentioned targets. All of them with the exception of his most important target – Robert Stewart – had he failed with his plots for that one in his mind 'crucial elimination!'

And after fourteen weeks, that was when Robert Stewart had his Final Showdown with his equally-categorised 'nemesis' Domenico Armando in Rome, Italy.

Robert Stewart and his cavalry stormed the enemy's Australian hideout much previously (once they overpowered all of Domenico's gunmen outside), and found he had disappeared with all his children and everyone else present inside, leaving only an isolated underground empty compound with a labyrinth of many mazes of tunnels they located, but once each one of them was searched, Domenico Armando was never found. They searched all the exits such tunnels led to outside via trap doors, but found Domenico and all his people were long gone! Nowhere in sight! He had escaped, yet again! They missed him by only a hair's-breadth! Their search for Domenico in Australia turned into a dead end on all counts!

It took longer than three months for Robert to finally track down his enemy once again. That one fateful encounter proved to be the climactic battle of all battles they shared against the other!

In the Grand Finale of that final struggle or contest between them which took place in Rome, Italy - Robert was the only survivor that day out of the two of them. The battle was won. The enemy had lost. The Chess Player was crushed in defeat! His body was smashed by a riddle of bullets! His dead corpse lay on the ground before them all for the entire world to see and hear – and breathe freely again!

The war between Robert Stewart and Domenico Armando was finally over!

Domenico Armando was predicted to never rise again – because if he had – God help the world – and God help Robert Stewart!

At the end of the day, following the burials of all the dead, was there really any other way to view the situation...?

DETECTIVE'S INVESTIGATIONS INTO THE MYSTERIES OF THE WORLD: SECRETS UNRAVELLED

THE LAZZARO REPORT

Sometimes the truth can be accessed through what a good cop calls 'gut instincts' – rather than simply relying on scientific evidence alone. Science can be manipulated just as evidence can be manufactured to achieve even diabolical means and conclusions. Cop instincts on the other hand can be more reliable than so-called facts.

He would now call himself Lazzaro. Lazzaro in Italian meant Lazarus; rising from the dead. And that was exactly what the man who once called himself, the Chess Player had done. He rose from the dead. He rose from all those bullets fired into him in Rome, Italy. Because the man who was shot in Rome, Italy was truly not the same man who now called himself, Lazzaro; a new alias he assumed from his former code name dubbed, the Chess Player; otherwise known as Domenico Armando.

The problem now was that the Chess Player would finally wake up to learn that another three of his children had been killed during his absence or forced absence.

I knew he never attended that meeting in Rome, Italy because he was physically unable to.

Domenico would never allow his children to attend such a meeting on their own without him present with them, in himself, to protect them. So the only way Domenico Armando would not attend was if his proven health crisis did not permit it; if he had a fainting spell, a seizure – which forbid him from attending that day.

Then the question remained: if that person in Rome who everyone thought was Domenico (shot to death), was in fact really not Domenico Armando – then who was he?

The answer to that lied in the files we confiscated in Armando's compound in the Caribbean which revealed his entire life's work: his achievements, his ambitious plans and his own handwritten journal we (the police) managed to take possession of before Armando had been able to hide such incriminating information from us, or even destroy all copies, so we would never know.

But we got to them first. His files labelled, 'The Revenge Project', 'The Robert Stewart File', and extensive documents into his own medical research notes he conducted himself, to attempt to be the first man alive to cure, what was in fact regarded as an 'inoperable-incurable' brain tumour!

I uncovered the evidence of the truth once I ordered my people to run an extensive DNA analysis of the corpse in Rome, Italy otherwise thought to be Domenico Armando.

Fast-track DNA tests confirmed the truth to us. They confirmed that the dead corpse before us who resembled Domenico Armando was in fact one of the many 'body doubles' of the yet breathing terrorist. Blood and saliva samples were taken of the corpse. We already had Armando's genetic profile stored away for comparison. During our investigations against him as the Chess Player, we extracted DNA samples from his toothbrush, and cups and forks he drank and ate from.

After that ambush in Rome, we had access to two of Armando's sons. Their genetic profiles matched our original records we also stored of them. Now the way we determined whether that corpse in Rome was Domenico Armando was to compare the newly-extracted DNA samples of the would-be Domenico corpse on his sons' Y-chromosomes; as this male sex chromosome was passed directly from father to son; so technically if that corpse was really Domenico, it should match. But it didn't.

I also knew what Domenico Armando was truly capable of, not only from my own personal experience with him, but through the target's own handwritten disclosures, jotted down extensive confessions in his own handwriting in diaries we located. Which revealed truths that otherwise would be considered science fiction! But we uncovered that money and people's immorality could make the impossible seem possible.

Domenico Armando in fact could make someone look like someone else using plastic surgery.

And the DNA tests I ordered be run on the corpse in Rome proved that that corpse who looked like Domenico was in fact not Domenico. It was someone else made to look like him. A man created as a backup or ordered created by his own son D.J. also prior his death.

Domenico Armando wrote in his own diary (we confiscated) that the son who once tried to kill him, then went to great lengths to try and save his life from us (the authorities).

Domenico mentioned in his journal that his son had approached the Armando family scientists to help him prevent his father from ever being found; thus the creation of a body double, an imposter, a decoy.

The DNA tests we ran on that so-called Domenico Armando corpse in Rome confirmed that it was a body double. It was not our man: the Chess Player-Domenico Armando-now Lazzaro!

Domenico also communicated his thoughts in writing concerning his extensive research into medicine. He also wrote down his revenge plans against me. He noted his big plans against the world for the sake of getting back at one man: me-myself-Robert Stewart!

And in regards to his plans for me, I knew when he woke up from his medically induced coma after suffering seizures – and once he was informed of his three children's deaths by the police, that all hell would break loose. There would be a war on the streets. He would declare a war against the police, the government, innocent civilians, the entire United States and then look to burn the entire world to the ground at whatever cost!

I had to use psychology here to figure out what his next move would be in precise detail. I had to put myself in his shoes. I had to think like him. I knew him well. And now I had to act as if I was Lazzaro. What would he do? What I was sure of, was that whatever the enemy planned would be of a gross nature. I knew it would be shocking. It would be unleashed in lightning speed and in a very startling fashion.

Basically, it would be my family for his family. He would blame me for the loss of his family. And I began to see the changes which were taking place around me thereafter.

I was being watched. I knew my family was being watched.

The enemy planned a camera outside my house. He was stalking me. He put me under surveillance. He used his rogue people to tail me and even give me constant prank phone calls.

This became a serious incident by a Federal government department called the SIA of harassment and invasion of privacy and spying on my home.

The enemy was using a government department I was recently affiliated with in order to now have them become my enemy. Instead of working with me as always, they began to join forces with the very scum they were previously encouraged to eradicate.

It became the rebirth of the enemy's usual course of action: out with the old, in with the new. It was his modus operandi. To infiltrate and takeover what became a threat to him.

After the death of former SIA Chief Lloyd McKenzie, the government department was being run by a new boss called, Maxwell Hawker. Maxwell Hawker was running the agency into the ground. All the old people of the agency met with one fatal accident after the other. They were killed one by one in their homes, in their cars, out on the street – and their houses were all blown up, killing their entire families in the terrible

401

blasts. The enemy had replaced the good with his people, the bad. This was the sign that the enemy had woken up from his coma once again. And now he would take justice into his hands once more.

Now that he had infiltrated what was the most effective and honourable government department in the United States, he would use this powerful institution to replace his now dead army – in order to do his bidding for him.

And I became his greatest target. I quickly became the target of a very serious criminal matter concerning harassment of myself which had involved my family since the turn of the New Year 1990. This incident soared for over four weeks.

And I knew that once this threat against me began, it would relentlessly proceed right through to the day I was assassinated too. But the enemy was adamant in playing his games with me-Robert Stewart before he delivered his final deathblow! It became the usual cat-and-mouse game between us. It was just a question of who would destroy the other first.

Since his wretched influence had now reached into the SIA agency, I strongly felt that the enemy would use these people to intentionally try and have me framed for something I was never guilty of, something I never was even suspected of prior to the SIA's allegiance with the enemy.

And such lies would no doubt warrant such government tailers of me being followed and harassed incessantly from that point on.

Because from that moment, I was being followed in every road I took, such cars turning where I was turning! Constantly being given bogus phone calls at home, where my phone number was a private number and no one, but the SIA knew those details. Where I was constantly receiving such prank phone calls by people portraying themselves as something they were not, such as finance companies to try to extract personal information from me! I was being harassed even when I was at work and being followed even when I was conducting police stakeouts on targets. This posed more than just a security risk. This put society as a whole in great jeopardy!

With the SIA in his pocket now serving as his ally, the enemy felt as safe as he could to then orchestrate a corrupt plan of revenge based on deception, lies, manipulations and conspiracies hoping that Robert Stewart would eventually collapse and die from the stress of it all. And what was even more of a crime was that the enemy had been responsible for over a thousand good agents being killed off inside that agency in such a short time frame once he woke up from his coma! He killed these masses of law enforcers and their entire families with a click of his fingers so quickly that no one could stop it on time!

For I could not take this up with the SIA, because I knew it was the SIA and their now run criminal links in fact involved in harassing me at the behest of the real enemy in all this. Their entire modi operandi revolved around dishonesty, lies, deceit, manipulations and now murder; mass murder. They would be the last people I would approach!

For every trip I took in my car, I noticed tails behind me. I sensed it. I was being followed by standard government tinted-windowed Holden Commodore vehicles; an army of them. I could see them inside their vehicles whenever I entered a lane parallel to them. The SIA rogues then turned their heads to glance at my direction in a lane next to me and when I turned to their directions, they turned away, and glanced at their dashboards as if they're staring at a laptop. This was the same scenario with all the tailers.

Such tailers were not legitimate tailers of the system. They were in fact a legion of lowlife criminal pals of that evil man who had risen back from the grave to unleash all-hell upon the world now labelled, Lazzaro!

What the SIA rogues were doing was not part of a legitimate investigation, but their actions instead amounted to pure harassment!

Another case where I was being followed within one week after the New Year of 1990 was once on Horsham Road. It was the road you drive to before reaching my house. Where I noticed such a Holden Commodore vehicle was parked at the side of the road. As soon as I approached passed it, it signalled its left indicator and eventually veered into the lane from the right behind me. But by the time it got into the lane, it was several cars behind me. My eyes were constantly glued to my vehicle's rear-view mirror. Then I did a U-turn at the intersection of Cult and Horsham Roads, which was halfway up Horsham Road and double-backed all the way back down Horsham Road again where I came from, round the roundabout and came back again, did another U-turn at Cult and Horsham Roads, then at the Horsham Road roundabout again, driving in what you can say in circles, from one end to the other. And I did this pattern of behaviour for about five times and this Holden Commodore vehicle was also doubling-back from the other side of the road at a higher speed to tail me. Where each time I U-turned-it U-turned in circles as well on Horsham Road. And after about five times it stopped and disappeared somewhere on Swans Road, a side street exit off Horsham. And I finally went home up Cult Road to 10th Avenue, the road of my residence.

What transpired from all this was that I was being followed, I was receiving prank phone calls - and at night hearing footsteps and voices trailing behind my house. These were the events which I noticed occurring since the first week of January 1990 right through to weeks thereafter, before my own

SECRET UNDERCOVER investigation into the hideous affair put a stop to it, COLD!

For weeks I played along with my stalkers. I wanted to catch all of them in the act. So I went along with their charade. I played it cool. I saw their movements and took note of all the inventory details of what I saw.

I also enlisted the services of the two usual people I could always turn to and trust in order to conduct an undercover sting operation of my own: they were my police partner John McCallum and my brother, Paul Stewart.

I used Paul and John to assist me in running a tally and tallies of all the vehicles circling the street of my house. They were armed with cameras and notepads. They would take snapshots of all the vehicles driving in what you could describe as visible patterns of behaviour of their own around my neighbourhood. They would jot down number plates and take snapshots of the drivers. If the tinted-windowed vehicles made it difficult for us to identify the drivers thoroughly, the police lab could blow up the developed films adjusting the brightness and contrast until we were able to perfectly identify all the drivers-and rogues involved.

I knew the SIA henchmen would not jot down their illegal movements in this regard as was the usual standard procedure for any government operative operating out in the field, to record all their movements in a log book. So whatever the case, in order to obtain the evidence necessary against all these perpetrators, we would have to catch them all in the act of their criminal activities red-handed.

Bank account records were also checked as well as safety deposit boxes being located and traced of all the henchmen as well as the new head of the SIA, named Maxwell Hawker. Hefty bribes and payoffs being deposited secretly into their accounts, some received under front names, were all identified!

The tallies of all the stalking vehicles used which were checked; with records being cross-filed, matched the same vehicles hired by the criminal elements that had penetrated the SIA; and the prank phone calls received were traced by my phone company contact to the offices and local SIA branches across New York City. The destination in which its new leader Maxwell Hawker had relocated to (from Washington), in order to supervise and carry out his thorough instructions concerning the Stewart family, orders from his own real secret superior, Lazzaro!

The evidence was mounted. I got what I needed. I got all the names of the guilty perpetrators operating within the government department. I got them cold!

Their harassment/stalking/corruption rackets would be smashed.

Their little games were finally exposed to all the 'proper' authorities.

For whenever I made a trip for example from my place of residence in Brooklyn to the Bronx, or Queens, Manhattan or Long Island, such tailers began changing tactics. At first they were planted on my car's arse from the moment I left my driveway. Weeks later, they played more cautiously. I then realised that when I left my house, there were no stalking cars following me from my direct residence. But all of a sudden such vehicles showed up on roads at such set-up destinations I created as part of my investigation to catch them all in the act.

They followed me then in other boroughs of New York, wherever I was going; creeping up in the lane beside me; either a female or male driver glancing at me. Every time I suspected a car was the SIA, I turned in roads I didn't need to go into, side streets and saw them doing the same thing; turning where I was turning, inside their tinted-windowed late model type vehicles. And when I made it obvious that I noticed them by veering into a lane beside them, which could be done mostly on a not-so-busy highway, they stared at my direction, then face-down at their wheel or dashboard, as if they were glancing at a laptop, then they turned the other way and often disappeared into other side streets.

They knew where I was heading inside my car at all times, where I was going and how long I was there for via an obvious tracking device they planted inside my car, that had my vehicle marked on city maps on their computers for them to spot me and suddenly show up everywhere I went, without requiring to even be at close proximity to me at all times. (After of course breaking in my car and planting such a tracking device in there; concealing it well.) Just as, no doubt, the undercover rogue SIA agents then tried to conceal their visible white-coloured surveillance van usually parked during that period on the side of the road up the street of my house, in order to keep surveillance of my movements from home, via a planted camera pointed at my house to see what were my exact movements, so they could then inform their secret employer, Lazzaro!

Where at night the camera's visible orange-coloured, torch-lit beam could be shown pointing at the angle direction of my house, from high above telephone poles, metres down across the street of my residence; such beaming lights pointing sideways at the direction of my home were never there before I knew that the man who now called himself Lazzaro, had in fact risen back from the grave to unleash hell onto the world as we know it!

And this strong-lit beam was not shining on every night. But often throughout the weeks of January 1990, at randomly-picked nights, the glare was obvious from the front door of my house by tip-toeing on the highest step I could see it.

And I knew only one man was behind it: Lazzaro. He began his obsession with his enemy-me-Robert Stewart once again by watching my every movement, waiting to strike at me at the right time, whilst plotting and planning his next move with careful chessman precision!

Basically, I knew I had to get him before he got me! There was no room for failure in this. The entire world depended on it!

In the meantime, I knew that any contact I made to anyone in my car, even old acquaintances, would automatically have them made targets to harassment and eventual death as well as had my family been targeted during the course of all this, through constant day-by-day menacing phone calls for weeks on end.

The government agent stalkers had targeted my family as well with prank phone calls, always delivered by what I knew was the SIA in their front pretences. I told my family to just hang up on them!

I did not want to alarm my family with too many details at the time. Especially concerning the horrible resurrection of a man they yet considered dead as had the rest of the civilians in the world!

But in regards to the harassment my family received in the meantime, I knew that's what government department rogues did. They ring people up and ask questions and follow them with their video cameras! And the reason was for a final stroke of death by the enemy!

For anyone and everyone connected to me, especially my family, were made targets to harassment as well. A corrupt government department such as the SIA and all its co-conspirator links chose to fill in their miserable schedules by harassing Robert Stewart, thinking, just like their dodgy scumbag true employer, Lazzaro, that Robert Stewart would never win this round!

Perhaps they thought he'd be dead soon.

And naturally they thought they would get away with this very serious criminal matter!!! And of course repeat it to someone else and hence get away with it again and again and again!

The SIA under the new leadership of Maxwell Hawker and the undercover goons working for him, took it upon themselves to abuse the authority they were given, and run a mockery of their power and positions, where every member of society who did not serve them were the most disadvantaged - and became their greatest victims; because they-the SIA rogues believed that they were above the law. They believed that their real superior was eternally unstoppable!

Pick a crime, any crime – that was what the SIA then stood for. This was what the government agency had been reduced to once the wrong man took over the top job! They then stood for the open-season attacks to every innocent civilian in society, whilst at the same time they were handshaking and covering up the real criminal perpetrator who masterminded their entire criminal operation: Lazzaro!

Anyhow, throughout the period of their tyrannical reign of stalking and conspiracies, the SIA rogues followed one pattern of behaviour before they deviated from it altogether in order to attempt to throw me off-guard; they began to change tactics.

From a standard white-coloured Holden Commodore which they had used on me at first, they then began changing vehicles to a Ford Falcon XR6, and four-wheel-drive vehicles, different colours and thereafter using other vehicles thinking I wouldn't notice, when still the same vehicle was following me at every road I took; even when such a tinted-windowed vehicle from a close surveillance spot was parked across the road at one of my 'on duty' police stakeouts at the time being conducted in the Bronx. Then at the end of my shift, presuming to follow me where I was going; where I had often slowed down considerably to ten, twenty kilometres below the speed limit and entered another lane, until the car had no choice but to pass me. And when they realised I'm onto them, they grinned and kept going straight, when I turned into another road.

Though, all in all, this harassment business was not only about me. This was a very serious threat also directed at my family.

These people sought to attack my family as a means to get to me.

The SIA rogues targeted my family with incessant harassment antics through never-ending phone calls by supposed marketing and finance companies and any other dodgy front company they portrayed, in order to try to extract personal information from them. And no doubt they were being followed too.

The SIA also began such attacks and conspiracies then to try and get to my family. These criminals were even targeting my own family, especially when I was at work! All the while sending scumbags to my family home-the front door, and constantly having no business car signage nor business cards or any form of appearing legitimacy; such as solid identification, that was being established in the company they supposedly represented-and for years, via any corporate affairs background checks for starters; to ask my own family if they needed the pavement done at the cost of $3000, so they could finagle any excuse to even legitimately enter the house.

They failed with me, so they tried to attack my family by sending people in undercover pursuits to my family home and constantly giving them harassing phone calls concerning questions of their financial affairs; acting the part of a finance company, asking if they had a mortgage and what was the cost of their telephone and electricity and gas and water bills each month; claiming that they were from the travel company, asking if they wanted to plan a very expensive holiday. This sort of harassment had been going on for well over one month.

And it would have continued until we all became annihilated!

The day when the arrests were made against all the highly incriminated 298 widespread SIA criminal rogues, conducted in the second week of February 1990, Maxwell Hawker who headed the pack found himself cornered by a legion of police inside his New York stationed local office.

Maxwell Hawker was a fifty-year-old, distinguished-looking, grey-haired man of American descent. But he was a coward nonetheless. As soon as we approached him holding a search and arrest warrant with his name printed on the order, he rose from his wooden desk he was seated behind, quickly opened the middle desk drawer before his waist, and grabbed for a cyanide-loaded syringe. He lifted his right hand with the syringe to his head, and then quickly stabbed the needle end into the side of his neck, his thumb squeezing the plunger, until his body had absorbed all the poison into his system.

Maxwell Hawker could not take prison. He would rather die than spend one day in any slammer. He fell to the carpet ground, rolled on his back, and died within seconds, with his eyes wide open.

Following the enemy's SIA power being neutralised, all the rogues removed from the agency, I then put two-and-two together. The buck did not start and stop with Maxwell Hawker. Maxwell Hawker was only a front man. He was a tool being used by a greater fish in the sea. That fish was called Lazzaro or what was better known to the world as Domenico Armando. He was the real enemy behind it all.

And I also knew that Domenico Armando was running the entire 'revenge' operation close to me. Close to my location. Very close. Even closer than he'd anticipate I would guess!

Domenico had lost all his key people upon the New Year of 1990. He was not a man to trust his newly-amassed army regime which had consisted of Maxwell Hawker and hundreds of SIA rogues to take care of his primary enemy-me, whilst he remained commanding his new troop from far away.

No! Trust took years; many years to be earned.

I knew Domenico was positioned so close to me that I would even cross paths with him on a daily basis without knowing the man I met was actually him.

Or so he thought!

408

One of the strange occurrences which took place around my residence at that time, happened to a next-door neighbour of mine; one of them; in fact, this neighbour was reported taking a holiday. But I knew he did not leave his house with his family on any holiday.

I knew Domenico had arranged for him to leave his house vacant by ordering him and his family dead.

I checked flight records and there were none. The man never left for a holiday as Mr. Harold Cristos claimed, when he entered his house to take residence in a place so close to me, he thought I would never suspect.

It was Domenico Armando who took residence in that dead man's house under the assumed alias as the man's brother: Mr. Harold Cristos.

Lo and behold, the enemy was living right next door to my house.

The most wanted man in America was living next door his worst enemy: me: a cop!

He wore the most perfect disguise.

He was using a latex mask and a wig to disguise his face.

I wore a secret camera on my clothing. I took snapshots of his face and ran the film in the police computer. That face did not exist on any of our police records. I even cross-referenced checks with the FBI and Interpol. Again, no match!

No driver's licence, no birth certificate or Social Security records even were found matching that man's face or profile.

The former neighbour was later confirmed dead. And the former neighbour did have a brother and with that name! But he always lived overseas. He never visited America!

Domenico would have used that information for his benefit; because I found out through my secret investigations also into this matter, that the real brother had also suddenly disappeared from his birth place residence in France.

I knew that Domenico Armando would have ordered him dead too and his body mysteriously vanished as he had ordered my former friendly neighbour and his wife and three teenage children into the ground. And upon such deaths, the house right next door mine was made vacant for Domenico to enter that premises under the assumed alias of Mr. Harold Cristos.

Domenico Armando now resided in the house as the previous owner's brother.

I also knew that the real dead neighbour's brother was certainly nothing in facial resemblance to what Domenico Armando disguised himself to be.

The real Mr. Harold Cristos looked nothing as Domenico's latex mask disguise made him appear to be!

At night I heard footsteps standing on my house roof. As if my proven psychic powers detected that the man standing on my house roof was Lazzaro-the Chess Player-Domenico Armando. And Domenico chose a full moon evening to climb outside my house and put himself on top of the roof and hum to his powerful opera lyrics sounded inside his head as he would deliver his own theoretical plans for a type of diabolical payback against me-Robert Stewart; soon to be a practical measure of justice served!

Domenico Armando intentionally chose to live next to me, so close, as if he wanted to experience something of a new force taking place inside of him in the next phase of our cat-and-mouse game or battle or war as it were!

I was overwhelmed to have my worst enemy posted so close to me. He even rang me everyday and invited me to his house for a coffee and a chat.

He disguised his voice quite naturally. He disguised his face with a latex mask, wearing a white-haired wig. He used a cane to also disguise his walk.

There were no clues inside that house that led to anyone being able to connect him as Domenico Armando. No pictures of his family, no smell of tobacco he enjoyed smoking. No opera or symphonic piece being played; his favourite tune being Wagner's, Ride of the Valkyries.

He left no clue for anyone else to put two-and-two together and piece all the clues of the mysterious puzzle that he most certainly was.

But no matter what, I knew there was a private place inside that old house he now resided in where he smoked his favourite cigarettes, listened to his favourite symphonies, and carried pictures of his now four dead children.

Domenico spoke to me rather openly about subjects concerning world wars and the violence in the world and how everything around them was a mess. He played his part as the enthusiastic peacekeeping force well. He talked of wanting to see a better world!

He never showed any sadness, bitterness and anger to his losses incurred. He never even had approached me with any signs of vengeance in his soul against me.

Domenico Armando was a master of deception, a spectacular actor. And I played my part equally as calm. I gave no clues away to him that I knew who he was. I wanted to first keep him on ice, and continue to see him constantly. I wanted to know what his plans were before I would make my final move against him.

Domenico Armando had international connections. To arrest him prematurely may have undermined our chances in stopping great destructive plans he may already have in the works. I had to know everything he was planning. I had to not only stop him-and hard, but I had to stop his explosive plans I knew he had in the works for the entire world.

I wanted to secretly plant a bug inside his home via those invitations he gave me to visit him all alone inside his so-called brother's house he reported minding during that previous owner's absence. But something told me inside, as if unconsciously, that if I had planted a listening device in that house, I would give the game away.

The enemy was not silly enough to move so close to me without any contingencies up his sleeve. He was mad crazy, but certainly not stupid in any sense of the word. To underestimate his brilliant cunning was to invite danger and death to anyone who even contemplated lower-rating Domenico Armando.

It would put everyone in harm's way.

I knew Domenico would have great secret security precautions put in place. I knew if I planted listening devices inside his home prematurely, it would certainly give the game away, because he would most definitely find out about it through his canny eyes and ears posted around him - and much invisibly.

So what I needed to do right now was find out everything he planned against the world and its people. I needed to stop his plans and thus stop him in the process before he could execute such heinous schemes and cost anymore lives in the process.

This was not the time for hasty decisions and rash movements. We had to think of the bigger picture or else...!

THE MEDICAL DOSSIER

I was always curious as to how his medical research and treatments were going.

I recalled in the police confiscated Armando files that Domenico wrote in his journal that he thought all doctors were rip-off merchants, fraudsters, pranksters, money-grabbing gutless wimps and a pack of the worst legalised murderers in history. They could kill people and get away with it by all forms of cover-ups, stories, half-truths and innuendos.

Domenico had even revealed in his own handwritten notes we found that he would treat himself with Eastern medicine.

He would study medical procedures and research techniques to be applied himself.

But what amazed me all the same was his detailed references to using as a guideline the methods of a practitioner who was in fact one of the worst criminal doctors in the nation's history.

Domenico would study the methods of what was one of the worst medical practitioners in the country and then he would adopt the exact opposite technique and procedures, thinking that then he would be able to prevent his internal death sentence from eventuating.

The notes he made out were very detailed, very thorough and very accurate into the true diabolical methods this practitioner in question had used in his clinic, which claimed the lives over 8,000 patients in over thirty years of practice.

I knew the methods too, because I was the police officer who in fact investigated this practitioner's criminal dealings inside his clinic, which led to mass murder over the decades.

I was also robbed of bringing this man to justice, because the man who got to him first was Domenico Armando.

Domenico had killed him on the eve of my planned arrest procedures of this practitioner known as Professor Wu Yang.

And much like myself, Domenico detailed in writing all the methods Wu Yang had used in practice to in fact get away with the murder and monetary thefts of thousands of his patients.

Domenico Armando had studied the following detailed medical procedures very carefully.

This was what Wu Yang had done as a practitioner of medicine in the United States of America for over thirty years, as described by his numerous patient victims prior their deaths-resultant of the chronic side

412

effects endured by his treatments on them: Particularly in non-specific medical conditions, whereby health concerns were not evident in blood tests or X-rays, but were much in existence, and just as serious as those diseases which were solely diagnosed through blood, urine and visual X-ray machine screenings, Wu Yang sought to play on their reported 'mystery illnesses' with much delight for the monetary gains he had amassed from problems which were real, but blinded from proof of diagnoses from conventional medicine tools; Western medicine.

This meant that if science could not prove such people who went to his clinic as patients were in fact sick, then Wu Yang considered that equally so, the Western Law System as it stood could also not prove that his acupuncture treatments would also eventually kill them!

Wu Yang had failed to bother to correctly diagnose his patients' conditions when they first saw him at his clinic.

He also failed thereon to provide them with the appropriate treatments for their conditions.

That as a result, because of such incorrect treatments by him, it had not only cost his patients extreme financial losses inside his clinic in those periods as his patients, but as well opportunity costs in seeking incomes via adequate employments during those times - which otherwise could have been given to those who were in-between the ages of 18-65.

And even such treatments by him had the natures of their conditions worsen drastically, especially towards the last few weeks and months under his so-called care within those periods of weeks, months or even years as his patients.

Wu Yang had been in fact depriving his patients of proper solutions all along, backed with lies and on top of that false promises. And he even failed to advise them of proper avenues to obtain elsewhere, when he failed to correct such patient problems during their prolonged stays at his clinic; where many aspects of their conditions only worsened.

Also, such accurate diagnoses for such conditions, his patients had to find out elsewhere upon finally leaving the Wu Yang Clinic.

All along, Wu Yang not only failed to diagnose correctly all his patients' medical conditions, but he also failed to explain such details to them, whenever they questioned him of such important information.

And as a result of such 'improper' and 'incorrect' treatments weighed up in the end, had made his patients worse both externally and internally; where so many of them had to take high doses of vitamins just to be able to walk and talk - and higher doses from even weeks and/or months before the day they were finally able to leave the Wu Yang Clinic after weeks, months or even years as his patients.

Where as much time went by, his patients only required to visit the Wu Yang Clinic for treatments more often, instead of only needing to reduce them had his treatments been correct and proper after those weeks, months or years of so-called Wu Yang Specialist Treatments.

From the very first day his patients sought treatments with the Wu Yang Clinic, he failed to diagnose their conditions correctly.

He first diagnosed their conditions as some immune system disorder, then months after that, he diagnosed their conditions as some sort of mystery virus, when thereon it had taken even months after that before his patients would learn his findings were then branched into the nervous system. Which all this had occupied up to many months of lost working time and expense, in which so many of them had struggled to afford all along, due to the fact that for the longest time they were too ill to both obtain and thereon maintain work!

Wu Yang's treatments had put them in a chronic paralysing state of disastrous proportions!

Where at such times, in approximately up to six months it had taken before his final diagnoses took place on so many of them, he was not honest with those patients to tell them the truth even then that he didn't know what their medical complaints comprised of, nor had he questioned them of it.

He just sent them in the treatment rooms for either bogus or incorrect treatments in which he charged them for all the same, instead of listening to their complaints from the onset, had he bothered to diagnose their conditions even correctly much sooner than the (up to) six-month periods that it had originally taken.

And even after those prolonged six-month periods, he failed to grant them with the correct treatments for such continuously neglected and misdiagnosed medical conditions.

All along Wu Yang had been only helping his many patients' symptoms (but only just temporarily even), whilst the problems themselves kept getting worse.

And in the last several weeks and/or months as Wu Yang's patients, his treatments in such times were even unable to effectively help with even the symptoms, which otherwise had solely led such patients to believe that all along they were getting better for weeks, months or years they each spent as his patients - backed with his own misleading assurances given to each of them throughout those time frames.

Though in the end, when the problems themselves had grown chronically much worse, had that led so many of them to finally leave the Wu Yang Clinic!

Wu Yang, during the course of those prolonged periods of trapping his patients inside his clinic, had intentionally misled them in a time when they didn't know any better, upon so many of them having tried all other conventional means of medicine made available to them, which failed to even diagnose such non-specific conditions so many of them were burdened with.

Wu Yang clearly misled them 'all' to believe that his incorrect treatments, which were finally confirmed to them at the very least of being clearly improper all along - he claimed that such treatments were really only the most correct medical procedures for their conditions that there was.

Where masses of them in fact had been seeking treatments with him longer than what they each had such conditions!

Such conditions never had subsided their critical stages during Wu Yang's supposed expert and 'world-renowned' treatments, as opposed to treatments they should have been receiving properly, but elsewhere!

Wu Yang had intentionally set out to rip them off and mislead them from the very beginning.

He could have at least even advised his many patients of how to go about obtaining professional treatments elsewhere. Or just simply referred them to some expert to treat them in another clinic, instead of just keeping them as they had been during his so-called care - in at first, a stationary and much shortly thereafter, growing deteriorated states - and just prolonging and undermining hundreds and thousands of people's medical recoveries, whilst taking their monies, thousands of dollars he had from each of them - where instead of doing the right thing by them, and being more honest, he just kept them trapped inside his clinic and hooked onto his ill-fated forms of acupuncture, bore no regard to their complaints, as he only had taken large sums of their monies - and really after all that he had no ambition to help any one of them to recover.

Where as much time went by inside his clinic, the patients' conditions only deteriorated more and more, as they needed only to see him at a greater frequency; as all his treatments were doing was making them sicker and their general appearances subjected to looking half-well one day and then chronically ill the next.

Wu Yang offered his patients no long-term results in any positive direction, apart from temporarily relieving the symptoms.

Their general well-beings were only subjected to the cycle of no change, as they went from bad to worse then bad again, never subsiding the critical stages, as many aspects of their conditions had grown far more noticeably worse.

Wu Yang had not even once asked any of them to explain in detail how they felt, and what aspects of their conditions were still vastly troubling them. Nor had he even granted them the opportunities to be heard whenever they complained to him. Because to Wu Yang, his patients' concerns to him were obviously only trivial, as if he had always more important concerns than the welfare of his patients who he made pay him many thousands of dollars each - and even then, that wasn't enough for any long-term results from him - and after weeks, months or years each was subjected to under his so-called world-renowned care.

It was confirmed that all Wu Yang had done to each of his patients was manage to stuff up their livelihoods!

Every time each of the patients had questioned Wu Yang in regards to their conditions, or even complained of his ineffective treatments given to them, he responded to each of them by lowering his eyes and head to the floor and sighed in reluctance to open up disclosures on all details of their conditions in which they had a right to know. And whenever they complained, he even wouldn't give them a chance to be heard. He only snapped the same response to all of them individually, 'I know. I know your story.' But all along they were getting worse.

Wu Yang only intentionally held back such details from his patients, so it made it much harder in others diagnosing their conditions, if they couldn't explain such (in particular) non-specific problems properly to any outside second opinions they sought thereafter. Such intent by him was so he could no doubt have kept them all as patients inside his clinic longer to further feed his business.

And any consecutive complaints or questions they had for him, all Wu Yang had done was walk in the opposite direction as fast as he could, wearing a very evasive demeanour, always closemouthed on all such complaints or questions they each had to him - and also of the main details of their conditions' true diagnoses.

And Wu Yang even had the audacity to label many of his patients' conditions on more than one occasion as 'Schizophrenia', contradicting his previous diagnoses to them, whenever they asked him at times and he answered by saying to them individually the same story he told the rest of his patients whom encountered the ultimate worst of his treatments, that their conditions had no known medical name to it.

Upon then, he sought to even label an unethical-incorrect name at that.

An incorrect diagnosis by him as well, would have undermined their chances of obtaining even correct treatments elsewhere, had they listened to him and believed what he was actually saying.

Wu Yang even set out to not only deceive his patients, but sabotage them entirely when he tried to mislead each of them in the knowledge of their true conditions' most accurate diagnoses. As he deliberately, on more than one occasion apiece, even labelled so many of his patients' conditions as psychological, and not what the truth was for so many of them, being of a physical nature and natures.

He told them this, one at a time, whenever they hinted to him of wanting to see a specialist. He hinted to all of them individually to go and see a psychiatrist for confirmed 'physical' conditions, which was at the very least, a deliberately and most obviously unethical, even illegal act on his behalf - to deliberately misquote his own patients' conditions' true diagnoses. To try and undermine their chances as well to immediately obtain successful treatments elsewhere, as he deliberately had tried to confuse them all of their own conditions' correct diagnoses.

Where his obvious motives for that too were in hopes to even keep them all longer as his patients to further feed his own business!

All along the patients had been charged in their inabilities to even afford such high treatment costs by him. Not only considering how many times they each had to see him per week, but as well throughout such long periods of times many were kept hooked inside his death trap clinic, since the patients were too ill most of the time to either obtain or even maintain adequate work for long periods.

Where at best, many were forced to work on-and-off in small menial jobs on the side, as their conditions being kept in stationary-unmovable states at first, and then rapidly deteriorated and chronic life-and-death situations thereafter, as was the case by undertaking Wu Yang's treatments throughout their long stretches of being trapped inside his clinic and hooked onto his treatments; the patients found that Wu Yang had even undermined their chances in keeping any obtained jobs for long periods of times anyway.

Many of the patients even had to obtain a medical subsidy for such treatments from Social Security.

Wu Yang had filled out the necessary medical clarification forms a high number of the patients brought to him for them to be entitled to such benefits to be able to then afford his treatments.

But even on the medical clarification forms that each of his patients brought to him from the government department to fill out, he even failed to be completely truthful with the entire natures of their conditions' true diagnoses to the government as well.

And knowing that, Wu Yang, throughout the years and decades he practised medicine in the United States, had willingly taken his patients' monies, and Social Security's money provided to so many of them as a subsidy for such treatments, many thousands of dollars each, by keeping all his patients ill for years and as a consequence dependent on his needles.

Such government payouts, if through such periods he had given his patients the correct forms of treatments, which could have corrected their conditions as quickly as it could have otherwise been the case; then such government allowances given to them for treatments could have been spared and instead given to others who could have benefited more from really needing them.

Wu Yang had no regard whether his treatments had provided his patients 'ever' with permanent solutions.

He would have no doubt kept them all as patients of his, inside his clinic for the rest of their lives; at not only theirs, but the government's expense as well.

The patients had paid Wu Yang in excess of many thousands of dollars each for treatments that in the end had only made them all worse.

And after all that, upon requiring months and years of frequent treatments every week by him, the patients had to increase the amount of times they had to see him per week as time passed, instead of decreasing, had they gotten better of frequent 3-4-5 times a week treatments.

The patients' confirmed incorrect treatments by Wu Yang had not only ripped them off, from the opportunity cost in general that otherwise could have been provided to the patients had they recovered sooner, but he also had ripped off the government as well.

For all along the patients at least hoped (as well as backed with Wu Yang's misleading assurances) that they were getting better - until the last several weeks and/or months of treatments by him, when circulation problems became in fact drastically worse - which caused havoc in general - not only much-resembling physical paralysis, but as well much mental disorientation and inabilities to establish proper concentration.

This had forced the actual problems themselves to grow worse contradicting his previous assurances given to each of them all along.

But whenever the patients had stopped seeing him, for even a short time, the symptoms either came back just as bad or some even worse than before. This meant the problems themselves got worse under his care and not better as he was always trying to convince them of.

His treatments had created severe circulation blockages throughout. And when blood flow throughout the body was impaired, death was imminent!

Ordinarily, such chronic worsening would at least never have resulted if the doctor treating such conditions was in fact true to his word to be, just as well as Wu Yang's own misleading advertising claimed him to be, 'a world-renowned medical expert in his field'.

And during the course of such treatments the patients should have been well enough to be able to decrease the amount of treatments they needed per week, in just a few months, tops, at the most, and not have to only increase them as they all had to with Wu Yang after months and years of being stuck inside his clinic - which showed all along the problems themselves were growing much more chronic under his so-called care.

As all along Wu Yang had set out to mislead thousands of his patients into thinking that his treatments, as a so-called world-renowned doctor, were the most expert of all Eastern treatments that were available, by telling his patients all along, one-by-one, such comments, delivered in tones of a guarantee, 'Don't worry, we'll get you right.'

Such comments by him were nothing but further false assurances backed with his own highly-misleading advertising on the medically ill into thinking when other forms of conventional medicine failed on them, that if his acupuncture failed, then so too would all other forms of acupuncture and acupuncturists in general.

He gave such comments to his patients in tones of guarantees, even when their conditions were deteriorating rapidly.

Such dishonesty of Wu Yang's was at the cost of people's futures, and eventually, their very lives!

For the problems that worsened with the Wu Yang Clinic treatments were as such: the patients had developed very noticeable tic/twitching problems in the eyes and shoulders. And due to circulation blockages, they had developed chronic organ damage, particularly in the liver and the spleen functions were very weak due to the problems themselves growing worse under his care at the time; as well as chronic pains in their stomachs.

And due to their apparent symptoms, very severe at the time, such organ damage had been confirmed due to poor blood circulation and circulation blockages throughout their entire beings that became chronic, especially within the end of the last several weeks and/or months of his treatments.

Such patients incurred almost physical paralysis-type symptoms in all their muscles growing very weak, especially their arm movements at the time had become almost totally immobile and weak.

This resulted because circulation was impaired as such, producing much-resembling paralysis-type problems as those particularly experienced with the patients' arms and bodily movements becoming slower by intense muscle spasms and cramping as a resultant side effect of Wu Yang's treatments!

And also especially at the time within the last several weeks and/or months as his patients, such problem-worsening peaked mentally as well, causing mental disorientation and even poorer concentration towards the end too - as developing hair loss issues, all due to poor circulation problems growing much worse under the highly incorrect treatments they had received at the Wu Yang Clinic.

The patients were getting weaker by the day under the Wu Yang Clinic treatments. And even when many finally left the Wu Yang Clinic and sought second opinions thereafter, it was too late for all of them.

Even had there been one noble practitioner of medicine who roamed the streets of New York City they could not save the dying patients.

The second opinions checked the pulses of those patients who left the Wu Yang Clinic and found their pulses were extremely weak. They were too fast. Weak meaning too fast!

The problem was that to reverse bad acupuncture treatments was only possible via good acupuncture treatments. But undertaking proper acupuncture treatments meant going forward. Going forward in such former Wu Yang Clinic patients meant going again right through all the damage rendered on them by his treatments, in order to pass it all out.

And the symptoms would become a whole hell of a lot worse going up than what they even experienced via Wu Yang's treatments, which was going downhill. The patients simply were not strong enough to sustain that. And any attempts to try and correct their conditions had patients die in other acupuncturist treatment clinics; whereby these second opinions sometimes even took the rap for the patients' deaths inside their clinics; deaths which in fact Wu Yang was truly responsible for committing!

And all the while that wasn't enough to have Wu Yang admit to any of his patients that he was unable to not only correct their conditions long-term, but to even help them short-term, or even concede to refer them to someone else before it was all too late when no one in the world could help them!

Wu Yang instead seemed to enjoy stuffing up his patients; not only to them financially, but as well as to their very futures' expense!!!

For not only had thousands of these patients been grossly ripped off so obviously by Wu Yang, in general, weighing out the cost of the services he gave all of them compared to the much poor and worsening results in the end, but it also didn't matter to him, when in the beginning, during the first six weeks and/or up to six months of commencing such treatments with him, had he not even had the regard to reimburse any of them their monies they spent into his clinic during those periods, when they had all received obvious 'bogus' treatments by him too, on top of the generalised incorrect procedures that he began treating them with upon his final diagnoses thereafter!

Wu Yang had also used to so obviously rip them off in the beginning of their long stretches inside his clinic as his patients, by giving such people bogus treatments that were so obviously a display of gross and illegal misconduct on his part - because in the end of the treatments, when they rose from the treatment room couches, the patients turned pale and became light-headed, which was the obvious confirmed sign of bogus treatments by any acupuncturist – in which every patient familiar with acupuncture knows of.

Wu Yang did this deliberately and even charged his patients still in the end for those so obvious 'rip-off' treatments, which was clearly an attempt to sabotage their medical recoveries from the very beginning!

Even needles, especially acupuncture points inserted around his patients' ears, for the longest times, throughout their victimisations inside his clinic, had Wu Yang placed carelessly loosely, where they fell out even seconds after he had fixed the so-called treatment needles in such areas. And whenever the patients had complained of that to him, he said casually to each of them when it happened, 'When it's in, it doesn't matter'. Though if the needles had fallen out three seconds after the treatments began by inserting the treatment needles in such areas that was certainly the furthest thing from the truth!

At other acupuncture clinics, such acupuncture needles were free, unlike with Wu Yang. And if the needles he gave each of his patients grew however blunt after time, he should have replaced them free of charge - and not charged $10 for 10 needles, every month that they had to be replaced. Where in actuality, would 10 needles cost him more than a matter of cents?

Many of the patients for one, who had been kept too ill to either obtain or maintain work, had struggled to afford to even replace them, as Wu Yang made it impossible to afford not only his grossly expensive and hopeless medications, but his acupuncture treatments as well, considering that one only had to increase the amount of times needed to see him and not decrease such treatments over time had one gotten better under his clinic's care.

$10 more just on the purchase of 10 needles on top of the other brutally high expenses incurred by his clinic was going towards the purchase of vitamins and weight gain supplements in which masses of his patients had to take at higher doses than what was ordinarily recommended on such products' labels, even after months and/or years as patients with the Wu Yang Clinic, just to be able to walk and talk, due to circulation problems in general being so impaired by his treatments as they were.

Such extra medications the patients had taken, whether natural or drug-prescribed were really only temporary relief of symptoms' supplements, but in the end such supplements only prolonged their lives for a short time, but could not spare them from eventually dying from the horrible side effects they all endured as a result of Wu Yang's abusive forms of acupuncture treatments.

Wu Yang never explained to his patients other options they could have underwent outside his clinic, that he could have no doubt given to them if he was the slightest bit honest, or at least, even just confirmed sooner his own inability to correct their medical conditions.

Wu Yang instead said to them, individually, one at a time, with no other witnesses present, when their conditions had each taken a turn for the worse under his care, he only used the petty phrase, and on more than one occasion in the final weeks and months as his patients, telling them, 'At least I'm keeping you going.'

This was what he said to each of his patients more than once, as he had seen their conditions deteriorate indisputably before his very eyes - and even then would not budge even a shred of honesty to admit then and there that he couldn't help them. Or even explain to any of them, where was the best possible option for a solution that they had?

Instead, Wu Yang, whilst enjoying the high life at his patients' expenses, and the government's expense who subsidised part of their treatments' costs to him, expected them to accept that as the best possible 'outlook' they should ever expect in hopes for any recovery!

Where Wu Yang, instead of, as it's quoted by true Eastern Practising Manuals, 'helping to rebalance and encourage circulation through Eastern treatments to improve the body's own defence system and healing response,' as it was said to be the true definition of Eastern Practising Medicine - and instead of searching to correct the problems themselves, Wu Yang only targeted the symptoms to keep his patients needing to see him for the rest of their lives!

Upon such chronically worsening effects the patients had experienced under the Wu Yang Clinic treatments throughout such times, whenever they would complain to Wu Yang, his only response then to his patients, was in changing his usual unholy words of saying throughout, 'Don't worry, we'll get you right,' to only saying thereafter, at such times their conditions became much more deteriorated, 'At least I'm keeping you going.'

He began changing his previous so-called assurances from certainty and false hope to then no guarantees and absolutely no hope. And whenever he'd think he'd lose their business, he'd give each of them a supposed so-called guarantee again of saying, 'We'll get you right.'

After finally seeking treatments from other clinics, many of the former patients had returned to see Wu Yang once again, but only for one specific purpose in mind: to ask him to pay them their money back.

After all, they required the money to pay for treatments by other practitioners who were attempting to reverse the damage caused to them by Wu Yang's treatments.

And it made perfect sense that someone as Wu Yang, who showed deliberate negligence and a firm lack of conscience on his part, should forfeit all their monies given to him for treatments which were highly damaging at least, and give it to someone genuine and more deserving in the field of medicine. Someone who actually does his patients good.

But after each of them had asked Wu Yang for this he said, 'I won't pay you your money back because you should not have reported this to the Chinese Medicine Authorities!'

But their silence in that matter would only cause further patients to be destroyed by Wu Yang.

Wu Yang also said inside his private office to each of his former patients who demanded full reimbursements of funds paid into his clinic, 'I won't pay you your money back in case you require my services again!'

Wu Yang would also tell each of the patients that they were the only ones who ever complained against him.

He lied once again so obviously because lawyers they went to see concerning this matter confirmed to each of them that in fact thousands of patients had complained against Wu Yang.

And after Wu Yang had ripped off his many patients and made their conditions extremely worse, being a man with no formal qualifications in any field of medicine, though only claimed he had, he expected his former patients to go back to him and lose more money, grow more sick by his ill-conceived treatments and become more cheated by him, being a medical practitioner who was a con artist and a cheat and a liar who had messed up 'thousands' of people.

And not one of them was fortunate to find sufficient enough help to reverse such damage caused by Wu Yang.

Wu Yang had taken advantage of the sick by ripping them off and his treatments made people much worse. And the real irony was that people paid more money to such an unqualified acupuncturist, whilst the qualified charged less, because they chose to treat patients sincerely; whom possessed the knowledge and were not in the business because of the money alone, but they were in it because they genuinely wanted to help people get well.

423

Because they enjoyed their jobs and they enjoyed the success in bringing such a success to people's health.

When Wu Yang made a patient worse through his grossly corrupt and negligent treatments with lethal life-threatening side effects, he cast the blame on the patient, not himself.

But the patient was never to blame!

The patient sees a physician for help and if the physician cannot help, he must at least be honest enough to say so and help refer that patient to someone who can help.

Not just send him in the five-man and separately five-woman fitted acupuncture room, as was the case inside his clinic, as if it were some factory, day-after-day, month-after-month, year-after-year only so he could make his money to afford his luxurious lifestyle of expensive cars, expensive widespread misleading and extremely dishonest advertising all on the backs of the sick as Wu Yang had done, with no conscience - and until the patient became chronic.

And when the patient complained to him and complained of him to the proper authorities, he hid cowardly behind business contracts he made patients sign when they first saw him, which claimed in short that, 'he was not to be held responsible for his patients falling more ill or in fact worse under his treatments'.

Which in itself, such a contract alone given by only an acupuncturist proved that he had no formal qualifications whatsoever in the field of medicine and that he cared nothing for people, for the sick, his patients - and that he was only in the business wearing a white coat, pretending he was a doctor, only to make a 'quick buck' with his false advertising claiming him to be a 'World-Renowned Leader' of medicine.

The truth was that Wu Yang was nothing but a crooked fraud who gave a bad name to Chinese medicine in general.

Where after seeing him, masses of people lost faith in alternative medicine altogether and then they re-entered Western Orthodox Medicine in desperation to get well, but drug treatments was of no solution to problems either and mostly made problems worse whilst masking symptoms short-term.

Wu Yang insulted the Chinese community of medicine by his fraudulent and con man, lying deception and greatly corrupt actions to the New York City community of those who saw him. He was a charlatan of monumental proportions.

His medical certificates were discovered to be doctored fakes supposedly from China that he had fabricated upon his arrival into the United States over thirty years ago.

424

His clinic was only a business for him to make huge sums of money, not to help cure the sick.

His treatments made people 'extremely' ill, where they required to see him extremely often to maintain energy levels in which his treatments drastically reduced.

As all he did was solely contribute to the worsening of the problem, whilst using carefully-appointed acupuncture points to treat the symptoms to have people think that he was helping correct the problem.

Where people entered his clinic with one simple problem and they walked out with a rapidly approaching death sentence! A small problem suddenly became extremely large with greatly terrible symptoms never experienced before!

Not only had Wu Yang made his patients much worse in their times of seeing him, but he had taken great sums of their money also. And whenever they asked him for their money to be reimbursed by him back to their pockets where such money belonged, Wu Yang refused to return the money and pay back their funds to any of them as he also had said with unconscionable gist, 'Come back to me. No one can help your condition, but me. It's extremely complex. I really want to fix you!' As they eyed him sceptically, some had asked, 'Oh, you want to fix me do you? Even if you could, now why would you want to do that?' His reply was, 'Because you pose a challenge to me!'

Wu Yang was not only a fraud without conscience, but also he was in fact criminally 'EVIL!'

He preyed on people with money. He considered that people's hard-earned livings belonged to him. And in one instance he claimed that he never forced his patients to see him, which was the sole rational behind his defence strategy. Though in another instance he tried to con his patients to see him claiming he was the best in his field and the only one able to fix medical problems.

Where the government had kept him alive in Brooklyn, so how were people supposed to know what he really was if he was allowed to maintain his criminal enterprise and in medicine of all the dangerous practices there were next to narcotics dealings? - Where both practices had proven fatal to human health when conducted by the wrong hands.

And even after Wu Yang messed up his patients both medically and financially, he still tried to con his patients to return to him, so any complaints made by them against him would make the complainant appear as liars and himself continuously with a clean record in the authorities' conviction records.

Where should patients return to him, he would also win when he had the second perfect opportunity to make patients weaker so they could not fight him legally.

Where if they died which was his ultimate goal for him to achieve, as he tried to do with many of his former patients by even inviting them to return to his ill-knowledgeable and evil care after he already stuffed them up to a certain chronic point of almost fatal proportions at the time; where once a patient dies, then he wins again and again.

For Wu Yang continued to get away with his fraudulent money-making practices when no one ever could recover the damage he created to them physically and mentally, particularly in non-specific problems, to prove in 'legal eyes' what a true scumbag of society he really was; for he was very strong to the sick and very weak to the healthy.

Wu Yang had absolutely no conscience, no ethics and not a shred of human decency. He cared for no one but his own bank account, the money he made from the lives he destroyed.

And for over thirty years of practising medicine in the United States, Wu Yang laughed behind his patients and everyone's backs, because the law itself often-than-not resembled uncivilised and barbaric fashion to allow criminals as him (Wu Yang) great loopholes within the law to escape punishment for attempted murder and mass murder itself.

Wu Yang committed one of the worst offences imaginable by taking one's life from them and great sums of their money too and then saying to the authorities, 'I am legally bound by a contract to practise as I do.'

Through his treatments, Wu Yang made someone who appeared very normal suddenly appear as someone who had every infectious disease known to man. They lost extreme amounts of weight, their muscles became paralysed; blood circulation was so poor that their skin became a humiliating yellow and they lost the ability to even speak properly due to the extreme damage he created also to his patients' nervous systems. This in fact was an atrocity of torture committed to the American public, to people with medical problems which were otherwise 'extremely curable' by Eastern medicine!!!

Wu Yang, quite openly and blasphemously also swore that he ran his whole practice-a practice that revolved around deception, con artistry, fraud, stealing the health and money from the sick with the laws of a religious 'Buddha' in toe.

Wu Yang, through the physical, emotional and financial chaos he created to his patients, indeed was a major contributor to an unbalanced society.

Wu Yang also sent his primary accomplice and spy for him in his crimes, his long-serving senior receptionist named Gertrude to former patients' homes, to spy on them in her car parked outside such patients' homes, to see if such patients who had complained against him were still alive or dead, so they could not pursue their legal cases against him again in the future.

Gertrude conducted this spying racket inside her slightly tinted-windowed car. At first she was parked discreetly on the side down the road a couple of houses away from the patient's home, in a white-coloured sedan for hours there, from midmorning. Then when it became afternoon, she drove closer and parked directly opposite the driveway to the targeted house. She sat crouched inside her vehicle, onto the driver's seat, waiting and hoping for the correct piece of information to report back to her criminal employer named Wu Yang!

Wu Yang also admitted his own errors in knowledge and the consequences of those errors to patients who unknowingly saw him through the contract he made people sign when they first attended his clinic. He even admitted it in complex words through the worded briefing of that contract; where its complex words were also designed to cause trickery against patients who began treatments with him.

****

All in all, it was certainly interesting when I-Robert Stewart had all of Wu Yang's medical records checked to see how many of those former patients of his were still alive? I even assumed all along when I raided his clinic that he may have destroyed such medical records to be used as evidence. But all former Wu Yang Clinic patients' complaints were lodged and filed at many law firms across the entire state of New York. Every lawyer I approached in this matter confirmed to me that the former Wu Yang patients' whom became clients of their law firms thereafter upon leaving his clinic, could not pursue further legal proceedings against Wu Yang for long because they-those former patients had all eventually died as a result of the poor treatments received by the Wu Yang Clinic.

I got the evidence I needed to arrest that man permanently. But on the eve of my planned justice-delivering order to be given, Wu Yang had mysteriously disappeared from circulation. He was later reported kidnapped and killed by Domenico Armando. His Brooklyn clinic was also blown up by the very same culprit.

And that concluded the Wu Yang Chronicles in which Domenico Armando had thoroughly studied in order to turn what was deadly medical methods into what could possibly save his own life from his growing mortal state.

Domenico Armando would strongly attempt to implement all the opposite medical procedures of his subject Wu Yang, in hopes to obtain a cure for his deadly abnormal cell growth inside his skull. Whether he was to become successful or not, was the six million dollar question!

But nonetheless, Domenico Armando planned to take that million-to-one shot and find out himself as a man with really nothing left to lose by simply trying!

THE REVENGE PROJECT

I did not wait for Domenico to invite me into his home the next evening.

After dinner with my pregnant wife and children next door the enemy's habitat, I invited myself into the enemy's domain.

I knocked on the door. No one answered. But the door was unlocked. So I entered inside the house and called, "Harold. Harold Cristos, where are you? It's Robert Stewart!"

I was posted inside the quite modern-looking living room; no one in sight.

After having dinner with my beautiful wife Cassandra who was now three months pregnant with our first child together, I was so happy that my family were happy and healthy. But at the same time I felt anxious and a tad frightened at losing them.

I still had not told them that Domenico was still alive. I mean, they would freak-out. They would panic.

My wife was pregnant. I did not want her to suffer the slightest bit of stress in her condition that would jeopardise both the lives of her and our child. So I kept that dark truth from her for now.

Only I-myself and police powers higher-up knew the truth. But we also kept it hidden from the newspapers. Because if truth be known at that point, not only would it cause a global panic, but the enemy would be all the more inclined to cast forward his murderous plans sooner rather than later, should he feel the pressure was on and his police pursuers were hot on his tail.

I felt that as long as I knew the truth and now as I knew where he was located, that Domenico would not be in such a hurry to 'destroy the world' if he thought he had no reason to rush forward his plans, if he had not ascertained that the authorities would close in on him and pose a threat to his deadly projects whilst in their preparatory stages to later become fully developed and soon be unleashed out into the world.

But in the back of my mind, I was immensely worried for my family and the innocent society I was paid to protect. Domenico was still a ticking time bomb. He could go off and detonate his explosive wrath to be unleashed globally at any time!

I was starting to lose patience. So that was why I invited myself this time to the enemy's habitat.

I wanted to see if I could uncover something, anything there that may expedite our plans to put an end to this craziness once and for all.

But as I was posted inside the living room, I saw the room was deserted. But I did hear distant voices from afar. It was a familiar old voice, no longer tainted by disguise. It was Domenico Armando. It was the shocking figure of the madman of all madmen himself, in the flesh! He this time wore a black-and-white silk-made maestro outfit. He had a baton in his hand. He was conducting to his favourite Wagner symphony, 'Ride of the Valkyries'. It was power music. The glorious effervescent composition was blaring from loudspeakers inside his office den. And he thrived on its piece like a crazy bull in heat!

Domenico exposed his normal face and mannerisms. The thought-to-be dying man had willed himself to a much energised state. And he certainly looked the perfect part of diabolical force and mysterious power. No disguises covering his face this time. He had a burning cigarette sitting in the real solid gold ashtray inside his den. He looked quite comfortable inside this average-sized house, which was ordinary in every aspect, certainly not posh or plush as his usual huge mansion situated in Brooklyn Heights, but now seeming abandoned. And he had one butler in toe, handing him a shot glass of cognac at his request from the small bar set up inside.

I was posted in the hallway outside the den situated on the other side of the house where all the activity was taking place; the house was filled with a maze of rooms and other hallways. Domenico was planted inside one of the rooms he furnished into his private office, but still it was rather plain-looking in measurement to the usual fully-fitted permanent housing properties he had previously lived inside. This meant that the enemy's lodgings inside these quarters was just of a temporary measure until he laid out his plans and moved himself to more permanent accommodations befitting his usual tastes and high standards of living.

The door of the private office den was left open by a crack and I peered inside from the crack outside the room, when I saw Domenico then wrap up his conductor's role he briefly partook until the symphonic piece had ended.

Domenico turned to his middle-aged Italian butler who seemed to be more than just a low-ranked paid servant.

The 45-year-old Italian henchman seemed to be Domenico's sudden replacement for his dead Counsellor Rex Higgins. I ascertained this as Domenico suddenly exploded words to him of his plans for the world.

Domenico Armando picked up an inch-thick-A4-sized file which lay on his wooden desk and shouted: "It is all here; copies of the detailed reports I have amassed of all the sorts of scum in this world; people such as Wu Yang.

"I have reread this file again to refresh my memory of what he did and I became enraged! These are the sorts of people living in this fucking world. People who torture the sick and steal from the disabled!" he cursed.

For a moment I witnessed what appeared to be a seeming compassionate side to the deadly beast. But the truth was that Domenico Armando had killed a whole hell of a lot more people than Wu Yang ever did. But the irony in all this was that Domenico was only concerned for the victims of another criminal, whilst ignoring the even greater crimes and wails from beyond at his own morgue-like killing sprees!

Domenico went on: "These are the sort of scum in this world, hmm, people who terrorise the helpless. The helpless who are then forced to turn to the world's leaders for help. HUH! Rubbish! Bullshit! Those people are not leaders! Every one of them who claim to have any important titles are all true failures! They are not worthy to have any such titles. How dare these fucks pretend that they have any form of importance? Because the truth is that they are all worthless worms of the ground! They don't deserve to belong in this world!

"They failed the world! They failed the people! They never protected the vulnerable! They only lied and deceived to the gullible of society in order to line their own wretched pockets! Yes. Undeniably, they have failed to protect the world from people such as Wu Yang! Which means those so-called leaders of the world are not true leaders. They are frauds and wankers; every fucking maggot one of them! And they will 'all' be replaced by someone like me who will protect the people from ever going through what they went through by every criminal practitioner in this world!

"The world is filled with jealous little people; such small-minded pettiness who worship what's disgustingly boring. Yes. They worship the dull, the dead and the dreary – whilst ignoring or belittling the great, the mighty and the exciting, such as me! And for what this world does, by allowing the Wu Yang's of society to breed their pollution into our homes and gardens, will result in a slaughterhouse to be unleashed by me NOW in their homes and THEIR gardens!

"I will burn this world to ashes. I will crush the bones of every person who walks this earth. I will squeeze the life out of them with my bare hands. I will break their skulls. I will spill their blood until they die!" he shouted with his fists clenched in the air.

Domenico then said in a more sorrowful tone: "Do you have any idea what it is like to wake up from a coma and hear that your children were killed in such a heinous fashion? Bullets fired into them in Rome by those fucking police!" He wept for a moment.

Domenico Armando took several deep breaths to contain his grief-stricken emotions. His sorrow then snapped mighty quickly into fierce rage as he glanced at his henchman dead in the eye and delivered the following orders: "Now this is the plan. It is time. I want every police officer in America to be executed. I want you to destroy every police station and send such buildings into the ground. Then the plan will be unleashed to the rest of

431

the world. I want the United States President to be brought to his knees. I want him dead! I want every religious leader and their followers in the ground. Everyone who follows any religion and law but mine will die!"

Domenico Armando then shouted the following words which echoed as bellows throughout the entire house as he further instructed: "Destroy the priests. Destroy the churches. I want everyone who calls themselves kings or queens eliminated; burn their husbands and wives and children at the stake. Destroy their houses. Burn their animals to the ground. Send off powerful missiles at all their livelihoods. Make them all perish! Destroy them all! Kill everyone who is a threat to my throne! There will be no kings or queens. No one will worship anyone, but me!

"I have earned this ruling. I am the one true Master. I am the one the world will follow and worship and listen to. Everyone else must die!

"Then I want Robert Stewart! I want to have him put in my jail cell. I also want you to get me the sizes of his wife and children's clothing. I will prepare a fresh new wardrobe for them. Prepare clothing for her unborn child as well. Get multiple sizes for both sexes, so we can be prepared if her child is a boy or a girl! It will be Robert's family for my family!

"Yes. Robert's wife will become my wife. And Robert Stewart will know what has happened and what has become of his family! A family who will learn to worship me as they have worshipped Robert! They will think of me as family too!

"And his beautiful wife Cassandra will learn to love me. I want to feel her caresses. I will make her seduce me with her beautiful body. I know she has such softness. I want to feel the touch of her skin. I will not rest until she gives herself to me: her mind, her soul and her beautiful body! I want her to nourish me and I will nourish her. She will have everything her heart desires. I will liberate every piece of gold, every piece of silver, every expensive diamond on earth; the world's most expensive jewellery which exists anywhere and I will hand them all to her as treasures.

"I will make her as passionate about me as I have suddenly become for her. As I will become the king of the world's throne, I will have the most beautiful woman sitting next to me on the alter overlooking the entire world. That woman is Cassandra! Yes. Everything I lost will be replaced by the possessions and the belongings of the very man who cost me everything. Yes, sir!

"Not only will Robert's wife become my wife, but his children will replace the children I have lost! Yes. Everything that man has cost me will be restored to me through his own possessions: his perfect family will replace the perfect family I also had, but who are now all dead! Yes. Prepare the most perfect mansion for us. They will be taken away to live with me forever! I will do it!

"So you go tonight after your late supper here and make all the arrangements for everything I have just told you. It will be done - and tonight. Yes. Tonight everything-all my plans will be cast forward and tomorrow the WORLD will be mine; because I have waited and I have suffered long enough. Now it is time that I become happy and triumphant once again! Yes. I am Lazzaro! And Lazzaro is Domenico Armando!"

****

I-me-Robert Stewart now knew the enemy's plans. Now it was time to move in before the enemy and his henchman commanded the criminal army regimes they controlled to do away with the millions-maybe billions of targets Domenico planned to claim around the world! And I was going to kill Domenico Armando before he went anywhere near my family!

I wore my secret microphone-camera on my clothes. I got everything I needed. Now the awaiting cavalry outside were automatically alerted.

As I spoke the police operation's code word signal which was 'checkmate', my microphone had picked up my transmitted words to the hundreds of standby police officers to swoop in the house and move in on Domenico. I did not have to give the order twice.

The cavalry broke down the front door of the target's house and stormed inside the building in droves and Domenico and his henchman were picked up by the army of police and dealt with accordingly.

It was on New Year's Day of 1990 when I was informed of the conclusive DNA results that the so-called Domenico Armando corpse in Rome was in fact not the man the police initially anticipated. He was a fake!

NOW a new round of DNA tests confirmed Domenico Armando's true identity.

Domenico Armando's trial was swift and his judgement was obvious. The last thing Domenico said to me when I saw him on death row after he was sentenced to die on the electric chair was, "So tell me Robert – are you going to get a front-row seat on the day of my execution?"

THE FIGURE OF DEATH

CHAPTER 1

The nasty, black-hearted, mean-spirited **Boss** was speaking over the phone from an anonymous location to his henchman, who had a loaded pistol pointed square at his target.

The henchman sat in the back seat of a large black limousine gaining proper control of the situation with his pistol in one hand, pointed at the kidnapped woman seated before him.

The henchman named Thomas held a phone in his other hand and spoke to the **Boss**.

He said in a serious tone of voice, but content in the fact that everything proceeded accordingly, "We got her, Boss. She's sitting right in front of me in the back of the limousine. The driver here should not be too long in arriving at your secret rendezvous point in the outskirts of New York!"

The henchman knew his boss would be pleased with the task of the target woman's kidnapping proceeding successfully.

But the henchman further gladdened his boss's heart by insisting, "Sir, we also have gotten possession of **'all'** your other targets. They have been crammed in another vehicle all on the way to be locked up at your secret destination!"

Thomas, the henchman, felt his boss's pleasure and delight being sounded in magnanimously great gestures over the vehicle's telephone he held in his hand, and then hung up the receiver once the news was broadcasted as instructed, much to the pleasure of the **Boss**.

The henchman then smiled at the terrified woman seated before him and said, "HE will be most glad to see you shortly!"

The petrified woman was restrained only by the sight of a very frightening gun pointed at her chest by this seeming crazy man seated before her. Her captor found it unnecessary to use any hand or leg restraints or blind her eyes with any fabric or cloth at this point.

The gun in himself was all that was needed to take possession of her quickly and then escort her directly and much promptly straight to his boss's possession, where she would then be made and much forced to belong, according to the **Boss**.

Thomas found it odd that his victim still displayed such a fearful look in her eyes. She was shaking. That was how scared out of her wits she was. But the coolly-eyed henchman insisted, "Please Cassandra, or should I say, Cassandra Stewart, please just accept the inevitable! Just accept your fate. The Boss will be most displeased by your demeanour right now, acting so sulky like a punished little schoolgirl. Just accept your fate and relax and enjoy the ride. It shouldn't be too much longer now!"

"Never!" she screamed in terror. "I will never accept this, your horrendous brand of hospitality! How dare you come into my house in broad daylight, first thing in the morning, and kidnap me and force me prisoner into this car like this here with you!" she shouted hysterically.

The henchman named Thomas laughed at her reaction. He looked like a bull, a bulky brute of a man, over six-feet tall. His face was ruggedly rough in appearance. His skin was ashen colour. His eyes were deviously callous. He indeed frightened the hell out of his subject. But despite his gravely dangerous appearance, he maintained his cool streak before his prey and insisted, "Scream, scream if you wish. No one can hear you. No one can help you now. So please calm down and as I said before, just accept your fate, the inevitable. Because from this moment on you are the Boss's property. You belong to him!"

"What are you saying? You cannot do this. Please let me go! Just stop the car and let me out. I promise, I won't say a word to anyone. I promise!" she begged in grave unimaginable fear.

But Thomas, yet coolly insisted, "You still don't understand the enormity of the situation, do you Cassandra? Your world is no longer out there. It is now with the Boss!"

"The Boss?" she asked at wits' end. "What do you mean the Boss? What are you saying? Who is the Boss?"

Thomas was a sadistic piece of work. His first reaction was a snake-resembling smile he gave to her. Indeed he enjoyed watching her squirm in terror before him. It made him feel big. It made him feel strong to overpower a defenceless woman as Cassandra. He thrived on controlling her; her sweetness, her beauty and her naivety, still not really accepting the reality of her inevitable destiny to be cast into his boss's overly-possessive web.

Thomas's smile now broke into laughter. She was a fragile little beauty queen this one, he thought to himself. No wonder the Boss had his eye on her. No wonder he wanted to possess her. And this equally nasty henchman, as sadistic as his boss, would enjoy every moment of forcing her to comply with her new demands. He would thrive on controlling this little Miss Prim and Proper goody two-shoes.

As soon as Thomas got over his diabolical laughing fit, he explained to his yet very frightened victim, "It means what it means, woman. Just sit tight and try to relax! You will find out who he is all in good time! Just don't worry your pretty little head over it; because the Boss wants you to look ever-so radiant when you arrive at his home. He doesn't want your sex-appeal tarnished in any way by tears or fears or any stress whatsoever!"

But Cassandra innocently still could not fathom how it was possible to be kidnapped like this from her home in broad daylight as she was. Such a horrendous action had indeed changed the course of her otherwise much harmonious life as she experienced for the past six months. But now, like that, with a click of a finger, by some evil person or thing, which was only referred to at present as the **Boss**, had her life taken a drastic turn for the worse at this point. The course of her otherwise peaceful and happy life had changed to a nightmarish state without warning. No words being given or signals being cast at her beforehand. She was taken by surprise and whisked away by this horrible and callous henchman to be delivered into the clutches of some monster she gathered her captor was. Yes, indeed, a monster who masterminded her fateful kidnapping this day. And all she knew about the man behind it all was that his people referred to him as the **Boss**!

But who was the Boss?

What was his name, his real name?

What did he want with her?

My God, she cried to herself. What does he want with the rest of my family?

She panicked now and shouted further at this cold man before her named Thomas, "My family, my family. When you were on the phone with that man, your superior you call the Boss, you told him that you had other targets being delivered to him in another vehicle at the same time as I was here with you! What did you mean by that? Who are they? Please don't tell me you also kidnapped the rest of my family?"

Thomas smiled again at her frightened mind playing tricks on her.

But were they really tricks?

"My husband!" Cassandra cried. "My beloved husband Robert; what have you done with Robert Stewart? Please don't tell me you hurt him? Please, answer me. What have you done to my family? What have you done to Robert?"

Thomas, yet with a slight sarcastic smile formed on his face, insisted, "All right, I tell you what. If you promise to be a good little girl, I will tell you. Is it a deal?"

Cassandra was desperate to know the fate of her precious loved ones. She took several deep breaths, wiped the emotions from her voice, and with her hands she scraped several tears from both her eyes and now said calmly with added composure in her tone of voice, "Yes, I promise. But please tell me… tell me the truth of what you did to my family? What did you do to my husband Robert Stewart?"

Thomas first clapped his hands together in an affirmative but not submissive gesture, before he would respond the following words to the woman before him, who may have acted now composed, but her eyes gave away her true emotions of feeling utter dread and panic at this moment.

But Thomas insisted that he would not deny her responses to such concerns. After all, he had the Boss to answer to. And if he delivered his boss's prize in such a messy state of fear and panic, his boss may surely feel that his mid-forties-aged henchman Thomas had not performed his task to the necessary perfection he demanded. And Thomas did not want to disappoint his mean-tempered boss in any way, shape or form; because if he ever had, he may in fact turn into the mere quivering jelly that resembled the very frightened lady who sat before him.

Thomas would then know what real fear was. He would certainly know what unbearable torture felt like. And that was something he truly was equally as frightened in never wanting to experience.

In him, that could never happen.

So Thomas quickly wiped the menacing grin off his face and answered the questions concerning her family with quickness and ease in a manner to compose her now rather than needle her. "Please, Cassandra, do not worry! The Boss has not harmed any member of your family. I can assure you of that. So believe me. Your husband is also in good health. We have been monitoring all of you Stewarts for quite some time. We waited this morning for your husband to go to work, and then that was when we made our move against you and the children, Ryan and Stephanie, and your newborn baby son Joseph!"

"Don't you dare hurt any of the children!" she snapped again emotionally.

But Thomas raised his hand at her in an appeasing gesture and said, "No one is going to hurt anyone, ok! If we wanted to hurt anyone, we could have. If we wanted to hurt your husband, we could have stormed your house with guns when we were inside and we could have taken him out. And that idiom does not mean out for a date. It means to be shot! But that was not the Boss's intention. It was not his plan. 'You bring them here safely and unharmed!' Those were his orders. Even your husband has not been touched. He has not been harmed. The Boss has not raised a finger at him."

"You mean as yet!" she cursed. "But you intend to hurt him, don't you? Don't you? ANSWER ME!" she shouted hysterically.

"The Boss does not make me privy to all his thoughts and not-so-distant future plans. I just follow his orders in real time as he presents them to me!" the henchman stated.

Cassandra, yet hysterical, insisted, "When Robert finds out what you and your hideous boss have done, he will move heaven and earth to find us, his family. And when he does, he will blow your world apart until he frees us

437

all from your clutches and then he will make you and your monster boss, whoever he is, pay with your wretched lives! You will not get away with this! You will not get away with any of it! He will find you! He will destroy you! All of you!"

Thomas now seemed worried and preoccupied all of a sudden by her revelation (in which he at this point became oblivious to), that he just kidnapped a cop's wife and children. He in fact just kidnapped what was New York City's best law-enforcement agent's family. He ignored the daunting reality of that initially, but now as that reality dawned on him, he felt a slight chill permeate into his bones all over his body, from head to foot at this moment. He tried to keep his fears under wraps from being seen by Cassandra at present. But all he could think of now was that the Boss better be a whole lot smarter and a whole lot tougher than Robert Stewart, in order to extricate himself from the repercussions of this fallout that will surely be the result of this ordeal from this point on. Because if his boss was even slightly weaker than Robert, well, the result of this affair was obvious: they were all finished! They were doomed and all hell would break loose in only a short space of time!

"Just keep calm and keep cool!" Thomas insisted.

Cassandra yet persisted with her initial questions relating to what all this was about. Who was behind it all - and most importantly, WHY?

What was the fascination they all had with the Stewarts, she could only wonder in herself. Then in desperation, she voiced her questions out loud, hoping that this man was not completely insane - and may in fact be driven to his senses and respond to her pleas in an affirmative manner. She asked in a yet demanding and desperate tone, "What is this all about? Who is the person you call the Boss? What does he want with us? Please answer my questions!"

Thomas yet maintained his solemn face which lost its venomous connotation a while ago during this detoured car ride to his boss's hideout, but he thought a bit before he would respond the answers to her questions she had a right to know. But his answers had to be on direct orders of what his boss allowed and disallowed him to say.

Thomas knew he could not reveal anything he was not permitted to at this point. Nor could he deny her anything which would scar that beautiful face of hers with any tears right now.

So Thomas thought long and hard in how to answer these questions without disappointing his boss, but at the same time, hopefully satisfying his victim's curiosity somewhat so she would stop crying and stop screaming. Hopefully she would be driven to a more relaxed mental atmosphere by what he said and what he could not say!

Thomas still held the gun at her, but he tried not to act threatening to her more than necessary. He lowered the gun and slightly swayed it away from her direction in order to show her that his intent was not to physically harm her. But in order to maintain complete control of the situation, he still held the gun in his hand as a security precaution.

She was after all a cop's wife. And Robert Stewart was not any ordinary cop.

No! Thomas thought.

That bastard was the best in the business. He was highly intelligent, extremely resourceful. He had more smarts than every other cop in the New York City Police Department put together. In fact, he considered that all other cops were mostly incompetent next to him. And above all else, Robert Stewart was dangerous to anyone and everyone who crossed him. That also included his wife Cassandra's kidnapper right now. The man behind it all, who called himself, the Boss!

Thomas considered his boss to be superior to any other man on earth. That was how much confidence he had in him. And shortly everything would be divulged to Cassandra. She would know how equally intelligent, clever, smart, resourceful and dangerous the Boss was; in the same level as her husband Robert!

So Thomas would reply in a manner of appeasing the subject Cassandra, but at the same time, not crossing his boss by giving away what he was not supposed to; and not crossing any strict boundaries at all; because the Boss wanted to surprise his lovely prisoner Cassandra. And by 'surprise', it meant that only the Boss himself was to divulge his identity to her when the time rose. And he wanted to do that personally.

Thomas finally decided his answers carefully. "Cassandra, everything will be fine. The children are being well taken care of. Yours and Robert's three-month-old son are also in expert hands. The Boss has a very well-trained nurse at his disposal that will look after young Joseph very well. So don't worry about that! That's all taken care of. As to what this is about. Well, I can only answer that question the same way as the answer I will give you concerning the Boss's identity. And that is, you will find out shortly, very soon. And you will know, when the Boss himself reveals that information to you. He will tell you shortly!"

"You are afraid of him, aren't you? He told you not to tell me that answer, didn't he? I assume the person in question is a man at least." Cassandra said in disgust. And when she saw his eyes flicker in uncontrollable admission to that last point she raised, she continued talking. "Who is that man? Yes. You are right! I will find out who he is and when I do, he will be sorry. Whether you tell me or not, I will find out who he is and then he will wish he had never committed this mass kidnapping crime of me and my family!"

Thomas briefly glanced at the male driver out front who nodded his head at him as he saw him in the rear-view mirror.

439

The driver, without any words being said by any of them knew what Thomas was thinking just by the expression of his eyes. And the silent nod meant that they would be arriving at their destination shortly.

The driver took many detours of his route prior his final destination, to ensure that they were not followed. He even, upon the Boss's instruction, made sure the limousine had phony plates registered under a phony name. And before Robert would find out anything, hopefully he would arrive safely and undetected at the Boss's secret residence outside New York.

But the fact that Cassandra was not blindfolded throughout the car ride was a bad sign; because she was allowed to see where she was being taken.

And if she was allowed to see where she was taken, it meant that the Boss would never allow her to tell anyone. And that meant that the Boss planned to never let her go! Both her and all of Robert's children!

Thomas took a deep breath for now but thought to himself: My dear Cassandra, how could you possibly entertain any ideas about challenging the Boss, when the United States government and all its armies combined could not even come close to outmatching him?

CHAPTER 2

The limousine pulled up into the gravel driveway of an ordinary-looking house within ten minutes later.

Cassandra was escorted inside the front door by Thomas the henchman, passing a number of armed guards on her journey inside.

She was taken into the fully-furnished but simple-looking living room area.

A pretty young lady servant entered inside dutifully in order to tend to her needs. "Would you like anything to eat or drink, Cassandra?"

Cassandra became alarmed at the fact that the servant whom she never met before knew her name instantly. But then she thought to herself, of course she would know. The Boss would have informed all his people of the arriving guests.

Cassandra replied equally as polite, "No, thank you. But can you please tell me where my family are? I know they were also being driven here. Have they arrived? Are they safe? Can I see them?"

Thomas who stood behind her, now with his weapon holstered on his right side shoulder holster just informed the servant quickly, "That will be all thanks Janet. You can go for now. When our guest becomes hungry we will call for you!"

The pretty young brunette nurse in her late twenties nodded and then left the room through the rear door she closed immediately upon her exit.

Thomas then invited Cassandra to sit down on the leather sofa couch behind her.

Cassandra was startled by being in the midst of foreign terrain and captured on foreign soil, in obviously enemy territory. She knew she had no authority to argue with the henchman's invitation which truly was more of a demand than a request.

So she sat down immediately without putting on any fight about it or displaying the slightest hesitation.

Regardless of her plight, the house was a comfortable outfit. But she noticed that the blinds and curtains were drawn. She understood why. Obviously the enemies who occupied this house wanted to make sure no one could take a sneak peek inside, especially those of the police variety and see exactly what was going on inside here and by whom.

Cassandra knew these bad guys would most certainly want to avoid anyone connected to the police variety - and especially avoid being seen by their expert surveillance equipment that could possibly catch a glimpse inside from even a mile away, such as via passing helicopters; hence the drawn drapes and curtains.

Thomas insisted to Cassandra, "Please stay here and don't try to escape because it is impossible. Men are posted outside every door and every window. And there are no phones allowed here. We have already confiscated your purse and checked your pockets before the limousine ride and are satisfied that you have nothing on you that could deem a threat. We will leave you here alone for now. And you are free to walk around the room. We will not place handcuffs or any restraints on your movements inside here. But you cannot leave the room or exit the premises in any way, shape or form.

"The Boss is upstairs resting inside his room for now. He will be with you shortly. But he did leave me a copy of something he would like you to read before he sees you. Something he thinks might make you understand the situation a lot clearer!" Thomas said as he pulled out a folded A4-sized small document from the inside of his blazer pocket and handed it to her gently.

The document was folded in a roll and held together by a rubber band.

Thomas's final words to her were: "Please Cassandra, relax and take it easy. Just read the **document letter**. I will leave you alone for now, but if you need anything, just knock on either of the two doors here and ask one of the guards who will remain posted outside this room. Right now I will leave you alone here to relax and read. And don't worry. Soon the Boss will be here and he will answer all your questions and put all your doubts to rest. Goodbye for now!"

CHAPTER 3

The document letter Cassandra had opened up was a copy of a letter addressed to her cop husband, Robert Stewart. She was given this letter to read right now. It was addressed three weeks ago. That was when Robert received it.

The letter went as follows:

1st December 1990

To: Commander Robert Stewart of the local Brooklyn Police Department, 25th division precinct station house, New York City.

Thank you for the kindness you showed me-Donnie and my mother Francesca Kensington inside your home over one year ago when we first met you.

I am writing to you concerning a complaint against a specialist in Orthodox Medicine called Anton Barton. He practises at two clinics. The address of the first is number 8, 112th Street, Brooklyn. The second is at number 12, 82nd Street in Queens.

Where I grant my permission for any and all investigative bodies I shall approach under the advisement of my lawyer, including the federal government, whom unknowingly subsidise the lifestyle to such a criminal through Medicare payouts to him for one, to study and make a copy each of any documentation in my medical files pertaining to and by Anton Barton, to be used as evidence. These documentations are to be found at such addresses previously mentioned and also to be obtained at the 116th Street Brooklyn Medical Clinic; and also at the Brooklyn Medical Surgery. Address is at 36th Street.

I was referred to Anton Barton by a Doctor Patrick Byron from the Brooklyn Medical Clinic in September the 12th 1990 for certain symptoms to diagnose a medical problem.

When I went to see Anton Barton, after explaining my symptoms to him, he began yawning constantly, and then he was asking questions of other symptoms unmentioned by me, which I admitted I had. Now my symptoms made obvious sense to him. But in the end, he wrote back to my GP at the time a letter claiming that my symptoms indicated such and such a malabsorption problem in the digestive system, though in conclusion to his letter, he indicated that it was all 'psychological'.

By saying so, he robbed me of treatments for a very uncomfortable problem that prolonged further my prospects of entering suitable employment due to my condition left untreated. My condition in fact later proved terminal, as I am now writing this letter from my sickbed situated at the Brooklyn Public Hospital. My sickbed will soon become my deathbed.

But before I was admitted to hospital, because of Anton Barton's deliberate mistreatment of me and his casual uncaring attitude to get to the bottom of my health crisis, which in fact was fatal, in the meantime, I was forced longer on Social Security benefits due to Anton Barton's unconscionable and corrupt actions of uncaring and deviousness and deliberate evil he displayed to me for no apparent reason.

Now, I see fit, in fact, I demand to all the appropriate authorities who handle such matters, to take all the action necessary so that such a doctor and doctors of the like, including Carl Boyd from the Brooklyn Medical Surgery and Yau Lun from the Brooklyn Medical Clinic, whom I dealt with thereafter Anton Barton's evil displayed to me, whom unscrupulously worked together to cover each other's lies in defence of Barton and themselves and their corrupt dealings in my case in particular - who view patients with physical problems, though to no regard of genuinely helping them, do not remain unpunished - those whom, arrogantly place patients in the too common category of 'psychological'.

Where I must say, it took a while after that time for me to find an appropriate doctor (which Barton did not bother to even advise me of such a route I must take, which only fate seemed to lead me to him). And this doctor had diagnosed my condition as a physical problem, similar to Anton Barton's initial diagnosis (of a problem in the digestive system, minus the psychological aspect of course).

But the crushing feeling I felt when tests after tests after tests were run, double-and-triple checking the final results, which all indicated that I had malignant cancer, which began in my brain and spread to my liver causing the digestive problems. And this was what Barton called psychological. He in fact tried to murder me and I don't know why?
I never met him before!
I never knew him!

But all I do know, was that if he even attempted to treat my physical issues and not the emotional aspects of the brain, it was confirmed to me by the staff inside the hospital now treating me, that not only would I have automatically found instant relief and great improvement of the problem swiftly, in which Anton Barton corruptly neglected to address, whilst even requesting Medicare payments afterwards, without a shred of conscience or regard on his part, as I was physically weak at the time due to my condition entering chronic; but my current doctors had also confirmed to me that if my condition was treated early enough, my brain cancer would not have spread to my other organs such as my liver, now resulting in my inevitable death sentence.

Not even had Anton Barton cared to grant me dietary advice to help even the symptoms, such as an appropriate Lactobacillus acidophilus formula, minerals and vitamins, in which I was informed of elsewhere that my symptoms reported warranted deficiencies in such supplements. Where the reason for such deficiencies was due to my digestive system in fact not absorbing correctly as I once had been, that was affecting the immune system, causing weight loss and recurrent cold symptoms, as well as other symptoms which deficiencies also in such supplements create, such as those associated with the nervous system and erupting cancers and so-called asthma - that since using, has in fact helped to alleviate my painful aches inside my digestive system, which at least has increased my appetite and helped me to withstand the extensive chemotherapy treatments I am receiving. But all this will not result in a cure. Because of Anton Barton's deliberate neglect of handling my case appropriately in the beginning, my condition, as it stands now, no matter what the doctors are trying to achieve, is terminal!

I only have some weeks left at most to live. That is why I must report this incident to you, Commander Robert Stewart, before it is too late and the guilty culprits get away with my murder.

However, what Anton Barton said was partially true. Yes, part of the problem I experienced was a 'malabsorption' problem, where I required to use a great deal of vitamins in the past and more so at present - particularly vitamins B and C. These natural supplements are helping me stay alert enough to write this report on my laptop my mother has given to me as I lay inside the hospital. The doctors there understand its necessity and have not once tried to stop me. Thank goodness for that. Because before I die, I want to tell you these things Commander Robert Stewart, in hopes that my death and all the other people who die at the hands of such doctors on a daily basis is not all in vain!

445

What was so bothersome to me was that when I went to see Anton Barton, for just that one time, he did not feel one bit of concern for my reported symptoms to him. And hence my general symptoms were many. My growing loss of weight was obvious, especially to him, a doctor of medicine. But in the end, he dismissed it all and just wrote me off onto the scrap heap without a second thought.

But why?

Was it because he is in his mid-sixties and the apparent generation gap between us via my much younger age, being in my late twenties; where now I won't even live 'till half that man's age.

At least he could have helped my symptoms and diagnosed my condition correctly – and even attempted to treat the actual cause for such symptoms.

But after I reported over two-dozen uncomfortable physical symptoms to him, he ruled it all as a state of mind. That perhaps I was crazy. I was making it up for some reason. But why would I do that? He never explained. And he said that all my aches and pains suddenly erupting in my brain were psychological. But this pain has now extended badly into my abdomen.

The truth of my condition was given no chance of a reprieve during its initial stages. And now it is all too late. The cancer has spread rapidly and my prognosis is death, within weeks at the most!

Now, if it was a psychological problem, then no doctor could treat it really, especially by treating a physical problem that was diagnosed by my symptoms' description at the time. And if it were a psychological problem, then certainly by treating a physical problem, there would be zero signs of improvement of even one of the symptoms at least, such as ability to eat some food as opposed to my inability to eat anything for a long duration beforehand.

My problem was harming my general constitution, causing loss of appetite and great weight loss to occur at an alarming rate.

But this was not enough to warrant treatment of or concern to be properly investigated by Anton Barton. He did not refer me for one test to confirm what is now confirmed to me; malignant cancer which formed inside of me. No. From the onset, he showed me no regard. He demonstrated pure negligence and uncaring and misdiagnosed my fatal condition I believe deliberately. And ruled what was a very dangerous problem, a problem which warranted treatment for immediately and urgently; he ruled all that inconsequential and just wrote back to my doctors at the time, that what I had was some 'crazy man syndrome'. That what I had, a deadly physical abnormal mass growing inside of me, pressing against nerves, causing me excruciating pains; he dismissed the seriousness of it all and just said that it was all psychological.

Anton Barton obviously understood my symptoms as my current doctors in hospital have. But Anton Barton, even in writing to such GP Clinic addresses mentioned on the first page of this letter, explained it, though in the end, he claimed it was a psychological problem; the corrupt cop-out cliché that so-called Western doctors keep giving to too many patients, when challenging symptoms they report are beyond that of a simple cold and flu.

And the government for one then wonders why so many people apply and remain for so long, sometimes even permanently, on sickness allowance benefits with doctors like that around who don't care to help anyone. These government payouts costs taxpayers a fortune yearly - and sometimes unnecessarily for those genuinely ill, who want to get back into the workforce, though due to misdiagnoses or simply deliberate neglect of treatment as Anton Barton provided with me, cannot.

And by the time those fortunate enough do however find appropriate alternative solutions, they find that due to Western doctors' initial neglect and misdiagnoses, such conditions take far longer to treat and stabilize than otherwise would have been the case, should people as Anton Barton even bothered to place patients in the right track, which costs taxpayers again more money for sickness allowance payouts being prolonged.

But in my case, the outcome was a whole lot more serious. How can any doctor willingly ignore a patient's dangerous strike with cancer? How can anyone take this so lightly? How can Anton Barton sleep at night knowing what he does? How does he kill and conspire to kill his patients so willingly and freely as if it is his sick right to do so? It is as if he enjoys making people succumb to excruciating pains. It is as if he is some sadistic man who can only feel joy within himself by tormenting his patients. And I was one of them he tormented and callously and cruelly so at that!

My case is rock bottom. It is the worst-case scenario. Malignant cancer in our day and age has no known medical cure. But perhaps it could have been cured if it was caught early. Anton Barton didn't care to stop it from spreading quickly as it had. He deliberately had been responsible for my admission into hospital as I write this letter to you. Now I am finding it hard to even walk on my own. I am stuck in bed all day in hospital.

My mother visits me everyday. And sometimes I am too weak to even type this letter. So instead, she writes it for me as I dictate to her what must be mentioned to you, Commander Robert Stewart.

447

My mother told me to make sure you receive the very first copy of this letter. She says, 'he is one of the only few people we can trust to enforce the law and bring justice to these injustices perpetuated by such cruel men upon people like you, my son, Donnie!'

And that was the real tragedy in this. When you question my doctors in the hospital where I currently am admitted, they will confirm that if my complaint was treated early, as Anton Barton should have, then I may not have been dying this very day. The cancer if caught early would surely not have been given the chance to spread.

That even very curable problems turn severe, even often enough fatal due to misdiagnoses, even deliberate incorrect treatments given by such doctors as Anton Barton, by using one drug to counterattack the drastic side effects of another drug already prescribed - and so forth, so patients keep going back to them to give them their Medicare Cards, only obtaining patient numbers to get Medicare payments from.

Where the government is paying hard-working taxpayers' money to such uncaring evil doctors for doing absolutely 'nothing' - and should one go public, you can wager a healthy bet that there would be countless people with experiences with such gutless drug-peddling doctors who would vouch for my complaint, having shared similar experiences themselves in Medicare-funded Western Medicine as I had with the highly-corrupt doctor called Anton Barton!

And after Anton Barton indicated his conclusive 'psychological' diagnosis of my 'entire' condition and symptoms, I rang him up not long after at his Brooklyn Practice, before I was admitted to hospital when my condition became very bad. Though I rang him before that time for some help of where I could seek a suitable solution for my problem that was only getting worse in time, in which he neglected to care to even treat or advise me of an appropriate path, as I needed to get back to work. And I was too ill to at the time. And I explained this to him, and he claimed to me over the phone that he would help, but I had to see a GP first, to have then the GP ring him up with my complaint.

And when I saw the GP, where this other GP called Carl Boyd (situated at the address mentioned on the first page of this letter at the Brooklyn Medical Surgery), whom examined symptoms I reported to him via his eyes and saw reasonable concern to warrant treatment of, Anton Barton claimed also to him that my condition was all psychological, even the asthmatic symptoms I reported to him initially, when he told me to see a GP. And he told the GP then cowardly behind my back (and not to my face, over the phone), that my symptoms reported were all psychological and even faxed

448

him a copy of his medical report letter that said as such also - so that all GPs would believe it coming from a so-called highly-renowned specialist diagnostician as Anton Barton was claimed to be. For it takes one with a psychological problem to accuse one of a psychological problem, especially so maliciously and without reason and gutlessly behind the patient's back.

Where thereafter, so-called doctors such as Carl Boyd and Yau Lun surely must have known of Anton Barton's evil schemes, particularly where I was concerned, though they began vouching for Anton Barton, when Yau Lun inside his clinic, whom when he offered me some natural treatments that hadn't worked for stomach acidity, had thereafter claimed with a devious and sardonic smile formed on his face that, 'Anton Barton wants you to see a psychiatrist'. And Carl Boyd claimed when I saw him thereafter, when I told him, 'You were treating me for asthma for one since I was a child, and Barton claimed even that was psychological. You know these specialists are stuffing people up!' Boyd replied, 'I know!' Though he did not bother to even assist me in searching for the truth to my condition correctly after each visit-over half a dozen from that time to date to him; he also just took my Medicare Card for doing absolutely nothing for me.

And to me all this stems as a serious breach of doctor-patient conduct. And I strongly believe that Anton Barton in particular is one of the very corrupt doctors in Western medicine. He is arrogant, without any shred of conscience, and totally does not care for his patients as I've seen him demonstrate black-heartedly to me. And I insist, with my dying breaths, in fact I won't let this alone, until all the necessary action that can be taken against such a criminal called Anton Barton, is taken.

I know that with you on this case, Commander Robert Stewart, I will be satisfied with the result and outcome. I know of your reputation. And I also know that you are perhaps the only person we can trust to do something concrete about serious matters as these pertaining to public safety and the lives of the community much in danger because of the displayed fraud and corruption by doctors as Anton Barton being unleashed upon his patients!

I have sent numerous copies to other authorities such as the government on all levels. But I do so with a heavy heart and a suspicious nature that not much will be done. And that is why the very first copy will be sent to you carefully and much secretly, Commander Stewart.

I also trust that you Commander Robert Stewart will make sure that such investigative authorities for this matter display adequate regard to seek the fullest and most deserving prosecution of such a man named, Anton

449

Barton. He is a very evil man. And everyone who sees him as a patient is really and truly taking their lives into their own hands. He is dangerous to them and to medicine in general.

In the meantime, I will also seek further legal advisement from my lawyer, until an adequate solution and result is undertaken to my complete satisfaction - and for the satisfaction of other patients who are in the same situation. And those who face the same situation that I was in at the time of seeing Anton Barton, so that this sort of criminal illegal action does not continue to happen unpunished to those genuinely ill, whom want to get on with their lives, though are unable to due to such doctors' deliberate neglects and acts of sabotage towards them, especially cowardly when their conditions are so chronic, that physically at the time, such doctors only ridicule instead of wanting to help.

In summary, such Western doctors like Anton Barton are deliberately destroying and in fact attempting to destroy people's lives by sending and even attempting to send patients with physical problems and physical-reported symptoms to psychiatrists. Where there is no real proof or linkage between the two major extremes. And by sending or attempting to send such patients to psychiatrists-where if drug treatments for the brain are undertaken for physical symptoms and physical causes, you can imagine the worsening aspects of the problems themselves that such lethal drugs with tremendous side effects for the stomach, kidneys, lung, heart and the liver for starters would only produce. It would most certainly be life-threatening and fatal. And that's what Anton Barton not only tried, but in fact had done to me. So what he did falls surely under the greatly illegal action of 'attempted murder' for now. But when I am dead, he will be guilty of murder! There is no two ways around it! And Carl Boyd and Yau Lun were aiding and abetting him in his corrupt dealings and the hypocritical way in which he carries himself as a supposed respected specialist!

Where with doctors who are ignorant, that's understandable for them to give the cop-out 'psychological' diagnosis, but also one has to consider, where is the proof that such problems as I reported were psychological? Even a psychiatrist would have to report irrational and insane behaviour stemmed from psychological disorders, the indistinction one has between right and wrong, to even allege a confirmation to a psychological diagnosis. Though how many people with psychological problems ever report physical symptoms beyond their control and present real symptoms of facial discoloration, obvious weight loss, loss of appetite, chronic knife-stabbing head and body pains and even asthma due to certain food intolerances given when the immune and digestive systems are at its worst forms?

Where to Western medicine bodies, even if a problem does not show up in the blood, it is either a psychological problem or it's irritable bowel syndrome or it's chronic fatigue syndrome. But where is the medicine to fix such problems? Even to treat them. Would Anton Barton genuinely present all his patients with them? I seriously doubt it. And the government tolerates such idiocy presented by such Western doctors and allows taxpayers to pay for their Medicare revenues continuously for doing absolutely nothing to patients but reduce their health even more so, with lethal immune system reducing and life-threatening prescribed chemical drugs with uncountable side effects, which costs the taxpayers even more when governments allow such doctors to only treat patient symptoms and not the cause, that keeps patients out of work even longer to be handed sickness allowances.

The Anton Barton's in Western medicine have only given me junk labels as diagnoses, but why hadn't they ever presented me with the medicine for such so-called labels? Because they know, I know, and anyone with common sense knows that such diagnoses don't even exist; they are a bunch of gutless crooked frauds and cowardly liars trying to cover their backsides only to keep their jobs.

Where even if anything happens to such patients with physical symptoms in which reveal nothing in blood tests, such doctors would only laugh, saying, 'Oh, he died of a psychological problem caused by stress and anxiety!' And such doctors still keep their jobs. The government yet issues them those Medicare Cards by patients and the deceased patient's file is closed; everything simple in a very neat package. There is no investigation; all Medicare-funded doctors vouch for the other, claiming that the patient died from a mental problem. And it's business as usual, then on to the next patient; or the next patient target; or victim.

Where to them (such despicable pretending doctors), no physical problem should cause stress, and if one is stressed, then everything boils down to a mental problem. Where all humans by nature suffer stress, but does it mean one requires the services of a psychiatrist, especially one with terminal cancer which my doctor can verify its cause is certainly not from Western medicine frauds' two favourite words, in which they have studied in university all those years to say, 'stress and anxiety!'

The Anton Barton's in Western medicine have done nothing for me - and the government had yet paid for this result of absolutely nothing given to me by Anton Barton, via my Medicare Card. How many patients must the Anton Barton's of the Western Medical Industry have to attempt to destroy on the backs of the taxpayers before something is done to stop them? Anton Barton in particular; the government ended up paying for a fee to him only

451

for giving me a lie of a diagnosis, with no medication for it to substantiate the accuracy to what he said.

Where also incorrect medication for an incorrect diagnosis - resulting in the worsening of all symptoms, would surely result in further proof that he lied and lied intentionally; such so-called doctors in the industry do nothing but attempt to destroy people's lives. I'm a prime example to that fact. And it's not too difficult particularly nowadays to find countless other examples.

All such names and labels given by the Anton Barton's of the medical industry to so-called conditions of patients do not bear proof to their existences. For what is psychological, irritable bowel and chronic fatigue syndrome? It is too general. And not based on the individual patient. They are just symptoms to a greater underlying problem, as was in my case, being cancer. For even ten patients with the same problem respond differently to different forms of treatments. And most sicknesses in the world, acute or chronic, show nothing in blood tests! Carl Boyd even admitted that to me when I questioned him. He also admitted that such problems can also equally present just as serious as those that do show themselves in blood tests, if left untreated.

Now those who are ignorant and completely foolish in the Western Medicine Industry, without a shred of diagnostic skills to their credit, who claim such unproven psychological diagnoses in particular to virtually every patient who sees them with symptoms ranging deeper than that of a simple cold or flu problem, at least one can say, how can you really argue with the fool who does not know any better? Who is just as I've indicated: ignorant.

But where Anton Barton was concerned, what he did to me was not out of ignorance. It was in fact a deliberate act of sabotage. It was illegal, gutless and highly criminal; depriving a patient of treatment or an avenue to obtain proper and correct treatments from. Because without treatment, my condition only becomes worse in time and the symptoms become more uncomfortable and difficult to handle beyond my control. And eventually it did become terminal.

And I emphasise, the symptoms I reported to Anton Barton made sense to him, particularly when he asked me questions to symptoms I experienced that I did not mention throughout, such as bad migraines and headaches. Not even had he bothered to adequately prescribe something to relieve those bad pains. He should have given me something, anything, to help the crushing pains in my head subside as I was constantly experiencing major headaches throughout that time. But no; he just wrote it all off as something inconsequential. He just lied and fabricated a story to see me succumb to the depths of misery and despair I am now currently subjected to.

Indeed, I have fallen into a hopeless situation, one in which there is no way out for me, ever! Too bad, I guess!

Anton Barton clearly knew what the real nature to my problem was, being brain cancer, as my current treating doctors in the Brooklyn Public Hospital know. But even in writing to such GP Clinics in Brooklyn, Anton Barton had claimed that some of my symptoms indicated some malabsorption problem with the digestion, though he conned and lied to naive GPs gullible enough to believe everything he says that it was all psychological with no explanation to warrant this.

Then such ignorant GPs began looking at me sideways from that moment on when I went to see them for help after that time, because they happened to believe or favour this so-called respectable specialist.

Now at least I have found doctors who diagnosed my condition correctly. But as I have stated throughout this letter, the necessary treatments in which my serious condition warranted from the onset at the time much urgently, which was neglected by Anton Burton; such neglect of his had become my true downfall. Now, it seems no one is able to help me. Where once I finally found these suitable doctors who could at least improve some symptoms for me, such as the crushing pains I experienced in my head, followed by my stomach, once the cancer had spread to my liver, and everyone could see the true nature of my condition, it's only then that GPs such as Carl Boyd would listen to me, when I rang them up from my sickbed here in hospital and I insisted that Anton Barton lied intentionally. For no psychological drug on earth would ever improve such things as I at least found improvements with, such as much-needed pain-relief medications I was given to numb the excruciating pains I was getting constantly, as my cancerous masses were growing at an alarming rate pressing on vital organs and nerves.

Commander Robert Stewart, I have presented you with such facts that indeed Anton Barton is not respectable at all, but in fact a highly deceptive liar with an extreme tendency for evil where his patients are concerned. He does not care for his patients as a doctor should and/or he only treats the ones he chooses to. Whatever or whoever they are. Possibly as mean-spirited, ugly and grotesque as him!

In any case, why would Anton Barton state in writing, that my symptoms reported some physical problem with the digestive system (which also was a cover-up diagnosis from the real state of affairs), then in the end of his report given to such GPs in order to attempt to deprive me completely from obtaining an accurate diagnosis and consecutively prompt accurate treatments thereafter, mixed with an accurate avenue to obtain those necessary correct treatments and access to seeking suitable assistance from my GP(s) at the time, lied to them that it was 'all' psychological?

Why did Anton Barton not even attempt to treat my digestive system at least, that could have given me some relief of symptoms at the time, by even prescribing such vitamins and minerals that he obviously knew I was deficient in from my reported symptoms, which I had found out from other means?

In hospital, my symptoms at least have been controlled in a short time, only in weeks compared to what Anton Barton did for me as well as those GPs mentioned, being absolutely nothing. And yet Medicare still pays for their livelihoods.

Anton Barton was paid by Medicare to literally do nothing for me. He deliberately deprived me of treatment so that I could be driven well to return back to work early, as he corruptly put me with who knows how many others who are perhaps all perfectly sane in the psychological category (with no explanation as to why he said that). That had me stick on sickness allowances indefinitely, which costs taxpayers great sums of money, instead of me contributing as usual to being a taxpayer. Where such sickness benefits provided for my condition throughout, could have been spared and provided to someone who really required it if he provided me with a genuine route early. And now my condition has gotten so bad that it will eventually kill me anytime now!

If Anton Barton (the supposed great diagnostician that GPs claim him to be), had advised me when I saw him on September the 12th 1990 this year then and there correctly of where I even could have went to obtain correct treatments from, which avenue to pursue, or more importantly, from whom – instead of as was the case of my being finally admitted to hospital off my own bat, when my condition became so bad that I struggled to even walk properly on my own - then my condition would not have worsened for months after that time until my final diagnosis via X-rays, which revealed the haunting truth of my real condition's diagnosis, which costed me more lost time and the taxpayers more expense. But it costed me more than just time alone. It costed me any hope for a recovery – EVER!

Where let me enforce, that if one has a psychological problem, better known as a mental problem, then no form of medicine can cure it, even help improve the problem, either in Eastern or Western medicine. Where in Western medicine, drugs for the brain would leave patients subdued as zombies, certainly not offering even the tiniest assistance in any of the symptoms experienced such as what I was presented with.

Anton Barton never wanted me to find any hope for a cure. He deliberately premeditated my death sentence to eventuate as it had this very day.

He never wanted me to get well so that I could get on with my life and function as normal again. No. Instead, he cold-heartedly calculated my demise as it stands today. I am a prisoner in my own body. I cannot function properly. I barely have enough strength to even eat on my own.

If what I had was truly a mental problem, then how did I succumb to this? How was I diagnosed with spreading malignancy cancers soon after my visit with Anton Barton, if it really was a psychological problem in which Anton Barton had deliberately lied it all to be. And put me in that category to attempt to destroy my life without reason. He has in fact destroyed my life! He has in actuality not only attempted murder, but in fact had orchestrated my murder very cruelly!

And Carl Boyd and Yau Lun were all in cahoots together on that note, covering their own backsides.

Yau Lun as Carl Boyd had claimed to me that, 'Anton Barton would certainly be one of the few people who would understand the real source to your symptoms!' Yau Lun also claimed, 'If Anton Barton can't help you, then no one else can. Just describe all your symptoms to him.'

Anton Barton was in fact guaranteed to understand my symptoms which was the sole reason why I even contemplated seeing him again, because no other GP was giving me any other guaranteed option, which was why Dr. Patrick Byron referred me to him to begin with after ruling certain things out first with blood tests; as Anton Barton had reportedly diagnosed many other basic and complex reported symptoms of patients in the past. And he had clearly understood my symptoms as well. But instead of helping me, he decided to sabotage me instead!

When people see a 'doctor', they are after the most 'obvious' solution, not an interrogation almost resembling some form of a third degree. Where the patient says white and the doctor says black. And why people have allowed the system to operate like this for decades, which only achieves countless complaints by patients being given false diagnoses, unnecessary prescribed medications with lethal side effects, neglect and corruption within the medical field makes absolutely no sense to me at all!

These people-these so-called doctors are labelled 'General Practitioners', which means they should understand the human pathology at a holistic point of view. Not just trained to or attempt to feed the field of psychiatry and psychology as an easy escape for them one too many times where they still make their money!

The real question is, what sort of inducements are these corrupt GPs being given when they refer so many patients with physical problems to psychiatrists? Could the most diabolical answer to that question ride on the fact that brain drugs make people very sick? They actually create more problems of a physical nature than any disease ever could. Then once the psychiatrist makes his or her money from the patients, they send such patients then back to GPs, to treat real physical problems only caused by the prescriptions of their organ-damaging psychiatric drugs. It was a classic example of bad business creating bad business for all ends of the medical industry. Where as a result, the corrupt GPs and the fraudulent psychiatrists are in fact profiting enormously from the other at the expense of the patient as well as the unknowing taxpayer!

On the same rational where GPs required full blood examinations to show proof of physical-reported symptoms, where is also the blood work to confirm first a psychological diagnosis prior their easily handing out of such brain medications instead? Where if they treat the body and not the brain as requested by patients, they might see a positive result happening. Either they're too stupid or do they just not give a damn? Logically, all things considered, it must be both!

Anton Barton, by trying to send me (as he and people like him had sent many others with physical-reported symptoms to a psychiatrist), was only in my worst interests. To in short try to sabotage me completely. These issues are what I will be seeking justice for against such words of dodging the issue and withholding valuable information through pretence and words of trickery and fraud directed by Anton Barton.

Patients' lives are at stake by grossly irresponsible practitioners such as Anton Barton. And such matters must never be ignored, especially when such doctors continuously evade the real issues in question and manipulate things for their own selfish convenience. And when these issues are continuously manipulated through lies, lame excuses and withholding valuable information, people's lives will continuously be destroyed by such doctors whom get away with everything corrupt they do, only to maintain their jobs.

So, as a consequence, I am seeking complete justice to be served in this matter against that corrupt and arrogant so-called specialist named Anton Barton! Because it is those so-called doctors as Anton Barton who are treating medicine, what is a very serious and necessary area in everyday life, as a game to toy with people's lives and toy unconscionably - who are giving 'Western medicine' as a whole, a terribly disgusting reputation!

456

For in conclusion, what Anton Barton did where I was concerned and who knows how many other patients of his, was a serious and highly improper and greatly illegal breach of doctor ethics and drastic attempt of sabotage on one's life.

Please Commander Robert Stewart; I want you to demand that the highest and most severe action that can be taken against such an evil practitioner of medicine is taken against him, if for anything, for the sake of any other people destined to stumble into that corrupt path of the Anton Barton's of the medical industry. And I know you will action my complaint straight from the heart – and you will not let this rest until suitable action to my complete satisfaction is assured.

In the meantime, whilst there is one breath left in me, I will be seeking advisement from my lawyer on this matter, even as I lay on my hospital bed, to ensure that every possible avenue that can be taken against such a corrupt and greatly evil man called Anton Barton, in the spirit of justice served, is taken!

Commander Robert Stewart: in trust I hand you the very first printed copy of this letter which includes all the necessary information you need for your thorough investigation.

Yours truly,

Donnie Kensington

Donnie Kensington

CHAPTER 4

For the past three weeks upon receiving his fresh copy of Donnie Kensington's official hardcopy complaint letter addressed at his station house office, Robert Stewart mounted a severe crackdown on the Western Medicine Industry right across New York City. His targets were not only the names mentioned in Donnie's letter, but his investigation also targeted those Western Medicine Authorities behind it all, such a board of corrupt medical practitioners who were members of its organization, who all ignored such complaints given to them by masses of patients such as Donnie Kensington - and kept mum on the whole sordid affairs!

Robert Stewart had established overwhelming evidence against Anton Barton. The Donnie Kensington story was certainly not an isolated incident. Not by a long shot! It was Robert's experience as a professional police officer, that if there was one reported crime against a criminal, there were always others. And in Anton Barton's case, the numbers of patient fatalities by his hands alone reached a mass number. There were stacks of them.

When Robert went to his Brooklyn clinic's office to officially arrest him on multiple counts of murder, Anton Barton was on his lunch break. He was seen eating a thick juicy steak alone, whilst sitting behind his desk inside his room. Anton Barton, for no good reason, seemed to want to resist arrest by threatening Robert and his police confederates with the very large sharp knife he used to slice his steak into consumable bits and pieces.

Upon threatening to stab the police with a knife, Robert and his confederate police officers took possession of their loaded guns in their hands and opened fire on the soon-to-become dead doctor in question.

Carl Boyd and Yau Lun with two hundred other GPs across New York City met with their downfalls not long after. They were each charged on conspiracy and multiple counts of murder - as well as had the entire Western Medicine Authorities' groups, which comprised of GPs of the like as its members, who covered up and protected their corrupt medical associates in a joint effort, to ensure that the truth of what they were 'all' doing and how they really made their money never saw the light of day.

Their efforts were foiled. The light had shone upon their criminal activities - and each dirty criminal practitioner of medicine was not only deregistered from ever practising medicine in the United States again, but most of them would never get their chance to even attempt it. They were each sentenced to very hefty prison terms – and it was predicted, many of them would not live long enough to ever see the light of day again!

Just as Robert Stewart spent the last few weeks devising the downfall of the Western Medicine criminal elements which penetrated inside its arena, he had spent much longer masterminding that of the Eastern Medicine Community.

In fact, Robert had spent the past year burying the dirty seeds of that field of medicine.

And it all began when the criminal antics of one of that field's dirtiest wrongdoers came to surface, with an even brighter light being shone on his activities, which then led to mass arrests being orchestrated upon the rest of the Eastern Medicine co-conspirators who descended into this country from the East - to begin a series of criminal money-making schemes which duped and tricked many thousands of people from right across New York City, who became their victim patients!

Out of all the complaints made against the dirtiest scoundrel of them all named Wu Yang, which was sent in legions to the Chinese Medicine Authorities, such authorities told each of the patient complainants to be patient, giving them hope that justice against this criminal named Wu Yang would occur.

But after months of waiting in false hope, the Chinese Medicine Authorities did nothing about the complaints. In fact, they just maintained Wu Yang's medical registration time and time again as legal and valid.

They kept him registered by offering him a loophole by saying that his crimes in their instances, in particular (such responses given to all of the patients, one by one), were committed without the onus of proof by any of those complainant patients. Because legally, in acupuncture, if no one died inside the acupuncture treatment room clinic couch during the treatment, and if they were able to get up after the acupuncture treatment finished and walk out of the clinic fine, then where was the proof that Wu Yang had in fact committed any wrongful action? In the eyes of the Chinese Medicine Authorities, it was claimed that Wu Yang was an honest practitioner of medicine being set up by jealous and racist members of the New York City community - who were picking on Asians because the Asians labelled themselves as the pioneers of medicine, something that the West could never really compete with. Those Chinese Medicine practitioners acted as if their presence from the East to the West should be welcomed and saluted instead of being criticized and ultimately condemned, justly so!

But Robert plugged that loophole by the simple 'coincidence factor', when so many of the patients who reported the same side effects by Wu Yang's treatments, which all resulted in their deaths. Coincidences could still become substantiated evidence in a court of law, if one pressed all the proper buttons as Robert had finagled quite expertly at that, assuming the role of cop, lawyer and psychologist - in order to burn those bastards at the stake for

459

their very devious ploy they orchestrated upon masses of citizens in the West who became their patients at one point!

So, in short, the New York City Chinese Medicine Practitioners Authorities had throughout the years, devised an evil scheme which ignored patients' complaints, in order to detract legal investigations also into their own money-making illegal schemes. So based on that, they simply allowed Wu Yang to practise medicine and get away with his multiple reported crimes to patients for decades, with no punishment at all.

Robert investigated the matter thoroughly of both the practitioners and those who ran the Chinese Medicine Authority groups.

Where following the Chinese Medicine Authorities' failures to do anything about such numerous complaints, Robert traced documented records of many of the former Wu Yang patient complainants then actually telephoning one of the Chinese Medicine Authorities' members, who took the calls of such patient complaints directed to the organisation. His name was Professor Samuel Fung (the very person who in fact initially encouraged such former Wu Yang patients to complain about Wu Yang to the Chinese Medicine Authorities to begin with). Details of the patients' directions in that regard were all documented and lodged by the patients in writing to their lawyers' offices across New York City.

Robert was able to retrieve it all. All the information he needed to shed light to the criminal acupuncturists' evil actions inflicted upon the community.

It seemed that Professor Samuel Fung further stated to each of the reporting former Wu Yang patients one by one at the time, that only one person complained against Wu Yang, meaning just them, to the Chinese Medicine Authorities, 'So we can't do anything.' And each of the patients had stated on different occasions, one by one, 'But have you checked any of the many existing New York City law firms' records, which my lawyer had confirmed to me that many patients had lodged masses of complaints in order to commence legal proceedings with them against Wu Yang over the years? But the patients all died before they could finalise any solid actions against him.' Professor Samuel Fung replied, 'It's not our job to chase these people. They should approach us!' Which was not a very caring attitude concerning the health of people!

Throughout his investigations, quite thorough at that, Robert deduced a very sinister conspiracy which lurked also within the Eastern field of medicine in New York City; a conspiracy which was in fact cast forward by so many corrupt practitioners, in epidemic proportions.

Robert concluded by his very extensive investigations into the medical corruption fields, that the Chinese Medicine Authorities (which also comprised of practising acupuncturists as its board members), clearly did not want to touch Wu Yang, because they were scared. They knew it would cause severe harm also to them by exposing Wu Yang's such atrocities to every authority that needed to know-to expose what he was really doing - for they practised as he had: Taking patients' monies - not caring if their treatments were negligent, corrupt or otherwise. For exposing this criminal wrongdoing by one of its members, would most certainly put their own similar money-making scams to the sick also under severe scrutiny. They did not want their money-making livelihoods jeopardised in any way. Hence, the ignoring of all the patients' complaints mixed with the false assurances given to them – and blended in with the railroading tactics in order to cover it all up from inside-out and back-to-front! After all, why was it that no one ever heard of anyone ever getting better through undertaking treatments by any of them?

Robert knew the patients had presented such Chinese Medicine Authorities with very serious complaints, which on their ends alone, had fallen under attempted murder. And eventually mass murder itself! Because every one of those countless patients who encountered the ultimate worse over the years because of Wu Yang had all eventually wound up dead. And the Chinese Medicine Authorities' responses were: 'Only one person complained to them!'

So in other words, they drummed up in their very sick and twisted minds, that the law was based upon the sole rationale in this country that murder and attempted murder was acceptable, particularly if only one of the victims had survived long enough to expose an entire complaint!

Those fiendish acupuncturist scoundrels entered into this country with dollar signs in their eyes and a very diabolical scheme embedded into all their black hearts. They figured that in the Western countries, the law could allow them to migrate into the West and grant them with the UNJUST privilege of making money by killing many people in such a way in which no one could prove anything: acupuncture medicine! They figured no one would be the wiser!

Robert Stewart was very keen on proving those ratbags wrong. In the end, he struck his powerful blows upon them with his mighty hands, bashing the law book on each of their heads forcefully, insisting that the law really would **not** allow them to get away with these atrocious crimes to which have resulted in countless deaths over the years, beginning with their wretched entrances upon American soil.

Wu Yang had killed thousands of Americans over the years - and Robert came to the damning conclusion of all of the guilty parties concerned, that Wu Yang only got away with it all, because the Chinese Medicine Practitioners Authorities, he genuinely and wholeheartedly believed, were as corrupt as Wu Yang was, to pass him registration after each of his documented crimes during the past several decades, showing no remorse, empathy, concern or emotion for the reported atrocities Wu Yang committed

461

in his practice, where those many thousands of patients were concerned, **"ESPECIALLY!"**

And whilst Wu Yang, throughout those decades, had maintained his deceitful con man advertising, even plastered on bulletin boards throughout the city, he, as well, had been, on numerous occasions, congratulated by senators for destroying people and making them sick to the point where they could not work and required unemployment assistance via Social Security benefits, costing taxpayers enormous amounts of money.

But this only became a short-term measure. Because the reality of it all was that all such patients who experienced Wu Yang's corruptive treatments eventually died in torturous agony.

And upon Robert's complete investigations into the nasty ordeal, he found that the great numbers of patient complaints lodged against Wu Yang, the thousands of them also handed to the Chinese Medicine Authorities throughout the years, were harshly ignored and nothing was done to obtain justice for such numerous masses of victims. And when Robert questioned the judicial system's legal firms, particularly throughout the State, heaps of lawyers had keenly attested to the visible hypocrisy of Wu Yang - and his insult to medicine in general – and his criminal dealings to the sick and his atrocious reputation!!!

Those fiendish doctors (which made up the group called the Chinese Medicine Authorities) who protected Wu Yang, were not only all found guilty in a court of law, each receiving hefty prison sentences for cheating the medical community, but also were found with equal complicity in cheating the Social Security system as well, by sabotaging people who wanted to work, forcing them to become ill and/or giving them intentional incorrect treatments so they could die!

Where the taxpayers' forked out the bill and these corrupt doctors had gotten away with attempted murder and murder itself and the law only tolerated it for many years!

The complaints concerning Wu Yang were extremely serious! It involved the health and welfare of many people left to chance, because of corrupt medical practitioners who entered such a field of medicine only for the inclinations to make large sums of money, despite the serious repercussions and side effects those ignorant, unconscionable and deliberately evil practitioners inflicted upon their patients.

Such foreigners thrived on the West just for that one unique purpose planted surreptitiously in their sick minds; given the weak laws in this country in that regard by former governments who in fact seemingly favoured such despicable and atrocious lawbreakers, who play God with people's lives, whilst taking their money and calling it their livelihoods!

462

Just like any other criminal, Wu Yang and his protectors inside the Chinese Medicine Authorities had adopted the same modi operandi of looking at people in the eye and lying! Wu Yang, just as his protectors in medicine, had informed each of the patient complainants in writing separately, that they were the only ones who ever complained against him. Aside from what their own lawyers had told them, absolutely contradicting Wu Yang's and the medical authorities' signed statements, such patients in their emotional traumas and outrage to such unjust defeats, had repeatedly telephoned the offices of the Chinese Medicine Authorities thereafter, the people they reported this Wu Yang incident to at the time, and cried for help. But no such help was given to them.

The patients then telephoned their lawyers and repeated that same story told to them by Wu Yang and the Chinese Medicine Authorities, cursing their lack of justice received. Their lawyers replied in responses to what Wu Yang and his protectors claimed, such blatant lies, confirming, 'That is not true!' And gave them no other details aside from the fact that they should call the police; but unfortunately, their own lawyers who informed them of the truth concerning Wu Yang and his protectors, still, at the same time, warned the patients that in a perfect world, the police should help them, but unfortunately, many police were not clever enough to understand such a story in which an acupuncturist and acupuncturists of the like had resulted in masses of people's deaths.

In fact, if truth be known, the corrupt practitioners of medicine across the whole world were responsible for more deaths upon people, than any and all of the worst forms of thugs combined, holding guns in their hands and squeezing triggers, shooting at masses of people had ever committed!

But attempting to convince all of the police in off-the-cuff remarks about this was an entire different matter altogether! The story just seemed too far-fetched even if it was completely true. But incompetence and ignorance was what the Wu Yang's of the world, particularly the medical world in the West, had thrived on to be operating inside the justice system, which included its police departments. And that was how these corrupt practitioners of medicine had gotten away with their murderous incidences for years and years and years on end!

Just as the victims' lawyers had explained to such former Wu Yang patients - the police would consider such a matter out of their usual jurisdiction, or some may not even care to do anything about it. And the partial reason why they would not care was because they would never understand that such a thing was possible or plausible in any way, shape or form whatsoever! The police could never appreciate the truth, the real cold-hard fact of the matter, that indeed, 'Medical Corruption was a Global Epidemic!' They would think just as Wu Yang expected all the Western

463

authorities to concede from the beginning of his arrival to the United States of America: that the patients were all looney-tunes and he (Wu Yang) was sane – and therefore he continues his money-making criminal exercise for a greater number of years, unscathed by anyone and everyone, including the good old American Justice System!

All in all, Wu Yang's responses and denials was not what was surprising! Wu Yang after all was a criminal and a hideous coward. Much like any other criminal, they would not admit to their crimes! That was to be expected! What was surprising however, what was unexpected by all the patients who had complained against this despicable and evil cowardly criminal named Wu Yang, was the simple fact that if it was not true - if as it was told to each one of them and each individual patient, which would no doubt be the same story Wu Yang would be feeding everyone who had complained against him, that they were the only ones who had ever complained against him; but if this story provided by Wu Yang, where each of them was concerned for example, what he told them all one at a time - if Wu Yang lied, and in fact if the truth remained that such individual patients were **not** the only ones to ever have complained against Wu Yang, then what the hell have those complaints been doing sitting there inside the offices of the Chinese Medicine Authorities in idle? And why were they not being forwarded to the proper authorities so that these further atrocities by Wu Yang to his patients could no longer be repeated? Why hadn't these complaints, the Chinese Medicine Authorities' records been accessed by any of the other external authorities approached in this matter, for the simple purpose, the much-necessary purpose to prevent further lives from being harmed by Wu Yang? Why had everyone kept silent in this matter? These were the groundbreaking questions; the main points in the argument. This was what became truly unacceptable! It was horrendous!
What the hell sort of people are in this country stationed in positions of authority? That was what the patients continuously were asking themselves.

Prior detailed written complaints being received by the Chinese Medicine Authorities, such people situated in those authoritative posts, when first undertaking casual conversations with each of the Wu Yang complainants, what were in fact the former Wu Yang patients, had all seemingly displayed eagerness to accept all complaints to them concerning Wu Yang.
But once they each received the fully documented printout details of what Wu Yang had committed against these patients, such complaints all matching similar scenarios by the numerous patients – the tones and the moods by those men and women bearing authority roles in those Chinese

medicine posts suddenly became nervous. The complaints it seemed were hitting a little too close to home. Because a lot of what the patients accused Wu Yang of committing also described their own hideous forms of wrongdoings perpetuated upon their own patient cliental. So, if they reprimanded Wu Yang and in fact assisted in his complete prosecution as was the right course of action to adhere to, many of such authorities in question, who were in fact board members within the Chinese Medicine Authority, who were all practitioners of medicine themselves, felt that one hanged in their group would mean they would all be hanged; those people who were all practising the same diabolical undertakings in each of their own clinics. And so was the reason for Wu Yang's freedom of operation for decades in all his criminal money-making dealings committed to the New York City community!

Following such exposés being mailed to their hands, corrupt Chinese Medicine Authority board members such as Professor Samuel Fung then all of a sudden lost all interest in doing anything about the written dossiers of incriminating facts. Professor Samuel Fung as all his colleagues would lie, would scheme, would run all circles around the complainants' eyes and ears and finagle any excuse and impossible reason for letting the complaints wither, decay and die in their hands.

'Yours is the only complaint against Wu Yang to the Chinese Medicine Authority. We saw no reason not to maintain his registration,' barked Professor Samuel Fung to each of the former Wu Yang patient complainants.

But prior receiving such detailed complaints, the man named Professor Samuel Fung who also migrated into this country from China, was all smiles, all encouraging and seemingly supportive in receiving the complaints by such poor and victimised, wrongly treated patients, the many thousands of them they became over the years.

Man, the Chinese Medicine Authorities quickly changed their tunes once they read what was in fact highly incriminating evidence which also described their own evil schemes in the West!

Prior receiving such formally written complaints, Samuel Fung even admitted to many of the high-strung complainants that he in fact dealt with patients who had complained against Wu Yang. Many of them then became patients inside his clinic. And he was the very same person who encouraged them, also in writing, to forward their complaints to the Chinese Medicine Authorities based in New York.

Where Samuel Fung on many occasions was the very first Chinese acupuncturist witness who saw the terrible state of conditions many of his new patients were in, many of them who had in fact been former patients of the Wu Yang Clinic over the years, prior their demises being fully met!

465

His written reports to that effect were also addressed to the patients and then later conveniently rebutted to everyone upon such patients dying inside Fung's clinic. To save his own skin, Fung had to then deny the truthfulness in what he said about Wu Yang. He feared he would be blamed for such patients' deaths. He feared that if it was documented that in fact 'acupuncture was proven to be a very dangerous game if performed by the wrong hands', then it also could be proven that he himself had literally ruined so many of his patients as well! So then everything became one giant conspiracy of everyone covering up the truthful mistakes of all of them operating in that field of medicine.

Robert Stewart quickly uncovered that the Chinese Medicine Authorities and all its board members were as corrupt as the criminal practitioners they received complaints from by so many patients over the years.

And by revealing the truth on one of its members would mean it would no doubt bring the flak down immediately on the rest of them who were profiting enormously by practising as Wu Yang had. They feared new laws could be brought in that would jeopardise that and restrict the rest of them from profiting as Wu Yang had, by deceiving their patients! It was due to this dishonest, unscrupulous and corrupt practise by so many acupuncturists, particularly in this country of the United States of America, whom lack the necessary knowledge and medical qualifications to treat patients correctly, and are in the alternative medicine field only to make money using their limited skills, no matter how much it hurts the patients and society as a whole, when people require longer absenteeism periods from work! And this was the fundamental reason why so many of their patients had not recovered EVER from even the simplest and most straightforward of medical problems!

And at first not even comprehending that simple fact, the desperate patients had sent further complaint letters about Wu Yang to the Chinese Medicine Authorities for a second time. To achieve only the same cover-up result in which they had originally obtained from the Chinese Medicine Authoritative Body that was enclosed to them! It was unskilful thinking on everyone's part. It was as preposterous as a Jew in the 1940s reporting a Nazi atrocity to Adolf Hitler himself! And then trying it again!

Though one vital revelation was uncovered throughout Robert Stewart's investigations into the hideous affair which became a landmark, a pure milestone into the real reasons why Wu Yang and the corrupt Chinese Medicine Authorities were so confident that the law would always protect them no matter what.

466

Robert Stewart again struck gold. He hit the nail on the head in this major case. The ugly truth had surfaced...FINALLY! He succeeded in accomplishing another great feat, another historical breakthrough!

The evidence accumulated by Robert Stewart was overpowering and overwhelming. He managed to finagle the arrests and prosecutions of not only every dirty acupuncturist killer who operated in New York City, but at the same time, he had nailed to the cross all those who protected them and covered up their dirty dealings, such as those board members who operated within the Chinese Medicine Authorities - and those higher up, who at the same time, protected this farce and fraudulent group of men and women which reached right to the doors of the White House in Washington, D.C. itself!

Robert Stewart accumulated further evidence of widespread corruption and bribery via protection rackets on all sides of the fence which reached to the door and the arrest of one of this country's most dirty presidents in its history.

Via bank account records checked, it seemed as though the dirty criminals in medicine were bribing high-placed political figures on all levels for years, including one of this country's presidents, in exchange for freedom against prosecution, at the same time as the former president and various senators were also bribing judges with smaller sums, in order to also acquit their own implicated staff members who were running illegal schemes for them, at their behest, for greater slices of the financial pie! Bribery which funded more illegal schemes of bribery all round! The arrests of all the guilty parties had truly shocked the country and all who occupied its households.

It seemed as though the former President of the United States Harold Mar, whose policies were only designed to hurt people who were not rich; whose policies favoured the criminal elements of society; who put economics over human lives; who gave criminals loopholes in the law to get away with their crimes, and a road map for such criminals to cover their tracks; the truth uncovered was no longer a question, but a certainty. It was found out to the world in cold hard fashion that the former President Harold Mar, also knew of all the reported complaints against Wu Yang by his patients to the Chinese Medicine Authorities and New York-based law firms, and in fact also helped to cover up the crimes of Wu Yang the day of March the 23rd 1981, over nine years ago to date, when he issued Wu Yang with a Centenary medal award during his one-term stint as President, before he was kicked out of office by the people in 1982, over eight years ago!

The President Harold Mar legislated and much created the issuing of the Centenary Medal Award. It was mostly issued, in his words: 'to citizens who made a substantial contribution to American society which improved the lives of people and their communities as a whole.'

In Wu Yang's case, the real bronze medal was issued to publicly commemorate him as 'one hell of a great practitioner of medicine.'

The President Mr. Harold Mar himself became Wu Yang's most personal and influential PR man. Through his words driven to the masses around the country, he was the major driving force which helped Wu Yang amass his large client base by those people in the community who were still very much in the dark of what it really meant to become a patient inside his clinic. Of how dangerous it truly was, not only to their bank accounts, but to their very lives in general!

With the United States President in his pocket, Wu Yang was laughing all the way to the bank.

And with Wu Yang raking in huge dollars, it also meant the president could also capitalise on large liquid change also being directed, all under the table of course, into his own pocket and much surreptitiously!

But little did his patients know at the time (until it was all too late), that Wu Yang was in fact not a great contributor to American society as the former president indicated.

The truth of the matter redefined the words 'hypocrisy' and 'deception' in the fiercest and most murderous of extremes!

Wu Yang was truly one of the worst criminals to ever hit American soil. He was one of the biggest frauds in America's history.

But what was even more devastating than all of this, was that Wu Yang was being protected by the most powerful man in the country at that time. He had a powerful politician, in fact, the head of this country vouching for him. Even promoting his medical practice which created more deaths inside his clinic in New York City during that four-year period of Mr. Harold Mar's presidency, than at any time during the almost four decades in total in which Wu Yang practised medicine in the United States of America!

Wu Yang was beyond a lawbreaker! Wu Yang was a barbaric, monstrous, vile and evil destroyer of many of his patients' lives who entered his clinic without knowing the real repercussions, and what it all meant to sign that bloody contract provided by him, prior to obtaining treatments by Wu Yang! And despite his victims' efforts, because of a criminal former Harold Mar led Republican government, headed by such a breeder of crime and evil named Harold Mar, Wu Yang had at that point, not only walked free, but he was also congratulated, his hand was shaken by various senators, he was applauded and publicly rewarded with Centenary medallions by one of this country's former Presidents, whilst his victims were left in a state of misfortunate chaos and mayhem which ultimately destroyed them all and killed them in gruesome fashion, but not until the flesh of their achy bones was stripped away, leaving but only an appearing skeletal figure as a result of

468

the dire consequences of Wu Yang's disastrous and incorrect forms of acupuncture treatments inflicted upon them all!

In Robert's mind, he was satisfied when justice against all the guilty parties was finally installed.

But the only thing that bothered him throughout this hideous affair was that Wu Yang's justice was met only by the hands of another major criminal. Robert so looked forward to prosecuting that scum Wu Yang with the system, his system. But if it were any consolation, Wu Yang did meet death as he deserved. Wu Yang was certainly no loss to humanity. In fact, his removal from circulation in such a fashion was still justice served! And New York City was a much safer environment for it!

CHAPTER 5

Cassandra Stewart gently laid the Donnie Kensington letter on her lap after she finished reading it as she sat on the leather couch, a prisoner of enemy captivity as it were.

But despite her dire predicament which became a painful reality she found difficult to endure, she could not help but feel deeply moved and very emotional concerning the contents of the Donnie Kensington demise. Her emotions were very genuine. She felt the tears in her eyes rolling onto her cheeks. She couldn't help but feel deeply bad for what had happened to a young man who she met only once over one year ago. It was seriously a cruel act of fate which hit such a person who should have been ordinarily at the prime of his life and beginning his life's journey into prosperity, but not what it actually became: the end of the course of his existence, cut down so unexpectedly and surprisingly with absolutely no forewarning at all.

She remembered the young man Donnie appearing so strong and vital when she saw him that one time inside her house with Robert. How was it possible for such a vital young man like that to be struck down so cruelly by a condition that indeed crippled him? And the rampant indecency of that horrible, horrible doctor who in fact took joy at his suffering and misery was completely despicable.

Cassandra could not help but weep at the dark revelation she just finished reading. She covered her face with her hands in order to try and contain her uncontrollable emotions at what she just learned. But at the same time, she did not know for the life of her why she was given the letter by this sadistic madman behind her kidnapping right now known as the Boss.

What was the meaning of this? She thought to herself. Why did he force me to read this? What does Donnie Kensington have to do with him? I just don't understand any of it. For the first time in my life I feel so confused.

Cassandra suddenly thought about the children Ryan and Stephanie. Where were they? This sinister madman wearing an equally sinister agenda concerning the Stewart family had those kids locked up somewhere in this house; and the baby. Yes, little Joseph, she thought to herself, her newborn son. Hers and Robert's baby boy just conceived a little over three months ago was also kidnapped and taken away from them in such hideous fashion. She thought of her husband Robert. What he must be going through at this moment. Oh, she missed him so much. She longed to feel the security and comfort of his embrace as surely as Robert wanted her back in his arms. She knew her husband well. Robert would be tearing the world apart in search for her and his children. He would intend to destroy every enemy who separated them this moment in order to get his family back - and to feel the beauty of his lovely wife entering into his arms again.

She thought constantly about her husband. She recalled Robert once telling her, 'Do you ever regret marrying a cop?'

Cassandra said jokingly, 'Everyday of my life. I mean, since I married you, our lives have been turned upside-down by one thing or another!'

Robert then embraced his wife and said softly in her ear, 'It was never my intention to ever bring danger to any of your lives as it unfortunately had been the case one too many times!'

And then she insisted solemnly, 'Robert. You don't need to apologise. I was only kidding around. You know I don't have any regrets about anything, especially our marriage!'

But Robert also became solemn in thought. 'I know. But unfortunately Cassandra, I am not joking about this. I became a cop because I had to clean up our streets from all those bad guys out there. But it was never my intention to put any of you in danger because of it. But admittedly, I have to say, that sometimes the bad guys will be out for revenge against me, because they see me as a threat to them. And they may stoop to whatever mean tactics they see necessary in order to remove that threat from them! But I promise you Cassandra, that I will always protect you and the children, the whole family from those nasty people out there! I promise you that!'

Cassandra always felt safe when her husband was around. She missed him as surely as he missed her right now. She knew he would definitely turn the city inside-out and upside-down to find both her and the children - and rescue them all from this evil force which has suddenly torn them apart and ripped away their seeming peaceful world as it had become the last several months. They were happy; especially after the birth of baby Joseph. But now, even the baby was taken away from his mother and father. Cassandra wept at that horrible thought too. How can anyone be so cold and cruel to take a baby from his parents like that? How can anyone be so cruel to tear apart a stable and happy family as hers?

Her mind could never stop thinking about her husband. Oh, Robert, the love of my life, please find us soon. And rescue us. Protect us and keep us safe! God, I hope you are all right. I hope these bad people have not harmed you in any way. What would the kids do if anything ever happened to you? What would become of our baby? He needs to know his father. He cannot grow up in this world without his great father around to guide him. We all need you, Robert! I need you. I cannot fathom life without you. Oh, please be safe! Please find us soon and free us from this EVIL that has separated us like this so unexpectedly, so surprisingly, so cruelly.

Cassandra then thought about the letter again. Yes, that fate of Donnie's was also so unexpected, so surprising and so cruel. Life seems to be

471

so fragile. There is just too much bad in the world. People's lives can be ended without any words. People's futures can be crushed without any warning. And that is why I have always accepted Robert's destiny, his course of action as a very good and very effective police officer. Because he needs to stop those mean and nasty people who have destroyed good men like Donnie - and now who have caused a major split in a great family as the Stewarts. Yes. I finally understand everything. I can only imagine with much heartache this world without good men like my great husband! The pendulum would be completely off-balance. Who would counter the terrorism which is inflicted by all those evil men if it weren't for heroes like Robert?

Cassandra then folded the letter in her lap neatly and unhelped, she cried in her hands again, "My God, Donnie. That letter was so sad. I don't know what to say about this. It is just not fair!"

"Indeed it is not, Cassandra!" A very deep voice cursed from aside her.

Cassandra became startled, deeply surprised by the strong familiar voice. She staggered back in her chair in fright. Cassandra's eyes quickly lifted away from her hands and turned to the direction of the voice which was very close to her. The figure of the man who spoke to her stood right next to her on the right of the sofa. But she heard no one entering. How did he enter this room so silently like that, without her seeing or hearing anything? He walked like the devil himself.

But that was not Cassandra's only great surprise. The even greater surprise became the shocking and heart-thumping revelation of the identity to that man who then stood before her. The man held a white-coloured silk handkerchief before her eyes. He insisted, "Take this and wipe your eyes. Believe me; I too feel such depths of emotion when I think of my wonderful son I never knew existed until recently!"

Cassandra in deep emotional turmoil stuttered for a moment. She could not speak. She was not only deeply surprised but frightened beyond words at the identity to the man before her. Her red lips were fumbling. She just could not put the words together for a while yet. She was struggling to gain control of her senses for moments. But when she did finally manage to speak, the words just blurted out, at the same time as she felt her heart skip several beats, as she became right this very moment, the most frightened woman in the world: "My God... My God... It cannot be... You are the Boss? You are the enemy?"

The strong man's voice surprisingly it seemed, attempted to assure her more than intimidate her as he pronounced the bitter truth to Cassandra Stewart at this very moment: "Yes, Cassandra. It is true! I am Domenico Armando. I am the Boss. And let me also pronounce to you this very day that I am back. And I will declare to you right here and right now that your husband this time has gone too far with me! Yes. He went too far this time,

472

indeed! He has crossed me very badly. And now I will cost him everything because of that. Yes. He will lose everything: his wife, his children, and his peace of mind: EVERYTHING!" he then shouted, "Yes, EVERYTHING!"

Cassandra still could not get her mind wrapped around one fundamental idea, the harsh premise of this bleak reality as it was identified to her so unimaginably right this very second: "But how? How is it possible? How can you be here? You are supposed to be–"

"Where?" the man interrupted very abruptly; Domenico who again wore his black-and-white favourite silk maestro outfit, but without a baton in his hand, just a handkerchief still held to her eyes had stated, then insisted, "Calm yourself and take the handkerchief."

Cassandra much frightened did as she was told.

Domenico Armando then finished his main point of reply. "Where? Were you going to say, on death row, hmm?"

Cassandra did not answer for now. She was too terrified.

Domenico then demanded her to respond: "ANSWER ME, DAMN IT!"

"Yes!" she stuttered.

Domenico now lowered the volume of his voice and insisted, "Yes, of course. But I am here to declare that it is my turn right now to gladly disappoint your husband on that matter. Hmm. Yes, the event of my escape was grand; it was violent, destructive, but necessary. I guess you want to know how it happened. Well, my dear Cassandra, I shall tell you!"

But first there was a knock outside the rear living room door and Domenico shouted: "Come in!"

The closed door was suddenly opened. It was Thomas. He entered inside whilst ushering another man to see the Boss. The second man was in his mid-thirties, ordinary-looking, wearing dark blue jeans, black steel-capped boots and a black T-shirt, who strolled to his eager superior in what, was in fact a much trancelike, zombie state. He did not speak. But Thomas insisted, "The job has been completed successfully!"

"So you supervised the performance?" asked Domenico.

Thomas smiled much pleased, "Yes. He used the untraceable gun with the silencer on it and shot the target twice in the heart. He's dead!"

Domenico's face also broke out in a smile. "Wonderful!" he cheered.

Cassandra, overhearing all this jumped to her feet in panic at the sight of this zombie-resembling man who was reported to have just committed murder. She began to stutter again, "My God... what... what... what is going on here? That man was a death row inmate. His name is Eric Grit. He was convicted of killing a total of thirty men, women and children with a knife. He cut out their intestines, their livers, hearts and kidneys and sent these organs anonymously to the police. Then they caught him. He was also sentenced to die. How...? How...? How can he be here?" she said, whilst experiencing the same fear and dread she had felt just moments before at seeing her family's worst enemy standing before her.

Domenico first placed two firm hands on Eric's shoulders and insisted, "You did good." He then faced Thomas and instructed, "Ok, Thomas, you can take him out of here. Take him to his resting quarters. He must be tired right now! And close the door to this living room on your way out!"

When Thomas and Eric left the room, Domenico replied to his female prisoner, "It is all right, Cassandra. He will not hurt you. Believe me. He is under my mercy. He is much under my control!"

Cassandra suddenly felt that the entire world was going crazy right now. She blurted out much confused, "I don't understand how any of this is possible. How can you and him be walking around here like that after a judge sentenced you both to be removed from the streets? And you said he killed someone!" she began to weep in panic, "Please don't tell me that you ordered him to kill Robert!"

Domenico first ushered her back to her couch. "Please sit down! No, Cassandra. He did not kill your husband. But he did kill the man you just mentioned. He killed the judge who sentenced me to the electric chair. Yes. Eric entered his home in Manhattan and shot him to death inside his own private study."

"My God!" she cursed.

"Yes. I suppose it was also justice for my son, my son Donnie. The son who I never knew existed until recently. I only found out about it because one of my people named Maxwell Hawker who was conveniently placed in a high government position granted me access to privileged government files; the very late Maxwell Hawker; another fine proposition cast into the grave, courtesy of your husband Robert. Yes. I knew your husband was aware of the truth concerning Donnie's paternity. But he kept it from me. As had my son's mother, Francesca. Yes. Francesca, Donnie's mother; that slut of a mother of his; I was denied access to my son because of her. That whore. She kept my son a secret from me all along. And now I will never be able to get to see my son ever. It is too late. I have lost my last remaining child and heir that remained in this world! He died in hospital three days ago and now it is payback for all my losses incurred. After his death, I cleared that debt owed to me by removing his mother from circulation. She deceived me. And she too met with bullets in her lying head. Her corpse was then fed to the alligators in medieval fashion!"

Cassandra was stunned beyond belief. But then her erupting anger overcame her initial overpowering fears and she said, "You are pure evil!"

Domenico ignored the insult and insisted, "And your husband is next, Cassandra. Yes. He is going to pay just like everyone else will pay for hurting me; BECAUSE NO ONE IS GOING TO GET AWAY THIS

TIME. No, my dear; they are all going to burn inside their coffins, screaming bloody murder for ever thinking that Domenico Armando was dead and done with. They will curse the day they ever underestimated Domenico Armando. You can believe that with your sweet lips, my beautiful and lovely prisoner, Cassandra Stewart!"

Cassandra now became struck by courage. "Hurting you? Is that the lie you are saying? That anyone hurt you? You have some twisted nerve, Domenico. My husband doesn't hurt anyone. You are the one who hurts people! And he will get you for this when he finds you!!!"

Domenico said coolly, "My dear lady, I will be the one to find him first. You don't have to worry about that! Yes. I am going to find all my enemies. Your husband is at the top of that list. Because let me tell you something, Cassandra. Let me repeat my words again and again and again to you: your husband has gone too far this time. Yes. He has gone too far. He has cost me my last remaining son. He cost me my world! He cost me my peace of mind! He cost me my sanity! He cost me the chance to save my Donnie. Yes. And because of that, he also cost me the opportunity to ever get to know him. If I was not locked up inside that hellhole for over six months, awaiting that ridiculous time and date for my appointment scheduled with death, then I could have helped my son. I could have saved him from death!"

"But Robert avenged what happened to Donnie. The doctor in question was shot and killed by the police!" Cassandra insisted.

Domenico nodded his head yet volcanically serious-faced, "Yes, I know. It was perhaps the only noble deed your husband has ever done for me! As well as ridding the earth from those syndicate animals who entered this country during the last several months when I was locked away. Yes. My absence left a vacuum in the underworld's power structure. So the main powerful leaders – one from Russia, another from the Middle East and another from Greece had entered this country during that time to try and takeover my territory. I suppose at least I should give credit where credit is due. Robert did end their quest quite recently. At least for once the police have done me a service when Robert and his cavalry cornered those animals and shot them down before they could do anything about taking over my former power lands!"

Cassandra wished to correct his wrongful assertions. "Domenico, you are very mistaken. Robert and the police did not shoot them dead for your benefit; it was for the benefit of society. Those people also tried to hurt him very badly."

Domenico knew the entire story. He briefly smiled in thought. "Yes. I know. And that tale indeed would be comical if not for its tragedy. I know what they wanted to do with your husband. I am also sure that Robert did not count on being famous when he sent me up the river. But nonetheless, he was promoted to Commander of Police for supposedly sending me to my death. But at the same time, he was also glorified by certain members of the underworld, such as those three syndicate leaders from Russia, Greece and the Middle East - who entered New York after feeling safe to do so, meaning once they thought I was finally removed as a roadblock to them. And following that, your husband had suddenly become glorified by those three animals in question in a surprising twist to that tale. They became obsessed with the very man who was able to get the Great Domenico Armando out of their way! So then they decided to work together in partnership for the sole purpose in accumulating something they called the **Prize**, meaning your husband. Yes. Robert Stewart became the famous **Prize** as they put it.

"They figured that with Robert on their side, they would be able to control every law-enforcement agency around the entire world. They would have unlimited freedom from police and government apprehension. They also figured that with Robert on their side, they could defeat any enemy army anywhere in the world. They also considered that with Robert on their side, they would become the richest and most powerful men in the world's history. And they were willing to go to any great lengths in order to possess your husband and make use of his great skills and talents. Yes. And then they planned to play with his mind, to put him under the knife, so to speak. So that he would forget who he was and begin his new life as their soldier. They also planned to kill you Cassandra and all of Robert's family, including his children and your baby; the baby of yours and Robert's. And they planned to do this, so that after his memory of his past has been wiped out and his orientation was driven only to events in their world, such men considered it necessary that nothing in this world connected to his past must remain in existence, meaning his family. To prevent the possibility of his old memories from his old life ever resurfacing, should he have ever come face to face with any of you again at some point in the future!"

Cassandra snapped, "But he uncovered their very sinister plot and he stopped them cold. He knew they were criminals who tried to takeover this town, which was why they entered it. And he stopped the three of them dead in their tracks before they could put their horrible scheme into practise!" she said proudly.

Domenico nodded also calmer. "Yes. The police shot them dead like those syndicate dogs deserved! I suppose that was also another plus for me, courtesy of the menacing police!"

"So how did you get out of death row or escape? And where are the rest of the children, my baby? I want to see them!" Cassandra cried.

Domenico responded simply, "And you will see them soon enough. But let me assure you that the children and your baby son are being well taken care of in another section of this house. But I suppose I will answer your question as to what I am doing here.

"I broke out of prison at 4:00 a.m. this morning. That was why your husband Robert left early this morning, shortly after he received the police call alerting him of the trouble down at the city's death row house. In order not to alarm you, he would not reveal anything until he went to investigate and was certain of what happened. And moments after he left the house, that was when my people stormed your home and took possession of both you and the children once Robert was distracted away from the scene. And we were able to snatch all of you before your husband had time to confirm the truth - and then put his entire family into protective custody.

"Yes. Even inside that wretched death row facility, I knew about my last remaining son's condition. He basically was struck with the same sort of cancer as me-his father. I was furious. I wanted to help him. But I was too late. Anyway, the escape was planned. Helicopters had circled above the prison house building which was detected on the surveillance monitors inside. Many of the prison guards then rushed outside to see what was happening, which worked to our purpose. The circling choppers caused a distraction. And this distraction lured many of those death row facility armed guards outside into the death trap which awaited them shortly thereafter. It was well executed and superb. Then the helicopters dropped large quantities of poison gas killing all the guards stationed outside. Then my armed foot soldiers in the vicinity wearing gas masks entered the prison facility, overpowering the remainder of the guards yet stationed inside – and my men began shooting open doors to cells and so forth with enough extra gas masks to hand to me and the rest of the death row inmates. I simply escaped that death row facility taking all the 23 death row inmates who were all locked up in different cells with me.

"We were flown away via several different choppers, enough to carry all of us to freedom."

Cassandra was devastated, "BUT WHY? Why would you also release those convicted serial murderers?"

Domenico replied, "I guess it was much in line with the very same rational as to why those syndicate leaders wanted possession of your husband's unique traits. I wanted those fiendish scums to also become my new trained killers. As you can see via Eric's performance earlier, my technique had worked to perfection. I gave him a dose of a unique drug which in fact works to invade the nervous system and paralyses the patient's will. Now he and the rest of them are subject to my control, my will. And they will simply become tools to help me take my revenge to which reaches across the entire world! Yes. I escaped and kidnapped all the death row inmate prisoners, taking them with me. I plan to transform them all into my killers and consecutively unleash them out into the world to do my bidding for me – and do away with all my enemies' first beginning in all parts of this country!"

477

"That is insane, Domenico! You are crazy! You will not get away with it!" Cassandra insisted.

"I already have!" Domenico demanded.

Cassandra became deeply sick by the thought: "And now because of Donnie, you are playing some sick plot of revenge against Robert?"

Domenico explained: "If that is how you wish to interpret it, then yes. It is revenge for the deaths of all my family which I hold your husband as directly responsible for all the events which cost me their lives. And soon Robert is going to feel what I want him to feel. He will think what I want him to think and then he will understand what I want him to understand. And that is the most unbearable emotional pain imaginable! He will feel the regret, the remorse, the power of great loss that he has caused me! That is why you and your children are here, Cassandra. It will be Robert's family for my family. Just as he cost me my precious loved ones, so too will he lose his precious articles of family and blood! Yes. I will indeed become this world's **Figure of Death**.

"But just as I have learnt about the identity to the son I never even knew existed, I still have yet to learn of the location of my grandson. Yes. Robert has been very clever in concealing that piece of information from me, because not even Maxwell Hawker was able to ascertain knowledge of that. His whereabouts is still a mystery to me. Your husband thinks he will keep him from me forever, hey. But I will locate him. You see, he is all I have left in this world that carries my blood, my genes. And I need to make him an Armando heir.

"I will replace my family with that family belonging to my bitterest nemesis - and at the same time, I will also rebuild my empire to even greater heights than it ever was. What is now completely destroyed. But your husband should never have underestimated me, Cassandra, because my empire is being rebuilt to great heights reaching right up to the sky – and it is being rebuilt very rapidly as we speak! And would you like to know how it is happening? Of course you do. Let me tell you.

"I call it: my unlimited money-making software. It is software that works very quickly. It is software that only trades on sure bets. It is like going to the casino and having the slot machines rigged to win every time you put coins in them. The software is capable of making unlimited money.

"And that is how I will rebuild my empire again very rapidly! Everything Robert took away from me will be restored. But this time my finances will grow even larger than ever. I will make more money than anyone else in this world could ever dream of. I am not talking millions or billions. I am talking multi-trillions.

"The world is my oyster. I am talking about world domination. With this software, I only need to invest a modest figure and my money keeps growing exponentially. It is infinite! You know how water comes easily when

478

you turn on a tap? Well, then, that is how easy this software will make money for whoever uses it. And only I will ever have access to it.

"This software will be the new key to rebuilding my even greater kingdom than ever before. And then... then, everything and everyone will belong to me; what I have in my possession is the most lucrative cash-making software in the world. With it in my grasp, there are no limitations to how much money I can make.

"The fact is, with this software that is now in my possession, I can make more money in one day than what one thousand Robert Stewart's can make in a lifetime. That is how great it is. As I said, this software trades only on sure bets. It has a 100% win rate and never loses anything, even in a most volatile market place. And it will double my money every time!

"So you see, with this software, money not only grows on trees as they say, but this software actually creates the trees in which the money grows! And it happens every day, day in and day out, forever and ever! That is how it works, like a chain reaction of nuclear proportions.

"I will now have more money than I know what to do with. But I need someone very special to share it all with. Money equals power. It is that simple. I liberated this software from a great engineer in this country. In crux, this software is designed to make money out of thin air. It is not crazy. It is true. This is how money is made all secretly by the richest people in the world.

"This software is simply software which trades on markets such as the derivatives market. And you know something. With this software, it will make so much money in one place, whilst draining liquid funds from all other avenues – and I will result in crushing and finally collapsing this country's economy. And once the American economy crumbles, it won't be long before the world economy is in a complete shambles. Businesses, large and small, will be facing bankruptcy. Banks will be forced to close their doors to potential customers who would never be able to afford to pay back loans with ruinous interest rates. And the world will be struck with the worst global recession in its history. One they will NEVER be able to get out of! This will be part of my national and global revenge against all those in America and the entire world who have hurt me! Especially those pigs in the American government!

"This software will result in me trading trillions everyday and profiting exponentially each time! And all I do is nothing. The computers are the machines which does it all for me; running the software. And all I do is sit back and make money, withdrawing what I want – when I want.

"Yes. I will takeover the world with this special computer software. I control most of the world's money-making systems which now flows through me.

"This software is generations ahead of its time. It is so advanced, that even the wealthy cannot begin to make as much as this software is making me. I will make more money than billionaires and even trillionaires. Because I will takeover their entire operations with this software, eliminating all my competition everywhere around the world!

"The software simply runs itself and it never dies. This software always bets on sure trades and the results are called the doubling-and-tripling effects; unlimited money. I am now crazy with joy. I want to spoil my loved ones with what I have.

"And now that I have also discovered the formula and the correct medical procedure to cure my illness, my possibilities right now are endless. They are boundless. They are infinite and eternal. It is as simple as that!" Domenico grabbed a palm-of-the-hand-sized box from the inside of his silk jacket pocket and waved it before Cassandra's face for a moment as he insisted, "With this box of top-of-the-line SEIRIN Acupuncture needles, I will choose the right points, dating back thousands of years in ancient medical scrolls to cure my cancer. Yes. With the knowledge of the right points in old acupuncture theories, any disease is curable. Yes, indeed!

"So tell me Cassandra, since you have been such an appreciative audience to me, what is it that I can do for you that will put a smile on that lovely face of yours?"

Cassandra replied to this madman she was forced, up until now, to listen to in silence, "If you won't let me see the children, then I want to see my husband. That is all I want! Please let me see him!"

Domenico grunted in gesture. "I see." Then he flicked his hand in the air approvingly and said, "Ok, Cassandra. If you want to see your husband, then your husband is exactly what I will bring you as long as you promise to cheer up, ok!"

She did not respond.

Domenico said almost expressionless, "All right. Since you insist on seeing your husband, I will instruct Thomas to bring him here. I will order him to find him, walk up to him and shoot him, and then voila – he will also become a very welcome guest in my domain!"

Cassandra rose from her couch in fright and shouted in panic, "Don't you hurt my husband!"

Domenico was amused. "Relax Cassandra, relax. It will only be a tranquiliser. I mean, what do you think? I should just call your husband and invite him here like that for one of our enjoyable rounds in a game of chess. No, my dear; your husband is a master combatant. He is in fact a one-man army. My mercenary men are all well-trained soldiers, but they are not suicidal. I don't think they would appreciate being put in the position to give up their lives so easily like that. But have no fear," he said deviously, with a careful plan up his sleeve. "You want to see Robert, well, let me tell you my dear. Bringing Robert here is indeed a very, very important part of the plan!"

Domenico then became much preoccupied in his next deadly agenda. He thought to himself: Yes, Robert Stewart! Bringing you here is of the utmost importance; because, our next meeting will be the beginning of your end. In fact, I am going to cause you more pain than you can ever imagine. Your pain will truly be hard to bear! And I cannot wait for that to all unfold. Yes. This very day will be the day for my justice being finally served against you. And like I explained to your lovely wife, no one is going to get away this time!!!

CHAPTER 6

Robert Stewart was posted on foot outside the gates of Domenico Armando's hideout with the entire New York City Police Department SWAT team cordoning the entire area with legions of men armed with heavy artillery, covering all sides of the building by 2:00 p.m. that afternoon.

Domenico viewed this with binoculars through a crack of his slightly opened curtains before a window inside his main living room area. And thought to himself: Damn it. Robert Stewart located the hideout. I wonder how he found out. Maybe he traced one of my men's tracks. Maybe he intercepted someone making a call somewhere. Or perhaps he traced Thomas to me and then realised this house was put in his late grandfather's name. Any scenario was possible. Perhaps someone even by mistake left some fingerprints at his home during the smuggling process of his wife and children inside his house earlier. Who knows?

Robert was standing behind a large white police van with his police partner, John McCallum. The van was used for cover in case the enemy's people began firing at them. Robert held a police rifle in his hand pointed at the target's house from his hiding spot and said to John, "In the right time we will be able to storm inside that place. Right now all we need is to see Armando poke his head out of the covers for just one second and we can shoot him down, overpower his men and rescue my family! Just one second is all I need and it will be over!"

"We'll get him, partner!" John assured him.

Robert insisted as time went by and no clean shot being given to their target, "Maybe I have to arrange somehow to get inside that house. Maybe we might have to open direct communications with Armando and see if he'll let me in. Surely he wants to get even with me more than he does anybody else. He is just using Cassandra and the kids to get to me. But if I can convince him somehow to let them go, maybe we can do a clean swap, a simple exchange; me for Cassandra and the kids."

John said, "Are you sure that will work?"

Robert replied, "Well, it's worth a shot. Then again, knowing the arrogant bastard Domenico is, he might just refuse the swap, but insist on holding me as well as my family captive in there. But that doesn't matter. Whilst my family is trapped inside there, we cannot open fire and blow that place up with Armando and all his men to pieces with our heavy artillery. So I think our best bet right now is if I can somehow convince him to let me inside and that way I'll have a better chance of freeing my family who are trapped in there."

John stated, "But you know Armando will not let you in wearing any weapon. I mean, he knows you. He wouldn't even let you walk in there with your ballpoint pen in your pocket. He knows your special training by the SIA. He knows you could turn any hard object into a dangerous weapon!"

Robert said coolly, "I don't need anything. Just my hands will be enough!" Robert whipped out his mobile phone from the inside of his navy blue jacket pocket and asked John for the number to Armando's house. John had it written down on his police pad in his pocket. John gave him the number as Robert pressed the digits onto his phone and dialled.

The phone on the other end answered. It wasn't Domenico. It was another man. Robert insisted, "This is Commander Robert Stewart. Just put Domenico Armando on the phone. I want to talk to him."

Within thirty seconds flat, Domenico Armando was on the other side of the phone. "Robert Stewart. It has been a while. How are you? I am glad you are here. Although I am not happy you brought an army of uninvited guests with you. This changes the game somewhat. But in any case, I was just about to come and collect you. It seems that you beat me to the punch by tracking down my location; very clever once again!"

Robert went straight to the point as a man who never liked beating around the bush. "How is Cassandra and my three children? You better not have hurt them in any way, Domenico!"

Domenico replied rather entertained, "Your family are perfectly healthy… for now. But it is up to you to make sure they remain that way, all right!"

Robert's voice cut through the phone like a knife, "What do you want?"

Domenico revealed in simple terms, "Well, I wanted to invite you here all along and that invitation still stands. I will let you in but on the condition that you enter alone and of course completely unarmed. The usual checks will be performed to ensure my orders are followed carefully, you understand?"

Robert said gladly that his plan was working so far, "Loud and clear. Ok. I want to see my wife and children. Let's get this underway!"

"Very well," Domenico insisted. "By the way, how have you been? I hope I haven't ruined your day too much by again breaking out of prison and then causing you much heartache in the aftermath of that!"

Robert smiled sardonically, "Now Domenico, how could you ruin anyone's day. You're welcome anyplace, anytime, you know that. We're always glad to see you."

Domenico chuckled, "Thank you very much for the sarcasm. The feelings are mutual, believe me. So, my very good friend; now that I am assured of your high spirits let us proceed with your entrance into my domain. I too cannot wait to see you. I have a great surprise for you!"

Robert said, yet maintaining his irony, but at the same time a tad of worry entered in the back of his mind, "Oh, I bet you do. I can't wait to see what it is!"

Robert knew there was going to be trouble, big trouble, upon his entrance inside the devil's castle. He felt he was walking into a trap. But his family was in there. He had to do whatever it took to free them. If that meant walking into a trap, well, he planned to deal with that and every Armando action with his own counter-attacking Stewart reaction!

CHAPTER 7

As soon as Robert Stewart was summoned inside the living room of the Armando hideout, isolated from his allies and completely alone, bearing no weapons on him, he was surrounded by many burly-looking enemy henchmen guards in one corner of the room, when Domenico stood aside his wife Cassandra and two children, Ryan and Stephanie all posted together at the other end.

In a quick surprising twist of anguish being unleashed without delay, Domenico then paced himself away from them to another corner and Robert's nightmarish experience began.

That was when three henchmen who stood in front of the row of legions of Armando bullies blocking Robert's path, then fired their weapons they held in their hands at Cassandra and the children.

It seemed to happen as expediently as dynamite exploding. After the gunfire was over, Cassandra and the children fell onto the hard wooden floor motionless.

Robert was struck by the greatest surprise of them all by Armando. At first he couldn't fathom what he just saw. His beloved family cut down in cold blood right before his eyes. What a cruel act of fate had befallen him.

The guards cleared a path enough for Robert to run as fast as he could towards his family and kneel in anguish before his wife and children's motionless bodies, lying onto the hard floor, eyes closed, after being cut down so cruelly as they were before his very eyes.

They didn't move. He assumed they were dead at first glance... just like that! No mercy!

Robert then overheard Domenico's barking venomously poisonous words being pronounced much bitterly from metres behind him: "How does it feel Robert? How does it feel to watch your family being shot down in cold blood like that? I have relived that memory of what you did to my family, my children in Rome every day since it happened, over and over again. You also robbed me of time spent with my now dead son Donnie. You denied me of ever knowing my last-remaining son on earth. Now I get to enjoy watching you suffer; watching you witness the joy and the light in your life being replaced by misery and death too. Yes. The joy of your family has been taken away from you as you have done to me! How does it feel, Robert Stewart? I want to know that you are suffering as I have suffered for many months thinking about the deaths of my family – and now you forced me to experience the tragic death of the very last son and would-be heir I had left in this world. So how does it feel, Robert? Are you suffering enough?"

Robert glanced at the lifeless bodies of his wife and children sprawled onto the ground before him as he knelt down to examine their seeming corpses. Robert quickly lost himself. He lost complete control of his emotions that instant.

Robert Stewart jumped onto his feet as if by a high-powered springboard. He grabbed the first person in his path with his arm squeezing around his neck in a headlock. And he twisted his body in expert precision until the target's neck snapped and Thomas fell to the ground instantly dead.

This all happened within seconds.

Robert struck the next target with his fist, a powerful killer blow. He sent his nose into his brain. And the next target Robert stabbed him with two knife-fingers extended expertly from his right hand and jabbed into both the henchman's eyes.

Before anymore fatalities could be performed, a striking voice was sounded in the background, overpowering the sudden commotion erupting inside the room.

It was Domenico Armando who ordered the rest of his men: "Shoot him! Shoot him now!"

And several of his men who had guns trained at Robert then fired their weapons and within a split second Robert's body was thrown onto the hard floor. And he was transformed into a corpse-like motionless state resembling his family who were shot down only moments earlier!

CHAPTER 8

Robert Stewart woke up inside a prison dungeon room facility two hours later. He was lying on his back onto the grey brick cold hard floor.

The dungeon room was made up of steel and brick. No windows. There was a great steel door out front that only flickered a tiny bit of light inside through a small, square-shaped peephole. The walls were made of brick. There was a small array of steel bars which was cemented into the centre of the concrete ceiling, shielding a small-sized sunroof above the top of the facility.

Initially, Robert never thought he would wake up alive. But it seemed as though Domenico ordered him to be shot with tranquilisers. And Robert knew his family were not dead either. They were only much temporarily incapacitated the same way as he had been. As they were lying on the ground earlier, he checked their pulses on the sides of their necks discreetly. There was life in them. But he was mad as hell that the enemy treated them that way. After all, they were innocent in all this. If Domenico had a grudge against him, he should have just vented that grudge on him-Robert alone. And not involve his family as he had. And that was why Robert well and truly hated Domenico right now with a bitter vengeance. That was why Robert attacked Armando's men so ferociously just some hours before.

Robert knew Domenico's plan was not to kill him or his family.

No.

Domenico wanted his family for himself and to make him suffer by that consequence.

What happened next was the master stroke that Robert used in order to free himself and his entire family from that madman's captivity.

Within an hour after he had woken up, an Armando guard entered his cell only to see Robert's feet suspended off the floor, with his trouser belt wrapped around his neck, whilst the buckle was tied around the steel bars stretched onto the ceiling.

The guard freaked-out. Damn. He hanged himself! The Boss is not going to be pleased one iota that his primary enemy has been let off the hook so easily.

As the guard neared him, Robert's eyes came to life and with his hard boot he kicked him in the head twice until the guard gave out a gasp and rolled onto the brick floor losing consciousness very quickly. Robert then untangled himself free. He performed a somersault manoeuvre until he was loose from his self-made restraint.

He took the guard's weapon and the keys he uncorked from his belt and left the cell, closing the door behind him, locking the guard inside with the liberated keys which dangled from a small chain.

NOW as he checked the loaded weapon in his hand, he began shooting every enemy in his sight - and took several more weapons from them so he wouldn't run out of ammunition in his great quest to free himself and his family from their harsh confinements.

Robert used the keys to open every door on his way out. He used the keys to open a padlock-bolted room outside the secret prison dungeon facility.

He saw his children Ryan and Stephanie huddled together inside. His baby son Joseph was inside a cradle. "Ok, kids. Let's go. Stick behind me!" Robert said to them. "Ryan, carry your brother baby Joseph securely as I intend to protect all of you with my life! Stick close behind me. I will shield you all when we come across trouble!"

Robert shot every guard in his way until he made it to the living room and saw Domenico inside still with his wife Cassandra.

Domenico was still preoccupied, studying the numbers of police men and women who surrounded every square inch of his current hiding place. There were stacks of them. He was unable to count all of them, that was how large a number of lawmen and lawwomen which swarmed his proximity at present; hundreds and hundreds of them. They brought in tanks, police dogs, heavy artillery of every sort and make up and choppers combing the entire area back and forth.

Domenico was still peeking through a curtain crack outside one of the windows. His back was facing Robert. He quickly turned around to face his enemy when Robert alerted him to his abrupt presence.

Domenico was surprised when he heard Robert calling out his name. Domenico was speechless as Robert cursed: "Domenico, I will kill you first before you go anywhere near my family again!"

Domenico fetched inside his blazer pocket, but before his hand could reach for his gun, Robert fired several shots into his chest.

Domenico fell onto the ground. Robert saw blood pouring out of him.

Robert quickly called out to his wife: "Come on, Cassandra. Let's go!"

Within 20 seconds, Robert was out of the house with his wife and children he shielded with his body and guided with both of his arms. Once they had all reached safety outside, Robert gave the order to the SWAT team: "Shoot! Fire the missiles! Blow the house up! Destroy Armando and all his men, RIGHT NOW!"

And within breakneck speed, the house that once occupied the devil and his henchmen had become a house of roaring flames and ash that burnt its entire existence and everyone inside it to the ground!

Robert placed his arms tightly around his entire family. His wife now held their baby in her arms. Robert was overwhelmed with joy that his family were all safe and sound. He then looked down at his baby son being rocked peacefully in his mother's arms and said: "Your father will always protect you Joseph. No matter what happens, I will always keep you, your mother and all my children safe from harm!"

Cassandra and the kids, Ryan and Stephanie, all felt safe once again being protected by the presence of the Great Robert Stewart.

Robert then led his entire family safely towards an awaiting police car and said: "Let's go home!"

Robert thought that this upcoming Christmas in three days' time and its consecutive New Year's celebrations would be as shattered as his last few. But this year he vowed it would be different. Because this holiday season would end in a new beginning for them all: the enemy was dead!

THE FINAL OFFENSIVE

Inside his underground fortification bomb shelter compound, beneath the blown-up ash remains of his former existing compound aboveground, the Titan was preparing full-scale military combat operations against his enemies.

"I will never die!" he cursed. "I will never succumb to death by any means and grant my dirty scum enemies a joyful gathering at my tomb. No, never. But my infinite achievements will truly mark the era of all my enemies' defeats. All of them and their crusading allies who choose to deliver me to ruins will succumb but instead to their bloody crushing deaths. My name will bear the title of conqueror. And the world is my conquest! I will reign forever! And as long as I reign, my only thoughts will be of triumph and victory. And in order to accomplish that, I will spill the blood of all who oppose me. And I will become the nightmare that all of them will never forget and never awaken from, nor will they ever recover from my brutal assault to be delivered against them all! I will execute everyone who is against me!"

Inside his secret underground steel-and-concrete hideaway, the Titan began planning, as per usual, his grand-scale vendettas. He began a symphonic orchestra of death-inflicting imaginings on an unprecedented scale, to be conducted inside his very powerful, but at the same time, unmercifully-cast and ruthlessly brutal mind.

The Titan planned to commit the greatest atrocity in the history of the evolution to man's existence. He planned to kill billions of people in his quest for supreme victory and security of his ascent to the top of the throne. His hierarchical ascension as ultimate king ruler over all which exists and all which had ever existed was in the works. Such supremacy he vowed, was his and his alone, in a world that he would strike with his ferocious blows, driven by an iron will to kill and kill and never stop killing, until all those he wanted removed from the earth, were in fact obliterated by his brutal strong clenched hands and fists alone!

The Titan would enforce his words again and again and again before his surrounding army troops gathered before him: "I will never die! I will never grant my enemies the satisfaction of seeing my corpse; NEVER. But instead, I will live with a joyful heart at the crushed and butchered corpses of all those who would otherwise wish to stab their swords into my heart and my soul! My achievements will be infinite! And that knowledge alone will drive the deadly swords instead into the guts of all the scourge and pestilence

490

in the world who think for one cold moment that they could ever win victory against me! And my name will mean the death of them all; the mass murder of the world. And that will be my very unique contribution to the world's history literature publications for all that will remain on this earth to see – and for all future generations to dwell on such a remarkable and historical factual knowledge of my infinite and supremely undefeatable being! That – and that alone – will bear my name!

"I am the conqueror. And the Titan will be what the world then calls me! I will dominate the earth. And everyone in it will be brought before me and sworn to a New World Order. One that is controlled by me! One that will be obeyed by only me! I will walk the streets and become enthralled in the people's cheers and chants and salutes of me and my name, bearing the mark of the greatest power they have ever known - and to which the world has ever seen! I will become eternal!

"But for that reality to be realized, first I must begin a war that will end all of civilization that belongs to my enemies! I must clean the earth of all the filth who is against my glory and whose existence in fact makes the world itself unglorified! Billions around the world, people of every nation, must be made extinct. And there must be no hole on this earth large enough or strong enough to withstand my powerful nuclear and atomic detonations targeted for them. And there must be no gas mask technologically advanced enough that my poisonous gas fumes to be unleashed upon them at the same time cannot penetrate, until such deadly substances enter their lungs, and paralyse their bodies completely, as the sight of my immortal being before them, will paralyse their minds and hearts and their entire wills, when they are forced to die before me in bitter agonies as they wished to end me just the same. I will smash them all to pieces as they even dared to contemplate any such vision of my corpse lying before their dirty shoes and feet!

"This next war I declare will not come to an end the way my enemies and their allies predict via my death. No. But it will end only with the extermination of my number one enemy - and all his allied forces and those people around him who choose to serve but HIM! I will live to see and bear witness to the execution and complete annihilation of all my world of spiteful enemies! This will be no game of chance. No. This will be a strategic assault delivered by me and unleashed by my forces on all angles of the hemisphere, until my arsenal strikes everyone on all ends of the globe, who are trying to see my corpse riddled with their own arsenal; arsenal that will prove powerless next to my own globally-advanced supremely powerful weaponry.

"With my eternal being and my iron will and undefeated character, I will find the world guilty of all atrocities they have taken it upon themselves to judge me with. And as a result, I-and-I alone, will sentence them all to the debris and garbage which made up the ingredients of their creations. I will send them back to the ground into the form that was used to create them at birth. I will turn their mortal beings back into dust. I will turn the fresh soil over all their dirty remains, until their filthy stench of dust and human diseases is made invisible and in a state with which ceases to exist forever and ever! The complete obliteration of all the filth and pollution which walks this earth with all their belongings; their families, their friends, their associates, towns, villages, states, territories and countries as a whole, which harboured such scum, will become my ultimate mission to accomplish in this world!

"And from that day forward, following the catastrophic defeats of all my enemies, the name of me, which will be forever held as highest in all the world's history books – the name the Titan will forever be imbedded into the skulls of all who remain in this world - and all who I will allow to live after I unleash my gigantic plans of mass destruction on all the soil that consumes this earth; such corrupted soil which has fed the seeds of human corruption and allowed such living germs to breathe life above it - and create a universe which has thus been created: one of infected disease-carrying stink bomb scum, which has placed their diseased penises into other diseased vaginas, that has ejaculated sperm into the uterus, resulting in a birth, in fact an evolutionary epidemic of the sort of world which exists today: a world overcome and overpopulated by the seeds of their fathers and mothers which bore them: seeds of the most contemptible and disloyal stinky filthy kind, which has resulted on what we hear every time we watch the 6 o'clock newscasts: that is a world which bears the seeds of corruption, which has filled our earth with such scum criminal-inflicting men and women – or should I say - such insults to the superior male and lovely female forms!

"The misery which such people have inflicted upon me, will be inflicted back onto them a thousand-fold! My attacks on them will be fuelled by my rage against them. And the world will bear witness to what happens when anyone wishes to put their miserable existences against my supreme being, which will forever reign upon them! This war will last for days, weeks, months, even years, if that is what it takes – until I stamp out all political, economic and social opposition to me! The world will be struck by my hands of complete demolition against all my enemies and all those around them which sustains their lives. I will turn what brings them life into what they will become – dust. All the seeds of fruit and vegetables they plant to give them life will be destroyed. Those who do not first die from my high-powered arsenal, will first die from thirst and starvation, as a result of my unleashing a cease-to-exist policy against all the water and crops they use to give them life into their miserable beings! That will be my personal and most ultimate triumph against this horrible filthy planet which dared cast their lives against that of the great and almighty Titan!

"I am the magician! I am the saviour, the hero, the greatest general the world has ever seen! I will save this earth finally from such pestilence, whose sole existences indeed threaten its entire well-being and livelihood! I

492

will stop them, such human filth! I will stop their plans of world corruption by in fact sending the world collapsing onto their skulls - and crushing their entire beings into this earth, with which had unjustly ever granted them the privilege to ever be born, a privilege not one of them had ever... ever deserved!"

The Titan, aka Domenico Armando, spent three months underground the bombed ruins of his last sighting on the outskirts of New York City. On the evening of the 23rd of March 1991, the infamous tyrant put together his complete plans of mass destruction. It was evident that Domenico Armando became a man completely desperate to win in the end of his life of already unleashed destruction and death being inflicted on a grand scale! Domenico was at the end of his rope now. He wanted things to move swiftly.

The incident of his shooting by Robert Stewart that day left him paralysed from the waist down. One of the bullets fired into his chest lodged into his spine which caused his legs now to become immobile. He commanded his army regime secretly underground whilst trapped onto a wheelchair.

Robert Stewart's shooting of him was bad, but not mortal as he hoped. Domenico fell to the ground that instant. Robert ran outside the former building aboveground, rescuing his wife and children to safety as the proverbial white knight he was indeed thought to be.

But in the hurried successful escape attempt, Robert did not know at the time that Domenico was not only still alive, but that Domenico Armando had secured a swift escape route inside, in which he managed to crawl into, only seconds before Robert gave the order to his SWAT team comrades to, "Blow the place up with Armando and all his men!"

Domenico Armando, in severe agonizing pain, only moments from losing consciousness, had still managed to crawl onto the hard wooden floor of the house living room using his hands and elbows, until he managed to reach the secret trap door situated inside, beneath a small rug covering a segment of the wooden floor.

Domenico removed a remote control from his blazer pocket which activated the secure lock, thus enabling him to push the trap door open by pressing the wooden hinged platform in a downward position - and then he threw himself down the hole, missing the stairs and collapsing onto the concrete one hundred feet below, at the same time he depressed a red button on his remote control still in his hand, which then closed the trap door that was disguised by wood panel on the surface, but made of fireproof steel in the middle. Then the bomb blasts went off destroying the house aboveground, as Domenico made it out of there, plunging himself to safety in the nick of time.

Domenico Armando proved himself as a man with nine lives. And the fact that he cheated death by Robert's bullets and escaped death by the SWAT team arsenal, solidified in his mind that his life was special – and as if by some divine right – the fact that he survived such extraordinary odds, he took it as a sign from destiny that he was born to rule over all - and his right to destroy all was thus sealed as an act of fate!

Inside his secretly-installed bomb shelter that was replicated into a palace compound, Domenico shouted and screamed for help. "Come. Come. Come quickly. Where are you doctors? Come quickly. Look at what my enemies have done to me! All is lost. They have taken everything from me! Look at what they have done. I cannot feel my legs. I cannot move my feet and legs. Quick. Quick. Quickly hurry to me before I die and all is lost. Hurry and give me necessary medical care before I die! Come on. Where are you?"

Eventually Domenico's people had located him. And when they had, he was rushed to their underground Medical Emergency Room fitted inside, prepped for surgery. The surgery was successful enough in removing the bullets from his body, but the scars left behind from that ordeal became a major confirmation to his bitterly fuelled and unquenched rage inside of him, which led him to his path of mass destruction this day. His paralysis became a constant black memory for him of that ordeal. It was a constant reminder of his number one enemy who he blamed responsible for not only the deaths of all his children, but the destruction of his entire kingdom now blown to smoke by the arsenal of such an enemy's allies – and Robert Stewart's now successful attempts, or so he thought, in immobilizing the great dictator by delivering to him right now a life of paralysis.

But Domenico's iron will much stemmed from his rage. And his rage meant a great need for revenge right now. He swore an oath to his staff before him: "I will walk again! You hear me? I am Domenico Armando. You better believe that I will get off this chair one day soon!" His determination was awe-inspiring. And equally as ambitious were his plans to get back at the world at large and cost them all what he had lost this very day. But he would cost them more! He planned to cost those fucking bastards their very fucking lives too as they intended, though only failed to cost him his! He wanted to end all of Western civilization with Europe and the East, mixed with the Middle East, everything-everywhere as part of his plans for demolition on a complete grand scale!

Domenico Armando felt no compassion, no mercy and no second thoughts, nor any consideration for any and all the lives he planned to destroy as part of his payback conspiracies. His mind was now programmed for one objective: that was to kill and kill and keep killing - until there was no one left on the outside to which meant nothing to him.

Domenico Armando spent three months inside his inconspicuous underground bomb shelter hideout, he used as his final place of refuge from all those who targeted him in the world. As he stayed in such fully-furnished quarters, he spent his time recovering from his injuries sustained as a result from his shooting incident - and planning for the end of his life's struggles. He planned for the end of all existences which he deemed a threat to him. He declared that as they-those fiends out there in this world had done his family in - that they would never succeed in putting the final stake into his heart. He vowed that he-and-he alone would become the last man standing in this bitter war which flared between Robert Stewart and Domenico Armando.

Domenico was situated thirty metres below the ground, protected by his well-armed group of guards and by four-metre thick concrete walls; the bombproof compound which truly managed to save his life from the severe unleashing of explosive artillery that was fired aboveground some months ago.

Now Domenico declared that that simple fact of his life yet cheating and defying death once again became a special sign to him, his surely divine right to exercise his will at any cost. He felt that he was something special, that was protected and shielded from all ill occurrences around him, and to which what was directed upon him. He now felt that his life meant a great purpose whilst everybody else's was subjected to meaningless nothingness; just a world of expendable clowns in comparison to his special existence!

NOW, Domenico Armando gathered his closest henchmen aids around him. From inside his secretly protected concrete bomb shelter, he commanded his troops to inflict his will of complete annihilation of billions of people around the world. He instructed them on where to purchase the weaponry and bombs to use, mainly from Middle Eastern suppliers, and then to smuggle such nuclear arsenal into all parts of the world, ready for his final instructions by radio to have them all detonate. He vowed: "This will be the final end! This time my powerful offensive will cause all the world below my enemies' feet to be blown to hell - and what will remain will resemble the primitive ages. But do not despair. It will not take us forever to rebuild the earth's monuments and plant new seeds for its crops, once we have sacrificed all our enemies and what brings them life; of course not.

"And no rally by any opposing force made against us to holdout our attacks will be successful. And Robert Stewart will never be able to assemble himself with his allies against us ever again. He will never be able to stop my plans of turning this earth back to dust on time! His objective was always to take down my kingdom. But just as he has destroyed my world, I will destroy his world but only to an irreversible degree. He will fail in any attempts to ever launch a large-scale offensive against me ever again. Because this time, I will attack before he has a chance to know what is going on around him. This time I will smoke him out before he can ever plan to do the same to me! Because my friends, this time, I have the true element of surprise at bay. I have the element of real surprise.

"You see, Robert does not even know that I am still alive. No, no, no, no! He thinks his foolish heroic antics aboveground three months ago had resulted in my untimely demise. But my old friend Robert Stewart is in for the shock of his life when he witnesses all that was-will no longer be in existence. He will realize it when his guard is at its lowest point. And what better way for him to be taken by surprise, when we start attacking at a time that he is in fact at his most unsuspecting. He thinks I am dead. But once my plans for complete demolition of all man and buildings and crops and water supplies to my enemies is unleashed, Robert, well, if he finally figures out the truth, it will only be done when it is too late for him to be able to do anything about it! That, friends, is a guarantee! Artillery and weapons of mass destruction will be ordered to be fired left, right and centre quite relentlessly. I will direct this battle against the world right from these quarters here. This will be my Command Post until the complete destruction of the world of my enemies at large has been fulfilled!

"Yes. Robert Stewart has caused me much harm and the bulk of my manpower and resources has been lost. But despite such setbacks, Robert Stewart's delusions in thinking that I, the Titan's days becoming ever numbered were a great miscalculation on his part. Because, friends – I will never accept defeat! I will NEVER accept death! I will never accept anything apart from a complete victory from all this turmoil which has been directed towards me! I will extricate myself from this onslaught - and I will rectify the Armando kingdom to be the great powerful institution that it once was – and then I will bring hell to the world at large. I will be the magician who resurrects himself from the grave - and unleashes retribution onto his masses of enemies to which the world has never been dealt with before.

"Yes. Robert Stewart had fought me long and hard. His ambition was to render me and my army regime immobile, a hopeless situation. But shortly it will become evident to everyone-evident to the entire fucking world that Robert Stewart failed in his quest and quests to render me gone-finished-incapacitated, dead. Because I will now turn things around, and believe me, it will be him who will suffer the grief-stricken sorrow of loss after loss after loss all around him, beginning with all his allies in Washington, D.C. Yes, the White House. We must destroy everyone inside there and the building itself - and all who can assist Robert Stewart in his quest against me and all that belongs to me! Washington, D.C., must be made to cease to exist with the White House and all its government departments. We must strike there first. Right there into the heart of this country! Then Robert will have no allies to help him win his fight against me. Because when I first remove all those who support him in allegiance, then I will make my final move to smash Robert Stewart to pieces! I will hurt him and I will squeeze the life out of him with my bare hands!" he shouted, with fists clenched together in the air as if he pictured Robert Stewart standing in front of him, his throat now cast into his hands, the Titan squeezing and squeezing and skinning the fucking destructive life out of his entire fucking being!

"Yes, my friend Robert Stewart!" he cursed such words. Domenico always referred to his bitter staunchest enemy as 'friend'. A term he used in the most sarcastic of ways which had a true double meaning. Whenever he referred to Robert Stewart as 'friend', it meant hard-core adversary, bitter opponent and his most hated enemy on the face of this scorch-filled earth in his mind. He went on: "Robert Stewart, my 'friend', you will never get away from my war to be unleashed against you. Don't even think of escaping like some meaningless refugee, because it is no use. There will be no escape for you or any of your little average soldiers. Because everywhere in this entire world will become a battleground. There will be nowhere for you to go. Nowhere to run and no rock big enough to hide under from my powerful arsenal that will strike all ends of the globe and all at once. You will indeed become witness to what hell on earth truly means, my 'friend' Robert Stewart! Yes. This will become the great Domenico Armando's final act. **The Final Offensive**, if you will! That is something you can bet on, my 'friend'. And there will be no escape from it-from any of it! You will see. Yes. You will see with your last fucking breath, you irritating son of a bitch who has cost me everything that is dear to me.

"You cost me everything that I held dearest to my heart and my soul. YOU Stewart are now going to be caught up in one gigantic fiery hell on earth after another, until you feel your heart collapsing into your stomach from the unimaginable pressure and stress I will bring to your miserable life and your hellish existence, you despicable fucking bastard that marks the name of Robert Stewart! And my war will never be over until large parts-in fact all the general population of your scummy world is brought into the brink of the Stone Age. You will all be made to crumble into the mud-in dust, which is what I will turn all your mortal beings into once you get a taste of my superior arsenal to be detonated against you all! Yes.

"Meanwhile, I will gloss over the entire World Map I hold in my hands as I strategically plan my greatest assault against the earth in all its major cities, towns, villages… I will plant nuclear weapons in all such areas, covering all the countries across the globe in my complete wipe out plans against the earth and all the worms who occupy it-worms who will all cease to exist very, very soon. Yes. With what I have planned for you all, there will be no glimmer of hope for any of you to extricate yourselves out of this. There will be no hope for your survivals. Yes. With the World Map in my hands, my very being encompasses all that belongs on earth today-and all that will be gone by tomorrow. I will recruit a high-calibre team of soldiers who will never suffer from any war-weary syndrome; because they will carry out my orders of destruction to the letter. They will all do everything I tell them without question. They will be groomed to never become tired in the face of battle. And they will wear no scars from the absolute acts of destructive warfare operations they will be forced to unleash at my behest-my will-my demands. Demands which will be carried out without question, without debate and absolutely no hesitation whatsoever! They will carry out the Titan's Final Revenge against the world he now currently loathes with every might and every force of his immortal being!

"Yes, Robert Stewart; you hear that? I am immortal, you bastard. The rest of you are mortals! But not me! No, no, no, no, nooooooooooooooo!" he shouted. "I cannot die. I cannot be defeated. Hear that! Understand that! And accept that you bloody fool, Robert Stewart! And remember also that both the endurance of you-yourself and your cavalry will run out as surely before my plans are even partially met. But me-yes, I and my team will never puff out. My soldiers' oaths to me will bind them to the instruction manual which I have mastered by my own hands, titled 'Victory', yes, The Complete Victory Manual.

"You see, as my men follow my training methods into the battlefields across the globe, they will be trained to destroy all who is deemed the opposition - and to win victory to me-their great Titan. And at the same time as they storm the battlegrounds with their artillery, they will know the meaning of unflinching attacks - and orchestrating unending duels against your clumsy people and their armies. Your men can only puff out in tiresome bouts of fatigue and injuries. But my men are trained like superhuman robots who do not know the definition of fatigue and losing a fight. Yes, my friend Robert Stewart! That is the difference between my tireless army and your tiresome weak and ineffective regime! Indeed. Your troops are not fit enough to take action against my men. Nooooooooooooo! Never! I will first attack this country's capital; its heartland in Washington, D.C.

"And you my friend Robert Stewart, both you and your clowns you call soldiers, will never be able to put so much as a dent against me and my final plans against you all! You will never be able to ward off such forceful attacks I will unleash against you all; the whole fucking world. You hear that Stewart! Hear it my friend. Hear it well, with your dying breaths. The dying breaths of both you and all your mentally and physically weak American army regiments!

"YOU cannot keep up with me! You cannot outrun me even after you have put me in a wheelchair. Even then I can still beat you! I can outmatch you anytime, anyplace - both mentally and physically. But what you have done to me, Robert Stewart, is just a slight inconvenience, only a temporary measure; because I will rise again. I will stand up off this chair and

I will walk over you. I will run you down Robert Stewart! I will put you into the ground my friend. And I will do this personally! Yes. I have instructed my people to spare your life by their hands, because they are ordered to deliver you here to me for our most certain final confrontation. Yes. It will be the true Duel of Titans.

"Because I want to fight you Robert Stewart; I want to beat the very life out of you personally with my bare hands! I want to smash you to pieces. I want to indulge in the sight of your very blood spilling out of every corner of your mortal being – and I want to witness that sight as well as relish in the sounds of your screams right before my very eyes and ears. Yes. I will not be denied that final reward; because it is destiny; because it is fate; and because I am special. That is why I am still alive today. The simple reality of my existence is something that I must consider as a divine right. Because I am better than everyone else, including you Robert Stewart. Like I said before, I am immortal! I am forever! What are you? You are nothing but a freak show compared to me. You are a meaningless little mortal.

"But me-yes me, I am destiny. I am forever! I am GOD! Yes. I am the GOD of earth. That is what I am. I am the ruler of all living things! I am the supernatural! The rest of you are flies and mosquitoes to be smashed with my fists and crushed with my feet at my will. Yes. At my fucking will! At my will, you will all be crushed to crusty sand dunes and dusty land clouds on the side of an unmade road. Yes Robert. This is no propaganda. This is real. And any defensive acts by you will be considered absurd in competition against me-the one true ruler of the globe and all things living and dead! You understand that Robert? I am the ruler of all that is living and all that will be made dead! Which means that you will be controlled by me and your life on earth will be made to suffer by me as you live and breathe here on earth – just as equally as your life will succumb to everlasting damnation by my attacks and punishment to be delivered against you in the hereafter.

"I will punish you forever. You will be haunted by my fury for all of eternity, both in flesh on earth and then in spirit in the hereafter, you son of a bitch. Because I am God; only God can survive bullets and explosions. Only God can survive what I have survived. I am divine! I am everlasting. I am supernatural! I am forever and ever! And you will be forever and ever enslaved by me, Robert Stewart. I curse your life on earth. And I curse your eternal soul.

"You will never know the meaning of peace again. You will never succumb to the desires of fondling your wife's breasts in your marital bed again. As you have cost me my women, so you too shall never find pleasure in the arms of your delectable wife ever again. No. Robert Stewart. I will cost you everything. Including indulging yourself in extreme sexual pleasures by touching your wife's breasts and tasting her moist aromatically love-scented vagina! You will never know love again, because I will take it all away from you. I will punish you for all of eternity. You think I am dead and your life is safe, hmmm? How can you possibly think that Robert Stewart? How can you think that you could kill me? How can you think that any bullet or bomb can kill me? I am special! I am divine! I am truly not from this earth! I have survived all what I have survived because I am GOD! I am the ruler of all things great and small. And just as I can allow peace and prosperity, I have the power-the divine right-and the eternal fortitude to take it all away!

"And you Stewart-you Robert Stewart are within my sights. You will never kiss your wife again. You will never experience the pleasure of orgasming inside her precious vagina again, because I will take her from you just as you took my wife from me. You will know pain. You will know suffering. You will know what it is like to cry blood! You will be brought to me to experience all the same suffering in which you have inflicted upon me. Because now it is my turn to be on the offensive!

"You have paralysed me to the point that I cannot indulge in the beauty of a woman again. You have brought extreme pain to me whilst at the same time you think you will be able to lay every night with your wife in a world in which you have envisioned in your very warped and foolish mind that is now safe and peaceful without the menacing Domenico Armando around to fuck you up any further. You are wrong, Robert Stewart, because I am still around. And I do not permit you to perform acts in which you have prevented me from performing.

"I disapprove of your actions of engaging in sexual conduct with your wife as you have forced me onto this chair, unable to satisfy my own longings of sweet female companionship. I forbid you Robert! Get off her! Get away from her vagina… You cannot indulge anymore. I am God. I forbid you to laugh, to have sexual pleasure from a woman to which your actions have prohibited me-your own God-the creator and ruler of all things great and small to indulge in. You have shot me. You have paralysed me. I cannot enter another woman, so I do not permit you to laugh or enter your wife's juicy and succulent sweet-scented vagina.

"YOU must suffer as you have made me suffer. If I cannot laugh, you must not laugh. If I cannot orgasm, you can never experience the pleasure of orgasm again. You have hurt me. You have defied me! You have insulted your God-ME! You must face the consequences! You must face your punishment! I will destroy you, Robert Stewart. You cannot be happy right now as I am here miserable. No. You cannot go to work, win cases, get promoted, then go home and have dinner with your family, your children, and then lead your wife to the bedroom and fuck her senseless. No.

"If I cannot fuck a woman, then neither will you. You do not deserve any happiness to which you have cost me. All my children are dead! My wife and mistresses are gone. I am paralysed. I cannot be with another woman as I am right now-as you have made me to be. And you think that my misery means your happiness? You think that my destruction means your success? NEVER! You hear me, Robert Stewart? Never! I am God. I command you to suffer! I curse the very manhood to which you use on your wife to give you sexual pleasure. I curse you to a life of abstinence as you have forced upon me. You listen to me, Robert. You are not permitted to touch your wife again! I do not permit you to enter your wife anymore. You hear me, Robert? I am God! Do as I tell you.

"I am the creator of all things. You must obey me, Robert. You must do as I tell you. Get away from her. Get away. You do not deserve her. Just don't touch her anymore! I condemn you to eternal suffering. You must cry as you have made me-your God cry. You will weep as I weep! You will abstain from any sexual contact with Cassandra as you have forced me to abstain from the beauty of the female breasts and vagina. You have defied me! Stop it! Stop entering your wife! I know what you are doing right now in the bedroom! Stop it, you bastard! You cannot take pleasure in any activity to which you have forbid your God to partake in. I am God. And you have made me weep. It is not fair-it is not right for the great God Domenico Armando, ruler of all things, to succumb to misery at the same time as those mistakes of creation by my hands are profiting from all I have given to the world! No. Get away from her! Stop kissing your wife! Stop fondling her naked body. Stop entering her. I forbid it. You hear me, Robert Stewart! I forbid it! Get off her! Get away! Get away, you son of a bitch, fucking bastard! I can instinctively feel your activities. I can sense what you are doing as if my soldiers-my angels are reporting it to me-to my mind. Stop it, Robert Stewart! Stop it! Nooooooooooo!"

Domenico Armando considered Robert Stewart's defiance of his ruling to abstain from any and all sexual contact with his wife Cassandra utterly intolerable. So Domenico had no choice in himself but to resort to drastic measures in order to ensure that Robert would be unable to indulge in any form of orgasmic pleasure with his goddess-resembling wife Cassandra.

Domenico, as he sat on his wheelchair inside his main War Planning Room of his underground bomb shelter compound, before a huge desk which contained a large map of the world for his final plans of global destruction, he looked up at all his trusted personnel who surrounded him. Such men looked at him in deep astonished shock. Domenico indeed managed to startle them quite frantically via his recent performance of such ludicrously insane word deliveries and the proclamations to such manner of their delivery, its innuendos and maniacal sideshows had his men eye him quite startled. They were in fact subjected to becoming a sight of jaw-dropping, almost comical dumbfounded speechless frightened figures at the sight of Domenico and his quite bizarre, if not, just blatant weird demonstrations he just displayed before his men, whom appeared scared as hell to even interrupt Domenico from his earlier insane whirls of explosive rants and lunatic ravings out loud.

But anyhow, Domenico seemed better now. He took a deep breath and glanced around the desk at all his standing men looking down on him as if he was some mentally deranged misfit. Domenico ordered to them: "Look away. What the hell are you all staring at, you fools? What am I, do you think? Some crazy case study for you amateurs to examine as if you were intern doctors trying to diagnose a new disease! So just look away!"

Domenico found it insulting that he should be stared at this way! So as they all moved their eyes to the floor out of his depth, Domenico then turned to one of the men, he called Harold. He said, "Yes, you, Harold. You don't need to back off! Come a little closer. After all, I know you too hate Robert Stewart! So that is why I am assigning you with this special delicate task of ensuring that Robert meanwhile cannot partake in anymore pleasure activities whatsoever, meaning with his wife!"

Harold edged forward to his boss with a bent ear facing down close to receive his master's fervent instruction.

Harold was certainly no fan of Robert Stewart's and for good reason. His name was Harold. In fact, his full name was Harold Mar. Yes. Harold Mar. He was in fact one of this country's former United States Presidents. President Harold Mar as he was once called, almost ten years ago.

Robert had recently nailed Harold to the wall for his past sins. Harold was also keen to take revenge against Robert. That was why Domenico had rescued Harold from his condemned fate by the hands of their mutual enemy, named Robert Stewart.

Robert's actions against the former country's president had in fact resulted in Harold Mar being sentenced to life in prison, the maximum-security facility in the state of New York.

Domenico was always a man who thrived on recruiting specific talent who shared a mutual interest. That current shared interest revolved around one man: one name: Robert Stewart. And the mutual feelings shared by the two of them were hatred for that specific cop in question - and a thirst for wanting to inflict extreme pain upon him.

Harold Mar spent over four months in prison. From a man running the country, he became a man running the harshest federal prison in the state of New York. What did running the prison mean? It simply meant that Harold Mar found himself as a type of ringleader in such a facility. Many of the criminals in there in fact held the former president in a ridiculous sort of high regard. Because as president of the United States, Harold Mar was a true ratbag; a ratbag who in fact protected ratbags of the like across the country. His single-term show as president spelled free reign to all criminals at the detriment of the United States of America. He basically ignored all crimes in which he could; as president, he never enforced the law. There was no regulatory legislation policies imposed in crime prevention. Instead, he seemed to favour deregulating the entire justice system which caused hell to be unleashed upon the police, but caused the criminals to prosper. For that, criminals at large who operated in the United States during that period favoured Harold Mar, at the same time, just as any do-gooder civilian and the police despised the hell out of the scum.

Harold Mar knew enough about society and the mechanics of becoming a different sort of president simply by understanding the characters of the masses, or the weaknesses of enough people he thought he could prey upon in exchange to secure their votes. By weakening the laws of the justice system against prosecution to such criminals, Harold Mar believed he could accumulate hefty bribes through such unscrupulous individuals in the country, all under the table and surreptitiously of course, at the same time as he believed that most of the country who were either corrupt or who could become accustomed to a life of corruption, may in fact vote for him quite easily if they found he was one of the only few presidents during their generation who could assist them in escaping prosecution.

The fiendish Harold Mar was mistaken!

His ambitions to win even a second term in office were shattered!

His criminal immoral ways cost him the second election in a landslide defeat against him.

Harold Mar's presidency was so corrupt-driven that he became simply a symbol of chaos, mayhem and destruction to the entire democratic way of life for the American people.

Harold Mar in fact was the most divisive president in the country's history. He turned the rich against the poor and vice versa. His racist, prejudice ideology turned Americans against all migrants. His Immigration Policies were soon driven to stop any migrant from entering the United States as permanent residents to live. And such philosophy caused constant bashings and threats against a lot of the migrant population already residing in the country.

Harold Mar also hated Medicare. He hated the unemployed. He hated the poverty-stricken members of the community he would usually verbally beat up as deadbeats and wastes of oxygen that should all be sent to concentration camps. He hated the disabled. He often would say in private to his colleagues, 'What the hell is their use? Why should we fork out taxpayers' money to assist them medically? They can't work. They can't bribe me. They are of no benefit to me! They should be slaughtered!'

Harold Mar in four years as president caused the country so much social, political and economic damage that the country was still recovering from the ordeal of his presidency almost ten years later. Harold Mar's Industrial Relations Policies had turned bosses against workers and vice versa. He destroyed working conditions for employees by forcing such workers to sign individual contracts which stripped them of any fairness in the workplace and significantly contributed to reducing their wages. On a Social Justice Level, he turned masses of people against the police. Constantly the police were getting gang bashed, knifed, attacked with broken glass from alcohol beer and spirit bottles and threatened with bodily harm even on sightings by such people, whilst these official constabulary lawmen and lawwomen were conducting their foot patrol rounds in all various districts across the nation. In the eyes of the unscrupulous hoods in the country they thought: 'Harold Mar is our president. His laws are designed to favour us and protect us from the law. So how dare you pigs try to arrest us? You don't fuck with us, you snot-nosed pigs or we'll damage you. We answer to our president, not you pig police. So either you fuck off from us and get stuffed and leave us alone or we will invoke the Harry Truman doctrine of 'massive retaliation' against you turds; got that!'

And that was the resultant negative impact on American society of having someone as corrupt, immoral and dangerously callous as Harold Mar as the country's president. Chaos ensued; where even the bad guys began attacking the bad guys, their rivals. The country became a war zone, a breeding ground for anarchy. And even the derelict arsehole hoods of the country, who favoured that equally clueless dumbshit walking disaster area President Harold Mar, soon realized that Harold Mar's policies, resulted in all-out anarchy being imposed on everyone on a grand scale without exception. It was too realised that suddenly that fraudulent president became a danger to even the hoods of the community, which then resulted in everyone turning against the once criminal-favoured Republican leader, costing him from winning another term in office.

But whilst he served his time in prison, Harold Mar was still looked upon favourably by many of the dangerous crooks who shared prison time with him inside the same facility. After all, they knew he was one of them, using his power once upon a time to make their lives easier, in exchange for a bribe and some perks. So Harold Mar fortunately never had to worry about being raped, sodomized, bashed or killed by a gang of black inmates or white inmates for that matter for any past indiscretions against them.

No. But the former president sure hated laundry duty. From running the country, he was then subjected to manufacturing fucking number plates, he thought with scorn. And the man behind it all was seriously a name he loathed with extreme vigour and contempt. The name Robert Stewart rang in his ears like a curse, as he was carrying a mop and bucket being ordered to clean up any and all crap stains on the entire prison house walls, floors – and the dreadful toilet area. Fuck that made me puke, he also thought to himself. From running the country, I was reduced to wiping prisoners' piss and shit splatters around the dunny, he cursed out loud. Fuck you, Robert Stewart! Fuck you for this. He was often heard saying.

504

Eventually word of the president's extreme frustrations spread around the entire prison facility, until one of the prison guard Titan moles got wind and approached the corrupt former president with a proposition by the Titan: 'How would you like to get the fuck out of here and secure your revenge against Robert Stewart at the same time?'

Of course Harold Mar was interested. 'But how will it be done, how will it be done?' he asked naively.

The Titan-taught prison guard coached him in the true art of deception which made Harold Mar's attempts of criminal dealings look like a production in Romper Room in comparison. The mole prison guard ushered him to a quiet place in the prison facility. A place where no other witnesses were present and no surveillance cameras could snoop in to the gossip between them.

The guard held a small-sized white drug tablet before the former country chief and said, 'Just swallow this tablet. It will make you appear dead long enough for us to get you out of here legitimately and safely to the Titan's secret quarters. Don't worry. The drug will stop your heart only long enough for the doctors to pronounce you dead. Then when you are safely out of here as a would-be corpse, we'll inject another drug into your arm to counter the effects of this one which will arrange for your death certificate to be issued – and by that time, you will be safely taken into the bosom of the Titan. Ok. So don't worry!'

The ex-president of the country remarkably was not worried. Even if the drug had somehow managed to kill him even accidently, he certainly would not even care. Because in himself, the humiliation of prison and all that prison life endured for a man of his former stature especially, was a worse punishment than any immediate death sentence could present to him.

So, in essence, the drug worked well – and much like his new boss, the Titan - both Harold Mar and Domenico Armando were at this time considered by the world to be: two dead maniacs who got what they deserved by Robert Stewart!

Anyhow, Domenico Armando spoke to the former president of his harsh plans he had against Robert Stewart. It was a delicate assignment and he wanted someone as capable as the former US President to carry out such plans for him, personally. "Don't worry," Domenico assured him. "We'll have you fitted up with all the proper disguises so no one will recognise you. But I need you to enter Robert's house and put my special plan against him into effect. Let me tell you what it is about!"

The sixty-year-old, white-haired, shifty-eyed, medium-built former president was all eagerness, as the Titan would pronounce this second, his master plan to him concerning their mutual enemy, Robert Stewart!

505

Domenico said mean-spiritedly, "You know, it makes me unhappy that Robert is able to... how shall I say... quite candidly... look... I don't want Robert to be able to fuck his wife anymore. So I want drastic actions to be put in place to ensure that he cannot anymore... you know... fuck her!"

The ex-president portrayed signs of complete eagerness as he remarked, "Tell me what you want me to do, Master. Tell me what you want me to do!"

Domenico replied, "All right. This is a delicate measure. You know a delicate assignment; a very sensitive task. So I want put in place certain actions that will make sure that Robert is unable to engage in any further sexual conduct with his wife. So, this is what I want done: Now, Cassandra cannot satisfy her husband in the bedroom, if, how shall I put it, she has suddenly lost her marbles... you know... if we alter her state of mind, to make her somewhat temporarily crazy, until we remove Robert from the picture, so to speak! Let me be extremely clear. I want his wife driven to a state of insanity so that even Robert cannot recognise her, let alone, be able to partake in any further sexual encounters with her. And the way it will be done is as follows: when she is alone in the house of both hers and Robert's, I want her to be shown images of me, you know via secretly-planted hologram technology. And that is where you come in.

"I want you to plant the projector equipment well and discreetly inside Robert Stewart's house. And make sure you are not seen. This equipment will suit my purpose quite nicely. I will be heard talking to Cassandra when she is alone inside the house with no one around. You know, in an attempt to drive her crazy as only an image of me can do. My voice will order her to pack her things at once as I want to marry her. That she has no choice but to leave Robert and come and live with me. I will tell her that I will take the children and plan to snatch her baby once more - and that if she wants to ever see them again, she will have no choice in the matter but to cater to my demands. She has to come and live with me. You know, it will be an ultimatum. She will definitely have no choice. She has to leave Robert! 'You will marry me Cassandra! I will take you away from Robert! Your husband's children will belong to me! I am coming after your husband! Quickly get ready. Pack your things; I'm coming for you too! Hurry up and be ready for me when I pay you a visit!'

"You know, when she sees and hears the image and the voice of a man believed to be dead, she will think she is losing her mind. She will report this to Robert, and before long, even Robert will be forced to question his wife's sanity and her sudden declining state of mind. She will be driven to the depths of such fear, panic and paranoia by such images, that I am sure she will have more pressing concerns to deal with than entering the bed of both her and her husband - and entertaining any further acts of lovemaking against my wishes. So yes, I, the creator, must play God with their lives in order to

506

separate them long enough until I can destroy Robert and leave the path clear for me – in order for me this time to claim his wife and children as my own, forever and ever!

"I know, I know what you are thinking. I am trapped in this chair. But my friend, Mr. President, as you were once called; I want you to look into my eyes and understand that I am the creator of all things living and all things dead; that means, I am God. And today I may be subjected to a wheelchair, courtesy of our mutual enemy Robert Stewart, but tomorrow, I will rise again and I will walk; because I am special. I am supernatural! And I-and-I alone am a miracle worker, which the rest of you ordinary people could not possibly understand. But suffice it to say, that once I remove Robert from the picture, and once I am able to walk again, and the energy below my waist is completely restored, then Cassandra will in fact join me in bed each and every morning, afternoon and evening. Her name will cease to exist as Cassandra Stewart. But instead it will become Cassandra Armando. And she will become my wife through and through, forever and ever. Because I am a miracle worker and I am the creator of all things and all happenings in this world! I can make the impossible happen. Please don't ever forget that or you may not only offend me, but you will disappoint me – and I am sure you never want that to happen. Because just as my rewards to loyalty are great, so too are my punishments for disloyalty around me. And never forget that either.

"And once Cassandra is with me, we will blow up that house of Cassandra and Robert's and erase any past memories of her life with him as if it had never even existed, understood! I want you to hear all my plans. Then when you understand everything to the minutest detail, we will put in motion the first phase which is to ensure that Robert cannot ever share his bed with Cassandra again. Because make no mistake, she will be with me, Harold. She will be mine, whether she likes it or not. After I make love to her and show her what true love is, I am sure she will like it. I am positive of that; because I am God. I can make anything happen. I can snap my fingers and make anyone think and do as I wish them to!"

Domenico Armando realized that his state of paralysis was a sign of a weakened leader before his loyal henchmen posted before him. He could see it in their eyes whenever he spoke to them and commanded them of his detailed instructions concerning the world's complete demolition of all living things and all what consumed it, meaning buildings. But Domenico was determined to rise off his chair soon, very soon, and he knew that miracle in itself, that display of his much believed supernatural qualities, would restore confidence back to his seeming not-very-confident henchmen situated before him.

He studied their eyes, and through the many eyes of dismay he witnessed all around him, he could read their minds much in contrast to what

507

he wanted them to believe. But he shouted to them all in a yet existing extremely powerful voice and insisted: "I will win the war, you hear me, you derelicts! I will win the war! All my enemies will face defeat. Not me! But my enemies! Don't you ever doubt that for even one moment! Or I will be sore at all of you. And you do not want to disappoint me and face my vengeful wrath as my enemies, especially Robert Stewart will soon face - understand?

"So you better get it in your heads right now and transform the look of a lack of confidence to utter convincing belief in me that the war will be won. My goals will become victorious. I will win. And the enemy, Robert Stewart, and all those in the world who he sees as allies, will also be brought down to destruction. They will all fall to the ground and be made extinct. Remember that. And believe it, or so help you all, I will force you to believe in that one truth, one way or another. So kindly do not test me, or there will become a line of dead Robert Stewart's planted right here in this room before my very shoes!"

Domenico Armando had planned and plotted his vast attack for three months now. He wished to wait no more in unleashing his wholesale offensive against the entire world. He wanted all his men planted in all sections of the United States as well as every city, village, state and country across the entire globe, all in readiness, for his final order to open fire on all things living and all people breathing.

But years of war against Robert Stewart had not proceeded without any battle scars left behind. Besides his currently endured disability and handicap which left him confined to a wheelchair right now, his months of planning his revenge on a global scale, mixed with his growing hatred for Robert, had left further marks and battle scars upon Domenico.

Domenico would never accept his fate as being paralysed for life in a wheelchair. For accepting that was as shameful as accepting his imminent and much humiliating defeat by the hands of the one man in the world he loathed the most: Police Chief Commissioner Robert Stewart!

Yes, he scorned in thought; after it was believed that Domenico died three months ago in those bomb blasts above his head, that bastard son of a bitch devious man Robert Stewart was then promoted to Chief of Police. What a mark of blackness! Domenico cursed constantly in thought. The day that bastard Robert Stewart crippled me from the waist down, he also gets to celebrate that unholy day as the day for his ultimate promotion to Chief of Police! That was the blackest day in the history of this country, Domenico scorned to himself. But where does that fiendish man Robert Stewart think he will go further next, hmm. Because I will soon rewrite history – and the day in question will be erased from all the records, and my own day will be marked on the calendar as the day I sought my wholesale retributions against the world at large, finishing with that piece of garbage named Robert Stewart!

But despite his supernatural myths he proclaimed of himself before his troop inside his underground bomb shelter, Domenico Armando indeed was a man who appeared at his worst. He was a weakened broken man, a mess. He could not use his legs. And as a result, he could not exercise for months. He looked diminished, less muscular.

In fact, he resembled a wreck. He had aged terribly. His brain tumour seizures were getting worse. In the explosions which took place above ground three months ago, all accurate theories he researched and located in old ancient medical scrolls of how to cure himself from his inoperable brain tumour were destroyed in the bomb blasts. His ingenious stock market software was also blown up. 'I should have forecasted what was to happen sooner. As a consequence, I should have placed such precious articles of mine inside this secure bombproof facility for safekeeping. But now everything is lost. All my great research and uncovered secrets turned to ash, because of that bastard Robert Stewart. That man has truly cost me everything sacred. But I cannot let my people know about any chinks in my armour. No. All humans by nature are treacherous. I must forever remain strong and almighty before them. Because if I even hint that I may very well die soon, they may be less inclined to follow my orders of complete destruction against all my enemies on the outside. They may even betray me. I must maintain the facade! I must appear supernatural before them. And above all else, I must live long enough until my plans to wipe out all my enemies have been accomplished successfully. Then... then... who gives a shit what anyone thinks.

'Those bastards who claim to be loyal to me here and now can all be sent to blow up in hell and perish just like the rest of my enemies on the outside, for all I care. But for now, I must maintain my supernatural facade. I must have my people follow my orders carefully and precisely. Then once they have outlived their usefulness to me, and completed my bidding for me, then I will eliminate all of them as their eyes constantly betray me. I must destroy them all too with the rest before they have a chance to betray me with more than their eyes... but they may betray me at a practical level if given the chance. So first I will maintain the act before them... then I will arrange for their deaths. I will order all of them to be eliminated once they have first done what I want them to do.

'It is a pity that such drastic measures must be taken, but at the end of the day, all of humanity's contagious disloyalty which stretches to all man, even those directly serving me, must all be made extinct before they have a chance to perform the ultimate act of disloyalty, which is to betray me-their God! Yes!' he thought to himself.

509

But now Domenico's health on all levels was diminishing. He did not look the same despite his acts and pretences to the contrary. His men noticed this but were too scared to speak out openly about it, not only among themselves, but especially before their master. They were frightened that even if they uttered among themselves the words of how bad Domenico looked, that one of them, possibly a spy, may report such considered treacherous overtones to their master, and Domenico Armando would then surely order them dead then and there on the spot!

But as he was seated on his wheelchair, and confined to it all the time, Domenico was certainly a diminished man. He surely did not resemble the once vital robust man of great charisma and force he was known to be. Even his back became curved from sitting in that damn wheelchair. His back no longer erect like a straight arrow anymore, but becoming bent. In fact, Domenico's entire appearance, his bad posture, his lean drawn face, his indented but still maniacal and delusional eyes was shocking to his people. He just looked terrible! His back became hunched, his eyes sunken in and dull, and his face became devoid of all colour. A white-yellowish appearance which was a mixture of his overall deteriorating health, to the fact that he was confined in underground seclusion for months, not ever seeing the outside sunshine once during that twelve-week period.

Domenico's magically ever-powerful appearance and powerful voice were always trademarks which commanded authority and made such a great impression on all those who served him, but now that former self of his was dead. What was left was a mere ghost, a broken vessel rapidly transformed into a skeletal scarecrow. And on top of all that, his brain tumour seizures were getting worse and worse than ever before. Constantly he shouted in pain whenever he was struck with seizures. And standby doctors had readied-morphine syringes to inject his arms with on a several-times-a-day basis. It was remarkable that old hag of a dog was still breathing; these were the thoughts many were forced to concede, but only in their own individual minds, much secretly of course.

Perhaps everyone inside this room just hoped the old resembling lizard would just finally croak, meaning to die. Then they would not have to stomach the ruthless tyrant's mass destructive plans he had in store for the world any longer. In fact, Domenico's death was a sure-fire way of escaping it all. But as they may have hoped for his death - the older, sicker and uglier he looked, the more frightening his barks and orders became. The son of a bitch rat bastard was certainly becoming delusional and less focused with every passing second. He actually thought he was God. He actually thought that his team of expert assassins who surrounded him day and night guarding him actually believed it. If that were the case, then the once brilliant Domenico

510

Armando brain had certainly transformed to a man of complete and utter fucking stupidity, many were forced to concede individually in their minds.

But just as Domenico played pretentious games with them, at the same time, his men were covering their true emotions from Domenico equally as expertly. Just as Domenico planned to kill them once they outlived their usefulness to him, they too only hoped Domenico would die before they were ordered to bomb countries of the world in a fashion that would make Hitler's Holocaust seem small-scale in comparison. Just fucking die you monstrously brutal piece of shit, many thought to themselves, whilst maintaining the ever-so caring and attentive facades of loyal soldiers and warriors before this mentally and physically sick lunatic, who now referred to himself as the Titan!

Domenico Armando in fact never planned to honour his men or reward them in any way upon completion of his plans of global destruction. No. Domenico only planned to have them all meet death the same way as he ordered them to kill every one of his enemies across the entire world for him; especially that man who still, with much delusional vigour, called himself Mr. President.

That scum, he thought to himself. I will blow that fuckwit insult of a president straight into hell with the rest of them, once he has outlived his usefulness to me! Does that dumb cunt of a failed leader seriously think he will get away with all to what he has done as president of this country; no, sir. That piece of shit has betrayed everyone, including me! The fact that he does not realize it proves how really stupid and dopey that old son of a bitch truly is!

That fucking bastard cocksucker was behind the ludicrously insane policies in this nation which allowed such criminal doctors in all fields to flourish in this country, whom ultimately cost me the lives of one daughter and my son. My son, Donnie! Oh, my son. You are never far from my thoughts! How I would have loved to meet with you even just once and comfort you in your time of grief. Oh, my son. I have been robbed as much as you have from knowing your father and how much he loved you. If only you had any idea what extremes I would have gone to in order to save your life from such an untimely tragedy which had befallen you! If only you knew!

I would have ordered the deaths of a million men if that's what it took to save you my son. I would have blown up entire countries just to have you here with me this day. But now it is all too late! You are dead! And my grief for that loss will haunt me for the rest of my days! But that scum behind yours and my precious Annemarie's death – the scum who helped such corruption in all of medicine flourish and torture its patients, as they tortured such children of mine, will be destroyed once I have outlived my plans of complete destruction to befall this wicked crime-ridden world of ours. A world with no morals! A world with not one man in it who has the courage to do what is right for people like you, my dead children. No. That scum former American president is going to pay dearly very soon! He has betrayed me and all my family and its loved ones. He will be tortured gruesomely in the end. And then I will blow him up right with the rest of the filth on this earth. That my children is my guarantee to you!

As I mourn your deaths daily, my heart and my mind at the same time is filled with fire and rage to be unleashed upon this hellish existence we call a world. It is a horrible earth without justice. But do not fret my dearly departed dead children. Your deaths will be completely avenged by my hands. And mine alone. And I will light candles for you all daily in memory of your precious lives. And I will forever work to rewrite the wrongs of your deaths! I will never forget you all! And I will never forget all my enemies who were responsible for taking you all from me. No. They are all as good as history! Gone! Finished! Dead! Yes. Dead! Dead! Dead! Dead! Dead! And dead again!

Domenico's plans of grandeur and conquering and ultimately taking over the world, were truly seen as a farce by his armies of delegates who constantly surrounded him. Domenico tried to hide his true state of health by talking big, sounding strong, but his growing frail appearance gave the true state of his mortal being away at every sight of his weakened and constantly weakening appearance. He was thinner, leaner. He was not dressed as immaculately as he was accustomed to. His usual attire of expensive Italian suits or silk robes were not worn for months. Instead, he wore what appeared to be old coats which looked wrinkled all over, the collars turned up instead of sitting firmly down in tidy fashion.

Domenico's entire dress sense at present indeed matched his state of health: declined and tattered! But Domenico was still adamant to live out his plans of total anarchy and unleashing his revolution against all who lived, both man and objects, large and small - no larger than Robert Stewart - and in his eyes, no smaller than that scum who was situated right before him at this moment who still called himself, Mr. President, even though that freak show of a leader was booted out of office years ago, and only after serving just one term in the so-called Oval Office of the White House! Ahh, where does that low-class rat think he will go after my revenge is complete, hmm? I tell you, it will be nowhere but to his damn grave! He kept telling himself.

Right now, Domenico was on a critical mission. He knew this was his last opportunity and his final chance to end it all concerning his enemies. To see them all dead before he himself finally died. But he did not want his entourage of war-fighting captains and soldiers who were summoned before him at present to know the truth of his mortality. So he constantly played the game by pronouncing untruths before them all time after time after time: I am GOD. I am the ruler of all things! I am immortal. The world will die, but I… I will be forever in power. I cannot be defeated! I cannot be killed! I have survived countless hostile attacks. I have survived much onslaught thrown my way! But I am God. I cannot be killed by any man, bullet or explosive device! No. I am the greatest of the great! Everyone else are small ants compared to me. Those ants will be stepped on and squashed by my very shoes into the cement and the dirty ground they choose to walk on and live.

Domenico considered that everyone was stupid next to him. He considered that if he kept repeating his big lies even before his own would-be loyal armies gathered before him, that eventually they would believe every word he said, especially such false proclamations that he was, God and the ruler of all things!

They will believe me. They will destroy everyone for me! They will obey no one but me. He thought such vivid nonsense to himself over and over again, as if to psyche himself into even believing something untrue and remotely positive, in order to escape the thought of his own dire circumstances. Thus, he was even led to self-delusions and tricking his own mind into false sense of securities, at the same time that he intended to fool all those around him.

But were they fooled?

Were they truly loyal?

Did they really want to carry out this madman's plans for complete destruction, or were they too playing the same games their Titan Master had orchestrated before them all?

Domenico Armando looked like crap to all of his people. He was unrecognizable to the powerhouse of magical charisma and unequalled commanding presence he portrayed, during the peak of his reign at all times of his former glory.

When Domenico ordered them all to kill and destroy millions and billions of people across the world, of those he labelled 'his enemies' - such armies of people close to him were only forced to consciously look at this man with a look on their faces as if he were out of his mind. As if he was delusional, not meaning what he was saying. Because such strong commands were no longer being given by an equally strong commanding presence of earlier times; but such strong orders were now being given by someone who was in fact appearing to be directly disproportionate to such words. Domenico looked like a weakened, broken, desperate man who could not even command a troop in battle. Such a weakened man certainly appeared to hold no conviction to his ever-so-powerful words of killing on a grand scale he thus attempted to command his expert troops all around him to commit.

In their minds, Domenico looked like some weak lunatic, talking crazy; sounding like his brain had become devoid of all power and reason, but wanted to sound authoritarian-like to all those beneath him. It became a joke.

Domenico looked up at them as he was forced paralysed on his wheelchair. His back was hunched, his neck was hunched from sitting down and staring down at his World Map of targets nonstop for months, his eyes still appeared powerful, but more so mixed with pain and grief and fatigue. His eyes looked tired and they were watery. And his voice was strained. A weak man barking strong orders, his men thought individually to themselves, but as no one of them vocalized to the other such thoughts, remarkably they had all thought the same thing.

It was as if they were receiving orders from a man whose bark was certainly stronger than his bite. They just appeared not to take this ailing man seriously anymore. But they were still fearful from committing any open displays of mutiny or disloyalty against him. So they all played their own charades of nodding their heads dutifully to his every crazy instruction – but at the same time, they hoped and prayed that this irritating monstrous scarecrow-figured man would just soon croak into eternity, before the time came when they had to put his wretched maniacal plans into full effect!

But just as they pretended absolute loyalty to their Titan Master, at the same time, Domenico Armando acted out the pretence of his own immortality before them: "I am going to bring salvation to the world! All that will be in the present and the future and all that will be forgotten in the past will be because of me and my absolute powers! I am greater than all leaders before me. And I will create the greatest power the world has ever seen! We will be victorious! We will enter combat operations tomorrow. And after tomorrow, I will be the chief commander of all that reigns and all which I allow to reign beneath me! This world is currently filled with many disease-ridden humans. But our high-powered arsenal will be the ultimate medicine to completely cleanse and cure the filth of disease and pestilence from our land and soil! Our actions beginning tomorrow will save the earth from being overrun by such contagious human conditions! Yes. I will be the saviour! I am the magician. I am God, the creator of all things! And you people before me here this day are my loyal followers. Dare I say - my faithful disciples!"

Domenico Armando had briefed his men on his precise orders as a daily ritual. He wanted to make sure that his plans of obliterating the masses of his enemies went without error; went without overlooking even the tiniest - most minute - detail. He would cover new ground and old ground before them repetitively, until they understood every sordid detail as second nature. He claimed, "This war is the beginning of the end for all that stands at odds with us-with me!" He used the word 'us' consistently, in order to coerce his people that eliminating the world's enemies was necessary for their survival as it was for his own. So they would all benefit and participate wholeheartedly right through to the bloody end. But in himself, Domenico was the only one who stood to benefit from such drastic actions; because he planned to takedown all his men in the aftermath of it all. But he kept that ace tightly concealed up his sleeve from their complete comprehension of the deadly matter of fact!

Domenico's teachings and instructions took place inside his War Preparations Operating Room of his underground bomb shelter complex. It was fully-fitted with advanced technology and high-tech computers with luxurious furnishings all round the spacious room.

NOW in view of the World Map before them, which was laid out flat before Domenico's huge desk, he ensured his people were kept abreast of the entire military operation to be unleashed upon the world very soon. He placed red pen underline marks on all areas across the globe he wanted targeted with planted bombs of a nuclear kind.

The briefings took place only inside this underground facility for reasons of confidentiality and of course for maintaining the Titan's safety and security from outside apprehension. "It is very important that no one find out that I am still alive meanwhile, because that would tip off our enemy Robert Stewart, who will understand what my thoughts and plans are before I am ready to let him know. You know - when it is too late for him to do anything about it! And meanwhile, I want no warnings given to him of any sort. We must maintain the element of surprise when we strike, and give no opportunity for our enemies to counterattack any successfully offensive strike against us, with their allies."

Domenico had spread out the great map of the world across his large wooden desk and made sure that he maintained everyone's attention as he indicated rather fervently, whilst pointing across all areas of the map's vicinity with his fingers, "We attack here, and we attack here. We attack there and there and there!" And so it went on countless times. "We'll catch them all with their pants down by maintaining the element of surprise. No one will be ready for it when the arsenal is presented to them in full-scale military combat style. They will be attacked and dead before they can so much as even scream a warning over any communications device, to alert any of their interstate and national neighbours of World War being declared against everyone."

Only Domenico was seated inside the War Room. All his men were forced to stand and remain alert and to rehearse carefully every instruction given to them right through to the finest detail. "Everyone must become an expert in theory before they can pull out their guns in practical measures of combat. So listen and learn!" he barked in order to them all.

All in all, Domenico's war-time captains and soldiers present with him, did not dare rebuke his plans to his face nor openly contradict

Domenico's insane ideas of murderous grandeur in any way. They just maintained their acts of nodding their heads in agreement without any words spoken.

Domenico kept teaching them the art of combat. He also continuously warned his people of their number one enemy's cunning. "Ahh, Robert Stewart! Remember, my loyal men. Robert is a man never to be underestimated at whatever cost. Yes. We will hate him, but remember, never allow your hatred for the man to cloud your sound judgements. Always be prepared for everything; because I did not end up in this condition of mine by battling an idiot. No. Robert Stewart is just as capable and resourceful as anyone in this room. This is simply a game of who will strike first. That is why it is imperative that our enemy never finds out that I am still alive. Because then our element of surprise will become foiled. And he cannot be given any chance to strike back and interfere with my plans for a complete global wipe out of all my contemptible enemies across the whole world! We must always be prepared to entertain notions of counter-campaigns, just in case our enemy catches wind of anything before all the deaths of our targets have been cast forward. We must be on full alert and ready at all times! Remember, the element of surprise with which we intend on striking our enemies is in fact something we too must heed carefully by planning against. We too must be prepared against being caught off-guard by such an enemy! We can never afford to be taken by surprise by Robert, or then my plans for a total destruction against all my enemies will be marred. And that is something that can never eventuate, all right!"

Domenico kept putting on grand shows and displays of his eminent authority before his men. He tried to overshadow the weakened appearance of his demeanour by constantly demonstrating powerful episodes of his rants before them. He simply did not want his people to think that he was as dim as he seemed. No. He would act in such a powerful authoritative way, so that his men standing before him would have no choice but to concede that Domenico Armando, the Titan was surely in full control of his mental faculties - and his brain power was as great as it ever was. He had to portray himself as an eternal leader as he was always considered during the days of his former glory!

Domenico constantly insisted before his men: "My ideology is the only ideology that works. I am correct and everybody else is wrong. Never forget that and never deviate even a crumb from my teachings installed upon you all this day; because we will win the war of grand total destruction only if my orders are carried out to the letter - understand? I am not paying you people to be creative. Because then you will fail. What I am asking and telling each of you is to become A-grade pupils and followers to all my instructions in The Art of Combat presented to you this day. Because then and only then will victory be assured against all our enemies!"

Domenico's views were fixed. His mind was rigid and no one in the world could persuade him otherwise, against his every damaging thought and every anarchist action. Domenico simply believed that only he knew everything, and he knew how to finagle the mechanics of operating every piece of machinery in all areas of life, particularly that of war. And he would not allow anyone to dispute him or persuade him otherwise, since his people were not even given permission to speak at him, just to listen in strict silence and carry out his orders equally in strict obedience.

Domenico remained pigheaded and stubborn to even any of the frontline troops' asking for improvisations and more surrounding backup regiments, should they run into any trouble when conducting open warfare operations out into the field commencing tomorrow. Should one request, especially for additional reinforcements to be made at such time, Domenico would only reply, 'Just follow my orders without question and you will be all right. Deviate from anything-any part of my training methods and you will all deserve to die with the rest of my enemies out there, ok!'

The Armando lackeys knew Domenico well enough to know that when their Master made a decision, they had to follow it doggedly; because Domenico Armando was a man who never changed his mind. He never reneged on a deal. And he sure as hell never allowed anyone to debate him on any detail of his instructions to be carried out.

Domenico insisted, "As your master is a professional, so too must I demand that my soldiers also become professionals. I will not tolerate inexperienced, ill-behaved and insubordinate juvenile recruits. Because such people will only slow us down and jeopardize the success of the mission. Such people must be made our targets, certainly not our allies! I need professional outfits and expert units in case we need to deploy a specialized counterattack operation, in the event that our enemy is somehow waiting in the wings for us. I know, I know. Perhaps it is paranoia taking over. But you must never forget that just as the element of surprise is our greatest combat strategy, so too, we must always be on guard in case we become the very recipients to such a ploy then targeted against us, hmm. Understand? Very good!"

Domenico suddenly felt invigorated. He insisted, "So be ready for our victory; because we will win this war. I know we will. Anyone here or elsewhere who thinks that we will not win the battle and the war itself is lying to you. He or they know nothing. So ignore them and listen to me and only trust me; because I know everything better than everyone else. The rest could hardly differentiate the dissimilarity between a knife and a fork, let alone trying to find ways to strategically and militarily defeat an enemy, especially one as bitter such as Robert Stewart! Yes. This will be the final campaign of our lives. And even if the fighting gets too tough for our enemies and they start approaching you with any flags for surrender - just shoot them. This is a war where no prisoners are allowed. No reprieves, no compassion, and absolutely no leeway for anyone to escape my plans for death to be inflicted upon them all!

"So just follow my lead and do as I say without any deviation from any of it; because only I control the levers of war. And only I command you; no one else. Not even yourselves and your thoughts must you trust. Your job is to do as I say and put your entire lives in my hands – then we will be assured complete victory. And once you are all in the battlefield, I-and-I alone will give you constant orders by telephone and radio. Listen to no one else but me. You will not be conducting your own war out there as you see fit. You are merely to follow my instructions and any improvisations necessary will only be carried out by me. Not you, but me. So your job is to constantly keep me up to date and abreast of all successes and any obstacles you may face along the course of our very acts of war declarations.

"And I will assist you with the field map spread out in front of me, alerting you on any further instructions for the offensive and counterattack procedures if or when necessary, should any of you face such difficulties down the line, prior our complete success in the war goals and missions set out before us!

"So please remember, victory must come to fruition. I will not accept my hopes for a win of this war on all fronts to be shattered by any of you. My objective is now within reach. I can feel the vibes of my divine right to kill all opposition at my behest. It is my supreme being that has been cast on this earth, in order to fix the world and to cleanse our lands and soils of all to which has contaminated it. We will encircle all our enemies with our arsenal. And once they are encircled, they will be in a stalemate, much trapped by our weaponry. There will be no way out for them. No escape from the detonations and bomb blasts which will ensue, to rid us all from their entire existences as if they never even belonged here to begin with.

"Then we will strike our final blows to bring about a checkmate against our targets! We will cut off their water, food and military arms supplies. We will destroy their crops. We will block their attempts to strike us back by destroying all their supply routes, from food to roads to ammunition, to anyone who is in allegiance to them, much opposed to us. Our enemies will have nothing left to fight us with. And even before my friend Robert Stewart knows what hit him; our artillery will start shelling the entire world around him. He will be dumbstruck by our vicious assault against him. We will be prepared also in case our enemy wishes to launch any Allied Air Raids against us. We must cover all bases and be prepared for every eventuality before such obstacles can unfold within our paths. Our shells must strike at all city centres of the globe without any warning given to our enemies beforehand. They must be taken by complete surprise. That way, even if they did have time to lift a weapon against us, that beautiful 'element of surprise' factor will startle them to such extremes, that their trembling hands would not even be able to lift a gun and aim it effectively at us, before we strike them all down first and foremost and much successfully.

"Yes. So by tomorrow, I want to be able to look at my World Map and be able to systematically cross out all the cities and states which currently exist on these maps; whereby following the detonation of all our powerful bombs, will then cease to exist on the globe. Then once the World Map is no longer divided into such countries, then I... I can reinvent the wheel so to speak, and I will unite all the lands left over previously divided into East, West, South and Northern country areas of such regions - and I will become the one and only World Leader which unites the entire world as one, to follow but their only existing true leader. And that is me, their God. The creator of all things! I will create a New World Order controlled by a Global Leader of all nations, no longer separated and divided by countries or Presidents and Prime Ministers and so forth. But everything will be as One. And that One World will be controlled only by one leader. And that is the man sitting before you all today: the God, creator of all things. And then branded as the uniter of all things!

"Yes. I cannot wait for tomorrow. It will be a great day for us all. And what a beautiful surprise it will be for the world, when they awaken by the sounds of our machine gun shells fired at them. So the question is, how long will the war last? When will our military operations end? The answer to that my friends is when every last enemy of mine is smashed to pieces and cast into the ground; however long it takes. There is no definitive answer for this. Nor will I insult anyone in this room by presenting you all with a phony standard answer, which was and is the usual protocol presented by all the phony leaders who currently occupy our world to their people. The war will go on until the end. And the end means, when there is nothing left on this earth for anyone to survive. And the end finally means, when there is no one left on this earth any longer needed to be removed! That is our enemies.

"And once all our enemies fall to the ground dead as ashes, then we can officially declare that the war is won in favour of our side - and that we have outlived our goals to become the one New World Power controlled by me. So in order to defeat our enemies, we must be orderly. And in the state of panic and confusion we inflict upon our enemies, we will make them disorderly. That way, we can defeat them easily. Like I keep saying, remember, the element of surprise! And remember, your orders are to fight and to win. Anyone who deviates from my instructions or even attempts to retreat anywhere for cover will be considered the enemy. And those guilty people will be dealt with as the rest of our targets will be! Understand that. Accept that! Burn those words vividly into your brains! And never forget it! Anyone who does not obey my instructions unconditionally will meet with death instantaneously as well!"

Domenico Armando understood that in his global massacre operations to be inflicted, there would be a fierce resistance to his efforts primarily by Robert Stewart and his law-enforcement allies. But Domenico was confident that he could run them all down and defeat every anti-Armando effort thrown against him. He simply instructed his people to triple their efforts against the enemies. To arm themselves with more powerful artillery than the opposition, and with that effort cast forward, the Armando army legions should certainly win out in the end. He ordered: "We will begin house-to-house fighting – country against country will ensue. And no matter how difficult it gets out there amidst the gunfire, the rabble, confusion and counterattacks by the enemy's Allied Resistance Forces, you are all to follow and obey my instructions fully. We will fight to the bloody end. We will prove the impossible. The war will be won in our favour. I will accept no other option. So do not let me down, any of you!

"I expect all of you to back me with your lives! You are to show me your full commitment out in the battlefields and you are not to return to me failing! It will be better for anyone who lets me down, to die out in the field of combat operations than return here at any time thereafter and face my wrath. Because I can assure you: that anything Robert Stewart and his allies can do to you will seem as pie in the sky compared to what I will do to anyone who lets me down from tomorrow onward! Because failing me will be very costly; it would mean signing your own death sentence! There will be no way out of that for anyone. So don't even think of seeking salvation elsewhere by taking flight to remote regions of the world; because no one can escape me. I will always find my prey! No matter what it takes, I will fight the final battle to the bitter end!

"You will either win in the battle against our enemies or you will fall in the battle. I suggest you do whatever it takes to win this war; because no one of you really has any other option but to fight and bring me victory. Things can end very well if you follow my lead and not take up your roles like blind rats in a maze. We will win against our enemies! We will win against Robert Stewart! There is no other choice. We are the ultimate powerhouse. No other force on this earth can compete with us! No one else can win against us! We must defeat them! We must cost them everything! Yes. Tomorrow it will be all over for Robert Stewart and his world of fools!"

Domenico then turned his eyes away from his people and stared through each and every one of them in preoccupied thought in which he had not kept it a secret, but he was very outspoken to such vivid proclamations against one specific target in mind, as he shouted in a volcanic rage displayed before his audience scattered around him. The product of his rage was but one single enemy running ragged inside his mind as he barked his shockingly frightening words: "I will startle you with the first round being sounded from the thunder of my guns! That will be only the beginning! Yes, Robert Stewart; Domenico Armando is expecting you! Domenico Armando is longing to cast his bullets in you with a vengeful heart. I am waiting for you! I am coming for you! Can you feel it? Are you scared Robert Stewart? Can you feel that the worst is imminent? My armies will soon be advancing closer and closer to your direction. There will be nowhere for you to run or hide from what I have planned against you! Yes, behold my friend; the conditions of your existence will soon become chaotic. Come tomorrow, I will have you and your world under siege! That will be the final blow which marks the beginning of your end! My war will eliminate all your people. It will be a horrific sight for you. I will orchestrate the terms which dictate the end of civilization! Nothing but rubble and dead corpses will remain! Your existence Robert Stewart will only become a dark relic of history!"

Domenico Armando then clenched his bony hands into fists and used all his might to straighten the hunch on his back and neck - and continued to stare at the wall passed his audience and envisioned thoughts of the Grand Finale. "Yes. And once I win the war and totally destroy Robert Stewart, then I will take his wife Cassandra to become my lover! She will become betrothed to me before the entire public eye. And she will be forced to do it willingly. She will abide even if it is against her will. She will remove all petty thoughts from her former life and her times with Robert; for I will flood her memory with new and better times. She will become my ultimate real fantasy. She will naturally come to realize the hopelessness of her former life, and be forced to succumb to her new life driven into my arms. I will walk again. I will carry her to my bedroom. I will remove all her clothes and indulge in my fantasies of kissing her breasts and her vagina and then her entire body all over. She will be mine. It is as if I can already taste her sweet aroma.

"And that is where you come in Harold Mar. You must carry out my plans first and foremost to drive a wedge between Robert and his wife. She is not to sleep with him again. I want her to succumb to a period of abstinence. Then she will come to me very randy, begging me to give her what she needs. And I will gladly oblige her in the bedroom. Yes. Indeed I will. And she will not resist me; because she will learn very quickly her options. And they are to either love me or to die at my orders. She will be with no man but me. And if she refuses me, she will suffer the consequences. And she will meet the death sentence. Because anyone who refuses me, automatically dictates their own sentence!

"Her options to consider must not be taken lightly. Either she lives with me or she will die without anyone or anything by her side! In the end, I have no doubt what her decision will be. In fact, I forecast she will make the admirable choice in choosing to be my lover to the end! And she will do it once she realizes that for the first time in her life, she will also obtain the same focus and limelight as her new and gifted husband. She will become the Queen among Queens, as opposed to what she is now: an insignificant lawyer married to a wretched man who happens to be my number one enemy!

"And the only way she will ever have a chance to change her dismal fortunes is to accept the ultimate invitation into my throne as my ultimate mistress! At least then she can go down in history as something: the mistress to the ultimate hero on earth. As opposed to what she currently faces: going down in history as a widow to my bitterest nemesis! It will be this simple idea that will give her the necessary courage to make the right decision in choosing life with me - and not death as her soon late husband!

"Yes, Cassandra; you need to make the right decision. She must choose me! I need her by my side. I need to feel her body next to mine. She is the only woman who I know I can adore completely. The rest are just simple women. But her, well, she is a real woman who is designed for a real man like me. She must forget her husband and accept me as a more suitable replacement!

"Yes, my dear Cassandra. One way or another, our destinies will be linked for all eternity. So do not fight it. Only accept it! It will be better for you that way. How can you allow yourself to be killed instead of choosing to spend the rest of your days in bliss with me? How? You simply cannot! You must not! I forbid you as I surely forbid you from any further betrayals to me by sleeping with your damn current husband. You must choose wisely, Cassandra! You must be strong! You must be smart! You must take my hand and save yourself from death. It would be such a pity to have to harm such beauty as yours. Believe me... please believe Cassandra... I do not want to hurt you. It would pain me to harm that beauty of yours in any way. So just say yes. Choose me. Choose life and I will spend the rest of my days making love to you! It is simple. There can be no stress! Just say yes. Make it instinctual. Make the invitation even sensual! Do not protest! Life must surely be better than death! You will become the First Lady to the First World Order run by me!

"So Cassandra; let me penetrate you - and believe me - you will not be left wanting! Pleasure me, but do not pleasure your current husband. He does not deserve a beauty such as yours! Only I do. Let me show you how happy I can make you. Whatever you have now is just false happiness. But I can offer you the most genuine and sincere form of happiness. Let me show you!"

Domenico Armando in fact right now resembled a machine that was programmed for one thing: death. He wanted to bring destruction to everyone and no one could change the inner workings of his yet very powerful strong mind. When he gave an order, it was to be obeyed without question in such dictatorial fashion, that even his men who had misgivings in carrying out such heinous plans, knew they were all trapped in the Armando web. They were all but forced to abide by rules given by such a maniac or in fact face extinction by the very same menace.

They were surely trapped. If they carried out the orders of this very twisted man sitting before them onto his wheelchair, they knew they faced imminent death by Robert and his allies – and if they refused to follow such orders, they would also face obliteration by Domenico's hands. Some in their minds cursed the world for failing to eliminate such a global threat of unequalled proportions in the history of civilization. They cursed everyone who failed in their quests to crucify and condemn this heinous man yet living before them; because his life meant the death and destruction of not only The Free World, but the eventual extinction of those planted all around him.

Domenico Armando was delusional. He was mad. He still thought that he knew everything. He thought he could defeat the entire world's armies. And he was quite willing to send his men into the ground in the process of attempting to prove that very point. It was a suicide mission and the most brutal human sacrifice of masses of lives imaginable! The son of a bitch, they cursed within themselves. Domenico acted as if the war to be won by him was a fait accompli. He was truly out of his mind. He was giving them instructions in theory which would simply result in anarchy once put into practice.

Such orders would result in their deaths surely from day one. But they feared Domenico. No one could reason with him. No one could question him and his crazy orders or debate him. Surely they were not even permitted to utter two words against his dismal plans without facing immediate execution.

Oh, how they wished he would just drop dead right now and end the fear that had overwhelmed their entire beings right this moment in time! Oh, how they wanted him to just collapse out of that wheelchair of his and die like the swine he was. He talked as if he would be the king of the world. The freak was paralysed. It was assured that his paralysis was permanent. But here he was, acting as if he would get up off that chair within hours and reclaim his notoriety among all nations of the globe, and whisk his beloved Cassandra into his arms and make another race of bad babies to be bred by him!

The guy was completely insane. He was giving orders of war in theory, which when put into practice out there into the battlefield, would ultimately destroy all their lives! He didn't care. "Just follow my orders and win. And don't come back unless you do win!" he kept barking. It was a farce. It was a sham. It was completely mad to even attempt such a feat of global destruction as this monster perpetuated in his very dark skull. It was sure as hell that Domenico Armando had to be stopped before tomorrow came.

In themselves, they could not participate in such a wicked scheme of unprecedented magnitude at this crazy man's whim, which would also end the lives of all of them quite instantaneously. They wanted Domenico out of their lives. But how were they going to do it? That hunchbacked cripple was still a menace to everyone. No matter if he was disabled, they still feared him. But how could they finally get rid of him before midnight came and they were ordered to carry out his dark schemes of mass destruction to be declared against the whole world? They did not have much time. Whatever needed to be done had to be done quickly or else they were all doomed.

The sicker Domenico got may have weakened him physically, but unfortunately his mental willpower was not broken. His mental faculties and determination were intact without even a dent. His brain was forever programmed for destruction. Nothing and no one could ever change that powerful and dangerous mindset of his. This final mission as Domenico put it was indeed a game of the highest stakes possible!

They knew that Domenico had no regard whatsoever if his men would perish in such an ill-fated failed battle of his as it were. It was as if he was deliberating sending them all into the hands of death by their enemies, pretending that he would win the war, which they knew he surely could not, especially in his weakened position at present. Domenico was willing to send thousands and thousands of soldiers to die in his battle against the world! It was nuts! Complete madness beyond description. One man meant the death of all of civilisation. How could this be allowed to pass?

Domenico talked of his final victory, but his people knew the truth. Whatever war he waged, would only result in an ultimate defeat. They then thought of abandoning this monster padrone of theirs. But in order for that to be done, the monstrously evil dictator first had to be deposed! Because if they entered battle tomorrow, they knew they would not only never live to see the end of that war alive, but they would not even survive the first day of launching their first offensive against their opponents!

But Domenico's omnipotence seemed forever sustained. His men around him were shaking inside, but the fanatical Domenico, despite his frail appearance on the outside, seemed as strong as steel on the inside. He was forever unwavering in his vendettas to be cast forward. And he planned for all his people to fight with no defiance, but only showing unyielding determination in order to grant him victory; to defend his cause by unleashing mass destruction against his enemies. Or, in the event of any failures, mishaps or open resistances demonstrated by his army troops, he wanted his captains in command of the war effort, to deliver him all the corpses of defiant soldiers before him, so he could then plan to scorn them even as they lay dead at his feet!

The situation Domenico Armando had presently faced became inconsequential to all those supposed loyal allies of his. In their minds, their own survival became paramount above all else, including the Titan's!

As it stood, the people stationed closest to Domenico Armando, became startled by his inhumane ideology and scarred emotionally by the horrible crimes they were then forced to partake in, which would ultimately cost them their lives! They wanted to oppose his oppression also inflicted upon them.

Domenico's plans of destruction on a global scale also meant that their families and loved ones would also be caught in the crossfire. Domenico did not care for them or their families. So now what ensued in each of their minds, was one final solution - which was how to rid themselves of this menace before them before it was too late - and they all died on top of those masses of people he targeted from areas across the entire globe.

What resulted from such thoughts was clear-cut: It became a plot amongst themselves to finally kill Domenico Armando!

Domenico must not be given his final chance to inflict carnage and devastation upon The Free World. He had to be killed before midnight tonight. Because from midnight onwards, should his life yet remain among the living, it would surely mean the end of civilisation at an entirety.

So now the men who were ordered to kill for Domenico, became the very conspirators who planned to kill their awful padrone!

These men now felt themselves victims of their own boss's ill will. They did not want to be held responsible for the actions of their master ruler. And so they decided to finally grab their one chance of escaping such a fate by doing something drastic about it. Domenico was a sick man in a wheelchair. Surely this was the most opportune time to overpower him and overthrow his sick and twisted reign which ruled over all of them. They were now planted very close to him. They should be able to finally finagle his end as justice begged for it…finally to eventuate!

They became quite willing participants to openly commit treason against their supreme leader, if it meant saving themselves and preventing the world from being driven back to the primitive Stone Age, which would result by the mass killings Domenico planned to be launched against his enemies, that would also end up in the thirst and starvation of their loved ones as a result of his intense bombing raid genocides planned after midnight, tonight, which would surely destroy all food and water supplies for anyone to be able to survive.

The henchmen now seemed intent on breaking their tyrant ruler's otherwise impenetrable barriers he created, which otherwise silenced them, and all others, from any outspoken and firm acts of opposition against him and his causes. They wanted to finally put a stop to a man to whom ordinarily had forever seemed unstoppable!

In their minds, they had to break down the walls of resistance in which Domenico had created for decades, which secured his power as that of the elite autocratic ruler, overshadowing all forms of democracy from penetrating his world. And now the Leader's own army began to conspire against him, when enough was enough!

No wonder Robert Stewart hunted him down relentlessly for years. Domenico Armando was a barbaric animal. And he had the audacity to call Robert names. But all Robert Stewart was guilty of was in wanting to obtain the Nobel Peace Prize of being the one who lodged the fine silver bullet between that wicked man's watery desperate-looking eyes.

Robert was right in his intent to crush, destroy and kill that tyrant, they now conceded.

They also felt the same depths of hatred for the very man who now called himself Titan! The tyrant's judgement and his sanity were severely questioned by even those people closest to him now.

The madman was setting his sights across the borders of all shores of the globe. He wanted to take over everyone and everything across all lands and all shores of the world! He could not be allowed to proceed with his dark-hearted scheme. He had to be killed before midnight tonight!

And the plan was now under way in how to proceed with such a delicate act! They had to unite under one common cause: destroying Domenico Armando once and for all!

Domenico must be killed before he gives the final go-ahead of his plans to make war against the world!

They had to figure out the best way to rid themselves of Domenico Armando and his evil regime!

They wanted to assassinate him right here and right now!

But the question was: HOW TO FINALLY KILL THE WORST CRIMINAL ALIVE WHO HAD DEFIED THE ODDS BEFORE?

They were confident it could be done successfully!

The coup would take place!

There was no room for failure this time!

Because if the co-conspirators failed in their plot for Domenico's final assassination, Domenico Armando would crush them as he sought to crush the lifeblood of the world.

The ever-growing resistance to the dictator's throne and philosophy now came close to home. His once loyal inner circle now became crumbling before his very eyes.

The end of Domenico Armando must be realised!

If Domenico was not killed – and if he did not win the war on the outside, he was sure to take revenge against all those who failed him.

And those closest to him knew the war could not be won, especially with Domenico's current diminished capacity, and most of his manpower and resources already accounted for by the previous police raids launched against him.

So before the Armando war was lost and he got his chance to unleash all-hell upon them, they now decided to 'finish' that tyrant off; meaning to eliminate him. To blow him away in his most vulnerable seated spot! Because as long as Domenico Armando remained alive, their lives all hung in the balance!

Domenico's inner circle refused to follow him into the depths of ruin.

Not only was Domenico hated by those he persecuted, but now he was equally despised by those closest to him.

As many others had failed to kill him, such soldiers posted before him at present planned to finally succeed in unleashing the last breath of this evil genius.

Domenico had always relied on a ruthless and carefully groomed loyal band of well-trained fighter protectors and muscle around him. These men had constantly carried out his instructions to wipe out his opposition at the same time as they worked fervently to protect him and secure their meal ticket.

But times had changed.

His most loyal inner core were dead and buried by law-enforcement groups, and the newly-recruited team who took over, would not put-up with this wretched man's killing field orders for long.

They rebelled.

They rapidly had proven to exhibit the exact opposite qualities of his old regime: now proving complete disloyalty.

They would overthrow this brutal leader.

They would literally drive the stake into his black heart and twist it ferociously, revelling in his startled screams, in eagerness to watch his final moments, as he was thrown onto the ground struggling to keep alive, as he gasped for his final breaths.

They would then dance on his death tomb!

But now as they had their firm decisions fixed into their minds to end this heinous tyrant's life, they first wanted to humiliate him as he humiliated so many others before persecuting, beating, intensely torturing and killing them!

On the 23rd of March 1991, the Army Resistance to the Armando throne was cast forward in full force.

"You're not the only one who is able to play games, Domenico!" cursed the man he had called Harold Mar.

Domenico Armando raised his head from a mass of a hunched neck and his desperate leaking watery eyes now turned to intense rage as he shouted, "How dare you talk to me without being asked. What the hell are you saying, you idiot?"

His so-called henchman replied, "We are all turning against you, Domenico. We will not carry out your plans to destroy the world!"

Domenico became stunned in a mixture of shock and fury as he barked in an abrupt response, "How dare you defy me! How dare you question me! How dare you mock me in front of my people like this! What do you mean?"

The man thought-to-be Harold Mar replied rather coolly, "We are all gathered here under false pretences with the intent to overthrow your sick arse to the wolves, you arrogant, old, mentally and physically sick son of a bitch!"

Domenico would not tolerate any dissent amongst his regime. He quickly turned his head to face the twelve men who gathered around him right now inside his high-tech furnished War Preparations Room and shouted commands of death orders to his troop, "Grab him. He is a traitor. He has committed treachery before me right now. String him up and hang him! Run him down! Put a knife into his stomach. Break his neck. Cut out his tongue! Amputate his hands and feet. Mutilate him to pieces for such words of mutiny against me! Butcher him to shreds. Shoot him right now. Let me see it!"

But his troop of men just stood there staring at Domenico without acting out his orders.

"Do as you are told!" Domenico furiously insisted. "What are you waiting for? I am your leader. I am your boss. You will obey me right now, on the double. Pull out your guns and shoot him!"

The pretentious Harold Mar stood before the ailing old man who was confined in a wheelchair, raised his head for a moment and laughed, "You are not in charge anymore Domenico. I am. They follow my orders, not yours." The man thought of as the former Mr. President, then commanded the troop with orders contradicting the dopey-looking, morphine-dependent Domenico. He ordered: "Pull out your weapons and aim them at Domenico.

Point them directly between his eyes! We want no near misses of vital organs this time!"

The manoeuvres were swiftly performed in soldier-like gestures as the men carried out their tasks expertly, when the entire twelve members of the cavalry had guns suddenly trained at the centre of Domenico's eyebrows. The man, thought-to-be Harold Mar, also whipped out his revolver too from his shoulder holster that was concealed beneath a black leather jacket and steadied his perfect aim between Domenico's eyes as all the others.

Domenico Armando was overcome by a very animated emotional surprise right now as he shouted in panic, "What the hell is going on here? Why are you idiots listening to him and pointing your revolvers at me? Do as you are told. Shoot Harold Mar!"

But his main prey right now wished to make his statement in a frightening declaration before Domenico. He maintained his steady right hand, holding the pistol at Domenico, at the same time as his left hand had arched swiftly across his face, moving to the top of his head. He removed his elaborate disguise quite rapidly. First the white-haired wig and then the very lifelike, very real Harold Mar resembling latex mask from his face, also losing the expertly disguised ex-president's silly voice impersonation - and revealed himself as the man Domenico Armando truly hated most in the world all along. He showed himself as Robert Stewart, who managed to infiltrate his organization very expertly, and overpower his usual army of protectors and replace them all with his people.

Robert Stewart nodded his head to the rest of his team, who also removed their perfect disguises and revealed themselves as members of the New York City Police Department to which he now presided over as Police Chief Commissioner.

Among the group of men was his usual police partner, now the promoted Commander John McCallum. And his brother Paul, also present, who was licensed to carry a firearm via his detective work.

As the masks and wigs were removed from all their faces, Domenico's jaw suddenly hung down, his mouth wide-open as he experienced the deepest shock of his life and knew the end was near. He suddenly had another seizure attack which abruptly exploded inside his skull. He raised his hands at the sides of his head, to attempt to soothe the excruciating pains which erupted across his brain, and he shouted in terror also at the shocking impact of his rapidly-forming multiple seizures taking full hold of him this time, as he uncontrollably staggered back in his wheelchair too far and too quickly, causing it to tilt over backwards.

Domenico rolled onto the hard ground after first crashing on his head, his body then striking hard wooden floor, as he groaned onto his hands and paralysed legs in the worst painful episodes of seizures he had experienced, since his brain tumour diagnosis almost two years ago.

Domenico had succumbed to blurred vision. His eyes could no longer focus properly at his enemies surrounding him. His brain became completely fogged. All he experienced right this very moment was intense pain and dire shock.

He could no longer talk. He was only stuttering. His tones were incomprehensible. His screams were louder. His fears experienced at this moment for the first time in his life overcame him. He rapidly lost his eyesight completely. From blurred glimpses of his enemies stationed all around him, he now could no longer see anything but blackness. He shouted echoes of terror. His pains inside his skull were driven by more intense and intolerable seizure episodes. Domenico's mouth then became wide-open, as if struck by the worst fear and surprise imaginable, due to the untimely thumping hammer beatings erupting inside his brain, one after the other, and all at the same time, mixed with the same sick feelings of utter shock and dread, in which he experienced only moments before, at the discovery that his primary enemy had managed to expertly infiltrate his fortress - and bring a final checkmate defeat to his vast extraordinary plans of death to the world!

But Domenico's jaw hung down in desperation to cling onto life itself, as he felt a great struggle to gain any further breaths. He was suffocating from the experienced grenades which erupted inside his head. His breaths were shallower. He could not breathe for much longer. Domenico Armando, in his final quest to sustain life, if only to live out his great vision of mass murder, was instead, taken by the very surprise he planned to unleash onto the world at large; the surprise of shock itself which caused his brain to haemorrhage. He had time for one final stroke. And that stroke ended his life, before any bullets were ordered to cease such a wicked life from the world's existence.

But this time the death of that man had to be confirmed.

Robert's brother Paul Stewart made one final unrehearsed movement concerning their target. And he strode toward the deceased Domenico, holding a large sword blade he removed from behind the evil man's corpse, which was situated on the back of the room's wall, held in place by a specially-made wooden frame.

Paul then stood before Domenico's corpse holding the large and heavy sword in his hand. He raised the gleaming silver blade high above his head and sent it perfectly arched around the former dictator's neck, severing his head clean off his body. Paul then displayed a brief rage at the beheaded target, and sent his steel-capped boot kicking the severed head into the wall, as a sign of a more personal disrespect for the man. Kicking his head as a ball into the wall, put a stamp of the final humiliation and degradation he wanted to bring to the very man who cost the world and the Stewart family so much endless grief.

Now, Domenico Armando's life would end as his reign of terror began: in the same measure of grief he had inflicted. The justice against Armando was finally fulfilled. It was truly the end of an era! With the death of one of history's worst dictators, today marked a holy day where justice was truly served on all fronts.

The justice by Robert Stewart's brilliant cunning, overshadowing the enemy's tarnished mindset, which was driven to illogical irrationality in the final course of his destructive wretched life, mixed with the justice of nature that finally caught up with him, had, in its totality, brought that evil wicked man to his end... at last!

Robert Stewart could now wrap-up his final report attached to the confirmed death certificate to be issued against what was the world's most dangerous enemy to date. He shook his brother's hand and would not even question nor debate Paul's uncalled-for, but at the same time, much understandable final actions delivered against the target, all last minute.

Robert and all his police personnel stationed before him could only congratulate each other on a true job well done. Their infiltration scheme worked perfectly. This was the workings of an effective police unit at its best!

And it all began when Robert received a police call yesterday morning from John McCallum at 8:00 a.m. at his home, concerning information that his brother Paul had been arrested inside of Brooklyn for wilfully speeding, allegedly. The police officer on car patrol duty in hot pursuit of Paul, then finally caught up with him, as he was on the verge of exiting the borough's border lines. But the arresting officer never asked why he was speeding fifty kilometres over the speed limit. He just hauled him out of his vehicle, forced his hands behind his back and cuffed him.

The police officer forced Paul to abandon his civilian vehicle left parked at the side of the road, then pushed him roughly into the back of his police car and drove him to the station house and booked him.

Within fifty minutes after his arrest, whilst he lay inside the prison lock-up facility, Paul Stewart was beaten up by three of the prisoners.

Fortunately Robert came at the scene on time. He stopped the fight before his brother was killed, which was surely the intent of the prisoners to kill him.

Robert instructed one of the jail guards at the scene to open his brother's cell he was forced to share with three other inmates – and once the cell door was unlocked, Robert proceeded to attack the three prisoners. Robert wanted to kill them. But two prison guards on duty interceded and broke off Robert's attempts.

Fortunately, Paul got off lucky; just a few bruises on his face, but no broken bones. Some ice would heal the bruises, but he felt all right enough to skip admission to the hospital. He would recover in no time following his immediate release from jail.

When his brother informed him that he was arrested trying to get away from a tailing vehicle containing two unidentified men with guns chasing him, Robert then insisted that that cop who arrested his brother with no questions asked be put under the microscope. He wanted to bust the son of a bitch. But within three hours of commencing his investigation against the culprit, the arresting police officer was reported shooting himself with his own gun in the head. He died inside his police car, last located outside his usual Brooklyn jurisdiction, but his dead body was found in the Bronx. His police car parked on an isolated dirt road.

Paul informed his brother that the car tailing him contained no registration number plates. The hoods trying to kill him for no good reason remained unidentified. They got away as that middle-aged cop emerged at the scene after him. They were obviously Armando plants who began their next reign of terror against the Stewart family, orders of the previously alive Domenico!

Robert also wanted to know why his brother was put in a cell with three dangerous hoods, whose sole intents were to harm him (no doubt also on orders from Domenico). The prison guards on duty became suspect. One of them, who authorized Paul's detainment inside such a death trap located at the 18th precinct station house lock-up facility in Brooklyn, was also traced as working part-time at the main maximum-security prison facility in New York.

Robert tailed the guard. But whilst he was still on duty at the 18th precinct jail house, Robert planted a discreet microphone on his prison blazer uniform; the microphone was attached like Velcro. He first questioned him concerning his brother's arrest rather subtly. Then in the end, once given run-around answers, Robert casually shook his hand - and using his other hand, he tapped him on the shoulder in a friendly-like gesture, thus planting the Velcro-glued small dot microphone inconspicuously onto his prison guard uniform, his jacket.

Robert intercepted a secret meeting that night then at the prison guard's part-time job at the maximum-security prison house in the state of New York, between that 40-year-old American guard in question, and surprise-of-all-surprises, former President Harold Mar.

The plan for his escape to Domenico's secret quarters was discussed. The reason was: to help Domenico take his revenge out on his number one enemy: Robert Stewart.

Robert and his team caught up with them outside the building after the escape was finalised; they were seen entering inside an awaiting ambulance vehicle parked in the prison's ambulance parking bay containing Armando stooges. Robert was not required to return the ex-president to his cell. Because Harold Mar had a bad reaction to the drug he was given.

Apparently, he had some liver disorder which was unable to tolerate the drug's effects inside his system and his heart gave way. Harold Mar could not be revived. His heart had completely stopped permanently. He died from the side effects to the drug given to him in order to fake his death, which was necessary to ensure his escape. Robert arrested all the ambulance personnel, including the crooked prison guard, who not only was behind his brother's attempted murder, but also who carried out Domenico's plans for Harold Mar's escape.

Robert held them under private guard in a local SIA safe house pending the whereabouts of Domenico being determined. Robert ferociously questioned the crooked guard and his pretentious ambulance co-conspirators until they were forced to give him the details to Domenico's location and how to get to him.

That was when Robert used his scientific laboratory contacts in the FBI, to have the latex mask disguise of Harold Mar be made out in the exact likeness of his face - and other disguises matching the faces and profiles of all the arrested henchmen, who were reportedly all to meet Domenico inside his secret bomb shelter to carry out his orders. But instead of those henchmen meeting their master as planned, an elaborate switch was orchestrated for the sole purpose to ending the life of the nation's greatest threat!

So Robert would make sure that none of the Armando lackeys would attend that gathering. Instead, Robert Stewart and his police cavalry would replace the Armando henchmen, in a grand plot to infiltrate the Armando secret fortress, and smoke the tyrant out from circulation, once and for all.

In the meantime, Harold Mar's death was kept secret from the media, just as the arrests of all the Armando henchmen would be made top secret. The henchmen were held in custody inside the local SIA safe house in the city, until after the police operation to get Domenico was finalized. Because Domenico could not be tipped off on any such arrests made, including Harold Mar's untimely demise, or else their secret police operation to smoke Domenico out from hiding would come to a crashing halt.

So, upon Domenico's apprehension and death, the transfer of Domenico's former henchmen from the SIA safe house, to the local jail facility was in effect. And Harold Mar's confirmed death was also made public.

And those were the events which led to the police operation 'Spearhead', being cast into action successfully, against the greatest tyrant who resided at close proximity to the city, underground, whilst plotting the deaths of multitudes of people in his quest to achieve immortality.

The threat was real!
But this time: the enemy's death was also real.

It was true this time!

Domenico Armando was a threat to humanity no longer!
It was truly an end of an era!

And in the aftermath, Robert Stewart and the entire Stewart clan could breathe a sigh of relief in the confirmation to it all.

Robert Stewart and the New York City Police Department participants in the enemy's successful apprehension and death each received medals for bravery and commendation by the Mayor of New York City.

Bringing one of the worst threats to civilisation to his end was indeed a proud day for successful law enforcement!

www.ingramcontent.com/pod-product-compliance
Lightning Source LLC
Chambersburg PA
CBHW031022030726
47497CB00004B/968